HUNTING HER BOX SET #1

EDEN SUMMERS

Copyright © 2020 by Eden Summers

This book is a work of fiction. The names, characters, places, and incidents are products of the writer's imagination or have been used fictitiously and are not to be construed as real. Any resemblance to persons, living or dead, actual events, locales or organizations is entirely coincidental.

All rights reserved. With the exception of quotes used in reviews, this book may not be reproduced or used in whole or in part by any means existing without written permission from the author.

The author acknowledges the trademarked status and trademark owners of various products referenced in this work of fiction, which have been used without permission. The publication/use of these trademarks is not authorized, associated with, or sponsored by the trademark owners.

HUNTER

1

HER

The weight of a psychopath's gaze rests heavy at the back of my neck. He's watching me, stalking me, probably already fantasizing about how my bones will break under his fists.

I fight to contain a smile and cross my legs, allowing the hem of my skin-tight skirt to hitch higher along my thighs.

Every move I make is strategic, every slow blink, every bated breath, every swipe of my lace glove-covered fingers along my exposed neck.

I've practiced this a million times. I always do, because this needs to be perfect. Second chances are for the unprepared, and I'm anything but.

My auburn wig is for his benefit—the brown contact lenses, bright red lipstick, and fuck-me boots, too. Tonight, I'm an actress, and my role is that of a novice escort—his ultimate temptation.

I stir the toothpick-speared olive around in my martini glass, feigning loneliness.

My mark, Dan Roberts, has to be beside himself with interest, salivating, his palms itching, his cock hardening. He's picturing his hands around my throat, anticipating how hard he'd have to squeeze, and for how long, before I lost consciousness.

I know this because I've watched him for weeks. He's become predictable. All those nights spent in the shadows, stalking him as he stalked other women, has paid off. And it could've been just as easy for the local Portland police to track his crimes, if they'd bothered to take the word of numerous beaten women over the statement from a rich senator's son.

Only they didn't.

Their pockets had been lined with so much green that the evidence didn't matter anymore. Fake alibis were taken as legitimate accounts. Photographs of beaten, bruised, and broken bodies were discarded, just like good ol' Danny boy had done with the women he'd tormented once he'd gained his sadistic fix.

This man is a criminal.

A vile waste of oxygen.

A pathetic piece of garbage.

And apparently, I'm the only one with enough devotion to take out the trash.

From the corner of my eye, I see him approach, stopping directly beside my perch on a cracked leather stool. He jerks his chin at the young female bartender and slides his hand over the scratched wooden bar. "Whiskey." His voice is loud, with an undertone of control.

He loves control.

Lives for it.

I glance at him from the corner of my eye and see no beauty in what people have described as a handsome man. His pale skin is smooth, his raven hair clean-cut and combed. Dark eyelashes frame what I know are deep brown irises, and his lips are lush and inviting. Or they would be, if I didn't know he was a few Froot Loops short of a carton.

I scoot forward on my stool to place my drink on the bar, but deliberately miss my target. The glass topples, the liquid racing toward the man's hand.

I lunge for his wrist, pushing it out of the way to save his immaculate suit, and exaggerate my loss of balance. I topple, my shoulder ramming into him, my stool knocking his. "Oh, my gosh. I'm so sorry."

He turns, those strong, destructive hands clutching my upper arms to stabilize me and my seat. "Are you okay?"

"Yeah." I lick my lower lip, quick, panicked, and nod. "I was trying to stop your jacket from getting wet and made an even bigger fool of myself."

"You're not a fool." He releases his grip and rights my martini glass as the bartender mops up the mess. "Let me replace your drink." Dan turns to the woman behind the bar, not waiting for my response. "When you're done, can you get her another martini?"

"Sure. Just give me a few seconds."

I remain still, the screaming euphoria of celebration contained to the inner walls of my mind. My plan is working. The foundation has been laid.

"Thanks." I grin. "That's kind of you."

"Not entirely. There's a catch to my generosity." He shoots me a glance, his lips kicked at one side. "You have to promise to sit with me until you finish your drink." His gaze slithers down my body, curving over my breasts, my hips, then lower, all the way to my exposed calves.

I will my cheeks to blush. I will them and will them, but alas, I'm not that fucking demure. Instead, I lower my gaze and bat my lashes. "Actually, I don't think that's a good idea. I'm…working." I hitch the strap of my small clutch higher on my shoulder. "It's my first night. I was told to always stay near the bar unless I have an offer."

His thoughts practically crackle in my head. He's thinking how easy this is. How perfect. How serendipitous.

You bet it is, buddy.

"Working?" he muses, palming the two drinks the bartender slides toward him.

"Yeah." I nibble my lower lip, exaggerating my vulnerable, virginal escort role. "I bet everyone can see how nervous I am."

I glance around the dilapidated bar. Nobody pays me attention. It's like my favorite drinking hole on the other side of the city—frequented by depressed drunkards too liquored to notice if it's day or night.

"Maybe a tiny bit." He chuckles, and I try not to cringe at his equally fake facade. "Come on." He swings out an arm, his whiskey pointing the way to one of the free booths in the back corner. "It's only one drink. I won't take up too much of your time." He winks. "Unless you want me to."

I continue to devour my bottom lip. It's my go-to move. And from the way he keeps glancing at my mouth, it must be working a charm.

"I guess one drink can't hurt." I scoot from my stool, grasp the martini glass he offers, and saunter myself to our private destination with the predator close at my back.

My skirt hitches higher with every step, the material creeping teasingly closer to my lace panties, until I slide into the booth.

"Get yourself settled." Dan places his whiskey on the table, his free hand twitching at his side. "I need to excuse myself for a moment."

"Okay." I sip from my glass, watching him over the rim as he strides to the restrooms.

He may be heading for the bathroom, but I know his main objective isn't to use the facilities. He needs to calm himself. To lessen the adrenaline spurring him to make snap decisions.

Day to day, he can fool the average Joe. From my time watching him, I've learned he gets careless when close to obtaining a fix. He turns into a stereotypical addict—jittery, breathless, and unable to control the need to rush to the finish line.

I've triggered his game.

There's no turning back.

He wants me. Needs me. He's hungry for my screams, and that's okay, because I'm just as hungry for his.

This man, although vile and psychotic, is actually quite special. He's not just the focus of another one of my retribution projects. He's more. Much more.

This smug piece of shit could be the key I've spent ten years searching for. He could quite possibly be my Holy Grail.

With a lazy glance around the room, I open the tiny baggie stuck to the inside of my blouse cuff and rest my fingers on the rim of his glass. Fine white powder falls over my palm and into the liquor, the Rohypnol dancing through the liquid with such choreographed perfection I can't hold back a smirk.

The sight is beautiful. Peaceful. Karma in motion.

I dust my gloves gently, brushing off the evidence, then bite the olive from my toothpick and give the concoction a stir. In seconds, the betrayal disappears, dissipating into sweet nothingness.

Every inch of me thrums, pulsing and throbbing from the inside out. The enjoyment only increases when the door to the men's bathroom opens and Dan strides forward with a wicked grin.

He thinks he's good, and I've gotta give it to him, when it comes to being a sadistic son-of-a-bitch, he's a real winner. What he doesn't realize is that when revenge is the aim, I'm the motherfucking queen.

Years of experience flow through my veins. Retribution is my specialty.

I discreetly flick away the toothpick and paste on a chaste smile as he reaches the booth.

"Everything okay?" I ask as he hovers at the end of my seat, his forehead beading with sweat, his gaze darting around the room.

"Let's get out of here."

"Leave?" A twinge of panic unfurls in my belly, and I shove it down with a sip of gin. I'm the one in control here. Not him. "I can't. I'm working, and you haven't even started your drink."

He grasps his glass and downs the contents in two large gulps.

Big mistake, Danny. Fucking huge.

I release a girlie laugh, the sound obnoxious to my ears. "You're eager."

"I guess I can't help myself. You're a beautiful woman who's nervous about her first gig. My gentlemanly nature means I'm obliged to ease your burden."

I take another sip, a tiny one to ensure I remain level-headed. "And how will you do that?"

"By being your first customer."

Ding, ding, ding. Jackpot.

"Oh." My response is shy, but no matter how hard I try, I still can't get my cheeks to heat. "I wasn't expecting that."

He reaches out a hand. "Come on. Let's go."

"Wait." I can't leave. Not yet. The drugs need time to start their numbing goodness. "We haven't discussed payment."

He reaches for his back pocket and pulls out a wallet. "Name your price."

"That depends on the service."

He retrieves a stack of bills and places them on the table. "Is this enough for a few hours?"

My lips part as I pretend to be gobsmacked by his generosity. In reality, I'm scrambling to stall. "Yeah." I slide my fingers over the money, drag it toward me, then slip it into my clutch. "That's more than enough."

"Come on, then."

He raises his hand again, and I stare. It's still too soon. Too quick. If I leave now, I'll have to think on my feet to slow down this sequence, and although I'm shit-hot and shiny when it comes to this, I'd prefer not to take unnecessary chances on such a special project.

"Can I finish my drink first?"

His mask of charismatic charm falters with the narrowing of his gaze. "I don't have all night, sweetheart."

"Right." *Fuck you.* "Of course not."

I slide from the booth, ignoring his offered hand, and lead the way outside into the chilly night air. "Maybe I should buy a bottle of something to celebrate." I spin back to face the door, only to be stopped by his large frame sliding in front of me.

"I know you're nervous, but we don't need it." His rush for a fix has risen to fever-pitch. His eyes are glazed, his cheeks flushed.

"It'll only take a second." I sidestep, and he shadows me.

"I've got whatever you need back at my place." He walks forward, and I'm forced to retreat. One step. Two.

I raise my hand, placing it on his chest as I plant my feet. "I'm sorry, I'm going about this all wrong. We haven't even discussed logistics." *Stall, stall, stall.* "I have a room within walking distance. It's small and simple and does the job. I'd just prefer if we had something to break the ice when we get there. Maybe a bottle of wine or some whiskey. I know a lot of body parts that taste better when moistened with liquor."

Those plump lips smile down at me, and I see the expression for the threat it is. "With you, sweetheart, I don't want booze."

He grabs my hand in a tight grip, and it takes all my strength not to knee him in the groin like my intuition demands.

"Now, come on." He tugs me along the footpath, toward the parking lot. "My car is down here."

"We don't need to drive. My hotel is literally at the end of the block. It's an easy walk."

"I'm not interested in walking." He tries to charm me with a playboy sparkle in his eyes. "And my place is warm and clean. Not some seedy hotel on the wrong side of town."

If I get in his car, we won't make it to his Lake Oswego home. I'll be driven to an isolated industrial area where he'll try to beat me, rape me, then leave me battered and barely breathing on the side of the road.

No, thank you, Danny boy.

"I appreciate the offer, but I insist on my hotel." I pull my hand away. "Neutral ground, ya know?"

His nostrils flare, and I wonder if he'll drop this bullshit act and drag me, hair first, to his getaway car.

"It's decent accommodation," I exaggerate with a flash of my pearly whites. "You'll like it."

"It's the car or nothing."

My chest tightens. Fear and anxiety collide in a mass of tangled emotions. I can't throw away my one and only shot at this.

At *him*.

But I can't get in that car either. Not now. Not even with the looming promise of his Rohypnol-induced impairment.

Confinement in a small space would mean my fun would end and his would begin. I'd lose my advantage and he'd gain the upper hand. His strength against my strategy.

I have to stick to my plan or let him walk.

God, I don't want to let this fucker walk.

"Then I guess this is where we part ways." My face falls, and I don't need to fake a stricken expression. I'm on the verge of heartbreak, devastated at the thought of this guy getting away, not only with what he's done, but with the information I desperately need. "See ya, handsome."

I give him a timid finger wave and the chance to demand a refund before I turn in the direction of my hotel. I take slow steps, and his pursuing footfalls don't hit my ears. He's not following. I guess he's too frustrated to even ask for his cash.

Shit.

Four weeks of meticulous preparation disintegrate into painful splinters, each one penetrating my skin to exacerbate the failure.

This guy deserved what I had planned. He'd earned it over months, possibly years, of brutality. But losing the connection to my past tears me apart, limb by limb, nerve by nerve.

Anger boils my blood, the potency so rich my throat tightens with the need to scream. I can't turn back.

I *can't*.

Getting in his car is too dangerous. The drugs might not kick in for another twenty minutes. Maybe more. He'd easily overpower me. I'm not stupid enough to believe my years of self-defense, martial arts, and boxing classes could save my ass in a confined space, up against a deranged psychopath.

The knife in my boot is insurance, but I'm not infallible.

I grind my teeth to the point of pain as I trudge the eight-minute walk to the sleazy, pay-by-the-hour hotel, with its flickering red 'Vacancy' sign.

What the hell am I going to do?

I may never get another chance to find Jacob. I've failed. Again. And not only on a personal level, but all those women Dan has abused won't get a vicarious taste of vengeance.

How have I messed this up?

Was the meticulous preparation not enough?

Should I have watched him for longer?

Could I have tried harder?

Risked more?

Fuck.

I pull the hotel key from my clutch and stride to door fifteen—the last room in the single-story complex. I slide my key into the flimsy lock, preparing to lick my wounds in private, when the noisy crunch of asphalt alerts me to a vehicle entering the parking lot. My heart kicks. A sixth sense sends goosebumps erupting along my arms. Or maybe it's optimism.

I want this.

I want it enough that each breath hitches in my throat.

I glance over my shoulder, my limbs throbbing, and come face to face with the impeccable good fortune that stares back at me.

2

HER

I paste a surprised look on my face, placing my mental celebration on hold.

Dan cuts the engine, slides from the car, then slams the door shut.

"You changed your mind?" I ask.

"Yeah." He stalks toward me, his smile stiff. "I did."

I unlock the hotel door and push it wide, allowing him to proceed. "After you."

He doesn't respond as he strides inside, not bothering to scope his surroundings. This smug piece of shit thinks he's invincible, and I can't wait to prove him wrong.

He slumps onto the well-worn bed, the cheap springs squeaking with his heavy weight. A frown spreads across his forehead as he stares blankly at the tiny kitchenette in front of him.

Could my buddy Rohypnol have given him a friendly nudge of disorientation?

"You okay?" I purr, closing the door to the world.

"Yeah." He clears his throat. "You got a glass of water or something?"

"Sure." I saunter to the sink, and the hair on my neck tingles as my back faces him.

Limit vulnerabilities.

Stay alert.

He pushes to his feet while I begin filling a cloudy glass with tap water. Every inch of me is tense, ready to attack, but I continue the monotonous actions, turning the tap off slowly and drying my hands on a dirty dish rag.

I swing around. He paces near the door. Like a caged dog, he wants out, but there is no *out*. Not until I have what I want.

"Here." I hand over the drink and point to the sturdy wooden chair strategically placed between the bed and the stained sofa. "Have a seat and I'll make you feel comfortable."

He takes large gulps of the water, the deep grooves of his frown still intact when he hands back the empty glass. "No." He shakes his head in a mix of confusion and agitation. "Let's go. I'll take you somewhere better than this."

"We have all we need right here." I grab his wrist and lead him forward, guiding him to sit in the hot seat. "I've been practicing something for a while, and I really want to see what you think. Call it an added bonus, if you like."

I place the glass on the unsteady bedside table and slide my hand under the pillow on the bed. He watches as I produce a handful of thick, red ribbon. I sway my hips to imaginary music on my return and let the long lengths of material fall to the floor, dragging behind me.

"This room is a dump," he mutters. "We need to go to my place." He grips the armrests, preparing to stand.

"Don't." I lean over and get in his face. "It will be fun to have sex in here. It adds to the fantasy." I inch closer, his stale breath brushing my lips. "I'm the weak woman in distress, and you're the wealthy, charming man here to save me. But every fantasy has to be earned. Let me earn this. After that, I'll go wherever you want."

His jaw tightens. His features harden. "You've got five minutes."

"I can work with that." It isn't a lie. Once he's tied, his ability to negotiate is over. The game is won. All that's left is the celebration.

I hold his right wrist to the armrest and begin binding it to the wood with my ribbons.

"What the fuck are you doing?" He lashes out, gripping a fistful of my hair—my wig.

I gasp, feigning fear when the reality is anger shooting through my body. "It's a part of the show," I plead. "I just—"

A rustle of noise sounds from the back of the room. In the bathroom. *No*, it must be right outside the window, in the alley. My escape route.

The potential for someone to overhear freezes my blood. It seems to have the same effect on Dan because he releases my hair and scowls at me.

"Hurry up and do your thing." A slur mars his words. "Then we leave."

I nod, quick and sharp, ever the eager escort, and continue binding one wrist to the armrest, then the other. Next, I kneel between his spread legs, sliding my palm over his crotch as I lower. There's no hardened cock behind that zipper, no erection, no arousal. Not surprising. He won't get turned on again until he's in control. Not until he's inflicting pain.

I bat my fake lashes at him and tie his ankles to the chair legs, tightening the last knot against his leg with all my strength.

"*Jesus.*" He tries to kick me and fails under the restriction. "Stupid bitch. That fucking hurt."

I cluck my tongue, stand, and leisurely walk to the bathroom to close the door on anyone in the alley who may plan to snoop on my pleasure. "You're really showing your true colors now, Danny boy."

His face slackens.

I let the situation sink in—my familiarity, his vulnerability.

Warring emotions spread across his face, from confusion to annoyance, then more confusion. "Who are you?"

I shrug and stroll back to stand before him. "Consider me a business partner. We're going to work together tonight."

"Is that right?" His narrowed gaze holds mine as he tugs at his wrist bindings. "Well, I'm more than happy to help a pretty lady. But you might want to untie me. We can't work together if I'm stuck like this."

"You'll do just fine where you are." I move to the bed and drop to a knee to retrieve the folder I stashed under the ensemble. "It's very easy, actually. All I need are a few answers to some really simple questions."

"*Ha.*" He grins. "If you're after information, I'll tell you what I've told everyone else. You're not getting anything until I get paid."

"I'm sorry, but that deal isn't going to work for me. I'll have to convince you to try this my way." It's my turn to smile, the curve of my lips gentle with the slightest hint of cocky menace.

"And what's stopping me from yelling for help?"

"I think the most influential answer is my ability to cut your dick off and dive out the back window before anyone finds the room key."

He snarls.

"There are many more reasons," I continue. "Like, what will Daddy think when another escort makes claims of sexual assault? I don't think the senator will appreciate an additional scandal where you're concerned."

"You fucking cunt."

I chuckle. If only he knew.

"Now, as I was saying. It's very simple." I slide out an image hidden inside the folder and hold it up. "This guy," I point to the man standing beside Dan in the candid photo, "I need to find out where he is."

He doesn't glance at the image, doesn't even acknowledge it. "Sorry. I can't help you."

I inhale slowly and smile. "You sure?"

"Yep."

I nod, shrug, then slam my elbow against his cheek.

His head jolts to the side. His shouted curse fills the room.

"How 'bout now, Dan?"

"You're going to die." He bucks in the chair. "I'll fucking kill you with my bare hands."

I lunge, grasping his throat in a tight grip as I glare. "Let's get one thing straight. You might think you're tough as nails because you hurt defenseless women, but I spend my days fucking up ruthless men. I will cut you. Flay you. I'll slice you open and wear your intestines like a fucking necklace to your own funeral unless I get what I want."

I release my hold and step back.

We're both panting, our chests heaving. Dan glares from under his lashes, his lids heavy. "Something is wrong. I feel like I'm going to pass out."

"That would be the Rohypnol I gave you back at the bar. It's only going to get worse."

His eyes widen.

"It also means we're on a tight schedule. So, tell me." I raise the photo and wait until his attention strays to the image. "The guy standing beside you, where can I find him?"

He squints, his fingers gripping into the chair. "Like I said, I don't know him."

"Danny, Danny, Danny." I cluck my tongue as I return to the bed. I slide my hand under the pillow and pull out a knuckle duster. He watches my return with narrowed eyes as I slide the shiny metal down my glove-covered fingers, then cock my fist.

"Wait," he snarls. "That photo was taken two years ago."

"Where?"

"I don't know. It was a rented property. Some mansion on the outskirts."

"The outskirts of Portland?" My words flow in an excited rush. "Here?"

"Yeah. Here."

"And you spoke to this guy? What were you doing with him? Have you seen him since? And who rented the property?" I fire questions, hoping to maintain the momentum.

He shakes his head, his brows furrowed. "It was a party. A celebration. I only went to pick up a package."

"What sort of package?"

His chin lifts. "Laundry," he grates.

AKA drugs? What a naughty, naughty senator's son.

"And this guy" I tap the man standing next to him in the photo, "is that who you got the package from?"

He jolts his wrists. "Yes. *Christ*. Who the fuck are you? You're getting yourself messed up in some pretty heavy shit, sweetheart."

"Why don't you let me worry about that." I only need the briefest grasp of information. That's all it will take to make another connection. Another lead. "Do you know his name?"

"I can't remember."

Liar.

"Think, Danny." I drop the photo and lean forward to grip his junk. "Think hard."

He winces, but the severity of my hold isn't evident in his features. The drugs must be providing a numbing effect.

I squeeze tighter and twist, achieving a grunt.

"Zander. Zeke. Zack. *Fuck*. I can't remember. Last name was Vaughn."

"Are you sure?" I point to the photo. "You're telling me this guy goes by the name Vaughn?"

"Yeah," he grates. "That's exactly what I'm saying, bitch."

My heart pounds, the inspired reverberations ebbing all the way into my stomach. I can work with a name. That's all I need to inch another step closer to Jacob.

I release his dick. "If you're lying to me…"

His head lolls back. "Too fucking tired to lie."

"Okay. Good." Tingling optimism makes me believe him.

"Are you going to let me go now?" His blinks are slow. Sluggish.

I'm running out of time. "We're just getting started."

He scoffs, opens his mouth, and yells, "*Help.*"

Jesus. I slam the heel of my palm into his nose, cutting off the call, then lunge for the bed. In seconds, I've retrieved the gag from under the pillow and have it pressed to his mouth.

His head thrashes, and he yells through clenched lips as I increase the pressure, banging and smacking the hard ball gag until he relents and opens for me with a growl.

"Good boy." I tighten the strap behind his head, then come back to stand in front of him, admiring my handiwork. "Revenge is such a pretty picture."

He's yelling, mumbling, whimpering behind the gag. Rage glares back at me, but it's a wavering emotion. A sleepy anger that dissipates. He no longer tests his bonds, the mind-numbing drugs making the situation more acceptable.

That won't last long.

"Now that we have the photo out of the way, I want you to know I've been watching you for quite some time." I hope to reignite his fear or maybe a bit of panic. Instead, he looks straight through me. "You enjoy hurting women, don't you?"

He releases a half-hearted chuckle, his eyes twinkling the slightest bit.

"Beating them. Raping them." I grab his hair and yank. "You prey on those weaker than you."

His eyes brighten in bliss. In memory. He's reliving what he's done in that twisted mind of his. Even with his life at my mercy, he's enjoying his accomplishments. But then his eyes close.

Oh, no, he isn't going to take a nap on my watch. It's time to fast-forward the festivities.

"Hey." I slap him. "You've gotta stay awake for this." I'm hell-bent on retribution, but I'm not going to beat the unconscious.

He mumbles, over and over, the same cadence, the same indecipherable syllables. I'm curious enough to lower the gag and give him a chance to confess his sins.

"What's your name, bitch?" he slurs, his eyes still closed. "I want to know what to whisper in your ear when I'm raping you raw."

"Oh, honey." I reposition the knuckle dusters, pressing them lower on my fingers. "Threats don't work well with me."

"You touch me again and I kill everyone you love."

"I wish you the best of luck."

His eyes open, but he's not there. Not really. I doubt he'll remember any of this tomorrow. He'll only have the physical pain to taunt his unclear memory.

I run the cold metal on my hand along his jaw. "Maybe I should cut out your tongue to stop your sweet-talkin' ways?"

He spits at me, the projectile not making the distance. "You're dead."

"Not yet. So, while we're both alive and kicking, I'm going to give you a refresher on the lives you've ruined." I shove the gag back in place and clench my fist. "Cassidy Trelore, twenty-six, broken ribs, broken jaw."

I cock my arm, my limbs heating with approaching euphoria. Then I swing, launching my fist into his ribs. A muffled grunt is my reward.

"Melissa Taylor, twenty-eight, swollen lip, two black eyes, and eight facial fractures." This punch I aim at the middle of his face, cracking cartilage and distorting his nose.

He yells.

Everything inside me tingles in celebration while rivulets of scarlet blood seep from his nostrils toward his mouth.

I continue, naming the women he's assaulted, along with his long list of offences. Each time I land a blow harder than the last, until his face is a masterpiece of reds, maroons, and puffy, swollen skin.

Bree Foster. Carla Kane. Zoey Day. Amanda Scupin.

"Do you like feeling vulnerable, Dan?" I stand in front of him, cupping his clean-shaven cheek in my palm while I run the steel down the other. "Do you like knowing I'm hurting you, the same way you hurt those women?"

His eyes roll, and my stomach swells with disappointment. He's tapping out. Already. Weak fucker.

Then again, I did give him a healthy dose of powdered goodness.

"That's the downside of the drugs." I sigh. "That, and the unlikelihood you'll remember this tomorrow. But I want you to try, Danny boy. I want you to try real hard. Can you do that for me?"

His head slumps forward, a barely conscious affirmation.

I lean in, place my lips near his ear, and close my eyes as I breathe victory deep into my lungs. "Good, because I never want you to forget the night karma finally caught up with you."

3

HER

I leave Dan tied to the chair, drool seeping from around the gag while he slumps forward in unconsciousness. Every inch of me that was numb and emotionless the day before is thrumming with the enthusiasm of a cheerleader at a pep rally.

The buzz spurs me on as I slip through the bathroom window with a pack of my belongings strapped on my back, and strut my cheap fuck-me heels as far as they will take me.

My journey home lasts longer than my magical moments with Dan. I walk a lot of miles, catch two different cabs, and slink down numerous dark alleys to dispose of every item of my costume in a different location.

By the time I reach the bar across the street from my apartment, I'm dressed in my favorite pair of denim jeans, a tight, long-sleeve, plunging top, and my strappy stiletto heels.

The lack of warm clothing isn't appropriate for the January chill, but that's what adrenaline is for. Right? That, and the promise of a stiff drink once I get inside.

I open the door to Atomic Buzz—a drinking hole with nowhere near the edginess or allure of its name—and Brent, the owner, grins at me.

"You're lucky, Steph. I was thinking about closing early."

I glance around, my attention skating over the two elderly guys playing poker near the front window, then around the soulless room to the couple whispering sweet nothings at a table in the far corner.

"And ruin the atomic buzz you've got going?" I ruffle the long blonde strands of my hair, trying to work out the stiffness left from the nasty wig. "It looks like you've doubled your clientele since I was here last."

"Almost." He snickers. "What are you drinking tonight?"

I throw my pack to the floor and slide onto a swiveling seat, resting my hands on the sticky wood of the bar. "Whiskey, neat. Thanks."

Brent raises his brows as he reaches for Johnny Walker, then slides me a filled glass.

Yeah, I know, it's a sick-fuck move picking Dan Roberts' drink of choice, but I'm in a sick-fuck kind of mood.

"I'm celebrating a job well done," I clarify.

"What job was it this time?" He eyes me with interest, as if he's actually invested in my life. Nobody else looks at me like that. No one has in years. I make sure of it.

"The professor had us researching the growing number of assault and rape cases tied to solicitation."

I sometimes wish I could tell him the truth—that I don't work as a research assistant for a college professor who specializes in violent crimes. Having one person in this world to confide in could be a game changer. But trust issues are one of my many colorful traits.

"Which means we're on to a new project by the end of the week." I raise my glass in a silent toast, then take a sip.

"Well, congratulations on having finished studying that fucked up shit." He gives me a grim smile. "You know, my sugar daddy offer still stands whenever you want to quit that horrible job and let me take care of you."

I laugh. "Brent, you've only mastered the daddy part. When you get the sugar, let me know."

The door to the bar opens, and we glance to the guy making his way toward us. His face is turned as he scopes the room, but the black jeans and matching leather jacket tell me he's got enough self-respect not to be seen in a place like this.

"Think he's lost?" Brent asks.

"Without a doubt." I return to my drink, cupping it in both hands. "I'll bet you five bucks he asks for directions out of this hellhole."

"You have such little faith in my fine establishment."

I sip casually, enjoying my salute to Danny boy as the newcomer sits two chairs away, teasing my peripheral vision.

"What can I get you?"

"A Corona." His voice is low and subtle, barely a whisper of response, yet masculine enough for me to appreciate.

"Comin' right up." Brent shoots me a look as he grabs a bottle from the fridge beneath the counter, his eyes wide in exaggerated surprise before he returns his focus to the new guy. "You a local?"

"No."

"What brings you here?"

There's a huff, a pause, then a muttered, "Life."

Brent twists the cap on the bottle, hands it over, and returns to his leaning post against the back counter. "Steph, look at me."

I frown, because I'm already looking at him.

"This guy is perfect for you. He's quiet and unresponsive, just how you like 'em."

I chuckle, roll my eyes, and raise my empty glass. "You need to spend less time focused on my sex life, and more on pouring drinks."

I chance a glance at my anti-social neighbor and take in his profile. His lips are tight. His jaw, too. There's a wealth of hostility vibrating from him. Even the dark stubble hugging his cheeks has a rough fuck-off vibe as wisps of hair shadow his eyes.

"Where you stayin'?" Brent asks, ignoring the tension.

"Do you always ask this many questions?" the guy drawls, the words smoothly gliding over his tongue to polish his annoyance.

"Yes," I answer. "He does."

Brent laughs. "This pretty little thing," he jerks his head at me, "came in years ago with the same aversion to conversation. Took me eight months to get a name out of her."

A name that isn't even mine.

I ignore the guilt and swivel my chair to face Mr. Reluctant. "You're better off spilling your guts. Just blurt it out. Divulge it all. It'll save the monotony of repeating all those monosyllabic answers."

He glances my way, dissolving my guilt with eyes so clear and hazel I'm caught off guard.

Whoa. Profile view was confronting. Front view? Equally so, with an added hint of panty-melting gorgeous.

Those lips are full and dark. His stare is fierce. The tense features make me want to lick his face, or slap it, just to see how he'd react.

"You know what?" Brent grasps the whiskey bottle and pours me another drink. "You two are perfect for each other. Silent, secretive, and socially awkward."

I hold in a snort and incline my head. "He's right. He just nailed my Tinder bio." Not that I use Tinder—I can get my kicks on my own, thank you very much—but I know at the very least Brent will get a chuckle from my sass.

What I don't expect is the slight tilt to the stranger's lips. The tiniest lift revealing a dimple in his left cheek. It's devious, devilish, and undeniably delicious on such a rough and intense face.

"He's not going to give up, is he?" he asks.

I shake my head. "Not if you plan on staying here."

His focus doesn't waver. "Then maybe you could lead the way to another bar that doesn't pester clientele."

I'm not usually caught off guard, but this man has claimed that response from me twice in less than a few minutes.

"Hey, now." Brent raises his voice. "I'm just being welcom—"

"I'm fucking with you." Hazel eyes hold mine as this stranger gifts me with the slightest hint of a grin.

I stare for longer than I should, trying to come to terms with all the conflicting aspects of the sight before me. There's something different about him. Something intriguing. Then again, I'm still high on adrenaline, which makes all my responses unreliable.

"So…" Brent clears his throat, breaking my train of thought. "In answer to my question…"

The stranger reverts to his scowl, a blatant sign he's annoyed at being dragged back into the game of Twenty Questions. "My sister got knocked up by a lowlife with a heavy hand. He ended up leaving her as soon as my nephew was born. To help her out, I quit my job, packed my things, and drove here."

"That's…" I want to say unbelievable, because it is. Men like him don't exist. They aren't real. Not in my world. "…admirable."

He shrugs and palms his beer, taking a long pull. "She doesn't know yet. I only got into town tonight."

"Well, I hope you find the lowlife piece-of-shit and give him a dose of his own medicine." I don't realize what I've said until the words are out there, announcing my hunger for vengeance.

He narrows his gaze, looking at me with such intensity I feel his questions sink inside my chest to tinker with my pulse.

"I'm not the violent type," he murmurs.

My heart flutters.

Clearly, I'm not used to men who don't think with their fists. My world revolves around violence. My past, my present, and my future all mesh into nothing but bloodshed and suffering.

This man is a breath of fresh, crisp air against my tarnished lungs. If I had any hopes for my life, any maternal or romantic plans, I might have been tempted to sink my hook and reel him in.

Here fishy, fishy.

I grasp my whiskey and fight not to guzzle it down. "How old is your nephew?"

"Eight weeks."

There's no pause. Not even a slight frown as he recalls the timeline. This guy is fully invested in his family, and I'm a smidge jealous. I used to be surrounded by people like him. Good people. Loving people. But they never looked this severe or harsh. I can feel him scrutinizing me, studying me, just like I was doing with him.

"See what I've done here?" Brent interrupts. "My pestering has started a conversation. If it wasn't for me, you two would be sitting in silence."

"Silence is good." The stranger swirls his beer with a lazy flick of his wrist. "Silence is comfortable."

"Silence is honest," I add, gaining another fierce stare.

He inclines his head.

Again, my gaze is glued to his. I can't help it. There's something about him that demands attention. Something dark, like I'm used to, and also something promising, which is entirely new to me. I suddenly feel like I want to climb his broad chest and ride his face for hours.

Not a good idea.

I turn back to the bar and ignore my nagging libido as the chatter continues without me. Brent returns to his questioning antics while the stranger resumes his monosyllabic answers.

Their conversation washes over me, sweeping away the brutal parts of the night to replace them with something basic and easy. Something suburban and casual. I concentrate, trying to learn more about him, but my adrenaline-filled brain is darting, looking for a hook to clasp onto.

Unfortunately, it snags onto my attraction. The sexiness.

My heart pounds harder with each muttered word. The minutes tick by with building lust. I glance to the large hands encasing his beer, the thick fingers, the tanned skin.

Hands are my downfall. My Achilles' heel. I can picture his grip around my throat. Clasping my flesh. Burying deep. A shudder slips through me.

Damn it.

I'm due to get laid. That's all. What is the cobweb tally at now? Two months? Three? And my last conquest ended up being more of an unwilling victim. He hadn't realized I was leading him into a sexual research situation and did a runner when I donned my newly purchased dominatrix attire.

But a woman's gotta try these things. I'm inquisitive by nature. Stepping outside the box is what I do. It's how I learn, and grow…and realize my error of spending five hundred dollars on black leather items, including a high-neck bralette and matching web garter.

"How about you, Steph?"

"Hmm?" I blink up at Brent and take another sip of alcoholic goodness. "What did I miss?"

"Laboring work. Do you know of any construction sites in this area?"

Construction? Laboring? Of course this broad temptation has a body built for sin under his jacket.

"Sorry." I shake my head and keep my gaze straight ahead. *Sip, sip, sip.* "Maybe a temp agency could help."

Brent leans into my line of sight, his lips lifting in a knowing smile. "What's wrong?"

I raise my glass. "I'm almost out of liquor."

It's no secret I like to get my sexy on, and my lovely bartender buddy probably thinks I'm too scared to get freaky with this Hulk-like Adonis.

That isn't the case.

Tonight is for celebration, and I don't feel like a sexual rejection to tarnish the memory. The insults from my last escapade are still raw.

That's a whole lot of spandex, sugar.

It wasn't spandex, asshole. It was expensive, supple matte black leather with gunmetal buckles.

Brent fakes a yawn as he refills my glass. "I think I might call last drinks."

I glare, and his eyes beam back at me, taunting—*matchmaker, matchmaker, make me a match.*

Does he think I'm too timid to sleep with this guy? Really? My sexual appetite is more likely to indicate I'll swallow the sexy stranger whole.

"Yeah," my drinking partner agrees. "I guess I better make a move."

I glance at him, and he's right there staring back at me, strumming my pussy with his caged emotions.

"Do you want to get out of here?" he asks, passive as fuck.

The question not only surprises me, it lassos my womb and squeezes tight. I'm flustered, which is out of character, and I'm also aroused, which isn't all that surprising.

"Yes." I throw back the last of my drink and stand. "But I'm leaving on my own."

Apparently, the mix of adrenaline and whiskey has made me reckless. I'm a panty slip away from taking this guy home. This devilishly sexy man with his shadowy intrigue and penetrating eyes. My heart palpitates. My sternum itches. I want to drag him to my apartment by his dick. I would strip him. Devour him.

Not tonight, Satan. Not tonight.

I need to focus. Regroup. I have a lead to chase tomorrow, and I don't want anything else stealing my attention.

I pull my pack from the floor and scrounge for my purse, only to have the stranger shake his head.

"I've got it." He reaches inside his jacket, pulls out a money clip, and slides a stack of bills across the bar. "This should be enough for both of us."

It is.

More than enough.

I don't know how to respond. I'm uncomfortable with being indebted. I'm also charmed by his generosity. "Thank you."

He grasps his drink, not paying me attention as he raises the bottle. "Don't mention it."

It isn't a gentlemanly request. It's a statement. A demand that I ignore his kindness. It's entirely gruff and anti-social. It's how I usually act—my MO outside of this bar and away from the one man I speak to. It's so familiar I can't help smiling.

This man is me.

"Well..." I beat my desire back with a studded bat. "It was nice meeting you."

He scans me with a quick appreciative stare, from eyes to heels and back again. "I assure you, the pleasure was all mine." There's no inflection in his tone, no excitement, and definitely none of this pleasure he speaks of. But I believe him anyway.

I tingle in places that aren't usually susceptible to flattery. I crave more of his scrutiny. I want all of his attention.

Shit.

I clear my throat to break the trance and sling my pack over one shoulder. "I'll catch you later, Brent."

I don't glance in the bartender's direction. I focus on the door, my head high, and eat up the space between me and necessary fresh air. I fight temptation like a pro, striding my seductive heels toward my escape, until I hear the squeak of a bar seat.

"I'm out of here, too."

That voice slays me. The lethargy. The masculinity.

I pause and glance over my shoulder to see my fantasy approaching, the slightest tweak to his mouth a threat and a taunt, all in one. I should run. Fast. But all the cautionary thoughts are being smothered by the heavy weight of attraction.

There's a hum.

A zing.

It slides down my spine, tightens my nipples, and contracts my pussy in the most delicious squeeze. I'm already convinced this guy could make me come like a runaway freight train, leaving me devastated and deliciously broken.

I want that pleasure. I want the pain, too.

He raises a cocky brow. "You waiting for me, princess?"

Princess? "Seems more like you're following."

"Maybe." He shrugs. "Is that a problem?"

There is much more to his question than the issue of him tailing me. It's about vulnerability. Susceptibility. Deliciously dreamy carnality.

And yes, it's a major problem. Huge. My normally infallible caution is wavering like a leaf in a hurricane. But I can't voice a protest. The words aren't there. Not the right ones. Only those that will be so very, very wrong. "I guess that depends on what you want to achieve."

Thoughts dance behind those lazy eyes, and I want to know them all. I itch to hear his secrets. His darkest desires. I need to know his plans for me, and I want the explanation to come in erotic Technicolor.

"I want everything." His voice is low—pure sex and seduction.

My pussy twists in knots. There's no denying the inevitable. I'm going to succumb. This zing is too vibrant to ignore. I can already taste him on my tongue. The alcohol. The sweat.

I sigh, resigned to my fate. "Then, no, I guess it's no problem at all."

4

HER

I lead the way across the room, the stranger an inch behind me. When I press my palm against the cold glass of the door, apprehension sinks its teeth deep into my flesh.

I pause, suck in a breath, and attempt to tune out my lust in an effort to listen to my instincts. This is the second time I've led a stranger from a seedy bar with the promise of sex, all in the space of a few hours.

The first didn't work well for Danny boy, and although I crept from that hotel room with a crazy-bitch smile on my face, I need to make sure I don't end up being the victim in this scenario.

"Problem?" The question is murmured with slight humor near my ear. "Don't tell me you've changed your mind already."

I glance over my shoulder and his face is a breath away. He's a mountain of a man up close. Thick and strong in the shoulders, with a heavy hand that lands beside mine on the door.

"Do I look like the type of woman who makes mistakes?" It's not a flirty tease. He needs to know I own my shit. All day. Every day.

He ponders the question, or maybe just me in general, and rakes his teeth over his lower lip. He gives an almost imperceptible shake of his head. "No. But there's always a first, and I have a feeling I'm going to be a special kind of mistake."

He's a cocky son-of-a-bitch, and damn, his confidence has latched onto my ovaries, and I don't want it to let go until we are both double-digits deep in orgasms.

"Promises, promises." I push the door and walk ahead, not stopping until we reach the edge of the sidewalk. "I live over there." I jerk my chin toward the looming apartment building across the street with the solitary streetlight that illuminates years of neglect. The old, block construction isn't inviting in the slightest. It's cheap and nasty. Just the way I like it.

All the obvious downfalls are the reasons I consider myself lucky to live there. Nobody inside the dark and dirty walls has enough time or money to bother snooping on their neighbors. Most are too busy keeping their own heads above water with day-to-day life. I come and go without notice, not having made any friends in the years I've rented the studio apartment.

"Lead the way."

A firm hand lands on the low of my back, beneath my pack, the touch warm against the thin cotton of my top. I straighten, stiffen, and suck in a deep breath at the tumbles taking over my stomach.

I wait for a passing car, then step onto the asphalt, bringing us closer and closer to approaching bliss. He's glancing around, scoping the area as I enter the pin code into the building's outdated security panel. The one-two-three-four access code is a poor excuse for protection, but in this crime-riddled area it's the thought that counts, right?

I'm only glad the lobby doesn't smell like urine and stale beer today. It means I can pretend this cheap-ass building has a modicum of decency, when clearly, everyone who lives here knows better.

Another few feet of tense silence and we're at the rickety death trap of an elevator. I shove my finger against the call button, and the doors jolt open. He follows, moving to the opposite side of the small space as I lean against the wall, my arms spread against the thin waist-high railing.

He mimics me, arms spread, ankles crossed, and watches while I press the button to floor three. Neither one of us moves, or talks. He barely bats an eye until those doors close. Then he pushes from the wall and eats the space between us in two predatory steps.

I hold my breath, my tingles turning into wildfire as he walks into me. Not up to me. *Into me.*

His hips bump mine. He parts my legs with an aggressive shove of his knee. The silence and staring continue, no words, only actions as he wraps a menacing hand around the back of my neck and grips tight.

Fear jolts through my chest, making me immobile. He's animalistic, not an ounce of warmth in his expression.

I don't know this man. Not his name, not his age, not his hobbies or life goals. He's a complete stranger who has me pinned inside an enclosed space, his strong, calloused hands holding me hostage.

"You look nervous," he growls close to my lips.

I should back out, cut and run from this careless idea. But my heart loses the panicked beat and produces something more adrenaline-based.

I want him. I *need* him. To make the sterile parts of tonight that hover on the edge of my awareness a little less harsh. To make life exciting for all the right reasons instead of those that are wrong.

I lean closer, taunting him with a look I hope is equally as devilish as his own. "You're the one who should be nervous."

His chuckle is barely audible. "It's not my style."

"Mine either."

His fingers clench tighter, as if he's daring me to back out. I won't. Other women might be inclined to run. I still want to ride him and tame the wild beast barely contained in those eyes.

The elevator bounces to a stop and the doors open. He backs away, and I ignore the chill seeping into me as I lead the way onto the threadbare hall carpet.

My door is at the end, the very last room on the left. I sling the pack off my shoulder and pull my keys from the internal Velcro compartment, ignoring any curiosity he might have as I start working on my door.

I have three locks, the last a pin-code-operated deadbolt that is more high-tech than the entire building's security. There's also the small motion-activated camera beaming down at us from above the doorframe.

"Have a problem with break-ins?" he asks.

I cover the keypad, tap in the code—six, five, three, nine—and shove the door wide. "Nope. Not a one."

I'm smart and pre-emptive when it comes to protection. This stranger at my back is a risk, but my blade is hidden in a strap below my breasts, mace is in my pack, and there's a myriad of hidden weapons at my disposal inside this apartment.

I flick on the light, illuminating my studio space that is practically in a different dimension from the rest of the building. The paintings on the walls are huge masterpieces. The kitchen is filled with shiny new appliances. The floor is the finest polished wood.

I've got family money. A whole heap of it. So, I live in comfort. I just choose to do it in a shitty building. I've learned it is easier to blend into the rat race than the wealthy elite.

But I don't get any of those reactions from him. I can't hear his shock, or sense his surprise. Instead, his heavy footfalls approach, his large body pressing into mine, pushing me into the back of the sofa.

A rough hand shoves into my hair, pulling my head to the side, his mouth moving to my neck. "What's a woman like you doing in a building like this, princess?" His voice vibrates along my carotid, killing me slowly.

The endearment is a special gift of misguided appraisal.

He thinks I'm a princess. How cute. Or maybe he's being sarcastic. If so, he gets a gold star.

He sucks on my skin, and I moan. I'm completely unfamiliar with the acute vibrations taking over my insides. So unfamiliar I don't want to speak for fear my voice might make it vanish.

"Who are you?" he murmurs.

I shake my head and nuzzle my ass against his crotch. He's hard and thick, his erection an adamant force behind his zipper.

I swing around, needing those lips on mine.

He sates me immediately, taking my mouth with a harshness I don't anticipate. I'm used to soft kisses. Kind and timid. This is profoundly better. A fierce, punishing collision of lips and teeth and tongues.

His hands find my hips and he grinds into me, teasing me with anticipation. "Who are you, Steph?" He holds my gaze, those eyes as questioning as his words.

"I'm a memory you're going to treasure forever." I grip his shirt and pull him forward, demanding more of his mouth.

I can't get enough. Maybe it's the way he scares me the slightest bit. The ferocity. The confidence. Or maybe it's narcissistic, because his harshness kind of reminds me of myself. Either way, I'm scrambling for more.

I want. I want. I want.

I glide my hands under his shirt and place my palms on the warmth of his stomach. Another moan escapes me. The ripples of his muscles are like an ocean under my fingers, moving and changing as his hands slide down my back and squeeze my ass.

He's so fucking strong, and I want that strength coiled around me, controlling me. I crave his temporary ownership. Instead of always being the one in command, in charge and under pressure, I want to be owned. To be a puppet instead of a puppeteer.

I claw at those muscles, working my way up his stomach and down his ribs. His masterful lips continue to overwhelm me, his tongue increasing its pace and severity.

My panties are wet, soaked, and my pussy clenches, demanding to be filled. I push my hands farther, learning more of him as I glide them around his back.

I'm about to release another moan at all the overwhelming perfection when my fingertips brush a hard object protruding from the waistband of his jeans.

He stiffens. I do the same.

He tries to recover by continuing the kiss, and I pull away, my fingers still touching the object that is undoubtedly a gun.

I wait for a response to all the questions going through my head, but he gives me nothing. No explanation. No apology. Only the lazy bat of his lashes over steely, lust-glazed eyes.

I inch closer and wrap my hand around the grip. He responds with the raise of his chin and the slightest narrowing of his gaze.

"Why does a non-violent man need a gun?"

"It's a bad neighborhood."

I incline my head, my heart beating rapidly in a mix of fear and arousal. I want to believe him—really, I do—but a lack of ignorance makes it impossible.

I weave my free hand around to sit on his chest, then shove him back while pulling the weapon from his waistband.

He goes with the flow, gifting me with a few retreating steps when we both know he could've tried to hardball his way out of the situation.

"A Walther P22? Nice." It's a serious gun. A seriously scary gun for someone who claims to avoid violence.

I eject the clip, shove it in my pocket, then pull back the slider. "Oh." I release a sardonic chuckle. "And a live one in the chamber. Aren't you a wealth of surprises?"

I guess it could be worse. The clip could be half empty.

He grins, but there's no humor in the expression. "And you sure know your way around a gun."

I shrug and lob the lone bullet his way. "Like you said, it's a bad neighborhood."

He catches the round without breaking my gaze, then again when I throw him the clip.

"Leave."

"You're kicking me out?" He scowls.

"You bet your perfectly sculpted ass I am." He's more like me than I realized—confident around guns, proficient in lies. I can no longer ignore the warning signs that highlight a dangerous man.

His jaw ticks, and those dazzling eyes are back in predator mode.

"Unless you want to play How Many Weapons Does She Have Stashed Within Arm's Reach." I grin. "That really is a fun game."

"Fine." He holds out a hand. "I'll leave."

I stare at his upturned palm and raise a brow. "If you're waiting for a high-five, you've assumed the wrong position."

"I'm waiting for my gun."

"Well, then, it looks like you're gonna luck out twice tonight." I jerk my chin toward the door. "Go. I'll throw it down once you're outside the building."

His hand falls to his side, fisting into a white-knuckled grip. "You're going to throw my gun from a third-story window?"

The upward twist of my mouth isn't friendly. "I hope you're a good catch."

He licks his lower lip, and I'm sure it's supposed to be a threatening gesture with those squinted eyes, but I'm over here still drowning in the gushing wetness of my panties.

I want to hate-fuck him right now. Hate-fuck him so damn hard. Unfortunately, I realize my safety is more important than indulging in my deranged fantasies. And yes, it's a seriously slow reaction I'm not overly proud of.

"Until next time." His mouth has the slightest incline, an almost imperceptible grin, as he turns for the door.

"Oh, sweetie, there's not going to be a next time."

He glances over his shoulder and smirks. "We'll see."

5

HIM

I stalk through the lobby, pissed as all hell that I've severely fucked up this situation. Tonight wasn't supposed to be difficult. The plan had been a straight line of simplicity. A fucking breeze.

Then *she* had happened. The distraction. The complication.

"*Shit.*" The curse bites through my clenched teeth, bitter and aggressive. "Such a fucking mess."

I have a million different things to do tonight, and one of them shouldn't have been the hot blonde with the sassy mouth. But that's where I've been, in her apartment, ready to fuck her.

I move along the sidewalk, toward the streetlight, my neck craning as I focus on her window—third one up, last along the wall. She isn't there. Not yet. So I stop, arms crossed, and wait.

Then I wait some fucking more, because she sure as shit isn't in a hurry to return my gun.

I'm about to start searching the street for a rock when the glass pane slides upward and her grin comes into view.

She sticks her head out the window, light blonde hair cascading over slim shoulders, those perky tits looking lush and inviting from yet another angle.

Her eyes hold a wicked gleam, and that sexy mouth is a lip-lick away from begging to blow me. There's no denying she still wants my dick. It's written all over her seductive face. Problem is, I can't ditch the stiffness in my pants to pretend I feel any different. My arms throb with my barely contained restraint. I can still feel her hair around my knuckles, can still smell the vanilla scent.

"Ready?" She dangles the gun, holding it lazily by the grip.

"Born ready."

She smiles—she probably gives a sadistic chuckle, and I'm too far away to hear it

—then drops my weapon. I watch her watching me until the split millisecond before the gun reaches my hands. Then I'm all business, loading, locking, and placing the P22 back into the ass of my waistband.

"Thanks for the memories," she calls out, then ducks her head inside and slides the window shut.

I focus on the square of glass for longer than I should. Glaring, still seeing her even though she's already gone. Damn that sassy mouth.

Who the fuck is she, anyway? *Steph*, the bartender called her. Stephanie. AKA The Whirlwind Who Became A Bigger Obstacle With Each Passing Second.

She's a loose end, but I can't convince myself to tie that knot tonight. I'll see her again. I'll resolve whatever we need to resolve soon enough. In the meantime, I will pave the way for resolution and return to the regular broadcast of my shit-show life.

I make for the bar, my softening cock leading the way across the deserted street. Behind me, I hear another slide of the window, then her authoritative, *"Hey."*

I pause, my ego taking a few seconds to enjoy her continued interest, then shoot a glance over my shoulder.

"Do you want a tip for future conquests?" she asks.

A tip? This woman wants to give *me* a tip? There's no denying we're both hooked in this impromptu game, but it's clear she has a misconception on what role she's playing.

I shrug. "Sure."

"The only thing a woman wants to find hard in a guy's pants is his dick. Ditch the gun next time."

I grin. I can't fucking help it. That mouth of hers is going to get us both in trouble. Then again, maybe it saved her. "There's going to be a next time?"

She laughs and slams the window closed again, but she's still there, still watching, still holding my gaze with those bewitching eyes.

I shake my head, trying to shake her off, too, and continue across the road to the shitty bar with the catchy name. I don't look back as I shove my way through the front door. I don't need to. I know she's watching. I can feel her stare at the base of my neck.

The same five people are inside. The two men playing cards, the couple in the far corner, and the bartender, who is eying me, probably trying to figure out if I hurt his girl or ended the night in a sexually premature fashion.

"She kicked me out," I admit as I slide onto a bar seat.

His jaw is tight as he throws a bar coaster toward me, the flimsy cardboard skittering along the scuffed wood. "Well, I didn't see that coming."

Funnily enough, neither had I. People rarely catch me off guard. Women never do. Until now.

"Want another drink?" The offer lacks kindness. I'm sure he's annoyed at me for hurting her, and I appreciate his loyalty. It's something I can exploit to get answers to my growing list of questions.

"Yeah. Whiskey." I'd already had a taste for it on her tongue, and fuck me for needing more.

His eyes narrow as he grabs the liquor bottle and begins to pour. He tries to stare me down, and I oblige because it's in my best interest to play the remorseful role.

"I know I messed up." I focus on the coaster, fiddling with the edge like a remorseful motherfucker.

He places my drink in front of me and holds tight until I meet his gaze. "What'd you do?"

"It was nothing."

"Obviously it was something to her."

"Yeah." I concede with a nod and decide to dive straight into the truth. "She found out I was carrying. It scared her off."

He releases my glass and steps back. A clear retreat. "I don't blame her."

"Neither do I. But come on, man." I play it cool. "I'm from the country, and when my sister calls to say this guy of hers is beating her and threatening her with a gun, how am I going to defend her and her kid? I'm not going to apologize for wanting to protect my family. I know how crazy you city people are."

He holds my focus, reading me. "Oh, well." He shrugs. "You can't win 'em all."

I nod. "I know, but she was different. Believe it or not, I actually like her. The woman's a spitfire."

He chuckles, eating up my attraction like a lovesick fool. "She sure is. If I was ten years younger…"

I force a laugh. "Any idea how I can get a second chance?" I raise my glass and take a sip. "She doesn't seem the type to appreciate me waiting out in front of her building in an attempt to see her again."

"Hmm." He leans against the back counter and crosses his arms over his chest. "That's a tough one."

I reach into my jacket, pull out my money clip, and flick over two fifty-dollar bills. "You can't happen to tell me some of her usual hangouts, can you?" I place the money on the sticky bar and slide it over.

His eyes narrow on my hand, then my face. "You bribing me, son?"

"I'm willing to do whatever it takes to get a second chance."

His lips thin. His shoulders straighten. "Your money is no good to me."

Bullshit. The guy might want to believe he's above the incentive, but his darting eyes tell a whole different story.

"You sure?" I hide my growing annoyance behind a relaxed tone. I don't have time for this shit. Not for him. Not for her. If Brent isn't careful, I'll lose my patience, and nobody wants that. "Come on. Just let me know where she hangs out."

He sighs, the first sign of a slight buckle in his resolve. "I don't know much about her. Only a few things I've learned here and there from regulars who talk a lot of shit. So, I'd suggest your money would be better spent getting a decent meal at the Hot Wok at the end of the street." He glances away. "On a Thursday night…at around seven o'clock."

I hide my smirk behind another sip of whiskey.

"And if you're new to the area, you should check out the boxing club six blocks south of here. I think they have classes Monday, Wednesday, and Friday mornings."

Wednesday—*tomorrow*.

I tilt my glass at him in appreciation. "Thanks."

His gaze narrows. "If you fuck with her—"

"I know." I should laugh. If the threat had come from anyone else, I would.

"You do right by her. Even if she isn't interested in what you've got to offer."

"I will." The lies come easily. They always have.

I throw back the remaining liquid, then slide the glass toward him. "Thanks for the drink." I stand, leaving the bills on the counter.

"Take the money with you. You left more than enough earlier."

"Keep it for next time. I have a feeling we'll be seeing more of each other."

He chuckles. "Only if you're lucky."

"Yeah." Or more specifically, if she's unlucky.

I walk outside, unable to help myself as I glance at the building across the street. The third-floor window. I expect to see her there, watching, waiting, and I'm ashamed to admit I'm disappointed she isn't.

She thinks the game is over. That the hook-up failed, and we've gone our separate ways.

In reality, our time together has just begun. The two of us are going to get to know one another, whether she likes it or not. And that's not my fault. It's all on her—her decisions, her actions. Her damn sassy mouth.

I continue along the road, down the side street, to my car. I climb in and snatch my phone from the glove compartment.

Three missed calls, all from Decker, but he's not the person I need to speak to first.

I dial Torian, and I'm not surprised when he doesn't answer. The fucker would be sleeping like a baby while I worked. His voicemail cuts in, and the beep sounds without a welcome message.

"Hey, Torian. There's been a complication." I swallow over the bitter taste of temporary failure. "It means a slight delay in the timeline, but I'll call once I'm done."

I hang up, knowing he won't give a shit about details, and call Decker.

"Where the fuck are you?" he demands in greeting. "You were supposed to check in over an hour ago."

"There was a change of plan."

"What change?"

"A snag with the job. I had to follow a lead."

"You're not a fucking detective. You do your job, get the hell out of there, *then call me.*"

I start the ignition and do a U-turn, going in the opposite direction of where I need to be. "You worried about me, pumpkin?"

"Stressed," he growls. "I was stressed. Big difference."

"That's cute, Deck. Real cute." I creep my car to the intersection and glance up at her building. Her window. She's there, standing to the side of the frame, trying to remain out of view as she peers down at the bar.

My dick pulses, and I'm not sure I even know what I want from her anymore. I should go back up there and finish what I started. I should end this tonight.

But I can't force this. For once, I don't want to.

"Fuck you, *Hunt*." He snaps my nickname, making it sound like a curse. "So, you've quit working for the night? Is this you calling to punch your card?"

"No. I haven't started." I shouldn't give a shit that she's up there waiting for a glimpse of me, but I do. I shouldn't want to draw her attention, but I itch to do that, too. "I only called because I need you to do a background search on someone."

"You haven't started? You checked out hours ago. What the fuck is going on?"

"Focus." It's a warning to us both. I tear my gaze from her silhouette and turn onto her street, driving away from her building. "The name is Stephanie. She lives at apartment nineteen, level three, six-five-nine Belldore Street." I pause, waiting for confirmation that doesn't come. "Did you get all that?"

"All that? You haven't given me much to go on."

"It's enough. Once you start digging, you'll find more." He always does.

"And what am I digging for, exactly?"

"Anything and everything." I want it all. I *need* it all. "And make sure you get started right away."

"Yeah, I got it."

"I mean tonight, Decker. Now. This is your main priority."

"Why? What happened?"

She happened. Long hair, slim legs, sassy blue eyes, and ruby lips I want stretched around my dick. And they are only the physical attributes. I know once I delve into that mind of hers, the fucked-up shit I find will be even more impressive. "It's nothing you need to worry about."

"Right." He huffs. "I don't need to worry at all."

"It's just stress, remember?"

"You know, it's no coincidence your nickname rhymes with cunt."

I grin. "I'll call you when I'm done."

6

HER

I pound the pavement, jogging the six blocks to the mid-morning boxing class due to start in less than five minutes.

I should've been up early to start my research on the names Dan gave me. Instead, I slept in, which is out of the ordinary. Being kept awake until three a.m. with a rabid case of insomnia is also an anomaly. And only one person carries the blame.

Hazel eyes haunted me all night. *No*, they didn't haunt. They taunted. Teased. I hadn't been able to get my pounding heartrate to lessen, which made relaxation impossible. I'd tossed and turned, each movement reminding me of the feel of a dominant man against my skin.

I don't even know his name.

It could be Bob or Jim or something equally lustless. Whereas I currently imagine calling out Ryder or Heath or Drew in the height of passion.

I could scream the fuck out of Heath.

Jim? Not so much.

I push through the door to the boxing class and haul the pack off my back to scrounge inside, pulling out my black and white sparring gloves and matching defending pads.

"You're late." Adam, my instructor, raises his voice as I walk across the room and dump my backpack on the floor. "We've got even numbers today. So hurry up and pair with the new guy."

"New guy?" I scrunch my face accordingly.

Fuck the new guy. I always work out with Adam. He's the only one with enough respect and guts to challenge me.

"You'll be fine." He juts his chin to the left and I follow the direction, already glaring in the hopes my intimidating squint will earn me a place back beside my rightful partner.

"Oh, hell no." The words whisper from my mouth as my attention fixes on yet another anomaly.

He's here. My insomnia-inducing, weapon-wielding fantasy is throwing air jabs like the rest of the class, his remarkably cut muscles on display through his white sports tank and mid-thigh black shorts.

He meets my glare with soulless, excitement-starved eyes. Yet, every part of me notices every part of him. Not only the taunting lack of familiarity in his expression, but his tauntingly sexy body, too. Every damn inch of my sweaty, heated skin is well aware there isn't an ounce of unsculpted flesh anywhere to be seen on this man. Not on his thighs. Not on his arms. And I'd bet my life, not on his ass, either.

There's definitely no gun hidden on him today, but this time it doesn't matter. The guy is a weapon in himself. A lethal assassin. At least where my pussy is concerned. This visual inspection is slaying my cooch. It's brutal and unwarranted and entirely thrilling.

I stride toward him, masking the need to salivate as if my life depends on it. "You following me again?"

He keeps jabbing at the air as a subtle grin kicks at one side of his lips. "That's a little paranoid, seeing as though I was here first, and this place isn't even in your suburb."

That's the exact reason I've been coming here for the last three months. It isn't somewhere anyone would expect me to be. I bypass two similar classes on the run here. I even jog additional miles, sometimes doubling back on myself, to ensure nobody follows.

So, yes, I do wave the paranoid flag with pride. But that doesn't mean he isn't tailing me.

"You're serious?" His lips thin, and he stops jabbing the air to stand at his full domineering height.

I drop my gloves to the floor and cross my arms over my chest in response. *Don't loom over me, asshole.*

He scoffs, the sound barely audible as he shakes his head. "No, princess, I'm not following you. But after seeing you in those curve hugging clothes, a guy might just change his plans." His interest stalks my active-wear, flittering over my body like a physical caress. Ankles to chest.

I want to tell him to stop, to back the fuck off, but there's something about the lazy way he appraises me that encourages stupid decisions.

"Thanks, buddy," I reply with a luscious amount of sarcasm. "It's actually funny you mention my outfit, because when I got dressed this morning I thought to myself, 'Hey, if I'm lucky enough to run into that random guy I met in the bar, who just so happened to bring a gun into my apartment, what would be the best outfit I could wear to impress him?' And these were the clothes I pulled out."

"I'm sensing a little hostility."

I raise a brow. "Really?"

He's different today. Tired. I don't like that I want to know why. I don't like much at all about this guy turning up in my life, only his eyes…and his grin…and his confidence, his muscles, the way he kisses…

Shit. I like too damn much about this man.

"You brought a lethal weapon into my apartment. Of course there's hostility." I take my position beside him and fall into routine.

Jab, jab, jab.

Jab, jab, jab.

He does the same, those sculpted arms assailing my peripheral vision.

"I can't believe you're still hung up on me having a gun," he mutters under his breath.

"For starters, it happened less than twenty-four hours ago. And second, no, I'm not hung up on you having a gun. I'm hung up on you bringing it into my apartment. Into *my home.*"

"Would it make you feel better if I apologized?"

I freeze, entirely surprised by the question, because, yeah, a sincere apology and explanation would help this situation. But I'm beginning to think a clean-up crew for this mess would be more dangerous than my annoyance.

I don't want to like this guy. Nope. He is already too far under my skin. Continuing dialogue would be a mistake.

"Forget it," I mutter. I train my gaze straight ahead, determined to focus on getting the workout I need, not the workout he could give me.

"Time to pair up," Adam calls. "One throwing punches, one holding pads. I want to see jab, cross, hook. Jab, cross, hook."

I reach for the gloves at my feet, not giving him the option of who will punch first. I need to swing the frustration from my body. To jab, cross, hook this shit out of my system.

"I guess I'll hold the pads to start off," he grumbles.

I glare. At him. At myself. At everything that seems out of place and abnormal. I don't like this. I'm not comfortable with the human interaction or how much I'm beginning to enjoy it.

Every time our eyes meet, that zing hits me.

I loathe it.

"So…" He pulls the worn class pads onto his hands and holds them at chest height. "You don't want an apology, but would it help if I told you I took your advice?"

"My advice?" I throw a hard jab, and he jolts.

He recovers quickly and gives me a game-on smirk. "Yeah. You told me to ditch the gun. Which I did."

I ignore him and throw a cross, packing all my strength into the swing. This time, he doesn't flinch. He barely moves.

"And I can assure you, the only thing hard in these pants is my dick."

A mental image assails me, and I have no idea why my imagination has overcompensated in the package department. Huge man, huge dick. It seems proportionate, but I don't want that visual.

Nope.

It's difficult enough concentrating on throwing a powerful hook without my pussy contracting with his every word.

"Jab, cross," I hiss as I complete the actions. "Hook." I throw everything I have into those punches, driving him backward.

Jab, cross, hook.

Jab, cross, hook.

"Whoa," Adam calls out, coming to my side. "Ease up, Emma. I don't want you scaring away the new guy."

Shit.

I ignore the narrowing hazel eyes staring back at me from my boxing partner and force myself to calm down.

Adam gives a disapproving shake of his head and moves on to the next pair.

Jab, cross, hook.

Jab, cross, hook.

Jab, cross, hook.

"Emma?" The stranger's steely gaze questions me more than the deeply murmured word.

"Concentrate." I cross higher, making him duck to avoid an impact to the face.

"I thought your name was Steph." He crouches, bringing our eyes level.

I hide my apprehension behind a scowl. "Emma Stephens. Some people shorten my surname and use it as a nickname."

Jab, cross, hook.

Jab, cross, hook.

The intensity in his expression increases, and I don't appreciate the scrutiny. I can't blame him for the disbelief. The explanation was poor, especially for my standards. Usually, I'm quick on my feet, mentally speaking.

Today? Not so much.

"Okay, everyone," Adam yells. "Switch places."

I throw my gloves to the floor and pull on a set of pads. Once I'm standing straight and ready, the asshole hits me with a jab worthy of knocking a lesser woman on her ass. I stumble, and he smirks at me.

"Sorry. I'll go easier on you."

"Don't you fucking dare." I hold my hands in place, preparing for the cross. This one is equally hard, but at least I'm ready. The hook, on the other hand, makes me stumble sideways.

He watches me with each swing, staring into me, holding me captive. The physical exertion and mental games make my heart pound incredibly hard. I start to pant, my breaths short and sharp, almost to the point of hyperventilation.

He doesn't question me anymore, not in words, but those eyes seek answers. They're digging deep, seeing things I don't want him to see.

"Stop it," I growl.

He chuckles, soft and oh-so low. "Stop what? Do you need me to throw softer punches?"

"You know what I'm talking about."

Jab, cross, hook.

Jab, cross, hook.

The more he moves, the more sweat beads his skin, making those muscles glisten.

"Get a drink, guys."

I slump at Adam's instruction, dropping the pads to the floor as I hunch, all my muscles squealing in agony.

"You did well." My tormentor pats me on the back, his actions and words equally derisive.

Fuck him. Fuck him for starving my libido. Fuck him for the insomnia. And fuck him for playing mind games.

He's messing with me, and he already knows enough to entice him to snoop. I straighten, my nostrils whistling like a damn bull with my labored breathing as Muscle Man stands at my side.

"What's wrong?" His grated whisper brushes my ear. "You look livid…and let me tell you, it's sexy as fuck."

A shudder jolts through me, the vibration culminating in my nipples.

Something isn't right. I don't know what it is. I can't see through his brain-numbing fog to understand it.

It's intuition that tells me to get out of here. I lean over, scoop my gloves and pads off the floor, and walk for my backpack. I rip the bag open, the zipper grinding under the pressure. I shove my stuff inside and haul it over my shoulder before stalking to the door.

Nobody tries to stop me. I have no friends here. No one knows me.

I push outside, and cold air hits my cheeks, bringing clarity. As cute as it was to think I had a similar personality to this guy, we are nothing alike. We never will be.

I'm not normal. Not my past and not my future. I don't fit in, and I don't want to. I need to remain under the radar, and it feels like this guy has nailed a neon sign on my ass.

I start down the sidewalk and hear the door push open behind me.

"Wait."

His demand has no effect on me.

Liar.

Of course it does. I want to plant my feet and confront the hell out of him. I want to ask him why he's hassling me, why he's paying attention when I've skated by unnoticed for so long. I want to know why the hell I'm torn with every action and every word where he's concerned.

And I seriously want to know why I can't stop picturing the size of his dick and how good it would feel down the back of my throat.

I keep walking, getting as far away from stupidity and craziness as I can. Even now, I'm hoping he follows, and I don't know why.

Why? *Fuck.* Why?

I don't understand. Nothing makes sense, and still, the feeling is a nagging force trying to break free from my chest.

I want him to continue, and I need him to stop.

"*Wait.*" This time the request is growled in the deepest command.

I start to jog, making my way along the street, past the fruit vendor and up to the second-hand store when strong fingers grab my elbow, pulling me to a stop.

"Why did you run out?" His frown bears down on me. "I thought we were having fun."

"*You* were having fun. This isn't enjoyable for me." It's messy and chaotic.

"We had chemistry last night." He releases my arm. "It'd be a shame to let it go to waste."

"We also had a lot of alcohol."

He scowls. "You weren't drunk, and neither was I."

He's right, and I can't bring myself to admit it. I've gone years without an emotional link to anyone apart from my friendly bartender. I've been alone and strong. Now I feel weak with my need for…*something*. I can't even pinpoint my attraction to this man. It's just there, hovering like a gas cloud.

"Let me buy you a drink tonight." There's still no enthusiasm ebbing from him. Not even the slightest glimpse.

Why is that entirely endearing?

I scoff. Maybe because he's the polar opposite to the last guy I dated. My stomach hollows at the reminder, and I push out a heavy breath to wash it away.

"I'm not much of a drinker." I tear my gaze from his and focus on the second-hand televisions playing in the window, my lack of interest raking over sitcom reruns and numerous news feeds. "Last night was a one-off."

"Then dinner. We can go to that wok place at the end of your block."

I'm about to decline the offer when a news flash crosses one of the television screens.

Senator's Son Found Dead.

I blink through the hallucination, trying to make the words disappear.

My heart stutters, and my world narrows to those four words. *Senator's. Son. Found. Dead.* Then Dan Roberts' face takes center stage.

Numbness seeps into my limbs, and the sound of the busy sidewalk disappears—the street traffic, too. My pulse echoes in my ears. There's only my thundering heartbeats and that news headline.

Pounding arrhythmia and panic.

Fear and hysteria.

I've killed a man?

I shake my head. *No.* I've never killed anyone, even though there have been numerous people who've tempted my restraint. I am the self-appointed person who gives criminals a dose of their own medicine when the legal system fails to provide punishment. I give victims revenge, and assholes a chance to change their ways.

I don't do death.

That is for a higher power to decide.

"What's wrong?" That voice sounds near my ear, and I squeeze my eyes shut to find focus. "Are you okay?"

I breathe through the delirium and finally blink to find him staring down at me, his forehead wrinkled, his lips tight.

"I'm good," I whisper. Then louder, "Just light-headed from the exercise."

"You need food." He scrutinizes me, reading me, and my cheeks heat under his surveillance. Under my guilt.

I step back. "I need to get home."

"No." He follows, matching me step for step. "Tell me what's going on."

I glance back at the television, finding the breaking news replaced with some sort of telenovela. Maybe it was a figment of my imagination. Maybe I'm losing my ever-loving mind.

"*Just leave me alone.*" I run, sprint, ditching him somewhere along the way.

I don't stop. I reach the end of the block, then the next, and the next. I don't glance at the cars that blare their horns as I cross numerous streets. I don't pause. Yet, I can't outrun the nightmare clipping at my heels.

I don't kill people. I couldn't bring myself to do so. No matter how vile or disgusting a criminal's actions are, I always make the punishment singular. I contain the pain to the guilty party. Because once that life is snuffed, an intricate web of people become affected.

The parents who live for their only son are devastated. Those nieces and nephews who dote on their uncle are heartbroken. The innocent sisters and brothers are filled with anger and confusion.

I can't be the person who inflicts that pain.

Maybe it's already too late.

Maybe I already am a murderer.

Fuck. I should've dug deeper into my research on Dan. There could've been a heart condition. An allergy to Rohypnol. *Hell.* He could've choked or had trouble breathing after I fled.

Oh, God, I'm going to throw up.

I push my legs even harder, reaching the corner of my building with shaky thighs, my chest heaving, and there he is, leaning against a black Chevrolet parked in the loading zone.

A sexy car for a sexy son-of-a-bitch.

"What the hell is going on?" He strides toward me, a thick black sweater now hugging his upper body.

"Stop following me." I sniff, my nose leaking from the vigorous exercise. "Get out of here."

"You took off after saying you were light-headed. I wanted to make sure you were all right. Clearly, you're not."

"Clearly?" I swipe at my stupid nose with my wrist.

He moves in front of me, his gaze softer, on the verge of kindness. "You look like you're about to cry."

I straighten and blink through his ignorance. "You're an idiot." I won't cry over Dan. I refuse. My nose tingles due to exertion. My eyes burn because…damned if I know, but it isn't from building tears.

I sidestep and hustle for the front doors, entering the pin code through blurry vision. He's at my back before I'm inside, and I no longer have the strength to tell him to leave.

"At least let me call someone. A friend. Or family."

A harsh laugh escapes my lips. There is nobody here for me. No friends. No family. Nobody and no one at all. Not a single soul.

I make it to the elevator and press the button. The doors open, and he follows me inside, always following, always there.

I slump into the corner, my arms hugging my chest.

"Give me your phone." The stranger holds out a hand while he presses the button for my floor with the other. "I'll call someone to come look after you."

I ignore him, too focused on Dan's face as it takes over my mind. The snide smile, the laugh, the voice. The feel of his ribs breaking beneath my fist. The crack of his jaw. The sound of his muffled shouts.

I press a hand to my mouth and the other to the elevator wall to hold myself upright. The floor jolts to a stop, and bile rushes up my throat, demanding to be free.

Please let me make it to the bathroom.

I lunge for the doors, pull them apart, and sprint for my apartment. I'm blinded by horrible images as I release deadbolts and enter the pin code. Dan's hair, his eyes, his mouth. I can see it all.

What's your name, bitch?

I shove inside my apartment, dump my backpack, and rush to the toilet. There's barely enough time to collapse to my knees before the contents of my stomach leave me in a heaving purge.

Through the rise of bile and partly digested toast, the face of a murdered man stares back at me. Haunting me.

I want to know what to whisper in your ear when I'm raping you raw.

I grip the toilet, my stomach convulsing over and over and over again until there's nothing left to give.

"Are you still going to tell me nothing's wrong?"

That voice pulls me from the panic, stripping away the memories of one man and replacing them with another. I wipe a hand across my mouth and glance over my shoulder, finding him leaning against the doorway.

"Get out." I push to shaky feet, flush my breakfast, and reach for the cabinet to pull out my toothbrush and paste.

"Did you know the guy?"

I rinse my mouth with water, load up my brush, and begin scrubbing. "*Leave.*" I scour the vomit from my mouth, cleaning my tongue and teeth and everywhere in between.

"The guy on the television," he clarifies. "The senator's son."

No, I didn't know him. He was a stranger, even after I killed him. I grasp the counter and focus on my reflection in the mirror. I'm pale, my eyes wild, with strands of hair stuck to the sweat on my cheeks.

"Was he a friend of yours?"

"*Shut up.*" My head throbs with each beat of my pulse. I can't think. It hurts to breathe. I start for the door, needing space, needing room. I try to push by him, and he doesn't budge. "Get out of my way."

He doesn't. Instead, he shoves from the frame, stands tall, and stares me down.

"I said, *move*."

He squares his jaw, preparing for a fight I'm more than willing to give. I have to get this toxic sludge out of my system, and thrusting it out is the only way I know how.

I cock my fist and swing, already anticipating the painful contact that never comes. He ducks, weaves, and steps back in a flash of movement that makes my head spin. I swing again and again, each attack thwarted by his quick reflexes.

I keep advancing, keep punching, keep trying to distract myself from reality.

I pounce forward. *Jab. Cross. Hook.* My knuckles graze his chin. Almost impact.

His eyes narrow and that harsh face hardens. "Enough."

I can't stop. My arms have a mind of their own. I can't control my thoughts. Not the blinding flashbacks of what I did to Dan, or the snapshots of what he'd done to other women.

I swing again, and this time the ferocious intruder grabs my wrist, wrenching it down and twisting. I'm spun in a circle until my back is plastered against his front, his other arm smothering my chest. He holds me in place, trapping me while I hyperventilate.

"I said, enough," he growls in my ear.

I whimper and sag against him, my heavy breathing lessening in the long, silent moments he holds me.

"Was he your lover?"

"What?" I struggle to break free and fail. "*No.* He was a disgusting excuse for a man who deserved to die long ago."

The truth shocks me. But it *is* the truth.

"Then why the breakdown?"

"It isn't a breakdown." Now I'm lying, because the reality is, I'm scared. I'm terrified of being sent to prison. Not because of what could happen to me once trapped inside. I'm petrified I'll die behind bars while the person who destroyed my family runs free.

I can't fail them.

I refuse.

"So, storming out of boxing class, running away from a conversation, and then violently vomiting is a common thing for you?" He scoffs against my neck, making me shiver. "I guess my first impression was wrong. Here I was thinking you had a massive set of balls."

"I don't need balls." I buck against him, and the faintest hint of his erection has me sucking in a sharp breath. "But it's nice to know you were thinking I had a set to match your own. Is that what turns you on? My massive balls?"

"No." His laughter is low and sinister, barely audible as it flitters over my neck. "I'll be honest and say everything about you turned me on last night."

Those mind-numbing tingles sink deeper inside me. My arms, my legs, even my toes buzz from the potential distraction.

"Everything about you *still* turns me on," he whispers.

I close my eyes, sinking under his confounding spell. He's not begging me for sex. There's no passion. No heat or urgency. His words are cold and emotionless, yet still coated with a devilishly seductive edge I can't ignore.

I need to learn to ignore it.

He knows where I live, which wouldn't be an issue due to my security measures if he'd become the one-night-stand I intended him to be. But now he also knows I've lied about my name. I've told him I have weapons stashed in my apartment. And he's aware of two of my regular haunts—Atomic Buzz and the boxing class I now have to quit taking.

He's chipping away at my privacy, and I need those pieces back.

I wiggle in an attempt to break free and ignore the heavy weight of disappointment when he lets me go. I face him, and the simplicity of what stares back at me turns my insides to mush.

He's not smiling. No, those lips are a flat line. His arms fall limp at his sides. There's no warmth or seduction. No cocky smirk. Just him. Just eyes that sink into me, whispering promises beyond my wildest fantasies.

Everything about you still turns me on.

His confession washes away the panic, and in its place, arousal blooms.

He stalks toward me, and I hold my ground, tilting my head to maintain contact with those predatory eyes. He brings us foot to foot, almost hip to hip. The looming wall of a man stands before me, expressionless, emotionless, apart from all the devastatingly calm superiority.

My mouth salivates.

His hand snaps up, aiming for my chin, but I smack it away. He grins, tries again, and fails after another one of my slaps.

My turn, big guy.

I launch my hand at his throat. He doesn't defend himself. He stands there, letting me wrap my fingers around his neck as his eyes flash. I'm taunting a bear. Poking the giant. I wonder if he'll crush me, mentally or physically.

"We can spar all you like." His offer brings chills. "But I'm sure you'd prefer it without any clothes on."

The temptation of his statement wraps around my chest. *Squeeze, squeeze, squeeze.* He's right. So painfully, unbelievably right.

"No." My grasp on this situation is slipping, sliding. My fingers grip the cliff's edge, but the ground crumbles beneath my grasp. "Get out, before I make you leave." The demand clogs my throat, coming out in a garbled mess.

"You don't want that."

"Don't I?" Fuck him and his incredibly clear insight. "Will my knee in your junk prove otherwise? Or maybe you need my fist in your face."

"Have at it, princess. I'm no stranger to pain."

7

HER

I BELIEVE HIM.

I think that's where our connection lies—in pain. He's been through it. Battled it. The evidence is clear in his emotional scars. The sterility. The harsh communication.

We're two tortured souls who've found each other by chance. And maybe all I need is to get my fill of him so I can cut this connection and go on my merry way. I only want what's between his thighs. The cheap thrill. That hard, generous length. And I bet my life he feels the same about my snatch.

Once this hot and sweaty masterpiece takes place, I will pull his ripcord and fast-track him in the opposite direction.

Toodaloo, motherfucker.

No emotion. No more attachment.

His lips curve, his growing smirk alluding to that slight dimple in his left cheek. My fingertips scratch over the rough stubble of his jaw. Harsh, yet too damn inviting.

My tongue snakes out, gliding over my tingling lower lip. My body is out of control. My heart vibrates beneath my ribs, my pulse pounds, my stomach flutters with a mass of tickling butterflies.

I release his throat, my fingers gliding over his neck, his chest, before dropping to my side.

I can't do this.

I can't continue, and I can't stop.

He steps back, kicking off his shoes, then grips the hem of his sweater and tank, and pulls them over his head, exposing more sculpted flesh. Not only muscles, but scars. His body is a canvas of brutality, with inch-long lines of puckered skin across his rib cage and a circular mark above his right hip.

He watches me watching him, wordlessly, almost breathlessly.

"You're accident-prone," I murmur.

"I guess I am."

"But still not the violent type, right?" I meet his gaze.

"Definitely not." His eyes glimmer with the slightest tease. "I hate the stuff."

I'd be a blind fool not to pick up on his sarcasm. It's there. *Right there.* In his grin, in his intensity, in the almost scary way he controls me without even knowing it.

Oh, God. I'm dancing with the devil.

And I love it.

He's dangerous. There's no doubt. And those *non-violent* scars around his ribs look awfully similar to stab wounds. The circular mark above his hip speaks of a bullet injury. Or maybe that's just my imagination talking, and they're only construction injuries. Laboring accidents.

Either way, I should pull his ripcord now. I should seriously give him a merry finger-wave as I boot his ass out the door.

I should. I should. I should.

Instead, need wraps itself around me, pulling my limbs, crushing my chest. For once, I feel... I just *feel*. I'm not hollow. I'm not adrift. This man has me tethered to something, his presence keeping my feet on solid ground.

"Come here," he growls.

There are mere feet of space between us, but he demands my submission. He wants me to succumb.

I can't deny his request. I inch forward, my chin lifting to keep our gazes connected.

"Good," he purrs, slicing a hand around my hip to drag me into his body.

I gasp, and he steals the sound with his mouth, his lips overtaking mine, his tongue delving deep. He kisses me into mindlessness, those strong arms wrapping around me, his hands gliding down my back to cup my ass. He lifts me in a callous jerk, positioning my pubic bone against his hard cock.

I spread my legs, wrapping my thighs around his waist to grind against him. Warmth flood my pussy, my body eagerly preparing for pleasure. There's never been a better feeling. A greater sensation.

I wrap my arms around his head, tangling my fingers in his hair. His scent is seduction, rich from aftershave and etched in sweat and virility. His kisses are strong, and yet there's a slight glimmer of softness. The most delicate swipe of affection.

My heart hurts. I don't want it to, but it does. It clenches. It weeps.

"Fuck me," I demand into his mouth.

He growls and strides toward the other side of the room. My bed. He climbs onto the mattress, still holding me, still kissing me, then guides me to lie down as he kneels between my spread thighs.

The sight is profound. His eyes are wild. Carnal. His broad chest heaves with energized breaths. Veins pulse from his carved arms.

I visualize his dick again, the generous size taunting my mind. I'm going to be disappointed. I just know it.

He shoves down his shorts, his underwear, and his thick cock is revealed. The length is above average, but the girth... My God.

I suck in a breath and my pussy clenches. Nope, not disappointed at all. I want to learn every inch of that hardness. I want it everywhere. Anywhere.

"You got protection?"

I nod and swallow to ease my drying mouth. "Top drawer."

He leans over me, pulls open my nightstand, and retrieves a loose condom. He's efficient. There's no hesitation. No reluctance. He rips open the packet, sheaths his length, and stares down at me. "Take off your clothes."

I ponder a protest. Playing hardball could be fun, but I'm too far gone for games. I tug the long-sleeve top over my head and wiggle my ass out of my tight sports pants to lie before him in my underwear.

"I said, take it off before I rip it off."

My stomach flips, and again, I contemplate dissent. This time it's for my protection. To keep a buffer between me and all the feels. I want him too much. Not only his lust, but the distraction. The connection. The reprieve from reality.

"Fine. Keep them on." His hands snake up my inner thighs, reaching my black lace panties. He grips the crotch, his fingers prodding, tugging, until the material tears. He stares down at me, his nostrils flaring, his teeth digging into his lower lip in a show of pure restrained aggression. "I hope you like it rough."

I shudder. "And what if I don't?"

His gaze glides to mine as a lone finger parts my slick folds. "Then I'll enjoy changing your mind."

That finger breeches my entrance, sliding inside me. It's a tease, the slightest penetration leaving me anticipating the considerable size of his dick. His free hand slides over my stomach, the callouses on his palms scratching, marking my skin.

He grasps the front of my bra, yanking the cups to the sides. I'm exposed to him, the dislodged material plumping my breasts, creating a mass of impressive cleavage.

"I'll have fun breaking you in."

I push to my elbows and clench my pussy around the lone digit. "You're too late to break anything."

His brows furrow, and I lean up to wrap my arm around his neck, pulling him down to me before he can question my response.

"Fuck me," I whisper in his ear and lick his neck. He's salty, the lingering sweat sinking into my tongue like an aphrodisiac.

He snarls and jerks his hips, the head of his cock finding my entrance. I feel his hand down there, positioning his length, then in one harsh thrust, he's deep inside me, stretching my muscles, blinding me with pleasure and the slightest twinge of torture. I moan, clinging to his neck as he shoves into me. Pulse after pulse. Slam after slam.

"*Fuck.*" His curse is ferocious, his movements merciless. He rests his forehead against mine, looking me in the eye. "Who are you?"

"Your fantasy," I tease with a kiss, digging my nails into his shoulders.

"No shit." He bites my lower lip, then sucks it into his mouth. "A fucking nightmare, too."

"I sure am." I chuckle.

He grins, exposing his dimple, and a softness in his eyes I've never seen before. It's beautiful. Frighteningly so. For a second, I pause, taking in his complexity. The calm of his smile against his hard penetration.

"I thought you were going to be rough."

He bites my lip again, this time harder. "I thought it was better not to scare you."

"Or you turned into a pussy."

"Yeah?" He raises a brow and slams into me. "You really think so?" He snakes his hand behind my neck and grips my ponytail, tugging my head back. My breasts thrust toward him. My eyes roll.

Pleasure. So much pleasure.

His mouth trails a path from my cheek to my shoulder, then my chest. His kisses become stronger. Harder. I squeal as he sucks on my skin. *Shit*. He's leaving marks, tattooing me with his domination.

"Too much for you? 'Cause I haven't even started," he murmurs against the side of my breast, his hips still bucking, fucking the life out of me. Or maybe he's fucking life back into me.

I don't want that. I don't want change. I need this sterile existence. "No. Not enough." I need the harsh detachment to keep me sane.

I shove at his chest and buck my hips, encouraging him to roll. We tumble, switching positions, me on top, his muscled body beneath me.

"Better?" He raises a brow in question.

I nod. His cock sinks deeper, stretching me farther. "Mmmhmm."

He cups my breasts, his fingers digging into flesh. I ride him, my hands splayed on his hard chest. All my muscles are tense, taut from the build of bliss. Then my foot twinges. A cramp strikes. "*Shit*."

"What?" He scowls.

"I've got a cramp."

"Not my fucking problem." His words are rough, but his lips curve in a tease.

No, it isn't his problem, but he pushes to sit, his hand sliding over my thigh, my calf, my heel. He curls my toes in his fist and the pain increases. He doesn't stop fucking me; he continues the rhythmic pulse of his hips, the stimulation gradually fighting back as the cramp subsides.

"Better?" His eyes hold something that threatens to weaken me. Something that cracks my ribs apart in an attempt to touch my heart.

"Yeah." I glance away and bury my head in his shoulder.

His hands find my ass as he continues to sit, our chests plastered together, our sweat mingling. He guides my movements, making me grind against the dick nestled deep inside me. The friction teases my clit, the pleasure pulsing through me from my core, to my stomach, to my breasts.

"For a fucking temptress, your pussy is as tight as a virgin's."

I close my eyes and smile. "You're so sweet."

He chuckles, digging his fingers deeper into my ass. Tomorrow, I'll have a roadmap of marks on my body. A treasure trove of carnal memories.

He leans down, his mouth latching onto my nipple. He sucks. He grinds. He thrusts. Every movement catapults me toward an edge I'll happily dive over.

"Tell me your name. I want to shout it when I come."

I shake my head. I'm already close. I need to focus.

He growls, "Tell me." The rough texture of his tongue swipes my breast, trailing my areola.

"Oh, God, don't stop." I want more. I need more.

"Then tell me."

I pulse faster, my orgasm within reach. He groans, and the delicious sound acts as a trigger.

My pussy contracts, pulsing over and over. Wave after wave of ecstasy pummels me from the inside out. Drowning and re-energizing at the same time. I moan, longer, louder. "Yes. Yes. *Yes*."

"Damn you," he growls, pistoning his hips.

I slowly blink through the shattering peak, my mind and body tangled in a delicious web of delirium and euphoria.

Each change in his expression becomes a memorable snapshot I vow to never forget. He shouts his release, his fingers creating scars—emotional and physical. That beautifully rugged face contorts. Sweat beads his skin. Wisps of hair cover his eyes as his forehead scrunches.

I watch, enraptured, as his pleasure takes hold, and I thrive on him succumbing. For once, he's not in control. He's weak. He's human.

My chest tightens in excitement, as if I've won a battle. But what could I have won other than a temporary distraction?

His shoulders slump, and his grip loosens. The emotionless face I've grown accustomed to returns along with his steady breathing. I stare at the stranger poised between my thighs, unable to look away from the lazy intensity staring at me.

"Who are you?" he murmurs, resting back on one hand.

I snap out of the lust haze and command myself to focus. "I've already told you."

"You haven't told me a damn thing."

"Then maybe it's none of your business."

His nostrils flare, and I'm equally annoyed and turned on by his anger. "Is it a crime to want to know your fucking name?"

Yes. He shouldn't need to know. I certainly have no interest in learning his.

"It's Emma." I scowl. "You already know that."

"Bullshit," he grates.

I pull back with the evaporation of ecstasy. So much for a distraction. The memory of how I got here floods back. The images of Dan assail me, creating revulsion.

I crawl off him, my body immediately missing his, and move to sit on the edge of the mattress. I lean over, massaging my forehead as my mind rambles unwanted thoughts.

How did I get here?

I was happy once. Loving. Optimistic. I didn't have a care in the world. Then Jacob changed everything, instigating a domino effect I had no control over. I functioned with continued detachment. I lived for one thing, and one thing only. And this is what I've become.

All the fulfilment I experienced moments ago washes out like a tide, and hollow disgust flows in with the force of a tsunami. I've just had sex. Mind-blowing, limb-shaking sex. Mere minutes after finding out I'm a murderer.

Who have I become?

"You should leave." My statement is strong, belying the already fractured parts of me which fragment into tinier slivers.

I stay silent, waiting for a protest that doesn't come.

The mattress jolts with his shifting weight, then he's gone, moving away from the bed, his padded footsteps retreating. His clothes rustle. His shoes thud against the floor.

"Emma… Stephanie… Whatever the hell your name is, I want to see you again." Each word is growled harsher than the last. "Tonight. At the bar."

I grab my pillow and drag it to my chest. I won't succumb again. I need to pull my shit together, not spread it out for the world to see. I have to figure out what to do now that I'm one of those people I usually fight to punish. And now, more than ever, I have to gain retribution for what has been done to my family before I become the focus of someone else's vengeance. Or worse—trapped behind bars.

"Do you hear me?" he asks.

I nod. "Yeah. I hear you."

But hearing him doesn't mean I'm listening.

8

HER

I don't meet him that night. Or the next. Or the one after that.

Too many nights pass with me sitting by the window watching him enter Atomic Buzz. But he's always there, always looking up at my window before he walks inside, and always glancing toward my position in the shadows when he leaves hours later.

I've tried to focus. I've pulled out all the memories I have on Jacob from the box hidden beneath the floorboards under my bed. I've scattered the newspaper clippings, the grainy photos, the family tree, and covered my living room floor, my coffee table, and the sofa.

Those papers have lain untouched for days.

I've attempted to find dirt on the name Dan mentioned—Vaughn. Zeke or Zander or Zack. Nothing comes up. Jacob York had successfully disappeared, and this new Vaughn alias is a ghost. Or maybe the lead was a lie.

Either way, it cost Dan his life and has now trapped me in a tighter cage of paranoia. I haven't left my apartment in days. I'm constantly alert, always on the lookout for anyone suspicious approaching my building. I reach for my gun whenever my phone vibrates with a notification that my door surveillance camera has been triggered. And sleep… Well, let's just say sleep and I aren't friends anymore.

I need to get a grip, but there's no grounding here. Each day that inches closer to Dan's funeral compacts the emotional instability clogging my veins. I've followed the investigation. Doctors say he suffered a dissected carotid artery from a blunt force trauma that led to a blood clot being carried to the brain.

The blunt force trauma was from me.

His death was a result of the injuries I'd inflicted.

He literally died at my hands, and as I look down at my palms, I can see the damage I've caused. My fingers seem savage. Less feminine, and now tarnished with brutality.

HUNTER

His funeral will be held the day after tomorrow, and I can't stomach the mental images my overly creative mind conjures. All those people who will mourn a depraved man. All the tears. All that misplaced heartache.

He should've lived to endure his punishment.

I drag my gaze back outside and stare at Brent's bar. Thoughts of the mystery man are the only thing capable of temporarily wiping away the anger. Even when he's not there, I can see him walking through those doors, glancing up at me.

I need to get a grip. *No.* I have to escape and clear my head. Even if just for a day.

I shove from the window ledge, grab my coat, and leave my apartment for the first time in days. I linger in the lobby, stalking the sidewalk like a deranged mental patient as I scan the roads and sidewalk for police. A suspect hasn't been announced yet, but that doesn't mean they don't have one.

I could be on any number of radars—authorities and Dan's family.

I slip outside, the weight of a million stares on my shoulders even though fewer than ten people are in sight. I hustle across the road, my jacket collar high and my head low as I enter Atomic Buzz.

Inside, I'm relieved there's only two of the regulars drinking away their sorrows. I approach the bar and slide onto a seat. "Hey, Brent."

He pauses in the middle of stacking racks of glasses on the far counter and turns my way. "You're back twice in one month. What did I do to earn the honor?"

"I actually came to ask a favor."

He places the rack down and dusts his hands. "What's up?"

A lump forms in my throat. I hadn't realized asking for help would be difficult. Favors build connections, and I seem to be making too many of them lately.

"I know it's late notice, but can I borrow your car tomorrow?"

"You heading back to Seattle to see your family?"

The lump grows, increasing the need to swallow.

He remembers. Of course he does. He listens to every word I say. He cares about me, even when he shouldn't.

"Yeah. Just a quick day trip. I'll have your car back before you close tomorrow night. I'll make sure to fill it with gas and give you cash for the cab rides you'll need while I'm gone."

"Don't worry about the money. You know you can borrow anything you want, whenever you like."

I nod and lower my gaze in an attempt to ditch his lingering stare.

"You look tired," he adds. "Is everything okay?"

"Yep," I answer without thought. "I just didn't want to rent a car at late notice. By the time I get to the lot and find—"

"I'm not talking about the car."

I assumed as much.

I paste on a confident smile and lift my gaze. "Everything is super-dooper perfect. I couldn't be better."

Go hard or go home, right?

His eyes narrow, not buying my bullshit, and I hold the expression like a motherfucker, unwilling to lose this battle. I can't handle his concern on top of everything else. I simply can't.

Eventually, he nods. "Have you seen that man of yours is hanging around a lot? I think I've doubled my income this week because of him alone."

I scowl. Maybe I should've held more interest in learning mystery man's name because calling him 'my man' isn't a trend I'm down with. "He's not mine."

Brent shrugs and grabs a liquor bottle from under the bar. He pours a nip, then grabs another bottle and another, finally filling it with soda before he slides the concoction toward me. "It sure looked that way when he left your building last week."

Last week? Geez, I've been hermitting my life away for longer than I thought. "I kicked him out the night we left here together."

"I know." He gives a conniving smile. "He told me."

"He did?" I shuffle forward, not realizing my mistake of showing my piqued interest until it's too late. And now I can't be bothered hiding my intrigue. "What did he say?"

That smile turns to a grin. "He told me he likes you. That you were different. But he also said he wouldn't apologize for carrying a gun because he was here to protect his family."

"He told you about the gun?" *Christ.* The guy acts as if every word he utters is a secret, yet he happily blurts the details to Brent. Maybe the whole recluse act is just that—an act to hold my interest. "I don't believe it."

"What part don't you believe?" he asks.

I don't want to believe any of it. I don't need to think about him liking me when he's already become my only comforting thought through this hellish week. I don't want my opinion of his gun to change, either. I've made a lot of my judgements about him based on his sinister intent with a deadly weapon. I've branded him dangerous because of that firearm.

If he only carried to protect his sister…

If he truly is a non-violent man…

"*Fuck*," I mutter under my breath.

"What now?"

"Nothing." I grasp the drink and sip. Tomorrow can't come soon enough.

"He seems like a genuine guy."

Genuine? In what? To me, the guy seems genuinely bad news. Genuinely toxic to my concentration. Genuinely a huge fucking mistake with his overly inquisitive nature.

I transition from a sip to a gulp, chugging the alcohol until it's all gone. "This isn't a conversation we're going to have." I push my glass toward him and slide off the chair. "Is it still okay to borrow your car?"

Brent chuckles and retrieves a set of keys from a hook on the back wall. "Sure." He lobs the prize at me. "Drive safe."

I catch the offering, along with a relaxing sense of relief at the enabling escapism. "Thanks."

I pull out the cash I've stashed in my jeans and place it on the bar. "For the cab rides and the drink."

"You know I don't want your money."

"And you know I don't want to hear your protests." I kinda love this guy. He's my only friend, no matter how disillusioned he is by the lies I've told. "I'll return the keys as soon as I get back."

"Don't rush. I can deal without a car if you need it longer."

"You're too damn good to me." I wink at him and make for the door, energized to get out of this city for a while. I'll leave before daybreak, clear my head with the three-hour drive, lick old wounds while I visit my family, then return home with a plan for the future.

I push open the door to the street, and the heavy glass falls away under the hand pulling from the other side.

"Hey." The deep, familiar voice slays me. Grips me. Punishes me.

I ignore the temptation to fall into lust and continue onto the sidewalk, only chancing a brief glance at my mystery man.

A brief glance is all it takes for his image to sear my retinas—worn, ripped jeans, a black jacket with the cuffs hitched a few inches up his tanned forearms, and a white T-shirt beneath that hugs his chest. "You're drinking earlier than usual tonight."

He releases the door, remaining outside as I pivot my attention toward the curb and watch for traffic. The light crunch of his steps follows me. Intuition tells me he's a foot away. I can feel him. Sense him. His interest raises the hair on the back of my neck and makes me shudder.

"You been watching me, princess?"

Fuck. *Fuck.*

"It's okay," he murmurs. "I don't mind the attention."

I roll my eyes and turn to face him. "I've gotta go."

In a blink, the subtle humor glistening in those hazel irises is gone, and a delicious scowl takes its place. "You're not going to join me for a drink?"

"Not tonight." Not any night. Not when my stomach turns in knots whenever he's close. I step onto the road, wait for a passing car, then jog to my side of the street. I'm yanking at my own ripcord, trying to fast-track my departure, but my heart is thumping in excitement, ignoring the inevitable crash and burn that will happen if I don't get out of here.

"Then when?" The question comes from right behind me. "What's got you in such a hurry to leave...again?"

Shit.

"I've got a big day tomorrow. I need to get up early." I reach my building and enter the pin code into the keypad. The panel beeps, the lock clicks in release, and I pull the door wide, only to have his fierce hand push it shut.

I stiffen, all my muscles frozen and humming as I drown under his intense stare.

"What are you doing tomorrow?" he asks.

I sigh and fight the good fight, trying not to lick my lower lip to give him the encouragement we both crave. "I'm heading out of town."

"Oh, yeah?" He raises a brow. "Where are you headed?"

Far away from his questions, his interest, and his temptation. I can't keep encouraging the distraction. As much as I want to deny it, I thoroughly enjoy his attention. I'm suffocating in my need to breathe him deep, and not just into my lungs—into my life.

I shouldn't have to remind myself it's imperative to lay low and focus. The police are looking for me, whether they know it or not. And I have to find Jacob before karma deals me a heavy punishment.

But this man sees more than he should. Those hands touch more than I want to allow. And whatever is going on in that mind of his is sure to create havoc.

No more.

I hitch my chin high. "I'm visiting my boyfriend."

How do you like them apples?

The tight clench of his jaw is a blatant sign he doesn't like my apples at all.

"Is that right?" he snarls.

"Yep."

His nostrils flare, and he licks his lower lip in such a delightfully slow roll of predatory intent that I have to squeeze my thighs together to stem the growing throb.

"And this boyfriend of yours, does he mind that you're fucking me?"

Chills. So many chills.

"Fucked," I clarify. "We did it once, and it was a mistake."

He steps closer, looming over me. "That's not the vibe I'm getting."

I squeak internally. On the outside, I stare like a motherfucker. "Really?" I inch into him, straightening my shoulders, raising my chin. "You're looming over me, glaring. To me, the only vibe here is threatening."

He flashes a smirk. "And I bet you're wet as hell because of it."

Touché, asshole.

I turn my back and re-enter the pin code into the keypad. "I'm sorry, but I'm not interested."

The panel beeps, the lock releases, but he's pressed into me before I can reach for the door, his thighs nestled behind mine, his chest against my back.

"Say it to my face," he demands.

My heart races, the rapid beat out of control. I swallow, knowing a believable declaration will be difficult to achieve. Hard, because this prick has my ovaries in his tight-fisted grip, but not impossible.

I turn, my brows raised in superiority. "I. Don't. Want. You."

I plaster myself to the wall, hoping for distance. He's hot. Scorching. Every inch of his body pressed into mine is an inch of heavenly connection.

He leans closer, his breath warming my lips. "Bullshit."

I want to succumb, to surrender to his erotic distraction but…

He strips the decision away from me, charging forward, taking my mouth with his. He steals my breath, his tongue swiping my lips to demand immediate entrance.

Goddamnit.

I can't deny him. I can't deny myself. I'm going down with this ship. Going down faster and harder than a cheerleader on prom night.

I grip his jacket, kissing him as if my life depends on the enthusiasm I place into our contact.

He growls, the rumble of his chest vibrating through me. He pushes me harder into the wall and grips my hips, his fingers digging into my jeans. His erection grinds against my pubic bone, making me want to beg.

No matter how risky or careless or insane, I want this man. I need him, if only to uplift me for those few short moments before I come crashing back down.

He retreats, retracting his devilish affection in a slap of withdrawal. His heavy breathing brushes my lips, my chin, my cheeks. Those fingers continue to dig into me. The light from inside highlights the flecks of color in his eyes, the greens, the browns as he stares at me with such sweet bewilderment that I know he thinks this is crazy, too.

I've kicked him out of my apartment and thrown his gun out a window. I've vomited in front of him, then launched into attack mode, before falling into bed in a mass of our tangled limbs.

This doesn't make sense. It's not what attraction is supposed to be. But attraction is what it is.

"Lie to me again," he murmurs. "Tell me you don't want me."

My heart climbs into my throat, restricting, suffocating.

"Yeah, I didn't think you could," he taunts, releasing my hips. His fingers find the waistband of my jeans, unclasping the button, lowering the zipper. A hand delves into my pants, beneath my panties, sliding straight to my pussy.

I gasp, not in shock, in undiluted pleasure. Everything tingles. Vibrates.

"For someone who doesn't want me, you sure are wet."

His fingers plunge inside me, two or three, I'm not sure. I'm too focused on grasping his shoulders to stop myself from crumpling to the floor. He twists, pulses, strokes. He pulls no stops in his masterful manipulation as he peers down at me, stalking my expression.

I want to succumb, not just physically, but emotionally, too. I want to admit how I feel. To tell him the tiny morsels of time in his presence are like a feast to my starving soul.

I sink my teeth into my lower lip, caging those words inside.

"You fucking want me," he snarls. "I bet you want me more than any other guy."

I close my eyes and grip him tight. Those talented fingers don't stop moving. The heat of his stare doesn't fade.

I'm falling, yet soaring. I'm hurting, yet drowning in the most exquisite pleasure. There's no life. No past. No future.

There's only now. Only ecstasy. Only sexual possibility.

We should take this upstairs. We could. If only my secrets weren't scattered over the floor in a mass of devastation.

The door swings open in a swoosh of noise and displaced air. I snap my eyes open and freeze when I see a woman standing there, gaping.

Mystery man shoves his shoulder into the wall, plastering his body to mine. He covers me, hiding what he's doing without stopping the pulse of his fingers for even a second.

"Get out of here," he snarls at her.

Protective. Oh, so protective.

I could swoon. Instead, my body trembles. I know nothing about this man, and yet he slays me. "Tell me your name."

His fingers plunge deeper as he holds my gaze. "Why? You've never shown any interest before."

I pant, my breathing fractured. "Well, I'm interested now." I need something to call him. Something other than '*my* mystery man.' I have to dissociate him from being mine at all.

He releases a barely audible chuckle. "If I tell you my name, will you promise to scream it when I make you come?"

I shake my head. "No." No way in hell. I'm out in the open, probably in view of Brent and those drunks who would be getting the show of their life. Not to mention the current state of my soaked panties is already a big enough compliment to satisfy even the largest ego. "I won't."

His fingers stop moving in a harsh threat. "Then whisper it for only me to hear."

Oh, God. My restraint snaps, and I moan in agreement. There's no will to deny him. Not when it's a mere whisper of surrender.

"Promise." His thumb flicks over my clit, igniting a pulse of wildfire.

"I will," I blurt. "I promise."

"Good." He leans closer, the rough stubble of his cheek brushing mine. His lips gently slide over my ear. "You can call me Hunter."

I whimper.

Hunter.

What a fucking seductive name. So much better than Jim or Jeff or Bill.

He twists those fingers, deeper, faster, the pad of his thumb pressing harder on my clit.

"Hunter," I whisper in warning. I'm close, nudging the precipice.

He inches back and gazes down at me, his eyes intent, his lips tight. God, I want to fuck him. I want to pull him close and kiss and kiss and kiss until I feel my soul return.

"What, princess?"

"Hunter." I can't say anything else. I can't think anything else. "Oh, God, *Hunter.*"

I close my eyes and rest my head against the wall as my pussy clamps tight. My core contracts over and over, the height of bliss hitting me as he leans his body into mine to keep me upright.

He doesn't stop fingering me. Those digits pulse. His thumb continues to work my clit.

I cling to him, my mouth finding his neck, my teeth digging into his flesh. I taste. I feel. I become invigorated. All because of this man.

The realization lessens the bliss, guiding me down from my peak in a gentle descent. I whimper as he holds me in one arm, his other hand still filling me.

"You done?" he murmurs.

My voice is lost to pleasure, my throat too tight to speak. I nod and meet his taut expression, noticing the wild, restrained lust in those harsh eyes.

"Good." He pulls away and steps back. His jaw ticks as he adjusts his cock, the thick outline of his erection bulging at his zipper. Then, without a goodbye, he turns and walks away muttering, "Tell your boyfriend I said hi."

9

HIM

I stride across the street, holding back the need to shove my fist against something that will break bone. She's playing me, I know that, but I still listen to her lies like a man starved of sound.

Problem is, I can't tell what's the truth and what's bullshit. Decker couldn't get a trail on her. Her apartment is owned by Brent Hendrix—the fucking bartender. Even the utilities are in his name. There are no ties to a Stephanie or Emma Stephens. She has to be paying him in cash to make sure she doesn't leave breadcrumbs.

But I'll find one.

Tomorrow.

I would bet my left nut she's not going to Seattle to meet a guy. I refuse to believe she's fucking me with a boyfriend a few hours away. But even with my nut on the line, the slightest doubt has furious jealousy streaming through my veins.

I want to kill this lover of hers. Real or imaginary.

The feel of her body against mine has become torture. The vanilla scent of her, too. All sweet and feminine. She's pliable to my touch, molding into me like butter, yet tough as nails at the same time.

So many conflicting aspects. A fucking kaleidoscope. Or maybe that's what she wants me to see. Smoke and mirrors.

I storm inside Atomic Buzz, slap my palms on the bar, and demand, "Scotch."

Brent glowers at me and prepares the drink. "Bad day?"

"You could say that." Every day has been a mix of heaven and hell since this woman walked into my life. I can't stop thinking about her—who she is, what she does, and why we've been brought together.

"Have you ever heard her talk about a boyfriend?" The question escapes my mouth without thought, making me sound like a needy little bitch.

"Steph?" Brent frowns.

"Yeah." I guess we'll stick with that for now because I don't believe her real name is Emma, either.

"No. Not at all. She doesn't share that shit with me."

So, having another dick on the side is a possibility. Great. Fucking perfect.

He hands over my scotch.

I throw down some bills before snatching the alcohol from the bar to go sit in the far corner of the room. Yeah, I'm sulking. For fuck's sake.

I need to leave, but I'm stuck here maintaining the charade that I showed up to get a drink, when I was actually stalking a woman who just left her apartment for the first time in days.

Impeccable timing is my only advantage, which Decker gained by hacking the video surveillance outside her apartment door. It seemed to be the only hole in her secretive existence—she logs into her online feed via her neighbor's unsecured internet.

So I have nothing on her—no name, no insight, no fucking clue—but I get notifications when there's motion around her door and a crystal-clear, black-and-white view of when she comes and goes.

Like right now. My cell vibrates in my jacket, and I already know it will be her. I tap into the video app to see her standing in the hall of her building. She enters the pin code to her apartment and releases the locks. I clench my cell as she opens the door, then she walks inside, out of sight, but still visible enough in my mind to make my dick pulse.

I should be doing a million other things. I should be on the other side of the city, preparing for an impromptu trip to Seattle.

Fuck.

I'm over a week late getting back to Torian. I've dodged his calls for days, which means I'm a heartbeat away from a gun-barrel prostate exam if I don't pull my shit together.

I gulp the cheap scotch and flick through my cell screen to call Decker. It's time to level-up our game.

He answers on the second ring with a chipper, "How can I be of assistance, fuck face?"

"Listen up." I'm not in the mood for his shit. Not that I ever have been. "I need you to be on the road tomorrow."

"Okay… Where's the party?"

I scan the bar, making sure nobody is paying me attention, and lower my voice. "Seattle."

"Who are we dealing with?"

Her. The woman who drives me mindless with curiosity and hunger. "We're still on the same project. Nothing has ch—"

"Are you serious?" He chuckles. "Torian is right. You're slipping."

Every muscle snaps taut. "When did you speak to Torian?"

"He called a few days ago wanting an update because you won't answer your cell."

Fucking hell. "What did you say?"

"What could I say? You haven't told me shit."

If Torian took the time to call, he would've pushed, demanded, threatened. He wasn't the type to walk away empty-handed.

"*What did you tell him?*" I repeat, my tone lethal.

"I said you were following some lead on a woman. That she's tied to Dan somehow… Which is only an assumption at this point, because it marks the time you dove headfirst into this weirdness."

I suck in a breath and hold it until it threatens to break my restraint. "Did you give him any specifics? Did you say anything that could lead to her?"

He gives a derisive scoff. "How is he going to find out who she is when I can't?"

Jesus. It's not about finding out who she is. Torian won't give a shit. If he knows about her, he'll do what I should've done days ago—get the information she has via whatever means necessary.

"Look," Decker starts, "I thought I was covering your ass. What was I supposed to do? Fabricate a story when I have no clue what's going on? We both know he'd lose his shit if he found out I was lying. And as much as I love you, buddy, it's not enough to take the fall when it comes to that crazy motherfucker."

No shit. Why does he think I didn't answer my phone? I don't need the drama.

I down the remaining scotch and breathe slowly to lessen the aggression pounding at my temples.

"What's going on, Hunt? Who is this chick?"

"I don't have a clue." It's the truth. "I know she was in that hotel room. She beat the fuck out of him, and I'm pretty sure she gained our information while doing it."

There's a pause. A silent criticism. "Why the hell didn't you tell me?"

Good question. The jury is out on that one. "Why did I need to? Would you have worked harder? Have you half-assed the background check because I didn't give you enough info?"

I'm a weak prick, trying to distract him from the more important questions, like, why didn't I get what I needed that first night? Why didn't this end back then? And why did I let it continue?

"I've done everything I can," he grates. "I don't half-ass anything, asshole, and you know it."

I do. But I don't regret the diversion. "Then you don't need specifics. You need to work with what I give you and remember who pays you. Me. Not Torian."

"Please tell me you're not sleeping with her." His plea is almost inaudible and followed with more criticizing silence. "Fuck, Hunt. You are, aren't you?"

I rest my glass on the table and massage my temples between my thumb and middle finger. I can't answer him. *No*. I don't need to.

"Are you still there, asshole?" he snaps. "What the fuck is going on?"

I don't know. I'm so lost in her I can't tell when common sense ended and obsession began. It wasn't supposed to go down like this. It started as a bit of fun. I was messing with the cocky bombshell with the sassy mouth. Then she flipped the fucking board on me and started to beat me at my own game. She had me chasing my tail and second-guessing myself.

I *never* second-guess myself.

"You need to sort this out," he says. "And fast. Torian isn't going to wait forever."

"I know." I fucking know. "I'm going to call him." I have no other choice. "I'll get in touch later with specifics for tomorrow."

"Yeah. I'll be waiting."

I shove from my chair and walk from the bar, not acknowledging Brent, who tracks my steps with his gaze. As I get outside, I glance up at her window, unable to break the habit.

She's there. I can feel her staring down at me, watching my movements with the same dedication I've shown watching hers.

I reach the end of the building, turn down the side street to my car, and start dialing Torian's number.

The call connects, and he greets with a, "About damn time you called." His tone is level, calm, but the man could turn on a dime.

"You got time to talk?" I ask.

"I'm at Devoured."

The call disconnects. One minute, conversation. The next, silence. It's not a bad connection. It's a demand to meet in person.

Fucking great.

I climb into my car and drive across town to his father's restaurant. I slow as I pass the front windows and see Torian inside, standing amongst a crowd of his family while he holds a young girl on one arm. His niece. His sisters are there, too, while a million other kids run around with balloons and streamers.

A private family function.

Fucking perfect.

I park my car and stalk inside, ignoring Carlos at the door, who quickly glances at Torian for approval to let me in.

The man of the moment inclines his head and grins at me as I approach. The slimy fucker is dressed in his typical designer suit, his brown hair immaculately styled, his face clean-shaven. The guy is young. Too fucking young to have the amount of power he carries under his belt. But he owns it, taking the authority in his stride.

I bypass his attractive younger sister along with the small army of children who have made his father's restaurant their bitch, and stop in front of Torian and the girl.

"Hunt." His smile remains in place, charismatic yet undeniably fake. I can see the anger hidden beneath the calm facade. I can sense the frustration, too. "I expected to see you sooner. You don't usually make me wait."

I ignore the little girl staring up at me and return his grin. His intimidation techniques don't work on me. They never have. Threats are only successful if you have something to lose, and Torian is well aware I've deliberately cut ties with anyone of value. "I told you I'd get in contact once the job was done."

"Why does it sound like you're about to tell me something I don't want to hear? Do you have what I need or not?"

"I'm still working on it."

His smile increases. Ignorant women would fall to their knees for that playboy charm, but I know the meaning of his expression. I know, and I refuse to give a shit. He leans down, placing his niece on her feet. "Go play with your friends, Stella."

"Okay, Unkie Cole." The girl skips away, her skirt swishing with every bounce.

He watches her, always smiling, always smug. "How are you still working on it when Dan is dead?"

"There was someone with him. A woman. I think she could be a lead to—"

"I didn't ask for a fucking lead. I asked for a name. *One* name. It wasn't a hard task."

I clench my teeth and look away in an attempt to control my temper. I'm not a failure. I won't accept being treated as one. "She beat him." I lower my voice. "Aren't you interested to find out why?"

"I'm only interested in the name. Why would I care about the whore who was with him before he died?"

"She's no whore."

"That's not what the detective tells me."

My pulse spikes, but I can understand where he's coming from. I'd assumed the same thing to begin with. "With a body like hers, she'd be stupid to work in a neighborhood well beneath her physical appeal. There has to be more to it than that."

She doesn't need to slum it for money. One look inside her apartment and I could tell she had cash. If she wanted to sell her body, she could easily do it with deep-pocketed men.

"Why are you wasting my time with assumptions, Hunt? Admit you've failed, and we can deal with the consequences."

"It's not an assumption, and I haven't fucking failed. She tortured him. And she's on the road tomorrow to meet someone in Seattle. I think she has contacts there." I drag my gaze back to meet his unfaltering stare. "If she was trying to keep him quiet, don't you want to know why? Don't you want to know if there are more players in this?"

Torian's eyes narrow. His lips flatten. He stares at me for long moments, scrutinizing, obviously strategizing. "Why do you care?"

"Money." That is the only acceptable answer. For me *and* him. "I'll get you more valuable information, and you can pay me for the extra work."

He laughs, long and hearty, as if I'm a fucking comedian. "Now that makes more sense. You've always been a money-hungry bastard." He inches forward to place his hand on my shoulder and guide me toward the front door. "And I appreciate you thinking outside the box. But do I need to reiterate how tired I am of waiting for a resolution on this?"

"It won't be much longer." I have no foundation for my promise. I'll just have to make it work. I'll have to move faster.

"Maybe you need help."

"No." I plant my feet and glare. "You gave this job to me, and I work alone."

"Really?" He taunts me with a smirk. "Does Decker know that?"

Decker is different. He helps from the outside. I never rely on him; I only ever lean. "Speaking of," I growl, "he's off-limits. You call him again, and we'll have a problem."

He laughs, but this time the facade cracks. The sound is sinister. Angered. "I wanted answers, and you wouldn't return my calls."

"Well, you have your answers now, so back off."

He squeezes my shoulder, the touch another threat. "I have nothing but your assurances, which mean little to me. In fact, I think I need to insist on someone else assisting you. I'll send Carlos to tag along."

I snap my gaze to those kids laughing and playing. I stare. I glare. I make sure they're at the front of my mind so I don't lose my shit. "You put a tail on me, and whoever it is will wind up face down in a dumpster."

A threat for a threat.

Torian chuckles and releases his hold, raising his hands in an act of surrender no sane person would believe. "Okay. Okay. I get it. You're invested in seeing this through. I can appreciate that."

"Thanks," I snarl.

We have worked together for years. We have been through more than most family members endure. But I have no doubt this man would cut ties in the blink of an eye. He also knows I'll do the same if pushed.

"I'll call you when I'm done." I stride ahead, a cautious throb tickling the back of my neck. I need to be finished with this job. I need to be done with it. With her.

"Hunt," Torian calls over the sound of celebrating children.

I stall, the cautious throb now taking over my limbs as I turn. "Yeah?"

"You've got forty-eight hours."

10

HER

I take Brent's car and head out of Portland before day breaks.

It's an easy drive tainted by the itch of paranoia. I stalk my rear-view mirror and pull over numerous times to make sure I'm not surrounded by the same cars. I also drive below the speed limit in an attempt to stay off the radar of any highway patrols.

Once I reach the outskirts of Seattle, I start to relax, and autopilot kicks in. I don't think about where I'm going until I'm in a familiar neighborhood, passing memories with each block.

Nostalgia tickles my senses as I slow through my old stomping ground. My elementary school looks the same, the brick building barely having aged over time. There's the track field I ran on. The mall I used to hang out at with my friends. My kindergarten teacher's house.

They all seem the same, and for a moment I feel the same, too.

The past engulfs me, returning me to another life where I was a different person. Back to the days when my only concerns were good grades and which party I would go to on the weekend.

I continue through traffic lights and streets, not stopping until I'm staring up at the thick metal gates which block my view from the prestigious property my family used to own.

It isn't the same vertical wrought-iron design my father installed. They've been replaced with horizontal ivory slats that attempt to cut me off from my childhood, but I still remember.

I can't forget how my sister told me to climb the property wall if I ever wanted to sneak out at night. I remember the smell of wisteria that lingered in the breeze every spring. I remember how my brother would run down the hall early each morning, waking me up with his enthusiasm to start the day.

I remember it all as if it were yesterday, even when it sometimes feels like a conjured fantasy. I want to get out and touch those walls that once encased a wealth of happiness, to peek into a yard which created laughter. But I can't.

I need to be careful. I won't risk being seen by people from my past. Not when they could drag my focus away from my goals with greater efficiency than Hunter already has.

I've started craving comfort again. Even the slightest human interaction. After a few brief encounters with a man I barely know, I've become foolishly charmed by the possibility of more.

Disconnecting from extended family has always been my hardest task. I've broken ties with anyone who previously took care of me. The aunts and uncles. The cousins and friends.

Leaving them behind was necessary for focus. I couldn't second-guess my endgame or the steps it would take to get there. I've become strong and determined with the sterility. I have no distractions.

The only things that matter are my parents and siblings, and the building fire they created inside me. They stoked the flames of retribution. That is why I am here. I need them to remind me of the promise I made ten years ago.

Them and only them.

I start the engine and continue along the road, passing the place where I fell off my bike and broke my arm, and the corner where I had my first kiss. After a quick detour for cheap takeout, I drive to the next suburb, toward the people I cherish most and love even more.

As I approach, remorse mixes with the digesting hamburger and fries now seated in my stomach. I've neglected my family for too long, and there's no excuse.

I approach another set of gates, these not quite as ostentatious as the last. They don't fit my mother's demand for flamboyance, or my father's appreciation for security. But the rich grass is immaculate, and I know Mom would love the scent of approaching rain in the air.

I pull over and climb out to face the devastating reunion. I keep my head low and try to ignore the uncomfortable scratching sensation at the back of my neck as I pass the first row of graves, then another, and another. I stop when I reach the seventh, and that hamburger threatens to make a comeback at the sight of the four identically shaped headstones standing before me, each with different text.

Stanley Carmichael. Emma Carmichael. Stephanie Carmichael. Thomas Carmichael.

I raise my chin, paste on a smile, and pretend I've got this.

"Hey, Mom. Dad." I scan the cemetery to make sure I don't have an audience to my one-sided conversation. Apart from a gray-haired woman yards and yards away, I'm alone. Like usual. I should be used to that by now.

"Sis. Baby Tom." My younger brother hated that nickname. He didn't like being seen as little or small. I'd only taunt him because it gave us the opportunity to tussle.

God, I miss tussling with him.

I kneel before them, my heart so heavy each beat feels certain to be my last. This is where I belong. Well, not exactly here. A few feet to the left, in the reserved space beside my brother. "I fucked up."

I swallow as a whisper of a chastisement brushes my mind. I hear their words, their voices, or maybe it's the approach of psychosis. I guess I'll find out sooner or later.

"I messed up bigtime." I stretch out along the grass and turn onto my back. I lie between them, my mom to my left, my dad to my right, as I blink up at the heavy clouds and let the chill of the ground seep through my coat. "I killed someone in my search to find Jacob."

Silence presses down on me, blanketing me in loneliness. It becomes hard to think. To breathe. To live. "I took his life, and now I know it's a race against time before karma catches up with me."

More whispered words fill my mind. Words of comfort and support. I have to believe it's them. I need to convince myself they're here, listening.

"The funeral is tomorrow." Dan will be laid to rest. His family will crumple, his friends will sob, and I have to accept the guilt.

My heart freezes beneath tightening ribs. I glance over my shoulder to my family, who have been reduced to stones amongst lush grass, and swallow through overwhelming dread. "I've become Jacob. I've done exactly what he did. And I don't know how to forgive myself."

Silence.

There are no comforting messages this time. I can't hear them. I can't feel them.

The bitter cold of loneliness digs deeper, and I curl into the fetal position, letting the frigidity take over. My stomach tumbles. Roll after roll of building self-loathing.

This is what I need to focus. I can't forget what I'm fighting for, what my goal is.

I close my eyes and focus on the image of Jacob in my mind. Young, blond, athletic.

I'd give anything to make him suffer. To restrain him the same way he did my family, and set his house on fire. I'd watch those flames melt his skin, and I wouldn't feel an ounce of remorse. I'd hear his screams, and I would smile. And he would scream. I know he would, just like I know my family did as they burned to death.

Bile launches up my throat.

I can't go back there. Not that far. It's too hard to leave.

I squeeze my lids tight and focus on relaxing. I have to calm myself. Think positive thoughts. I picture each muscle, one at a time, willing them to loosen. Toes. Calves. Thighs.

This is why I rarely return to Seattle. It took all my energy to commit to the future and not dwell in the torment of my past. Years dragged before I could break the habit of spending days in bed, cuddling my pillow as I sobbed with the need to wake up from this nightmare.

Relax. Hips. Stomach. Chest.

But I'd been so naive with Jacob. Entirely innocent. We'd been together for months. The perfect power couple—the jock and the loved socialite. I'd selfishly enjoyed the additional attention, not only from a dedicated boyfriend, but from my classmates who all decided they wanted to be me.

They didn't notice the changes in him like I did. They didn't see how his devotion turned into obsession. They didn't acknowledge his growing aggression.

Then again, even I found it hard to come to terms with him being capable of his horrific end game. And the actions of his wealthy parents who helped him escape police custody. I'm one-hundred percent certain his entire extended family assisted in the efforts to hide him from his punishment for all these years. That's why I won't feel shame or guilt at wanting him dead. He deserves it, and his family deserves to mourn the loss.

Fuck, woman, concentrate. Arms. Face. Mind.

My head becomes heavy, tempting me with sleep. Or maybe dragging me into approaching nightmares.

I never would've thought one simple, careless deception could cause such devastation. That a few simple words could be the difference between life and death.

I can't go to the party with you, Jacob. I have plans with my family.

I can taste the lie in my mouth, can feel it curl and twist around my tongue. I want to break up with him. I just don't know how. So, instead of going to that party, I walk to my best friend's house in the hope we can figure it out together.

I ignore his ten phone calls. I pretend he doesn't exist. But he ensures I'll never forget him.

The sound of wailing sirens follows me on the stroll home. Smoke billows in the distance. By the time I reach the bottom of my street I'm running, sprinting toward the bent and battered gates at the front of my property.

I search the yard, looking past fire engines and firemen in an attempt to find my parents and siblings. It's Friday night. My father always leaves work early. Stephanie is grounded for sneaking out to see her boyfriend. And my mom and Thomas are inseparable.

They're all home. But there's nothing to worry about because we have smoke alarms. Dad pays the alarm company to check them every spring. They would've gotten out. I'll find them around here somewhere. Maybe even in the back yard.

They've already located four bodies restrained in one of the downstairs rooms.

My heart lurches at the murmured words. I don't even know who they come from. The statement is just there, ringing in my ears, tearing at my soul.

No. I run for the front door, heat licking my skin, only to be dragged back. I scream. I sob. I crumple.

Don't be in there. Please, God, don't let them be in there.

I'm hauled onto the grass where some nameless, faceless woman yaps at me until I'm catatonic. *It will be okay. You're not alone. Do you want me to call a friend? A relative? Are you cold? Hungry?*

I remain still. Frozen in stone. I can already feel it—the isolating detachment, the brutal desolation.

I watch, in a daze as men rush around me, attempting to put out a blaze that burns my world to the ground. The fire crackles. Windows shatter. The sight before me doesn't make sense, not even the sense of overwhelming loss.

It's going to be okay, princess.

The familiar tone eats up my sorrow, and I snap my gaze to the left to find Hunter seated beside me. He's dressed in fireman's clothes. His face is smudged with soot. His skin is beaded with sweat.

Relief overwhelms me. There's no rhyme or reason. Not when hell has erupted around me.

What are you doing here?

I frown as he gives me that look of his. The one built of power, intent, and determination. I feel strengthened from the sight of him, from his mere presence. All I want to do is sit on his lap and curl into his arms like a child. To be protected and cared for. But I'll never be foolish enough to act on my desires. I'm already weak enough. The only way to grow strong is to detach myself from anything of value.

No car, no house, and definitely no loved ones.

Hunter, why are you here?

I repeat myself, over and over, as he sits there in silence. There's no more burning building. No dying family. The flames dwindle. The devastation evaporates. Everything fades. There's only him. Only me. Only faith and building assurance.

He leans close, his knee brushing mine. He reaches out a hand, his fingertips skimming my cheek. The zing that always accompanies his touch pummels my insides. I can breathe again. I can smile.

Tell me, I whisper. *Tell me why you're here.*

He smiles, sad but sure, those hazel eyes filling with promise and conviction.

I'm here because that's where you need me to be.

11

HIM

I crouch behind the headstone four rows back and listen to her mumble in her sleep. She's been lying on those graves for more than an hour, dead to the world. No pun intended.

My phone vibrates from the grass beside my thigh, the screen alighting with a notification from the walkie-talkie app. I shove my wireless earpiece back into place and click the button to make Decker's responses play automatically on arrival.

"Hunt, now I understand why you're so into her. She's morbid as fuck."

Prick.

From first thing this morning, this so-called friend has been a pain in my ass. He's commented on her tight jeans and the coat that apparently starves his view of her tits. He's criticized her driving, her mental stability, and her judgment for sleeping with me.

He's ogled her, made dirty comments and filthy promises. He's poked, teased, pushed, and I've withstood it all. But pretty soon I am going to break—his neck.

I press the response button on my screen and whisper, "Concentrate, motherfucker. Have you noted the names on those gravestones?"

"I'm all over it. Once we get home, I'll have answers for you."

Good. I'm running out of time.

"Do you think her tits are real?" Deck asks. "I've only seen her with a jacket on, but she looks too top-heavy for her figure."

I don't know where that piece of shit is hidden, but I raise a hand over my shoulder, above the shelter of my hiding place, and shoot him the bird.

Laughter echoes into my ear. "I think I've discovered a new favorite game. Teasing you about this chick is fun as hell."

I press the response button and mutter, "Teasing me will get you killed."

I chance a glance over the thick stone resting place of Doug Smith to find her lying in the exact same spot from ten minutes ago. She hasn't budged, only the cadence of her mumbled words has changed.

She's having a nightmare, and if she doesn't wake up soon she'll get soaked by the approaching black clouds.

"How long are we going to sit around playing with our dicks?" Decker asks.

I slump against the headstone and massage the bridge of my nose. "If you're playing with your dick," I whisper, "maybe consider cutting communication for a while."

"You know what I mean, lover boy. I'm happy to support your somnophilia, but I'm going to draw the line at spending the night in a cemetery."

"Somnophilia? What are you—"

"Hunter." Her voice cuts off my question.

I freeze. Not moving. Not breathing.

"*Hunter.*" This time it's a scream.

"Don't panic," Decker says in a rush. "She's still asleep… probably balls-deep in a nightmare about your tiny dick."

I ignore his blatant death wish and scour the ground for something to throw. I have to wake her up. Not because of the nightmare. Not because of the impending rain. I have to wake her because… *Fuck.* Just because.

I crawl to fetch a pebble a few feet away, then turn and launch it close in her direction. The projectile hits a nearby headstone with a thwack, and her legs jolt.

I slide back against my hiding place and wait as a drop of rain hits my cheek.

"Stay down. She's awake," Decker mumbles. "She's getting up."

Water hits my nose, my jacket, my jeans, the drips falling with lethargic frequency.

I clench my fists, fighting the need to see her, to read her expression and get a clue as to why she called my name. Was it really a nightmare? Does she know of my intentions? Can she feel me nearby?

I remain hidden, every inch of me on alert, as the rain settles in.

"She's on the move. Headed toward her car," Decker adds. "I'll be right behind her."

I hear a rush of footsteps, the release of a car door, and the thwack of it closing. There's the purr of an engine, then the crunch of loose asphalt.

I grab my phone and press the button to talk. "You better be all over her. Don't let her out of your sight."

"My pleasure."

Fucker.

I wait until the sound fades, then dash for my car parked outside the fence on the other side of the cemetery. I'm behind the wheel within minutes and speeding through the streets seconds later.

Adrenaline makes me her bitch—pounding heart, racing blood and all. I'm so entirely fucked up because I know this shit will end badly, and yet I still love the game of cat and mouse.

The trill of an incoming call from Decker hits my speakers, and I connect via Bluetooth. "Where are you?"

"She's driving toward the I-5. I think we're going home."

"Okay." *Fuck.* She hasn't met with anyone. Not even a goddamn boyfriend. "Stay on her, and let me know if you run into any trouble. I'll make sure to keep my distance."

I end the call and sink into my seat. This excursion hadn't been the epiphany of information I'd needed. I have the address of the house she stopped at when we first arrived, and the names on the headstones. But I expected revelations.

And now I have to rely on Decker to do more digging. He'll have less than a day before I have to quit playing nice with her to ensure I get the answers Torian needs.

She will hate me. Fight me. And I'm a perverted motherfucker for the way my cock pulses at the thought.

Over the passing miles, Decker keeps in contact, giving me updates when necessary. "We've reached the highway." "We're at Tacoma." "I just passed Olympia."

I follow, along with rain that switches from a light dusting to a heavy downpour and back again. I play out the conversation I'm going to have with her once this turns sour—the threats, the lies, her physical abuse.

My dick appreciates the mental stimulation, even though I'm not thrilled to be sporting wood on the I-5 with no relief in sight. Not for a few hours, at least. By then I'll be back in Portland in the shitty bar, waiting for her to arrive with Brent's keys. I just have to pass her somewhere in between now and then.

I have every intention of spending the night in her bed. I'll beg, borrow, and steal to get between those sheets. Or more accurately, I'll bluff, intimidate, and manipulate.

Old habits die hard.

Night descends, and boredom grows. The taillights in front of me brighten the highway like a switchboard, and I become tired of the radio silence. I haven't heard from Decker in more than forty minutes, which isn't normal.

I dictate a message, press send, then wait some more. Once another five minutes pass, I succumb to the update deprivation and place a call. "What's going on?"

"I'm not sure. I'm a little on edge thinking we might have a problem."

"What is it?" I press down on the accelerator.

"We could have a tail."

"And you didn't think to call me?" *Fuck.* "Where? What car?" I scan the passing vehicles, even though I have to be miles behind him.

"It's a black Mercedes. I noticed it a while ago, but it hung way back. Now he's being obvious. Every time she slows, he slows. If she speeds up, he's right there behind her."

"Have you got eyes on the driver?" I pass car after car, exceeding the speed limit without any shits given.

"I'll take a closer look."

There's silence, nothing but the slush of water beneath my tires.

"Damn it," he snarls.

"What?" My chest pounds, and I grip the steering wheel tighter.

"He's got tinted windows. I can't see dick. But he's retreating now that I'm riding side-saddle."

"Don't hound him. Keep back and watch. I don't want her thinking she's boxed in. I'm going to make a call and see if I know who's responsible."

"Torian?"

Yeah, fucking Torian. "I'll let you know."

I disconnect and make the new call.

"Good evening, Hunter."

"Have you lost your fucking mind?" I suck in a breath and let it out slowly. "You've got eyes on me, don't you?"

He laughs, and I have to force myself to remain calm. Decker comes into view up ahead, his white suburban in the middle lane, the fucking Merc farther ahead.

"You promised you wouldn't follow," I snap. "You gave me forty-eight hours."

"I made no promises. In fact, I think you were the one who made a pledge during that conversation. Something about a dumpster, if my memory serves."

"Did you think I was joking?"

"No, but I thought I'd send Carlos to investigate anyway."

"Well, your investigator is about to run my mark off the road."

"Maybe he's there as a friendly warning, too."

Breathe. Just fucking breathe.

"I get it, okay? You want answers, and you think I'm dragging my feet. Believe me, I understand. But this will pay off. You don't need to send your bitch to play hardball."

"Are you sure? Carlos says she hasn't met with anyone yet. I'll be interested to hear his full report once he returns."

"After all these years, you don't trust me? Come on, Torian. You either let me do this my way or you're on your own." I'm bluffing. I have no choice. "Commit to the forty-eight hours you gave me. Let me do my job."

The Merc's brake lights grow smaller with its gaining speed, and he cuts into the middle lane in front of Decker, closing in beside Steph.

"Torian…" My chest pounds. My temples, too. "You're going to blow this, and I'm so fucking close." To her. To this. To insanity. "What's the plan, anyway? You're losing your fucking mind if you want to run her off the road."

"Maybe that's necessary."

"For what reason?" I snap.

"To send a message. Or do you already get the picture?"

"I've got the fucking picture. Do I have forty-eight hours or not?"

"No. Now you're approaching twenty-four."

The line disconnects.

"*Fuck.*" My shout reverberates through the car. I can't get any closer. Not without letting her know I've been trailing her. All I can do is twiddle my fucking thumbs as this son-of-a-bitch veers closer and closer into her lane.

I call Decker.

"What do you want me to do?" he asks. "This guy is going to ram her."

"I know." And all I can do is watch. One look at me and the game is over. She can't see me here. I could claim it was a coincidence we ran into each other whenever she left her building. But being in the same place, more than an hour from her home, is a fucking stretch. "Slow down. Maybe he'll back off if you do."

"Okay. Got it."

The Merc veers for her again. Slow. Slow. Then fast, almost ramming into her. She swerves, the car fishtailing along the slippery road as her brake lights beam bright.

"*Stop*," I yell at Decker as I rapidly approach.

She hydroplanes, sliding one way, then the other, taking over the middle lane, then the third.

I slow, but I can't stop.

I can't fucking stop.

"Help her." I hold my breath as Decker slows in front of me, hanging back to stalk her movements.

I approach, getting closer and closer, while she careens off the road, along the soaked grass and puddles that spray water in every direction.

"Make sure she's okay." My pulse spikes as I pass. I'm fucking shaking. In anger or fear, I don't know.

"You've really got a thing for this chick, don't you?" Decker asks.

"Pretend I do and make sure you act accordingly." I stalk my rear-view mirror, watching as he pulls up beside her. "That means you touch her, you die."

He chuckles. "Although I'd love to make promises, sometimes the charm can't turn itself off."

"Touch her and die," I snarl.

"You're such an easy target these days."

His laughter echoes through the car until I disconnect the call.

I have to get over this shit. I'm nobody's bitch. Not hers. Not Torian's. And definitely not this fucker in front who thinks he can mess with my assignment.

I shove my foot against the gas, and the car kicks up a gear. Decker and Steph disappear in the distance of the mirror, and I force myself not to look back.

I crank up my music and let the rhythmic thump of rage take over. I'll catch up to this motherfucker and teach him a thing or two about road safety. I'll also ensure Torian doesn't get that report he's waiting on and make it clear I always fulfill my promises.

12

HER

I careen off the road, panic clogging my throat. I jolt in my seat as I bump along the grass median strip, hitting puddles that douse my windshield. The car slides sideways, completely out of control, along with the frantic beat of my pulse. I release the brake and try again, shoving my foot down hard.

The brakes grip. Tight. I keep my foot planted as I'm flung forward. The seatbelt finally locks, burning my neck and holding my chest in place. My forehead hits the steering wheel. Pain consumes my skull, and the world blurs.

For a moment, there's nothing. No movement. No sound. No panic. Just a blur.

"Jesus Christ." I close my eyes and breathe. Slow, calming breaths.

The rhythmic thump of the windshield wipers returns to my awareness. The light patter of rain, too. Cars pass, slushing water.

I'm safe. I'm safe. I'm safe. I chant the words over and over in my mind.

It was a careless road accident. A stupid goddamn mistake. That's all. There was no malicious intent. No hidden agenda. No asshole trying to kill me.

I open my eyes and swallow the need to crumple. For once, I wish I could be weak. I want someone else to fix my mess. To make everything okay again. I want the guilt over Dan to be gone. The pain over my family to ease. And I want Hunter.

I want him now.

Come on, bitch. Focus. Get your ass out of here.

I place the car in reverse, and a shadow creeps into my peripheral vision. A large, looming figure approaches my door. I lunge for the glove compartment and yank it open.

"Are you okay?" a man asks.

I pause in my reach for the gun hidden beneath road maps and glance over my shoulder. A guy stands at my window. His image is distorted through the droplets of rain against the glass, but I can still glimpse a relatively handsome face full of concern.

"I saw everything. Do you want me to call the cops?"

"*No.* I'm good." I straighten and wind the window down a crack, letting the chilled wet air gush in.

He smiles at me as rain hits his smooth honeyed skin and chocolate hair. "You sure? That old guy shouldn't be on the road."

"Old guy?"

He nods. "hair, thick glasses, golfer hat. He almost cut me off a few miles back."

The tightening in my lungs loosens. I can deal with the thought of an old-timer. It's the other possibilities that poke at my paranoia. "I didn't see who was driving."

"I don't think he saw much of anything either." He chuckles, but the humor quickly fades under his narrowing brown eyes. "You've got a bump." He points to his forehead. "Are you sure you're okay?"

"I'll be fine once I get back on the road."

He retreats a step and glances along the side of the car, his gaze low. "That might be a problem. Those wheels look pretty deep."

Shit. *Shit.* "*Shit.*" My frustration comes out in a rough shout. This is the karma I expected. The starting phase that will slowly morph into something big enough to drag me under its suffocating wing.

He flashes a sexy grin. It's gorgeous, filled with oozing amounts of charm. "Don't worry. I'll get you out of here. Why don't you put it in reverse and give it a try?"

A shiver runs down my neck. Not a welcome one. As physically appealing as this guy is, I don't want to be reliant on him. But being stuck on the side of the highway, in the middle of nowhere, is even less of a preference.

"Yeah..." I nod and wince at the renewed pain pounding through my head. "Okay."

I place the gearshift in reverse and slowly lower my foot on the accelerator. The wheels spin, whirring and sliding without traction. "Damn it."

"I'll give you a push."

He stalks for the front of the car, and I can't help my usual cautious analysis. He's tall. Way taller than I am. Thick arms, broad shoulders. In an attack, overpowering him would be difficult. In all honesty, it would be almost impossible without a substantial eye gouge or knee to the groin.

He stands before the beaming headlights, places his hands on the hood, and meets my gaze through the windshield. "Give it another try."

"Hold on a sec." I reach across the car, grab my gun from the glove compartment and my coat from the passenger seat. I hide the weapon inside the thick material and place them both in my lap.

I don't believe this guy's selfless act. I don't care that he's attractive, or kind, or charming. I'm not even sure I buy his account of the old guy not seeing me. I have no choice but to question everything.

"I'm ready now," I call out the window. "How about you?"

"Go for it."

I inch my foot down on the pedal. The wheels spin, whir. I hold my breath, my pulse increasing with each passing second. I can't stay out here. I can't wait for a tow. The piece-of-shit car has to move. There is no other choice.

Please, please, please.

The man roars as he pushes, his expression pinched, the material of his long-sleeve gray shirt growing damp and sticking to his biceps.

The car slides in and out of traction, moving sideways, farther and farther, before finally gripping. I exhale in a gush of relief and steer through bumpy, soaked grass.

The man follows, running after me, still pushing, until I pull the car to a stop parallel to the highway. He grins at me through the windshield, his chest heaving as he straightens, exposing more muscles hugged by his shirt and the faint hint of dark tattoos beneath.

He walks around the hood, shaking his feet, and returns to my window, his lips quirked in smug satisfaction.

"Thanks." I glance down at his soaked shoes and wince at the pants drenched from his ankles to his knees. "I'm sorry about your clothes."

"You don't happen to have a towel, do you?" He leans forward and looks in the car, scoping out the front and the back.

The chill returns, sliding down my neck, my spine. I slip my hand into my coat and palm my weapon. "No, unfortunately, I don't." I shouldn't be this jumpy, not when he clearly needs a towel, but distrust comes with the territory.

"No problem." He waves me away. "Where are you headed, anyway?"

None of your damn business. "Portland."

"Me, too. Do you want me to follow you in case you have any problems?"

"I'll be fine." My response is unintentionally growled, which only increases his grin.

"I'm not looking for a gratitude blow job, if that's what you're thinking. It's just that the roads are slippery, and it's harder to drive at night. Your wheel alignment might be messed up, too."

"I don't have much farther to go. And if I run into any problems, I have someone I can call."

"Okay. I'll get out of your hair, then." He reaches out a hand to shake.

I stare for longer than necessary, my heart pounding as I release my gun and clasp his offering. "Thanks again."

His palm engulfs mine, and he's warm despite the rain and cool temperature. He also grips my hand gently. Not weak, but not overpowering.

Those dark eyes turn somber, and I can see sympathy staring back at me. Or maybe it's an apology. I don't know either way, but he stares for longer than he should, his attention stealing parts of me that I want back.

I pull my hand away and paste on a smile. "It was nice meeting you."

"Likewise." He inclines his head and gives me a two-finger salute. "I'll see you around."

He walks away, and I watch my side mirror until he's inside his car. I wait. Then wait some more. He doesn't make a move to leave before me. In fact, he flashes his lights, instructing me to go first.

"Damn you." I pull onto the highway, trying to watch the road and the Good Samaritan who can't take a hint as he follows.

I pump the brakes to make sure they're in working order, then I press my foot down on the gas. I stop worrying about highway patrols and breaking the speed limit, and focus on ditching the guy behind me.

I REACH Atomic Buzz within fifty minutes and park in the alley out back before walking inside.

Brent is behind the bar with Hunter perched on a seat in front of him.

They both look toward me at the same time, and I shiver. It's easy to ignore Brent's gentle smile; I've seen it so many times before. What I can't tear my gaze away from is Hunter and the concern tightening his brows. His eyes narrow, taking me in, head to foot. The air in my lungs becomes heavy. My sternum throbs. I raise the collar on my coat in a vain attempt to shield myself.

Why does he have this effect on me? How does he have any affect?

I left town to gain distance from him, yet the physical miles seem to have brought me emotionally closer. My dream, and the fucked up message my subconscious tried to send, have me on the verge of weak, pathetic girliness.

"Thanks for the loan." I continue forward, forcing my attention to Brent, and lob the keys at him. "I appreciate it."

"No problem." He places the keys back on the hook. "How did the old girl run?"

"Like a dream." I lick my lower lip, trying to relieve the scorching heat of a predator's stare. "She's parked out the back. I even took her through the car wash so she looks all pretty." Truth be told, I'd had to hose off all the caked mud and grass to hide the evidence of my off-road adventure.

Hunter slides off his seat, and I stiffen as he approaches. Every inch of me is aware of him—my nerves, my pulse, my intuition.

"Are you okay?" His voice is low, yet strong.

That's what I need right now—strength, and lots of it.

What I wouldn't give to be a person who could crumple into a pool of exhausted tears and dramatic sobs. To have the freedom to be vulnerable and allow him to gather me in his arms and whisper words of comfort.

Like in the movies.

Like in a dream.

I grind my teeth, grinding away the weakness at the same time. "Yeah. Of course." I step back, needing distance from the eyes that narrow on my forehead. "Why wouldn't I be?" I lick my lower lip, then curse the action. "On second thought, don't answer that."

I need to break this… whatever it is—attraction, distraction, complication. "I've gotta go."

"You're not staying for a drink?" Brent asks.

"No, not tonight. I'm exhausted." I give them a lazy finger wave and turn for the door. Then I hear it—his footsteps. Hunter's pursuit.

My heart trembles with giddy excitement, and I wish it didn't. I wish I had some glimmer of control. But I'm completely lacking.

I reach the door, push outside, and stop as soon as I feel him approach behind me. "I can't do this tonight, Hunter. I'm too tired."

"Relax." He settles into me, his legs brushing the back of my thighs, his arm wrapping around my waist to place a gentle hand on my stomach. "I'm not looking for sex."

I don't move. I can't. I'm starved for his touch, my appetite too demanding to ignore.

"Are you hurt?" he murmurs.

I frown in confusion. "Why would I be hurt that you don't want to have sex with me? I just told you I'm too tired to deal with you tonight."

His breathy laughter sweeps over my neck, and he walks around to face me. His hand raises, slow and sure, his fingers pushing the hair from my forehead. "I'm talking about this." A gentle touch glides around the tender bump in pure, heart-melting torture. "But if you want to keep talking about sex…"

"No." I nudge him out of the way and walk to the curb to check for traffic. "I'm completely exhausted."

"Too exhausted for sex?" he asks. "I guess we skipped the whole dating thing and slid straight into being a married couple."

I can't hold back a smile. "Don't be a dick."

"Then don't be a pussy."

My humor fades. He's right. I need to toughen up. "Good night, Hunter."

I walk across the road and hitch my handbag higher on my shoulder.

The crunch of his steps follows. "I'm worried about you."

It's not the words that slay me. It's the tone. The pure concern. Ten years have passed since anyone has uttered words like that to me. Ten long, painful years.

"I bumped my head." I reach my building and face him. "It's no big deal."

He nods and his focus lowers, the seductive trail moving over my cheek, my jaw, to my neck. His brows snap tight, and his jaw ticks. "*Fuck.*"

"What?" I place a hand on my neck, to the place where the seatbelt had burned me. "Is it bad?"

"It's bad enough." He nudges my wrist away and scrutinizes the area. "What happened?"

"Nothing. Just let it go."

I continue to the building entrance and enter the pin code. The lock releases, and he pulls the door wide.

"Let *me* go," I clarify.

"I will. Once I check you over and make sure you're really okay."

I stand there, caught between two options, one sensible, one indulgent. "It's my neck and my head. That's all."

He nods. "Good. That means it won't take long."

He lathers me with his concern, pulling at the thinnest fibers of my control. He's figured me out and determined how much I crave him. He knows he's my weakness.

"You've got five minutes."

He smirks, and the sight should have me retracting my offer. It should...but it doesn't. He follows me into the elevator, down the third-floor hall, and into my apartment.

Oh, shit.

The box of my life secrets is still open with the pages scattered across the floor, over my coffee table, and along the sofa, like a mass of dirty laundry. I shoot a glance at Hunter and he's staring, taking it all in with those scanning eyes.

"Sorry about the mess." I dump my handbag on the floor and take slow, measured steps, forcing myself not to rush forward. "Help yourself to the coffee machine, or get whatever you want from the fridge."

"I'm good." He follows, stopping at my sofa to peer down at the skeletons now outside of my closet. "Do you need a hand?" He leans over and picks up a piece of paper.

"No." I lunge and snatch the newspaper article away. "It's confidential."

He infuriates me with a dubious raise of his brow.

I lose all pretense of calm and scramble, shifting the pages into piles to cover them from view. "I do research work for a university professor. He doesn't like when we discuss projects with outsiders."

"Outsiders?"

Shit. I sound like an idiot. "Yeah." I shrug. "He studies criminal psychology but already has enough issues of his own, ya know?"

He nods and focuses on the piles I've created, his neck slightly craned to peek at the information. "Seems interesting enough."

"Not really." I grab the last of my secrets from the floor and stack them on top of those on the sofa, then those on the coffee table. I shuffle until they're in a neat pile and then place them back in the box.

"There." I dust my hands and will my pulse to settle. "All done."

He continues to nod, lazy and contemplative.

"Now, where were we?" I wiggle the coat from my shoulders and drape it over the sofa. "You wanted me to prove I was fine, right?" I spread my arms wide, then tap my nose with each forefinger and do a twirl. "See? I'm perfect."

Again, he gives me a lethargic nod, and this time a smirk is added to the mix, as if he's agreeing that I'm perfect. "How did it happen?" He approaches with predatory steps. "Was it your boyfriend?"

I swallow, my mouth tingling. I want to lie. I want to lie so damn bad and tell him this fake boyfriend hurt me. *He hurt me because of you.*

Would Hunter care? Would he vow to protect me?

I suck in a deep breath and stand tall. I'm not going to succumb. Not again. "I had a slight car accident. I ran off the road."

He stops in front of me, almost toe to toe.

"I adore Brent, but his car is a piece of shit. The seatbelt didn't lock fast enough, and I hit my head on the steering wheel."

He remains calm. Always in control. "Are you hurt anywhere else?" His gaze scans me, across my hairline, along my jaw, down to the small V of my thin cotton sweater.

"I'm not hurt at all."

He grips my sweater and begins to lift.

"Hunter." I place my hands on top of his. "I'm not doing this now." No matter how adamantly my body voices a protest.

He meets my gaze, those hazel eyes strong and true. "I know."

He continues to lift my sweater, taking it over my head and dropping it to the floor. He captures my stare as he unbuttons my blouse from the top. I hold my breath as his knuckles brush the inside curve of my covered breasts, and I can't fight the need to swallow.

He glances down, and his jaw tenses.

I'm caught in a daze, transfixed by the way his hair falls gently over his forehead, as a lone finger streaks a line from my shoulder to my cleavage.

"You're hurt worse than you thought." That finger continues strumming my desire with its delicate caress. "Are you sure you're okay?"

"Hmm?" I glance down to the light pink line marking my chest. An extended war wound left from the seatbelt. "It's nothing. It doesn't even hurt."

My attraction is much more painful.

He ignores me, those fingers trailing farther along my buttons, this time leaving them in place. He reaches the hem and lifts, exposing my stomach.

I notice everything he does, the soft blinks, the slight narrowing of his stare. Every inch of me is in tune with every inch of him, the gentle rise of his chest, the bite of teeth into his lower lip.

He's beautiful. Harsh, yet stunning.

The pad of his thumb swipes my abdomen, the touch trailing above the waistband of my jeans in exquisite lethargy.

It's so light.

Too light.

Barely enough.

"There's the slightest mark here. You'll probably bruise tomorrow."

I don't care. Right now, I wouldn't mind if the morning brought the end of the world, as long as he didn't stop touching me.

"Is there anywhere else I need to check?" he asks.

Mmmhmm. There sure is, doctor.

"No." I clear my throat. "Is there anywhere on *you* that I need to check?"

His light chuckle is like melted chocolate and scented candles—the absolute perfect prelude to sex.

His eyes darken, growing devilish. "Maybe." He slides his hands over my ass, gently pulling me closer to grind into me.

I withhold a whimper, caging it inside my throbbing chest.

All I can think about is sex. Lots and lots of sex. Tangled sheets. Sweaty skin. Glistening muscles. Moaning. Screaming.

Oh, God, I could come already.

"You distract me," I admit.

"From what?"

I blink to awareness, realizing my stupidity. I've fought to keep him away from my secrets, only to stumble with the simple grind of his dick.

I'm slipping.

"Nothing." I shake my head.

He growls, his fingers digging into my ass. "I should've known better than to assume you'd ever share any insight into your life. You won't even tell me your fucking name."

He doesn't stem the aggression in his tone. I see it. I feel it, too. The threat should scare me. Instead, I crave it. I want more. "You know my name."

"Yeah." He scoffs. "It's Emma. Steph for short."

He retreats a step, and his withdrawal leaves me chilled. Icy. I want to reach out, to grasp, and tug, and pull. Instead, I hold my ground as he begins to pace.

"When are you going to tell me something real?" His question is a plea that hits the weaker parts of my resolve. "I want to hear the fucking truth for once."

I lift my chin, battling his emotional onslaught.

Don't falter. Don't break.

"Who are you running from?"

I shake my head. "I'm not running from anyone."

"Bullshit."

"It's true." I keep my hands at my sides, even though I want to reach out and reconnect. "I'm searching for someone. I've been searching for almost ten years."

His brows pull tight. He's assessing me, attempting to sift through the truth and lies. "Who?"

"An old friend. A boyfriend."

He releases a derisive laugh. "Another one?"

"No. Not another one." I inch back to rest my hip against the sofa when all I want to do is move toward him. Into him. "I lied about Seattle."

"Yeah?" He narrows his gaze. "Why?"

More stupid. So much stupid.

Stupid. Stupid. Stupid.

I look away. I can't do this. For normal people, this might be simple, giving answers to menial questions. For me, it's slicing open a vein and letting my soul rush out.

He advances, eating up my vision to cage me against the furniture. "Why?" he growls against my ear.

"Because I can't want this. You shouldn't be here."

"I don't want to be here either, Emma." He leans in, brushing his lips against my neck. "Steph..." He does it again, the next kiss lower. "Princess..." And lower, devouring the sensitive spot where my shoulder meets my neck. "I have a million things I need to do right now, and the only one I plan on doing is you."

He keeps his mouth in place, and each second is a dose of pleasured pain. A temptation and a punishment.

"Do you love him?" he murmurs.

My heart drops at his raw emotion. "Who?"

"This boyfriend you're chasing."

I clutch his shirt, twisting the fabric. Even the concept of loving Jacob makes me nauseated. "No. We have unfinished business. That's all."

"Then how can I help you find him?"

The nausea vanishes, the bile and hatred being replaced with the warmest gratitude. Then disappointment. "You can't. The only connection I had to him is now dead."

There's another pause, this one filled with tension. "The senator's son?"

I don't answer. He's seen enough of my dirty laundry for one night. "Can we talk about something else?"

He nods, scraping his teeth over my shoulder. Tickling. Teasing.

I breathe him in, letting the lingering scent of fading aftershave sink into my lungs. "On second thought, let's not talk at all."

13

HER

The next morning arrives with me having to claw my way out of the deepest depths of sleep. I sit up, the sheet falling from my chest to expose my nudity as sunlight bathes my room.

"Hey." Hunter clears his throat from beside me, his eyes closed. "You okay?"

"Yeah. Bad dream, that's all."

A nightmare.

I'd been at Dan's funeral, witnessing the pain I'd inflicted on innocent people as they stood sobbing around his grave.

I'd apologized, over and over, but nobody could hear me. The crying grew, building to a cacophony that pounded in my ears, until mourners began walking away. One by one, the crowd had dispersed, leaving a lone man to stand before the open hole in the ground.

Jacob.

"We're both the same now." He'd smirked at me. Fucking smirked.

I can't get the image out of my head. It's there, stalking me from every corner of my mind.

"Oh, shit," I whisper. It's a sign.

"What's wrong?" Hunter mutters.

"Nothing." I slide from the bed and tug my nightshirt from under my pillow. "Go back to sleep."

He groans and turns onto his stomach, planting his face into the mattress.

I pull the shirt over my head and stare vacantly across the apartment.

Jacob could be at the funeral. And yeah, maybe I am clutching at disintegrating straws here, but it is a possibility. One that makes my heart pound and my hands sweaty.

Could it be that easy? Could my actions toward Dan have led to what I've been searching for?

Maybe that's why he died. Dan had to so I could find Jacob. Instead of chasing him for the rest of my life, the asshole will come to me.

Fate and destiny have collided. It all makes sense now.

I could go to the church. *No.* The enclosed space will be tricky. I'll go to the cemetery instead and watch as the cars roll in. If I find my mark, I'll place a tracker on his vehicle and let the retribution begin.

I smile. I almost laugh.

Soon, I'll be free, and my family can rest in peace.

I rush on my toes to my wardrobe and inch the doors apart. I grab my handbag from the hook on the wall, place it on the floor, then kneel to open the plastic storage container stashed behind my coats.

I scrounge through the contents and pull out anything I might need.

GPS tracker—check.

Cable ties—check.

Silencer—check… Just in case.

I place them in my handbag and double-check my gun is there from yesterday.

Could I even pull the trigger at the funeral of a man I've murdered? *No.* I won't inflict more pain on these people. But I will arrive prepared.

I grab my black corporate dress off a hanger, then rush back to the bed and pull underwear from my drawer, along with my phone. With my handbag in one hand and clothes in the other, I sneak to the bathroom and close myself inside.

I do an Internet search on the funeral. The church service is at ten. *Shit.* I only have an hour before it starts, which gives me roughly an additional hour to get to the cemetery, right?

You'd think I'd know more about funerals, having lost my entire family, but I wasn't involved in planning that event. I'd been catatonic. All I remember is the walk down the aisle toward four matching coffins, each with a large adornment of lilies displayed on top.

My mother had never liked lilies.

Focus.

I dump my stuff on the floor, and have a record-breaking time trial in the shower. I spare five minutes on a rushed makeup attempt, two minutes for my hair, then I'm ready and pulling the bathroom door wide.

Hunter is seated in bed, his back against the headboard, his hands behind his head. I pause, gifting myself with the briefest visual indulgence. I fell asleep in those arms, against that Hulk-like chest, and I can't deny I want to do it again.

"Good morning." I grin, unable to hide my appreciation for last night's orgasm extravaganza. Hunter has a way with me, one that rocks my womb and has probably destroyed me for any other man.

"Morning." He takes me in with a visual sweep, over the stiff black dress that shadows every inch of my skin, from knees to collarbone to shoulder. It screams sophistication, but I can tell he sees the sex appeal. "You look nice."

"Thanks." I'm not a giddy person—at least, I wasn't until he showed up in my life. Now, I'm not so sure. "You look well rested."

"I am. For once." He jerks his chin at me. "Come here."

I struggle not to comply. My wants and needs wage war. "I can't. I have to leave."

His gentle appraisal transforms to tight scrutiny. "Where are you going?"

He flicks back the sheet, exposing his divine lower half before he slides from the mattress. He approaches, entirely naked, completely aroused, and I force myself to hold his gaze. "Where?" he repeats.

"A funeral."

The hint of fear slides through his features, a brief snap of flaring eyes and parting lips before he masks his concern. "Why?"

"I don't know," I lie. "For curiosity. For closure."

"You're talking about Dan Roberts, right?"

"Yeah…" I don't appreciate how intuitive he is. "How do you know him?"

"I knew *of* him. Everyone does. He was the crooked son of a senator. He had links to drugs and solicitation, among other shady shit." He stops in front of me, unabashed and unapologetic. "People who associate themselves with men like Dan are dangerous. They aren't people you want to be around. Even at a funeral."

"I don't plan on handing out business cards or networking with those in mourning. I just need to go. For me."

For my family.

He steps into me, draping his arm around my waist. "I don't want you there." He speaks against my lips, gifting me with light butterfly kisses until his words sink in.

I pull back and meet his gaze. There's no remorse over his dictate, no shame visible in his features. Only determination.

"You're overstepping," I whisper.

This thing between us, whatever it is, doesn't carry a noose. I'm not his woman to leash. I never will be.

"Then let me come with you. Let me drive you there. I don't even have to get out of the car. I'll just be close if you need me."

I shake my head. "I can't." I need to lay low. Not draw any attention. Police will be there, looking for the murderer, and I don't want to ping any radars.

"Let me put it this way, I'm going whether you like it or not." He steps back and walks for his clothes piled beside the bed. "We can do it the easy way, in the same car. Together." He snatches his jeans off the floor and tugs them on sans underwear. "Or you can be stubborn and get there on your own."

I ignore how he has to fold his dick like a full-grown anaconda to shove it inside his pants. I ignore and ignore, because at a time like this I shouldn't be thinking about him pretzel-ing his dick.

"Whatever you decide," he growls, "you won't be there alone."

No. "I need to do this on my own."

"And you will." He pulls his shirt over his head and straightens the material with the repeated brush of a hand. "I'll wait in the car."

"Don't push," I plead. "This is for me, Hunter. It's personal."

He tugs on his boots, rough and full of aggression. "I said I'd wait in the damn car."

I want to hate him. I probably would if the ride didn't make the travel component of my plan ten times easier. I'll have a base to spy from, unlike being left in the open if I catch a cab.

He strides for the door and pulls it wide. "You coming?"

I glare, not appreciating how he's manipulated the moment to become the offended party. He's the one stepping on *my* toes. Not the other way around.

"Yeah." I sigh and grab my coat from the rack. "I'm coming."

WE TRAVEL IN SILENCE. Hunter broods, while I plot.

I don't want anyone else affected by my actions. No one but Jacob. Which means I can't make a scene.

I need to focus on finding his car. That way, I can track him to his house, where the possibilities will be endless. I'll have more time to scheme. I'll have innumerable opportunities to make this perfect. And revenge will be so much sweeter if I don't rush.

I'll get my chance to make him suffer. To make him pay for stealing my family from me. For hurting them. Torturing them with flames and agony.

I dig my fingernails into my palm to distract myself.

I can't go back there. Not today.

Guilt tries to haunt me with each approaching mile toward Dan's final resting place. But I don't let that penetrate either.

It's time to step up to the plate with my A-game.

We approach the open black gates of the cemetery ahead of time, and I point to the side of the road. "Can you pull over here, please?"

"Outside?"

"Yeah. Just for now."

He veers to the curb and turns off the car, the silence growing thicker. He taps the steering wheel, winds down his window, and turns the radio on, then off again.

"Have you got something you want to say?" I ask.

He puts his arm out the window and drums his fingers against the door. "You know you can talk to me, right?" he mutters.

I sit forward in my seat as the hearse comes into view at the end of the road. "About what?"

"About anything."

Dan passes in front of us, the black coffin in full view. I swallow, my heart trembling. This is the first funeral I've been to since my family died. And the first where I've been the cause of the festivities.

I scan the passengers in the vehicle procession, searching for a familiar face.

"Did you hear me?" Hunter growls.

"Yeah. I heard you. But you're pushing too hard, too fast." In other words, I'm falling, too far, too soon. "You need to back off."

His response comes in the form of a white-knuckled grip around the steering wheel.

"Look... I don't do this." I wave a hand between us. "Ever. Not relationships. Not sleepovers. I'm used to being alone."

His jaw ticks. "I'm not familiar with fairytales either, princess. I'm trying my best here."

My lips curve at the description—a fairytale. If only. "Give me time, okay?"

He scoffs. "Yeah. All we need is time." He starts the push-button ignition and puts the car in drive. "Do you want me to follow?"

"Yeah... Thanks."

We pull in behind the last car and weave along the narrow, curving road through the cemetery. My pulse increases the farther we go, until we stop behind a mass of parked cars.

Mourners walk across the grass, the crowd milling around a grave in the distance. I can't distinguish faces from here. There are too many.

"I'm going to make my way to the burial site."

Hunter glares through the windshield as I open my door and slide out. He's angry with me, and I understand the frustration. But I can't let it get between me and Jacob.

"Wait," he grates. "Are you sure you're happy to go on your own?"

I should crack a joke. I want to. I've done everything on my own for so long that his question is comical. "I'm good." If only his concern didn't leave me thirsty for more. "Thanks for caring."

His nostrils flare, those fingers still gripping tight. I shake off the excess guilt, tug my handbag higher along my shoulder, and pull my sunglasses down to partially cover my face. "I'll be back soon."

I close the door and keep my head tipped toward the ground. I don't raise my gaze until I've inched my way into the outer ring of the intimate crowd.

Large framed pictures of a dead man are placed on the other side of Dan's coffin, which is poised above the hole in the ground. They stare, smiling, mocking, unsettling me. Two rows of seated guests whimper softly, the senator seated on the end, his head high, his face impassive.

The reality of my crime hits me, the blow landing heavy against my chest. I created this pain. I'm the cause of the heartache experienced by each and every one of these guests.

I let out a long breath and close my eyes. I'll pay for my sins soon enough. I know I will. Until then, I can only hope to drag another deserving criminal down with me.

I dance my gaze over the mourners as the priest begins the burial service. I pass over the sniffling women who dab their eyes and the array of men who barely show an ounce of emotion.

Kind words are spoken about an honorless man, lies are shared, and here I stand, searching for hope with none in sight.

I can't see Jacob. Not even anyone vaguely familiar to the teenager who has since grown into the man in the picture with Dan. I lean to the left to see hidden faces, then again to the right.

He's not here.

But he has to be. I can feel him through the building tension in my bones, my stomach, my heart. This moment is going to be the culmination of everything I've worked for. The years of searching and plotting. The nights of tears and torment.

He has to be here.

He has to be.

I inch forward to gain a better view of the people closest to me and scan the outer row of mourners. I swoop my gaze in a swaying arc, back and forth, until my attention latches onto a familiar profile to my left.

My heart stops.

I freeze.

But it's not Jacob. It's the Good Samaritan from yesterday. The one who helped me on the highway. His head is bowed, not in grief, but in conversation. He's talking to a GQ model-type on the far side of him, their lips moving in lazy chatter.

I pretend to focus straight ahead and watch from my peripheral vision.

The crowd becomes restless. The sobs and sniffles grow. Then I hear the mechanical whir of the coffin being lowered, and people break into category-three mourning.

The Samaritan and the hottie straighten, doing a half-hearted job of paying attention. They're definitely not close to the deceased. So, why are they here? Business, maybe? Are these the type of men Hunter warned me about?

I inch back. One step… Pause… Two.

The Samaritan's gaze lazily swings in my direction, then makes a direct hit.

I stiffen, and so does he. His lips part and his eyes widen, and I'm okay with the shock, because I feel it, too. But then he glances away, the action quick and panicked.

Why is *he* panicked?

A sudden case of vertigo hits, my world tilting. Is he a cop? A detective?

I rush to scour the mourning faces again, this time with more scrutiny. Am I being watched?

I place a protective palm over my handbag.

Oh, fuckity fuck. I'm in big trouble. Even bigger trouble than normal, seeing as though I have a handbag filled with premeditated craziness.

I glance over my shoulder to Hunter. He's getting out of the car, his gaze still on me as he shuts the door.

He knows. He can tell something is wrong. I'm not being paranoid anymore.

I take another step back, and the suspicious stranger turns away from me, as if trying to hide. Or at least pretending I don't exist.

It's too damn late for that, buddy.

I know he's up to something. I just don't know what that something is.

Mourners murmur amongst themselves, while others hug or stroll to their car.

I'm trapped in indecision, ready to run, but prepared to fight. I can't go down without Jacob. If this is the end of my freedom, then I need him to be right here with me.

I chance another glance at Hunter and find him striding toward me, shoulders back, chin high. He looks ready for battle, and that's exactly what I need. I want him to know how petrified I am. That I need him. That I'm ready for him to save me, today and from now on.

He slows as he approaches, his face set in stone, but when he reaches my side, he bends down and scoops something off the ground. "Excuse me, ma'am, I think you dropped something."

I frown as he straightens. There's no familiarity in the way he speaks to me. Surely, he can't still be holding a grudge from our earlier conversation.

He reaches out a closed hand, and instinctively I offer him my palm.

He places the clicker to his car in my hand and clasps his fingers over mine as he whispers, "Pretend you don't know me and get out of here. I'll find you later."

All I can do is blink, my heart hammering, my mind racing.

"Go." His touch falls and he walks away, toward the Samaritan.

I stand in stunned silence, growing colder and colder with each of his departing steps. I'm caught between the need to run and the need to understand. The desire to chase after him and the fear making me want to flee.

He keeps walking straight toward those men, and I can't look away. Not when he stops beside them. Not when he inclines his head in greeting.

And definitely not when one of them addresses him by name.

14

HIM

Her hand has the slightest tremble as I tell her to leave. I put that tremble there. I'm the cause of the slightly parted lips and the wide eyes I'm sure she's hiding behind those dark sunglasses.

I can feel Torian watching us. Watching every single thing I do.

I never should've brought her here. I should've faked a car breakdown or gotten us lost along the way. The only reason I didn't was because I needed to know who she was looking for. That one clue could've saved me. Saved *her*.

At least that was what I thought, until I found Decker and Torian standing less than a few feet away from her.

I walk toward them, trying to act casual when my insides are wound tight.

"Hunter," Torian greets. "Fancy seeing you here. Did you know the deceased?"

I ignore his poor excuse for a joke and turn my attention to Decker. "I guess the attendance today is a surprise for all."

His jaw tightens. He knows he's fucked up, but there's anger in that expression, too.

"Have you checked your messages lately?" he grates.

No. My phone has been in the car glove compartment since we returned from Seattle. "You know I rarely have my cell on me."

"That's true." Torian nods, unconcerned by the underlying tension in our conversation. "But it's a weak excuse for poor communication. I'm still waiting on an update on what happened yesterday."

I itch to glance over my shoulder and check to make sure Steph has gone. I know better, though. I can feel her attention burning the back of my neck. The good news is that Torian hasn't latched onto her. Carlos mustn't have taken any photos, and no photos means no familiarity or cause for concern. Yet.

She's in the clear. As long as I can figure out a way to keep her safe, while also extracting the information I need.

Once we get out of here, I will sit her down and have the tough conversation. I'll explain what's going on, and we'll clean this mess.

"I assumed you already had an update from Carlos." I flash Torian a cocky smirk. "How is your little bitch boy doing this morning?"

His left eye twitches the slightest bit. "I'll let you know once I hear from him."

"Yeah." I chuckle. "You do that."

Decker clears his throat. "Can you two measure your dicks somewhere else? This isn't the time or place."

"You're right." Torian watches as mourners move around us, walking to their vehicles, while a small group remain around the burial site. "We will discuss this later. I should go and give my condolences to the senator."

Relief expands in my chest as I wait for him to leave. Then something nudges my arm and the reprieve turns into panic as Steph steps into my periphery—the beautiful blonde hair, the smooth creamy skin.

She stops between me and Decker, and the guy stiffens. I can't help doing the same as she raises her sunglasses and gives a friendly smile.

"Fancy seeing you here." She pats us both on the arm. "Small world, right?"

Decker clears his throat and glances to me for guidance.

I have nothing. No direction. No response. Only dread.

"You all know each other." Her statement is calm and collected, belying the furious warrior I see flash in her eyes.

"Yes, sweetheart, we do." Torian reaches out a hand. "I'm sorry, I haven't had the pleasure of an introduction."

"I'm Steph." She raises her hand for him to shake and uses the other to lower her glasses into place.

"Steph," he repeats, letting her name linger between us like a warning. "I'm Cole, but call me Torian. It's lovely to meet you." He grasps her hand and looks at me as he brings her knuckles to his lips. "How do you know Decker and my Hunter?"

My Hunter.

He's digging my hole deeper, burying me.

"Oh, we go way back." She releases his hand and places it against her bag. "Don't we, Hunter?"

Torian glances between us, back and forth, putting puzzle pieces together.

"Yeah, I guess we do," I growl.

"We met when he came into town to look after his sister and nephew." She looks at me, and I can imagine those eyes glaring from behind her glasses.

She's pissed. Really pissed. And I could strangle her for it.

"Your sister?" Torian raises a brow. "All this time and I didn't know you had family in Portland."

She nods. "Oh, he definitely does. And he's very protective. Big and macho and mean. But..." She raises a cautionary finger. "He's *not* a violent man. Isn't that right, princess?"

Okay, now she's being downright derisive.

Torian breaks out in laughter, long and loud, not giving any respect to the people behind him who have just buried a loved one. "I like this woman. I really do." His gaze snaps to me. "I understand now."

No, he doesn't. He can't. Not when I struggle to understand it myself.

"Understand what?" She leans into me, shoulder to shoulder, all chummy and shit.

Torian continues to chuckle, making me well aware I've played right into his hand. "Hunter has been distracted lately. Now I understand the cause. You should've told me it was your family."

"Yep. Nothing but family," she drawls.

I dig my fingers into my palm, forcing down my anger while I try to determine if she's truly dim-witted or just has a death wish.

"Well, I better not waste any more of your time." She places her hand on my back, my gun. The touch is a message. A clear warning. "I'll leave you boys to your conversation."

I nod, one quick jerk of fucked up acknowledgement.

I want to grab her, keep her at my side, and never let her go. But she walks away, leaving me with a friend who looks as if he's having a heart attack and a man I'm beginning to want to see six feet under.

"She's a spitfire," Torian muses.

"Stay away from her." I keep my gaze trained on her until she stops at my car and opens the passenger door. "You're not going to touch her."

A dark brow raises over the frame of his sunglasses. "Is that so?"

"Yeah. That's so. As far as you're concerned, she's off-limits. I'm sorting this out."

His humor finally fades. "We had an agreement, Hunter. One you didn't fulfil."

"I still have a few more hours."

He inclines his head. "You're right." He flicks out his arm to check his watch. "But let's agree that once your time is up, she'll no longer be yours. She'll be mine."

I keep my mouth shut. I have to. I'm smart enough to know more threats won't work, and I can't find the composure to say anything else right now.

"I'm off to see the senator." Torian smirks in farewell. "We'll speak later."

I remain silent as he walks toward Dan's family, between the white outdoor chairs to the other side of the burial site.

"You should have called me," Decker mutters. "Now you're fucked."

"Thanks for the insight, asshole." I start walking backward, needing to get to Steph. "Why the fuck are you even here?"

"If you checked your phone, you'd know. I called over fifteen times."

"I left it in the car while—"

"—while you were fucking balls-deep in her snatch."

I clench my teeth, unable to deny the truth.

"I'm right, aren't I?" He raises his voice with the building distance between us. "Jesus Christ, *Hunt*. Fucking call me."

There he goes again, trying to make my name sound like cunt. "I will. As soon as I'm done with her."

HUNTER

I turn and stride toward Steph when all I want to do is run to her.

She's seated in the passenger seat, watching, waiting. She has to know what's coming isn't going to be pretty. The next instalment of this shit show is going to be epic, and she has front-row seats.

I reach the car, open the driver's door, and sink behind the wheel.

I don't look at her. I don't mention our fucked up situation. I don't say a word—not about the men I'm sure she's curious about, and not about the silenced gun she has in her hand, pointed in my direction.

15

HER

I'M FUCKED.

And not only am I fucked, I'm a goddamn idiot for thinking this Decker guy from the highway could be a cop when it now seems clear his intent was much more sinister.

My hunter, Torian had said.

He made it sound like a description, not a name, which made my blood run cold with possibilities. It hadn't been a slip of the tongue. His focus had been trained on me, waiting for a reaction. And he'd gotten one—a heart-palpitating, soul-screaming one I hope I was able to hide.

Hunter slides into the car, starts the engine, and doesn't acknowledge the weapon in my hand as he veers onto the narrow road and drives from the cemetery.

He's not daunted by the threat. He's probably used to it.

The detachment only increases the chill sinking into my bones, freezing every inch of me. In a perfect world, this would be the part where he divulged all his lies and begged for my forgiveness. But my world isn't perfect.

There is no knight in shining armor here.

I have to save myself.

He drives through the busy streets and onto the highway with neither of us breaking the silence. The voices in my head are already too deafening.

This is bad. This is so horribly, terribly bad, and I don't know how to make it stop. How could I have missed so much? I've probably missed everything. All the signs. All the clues.

He pulls onto an off-ramp, and I tap my heel against the floor, unable to hide my panic. The time for pretending I have this under control is gone. "Where are we going?"

"Somewhere we can talk." He continues into a rural area, his eyes trained on the road.

I glance around, to the diminishing houses and lack of cars. There are miles and miles of nothing but trees and long grass. Not one witness in sight. "Pull over."

"In a minute. It's not much farther."

My hand trembles as I raise the gun and place the barrel against his temple. "Pull. Over."

His fingers tighten on the steering wheel. I can't tear my gaze away from the palpable fury evident in his tight jaw and the rapid pulse in his neck. I'd known he was dangerous, and still I'd ignored the threat. My intuition escaped me, and I was left vulnerable to his manipulative charms.

Not anymore.

I press the gun harder and brace for him to snap. I'll pull the trigger if I have to. I have no choice. He'd said it himself—only dangerous people would be at Dan's funeral.

The car slows and veers onto the shoulder, the tires crunching under gravel. We stop. But it's not just the forward momentum. I cease breathing. Thinking. There's only white noise and the monotonous reminder of my mistakes.

"Get out." I withdraw the gun and point it at his chest, bracing for any sudden movement.

"You're not going to shoot me."

I laugh, and my stomach drops at how wrong he is. I won't stop fighting now. I won't let my heart mess with my objectives.

"*Out*," I snarl.

He glances at me, his eyes bleak with concern, one brow raised in condescension. A conflicting expression. Two warring emotions, despair, and disdain.

I have to focus on truth and not let the lies sway me. This man holds no concern. Not for me. Not for my life. And certainly not for the vendetta I have to achieve.

I divert the barrel to the right, one inch, maybe two, then squeeze the trigger.

Noise explodes around me, the burst of audible violence filling the confined space even with the silencer firmly affixed to the barrel.

Glass shatters his window and he jerks away, his eyes wide, wild, and threatening. The condescending brow disappears. His lips move, but I can't hear him. I can't hear anything apart from the deafening ring in my ears.

"*Out*." I hide my building hysteria behind a curl of my lip and open my door, the barrel now trained back on his chest.

His jaw ticks, all that rough stubble shifting while wisps of hair frame his eyes in an untamed mess.

He's still gorgeous. Brilliantly so. But I see through it now. I'm beginning to understand my self-sabotage and how far I've fallen.

He turns to get out, and I take the opportunity to pull the gun from the back of his jeans and throw it at my feet. He doesn't flinch, just slides from the seat, and closes the door behind him.

I follow on my side, round the hood, and fight the need to massage my aching temples.

He shoves a finger in his ear, wiggles it, then does the same to the other. "You're fucking crazy, do you know that?"

"Thanks for noticing." But he's wrong. I no longer feel crazy with my energetic lust for revenge. I'm hollow. The emptiness is irreparable.

"Oh, I fucking noticed, all right. And no doubt I'll have the friendly reminder for the rest of my life in the form of *damaged goddamn hearing*." He stretches his jaw, working it from side to side. "Don't ever do that again."

I want to laugh, to ridicule the concept that anything at all will happen between us ever again. Not sex. Not betrayal. Not backstabbing. But he'll learn that soon enough.

"Who are you?" I demand.

He straightens, growing taller as his lips press tight and his chin lifts. He tries to stare me down, and I don't understand how he can look at me like that. Without remorse or regret.

My throat constricts, growing tighter and tighter. Maybe his silence is a sign of guilt. But it's not enough. I need more. I need *something*. He played me. Humiliated me. Betrayed me. All the while seducing me with his strength and confidence.

"*Start talking*." I almost scream the words, and still he doesn't answer. "Otherwise, we do this the hard way." I lower the barrel, aim at his feet, and squeeze.

Bang.

He doesn't shift as dirt dances at his toes. Not a jump or a flinch. He's not scared of me. Not scared of guns or bullets or death.

"Goddamn it. *Tell me who you are.*" I raise the gun and storm toward him, aiming at his chest.

Still, he doesn't cringe, or cower, or recoil. He doesn't do anything. Not a damn thing, and it's killing me. Voices scream in my head, demanding answers, demanding punishment. I need him to react to what he's done. I need an acknowledgement of the devastation eating me from the inside out.

"*Tell. Me—*"

He lunges, grabs the silencer, and yanks down with a hard twist. I had a split second to pull the trigger, but I didn't.

I fucking didn't.

I squeal as my hand follows the movement, bending awkwardly. My fingers lose grip, and the weapon is wrenched from my hand. From powerful to powerless in the space of a heartbeat. In the blink of those menacing hazel eyes.

I retreat with quick backward steps that could easily turn into a sprint if I think he's going to shoot. I wait for him to turn the tables, to place me in his sights. Instead, he flicks on the safety and slides the gun down his leg, assisting it as it falls to the ground before he kicks it away.

We remain frozen in a stony standoff, matching each other glare for glare.

"You first," he mutters.

"No way in hell."

He runs a hand through his hair. "Fuck, you're stubborn about your stupid secrets."

"I can deal with being stubborn." What I can't deal with is being fooled by another man who only wants to hurt me. "You know, earlier, when I first saw the recognition between you and that guy I met yesterday, I thought you might be a cop." I swallow to ease my emotion-filled throat. "I thought maybe you'd been watching, waiting to arrest me, but you're not a cop, are you?"

He laughs, flashing his too perfect teeth and too perfect smile. "You're looking on the wrong side of the law, princess."

My throat threatens to close. Swallowing is no longer an option. "Okay…" I can figure this out. "Obviously, you know Dan Roberts. So, I assume you're a criminal. Maybe a lowlife dealer."

Or a pimp? A thief?

"I'm worse than that." His eyes harden, and I believe him.

He walks toward me, and I sidestep, making sure not to place additional space between me and the gun.

"A member of the mafia?" I ask.

He plants his feet and glares. "I'm the guy who finished the job you started."

I keep moving, walking in a circle as his explanation runs through my head. Over and over. He's deliberately playing more mind games, dragging this out to lengthen the torture.

Either that, or I'm truly not as smart as I once thought.

"Think about it, Steph," he taunts. "What were you doing the night I met you?"

No. I frown and shake my head. I'm not going to allow that train of thought to make sense. I can't.

"Come on now, princess," he murmurs. "You can say it."

I don't want to.

He steps forward, once, twice. A slow, sure stride that intensifies my panic.

"You killed him," I whisper.

I don't know if it's a question or a statement. It should be an adamant declaration. X marks this map like a neon sign in the dead of night. But I need it to be a question. And I desperately want the answer to be 'no.'

There's a slight pulse in his throat. The briefest glimpse of a hard swallow.

"Oh, my God." He *did* kill Dan.

I stand before him, legs numb, chest heavy, heartbroken. Relief doesn't flood me. I don't feel vindicated. Instead, bile churns in a mass production in my stomach because the harsh man I've fallen for isn't harsh at all. He is horrific.

"Why?" I'm still shaking, but now it's not just my head. It's my hands, my arms, my foundations.

I inch closer to the gun. It's right there, three feet to my left.

His gaze drops to the weapon, then returns to my face. "Don't do it."

I need to. I have to. He isn't going to let me walk. Obviously, I am stupid, but not *that* stupid.

He's poised to strike, every muscled inch of him taut and ready.

I lunge to the side, my hands sliding through dirt, my fingers grating over gravel. He dives after me, grips my ankle, and pulls. I scream as he drags me backward, then to my feet, and into his arms.

I'm plastered to him. Back to chest. Ass to crotch.

"I told you not to do that," he growls.

I kick. I scream. I thrash.

His hold tightens and he rushes forward, eating up the space to the car to press me into the cold metal. He smothers me, choking my strength under the heavy weight of memories.

He made me feel safe. He made me feel wanted. He made me *feel*. That is the worst part of all.

"Why?" I demand. "Why did you kill him?"

His breath brushes my neck. He's so close, he's under my skin. "Dan had a habit of finding useful information. But instead of handing it over to my contractor, he kept blackmailing for bigger sums of money. The guy was in a perfect position, hearing whispers from the police through his father. He could've gone far. Instead he got greedy."

"And greed deserves death?" I snarl.

"Greed, and assault, and rape, among other things." The growled words vibrate through my ribs. "I don't feel guilty in the slightest, princess. So don't try that shit on me."

"And what about framing me? Do you feel guilty about that?"

He stills. "I didn't frame you. I've done this enough times to know how to cover my ass. Nobody else has to take the fall."

Again, it isn't what I want to hear. I picture dead bodies at his feet. Innocent faces. Vacant eyes.

He steps back and I remain still, clinging to the car like it holds the answers to my problems. And maybe it does. The ignition fob is in the center console. Starting the engine and getting out of here is a button-click away.

"Look at me," he demands.

No. Not going to happen. I refuse to look into the eyes of a cold-blooded killer and feel attraction. And that's exactly what would happen if I met his gaze. I wouldn't be able to help it. I wouldn't be able to stop it.

"Steph, I need you to listen."

"I'm listening."

He sighs. "I didn't get the information I needed from Dan. I followed you instead, and by the time I went back to the hotel, he was already too fucked up to talk."

"What does that mean?" I stare out at the vacant fields, the miles of space between me and safety.

"I heard you interrogate him. I just didn't get specifics. I now need the information he gave you. And I need to know why you wanted it."

"I didn't get any information." Nothing his merry murderous crew would find useful, anyway.

"Don't lie to me." He grabs my elbow and tugs, making me face him. "He had the details on an informant, and I heard you asking him for a fucking name."

He presses into me, thigh to thigh, hip to hip. His hands land on either side of my head, a threatening stance, if only those eyes weren't slaying me.

I cluck my tongue at him. "That looming thing doesn't work anymore. Last time you did it, I got an orgasm, remember?"

His lips kick, slow and subtle. "You can this time, too. All you need to do is give me the name."

I fight a shudder. Fight and fight and fail. Tingles wrack my body, from collarbone to nipples and stomach. "No. Thanks."

"Come on, Steph. What did he tell you?"

"*Nothing*," I snap. "I didn't get a damn thing."

This man has already stripped me of too much—my dignity, my strength, my confidence. He won't steal the secrets of my past, too.

"Please." The plea is pained, almost believable. "I'm not joking. They're going to come after you. That man you met earlier—Torian—is a bad guy. Worse than Dan. Worse than me. Worse than any motherfucker you've ever met. But if you talk, I can help you."

I roll my eyes. "So this big, bad motherfucker lets me walk free if I talk?"

"I can protect you."

"Oh, goodie." I release a derisive chuckle. "Is this where I'm supposed to swoon?"

"No. This is where you tell me the fucking truth so both of us walk away from this unscathed."

I chuckle again, and this time it hurts. Pressure consumes my chest, moving higher, wider, deeper. "Too late," I whisper.

He lets out a heavy breath and leans in to rest the side of his head against mine. I want to fight for space, for freedom, but I can't when everything inside me still aches for proximity.

I need to believe in his torment. That the pain he's wrapping around me in tightening ribbons is real.

"I never meant for this shit to happen between us. I never meant to want you," he admits. "And now we're in a fucking mess, and the only way out is for you to tell me what you know."

"Then trust me when I say whatever information you're after, I didn't get."

"That's for me to decide."

He leans closer, those lips a breath away, his hips pressing harder. The thick length of his erection nestles against my pubic bone, and I freeze in disbelief.

This fucker is horny. And damn it, the thought of his arousal has the same effect on me. My nipples tingle. My pussy tightens.

"Tell me," he whispers against my neck.

His mouth trails my skin, leaving a path of goosebumps in its wake. He's a murderer. A killer. And I still want to kiss him. Taste him. Devour him.

I hate myself for the war waging inside me. The battle between sanity and stupidity. A ragged breath escapes my lips and he leans closer, our mouths almost touching.

"I'll protect you. I can promise that."

I crave the truth of those words, even when he's played me so many times already. I can't help bridging the space between us to sweep my mouth over his in a gentle glide.

He relaxes, all those muscles losing their tension. I don't want to enjoy this, but I do. The bliss sinks under my skin, flutters my heart, and warms my limbs.

I want more. I want everything.

Stupid. Stupid. Stupid.

I break the connection and pull back, sinking my teeth into my lower lip to stop the tingling throb.

"If I tell you, will you really protect me?" I ask.

"With my life."

I smile through my heartache and raise my hand to his hair. I guide the strands away from his eyes, brush my fingertips along the rough stubble of his jaw, then launch the heel of my palm into his Adam's apple.

He buckles, hunching over in an instant.

I give him a shove to escape the confinement of his body. He coughs, splutters, and swings out an arm, trying to catch me. I slap away his touch and run for the gun, leaning over to scoop it up before twirling back in his direction.

"Move away from the car," I yell.

He clears his throat, chokes, swallows. "Don't do this." His voice is raspy as he shakes his head.

"I'll shoot you if I have to." I flick off the safety and jerk the barrel in an instruction for him to move. "And this time I'll aim higher."

He backs away, the hand at his side balling into a fist as the other holds his throat. He continues to cough, to splutter. "They'll kill you."

"They'll have to find me first."

I'm good at hiding. I can do it a little longer. Then once I finish the unresolved business with Jacob, I'll run, because I'm good at that, too.

I open the driver's side door and slide inside, keeping my gaze on him the entire time.

"Don't be stupid." He hunches, hands on knees, looking over at me from beneath his lashes. "There's an easier way out of this."

"I appreciate the concern." I close the door, start the ignition, and shove the car into drive. "But I can look after myself."

16

HER

I don't know how I get back to my apartment. The drive is a whirlwind of adrenaline and hysteria until I'm sitting in his idling car in the loading zone in front of my building.

I cut the ignition, leave the key fob in the console, then sprint inside. That asshole deserves to have his car stolen, and so much more.

I enter the building pin code, shove open the door, and skip the elevator to sprint up the stairs two at a time.

Once I'm inside my apartment, I focus on getting back outside as soon as possible. My knife is placed in a leather holster and attached to my bra. A switchblade is inserted into my left boot. Mace goes into the right. My gun is shoved into the pocket I've sewn inside my coat.

I grab the stack of cash from the ice-cream tub in the freezer. Another from the sealed bag in the toilet cistern. Then the last from the hidden panel inside the bedside table bottom drawer.

Anything of value goes into my backpack. My laptop, my money, a change of clothes, and most importantly, the few treasured items from my family that I sifted through burning embers to find. The rest has to stay.

I place anything else I might want later—electronic devices, more weapons—into purple garbage bags and shove them down the disgusting trash chute in the hall. I can only hope they are still in the dumpster when I chance coming back to retrieve them.

I'm not going to hang around and load a damn truck. I don't even give myself five seconds to say goodbye to memories. Hunter isn't messing around, and neither can I.

I haul the pack onto my back and lock the door on my way out. I even grab my portable surveillance camera in the hall to take with me.

I run three blocks, catch the first cab I find, and ask the driver to take me as far away as possible. He cuts across town, and I get him to drive in circles for almost an hour to make sure I'm not being followed before I get out.

The sun starts to set as I walk miles and miles until I find a cheap motel with an easy escape route, pay cash in advance, and ask for a room that backs onto the alley.

The click of the door is deafening as I close myself into my new home. I don't bother to unpack. All I remove from the backpack is the surveillance camera, which I place in the window, the lens pointing outside.

Coiling tendrils of self-loathing wrap around my ankles and hold me in place. Failure threatens to drag me under.

All I can see is Hunter. All I can feel is his presence—his breath on my neck, his hands on my skin.

"Fuck you," I scream. "*Fuck you. Fuck you. Fuck you.*"

Someone bangs on the wall from the next room, and I scream louder. "*Fuck you, too.*"

I drag my feet to the bed and slump onto the mattress. My dress tightens around me like a straitjacket, constricting and choking. I yank at the zipper, drag it down, and throw the material across the room.

Sitting in my underwear doesn't help either because I still feel dirty.

Used.

God, I hate him. I hate his lies. I hate what he stands for. And most of all, I hate that I can't truly hate him at all. My building emotions aren't born of anger. They're weaker than that. I'm consumed with betrayal and pathetic heartbreak.

"Damn it to hell. I'm not this woman." I flop back on the bed. I *can't* be this woman.

Someone this weak and useless won't succeed in gaining revenge on the man who murdered her family. *No.* This woman will get herself killed by distraction. It's a certainty.

I shove a hand through my hair and stare at the ceiling.

At least I'm not a murderer. My conscience is clean in that regard, and yet the relief hasn't arrived. It felt so much better to have killed a man while another warmed my bed than it does now when I'm innocent and alone.

How pitiful is that?

I don't even know myself anymore.

I shake my head, but I'm unable to shake the train of thought.

I crawl up to the pillows and try to ignore how he's made me feel. I still have to get back to my apartment to retrieve the bags in the dumpster. I also have to get rent money to Brent somehow.

For now, though, I need to rest and recharge. I didn't sleep well last night, which is probably why I'm overly emotional.

I roll to my side and close my eyes. On instant replay, all the time I spent with Hunter comes rushing back. His face, his comfort, his promises.

All lies.

Every single breath he took in my presence was fake. And I am no closer to Jacob, either. Everything has turned to shit.

I drift, sleep dragging me under, then spitting me back out, over and over on a continuous loop. I dream about him. His voice murmurs, the words hazy. His mouth presses against mine and his lips curve in a smile while a possessive grip lands on my hip. I moan and clench my thighs.

I want you. God, why do I still want you?

He drifts away, disappearing into darkness.

I dream of my family. Of the past. Of the Samaritan—Decker—and the other threatening man from this morning—Torian. I toss and turn and finally give up hope of energizing rest when the sun begins to pound the back of my lids.

I groan, snuggle the pillow to my chest, and open my eyes.

Bright light beams down on me from the partly opened curtain. I sit up, frown, and narrow my gaze on the surveillance camera now pointed in my direction.

What...the...

I push onto my elbow. There's no way I focused the lens on the bed. I hadn't been *that* tired. I faced it in the other direction. Outside.

I flick back the covers and search for my phone. "Shit." I should've had it right beside me.

A sheet of paper swoops off the mattress, floating through the air with menacing grace as I cease moving. It drifts down to the pillows, laying gently beside me like a threatening plague.

I glance around the room, my senses heightened as I search for anything out of place. There's no movement, no unnatural sound. Nothing nudges my senses, only the camera bearing down on me and the note taunting me.

I reach across to the pillows and retrieve the paper to read the neat script—*Stop messing around and find a better place to hide.* I snap a hand over my mouth to hold in my fear.

He found me. He was in my fucking room.

I scamper from the bed and do another scan of my surroundings, over the television, across the windowsill, my gaze pausing on the door. A steak knife protrudes from the wood, a piece of paper stabbed beneath the blade. I rush toward it and pull the note free.

You're beautiful when you sleep.

My heart kicks, and I hate it. I hate it so much my tummy tumbles.

I crumple the message in my fist and throw it to the floor. I scramble to collect my belongings, the video camera, my phone, my dress. I pull on the only set of clothes I packed—a pair of black workout leggings, a loose top, and an even baggier hoodie.

I don't waste time hanging around. I get out of there and rush to catch the bus pulling to a stop at the end of the block.

"Please drive. Quick," I beg the middle-aged man behind the wheel. "Someone is following me."

The damsel-in-distress gig works most of the time, and now is no exception as the driver hastens to close the door and pull away from the curb.

Three people are on board, all of them watching me from their spaced positions throughout the rows of seats. A teenage girl. An elderly man. A woman in a business suit. I remain in the front of the bus, on a seat parallel with the aisle and close to the door.

I can keep an eye on my surroundings while I pull out my phone and log into my surveillance account. The damn device has been silenced since the funeral, which means I didn't get a notification when Hunter approached my room around four in the morning. He tested the door handle, then walked out of view.

I fast forward the video until the image tilts, turns, then I'm in the picture, half-naked on the bed. He walks away from the camera, toward me. I don't flinch in my sleep. I don't even stir as he looks down at me, without malice or anger. He stares, watching, waiting, while I lie vulnerable and exposed.

My heart crumples at the longing I see in his expression, even though I know it's not really there. It's a hallucination. A mirage. I glide my finger over the screen, touching what can no longer be truly touched and hate myself for the pathetic gesture.

Why didn't he hurt me? Why didn't he tie me up and demand the information he wants so badly?

He leans in, and I hold my breath as I watch him press his lips to mine.

"Holy shit." It wasn't a dream. He kissed me in my sleep, and I kissed him back.

Why? I don't understand his intent. Am I supposed to believe his actions are some sort of truce? Did he change the camera angle to showcase his incredible acting skills?

He places his notes around the room, not tiptoeing, with casual self-assurance, then he glances at the camera and those eyes meet mine.

Why is he doing this to me? Why am I letting him?

He keeps reeling me in, sinking his hooks into the vulnerable parts I thought I'd strengthened.

"Pull over at the next stop, please," I instruct the driver.

I log out of the feed, delete the app, and place my cell on the seat as the bus veers to the curb of an unfamiliar street.

"Thank you." I haul my pack onto my back and stand, leaving my phone behind. If Hunter placed a tracker in my cell, he could enjoy the excursion the day would bring, because I have no plans to participate in his game anymore.

I need to feel whole again. Free.

And so I run.

17

HER

I run for months. Well, it's actually only four weeks, but it feels like forever. Every time I crash in a new location, he finds me, and he always leaves a note.

Most of the time his messages are playful—*You're not good at this, are you? I like those pajamas. I'll see you tomorrow.*

And sometimes his words cut to the heart of me—*When this is over, you're mine.*

The dictatorship isn't as offensive as it should be. Nothing about this seems as offensive as it should be. Yet again, I've become a willing participant in his game.

I fall asleep each night with growing anticipation. I wake every morning to heart-pounding excitement. I search for his messages like an attention-starved fool, and each and every time I find one, my stomach soars.

At least it had, until five days ago.

That was when I extended the playing field and fled to a small bed and breakfast in Eagle Creek. He didn't follow. There hasn't been one note. Not a single word.

He's either lost interest, or something or someone made him stop.

"Are you thinking about him again, pet?"

I glance to my right, at Betty, the elderly lady who owns the bed and breakfast. She's kind enough. Smart, too. But her intuition is on-point, which makes the hair on the back of my neck stand on end. If she didn't cook like a master chef and feed me like I'd been homeless all my life, I would've cut and run after my first night.

"I'm not thinking about anyone." I rest my elbows on her porch railing and glance out at the glowing lights of Eagle Creek. It's nice here. Quiet. Which makes it difficult to dodge thoughts of Hunter.

"Have it your way." She moves to stand beside me, taking the same stance—elbows on the railing, her gaze straight ahead staring out into the night. "You've lost your hope, though. I can see it in your eyes."

Damn woman can't even see my eyes at the moment. It's dark out, and I'm not looking in her direction. Still, she's right.

What if Hunter has grown tired of playing?

The answer shouldn't matter. I shouldn't even ponder the question. Only I do. On repeat. All day. All night.

"Who needs hope when I can smell blueberry pie?" I shoot her a glance and raise a brow. "Hmm? You're going to feed me again, aren't you?"

She chuckles, her face gaining a mass of enviable laugh lines. This woman has experienced a lot of joy. Every single one of those wrinkles is a testament to her happiness. "I certainly will… If you promise to try to find that hope you showed up here with."

I sigh and turn back to the night. "It wasn't hope. It was a game." A silly challenge I spent too many nights playing.

"I know hope when I see it, and yours wasn't the type to revolve around a career or family. It was the type of love-filled hope that can only be inspired by a man."

Love?

Now *that* is a word capable of slamming the brakes on any conversation, as far as I'm concerned. "Did you get lost in the liquor cabinet again?"

She snickers. "Maybe. But I'm right, aren't I?"

"My life is too complicated for love. Or hope, for that matter." In my chest, there is a void where both emotions should be. An abyss. "It's just not for me."

"With that attitude, I'm sure you're right." She pats my shoulder with a gentle hand. "Now, how about that pie?"

"Yes, please." I'll agree to anything that will get her meddling insight out of my life. "Want me to make the green tea?"

"No, I've got it." She starts for the front door, the aged wooden planks creaking under her steps.

This place feels like a home. The constant delicious scent of food, the warmth, the conversation, and the inbuilt security of a German shepherd guard dog in the back yard and the tiny yap-yap Maltese inside. I didn't even bother setting up my camera here. Nothing could escape the attention of the canines.

It would be a great place for me to stay a while. To find that clarity and focus I need. But no matter how homey it is, I can't shake the uncomfortable feeling that I need to be somewhere else.

I *want* to be somewhere else.

I'm sure it's as simple as missing my apartment. And not having Brent nearby in case I get smothered with loneliness. I owe him rent money, too, which I really need to resolve. I never even got back to my apartment to fetch my belongings from the trash.

Or maybe I have to stop kidding myself and admit I'm growing insane without an update on Hunter. I need answers, and I want the good night's sleep I'll finally get once I have them.

I don't know if he's lying in wait, about to strike. I don't know if he's hurt or if he found someone else to play with. I don't know if Torian gave up on my so-called information.

"Betty." I walk after her and pull open the front door. "Do you mind if I use your phone?"

Brent will know something.

Maybe Hunter is still hanging around at the bar or scoping out my apartment.

"Are you calling that man of yours?" She raises her voice from the kitchen down the long hall.

"Of course. You know I always listen to your advice and jump to respond."

"You're a horrible liar."

No, I'm not. At least not when I want to be.

"Go ahead and use it," she calls "Just throw a few dollars in the jar on the table if it's long distance."

"Thank you." I stride for the small wooden stand beside the staircase leading to the second floor. The corded phone sits crowded among pens, paper, the money jar, car keys, receipts, and mail. It's the only place in this house that isn't immaculate.

I dial Brent's number from memory and lean against the banister while I wait. When the call connects, I straighten and stare down at the one-stop dumping ground of knickknacks as I picture his face.

"Atomic Buzz," Brent mutters.

My stomach tumbles at the sound of his voice. "Hey. It's Steph. How are you?"

The lengthening silence makes me wince. I can't blame him for not speaking to me. I've been a selfish bitch who only thinks of herself.

"I'm sorry," I whisper. "I know I left without a word, and that I'm late with rent money." He doesn't have a generous bank account like I do. And still, he's never been anything but generous to me. "I shouldn't have checked out without telling you. But I'm going to try to get back there to fix you up for what I owe. I just—"

"No. Don't." He cuts me off. "Forget it. I don't need it."

My chest squeezes. We both know he's lying.

"Please, Brent. I know I should've called sooner. I had to get out of town real quick. I didn't mean to fuck you over."

"Like I said, forget it," he growls at me. My only friend. My only connection to kindness and support.

"I get that you're angry. I deserve it. And I don't expect you to forgive me. But I'll travel back into Portland tonight." I'd have to find a ride available in the early hours of the morning for safety's sake. I can't go back now. It's only a little past ten, and people would be out and about. But I can return to Portland to make the delivery. No problem. "I'll get there after you close and slip the money under the door."

"I said *don't*." His tone is gruff. "I don't want to see you here again. Do you understand? Don't—"

His words are lost to rustling over the line. I hear a grunt. A muttered curse. Then more rustling.

"Brent?" I lower my gaze to the thick maroon carpet and stare blankly as I focus on sound. "*Brent?*"

"Forget what he said, pumpkin," another voice croons in my ear. A voice I can't pinpoint. It isn't one of the bar regulars. It isn't Hunter. It's someone else.

"Who is this?" I demand. "Put Brent back on the phone."

"Your bartender friend is unavailable right now. I think it's best if you come here and speak to him in person."

I swallow over the throb building behind my sternum. Someone is threatening Brent to get to me, and the stupid son-of-a-bitch tried to protect me. Save me.

"Are we clear?" the man asks. "Get back here now. No weapons. No cops. You've got an hour."

The call disconnects, leaving me with nothing but white noise and building panic. I drop my arm to my side, and the receiver slips from my fingertips to fall to the floor.

Is this Torian's doing? Or someone else?

I focus on the mess scattered across the small table. The pens. The receipts. The car keys. I have to get to Atomic Buzz, and I can't wait for a driver.

I shoot a glance down the empty hall, toward the sound of clattering plates and the clink of cutlery. I have to leave. Right now. I can't go upstairs for my few belongings. I can't say goodbye. The knife attached to my bra will have to be my only protection, because I don't want to ponder the danger it will put Brent in if I bring a gun.

I place my hand over the BMW car keys and clench my fingers around them.

Then I walk from the house and don't look back. Not even when the dogs start barking announcing their intuition of my betrayal.

The shiny black sedan is parked in the carport, the moonlight reflecting off the dark surface. I click the lock release, slide inside, and reverse out of the driveway, like stealing a car comes naturally to me. But it doesn't.

Remorse eats away at my chest. My lungs ache. I can picture the joy in Betty's features evaporating. The woman who provided me with a safe haven is now being punished.

"Goddamn it."

I drive to Portland, the miles passing as I break every speed limit. I reach my street and drive past the bar. It's almost eleven, well within open hours, but the lights are out and the closed sign hangs on the front door.

I continue forward, pretending someone's life isn't resting in the palm of my hands, and turn down a nearby side street. I flick off the headlights, inch into the darkness of a suburban driveway, and park behind a family wagon.

Whoever lives here will wake up to find Betty's BMW. They will have to report the incident, and get the car towed to be able to move their own vehicle.

The plan isn't foolproof, but it's the best I can come up with to get Betty's car back to her safe and sound, and as soon as possible.

I get out, lock the car, and creep toward for the street. I walk a block and a half until I reach the alley that leads to the back door of Atomic Buzz.

I don't have a plan. I don't even have confidence. All I have is the necessity to help someone who always helped me. Brent offered me his apartment years ago, when he had planned to move in there himself. He shared his life with me, when I never even told him my name. He gave me patience and generosity. He gave me friendship and solace.

It's time to repay the favor.

I inch across the back wall of the businesses along the alley and blend into the shadows. I take cautious steps, walking on the tips of my sneakers. I watch for litter and glass, making sure I don't make any sound when the crunch of a distant footfall comes from the street I just walked out of.

I slink deeper into the darkness and don't move. Another step approaches and another, becoming faster, harder. I shoot a glance over my shoulder to find a man running toward me, tall and broad, dressed in black with a baseball cap pulled low to cover his face.

Fuck.

I don't think. I sprint.

I make it ten steps before he hauls me off the ground by an arm around my waist while a hand slams across my mouth to cut off my scream.

"Shh," he whispers. "It's me."

His hard body presses into me. I recognize the scent, I remember the warmth, and for a second I feel safe.

My traitorous body relaxes, and Hunter removes his hand, tugging me toward the wall of the building. My chest hums at the reunion. I'm stupidly relieved to see him. Happiness wouldn't even be a stretch.

"What are you doing here?" I cling to the little hope that comes with his familiar face.

"I heard what was going on."

"And you're here to what? Thwart my efforts or help?"

He tugs me toward the opening to the alley, the streetlights exposing me to anyone who may be in the area.

"There's no helping this situation," he whispers. "If you go in there, they'll kill you."

"Who's they?"

"Torian and his men."

"Aren't you one of his men?" I ask.

"I'm a contractor. Big difference. He wants the information—"

"Then I'll tell him to his face that I don't have the name he needs."

"And he'll tear you limb from limb until you change your mind or die in the process."

My pulse pounds erratically in my throat. "Why is that your concern?" He gave up on me days ago. He cut and run.

"Quit the shit, Sarah. This thing between us isn't over."

Sarah.

He knows my name. My real name. The one I haven't uttered in years.

I release a silent breath of a chuckle, because if I don't, I'll crumple.

"It took a while, princess." He reaches for my hair, stroking the stray strands from my cheek. "But I finally figured you out."

I jerk away, unwilling to succumb to his allure even though that's all I've wanted to do for the past few weeks. "You're lucky, because I still know nothing about you."

"All you need to know right now is that I'm here to help. I'm going to get you out of here."

I frown. "What about Brent? How will you get him out?"

His lips press tight, and it's all the answer I need.

"No." I step back, toward Atomic Buzz. "I'm not leaving him."

"He's as good as dead, and you know it."

His comment slaps me across the face. Hard. I keep moving, hoping to distance myself from his words. From everything. I refuse to believe there's no way out. "I won't lose him, too."

"Shh." He follows, gripping me around the waist in a one-armed grab. "He's already gone."

"They gave me an hour," I argue. "I've still got time."

"To do what? Beg? Plead? They're not going to give a shit when you don't have the informant's name."

I keep shaking my head. I won't believe him. I refuse. "Then I go down with him." I couldn't die with my family, but maybe this is an honorable alternative because I sure as hell won't let another person die because of my decisions.

"Like hell," he growls, all protective and animalistic. He wants to help; that much is clear. I just need to convince him to do it my way.

"Please, Hunter." I grab his jacket, curling my fingers in the leather. "Help me."

His brows pull tight, and I see the conflict he tries to battle.

"*Please.*" I clutch tighter. "I'll do anything."

He lifts his chin as if accepting my terms and steps back to retrieve a phone from his jeans pocket. "Let me send a message to Decker and see if he can get his ass here."

Decker—the guy from the highway. I don't trust him. Then again, I don't have the luxury of trust at the moment.

"Okay." I nod, my hope building.

He presses buttons, then places his phone in his jacket and meets my eyes with a sad smile. "I guess we have to wait and—"

A bang splits the air. A pungent, ear-splitting gunshot that travels from the vicinity of Atomic Buzz.

I suck in a breath, but the air doesn't penetrate. I can't breathe. I gasp, trying to cling to positive thoughts, which flitter away in the chilled night air.

"We need to get out of here." Hunter steals my hand and pulls.

I hear him, yet the words don't sink in. They're distant. Faded. Everything is a mile away while I stand here in solitude, bathed in sorrow and drowning in guilt.

"Sarah." Hunter gets in my face and clutches my arms. "Look at me."

He's there, *right there*, and still, I can't focus. All I can see is Brent. Dead. Because of me. Because of what I've done.

"I n-need to get in there." I move to walk around him, only to have his hands grip tight.

"It's too late."

"No." I push at his chest. "He might not be dead. He could be hurt. We have to call the police… An ambulance."

He gives me a shake. "*It's too late.*"

I waiver like a rag doll in his grip. I can see the truth in his black eyes. I can see the pain and brutal honesty of what has happened.

"No," I whisper. Then louder with a thump against his chest. "*No.*"

His eyes widen and he spins me, hauling my body against his to drag me backward down the alley. I can't protest, not in movements, only in words. "*No. No. No.*"

He claps a hand over my mouth, holding me tighter. I tremble, my limbs shaking violently as shock takes over.

"I'm sorry," he whispers. "But we can't stay here."

Why not? My life no longer has value. All I do is hurt people. And although I may not have been responsible for Dan's death, Brent's blood is on my hands.

"Why?" I plead. "Why would they do this?"

"It doesn't matter right now." He speaks softly in my ear, in full control even though destruction follows our every step.

He takes me from the alley, where I finally find my feet, then holds my hand as I jog beside him. I'm not thinking. I can't. Otherwise, I'd be moving in the opposite direction. Toward Brent. Toward help. We go around a corner, onto the street I used to walk down to get my groceries, and he stops beside a car I've never seen before.

"Tell me you won't run back to the bar."

I meet his eyes, those deep, penetrating eyes that now hold a wealth of sympathy.

I shake my head. "I shouldn't leave him."

"He's already gone. You know that as well as I do." He implores me with a look filled with so much conviction I want to fall to my knees and sob. But I won't. I don't cry anymore. I haven't in ten years.

"Let me get you in the car." He slides a hand around my waist, as if I might fall, and leans to the side to open the passenger door. "Quick. The cops will be here any minute."

He guides me forward, into the seat, and fastens my belt in place. "Promise me you won't take off as soon as I leave your side."

I stare at nothingness while he hovers, unmoving.

"Where would I go?" I murmur. "I have nowhere left to run."

And no will to do it either.

18

HER

Hunter closes me in the car, rounds the hood, and then slides into his seat. He's gunning the engine in seconds, speeding through streets I can't bring into focus.

"It's going to be okay." He breaks the silence. "I'll make sure it is."

I hear guilt in his voice. The same strangling guilt that tightens around my throat.

"How did he know?" I ask, my gaze straying from one passing streetlight to the next. How would anyone know of my friendship with Brent? I rarely went to Atomic Buzz. I shared a few drinks once or twice a month. I paid rent in cash. Nobody knew how much that man meant to me, not even the man himself.

"Torian?" Hunter asks. "It wouldn't have taken much. Especially not when you borrowed Brent's car to go to Seattle."

"That's how you worked out my name, isn't it?" I drag my attention from the road and face him. "You followed me?" To Seattle. To my childhood home. To the cemetery.

"Yes."

One word. No elaboration.

I nod, no longer shocked by the depth of his betrayal. "Were you the asshole who ran me off the road?"

"No." He hits me with a two-second scowl, then returns his focus to the road. "I'm the asshole who showed that piece-of-shit a thing or two about manners."

"You killed him?" I can't find the will to care. I'm devoid of emotion. Completely lacking concern.

He remains quiet, shielding me from the truth.

"Hunter?"

"No, I didn't," he growls. "I could've. I should've. I even promised I would. But then I remembered how you reacted to Dan's death, and I didn't think you'd appreciate me taking a guy's life, despite what he did. I only inflicted the pain and threats necessary to make sure he wouldn't give Torian any valid information about you."

I frown, my brain taking too long to process any coherent thoughts. "Am I supposed to be flattered? Should I say thank you?"

He releases a derisive laugh. "No. Don't thank me, princess. I fucked him up enough to make him wish he was six feet under."

My chest loosens. Why?

I refuse to be charmed by his brutality. I won't be seduced by violence. And yet a part of me is comforted by the thought of his protective savagery.

I'm so irrational right now it's scary.

I glare and return my attention to the road, letting the hollow ache sink back in. He drives onto the highway, takes a familiar off-ramp, and then onto a desolate street.

"Where are we going?" I rest the side of my head against the glass. "Is this another ploy to get me away from civilization so you can kill me?"

"Yeah." He nods. "I trail you for weeks to make sure you're safe, save your ass from getting killed, only to slit your throat on a back road in the middle of nowhere."

"Smarter men have done stupider things."

He sighs. "I'm not going to hurt you, Sarah."

"Anymore, you mean?" The taunt slips from my lips without permission.

"Yeah," he murmurs. "Not anymore." The promise is barely spoken, yet filled with solemn conviction. I believe him. At least, I want to. I *need* to.

I have nobody. Nothing. And God, I'm beginning to hate it.

My immediate family is dead. My extended family are so distant they wouldn't even recognize me after all these years. My one friend has just been murdered. And tonight, I stole a car from the only other person who has acknowledged my pathetic existence.

"Why did you stop chasing me?" I ask, exacerbating my pitiful situation.

The car slows as he looks me in the eye. "You don't know? I thought you must have figured it out."

"No. Why would you think that? I've had no clue this entire time. I always used cash. I don't know how many times I got a new phone, only to throw it away days later. But you always found me. At least until I went to Eagle Creek."

"Because you stopped using your video surveillance." He turns his attention back to the road. "Without the feed, I had no idea where to look."

My mouth gapes. "You hacked my feed?"

How the hell did he do that? *When* did he do that?

He glances at me, and his lips kick at one side.

"You think this is funny?" I accuse.

He smirks. "No, I'm thinking that I'd love to slam my mouth against yours to taste your shock."

My heart stops, drops, and rolls. I'm burning. Blazing.

"Decker gained access to your account not long after we first met. It gave me the ability to track whenever you left your apartment."

"But..."

"You always stayed in cheap hotels with a window that faced the road. Without fail, you would point the camera at something Decker and I could search online. Either a road sign, a business name, or a landmark. You made it easy."

Until I moved into a bed and breakfast and started relying on Betty's dogs for security instead of my camera. "I thought you'd given up on playing games. I didn't think I'd see you again."

"No." He shakes his head. "I hadn't given up."

If my stomach wasn't currently in a battle with grief and attraction, I'd slowly devour the delicious bowl of his determination.

He flicks the car lights to high-beam, illuminating a stretch of road I recognize. "Is this…"

"The place you shot at me?" he taunts. "Yeah."

"Why are we back out here?"

He slows, approaching a dirt drive with a dilapidated wooden mailbox to the side, the faded number thirteen partially covered by overgrown shrubs.

"Who lives here?"

"I do. This is where I wanted to take you the day of the funeral."

"Why?" Surely, taking me to his house will expose vulnerabilities for a man with his profession. How does he trust me so easily? Or is this knowledge a bigger vulnerability for me? "Do you plan on keeping me here?"

"Keeping you?" He scoffs. "Can you stop assuming the worst for a second and focus on what you already know?"

"Which is?" I scan the front yard, with its imposing trees covering the ground in a canopy of black.

"I was supposed to hurt you, okay? But I didn't. I should've, and I chose not to. After wasting weeks sidestepping my contract, I'm not going to change my mind now."

"That's comforting," I drawl.

A house comes into view, the roof bathed in moonlight, along with the front porch that gives a slight hint to the wall of windows behind.

It looks nice. Modern and tidy, with no garden, only manicured lawns and sensor lights that flick on and temporarily blind me.

"Shit." I squint through my adjusting vision while he pulls into the garage.

The car turns off, and I sit, waiting for answers to questions that multiply. Why did he bring me here? Why did he save me tonight? What happens next? And the most poignant of all—"Why did all this happen, Hunter?" My voice is soft as I stare at his vacant garage wall. "Why didn't you ask me for information on day one? Why didn't you force it from me?" I turn to face him. "You're this cold-blooded killer who doesn't care about hurting people, so why didn't you use that against me?"

He focuses straight ahead, not meeting my gaze. "I don't know."

"Bullshit," I whisper. "You have an agenda. I know you do. I'm just not sure what it is."

"Come inside and I'll explain." He unfastens his belt and opens the driver's side door.

"Why? Why can't you do it here?"

"Because we both need a drink to settle the adrenaline." He slides from the seat and closes the door behind him. He walks around the hood, opens my door, and holds out a hand. "Come on. I'll tell you everything. Whatever you want to hear."

"Whatever I want to hear?" I raise a brow and swing my body around to face him. "Or the actual truth?"

"The truth. Okay?" He implores me with beseeching eyes, kicking me in the girlie parts with the thinly veiled emotion in his words. "I'm not going to lie to you again."

I tilt my head in scrutiny and my tongue sneaks out to moisten my dried lower lip. He watches the movement, his focus turning predatory in a snap. I can't resist that shit.

Why the hell can't I resist that shit?

"I'll follow you inside once you admit that Hunter isn't your real name."

"That's it?" He chuckles. "That's what you want to know first?"

I nod. It's a start.

"Okay. You got me. Hunter's not my real name."

"What is it?"

He hitches a thumb over my shoulder, pointing toward the door. "Follow me inside and I'll tell you."

"No." I glower. "Your name first."

He crouches between my bent legs, places his hands on my knees, and peers up at me. "It's Luke."

He could easily lie. I wouldn't know any different. But I believe him. I swear to God he's telling me the truth.

"You're not lying."

"No, I'm not, but nobody else around these parts knows my name. Not Decker. Not Torian. I'd like to keep it that way. Okay?"

"Then why tell me?" Why bring me here? Why do any of this?

"Because I want there to be trust between us."

I frown, not appreciating the momentary dip in my pulse. "I don't want to trust you."

"And I don't blame you for that."

His honesty is seductive. I guess seeing a major change in a man will have that affect. Or maybe it's like he said—I need to settle the adrenaline.

I scoot closer, his palms hitching higher up my thighs. My chest pounds with the need for comfort. My lips tingle at the thought of his kiss.

"I'm ready to go inside now," I whisper.

He nods and pushes to his feet, offering me a hand. I place my fingers against his and wince at how good it feels. There's strength in our connection. It doesn't make sense. But it's there. Buzzing. Tingling.

He leads me to the door, down the dark hall, then stops to flick on a light. A massive living area is exposed. Sofas, a dining table, a large television, and a sparkling kitchen. It's clean, stylish, and uncharacteristically homely.

I release his hand and take a few steps ahead, letting it all sink in. "Your home is nice."

"You sound surprised." He walks by me, into the kitchen to pull open one of the glossy white cupboards.

"I'm not familiar with the murderer stereotype. I guess I didn't expect it to be so…"

"Normal?" He grabs two scotch glasses and places them on the island counter. "I don't fit a stereotype, Sarah. And I'm not the horrible person you think I am. Not entirely, anyway."

I hope that's true. In fact, I'm banking on it.

"What do you want to drink?" He moves to a high cupboard above the stainless-steel, double-door fridge. "Scotch? Gin? I think I've got some vodka in here somewhere, too."

"No, thanks. The last thing I need is alcohol."

He frowns at me over his shoulder. "How about coffee?"

"Caffeine isn't a good idea either. I'm fine, really."

He grabs a bottle of scotch and returns to the island bench.

My grief returns, not only for Brent, but for myself. This murderous, manipulative man has a comforting, tidy home to return to. He has his shit together. He functions better than I do.

It isn't fair.

Nothing in this world is fair.

"I don't know what to do for you." His admission cuts me to the core. "Tell me what you need."

"I don't need anything," I lie. The reality is, I need everything. Anything. Something.

He places the bottle down on the counter and walks toward me. My heartrate increases with every step. I don't want him close. But I also want it so bad it hurts, ripping and slicing me to shreds from the inside out.

He stops in front of me, and I fight the need to touch him. To reach out and steal his strength. He raises a hand, his fingers drifting close.

"Please don't," I plead.

That hand descends, my heart falling along with it.

"Is that a directive for tonight?" he asks. "Or forever?"

"Forever would be the smart answer," I admit.

"But it's not what you want." This time he raises his hand and doesn't stop until those fingers are tangling in the loose strands that have fallen from my ponytail.

I turn my head away and his touch moves to my cheek, my jaw. He burns a trail along my skin, devastating my senses.

"He's all I had." I face him, his sympathy sinking its teeth into my ribs.

"You've got me."

"The man who kills for a living." I release a derisive laugh. "You know, I've actively tried to take down people like you." And yet I can't step away. Not even an inch. "You have no respect for life."

"That's not true."

"How can you say that with a straight face?"

His jaw hardens, and his nostrils flare. "Don't judge me until you know me." He stalks back to the kitchen, pouring himself a generous glass of scotch.

"Then tell me." I follow, slower, more cautious. "Have I got this murderous thing all wrong? Was Dan the only man you killed?"

He raises the glass, drinks the contents in three heavy swallows, then slams it down on the counter. He glares and pours himself another.

"Well?" I ask.

"He wasn't the first," he snarls. "And he won't be the last." He raises the glass again, this time staring at me over the rim as he takes a sip. "And what about you, princess? How innocent are you? I saw what you did to Dan. And what do you have planned for Jacob? I can't imagine you want to catch up on the good ol' days."

Of course he knows about Jacob. How can I still be surprised?

"Dan abused women habitually, and Jacob killed my family. Neither one of them is innocent."

He lets out a harsh laugh, then raises his brows and his glass, as if in toast. "Well, at least we have the same work ethic."

"Are you trying to tell me you've never hurt anyone innocent?"

His jaw ticks. "That's exactly what I'm saying. I may have killed a lot of people, but none of them were good."

"What about children?"

"Jesus Christ." He smacks the glass down and runs a hand through his hair. "I've never killed a fucking kid. I never will."

"Women?" I ask.

His chin lifts, almost imperceptibly, and he scowls at me. "One. Indirectly."

"How indirectly?" My pulse thunders in my throat as I wait for a reply.

A myriad of emotions flicker across his features—annoyance, regret, determination. "I killed her husband. A week later, she killed herself." He takes another sip, watching me. "Is there anything else you want to know?"

Yes. Everything.

"For now, I've just got one more question." I swallow. "Why did you save me tonight?"

19

HIM

I can't lie to her anymore. I'm done playing games. "I was there tonight because I needed to see you. I had to make sure you were all right."

Her gaze rakes over me, probably trying to weigh the truth against the fabrication. Her attention is like a touch—A slight sweep of gentle fingertips against my skin.

This is what I've missed, the addictive sensation that follows wherever she goes. Her scrutiny is like a drug. Without it, my insides scream and claw, begging to be sated.

"But you had no intention of saving Brent."

I stare her down, determined not to lie. "My first concern was your safety."

"Did you even message Decker to ask for help?"

"Yes." It was the truth. Kind of.

"And you left him to show up to an ambush?"

"No. I messaged him after I got you in the car." Again, truth. "A rental, I might add, seeing as though mine was stolen and stripped. Thank you very much."

Her lips kick at one side, but the satisfaction doesn't reach her eyes. It touches my dick, though, makes it fucking throb.

She lowers her gaze and stares at the kitchen counter. "So, that's it?" She shrugs. "You just wanted to start the cat-and-mouse chase all over again?"

"No. We're not doing that anymore. You need to stay with me until things die down."

She turns her back and faces the room. "And when do you think that will happen?"

My preference? Never. But the time for the finer intricacies of the truth will come later. "I don't know. Maybe a few months."

She doesn't respond with a sharp quip like I expect. Instead, she remains silent, her arms moving to wrap around her waist.

"Will you stay?" I round the island counter, edging closer. She's turned me into a needy little bitch, and I hate it. I hate every fucking minute of it, and still, I can't ditch the hold she has on me.

"I've got nowhere else to go," she murmurs. "The police will be looking for me by now."

"Because of Brent?" She doesn't need to worry about that.

"That…" She nods. "And the car I stole in an effort to get to the bar in a hurry."

I raise my brows, impressed. "Did anyone see you?"

"No, but it's obvious. I stole it from the B&B owner where I was staying. One minute I asked to use her phone, the next I was walking out her front door with her car keys in my hand."

Her tone is full of regret, making remorse punch me in the gut. I stride for her, eating up the distance between us so I can place my hands on her waist.

She doesn't flinch, doesn't protest. She lets me touch her, and fuck, am I thankful.

"What did you do with the car?"

"I parked it in someone's driveway. I thought maybe the person who lives there would call the cops in the morning."

"That's good," I whisper into her hair. "No harm. No foul. Right?"

She releases a barely audible scoff. "Yeah. Maybe. But I took off without packing my things. I left everything there. The few clothes I had. My purse."

Shit. "Your I.D?"

"No. I don't carry it. Only cash. I placed a few valuables and some money in a locked box a week ago, but apart from that…" She sighs, her shoulders falling. "I literally have nothing."

I rest my forehead into her hair and breathe her deep. The scent of flowers and candy slaughters me. "Can I show you something?"

"Why not?" She releases a heavy breath. "It's not like I'm going anywhere."

I slide my palm over her wrist and lower it to entwine our fingers. "It's down the other end of the house."

She stares where our hands meet, and I wait for a protest to the connection.

"Okay." She nods and meets my gaze.

I could fuck her right here. On the floor. Clothes on. Face pale. Eyes filled with sorrow. I fucking could. But would I regret it?

I doubt it.

She wants this as much as I do. Needs it.

Instead of succumbing, I start for the opposite side of the room, toward the far hall. She keeps her hand against mine, warm and gently clasping, until I stop before a closed door.

"Go on." I jerk my chin. "Open it."

She frowns as she releases my hand and steps forward to grip the handle. I can't hear her breathe. I can't hear anything but lust and anticipation rushing through my ears.

She twists the handle and inches into the bedroom, her gaze scanning the furniture —her bed, drawers, mirror, and television.

"You emptied my apartment," she whispers.

"I thought I owed you that much. Otherwise Torian would've sent someone to ransack it." There is a slip of truth in there somewhere.

"Did you go through my stuff?"

"Yeah." I don't even pause. That won't be the worst admission she hears from me tonight.

"Everything?" She shoots me a glower over her shoulder.

"From the kitchen cupboards, to your bathroom supplies, and all those pretty pieces of lingerie that turned my dick to stone." I smirk, without an ounce of remorse. "There's a black leather item in there somewhere that I wouldn't mind seeing again."

There had also been other things she wouldn't have wanted me to snoop through. Not just the sex toys, but the information. I'd found her hidden box of articles on Jacob after walking over the only creaking floorboard in her entire apartment.

I'd read every word in my car as she slept in cheap hotels. There were details on her, too. Snippets of her life the Seattle newspaper had catalogued after her family died. There were details on the sale of her childhood home and her bank accounts. I know it all. At least everything that has been written down on paper.

She kicks off her sneakers, pads to the far side of the bed, and pulls a pillow to her chest as she stands looking down at the mattress.

"It still smells like you," I murmur.

She shoots me an are-you-fucking-kidding look with one hike of her brow. "Smells a little like you, too."

I shrug. "I may have slept in here a time or two since you skipped town."

Her eyes narrow. "Liar."

"No lies here. I told you I missed you."

A flash of surprise passes across her features before she turns her back and slumps onto the bed.

"You don't believe me?" I start toward her, my steps slow.

"I don't know what to believe anymore." She buries her head in the pillow.

The need to bare my soul drags me forward. "I'm never going to lie to you again." It isn't a vain attempt to make her happy. It's a promise. A vow.

I had cause to lie before. Now my objective is keeping her here, and I know that will only happen if I give her the truth. The full truth.

She raises her face, and those pleading eyes are glazed, but she doesn't cry. Not one tear escapes. She's strong. Too fucking strong.

"There's something else I need to tell you, though." I force the words out, knowing this quiet moment will be over once I confess.

She blinks up at me and swallows. "I'm not going to like it, am I?"

"No, you're not."

She nods and lowers her attention to the floor. "Then don't tell me. Not yet. I need time to regroup or I'm going to break."

My chest hollows. I wasn't expecting to be denied. The reprieve is too damn good to be true. Any additional minute with her at my mercy is a blessing. A fucking gift. "You won't break."

She lets out a derisive laugh. "I'm glad you're confident."

I grab the pillow clutched in her arms and tug until she lets it go. Her hands fall to the mattress as I move forward bringing us toe to toe, her knees to mine.

"I won't let you break," I pledge, grasping her chin to drag her attention back to me.

Her eyes are bleak, the grief ebbing off her in a continuous onslaught. All I want to do is pull her into me and fuck some life back into her. To make everything better.

She stares, barely blinking, barely breathing.

I see my future in those eyes. In this woman. It's fucking crazy and unwanted, but it's there. It's been there from the first night she fucked me over and threw my gun out a third-story window, to right now, when I'd give anything to see her smile.

I can't stop thinking about her. I won't.

"Do you hear me?" I drag my thumb along her lower lip. "I won't let you break."

"You must be one tough guy to stop that from happening." She reaches out, her fingers latching onto my waistband. Her gaze turns determined, seductive, and it takes all my strength not to slam my mouth over hers.

"I can be whatever you need me to be."

She grabs my belt and yanks at the clasp. She's looking for something to take her mind off Brent, and my dick is enthusiastic to run interference.

I'm hard already. Crazy with rapidly building lust. I want to taste her pain, her anguish. I want to be there with her, letting it drag us both under instead of me watching from the sidelines.

She lowers my zipper and tugs my waistband down over my ass.

"You sure you want to do this?" Once this starts, I'll have no will to stop.

"Are you really asking me that?"

"Yeah, I'm fucking asking, and once I get an affirmation there's no turning back."

She yanks my jeans lower. My boxer briefs, too. My cock stands between us, pulsing as she licks her lower lip. She pulls and tugs until my jeans are at my knees, then places her hands on my thighs. I hold my breath as she leans in, her greedy little tongue snaking out to taste the tip of my cock.

Fuck.

I groan. That simple touch...that brief brush of connection... Damn her. She's killing me.

I grab a fistful of her hair and she moans, her eyes rolling as I tug her head back. I pull until her chin lifts, and her attention is all mine.

"Are you fucking sure you want to do this?" I snarl through my weakening restraint.

"Yes," she whispers. "I'm sure."

I tighten my grip, and her chin ascends. "I'll make you feel good," I promise.

"I don't want to feel good. All I need is a distraction, and that's what you've been every day since you walked into Atomic Buzz all those weeks ago."

"A distraction?" I wrap her hair around my knuckles and yank.

She gasps, and it's the sexiest sound I've ever heard.

"I'll take pleasure in distracting the fuck out of you, princess." I shove my fist forward, pushing her head toward my cock. She smirks up at me, but the emotion doesn't reach her eyes. She's still hollow. Still grief-stricken.

"What's your favorite type of distraction?" I hold her a lip-lick away from my shaft. "Oral? Anal? Or will my dick make that sweet pussy its bitch?"

"All of the above."

Fuck. I won't last. I'm already wound tight, my balls throbbing, my dick pulsing.

Her tongue stretches out, gently gliding along my shaft from base to tip in a swipe of devilish torture.

I release her hair and bend down to grip her thighs. I tip her onto her back, yanking the tight leggings down her incredible legs. Her panties are already wet, the crotch bathed in her arousal. She smells like a feast. One I'm ready to devour.

I tug the pants off, then her underwear, and fall to my knees, leaving her in the gray woolen sweater that is far too cute for the dirty things I want to do to her.

With rough hands, I shove her knees apart and slide my hands under her ass to bring her to the edge of the mattress. She glistens, the puffy pink flesh of her cunt ready and waiting.

I sink my head between her thighs, my tongue leading the way to her pussy. The first lick straight down her slit has us both moaning. I do it again and again, making her writhe, sending me insane.

"More," she demands.

I pull back and remove one hand from under her ass. I swirl my thumb through her slickness, sink it deep inside. I do it again and again until my digit is drenched, then I let my tongue take its place.

I torment that greedy little cunt, while I move my thumb to her ass to swirl the lubrication over the puckered hole.

She groans, wiggles, squirms while my dick seeps with pre-cum. I press harder, breeching her ass to sink my digit inside. She jolts and shoves her hands into my hair to hold my head in place, demanding more.

Normally, I'd smirk at a woman this eager, but I'm right there with her. *No*, I'm surpassing her. The need to sink my dick inside her heat makes me fucking mindless.

I clench my free hand around the flesh of her butt. My thumb pumps her ass, while my tongue laps up a treat. I'm on the edge, and the briefest lapse in concentration will have me blowing against the side of the bed.

"Fuck me," she cries. "Hurry up and fuck me."

She rocks her hips like a sexual goddess as I move my mouth to her clit and rub against it with my lower lip. I watch her, wanting to deny her just for a little while as I enjoy the erotic display.

I've never seen a sexier woman. I never will again. With her top half entirely covered, she's still a fantasy brought to life.

"Fuck. Me. Luke."

Jesus fucking Christ.

I dump her on the mattress and shove to my feet, prepared to punish her for using my real name.

"Don't say that again," I warn. Not because I don't want her to, because I can't risk anyone finding out if she grows used to saying it.

"Sorry." She grins and leans up on her elbows. *"Luke."*

I grasp her knees and lift, sending her toppling backward as I position her drenched pussy right in front of my cock.

She holds my gaze, her chest heaving, her breathing ragged. I impale her, sinking deep, shoving so fucking hard I feel the pleasure all the way to my bones.

She clenches the quilt and gasps. "Oh my God."

I pound into her. Over and over. I have to close my damn eyes because the sight before me is pure nirvana. But she's there, too, taunting me from behind closed lids.

I slide my hands along to her ass, lifting, arching her back higher, digging my fingers deep. Her scent is in my lungs, her taste is on my lips, and that perfect pussy is seconds from milking me dry.

"You're going to make me come," she pants.

I open my eyes, unable to deny myself. "Say my name," I demand.

"I thought you didn't want—"

"Say my fucking name."

I slam into her, over and over and over. Harder and harder and harder. She moans, the sound increasing while her thighs clench tight around my hips.

"Please, Luke," she cries out, her pussy massaging my dick. Pulsing and contracting. "I'm coming."

I shout as my release follows hers, my cum bursting free in relieving spurts.

I don't stop.

I can't.

I won't.

She keeps moaning, crying, those knuckles turning white as she grips the coverings. I've never wanted someone like this. I've never needed anyone like I need her.

I slam into her with each fading pulse of orgasm. Her pussy has exhausted me, chained and enslaved me.

I swallow while she pants, her gray woolen sweater tight against her breasts as her chest rises and falls. Her legs begin to relax. My thrusts slow. I've marked her thighs with my fingers and made her breathless from the way I fucked her. I've affected her, but it's not even close to the way she affects me.

"Don't say my name again," I murmur.

She nods, biting her lower lip, her lids heavy, her cheeks flushed.

I inch back, my cock leaving her heat, a trail of cum following in its wake.

Fuck.

Fuck.

Fuck.

"I'm sorry." I place her down on the bed and run a hand over my mouth. "I didn't mean for that to happen."

She frowns up at me, then awareness dawns and her eyes flare. *"Jesus. Fuck."*

"You wanted a distraction, right?" I drawl.

Her glower is a great indication that this situation isn't something we can joke about.

"Why is everything a complete disaster with you?" she accuses. "Everything falls to shit. Every single time."

It isn't sunshine and rainbows for me either. Sarah has brought me nothing but trouble and mind-numbing lust.

"Why the hell are we still doing this?" She pushes to her elbows and looks up at me as if I have the answer.

I don't.

I have no clue.

"I wish I knew." I pull up my jeans to cover my ass and stalk from the room, returning moments later with a damp washcloth.

She flops back onto the mattress and rests an arm over her face as I slide a hand between her thighs. I wipe the slickness from her legs, her mound, her slit.

My dick throbs with the possibility of round two. That greedy motherfucker.

"I'll deal with the morning-after pill tomorrow," she murmurs.

"Right." What if I don't want her to deal with it? *Fuck.* Am I really that desperate to have her locked in my life?

I place the cloth on her bedside table and turn off the light. She crawls across the mattress then pulls back the covers, her movements visible with the slight illumination from the living room.

I ditch my shoes and clothes to climb naked onto the mattress. I don't offer to give her privacy or space. She won't get either from me. No matter how hellish this is, I can't drag myself away.

I want her. Not just her body or her secrets. I want her trust. I want more. I want everything. Every touch. Every breath. I want to know she's mine, and I won't stop until I'm successful.

I slide in beside her and place my palm on her stomach, my lips on her shoulder.

I listen to her breathing and feel her stomach rise and fall. Every so often she sniffs, and it's the most vulnerable, emotional sound I've ever heard. She's caged all her anguish inside, not letting it break free.

"Why did you keep turning the camera around?" she whispers into the darkness. "Was it a hint to tell me I was disclosing my location?"

She turns to face me, and I briefly close my eyes to bite back the bliss of her snuggling into my chest.

I've never had this. Not the woman in my home. Not the cuddling or the after-sex conversation.

"It wasn't that at all."

"Then what was it?"

I remember my vow of honesty and bite back the need to lie as I meet her gaze. "I had to see you. Those hours before you woke were all I had."

She lowers her attention to focus on my chest. There's no other reaction. She isn't happy for my weakness. She isn't latching her claws in, scrambling for more. "Why didn't you interrogate me for the name of the informant?"

"Because I know you don't have it. After the funeral, Decker filled me in on what he'd dug up on you now that we have the names from the headstones in Seattle. I read about your family, which led to Jacob. There was a photo of him with Dan in your apartment." I glance over my shoulder to the room. "It's around here somewhere."

I turn back to her sad eyes and lazy appraisal. My mind tells me to cut and run, but my lungs ache for more. It's a constant fight between want and need. It has been for weeks. I think it will be for a long time to come.

She's hypnotizing. Mesmerizing. She's a damn dream, or maybe she's a nightmare. Either way, I'm not ready to wake up.

She burrows into me, resting her cheek to my chest. "You never kissed me again. Not after that first night."

My pulse thunders. "Did you want me to?"

Her head shakes the slightest bit. "No."

She stabs me through the ribs with that one word, creating a hole where my self-respect should be.

"But no matter how much I told myself I didn't want it," she whispers, "I needed it more than anything."

20

HER

I startle awake to the sound of a shrill, rhythmic beep coming from another room.

"What the hell is that?" I push from the cage of Hunter's arms and sit.

"Don't worry. It's just the motion detectors at the gate. Decker must be here."

"How do you know it's him?"

He slides from the bed and yanks his jeans on. "Nobody else knows where I live."

I ignore the monumental realization that I'm one of only two people trusted with this man's address, and glance over my shoulder to the bedside clock. "Why would he be here at three in the morning?"

"I don't know." He slides up his zipper and clasps the belt, the peaks and troughs of his abs highlighted with the gentle glow of light coming from the living room. "Stay in here while I deal with him."

He starts for the door, and my throat tightens at the thought of him leaving.

"Hunter?"

He pauses at the threshold and glances at me. "Yeah?"

"Can I trust Decker?" It's a stupid question. I can't even trust Hunter, despite my body being at his mercy. But I need his affirmation. In the quiet hours before I passed out, all I could think about was Brent and who, apart from me, was responsible for his death. "Could he have led Torian to Atomic Buzz?"

"No." His response is immediate, without contemplation. "You don't need to worry about him."

I clutch the sheet to my naked chest. "How can you be so sure?"

"We can talk about it later. When you're ready." He gives me a sad smile and closes the door behind him, imprisoning me with rabid contemplation.

If Hunter knows Decker isn't to blame, then he must also know who is.

I slide from the bed as the beeping stops, pulling my woolen sweater down to cover my ass. I hustle to the door, inch it open, and listen.

I don't hear anything. Not movement. Not conversation.

"Hunter?"

He doesn't answer.

My apprehension increases, tickling the back of my neck as I tiptoe down the hall and stop in the shadows before the opening to the living room. He isn't in sight. He's not inside.

Something flickers in my peripheral vision. I tilt my head to see him outside, shirtless, striding away from me across the lawn toward Decker, who gets out of the car I'd seen him in weeks ago on the highway.

I creep forward, not hiding, but also not making my presence known by positioning myself in line with one of the porch poles so Decker can't see my approach. I begin to hear words, some clear, some indecipherable. Nothing makes sense yet, not even when I reach the door and grasp the handle. Slowly, I plunge the lever, opening the door a crack.

"She's asleep," Hunter murmurs. "I don't want her disturbed."

Decker nods. "How did she take the news?"

"She doesn't know the half of it yet."

I inch to the side to see Decker's profile. He's frowning. No, it's a glare. "What half does she know?"

"It was her choice," Hunter snarls. "I was going to tell her, but she's been through a lot. It's her preference to wait until she calms down."

My cheeks heat at how weak I sound. They heat even more at the possibility of Hunter thinking I'm fragile. I shouldn't crave his praise, and still I itch to have him infatuated with me, the way I am with him. Mindless, crazed, and emotionally unstable, too.

Decker laughs, the sound caustic. "Do you hear yourself? I fucking know she's been through a lot. And you're too much of a chicken shit to tell her why. My God, man, when it comes to women, you're the dumbest asshole I know."

I push the door wider and tiptoe onto the porch, the chilled night air drifting under my sweater to touch the nakedness beneath.

"So, when are you going to tell her?"

"When she's ready."

"When she's ready or when you're ready?"

"*Jesus fucking Christ, Decker.*" Hunter runs a hand through his hair. "I said I would tell her, and I will."

I move closer, needing to be near him. That's all I want. I'm stronger when he's close. Even now, I grow emboldened, ready and capable of listening to whatever I need to hear as the door falls back to click in place.

Hunter stiffens. Decker pins me with a stare.

"You can tell me now." I walk across the porch, my uncovered feet tingling from the cold. "I'm ready to hear it."

Decker mutters something under his breath. A curse, maybe. But Hunter remains still, his back to me.

"What is it?" I walk down the three steps to the lawn. "What do I need to know?"

"Nice outfit." Decker clears his throat and stalks in my direction. "I'll meet you both inside."

"Why?" I ask. "Aren't you a part of this, too?"

"Oh, no." He raises his hands and shakes his head. "No, no, no. I follow orders. I don't make the plans. This is all on him."

I nod, trying to steel myself against the upcoming news. An ominous feeling creeps down my spine as he passes and goes inside.

Hunter doesn't face me. He stares into the darkness, silent in contemplation, or maybe it's annoyance over my interruption.

"Hunter?" I take one step, then another. "You can tell me now."

Finally, he turns, his head lowered, his gaze meeting mine through thick, dark lashes. "Torian wasn't in the bar with Brent."

My heart drops, and I force myself to nod. "Okay… Who was?"

His attention flicks toward the house. Toward Decker.

I swallow, coming to the conclusion that a predator is behind me. Inside the house. I move away from the porch, coming closer to my protector, and glance over my shoulder. "He killed Brent?"

"No. He didn't kill him."

"Then who did? And why was he there?" My words are garbled in a tangled mess as fear and the need for retribution rush through me.

"He made sure everything ran smoothly." Hunter straightens his shoulders as if preparing for an onslaught. "He controlled the situation for me from the inside."

He looks at me as if waiting for my comprehension to dawn, but there's no dawning here. I don't understand. I don't think I want to.

"I organized everything." His lips are downcast, his eyes grim. Everything about him screams remorse, and yet nothing makes sense.

"*You* arranged for Brent to be killed?" My tone is strong, belying the fissure cracking right through the heart of me.

He stares for long moments that drag on for an eternity. "Sarah, he's not dead."

Not. Dead.

A spark of excited relief bursts to life inside my chest. He's not dead. He…is not…dead.

I want to fall to my knees in thanks, but Hunter's unshifting look of stony remorse fizzles my relief. "Is he hurt?"

I retreat a step, needing space to think, only to freeze at the sound of the porch door opening. Decker walks outside, a large bowl cradled in one arm. He leans against the banister, watching me as his hand dives into the bowl, retrieving a pile of popcorn.

"*Son-of-a-bitch*," Hunter hisses. "We're not entertainment. Get the fuck inside."

Decker smiles, all toothy and wide, then snaps the handful of popcorn into his mouth.

Concentrate. Think.

Hunter arranged for Decker to be inside the bar.

"Is he hurt?" I repeat, standing my ground and squaring my shoulders. "I heard the gunshot. You wanted him dead."

"No. I wanted you scared. I wanted you vulnerable and in need of my help. When I told you I was messaging Decker, I did. I told him to fire a warning shot."

I snap my lips closed to stop a gasp escaping.

He wanted me back in Portland. He wanted me here.

"Is. He. Hurt?" I enunciate each word through clenched teeth.

"No." He shakes his head. "He's fine."

"A little pissed off that he got held at gunpoint," Decker clarifies. "And that I shot a hole in his wall. But yeah, fine."

"You're not helping," Hunter growls.

I blink slowly as rage and humiliation burn my eyes. "So much for no more lies."

He snaps to attention and takes a step forward. "I haven't lied since I promised you the truth. Since we arrived here."

What a privilege that must be to a snake like him.

I stand immobile. Heart heavy. Soul weary.

"I won't lie to you again, Sarah. Everything that has happened since we came here is real."

He means the fucking and maybe the brief admission that he wants me. But who doesn't want A-grade snatch?

Asshole.

My feelings had been more than that. So horribly, disturbingly immense.

"Say something," he begs.

That's a tough request, seeing as I'm tongue-tied with humiliation.

I owe him nothing. Not my anger. Not even my words. But I can give him one. "Goodbye."

I start for the house. I'll get changed, stuff a pair of clean underwear in my pocket, then run.

That's all I do now. Run. Flee.

Every step I've made since Hunter entered my life has been wrought with failure and disappointment. And yet I stupidly felt my emptiness lessen.

I take the three stairs onto the porch one at a time, calm and civil, while I scowl at Decker, who continues to eat popcorn like he's watching an Academy Award performance. I walk inside without a word, head straight for my doppelgänger bedroom, and change into a fresh pair of jeans from the clothes Hunter has stacked in the wardrobe.

I grab a few pairs of underwear from my bedside drawers, shoving them in my pockets, and lift my mattress to retrieve an old switchblade stored in a hole between the springs.

"You can't leave."

I straighten at the sound of his voice and lower the mattress back in place.

"You don't have any money on you. You don't have a phone."

I turn with a derisive smile and face him standing in the doorway. "No, and I don't even have my dignity, because you stole that from me, too. But I'll make it work."

He winces. "Let me explain."

"I don't want to hear it." I shove the blade into my pocket beside the already tightly compacted underwear. "All I want is for you to let me walk out of here without another confrontation."

"I can't do that." The words are murmured softly, in the deepest, richest tone.

I stride toward him—I'll stride straight through him if I have to—and he widens his stance, his shoulders broad, his arms hanging limp. He covers my escape.

"I'm not doing this with you again," I mutter. "Move."

He doesn't.

I continue forward and try to shove my way through. He stands like stone, his beseeching eyes tearing me apart.

"*Move*."

"Ask me why."

I close my eyes briefly, warding off the insincere heartbreak in his tone. "I don't need to."

I push at his arm, and he responds by getting right in my face. "Yes, you do. You need to know why I did it."

I pull away, thankful he allows the retreat. "I already know why. You love to play games. You love tormenting me. It's who you are. It's what you do."

He cringes.

"See?" I throw my arms wide and give a bitter laugh. "I'm right."

"Yeah. You are." He nods. "I loved playing our games."

My heart squeezes at the admission. I don't want to be right. No matter how obvious the answer, I wish and wish to be wrong.

"I lost you for five days. One minute, I knew where you were; the next you were gone." He leans in, but not toward my face. He moves to the side, his breath tickling my neck. "That first night, not knowing where you were…*Fucking. Killed. Me.*"

He enunciates those last words into my ear with such vehement passion my chest tightens. Sternum. Ribs. Lungs.

"I was scared." He moves closer. So close I can feel the heat emanating from his bare chest. "I thought you were hurt. Or that Torian changed his mind about the deal we made."

"What deal?" I pull away to meet his gaze.

"I practically sold my soul for your safety."

Lies. Lies. Lies.

I shake my head in disbelief.

"It's true." He looks me in the eye, undaunted by my skepticism. "There's trust between me and Torian, no matter how temperamental. So, I vouched for you, putting everything on the line to convince him I believed you when you said you knew nothing. But I wasn't entirely sure he would leave you alone. Then you disappeared, and I thought he was responsible. My panic only increased the longer you were gone. I was mindless, Sarah. You've got no idea how crazy I was searching for you."

"So you fooled me into thinking my one and only friend was murdered?"

He clenches his jaw, raises his chin. "Would you have come home with me for any other reason?"

I open my mouth, poised to respond.

"Think about it," he demands. "There's no way you would've gotten in my car if I'd asked. There's no way you would've let me fuck you, or stay in your bed. You wouldn't have crawled into my arms or spoken to me the way you have tonight."

My throat tightens at the reminder of how much I've given him. "That's a lot of effort to get laid, buddy."

His eyes narrow to harsh slits. "I can get laid any time, any place. This isn't about sex. This is about you and me. It's about not being able to fucking walk away." He sucks in a breath and lets it out in a heave. "You can't deny feeling the same. I know you do."

"What I feel is anger," I snarl. "I feel disgusted and played. I feel like every word that comes out of your mouth is nothing but a lie." I square my shoulders and get in his face, almost nose to nose. "I feel like you've won this battle, but never again. I'm done. For good."

I glare at him for long seconds, then stride around him, making it to the door.

"We're not done," he growls. "We're not finished here."

"Yes, we are." I continue into the hall, hating the distance I'm putting between us, but needing it, too.

"Sarah," he calls after me. "You can't leave."

I briefly close my eyes, pained by the way he says my name. Loving and loathing in immeasurable quantities.

"*Sarah*," he yells, his footsteps following me.

I stride through the living room, toward Decker, who now stands between me and the porch door.

"I know how to find Jacob."

Hunter's statement stops me in my tracks. I meet Decker's gaze, and there's no longer any humor in his features. His face is emotionless. Solemn. A picture-perfect portrait of the truth.

This isn't a lie.

No. I can't be fooled again. I can't let myself believe that the man who torments me knows where to find the man who ruined me.

"Stop it," I whisper.

"Believe me." His footfalls move closer. "I know where he is."

It shouldn't matter. It *can't* matter. Staying here is a bad decision, no matter the reason. I will my feet to move and hold my head high as I continue to the door.

"We can help you take him down," Decker adds. "That's what you want, isn't it? To get him back for—"

"*Shut up*," I scream. "Just shut the hell up, and quit playing me. I can't take this anymore."

I focus on the freedom waiting for me on the other side of the wall of glass. There is a peaceful truth that comes with solitude. A clarity of vision unmarred by the opinions of others.

Yes, it's lonely. But there is harmony in that, too.

I lived in that existence for a long time, going through the motions of life yet not really living. Not really feeling in my self-imposed isolation. Then Hunter showed up, obliterating my truth. He destroyed the peace. He blurred the bigger picture.

And I can't deny I liked it.

He creeps into the reflection in the glass, approaching from over my right shoulder to meet my gaze. "He works for Torian. He's a small-time dealer in Newport who comes back to Portland every few weeks to check in."

He's tempting me with the one thing I want, manipulating me because I've let him know all the right buttons to push. I close my eyes and simply listen. Not to Hunter. Not to Decker. I tune in to my intuition, hoping against all hope that it steers me in the right direction.

After all his lies, I can't stomach the thought of trusting him. And then I think about him kissing me. I remember his notes. I hear his emotional admissions—*I had to see you… You've got me… I sold my soul for your safety.*

There has to be truth in those moments. At least the slightest glimmer.

"I know you think I've been fucking with you," he murmurs. "But trust me, you've done shit to me, too."

I open my eyes and glare at him through the reflection. "I haven't done *anything* to you. Not one damn thing."

"That's where you're wrong. You've fucked with me since the first time I saw you with Roberts. You messed with my head. You made me lose sight of everything." He gives a sad smile. "All I see is you, Sarah."

"Stop it." I shove my hand through my loose hair, pulling tight. I need the pressure to stop building in my skull. I need relief. I need… *Fuck*. I don't know what I need anymore.

"Let me help you with Jacob." He takes a step closer.

"Don't." I scoot away and turn to face him. "If you move another step I'll…" What? Scratch his eyes out? Beat him? Cuss him to death? Maybe I could do all of the above.

"I followed you from the hotel room with Dan because I wanted to know who you were. I wanted to know why someone like you would be with a lowlife piece of shit."

"Bullshit," I spit. "You needed to find out what he told me."

"That was part of it, yes. But it didn't stop there. It never stops with you."

Oh, God. I'm succumbing. I want his lies. I crave the manipulation. Because even though his attention is fake, I keep convincing myself it's real. From the first night I met him, I saw things in this man that were never there—attraction, passion, protection.

None of it existed, yet the fiction weaves around me like tendrils of the finest silk, delicate and comforting in my denial.

"I needed to know more. Not just about Dan, about you." He remains a few feet away, somber with his deceptive conviction. "It got worse after we kissed. And then again when we fucked. Nothing made sense except my craving for more. It hasn't changed. Even when Torian was breathing down my neck. Even when you had a gun to my chest. And God knows it only got worse when Carlos ran you off the—"

"I need you to stop." My voice cracks and I give up the show of strength. "Please… Just stop."

"I can't. I've tried. When it comes to you, I don't have any control. I just want you, Sarah. That's all I know anymore."

I suck in a breath and glance to Decker, expecting a smirk or a grin at the very least. I get neither. His lips are tight, his brow furrowed. He's uncomfortable.

Well, goddamnit, so am I.

"I played you." Hunter moves toward me, stopping within reach. "And I get that you don't trust me. But I trust you."

He reaches out, and I stiffen as he grabs me by my jeans pocket and retrieves my knife. I watch in disbelief as he flicks it open and holds out the hilt for me to take.

"Do what you like," he offers. "Carve your name across my chest. Retaliate however you want."

"Jesus Christ," Decker mutters.

"I mean it." Hunter places the knife in my palm and wraps his hand around mine, raising the blade so the tip almost touches the skin across his ribs. "Do what you need to. Make this right."

My eyes are wide, my lips parted. He clutches my hand tight around the grip, and for the moment, I don't want to let go. I want to hurt him. I need to make him suffer.

I take a menacing step forward, and the tip of the blade pierces his skin.

I watch intently as his eyes flare, his jaw tenses, his chin lifts. I derive the slightest taste of justice from his pain, but the remorse hits me tenfold.

"Go on," he implores, his determination unwavering. "Do it."

I clench my fingers tighter, my throat closing. I increase the pressure, hoping for satisfaction to hit me by the bucket-load. But those hazel eyes… God, those eyes. They do things to me that the most malicious actions can't achieve. They strip my defenses. They strum my soul.

He sucks in a breath, and his grip loosens on my hand.

I glance down to find blood trailing over his stomach in a tiny rivulet to sink into the material of his black jeans.

"Get away from me." I scoot back out of his reach, and the knife falls from my fingers to clatter to the tiled floor.

"It's okay."

"No, it's not. Forgiveness doesn't come that easily. You have too much bullshit to make up for. No stab wound can amount to that."

"Then tell me how to fix this," he growls.

"How should I know?" I snap. "Haven't you heard the saying? You don't break a plate and expect an apology to make it better. You can glue it back together, but it's still not the same. The damage is already done."

"That's some philosophical genius, right there," Decker mumbles.

I ignore him, but Hunter's eyes flare with fury. "Fine. I'll give you space for now."

He turns to the kitchen and walks away, leaving me cold with the receding attention. Maybe I should've stabbed him after all.

Decker raises a brow as his gaze drops to Hunter's stomach. "You two are motherfucking crazy. I feel like I've just witnessed a satanic mating ritual."

"Nobody asked you to be here." Hunter rounds the island counter, grabs the scotch, and drinks from the bottle.

Blood seeps from the small cut against his ribs. He's never been more vicious with his harsh glare and flaring nostrils. He's never been more masculine. More fascinating. Alluring.

I march toward him, his eyes narrowing on me as I approach, and snatch the bottle from his hand. If I can't escape this torment, then I sure as hell won't let him do it via the reprieve of intoxication.

The asshole can suffer.

"Thanks." I turn away and storm to my new bedroom.

The last thing I hear as I close myself inside is Decker's laughter and his snickered, "You've got your hands full with that one."

21

HIM

I've been standing at the kitchen counter for hours, the sun now rising as I wait for Sarah to come out of her room.

She needs space, which I'm happy to give, since the window in her room can't be opened without a key. She can't run from me. At least not without me knowing.

"When do you plan on calling Torian?" Decker asks from his leaned position against the other side of the kitchen island.

"Not until she's ready."

"He's not going to be happy."

No shit. "I'll deal with it."

The soft click of an opening door sounds from down the hall, and Decker raises a brow. "How drunk do you think she is?"

Drunk enough to cause trouble would be my guess, especially since she isn't a drinker. Then again, she doesn't need to be drunk to cause problems.

Her padded footsteps approach, and I keep my focus straight ahead, on Decker, determined not to let my gaze rush after her like an eager little puppy.

"Want me to leave you two alone?" he asks.

"Really?" I glare. "Now you ask that?"

The asshole could've left us alone earlier, but oh no, he had to bear witness to my idiocy. He'll never let me live it down.

He smirks. "Better late than never."

I sigh as her slim figure nudges the edge of my sight from the start of the hall. She isn't dressed in the jeans she had on before. It's something less than that. Something I can't quite determine from my peripheral vision. I clench the kitchen counter behind me and grind my molars, determined not to take a proper look.

"I'm ready to hear what you know about Jacob." She continues forward, increasing the temptation.

"When was the last time you ate?" I finally succumb to the need to visually consume her.

Fuck.

She's wearing the shirt I had on last night. The one I left on the floor in her bedroom. Now it's covered in cuts and slices as if she's spent the last hours performing a voodoo ritual on me through the large material that dwarfs her body.

She stops at the far corner of the U-shaped kitchen, her arms crossing over her chest. "Right before I stole a car," she mutters, "to save a friend you pretended to murder in an effort to get me back in your bed."

Decker clears his throat to disguise a laugh.

Great. I walked straight into that one.

"Well, I'm starving." And after another night without sleep, I need caffeine. I shove from the counter and finally meet her gaze. She's tired, the dark smudges beneath her eyes making this tough woman appear fragile. "Get changed. We're going out for breakfast."

"I'm not going anywhere," she says softly with the undertone of her iron-clad determination.

I drag my focus away and scowl at Decker, because if I scowl at her, we are only going to fight again. "You need to focus before we talk. I'm not going to waste my time if you're drunk."

"As much as I would've loved the escapism, I didn't drink your damn scotch," she growls. "I only took it because I wanted to make sure you didn't either."

"How about I go out and get food while you two have some time alone?" Decker walks to the sofa and grabs his jacket. "You can settle your unresolved satanic rituals and be ready to eat once I get back."

I'm not going to bite. I'm not even going to increase my glare. I've learned it only spurs him on. "Don't forget the coffee."

He jerks his head in acknowledgement and leaves via the porch.

The click of the latching door is deafening, closing me in with her anger-filled silence. I don't know what she wants me to say to make this right. There probably isn't anything in the English language capable of reaching the level of apology she needs.

"I'm going to take a shower." I stalk from the kitchen, toward the hall in the opposite direction to Sarah.

"You're angry at *me* now?" she accuses.

"No." I'm tired. I'm frustrated.

"Good, because you have no right to be angry."

I pause and bite my tongue like a motherfucker. "Go get dressed, Sarah. Decker doesn't need to keep seeing you like that." The exposed thighs. Those nipples beading behind the thin material.

"Decker can kiss my ass."

I give a caustic laugh. "Be careful what you wish for. He's more than likely to give you what you want if you keep strutting around the house wearing next to nothing."

I continue down the hall and enter my room, not waiting for her to snap. I need a shower to clear my head. To wake me up. To wash her scent from my skin.

I undo my jeans button and lower the zipper when the door creaks wider. She's there again, stalking in my peripheral vision like a temptress. "Do you plan on joining me?"

"No," she whispers.

I shove my jeans down my legs, giving her an uncensored view of my hardening dick. "Then I suggest you get out of my room."

Her hungry gaze takes me in, her interest straying over my crotch, then quickly diverting to my stomach. "Do you need stitches?"

"Don't worry, princess. You barely scratched the surface."

She raises a brow. "Then maybe you should give me another try."

I heave out a tired breath. "You want to cut me again?"

I'll let her, if that's what it takes. I'll let her take whatever revenge she needs, because I deserve it. But my willingness to admit my mistakes won't last forever. My stubborn pride will see to that.

"No." She continues staring, not meeting my eyes as long moments pass. "I want you to prove this isn't another one of your games. I need you to convince me."

"How?" I approach her and she holds up a hand, instructing me to stop. "Look, Sarah, I don't do this shit. I don't *want* to do this shit. But I fought to get you back, and I apologized for my less-than-stellar tactics—"

"Less than stellar?" She balks. "Whispering behind someone's back is less than stellar. Conspiring against someone is less than stellar. But pretending to murder someone in an effort to get laid is a little beyond that, don't you think?"

I clamp my mouth shut, stifling a harsh response. I already told her this isn't about sex. If it was, I would've fucked her in every cheap-ass hotel in Portland. I wouldn't have merely watched her sleep. I would've woken her with my face between her thighs, my fingers in her cunt.

And I sure as hell wouldn't have let Decker see exactly how much of a vulnerability she is to me.

"Do you think I'd let you get away with stealing my car if this was only about sex?" I growl.

"Maybe this is retaliation for leaving the key fob in the console when I left the car unlocked in front of my building."

"You left the key?"

She beams an exaggerated smile.

Fuck this woman and my crazy infatuation that only seems to grow the longer she holds that expression. Even now, I want to laugh.

Laugh? She stole my goddamn car.

But none of that matters now. The only aim is convincing her this isn't all bullshit.

"How is exposing my home and my real name a retaliation? I've entrusted you with more information than I've ever entrusted with anyone. And you still don't get it. I don't know what else to tell you."

"Then don't tell me. Show me."

I frown. Is this some weird female fuckery? How the hell do I show her without words or the sex she claims this is about? Decker was right. I'm the dumbest asshole when it comes to women.

"If you care about me, you'll help me find Jacob—"

"I already promised I would," I growl.

She inclines her head. "*Then* you'll let me walk away."

I stiffen, my pulse spiking violently. "I can't do that."

I can't lose her. I don't know why; I just can't. Even the thought of it makes my chest tight. I already lost her once. I can't willingly do it again.

The determined gleam in her eyes transforms to a solemn stare of disappointment, and I hate it. I hate that she doesn't understand this shit is driving me to insanity. Isn't my inability to let her go enough? Doesn't that prove how much she means to me?

A woman has never come between me and my job before.

A woman has never stolen my focus and created havoc in my mind.

A woman has never controlled me. Not even a little bit. And certainly not with her level of effortless efficiency.

"Then this isn't about you caring for me. It's about you lusting after me." She pads from the room, her retreating steps fading down the hall as I stand in frustrated silence.

I wipe a rough hand over my face. Maybe she's right. Maybe it is lust. But even if it is, I still have no plan to let her go.

She wants revenge against a man who works for Torian. That won't come without consequences unless done strategically. Methodically. So, she needs me, no matter how much she refuses to admit it.

I mutter a string of curse words under my breath as I shove into my private bathroom, then lock myself inside and take a long shower. I take pleasure in the bite of pain as hot water breeches my cut. I take even more when I add soap to the mix. At least the distraction gives me a reprieve from thoughts of Sarah for a few short minutes.

I don't get out until the blood is washed from my skin and her scent no longer haunts me.

I should stay in my room until Decker returns. There needs to be a buffer between me and her. But as soon as I leave the bathroom, I pull on a clean pair of cargos and another black T-shirt, then stride right back down to the kitchen.

She's standing before the floor-to-ceiling windows, staring at my front yard. She's pulled her hair back into a high ponytail and is wearing tight leggings and the gray woolen sweater I fucked her in last night. The memory is a bitch—a haunting, conniving, sinister mistress that controls me like I'm a willing slave.

Problem is, she doesn't want me to be mastered. She doesn't want anything from me at all…apart from my dick.

I scowl, not appreciating the realization.

She doesn't hold the same fascination toward this thing between us that I do. For her, it's lust. Pure and simple.

I come up behind her, meeting her gaze in the reflection of the glass. She blinks back at me, no longer shooting spiteful daggers with her stare.

"Do you really want to walk after all this is said and done?"

She sucks in a deep breath and lowers her gaze.

She doesn't want to goddamn walk. She wants to continue this thing between us as much as I do—unwillingly and undeniably in equal measure.

"No," she whispers. "It's not what I want."

The admission makes a direct hit to my relief.

"It's what I need," she clarifies, stabbing the disappointment directly into my chest. "Because once I finish with Jacob, I'm going to need to find myself again. I'll have to start over and determine what I want from life."

"You want *me*."

She lets out a whisper of a laugh. "I do." She nods. "But that in itself isn't healthy. I doubt it ever can be. Not after everything that's happened."

An invisible weight rests heavily on my chest, growing more intense under her serene conviction. "Then I'll think about it."

"Really?" She turns, meeting my gaze with questioning eyes. "That means no following. No spying. No games. You need to let me move on with my life."

No checking in on her safety. No getting a fix from the distance between us by watching her sleep. No connection whatsoever.

I don't get it. I don't fucking understand why I want her so much. But even now, knowing she itches to run away from me, I can't stop wishing I had the words to make her stay.

"I said, I'll think about it." I step into her and wrap an arm around her waist. She doesn't flinch; she lets me hold her. "If that's what it takes to show you this isn't just about sex."

She licks her lower lip and then drags her teeth over the moistened temptation. There's no doubt she wants me. There's no doubt I could have her. Right here. Right now. On my living room floor.

"You don't get it. My concerns don't simply revolve around sex. They're more complicated than that."

"Then explain it to me."

Her shoulders slump as she releases a heavy breath. "The first boyfriend I ever had killed my entire family. He took everything from me, and I refused to let anyone into my life after that... Until you."

Until me, a replacement who was probably only a smidge better than her fucking psychotic ex.

"You've lied to me constantly," she continues. "You hacked my video surveillance. You followed me to another city and stole secrets I never would've shared. Then you pretended my only friend—"

"I get it." I don't need the reminder of my rap sheet.

I've maimed. I've tortured. I've killed. But never before have I felt the remorse I do right now.

She needs to learn to trust me. *Me*. A man who barely trusts himself.

She rests her forehead against my chest. "You have to give me space, Luke."

Not only does it sound like she wants space, it's fucking clear she might never want to see me again. She has the determination to move on, regardless of this connection. This dependence. This addiction.

I hold her tighter, both arms around her back.

I don't think I'm that strong. Not yet, anyway. Maybe I will be after she pisses me off a few more times. Maybe… Then again, it's highly doubtful when it hurts to fucking breathe unless she's in my arms.

I press my lips to her hair and close my eyes. "I'm not making any promises, but like I said, I'll think about it."

22

HER

The sound of a car approaches in the front yard. I close my eyes, not wanting to leave the warmth of Hunter's arms.

"Decker is here," he whispers into my hair.

I nod.

Once I step back, I know I have to focus. There will be no time for fluttering hearts and craving attention. I have to take control. But I loathe to move from his arms when I know this could be one of the last times I'll be here.

"I think you'll change your mind about us once this is all over," he whispers.

He still doesn't get it. This isn't about our attraction. If it was, I'd never leave his bed.

"I'm not going to change my mind." I can't. Not if I have any hope for a mentally stable future.

I suck in a breath, fill my lungs, and retreat from his embrace. I don't look at him. I turn to the glass and watch Decker approach with food bags and a tray of takeout coffee.

Hunter opens the door, lets him inside, then leads the way to the dining table.

"There are croissants, English muffins, and donuts, depending on your mood." Decker dumps the feast on the thick polished wood and pulls out a chair.

I take a seat across from him, while Hunter sits at the head of the table. Both of them focus on spreading the food and handing out coffee. Neither of them looks at me, as if fearing even a glance will bring up the topic we need to discuss.

Well, it's too late for avoidance.

"Tell me what you know about Jacob." I unwrap my croissant and take a large bite, the taste inspiring a hearty groan.

Hunter flicks me a casual glance, devoid of the feelings from our private moment. "He goes by the name Vaughn."

"Zack," Decker adds. "He's been working with Torian for years."

"Almost as long as I have." Hunter takes a sip of coffee, watching me over the rim of the cup.

"You know him?"

He nods. "We're not buddies, but yeah, I know him."

My appetite threatens to flee. "And you're still willing to help me take him down?"

"Yep." He takes another lazy sip of caffeine.

There's no concern. No building apprehension. Does he even understand my plans?

"You do realize I want him dead, right?" I glance at them both, expecting to see a glimmer of shock or foreboding. I find neither.

"I know." He places the coffee cup down and unwraps an English muffin. "It shouldn't be hard."

"Why is that?" I place my croissant on the paper wrapping, giving him my full attention.

"We're going to get someone else to do it."

"No." I scowl. "I don't want anyone else. I've waited ten yea—"

"Sending someone to meet their maker isn't all it's cracked up to be. You're not a murderer, princess."

I straighten my shoulders and want to snarl at how his gaze dips to my now thrusted breasts. "Let me worry about that."

"I can't. I won't." His attention returns to mine without remorse. "Do you really think you can look him in the eye and follow through with killing him?"

"Yes," I grate.

"And do you think you can spend the rest of your life seeing that face every time you close your eyes? Do you think you can live with his ghost haunting you? Always looking over your shoulder to see if the cops are following?"

"I handled you following me, didn't I?"

"That's nothing in comparison." His lip curls, but it isn't nice. It's cruel and derisive. "Have you forgotten what it felt like when you thought you killed Dan? Do you remember the nausea? Do you remember how you hid in your apartment for days?"

I remember.

But Dan was different. He didn't murder four people in cold blood. He didn't murder anyone. In comparison, Jacob turned my family to ash without remorse.

He didn't deserve this new life as Zack Vaughn. He didn't deserve a life at all.

"I. Can. Handle. It." I enunciate the words with vehemence.

I want the other Hunter back. The caring, pleasing one, not the harsh criminal who now sits in his place.

"And what if I don't want you to? What if I can't handle you handling it?"

The thick silence that follows his response is louder than our argument. Static rushes in my ears. My pulse pounds in my throat. I don't want this to be hard on him, but neither can I let him distract me from what I've strived for.

"Sarah..." Decker places his croissant down. "Let Torian do it for you. That way you're still responsible, but not held accountable, and he will fuck Vaughn up better than you ever could."

I drag my attention to him and frown. "Torian? Why would he kill Jacob for me?"

"Because that's exactly what he does to anyone who crosses him."

"I don't understand." I glance between them, back and forth, trying to work out the puzzle.

"You're going to tell him that Dan gave you the name of the informant."

I gasp at the simplicity of their scheme. "I'm going to tell him it was Jacob?"

"Vaughn," Decker corrects. "You need to make sure you get the name right."

I nod, my lips curling in an excited leer. "That sounds..." I want to say easy, but this is a murderous plot. Surely it can't be that simple. "Are you certain it will work?"

"No, not at all." Hunter pins me with a stern scowl. "Convincing Torian will be a bitch now that I've already promised him you know nothing. He won't appreciate me going back on my word. He'll be skeptical from the get go."

"Which means it's best if the news comes from you," Decker adds. "We'll take you to see him or—"

"We'll fucking call him first," Hunter growls. "And pray to God that's enough. I don't want you there with him."

My throat dries at the unwavering concern in his eyes.

"But all this will put you in a dangerous position, too, right?" I ask. "It makes your original promise a lie."

"Don't worry about me. You're the one we're concerned about."

"Concentrate on getting your story straight." Decker balls his trash and throws it at the open paper bag in the middle of the table. "We need to go over the details again and again and again until it's memorized. It will take days to get this right."

"That doesn't work for me." The sooner this is all over, the sooner I can remove the shackles of Jacob's strangling hold. I won't wait a minute longer than necessary to be free from him. "I don't need to practice. Not when the truth is so close to what happened with Dan in the first place. The story will be simple and without complication. He can either take it or leave it."

"And if he leaves it?" Hunter asks.

"Then I deal with Jacob the old-fashioned way."

"You mean the way that gets you killed?" He scoffs, smug and superior. "I should just do this on my own."

"Don't you dare take this from me," I snap. "He's not yours to kill."

I can't believe we're bickering about murder. We're fighting over who gets to end someone's life. If my high school self could see me now, she would literally pee her pants.

"She's right." Decker raises his voice. "We already discussed this. If Torian found out you smoked one of his dealers, your life wouldn't be worth living."

"And besides," I add, "you act as though I'm new to this, but I'm not. Dan wasn't the first guy I fucked with. I've done this before. Many times." I grab the edge of the table in both hands to hold back my frustration. "Do you remember the priest whose child-molesting case was dropped? Do you also remember that same priest was admitted to hospital with self-inflicted cuts to his genitals?"

"Oh, boy," Decker mumbles.

"They weren't self-inflicted," I clarify. "And the investment banker who signed all of his assets over to the ex-wife he physically abused? Do you think he did that out of the goodness of his heart? Or the school teacher who secretly filmed high school girls in the shower? Did you ever wonder why he made the sudden decision to join a monastery?" I stab a finger at my chest. "I did all that. And much more."

Decker grins. "Is it weird that I'm a little turned on right now?"

Hunter glares at me, obviously not appreciating his friend's enthusiasm. "Congratulations." He leans back in his chair and gives a slow clap. "And how much time did you spend planning those jobs?"

Asshole.

Trust him to cut right to the only flaw in this plan. "I know what I'm doing, Hunter. And I already have a story straight in my head. A real one. *The truth.* I'll tell him exactly what happened. The only thing I have to add is the few seconds where Dan told me the name."

He continues to eye me, his focus bordering on a glower.

"Look," I plead. "This isn't new to me, and it sure as hell doesn't daunt me. I've wanted this for too damn long not to be enthusiastic to get it done."

"Then tell us your story." He spreads his arms wide. "Why were you with Dan that night?"

"To make him stop assaulting women. He'd been beating prostitutes on a regular basis and leaving them for dead."

"And why was that your concern?" Decker asks.

"It should be everyone's concern. Vulnerable women were hurt, and he had no intention of stopping. The police wouldn't do a damn thing and nobody held his father accountable—"

"So you beat him?" Decker interrupts.

"Yes."

They continue to bombard me with questions, one after another, but my responses are confident and given with conviction. I know my story. The timeline is infallible. The account is legitimate. All I have to do is leave out the parts about Jacob.

"And why would Dan just give you Vaughn's name without you having to ask?" Hunter raises a brow. "Especially when he demanded a large sum of money from Torian for the information."

"Because Rohypnol can be a bitch." I keep my expression blank. "In the minutes before he passed out, he was so confused he blurted a whole diatribe of what I thought was useless information. He said his father would kill him if another scandal got out. Then he pleaded once more for me to let him go, and told me Vaughn was the name I wanted. That Vaughn was Torian's informant."

Hunter's nostrils flare as he glares at me in an intimidation tactic. Or is it legitimate anger? I'm not sure. He pushes from his seat and silently begins snatching used food wrappers from the table.

"Is that it?" I follow him with my gaze. "Are you done grilling me?"

"Not even close." He shoves garbage into the empty takeout bags. "We need to keep going over this."

I sigh and glance to Decker for support. "I told you I won't do this a million times. I know my story. It won't change."

Hunter slams his palms against the wood. "And I told you that convincing Torian won't be a fucking walk in the park. You're not ready until I say you are."

I close my eyes briefly and find calm. He's upset that I nailed my account of what happened, because once this is all over, he knows I'll leave him. I get it. Really, I do. But I'm not going to wait around until he feels all warm and fuzzy about this. That shit could take weeks.

"You're angry." I look up at him, trying to reiterate how important the culmination of this moment with Torian will be for me. "I need this, Hunter. I'm ready."

His nostrils flare.

"She's right," Decker murmurs. "She's got this."

"How the fuck do you know that?" Hunter snarls. "I promised Torian she knew nothing. Going back on my word will make him suspicious. He'll come at her from every angle—"

"You don't know that, either." Decker stands. "He might not even want to talk to her in person. Having the conversation over the phone might be enough, seeing as he already knows there's an informant. But no matter what he does, we can't prepare for the unknown. We can only bank on her story being straight. And it is."

I give Hunter a sad smile. I can see the concern in his glare. He's worried. On edge. "I can do this. I promise."

"Go on." Decker jerks his chin toward the kitchen. "Get your phone. Call him. This could be as simple as a ten-minute conversation."

Hunter doesn't move. Not apart from clenching his fists in a white-knuckle grip against the wood.

"Please, Hunter." I clasp my hands in prayer and bat my lashes softly for dramatic effect.

He rolls his eyes and snatches the trash-filled bag from the table to stalk to the kitchen. My belly tumbles as he grabs his phone off the counter, then strides back in my direction, then past to the porch door, and outside.

I don't know if I should give him space or follow. Chase after him, like he's always chased after me. Or remain in place, where it's safe and sterile from his affection.

"He's fucked up over you," Decker mutters. "Well and truly fucked."

I don't respond. I can't, not when I know what it feels like to be in Hunter's shoes. I feel exactly the same way. I experience it with every breath.

Hunter slumps onto the top step leading to the grass and stares off in the distance. He's picture perfect from this angle—the back view. The one where I can't see his massive scowl and harsh eyes. Looking at him front-on won't be as pretty—I know that. But I still want to be beside him.

I *always* want to be beside him.

"He won't call until you make him do it." Decker grabs the second bag of trash from the table and walks around me. "While you're here with him, he's going to try to protect you for as long as he can."

The beat of my heart quickens, in both sorrow and determination. There is always too much conflict when it comes to Hunter. We're opposing forces that continuously try to unite but consistently fail.

"I'll convince him." I drag my feet to the door and step onto the porch, the cool morning breeze sinking straight into me.

Hunter sits there cradling the phone in his hand with Torian's name displayed across the screen, the call waiting to be connected.

"Please call him," I beg.

His jaw ticks as he stares down at the device in his palm. "I need you to promise me you won't do anything stupid." His gaze flicks up at me, those gorgeous hazel eyes peering through dark lashes.

"Stupid is a really broad term. You might need to be more specific." I smile, but he doesn't reciprocate the expression.

Instead, he sighs. "I'm just as likely to stop you from doing something stupid as I am of convincing you to stay with me, aren't I?"

I sit down beside him, our arms brushing. "I've wanted this for ten years. It's the only thing I've wanted. Well… I spent months wishing for the impossible—that I would wake up from my nightmare and my family would all be surrounding me. Eventually, I got sick of kidding myself and I focused on something tangible. Something I could actually achieve. And this is it. My family deserves to be at rest knowing the person who murdered them isn't capable of hurting anyone else. *I* deserve to know that, too."

He glances down at his phone, and the seconds tick by with the peaceful chirp of birds in the trees above.

"Don't say a word while I talk to him." He gives me one last glance, then presses the call button.

I hold my breath as he puts the loud speaker on, and the *ring, ring, rings* sail through me like arrows. The call connects, and the briefest pause of silence makes my stomach turn.

"You're up early," Torian greets.

All the air leaves my lungs in a sudden rush of anxiety. It's time to start the game. Out-master. Out-strategize. Out-play.

Hunter places his hand on my thigh and gives a comforting squeeze. "I've got news."

"What sort of news?"

Hunter closes his eyes, his face etched in pain. "It turns out Steph obtained information from Dan after all."

Neither of them speaks for seconds that tick by like tortured years. Torian is skeptical. Already. This doesn't bode well.

"Is that so?" Torian asks.

"Yeah, that's so. But I'll let you talk to her about it. She's here with me now."

"I don't want to talk to her, Hunt." The tone is lethal. "I want to talk to you."

My heart seizes. I'm frozen. Hunter stiffens, too, his apprehension clear.

"You already told me she knew nothing," Torian continues. "If memory serves, you vowed it to me."

Hunter releases his hold on my leg and wipes a hand down his face. "I was wrong. Apparently, she was too scared to talk."

"Hmm." There's a wealth of judgmental disappointment in that one sound. "You've been wrong a lot lately."

"Once *isn't* a lot." Hunter shoves to his feet and walks onto the grass, stalking back and forth like a caged predator.

"Give me the name. Who is it?"

Hunter pauses and meets my gaze, his eyes filled with bitter sorrow. "It's your dealer in Newport. Dan told her it was Vaughn."

I bite my lower lip, my fingers tangling in the warm wool of my sweater. Torian doesn't believe him. I can feel it in the sinking sensation taking over my stomach.

Please. Please. Please.

"Okay. Now, I'm willing to talk to her."

Hunter nods. "Good. I'll put her on the line."

"No. We do this face to face."

The strong man before me snaps taut. His eyes widen, his lips part, before he finally bows his head. Defeated.

I'm not going to panic. Nope. We're still on track.

"Tell me when and where, and I'll make it happen."

"I've got plans this morning. I'll call you when I have time."

Sweet relief rushes through me as Hunter disconnects the call and places the device in his pants pocket. He remains on the grass, his brow furrowed in concern, his lips set in a tight line.

"This is good." I push to my feet. "We're moving forward."

I'd hoped Torian wouldn't want to see me. That all this could be fixed with a simple phone call. But after years of searching and scheming, that result wouldn't have given me closure.

I need to do this properly. To articulate my words with utter perfection to ensure my dance of victory is the sweetest imaginable. To see the hatred for Jacob in Torian's eyes and know he will punish my tormenter far greater than I could.

He approaches, climbing the step in front of me to wrap his arms around my waist. He tilts his chin, meeting my gaze. "Are you still confident?" His fingers rub up and down my back. Calming. Comforting.

"Yes. We've got this."

"*You've* got this," he corrects. "As much as I hate it, all the pressure is on your shoulders. I can only be by your side to help you through it."

"And I appreciate that." I drape my arms around his neck, wanting to stay like this for a while. Just the two of us. Just words. Not menacing actions.

"You know, you only have to ask, and I'll end this for you."

"No." I press my lips to his, breathing him in. "You're not killing anyone. Okay?" His risks are already too high without being held entirely responsible. "*Okay*, Hunter? Promise me."

He nods, his nose brushing mine. "I promise."

23

HER

I escaped to my room hours ago to catch up on sleep while we waited to hear from Torian. It took an hour before Hunter silently opened the door and crept in bed beside me.

I pretended to be asleep, not wanting to encourage the connection, but I had no intention of kicking him out. Not when the strength of his arms wrapped around me seems like a protecting force warding away the upcoming danger.

I even groaned a few times, feigning restlessness, so I could turn and snuggle farther into his chest.

Pathetic, I know.

I don't regret it.

Not even when Decker knocks on the door and walks inside the room, exposing my needy position.

"Torian is calling me." He flashes us his phone. "What should I do?"

"Answer it." Hunter sits up beside me, alert and ready for action while I struggle to shake my lethargy.

Decker nods and takes the call. "What's going on?"

There's a pause, and I lean on my elbow in an attempt to get a better view to read his expression.

"Yeah, I'm here with him." Decker keeps his focus on Hunter as he talks, a million and one silently relayed messages passing between them. "Yep. We'll be there."

He lowers the phone and disconnects the call. "We meet at Devoured."

"When?" Hunter asks.

"Now."

There's the slightest stiffening of Hunter's posture beside me. His anxiety is almost hidden.

"Right…" He slides from the mattress and turns to face me. "Are you still ready?"

"Yep." I move from the bed, hoping the nervous bubble of nausea threatening to burst from my throat isn't written all over my face. "But why did he call Decker and not you?"

"I guess he wants to know how deep this runs." Hunter starts for the door, and I quickly follow, pulling on my sneakers. "He's checking to see if I'm wasting his time with false information or if I've involved Decker because we mean business."

"So, it's a good thing?"

"I guess." Decker shrugs. "You can never tell with Torian."

The men lead the way out of the bedroom and down the hall. Decker grabs his jacket from the sofa while Hunter disappears into his room and comes back minutes later, shrugging into a leather jacket.

"We ready?" he asks.

"Yep." Decker starts for the hall leading to the garage. "Locked and loaded."

Shit. My lack of foresight is showing. "Do I need a weapon?"

"No. Torian will expect it from us, but might consider it a threat from you." Hunter gives me a sad smile. "It's best to go without."

"Don't worry." Decker shoots me a wink. "The big guy will be your shield and your weapon if you need it."

That's what I'm worried about.

"Ignore him." Hunter jerks his chin toward the garage. "Let's do this."

I follow them down to the rental car and climb in, Decker in the back with me riding shotgun, trying not to burst an artery with my elevated pulse.

We drive into the heart of Portland, and the closer we get to the imposing buildings and busy streets, the more my stomach tumbles. I'm not concerned so much for my own safety. I've thought about this day for too long to not be at peace with whatever could happen to me—good, bad, or horrendously ugly.

What doesn't sit right is what Hunter and Decker are risking for my personal vendetta. This has nothing to do with them. Yet, they're here, driving me to a meeting they organized, to deliver a plan they came up with.

"If something goes wrong," I speak to the window, unable to face them, "you need to turn on me. If he finds out I'm not telling the truth, do whatever you have to do. Make him believe you aren't a part of this. Just get yourselves out of there safely. Okay?"

They don't answer. There's no response bar the soft hum of the radio.

"Hunter?" I turn to him. "Are you listening?"

"We won't go down like that." He flicks his gaze to the rear-view mirror, glancing at Decker. "Will we?"

"No, siree. We go down with this ship," Decker adds. "In a blaze of glory and bloodshed, if necessary."

Hunter sighs and focuses back on the road. "There won't be any blaze of glory or sinking ship. This is going to work. And if Torian decides not to believe you, then that's his problem. Just don't change your story, no matter how strongly he doubts you."

"But if—"

"We're not discussing this, Sarah," he growls. "Stick to the plan, and stop jinxing us."

Right. I'm jinxing us.

I turn back to the window and hold my apprehension in check.

"This is it." Hunter slows, pulling the car to the curb.

I glance around, trying to find our destination.

"Across the road." Decker releases his belt and scoots toward the front seats. "The restaurant with the ugly motherfucker standing out front."

I lean forward, taking in the quaint building and the overweight Italian-looking man standing at the front door.

"You wanted to know who ran you off the road." Hunter taps his window, pointing at the 'ugly motherfucker.' "That's him. My buddy, Carlos."

My palms sweat. That guy has information on my past. Information that could get us killed once we walk inside the restaurant. "Aren't you worried he's told Torian about my past?"

"I wouldn't have risked bringing you here if I did. I know him. I know what he's like. He's more scared of me than his boss and too spineless to do anything about it. After what I did to him the day he went to Seattle, I promise he won't dare to cross me again."

I want to ask what happened that day. What exactly did Hunter do? But the walking stick and full arm of plaster on the man at the door is a great indication. Especially after all the weeks that have passed.

"Should I be worried about approaching him?" I try to hide the concern from my voice.

"With me by your side?" Decker scoffs. "No way."

Hunter grabs my hand and gives it a squeeze. "You don't need to worry at all. Okay?"

I nod, trusting him.

Actually trusting him.

I unfasten my belt and meet them outside the car, Hunter yet again reaching for my hand as we cross the road.

The man at the door leers at me as we approach, his dark eyes spiteful.

"Carlos," Hunter greets. "How's the arm?"

"Fuck you, asshole."

Hunter chuckles, entirely unconcerned, and continues into the restaurant, me by his side and Decker close at our back. We pass a mass of filled tables and chairs with couples dining, and push by a staff entrance to enter a quiet hall.

"His office is the one at the end." Hunter stops and turns to face me. "Just remember what we said. Keep it simple. Then this will all be over."

I nod.

He's making me nervous. His palm is clammy, and he keeps scrutinizing me. He's panicked, and it's rubbing off on me.

This is like any other job. If something goes wrong, I bend and adapt. Bend and adapt. I don't stop until I'm safely on the other side.

I can do this. Easy.

I lean on the tips of my toes and place a kiss on his lips. Chaste. Quick. When I lower, he scowls and weaves an arm around my waist, yanking me back into him.

"Is that all I get?" he snarls and slams his lips against mine as if in punishment. Harsh and strong and deep. He kisses me and kisses me, making the world disappear and my heart sizzle.

Decker clears his throat. "I guess we all get a little horny when it comes to life-threatening situations. But can we save the celebrations until after we escape the drug lord's lair?"

Hunter inches back and rests his forehead against mine.

"It's just a thought," Decker adds. "If you two want to keep going at it, I'll wait. S'all good."

"Remember what I said," Hunter whispers.

I nod. "I remember it all. Don't worry. I've been doing this for years."

"Not with Torian, you haven't. He'll act as though he's your best friend seconds before he tries to gun you down."

"Stop worrying." I step back. "You're making me nervous."

I walk away from him, continuing down the hall to stop in front of the door. I don't pause. I don't contemplate. I knock and wait for a muttered 'come in' before I turn the handle.

The man from the funeral sits behind an elegant wooden desk, pages upon pages of scattered paperwork spread before him. He leans back in his chair and greets us with a welcoming grin. "It's great to see you all again."

He stands, moves around the desk, and stops in front of me. "You'll have to forgive me, but I've forgotten your name." His hand brushes my bicep in a soft slide. It's gentle and kind. Not exactly the reception I anticipated.

"Steph," Hunter grates.

"Ahh, yes. The infamous Steph." His touch falls from my arm. "A devilish vixen with a pussy capable of tempting even the most heartless of men. Isn't that right, Hunter?"

"Let's keep it professional," Decker mutters.

"Of course." Torian leans back against his desk and crosses his feet at the ankles. Calm, cool, controlled. "So, tell me, Steph. You were with Dan the night he died, is that right?"

I chance one last glance at Hunter who inclines his head in encouragement, then I face Torian head on. "Yes. For about an hour."

"And why were you with him?"

"He'd been assaulting women, and nobody did anything about it. I took it upon myself to make him stop."

His eyes glisten with a hint of pride. At least that's what I think it is until he opens his mouth. "You murdered him selflessly? I don't know if I should consider that admirably noble or entirely bloodthirsty."

The assessment isn't a shock. The remark that I murdered Dan, is.

I keep my focus straight ahead, fighting not to show my renewed horror. I can't let this get to me. Not even if I am Dan's murderer. Not even if Hunter has lied to me. *Again.* Not even if this is all a set-up.

"She didn't kill him." The words are snarled from beside me. *"I did."*

"Really?" Torian cocks his head. "The investigator's timeline says otherwise."

I keep my chin high, my eyes focused.

Don't take the bait.

I pretend the news doesn't matter. That I'm so entirely heartless I don't even care. How can I when I'm about to cause another death?

"Don't believe him," Hunter mutters. "I swear to God he's messing with you."

I shouldn't look at him. I know I shouldn't. But my gaze goes rogue, taking in Hunter's tortured expression. My chest restricts. My throat tightens. I still believe him. I really do.

Torian chuckles. "Am I? I guess we'll never truly know."

"We know," Decker interrupts. "If Hunter says he did it, the only one who might have doubts is her, and you know it. Stop fucking around and ease up on her. You already know she was too scared to talk in the first place."

I remain quiet, reclaiming my focus while they bicker.

Torian walks around his desk and takes a seat, kicking his polished shoes onto the scattered papers. "So, you played vigilante with Dan," he muses. "When did Vaughn's name come up?"

"Once the Rohypnol kicked in, he lost his mind a little. He started blurting things that didn't make sense."

"What sort of things?"

I shrug. "He said something about not giving me information unless I paid him. But the more I hurt him, the more he talked. He laughed about what he did to those women. Then began to panic over what his father would do if another story broke. And he mentioned Vaughn taking everyone down. That he was the name everyone was after."

"And you're sure it was Vaughn?"

"Yes. I'm sure."

He nods, thoughts flickering in his eyes. "Are you aware that Vaughn has worked with me for a very long time?"

His tone changes. It has an edge now. A crisp bite of bitterness.

"What he is to you doesn't concern me," I answer honestly. "I'm only here to relay the information I was given. You can believe it or not. It doesn't matter to me."

He leans back in his chair, steepling his fingers in front of his chest. "Did he say anything else?"

"He said a lot of things. About how he would rape me raw—"

Hunter stiffens.

"He told me he would kill my family. He made numerous threats, and even tried to negotiate. But nothing else to do with Vaughn."

Torian stares at me, his gaze trekking my face with enough scrutiny to make me shiver. I want to elaborate, to place more intricate details into the story to make it more believable, but that's where problems would arise. More details mean more lies, and more lies mean a bigger chance of getting caught in my dishonesty.

He turns his focus to Hunter. "You know vouching for her again will have significant consequences if she changes her story for a second time."

I stiffen. I can't help it. The stakes shouldn't be this high. Not for him. Not for anyone but me. "Hold me fully responsible. And you can double or triple your consequences. It won't matter. My account won't change."

He keeps narrowed eyes on Hunter. "He's already vouched for you once. I need to make sure he isn't making another mistake."

"Yes," the grated agreement comes from my left. From the lips of a man who shouldn't have to risk anything for me. "I believe her."

Torian nods and sits forward to open his top drawer. My heart rushes into painful arrhythmia waiting for him to pull out a gun. Decker must think the same thing because he steps closer, his chest brushing against my back.

Instead, Torian pulls out a cell and scrolls through it without a care in the world. "Do you know Zack, Steph?"

"I'd never heard the name until Dan mentioned it." That is the God's honest truth.

He presses buttons, ignoring me, disregarding the information. He's not buying it. He's not even listening anymore.

Shit.

I glance at Hunter, but he's staring at Torian with intent, his jaw ticking. Watching. Waiting. Something has changed. Something I'm not aware of.

"Well…" Torian places the phone down and meets my gaze with a smile. "I appreciate the information."

That appreciation in his tone seems ominously fake.

"Good. Am I right in assuming you'll deal with the problem?" Hunter asks.

Torian sucks in a lazy breath and lets it out slowly. "Not yet. I want to make sure the information is authentic—"

"Authentic?" I glance at Hunter again, but his expression hasn't changed. He's still staring, chin high, shoulders straight. "How are you going to determine that?"

There's a knock at the door, and my throat constricts.

"Come in," Torian calls out.

The door opens, and Carlos limps inside, grinning. He's not the problem, though. It's the man who strolls in behind him and closes the door.

My heart stops.

I remember those blue eyes.

That sandy hair.

That confident gait.

I know.

I know.

Jacob turns from the door and follows Carlos, his steps faltering when his gaze reaches mine. He slows. Stops. Smirks. "Sarah?"

Everything burns. My limbs. Throat. Eyes. Heart. Oh, God, my heart. It threatens to take its final beat.

I stand tall, strong, and refuse to let the rage and rapidly building sorrow take over.

He's here. Right here. With his styled hair, expensive suit, and playboy looks that I itch to burn from his flesh.

"What the fuck is going on here?" Hunter moves to my right, unsuccessfully trying to block my view of the monster from my nightmares. But I can still see him, sense him, feel him. The hollow taint of what he's done wraps around me, tightening. Strangling.

"Pretend he's not here," Decker whispers in my ear. "Focus."

Focus. It's the one thing I can't do right now.

"Like I said, I need to authenticate the information, and what better way to do it than by asking the accused to come to Portland to stand trial?" Torian continues to steeple his fingers, his eyes sparkling with devious delight. "By the sound of it, we already have a flaw in your story, Steph… Or is it Sarah?"

"There's no flaw," Hunter snarls.

"What am I accused of?" Jacob asks.

"Breathe," Decker whispers in my ear. "Don't panic."

They all speak over one another, the voices garbled. I can't shake it off. I can't find the focus I need. Grief overwhelms me.

I'm failing. I'm failing. I'm failing.

"She claims Dan told her you are the informant who's been ratting to the police."

I swallow and find my voice. "It's not a claim."

"Like hell," Jacob snarls. "This bitch is setting me up because I killed her family."

"Is that true?" Torian's joker mask slips away under his deepening frown.

"You don't need to take my word for it." Jacob steps forward, pulling a cell from the inside pocket of his business suit jacket. "Look it up online. There are a million and one articles about what I did."

I'm fucked. No question.

Hunter grasps my hand, as if knowing I'm as good as dead. But I can't go down like this. I refuse to let Jacob walk out of here. No matter what it takes. No matter what the price. I have to turn this around.

I need to bend and adapt.

I drop Hunter's hand, gaining my independence, and paste on a smirk. "It's true. He did kill my family. But I haven't seen this man in ten years. I didn't know he was still alive or that he changed his name. To me, this is fate."

Karma.

The room erupts in vocal conflict. Jacob curses. Hunter defends me. Decker keeps whispering unnecessary motivation in my ear while Carlos grins.

"*Quiet,*" Torian shouts.

Hunter inches in front of me and widens his stance, parting his feet to act as a body shield. He knows what's going to happen. He senses it, and it isn't good.

Torian doesn't believe me. He knows I'm lying.

Jacob begins to chuckle, the sound of victory sinking under my skin like acid.

I rest my forehead on Hunter's shoulder blade and whisper a barely audible apology. I'm so sorry. So deeply, truly sorry as I place my hand on the low of his back, on the gun that always lies in wait.

He stiffens under my touch, fully aware of what's running through my mind. "It's okay," he murmurs.

He's certain he knows what I'm about to do. He knows the increased danger I will put us all in. He *knows*. And still, he doesn't try to stop me. He lets me know it's perfectly fine to risk his life. That he's here for me. Always willing to fight for me.

"I'm sorry, Torian," I say louder. "I don't expect you to understand." I reach under Hunter's jacket, remove the gun from his waistband and shove him forward, out of the way.

"*Stop*," Torian shouts.

But it's too late. I raise the barrel before anyone has time to reach for a weapon, Jacob's eyes widening in realization.

"For my family," I whisper, and pull the trigger.

Once.

Twice.

Three times.

And the last, for baby Thomas.

The bullets pepper his chest, jolting him with each impact. I breathe in his horror, delighting in his shock. I barely register Hunter stepping back into me, arms wide, returning to his role as human shield, while Decker smothers my back.

I'm sandwiched but all I can see is Jacob as he stumbles backward, collapsing to the floor, his hands clutching his chest in vain as blood soaks his clothes.

I hear shouts. Threats. My name. I hear instructions, but the words don't penetrate. The only thing seeping deep into my chest is victory. Relief. The bitter-sweet euphoria of vengeance.

Sarah, pay attention.

It's my father's voice, his guidance snapping me back to the present, to the room full of drawn guns.

Decker's is trained on Carlos. Carlos's on me. Torian's on Hunter. Mine on the wall, at the space where a murderer once stood.

"Her actions are justified," Hunter says in a rush. "He killed her family. You would've done the same."

Screams carry from down the hall. The rough scrape of chairs and scampering feet.

"Her justification means nothing when she brought this feud into my family's restaurant. She killed one of my men." Torian looms over his desk, the barrel of his gun aimed at Hunter's chest. "Step aside."

"Not going to happen."

"Do it." I push at Hunter's back. "Please."

He doesn't budge.

I could probably get another shot off and take Carlos down with me, but I wouldn't have a chance with Torian. He would kill my determined protector before Carlos hit the ground.

"Move, Hunter," I plead.

If at all possible, he grows an inch taller with his dominant stance. He's not going to let me take the fall.

"*Move.*" I shove at him with my free hand, only to have Decker's arm grab my wrist, plastering it to my side as he holds me in place.

"The police will be here any minute, Hunt. What's your next move?" Torian blurts. "How are you going to play this?"

"I take responsibility. I owe you. I'll do whatever you want. *Be* whatever you want. I'll stop being a contractor and instead become one of your bitch boys, like you've always wanted. We can work out the details at a later date."

"No." I plead. "This was my fault."

"Let him sort this out," Decker whispers in my ear. "He's got it under control."

"No." I elbow him in the ribs, breaking free of his grasp. I stalk around Hunter, only to be engulfed in his arms and drawn into his body

"Don't move," Torian demands, his barrel trained on my chest.

"She's mine," Hunter snarls, taking the gun from my hand. "My responsibility. My debt. You shoot her, and you won't live to take another breath."

Torian's eyes narrow. "Do you really want to threaten me?"

"No. No. *No.*" I scramble to turn to face Hunter. "Don't do this."

A shot blasts the air, and his hands fall. His eyes widen. His lips part. I frantically search his face for answers, my mind screaming, until I hear a thud behind him.

Carlos is on the floor, blood seeping from a perfectly circular hole in his forehead.

"You should've done that weeks ago," Torian mutters, lobbing his gun at Hunter. "Put it in Vaughn's hand. As far as you're all concerned, they killed each other."

I stand rooted in place as Hunter wipes the gun of fingerprints, then places it in Jacob's hand. He does the same with his weapon, placing it with Carlos.

"What's going on?" I whisper.

"It's over." Decker puts his hands on my shoulders. "He's got it worked out."

"He's got what worked out?"

The wail of sirens increases. All I can hear is noise, the panic and chaos increasing.

"She needs to get out of here." Torian strides around the desk. "She'll come with me. You two can stay."

Hunter nods.

He nods.

"What are you doing?" I walk to him, searching those harsh eyes.

"You need to go. I'll meet up with you later."

"No. I'm not leaving you." And I'm sure as hell not going to run into the sunset with the man who seconds ago wanted to kill me.

"Sarah." He leans in, bare inches from my face. "You're covered in gun residue, and so is Torian. You can't stay."

"No." I shake my head and cling to him. "I'm not going without you."

I can't. I *won't*. I thought I could walk away, but it's an impossibility. I want him. I *need* him.

He winces and glances over my shoulder. "I'm sorry."

I snap my gaze to Decker, but I'm too late. I have a split second to brace for the butt of the gun before pain explodes in my head. Then the world fades to black.

24

HER

I wake up on a plush, unfamiliar sofa, dressed in nothing but my underwear. My head pounds as if I've been at a month-long rave and there's a sore spot that throbs even harder near my temple.

It takes seconds to blink away the groggy confusion. To remember what happened. I don't move. I don't breathe.

I take in my surroundings—the sunlight streaming into the room, the expensive furniture, the scent of baked cookies or cake that makes my stomach growl.

Great. I killed a guy only to be abducted and stripped by Betty fucking Crocker.

"I think she's awake," a woman murmurs.

"About time."

The response chills my blood. It's Torian. I don't need to glance over the sofa to confirm, but I do. I sit up and find him in a million-dollar kitchen beside an equally stunning woman with sleek brown hair and mesmerizing blue eyes, just like him.

"Sleep well?" he taunts.

My head voices a protest, throbbing and pounding.

Decker knocked me out. At Hunter's instruction.

"Where is he?"

Torian raises a brow. "The surly one or his faithful sidekick?"

"Both," I snap, pushing to my feet, then wincing at the renewed burst of pain in my skull. "Where are they?"

"At the police station."

"Why?" Blood rushes from my head, the panic making me dizzy. "What's going on?"

"It's standard procedure for a witness of a double murder. At least it will be if they get released soon. Otherwise..." He shrugs. "Your friends might have to spend a generous amount of time in prison."

I reach for the sofa as my legs threaten to buckle.

"Don't be cruel," the woman chastises. "She's been through enough." She saunters toward me, her long, lean legs eating up the space between us. "It's only been a few hours. I'm sure they'll be back any minute now."

She continues by me to the pile of folded clothing on the coffee table. "Here." She picks up a pair of yoga pants and a baby blue sweater. "Put these on. They should fit. And your shoes are underneath the sofa."

I take the offering and pull them on with shaky arms. "Where are my clothes?"

"Incinerated," Torian mutters. "Just one of the many things I've done to cover your ass."

I wince, not appreciating the help, but thankful for it at the same time. I'm not naive to think his assistance is out of the kindness of his heart. I owe him now. Or worse, Hunter owes him.

That's a debt I need to clear.

"I'm sorry for involving you in this." I slide my feet into my sneakers and approach the kitchen. "And I beg you not to hold my actions against anyone but me."

He reaches for a mug and takes a drink. "You're worthless to me, little girl. Hunter, on the other hand, has been an asset I've wanted to control for quite some time."

"What will you do to him?"

He takes another sip of tea, or coffee, or marijuana-infused water for all I know, and stares at me over the rim of his mug.

"Please," I beg. "I need to know."

Will he be tortured? Beaten? What will happen to Decker? Will they be treated the same? Punished equally?

Hunter vowed on his life that I was telling the truth. It should've been my goddamn life.

Torian cocks a judgmental brow, probably disgusted by my show of weakness. "I've worked with Hunter for years. But it has always been on a contractual basis. Under his terms. He had the freedom to pick and choose when and if we worked together."

"And?"

"And he will no longer get to pick and choose. He will no longer be a contractor. He will be a valued part of my team that will fulfil any job I see fit."

Anguish overwhelms me. "You can't make him hurt innocent people." I shake my head. "You can't. Eventually, he'll turn on you. You'll always have to watch your back."

"Nobody in my world is innocent. We all have a cross to bear. Even you." His lips kick in a devilish grin. "And it's not as difficult as you might think to break a warrior's back. You just need to know his weakness."

He raises his mug and inclines his head, as if toasting my existence. Toasting the vulnerability I bring to Hunter's life.

"*Cole*," the woman reprimands. "Stop it." She walks by me, squeezing my arm as she passes. "Ignore him. My brother likes to be dramatic. But deep down, he loves Hunter. We all do."

Torian gives a barely audible chuckle. "I love the debt he now owes me, that's for sure."

"Enough," she demands. "The poor thing is petrified. Leave her be."

I'm not petrified.

I'm angry.

Unstable.

She walks into the kitchen and opens a cupboard under the black marble bench. "Would you like a coffee? Or maybe something stronger?"

"No, thanks." I lean forward, looking down a hall to my right. There's a door with light streaming through the frosted-glass panels. The front door, I'm sure.

"Making an escape plan?" Torian taunts. "Don't bother. I don't want you here as much as you don't want to be here. You're free to go."

I snap my gaze to his in disbelief, my heart thundering beneath tightened ribs. Is this a trick?

"Go on." He jerks his head toward the hall.

"You're safe to leave," the woman reiterates softly.

I stare at the door, at freedom, as a shadow darkens the frosted glass from the other side. A knock sounds, and I hold my breath, hoping it's Hunter.

"Come in," Torian yells.

There's a click of the latch, the air in my lungs congealing as I wait, impatiently, to see Decker walk inside, closing the door behind him.

Where the hell is Hunter?

I stalk toward him, stopping him halfway down the hall to throw my arms around him.

He stiffens, long seconds passing before he drapes his arms around me in an awkward reciprocation of the gesture. "Hey, tiger. How are you holding up?"

"I'm not sure yet. How about you?" I lean back to ask the question tightening my throat, but it lodges in my mouth as I acknowledge the extent of his drawn features. He looks exhausted, his skin pale.

"I'll be perfect once I catch some sleep." He winks at me.

I nod and wait for more, my gaze pleading for answers he doesn't seem to understand. "Please tell me where he is. What happened at the police station? Is he okay?" The onslaught bubbles from me in a garbled mess.

"You don't have to worry about a thing." He claps my shoulder and steps back. "Hunt took the fall, so you're all clear on murder one."

"What?" I stumble backward as he walks around me, continuing down the hall. Hunter took the fall? He confessed? "Why?"

Decker stops and turns back around to face me with a wince. "Sorry. Bad joke. He's outside paying the cab driver."

"He's here?" I swing around to the door as another shadow creeps over the glass, and seconds later Hunter walks inside.

"Oh, God." I rush for him, running the few feet of space separating us to engulf him in a body hug. He grunts with the impact, and I can't find the will to apologize. I wrap my arms around his neck, my legs around his waist, and bury my face in his neck.

"Hey, now, princess," he whispers. "It's okay."

I hold him tighter, squeezing until my muscles burn as his gentle arms wrap around my back.

"Come on now." His voice grows an authoritative edge and he pulls back, craning his neck to look at me. "It's over. He's gone."

"And you're not going to jail?"

"In your dreams, princess."

No. That's the last thing I want. I'm so unbelievably thankful for this man. Gratitude and respect flood me.

I cup his cheeks, his rough stubble teasing my palms as I take in every intricate detail of his harsh beauty. He's unbelievably gorgeous. Even more so now that I know him.

Trust him.

"Are you okay?" He rests his forehead against mine

"No."

He guides me to stand, keeping his hands on my hips as he scrutinizes me. "What is it?"

I glance down the hall, making sure we don't have an audience before I whisper, "What about Torian? What are you going to do about him?"

A half-hearted smile pulls at his lips. "Don't worry about him."

"But he practically said he's going to make you his bitch."

"He can't make me do anything." He leans in, placing his mouth deliciously close to my ear. "He knows he's nothing but another pull of the trigger if he gets on my bad side. As far as I'm concerned, he did us a solid today, and I'm thankful."

He retreats a step, his hands moving to my shoulders to give a gentle squeeze. The gesture is friendly, not affectionate. A goodbye, not a demand to stay by his side forever like I want.

He's pulling away from me, not just physically as he places farther space between us, but emotionally.

I frown. "What's going on?"

"I'm giving you what you need, Sarah." He sucks in a deep breath. "I'm letting you go."

My heart ceases to beat. My chest cracks open, exposing a hollow cavern.

"I won't follow," he continues. "I won't play any more games."

I should be relieved he's giving me what I asked for. He's giving me the space to get my life back on track, the solitude to regroup and reassess. But the celebratory emotions are non-existent.

I'm devastated.

Shattered.

"What about the police?" I ask. "What about the investigation?"

"You don't need to worry about either. As far as they're concerned, Jacob and Carlos killed each other, and you weren't even there."

"Go on." He jerks his head toward the door, his expression turning to stone. "I paid the cab driver to wait for you and drive you back to your apartment or wherever you want to go."

It's not my apartment. Not anymore. But that's the last thing on my mind.

"I'll organize a moving van and get your furniture back to you tomorrow."

I drag my gaze from him, unable to look him in the eye. "You might need to hold onto my things for a while longer. It's not my apartment anymore. Brent would've found someone else by now."

"I hope not," he murmurs. "Because I paid him to hold it for you weeks ago."

He did?

"I knew this would all work itself out sooner or later, and I didn't want you to lose your home," he answers my unspoken question. "You have nothing to worry about anymore, Sarah."

Nothing but loneliness and heartbreak.

I nod. "Right. I'll get going, then."

I don't move. I can't.

I want to stay. With him. With Decker. In this crazy life that not only tipped my world upside down but rocked my foundations. But maybe that's the adrenaline talking, or the pounding headache, or the lack of restful sleep.

He gives me a sad smile and swings out an arm to lead me to the door. He's calm. Stoic.

It tears me apart.

He pulls the door wide, giving me a view of the mansions and manicured gardens outside, along with the cab waiting in the drive.

How do I say goodbye to this man? The one who tricked me with his lies and won me over with his loyalty.

"Thank you for everything," I murmur.

"You're thanking me now?" He gives a subtle grin, that dimple stunning me with its exquisite allure.

"Yes. For what you did today, I'll be forever grateful."

He lowers his gaze, that grin turning somber. "Don't mention it."

I keep my head high, faking determination as I walk outside into the dimming late-afternoon sun, and approach the cab.

I don't want to leave, but it's the only thing I know. I'm always running, always seeking distance. I don't have any experience doing anything else. Staying and fighting for what my heart craves is a foreign concept I don't know how to battle.

"Wait," he calls.

I freeze, as if moving even an inch will stop him from trying to make me stay. My belly tumbles as his footsteps approach, then he grabs my hand and gently glides me around to face him.

My lungs seize as he leans in, placing the sweetest, softest, most flawless kiss on my tingling lips. I could die from the pleasure. From the affection and pure perfection.

Then he steps back, turns toward the house, and stalks away. "Goodbye, princess."

EPILOGUE

HER

One month later

I SAUNTER INTO ATOMIC BUZZ AND APPROACH BRENT BEHIND THE BAR.

"Your third visit this week," he drawls. "I don't know if I should be thankful for the company or concerned of impending alcoholism."

I roll my eyes and slide into my favorite seat. "I didn't realize I could become an alcoholic from two drinks a night."

"Everyone has to start somewhere." He grins at me and slides over a Long Island Iced Tea, my current drink of choice. "You're just a little slower at this than my regulars."

After I left Hunter a month ago, I came here. There had been nowhere else to go. I'd loathed the thought of spending another night in a hotel when I knew Hunter wouldn't come after me, and my apartment was nothing but empty space.

Brent had welcomed me back with open arms and a large amount of growled concern. He'd wanted to know what happened, and for the first time in ten years, I'd been willing to pour my heart out.

I told him everything.

Well, not *everything*.

I explained the situation with my family and went into detail about my search for the man who murdered them. He now knew that Hunter had helped me find Jacob, and thankfully he didn't pester me for more details when I gave vague references to why my time with both men had come to an end.

Brent looked after me for those first few days. He let me crash on his couch for a night, and helped the moving company place my furniture back in my apartment the next day when the truck arrived.

He became more than a friend in a short space of time, and quickly turned into someone I now consider family.

"How was the old duck today?" he asks, polishing the bar. "Did she make me any cookies?"

"The cookies are always mine, you know that." I smirk. "But she's good. We spent three hours in her kitchen while she unsuccessfully tried to teach me how to make a red velvet white trifle."

Brent snickers. "I guess you can't teach an old dog new tricks."

"I'm not old." I glare.

Betty had been another task on my newly made bucket list. It had taken me a week to work up the courage to return to Eagle Creek. When my cab pulled into her driveway, she had been standing on the porch, looking down on me as I stepped onto her lawn.

Turns out, she welcomed me back with just as much enthusiasm as Brent.

I crumpled in her arms. I actually had to fight not to sob like a little bitch. And as I explained my unworthy reasons for stealing her car, she filled my belly with coffee and homemade apple cake. She's been doing the same thing every Sunday for the last three weeks.

I've created a life and a home for myself in Portland, not just a place to hide.

The door to Atomic Buzz swooshes open, and Brent raises a brow at the newcomer. "I think this guy's lost. I bet you ten bucks he asks for directions."

"No way." I swirl my Long Island Iced Tea, not bothering to look over my shoulder. "I still owe you money from the last time we had this bet."

The time when Hunter had walked through that door.

The footfalls approach, and I cringe, not wanting my time with Brent to be interrupted with menial chitchat.

"What can I get you?" Brent lowers a hand to the fridge below the counter, waiting.

"A Corona." The voice is low and subtle, barely a whisper of a response.

My heart stops. It's him. The man I've dreamed about for nights on end.

From my peripheral vision, I see him slide onto a seat, leaving a vacant spot between us. Just like the first time we met.

"You lost?" Brent slides a coaster across the bar and places Hunter's beer bottle down on it.

"No."

"Looking for something in particular?" Brent taunts.

"Yeah."

I swallow over the tightening in my throat. "You're wasting your time with monosyllable answers," I whisper. "He'll keep pestering you until you divulge your deepest, darkest secrets."

"Is that so?" His voice washes over me, caressing all of my erogenous zones, touching all my newly formed strength and making me even stronger.

"Yep," Brent admits. "So, spit it out. What are you doing here?"

I succumb to my visual thirst and turn to face Hunter.

He looks good. Really good.

A charcoal shirt is molded to the muscles of his chest. Rough stubble hugs his jaw, and those eyes are exactly how I remember them. Although, they're not harsh like when we first met, but they're equally intense. Then there are his lips—pure temptation in motion, the slight curve lifting at one side in a half-hearted smile.

"My sister got knocked up by a lowlife with a heavy hand. He left her as soon as my nephew was born. So, I quit my job, packed my things, and drove here."

"That's…" I want to keep up the recap of our first night together, but my palpitating heart won't allow it. "That's not funny."

"Sorry." He cringes, and it's kinda cute to see him uncomfortable. "I actually thought you would've come to find me by now. But seeing as you didn't, I came to offer my support in whatever way you'll take it."

"Support?" My brows pull tight as his gaze rakes me, from my face, to my stomach, then back up again.

My breath catches. "You think I'm pregnant?"

"The last time we were together we weren't…"

Safe. Protected. I was supposed to get the morning after pill and forgot in the mad scramble to regain control in my life. "I'm not pregnant."

"Not…pregnant."

I don't think he means to parrot me. It seems more like shock. Maybe it's even disappointment building in those clear hazel eyes.

"I just thought…" He sighs and grasps his beer, taking one large gulp after another.

Brent clears his throat then fakes a dramatic yawn, again, like the first night I met Hunter. "I think I might have to call last drinks."

This time I don't glare. I can barely hold in a grin. His eyes are gleaming at me, taunting in their memory.

Matchmaker, matchmaker, make me a match.

"It's barely dark out," I drawl.

He shrugs.

Hunter downs the last of his beer. "He's right. I should get out of here and leave you alone like I promised."

He slides from his seat and pulls his wallet from the back pocket of his cargos to slap some bills on the bar.

I let him walk away and remind myself of how much I've grown without him.

I've found myself in his absence. I've almost become whole again. But until now, I wasn't sure if I was ready for the final puzzle piece. The biggest, brightest part of being happy.

"Wait," I call out.

He plants his feet. His back straightens.

Brent grins at me, a pride-filled, happiness-rich grin.

"You're supposed to follow me out of here, remember?" I grab my purse from the bar and scoot off my seat to stride toward him. My legs tingle. My belly flutters.

I walk past him to the door, then pause to glance over my shoulder. This time, the tweak of his mouth isn't a threat or a taunt. It's pure elation. Undiluted relief.

There's still a hum.

An absolutely amazing zing.

It slides down my spine, tightens my nipples, and contracts my pussy in a repeat of the exquisite squeeze from when we first met.

I was right when I anticipated that Hunter would devastate me and leave me deliciously broken. I was wrong, too. Because he also made me whole again.

"You waiting for me, princess?"

My heart does a goddamn flip. It's enough to make my knees weak and my stomach tumble. "I've been waiting for a month."

The humor flees his features. "Are you serious?" He approaches to settle in beside me, peering down at me with beseeching eyes.

"Sorry, I broke character." I grin. "I'm supposed to point out that you're following me, then you ask if that's a problem."

His brows pull tight, then finally, he gives a succinct nod. "Is it a problem that I plan on following you?"

I want to laugh. Goddamn it. The vibration consumes my chest. This man, this murderer, is following instructions to do a cheesy re-run of the first night we met. And I goddamn love it.

I love *him*.

A breath shudders from my lips, and I blink back the burn in my eyes. "I guess that depends on what you want to achieve."

My vision blurs as I wait for his response. I remember what he said the first time. I remember the exact words—*I want everything.*

"Hey..." His rough palm glides over my cheek, his gentle touch inspiring the first tear to fall.

I haven't cried in ten years. Not in sorrow. Not in pain. And definitely not in the overwhelming happiness currently sinking through every inch of my being.

"I want you to move in with me," he whispers. "I want you to be mine. I want you to be as in love with me as I am with you."

He takes my mouth in a forceful kiss, curling my toes, stroking my tongue with his before pulling back to rest his forehead against mine. "I still want everything, Sarah."

I nod, the movement jerky and uncontrolled. "Then, no, Luke. I guess it's no problem at all."

DECKER

PROLOGUE
DECKER

I stare at the blood on the floor, the liquid soaking the carpet and bathing my soul in sins.

I didn't cause the death at my feet, but the guilt taunts me regardless.

This isn't the happily-ever-after I expected for this meeting. I only wanted to help Hunter. And in return, I'd be helping the woman who has made a remarkable change in him. The same woman he knocked out minutes ago for her own safety, then watched in livid rage as Torian, the psychopath we're now indebted to, carried her from the scene of the crime, leaving us to deal with the aftermath.

I can't think straight through the whiplash.

One minute we had the upper hand, the next that same hand is shoved up our asses and Torian is playing ventriloquist with our lives.

It's a fucking disaster with consequences set to haunt me to my dying day, because now I'm trapped. Not in this office in the back of a prestigious restaurant, but in this world.

I'm no longer a spectator, dabbling from the sidelines.

Now I'm in the thick of it.

"Keep your mouth shut." Hunter gets in my face. "Neither of us saw what happened. We were talking. They were arguing. Then hell broke loose. You got it? If they ask for specifics, tell them you can't remember. Shock has fucked with your head."

I nod, because, seriously, shock *has* fucked with my head.

"*You got that?*" He grabs my bicep and gives me a shake.

"Yeah." I yank my arm free. "I've fucking got it."

The police close in, their indecipherable instructions booming from a loudspeaker near the front of the building.

"This is going to get messy." Hunter's comment is serious. Not one hint of a joke.

My attention drifts over the frontal lobe splattered across the floor before I drag my gaze to his. "Somehow I think we're past that point."

We predicted a mess. We knew getting out of here wouldn't be easy. But this... *This* —the lifeless bodies and the taint of gunpowder in the air—this shit is a whole different dimension from mess.

This fucked up disaster is beyond repair, and certainly beyond salvation.

It's the hole that keeps on digging.

The shitty gift that keeps on giving.

"*This is the police,*" a voice shouts. "*Is anyone in here?*"

"Yeah. Back here." Hunter jerks his head at me, silently asking if I'm holding myself together.

I nod, pretending this crap happens on a daily basis.

It's no skin off my nose.

I lie to the cops about double murders all the damn time.

Piece of cake.

The squishy crap on the rug that looks like brains isn't going to haunt me for years. Nope. I've already resolved that shit.

I'm chill.

Hunter narrows his eyes, and I can practically hear his thoughts. He's well aware one slip will land us both in prison where we'll have to hold our ankles during shower sessions until we're old and gray.

"We've got this," he murmurs. "Torian has cops in his pocket. He's not going to let us fry. So man the fuck up and keep it simple."

Eight hours later...

"They questioned you for a lot longer than they did with me." Hunter's stare pins me in place from the other side of the dining table. His words are a harsh accusation despite the lazy way he cradles the beer in his hands.

"Excuse me?" I take a sip of scotch and mimic his relaxed demeanor even though there's so much shit churning in my head I swear I'm a few brief contemplations from a stroke.

"The police station," he clarifies. "Your interview took twice as long as mine. Did you keep your mouth shut like a good little boy?"

"Yeah, I kept my mouth shut," I sneer. "But rumor has it that you didn't. The cops mentioned something about you sucking pole like it's going out of fashion, just so you could get out before dinner."

He grins, but it's not kind. It never is. "You're edgy. Did little Deckey sing like a canary?"

I glare and down a gulp of alcohol to stop myself from reaching across the table to smash his face against the thick polished wood. "Question my integrity one more time, asshole, see how far it gets you."

I didn't squeal on Torian. If I did, I would've been long gone hours ago instead of sitting in an unfamiliar house with the asshole breathing down my neck, claiming I'm his new poster boy for criminal activity.

Apparently, I work for him now.

I no longer report to Hunter. I'm not the big teddy bear's faithful sidekick who tags along on the occasional stakeout or hacks into some random joe's personal information.

I'm balls deep in Cole Torian's pocket.

His pathetic little bitch.

Yay, me.

Hunter leans forward and shoots a quick glance over his shoulder, checking on the man of the moment, who talks on his cell. Torian seems to be relaying the same fictional story to everyone in his employ—Jacob, aka his out-of-town drug runner, fatally shot his number one goon, Carlos, moments before the now-dead-guy inflicted a fatal shot of his own.

Implausible? Hell yes.

Will anyone dare to question him? Fuck no.

Nobody who knows his power and reach would be that stupid.

Hunter meets my gaze, his eyes intense as he murmurs, "Are you sure this is the life you want?"

"Oh, yeah," I seethe. "This shit is right up my alley."

I roll my eyes then return my scowl toward the living room. This house is dripping in dirty money—the artwork, the furnishings, the architecture. And it's not even Cole's house. It's his older sister, Layla's. The same sister who listened to the fictional murder story and didn't question its lunacy. Then she nodded like a good little puppy when her brother told her to go get her kid from a friend's house.

She's either scared out of her mind, or an obedient little doll.

I don't know which is worse.

"Have you thought about running?" Hunter whispers.

"Of course I have." I keep my voice low, making sure not to disturb the psychopath in the room. "But waiting for a bullet in the back of my brain for being a traitor isn't something that fills me with giddy excitement, ya know?"

"I'll help you run. You're stupid if you stay."

I scoff. "Jeez, Hunt, you always know how to make a guy feel special."

"I'm not joking. If you want out, say the word. It's now or never."

Maybe I should take him up on the offer.

Walk away. Start over someplace new.

But I'd have to leave all this behind. Every little bit. And not just the money. I'd have to forget what I've seen. What I've done.

I came looking for trouble. I wanted destruction.

Well, maybe not to this degree.

Back then I wasn't entirely stable. I wanted to be a part of this stupid game of chicken. Now I don't know what the hell I'm doing setting down roots in the middle of a minefield.

Torian falls silent, taking a gulp from his glass of gin and tonic before starting another call.

"Let me think on it." I push from my chair, grab my drink, and stalk outside the glass doors to get much needed fresh air on the back deck.

Hunt's right. If I don't jump ship now, I never will. Not unless it's in a body bag. And I guess that doesn't really matter much anymore, either.

My life doesn't have a high value these days.

I've got nothing. Nothing but this.

Yes, my family is out there somewhere—my parents are traveling the country in their camper van, trying to outrun their nightmares. My brother is living in the middle of desolate-as-fuck Oregon, basking in seclusion. And my sister is…

I huff out a breath.

I lost sight of Penny so fucking long ago. She's God knows where, doing God knows what, with God knows who. It's the unknown that kills me.

Nobody is waiting for me to drop by.

This, right here, right now, is all I have.

I lean against the wall of the house, one foot cocked against the brick while I drink the last of my scotch and curse myself for the stupid decision to give up smoking twelve months ago.

I'd give anything for a nicotine boost right now. And more scotch. And less of a death wish.

The slam of a door brings me to my feet, and I turn to find a woman stalking through the living room. Another Torian. I've seen her picture online. I've read about her in the papers—Keira, the youngest member of the crime-riddled family, at least before Layla's daughter, Stella, was born.

I cock my head, trying to hear the vehement words from the slim brunette, but I can only make out the vicious tone.

It's a showdown. Unhinged Barbie versus Satan in a suit. Not that it's a fair fight. Satan is entirely unfazed by the confrontation, while Barbie has blushed cheeks and disheveled hair, as if she's trekked her fingers through the long, dark strands a thousand times.

I step forward, not willing to miss a moment of the theatrics, and slowly inch the door open. There's the softest squeak of the hinge as her aggression batters the room, but she hears it, those rage-filled baby blues snapping in my direction.

She tries to stare me down, her petite frame so tightly wound I bet I could twist a stick up her ass and hear a music box melody come to life.

"Hey, sweet cheeks." I give a derisive finger wave. "Don't mind me. I couldn't hear the drama outside. It's much better from in here."

Torian ignores me. He should know me well enough by now to understand I'm not going to stop being a smartass just because he's got my balls in his fist.

He may own me, but he sure as fuck won't control me.

"Who is *he*?" Keira's gaze snaps to her brother.

"Decker," Torian mutters. "He works for us now."

She scoffs, the burst of menace turning into a bitter laugh. "And I bet he found out before I did, too."

"He was there, Keira. It's pretty hard to tell you about the incident before someone who witnessed it."

"Don't talk down to me, you smug piece of shit. I had to hear about a fatal shooting in my own family's restaurant on the *damn radio*. And when I tried calling you, *numerous times*, all I got was your message service."

"This is business. I had to make some calls before—"

"Oh, I know." Her eyes narrow to spiteful slits. "I got in contact with ten people in between my calls to you. *Ten people, Cole.* And all of them had already spoken to you. How can you keep me in the dark like this? You're risking my safety."

"I'm not risking a damn thing." His tone is sinister. "This had nothing to do with you. So, if or when I finally got around to calling, it would've been out of courtesy, not necessity."

"Courtesy?" Those pretty ruby lips flatten into a straight line. Her jaw ticks. "Who are you, Cole? I don't even know you anymore."

He inclines his head. "It's better that way."

She retreats, her face crumpling as she wraps her arms around her middle. Moments of heated silence pass, the tension building while Hunter and I watch in avid fascination.

The woman has brass balls, that's for sure.

As if hearing my thoughts, her gaze meets mine, those deep blue eyes shimmering with emotion, before she glares and focuses out the window. "Where's Layla?"

"She went to get Stella from a friend's house."

"Under your instruction, of course." She sniffs. "I bet you put her on lockdown, too. Are you the reason she wouldn't answer my calls? I swear to God, since Dad left, you've lost your fucking mind."

Torian takes a threatening step forward. "Watch your mouth. I'm growing tired of your bullshit."

"Fuck you, Cole. You can't tell me what to do."

"Can't I?" In a flash, his hand wraps around her throat.

I shove from my chair, and Hunter follows suit.

She doesn't flail. She barely reacts. Apart from the high tilt of her chin, nothing has changed. Venom still shoots from her gaze. There's no fear. No retreat.

"Let her go, Torian." I step toward them.

He gets in her face. "Pull yourself together," he repeats, this time softer, under control, as he releases his grip.

She doesn't whimper. There's barely a sag in her shoulders. Instead, she seems to take his demand on board, pulling her crazy into check.

"I'm getting another drink." Hunter starts for the kitchen, his leveled words and casual pace creating a calming buffer. "Who wants one?"

"Make mine a double." Torian turns his back on his sister and grabs his empty glass from the coffee table.

Life returns to normal.

Well, as normal as this fucked up existence can be, but I can't drag my gaze away from her. I can't stop waiting for the moment where she weakens. Where she breaks.

She doesn't.

It's fascinating.

She's fascinating.

She's also beautiful and strong, yet obviously harboring the same death wish that has coiled around my soul.

Her rampant breathing lessens, the warrior vanishing, and a picture of vulnerable perfection takes its place as she glances my way. This time when our eyes meet, she doesn't glare. There's no menace or spite in her gaze. I see confusion in the deep furrow of her brow.

But most of all, I see appreciation.

I see her thanks.

And it's the only reason I need to make me stay.

1

KEIRA

Four months later

I GLANCE AROUND MY FAMILY'S RESTAURANT, OVER THE STANDING GUESTS WHO MINGLE and laugh between each guzzle of expensive alcohol. They exude joy in their tailored suits and stylish dresses while filling their bellies with the finest cuisine.

It's what we do.

All part of the show.

I paste on a grin, playing my role. I appear humbled by their presence. Blessed by their support as I saunter around the room flaunting a halter-neck gown worth more than most people earn in a month.

I'm acting.

But so is my audience.

Their kindness is a facade. Their friendship a lie. Their happiness a bluff.

I don't doubt that each and every man in attendance would slaughter me and mine in a heartbeat if they thought they could get away with it. If they thought, for even a second, they could bring us down.

The women aren't any better. Their polite questions are made with sinister intent. Digging for information. Scrambling for leverage with every softly spoken word.

They're fake. From their personas to their smiles—none more so than mine.

"Can I have your attention, please?" I raise my champagne flute, my mask of charm perfectly in place as the chatter lessens. "I'd like you all to join me in a toast."

My focus strays to the reason for the engagement party—Hunter and Sarah—and for a moment I don't have to feign happiness, even though the man in question scowls at me.

The love between these two is one of the very few *real* things in my world. Their relationship isn't about rainbows and butterflies. It's dark and gritty. Pure and honest. At times, it's honestly fucking scary. But honest nonetheless.

They've created an unbreakable partnership amongst the threats and betrayal surrounding us. They beat the odds and have earned my admiration, along with the slightest case of jealousy.

"To Hunter and Sarah, may your upcoming marriage be filled with peace—" which is non-existent. "Love—" that will make you vulnerable. "And friends and family—" who can easily stab you in the back.

"To Hunter and Sarah," the guests echo, raising their glasses to drink away my poor excuse for a toast.

Finding the perfect sentiment to describe this moment is something I gave up on nights ago. We don't do perfection. We do manipulation and lies. Deceit and danger.

There are no fairytales here. Only wealth derived from the death of many and the demise of more.

A presence approaches behind me, making me stiffen.

A man.

No, *men*.

There's more than one, their proximity raising the hair on the back of my neck. But I show no fear. I can't. Not in a room filled with security and people I'm supposed to cherish.

I have to pretend I'm safe. Although we all know safety is another illusion.

"You're off your game, sis." Cole gives a friendly nudge to my elbow, washing away my discomfort with his gruff voice. "I thought you would've bored us for hours with a gushing speech about love and commitment."

I raise a brow in offense and wave a hand for him to continue forward. "Why don't you show me how it's done?"

He smirks, and for a moment I glimpse the devil. The determination and unwavering confidence in his gaze is unfathomable. But there's sterility, too.

He's not entirely present. He hasn't been for a while.

"I will." He strides ahead, wordlessly demanding everyone's attention.

Conversation dies a quick death under his muted authority. The crowd becomes enraptured, acting as if this man is their savior instead of the one threatening them to remain loyal.

"Thank you all for being here tonight." He indicates the not-so-happy couple with a tilt of his chin. Hunter glowers, his irritation unrestrained, while Sarah glares, her eyes narrowed to spiteful slits. "Although neither of them were enthusiastic about having an engagement party—"

"Slight understatement," the man at my back murmurs near my ear.

A shiver skitters down my spine. I know that voice. I've grown accustomed to the way it makes my pulse quicken.

No man has ever intrigued me the way Decker does.

"But through their adamant disapproval," Cole continues, "I knew this would be the perfect opportunity to bring us together. All of you were invited today because you're a part of the family. And right now, with our uncle still fighting for his life in hospital, we need to remain close."

My heart snags beneath tightening ribs. The flash of Uncle Richard's bruised and swollen face assails my mind. The broken arm. The cracked skull. The unrecognizable form in a crisp white hospital bed littered with cords and IVs.

It would've been more humane if he'd died. No man should've survived his injuries.

"Not only was his attack a blatant display of what others will do to try to tear us apart, it's also an act I can't ignore. I will fight for what's mine, and I will find everyone involved."

For the naive, Cole's speech could be considered protective and inspiring. To those who know him, it will be heard for the threat it is. It's a reminder to those in this room who have contemplated betrayal. A clear warning to anyone questioning their loyalties.

Remaining devoted is the only option for anyone who values the breath in their lungs.

At one time the sentiment frightened me, back when I was a child and the harsh words of a heartless father were something I whimsically hoped he'd outgrow.

I'm the one who outgrew the whimsy.

I adapted to my circumstances because there was no alternative. The weak don't survive here.

Mentally or physically.

"I will not stand idle and watch my family be destroyed. With Hunter and Sarah's engagement, we become stronger. We show outsiders how powerful we are when we work together."

I drown out my brother's words with another sip of champagne and scrutinize the vultures eagerly waiting for the scent of blood. They want Cole to expose a weakness. The slightest flaw.

"For a powerful man, Torian sure talks a lot of shit, don't you think?" Decker mutters.

I stifle a chuckle, my morbid thoughts being ripped away by his comic relief. "You can leave at any time," I murmur over my shoulder, not willing to make eye contact.

I know what I'll find in his expression, and it won't be the cold calculation I see from everyone else.

"Yeah... sure I can," he drawls. "With a bullet in the back of my skull as a parting gift."

I cringe, the visual hitting with vivid clarity.

"Besides, I couldn't leave you behind. You'd die of heartbreak. Sarah, too, for that matter. How could I live with the guilt?"

I roll my eyes. "Does your best friend know his fiancée is the only reason you stick around?"

"Of course. I tell him often."

I snort, earning the attention of my brother, who pauses mid-speech to shoot me a glower.

"*Sorry,*" I mouth.

Cole's hard gaze slips over my shoulder, his stare intensifying for a threatening moment, before he turns back to the crowd and continues his dictatorial speech.

"You're a bad influence," Decker mutters. "Nothing but trouble."

I bite my lower lip, my neck tingling with the need to face him.

I'm dying for another glimpse of that spectacularly fitted suit. The chocolate hair styled to perfection. The shadow of stubble along his jaw that begs for my touch, and eyes so dark and deep I could lose myself.

Sometimes I want to lose myself.

Instead, I have to ignore the escapism that comes when I'm around him. The playfulness. The banter. Getting mixed up in him isn't smart.

And I'm always smart.

"Stop playing games," I murmur.

He chuckles, the subtle sound smooth and too damn cocky. "Life is a game. If it isn't fun, what's the point in playing?"

There's a beat of silence where my heart lodges in my throat, then the crowd raises their glasses in unison. "To Hunter and Sarah."

I follow suit and take another sip of champagne, this one longer than the last.

Decker's scotch glass grazes my peripheral vision then disappears from view. I imagine his throat working over the liquor. The swipe of his tongue against his lower lip to lick away the moisture.

My mouth dries.

My skin prickles.

This man stokes to life a sexual appetite I've deliberately kept starved for years.

"I'm going to speak to the happy couple." I hold my head high and saunter away, not wanting to test myself more than necessary. His warmth fades, leaving me chilled. My fake smile returns, and the sterility of my existence along with it.

"You're hating every minute of this, aren't you?" I ask Sarah in greeting.

"Yes." She crosses her arms over her chest, fending off well wishes from guests with her hostile expression. "Do we look like the type to get giddy over an engagement party full of thugs?"

I cock my head in mock scrutiny. She's beautiful, and not merely in physical form. She can be brutal and kind in the same breath. Vicious and caring. This woman is truly remarkable. "Will you strangle me if I say you're not the type to get giddy over anything?"

Her lips twitch. "I'm not going to strangle you for an accurate assessment. But this —" She jerks her chin at the vultures. "This is in no way a reflection of what I'd like to be doing to celebrate our engagement. I have far more important things on my mind."

"She means fucking," Hunter adds, deadpan.

I grin. "Yeah, I figured."

"Torian is right, though." He pivots away from Sarah to watch my brother approach the bar. "Tonight was a good opportunity to get everyone together. We need to lock this shit down before the whole operation unravels."

He's referring to the attack on my uncle and how it makes our family hierarchy appear fragile. Especially when my father hasn't shown his face in months. We're teetering on shaky ground, but this isn't the first time. And it won't be the last.

"Has there been any news on who ran him down?" I hedge. "You know Cole doesn't tell me much."

"And that's for your own safety." Hunter's response is gruff. "He'll tell you what you need to know. *When* you need to know."

My pulse increases with the placation. I despise being seen as the clueless little princess. But perception is everything. "Would your fiancée accept that type of overbearing protection?"

He holds my gaze, his eyes narrowing.

We both know Sarah would demand complete transparency. If kept in the dark, that woman would create havoc. I'd love to hold a fraction of her warrior's reputation. To be known for strength instead of weakness. To be seen as an asset instead of a liability.

We are regarded in entirely different light, but in reality, we aren't all that different. At least, that's what I'd like to believe.

"I don't like secrets, do I, handsome?" Sarah places her hand on Hunter's chest and winks at me. "Don't worry. If I hear anything, I'll let you know."

He snags her wrist in a tight grip. "If you hear anything, you'll keep your mouth shut, woman."

She smirks. "Now you're just turning me on, big guy. Do you want to take this macho bullshit some place private?"

His nostrils flare.

"Speaking of being turned on..." Decker appears beside me. "Have I told you ladies how gorgeous you look tonight?"

Hunter releases Sarah's wrist and clenches his fist. "Don't push me, *Deck*."

"What did I do?" Decker holds up his hands in surrender. "It's not like I told them I'm going to be picturing them while I'm all alone in the shower. I actually restrained myself this time. What more do you want from me?"

Sarah rolls her eyes, and yet again, I can't help appreciating the lack of apprehension I feel around the joker beside me. Decker is a loose cannon. He's the guy who eases tension with his endless sarcasm. He's also the guy who will get himself killed for running his mouth.

I'm still trying to learn who he is. Piece by piece. Day by day.

I've witnessed a glimpse of honor and protection. But like all the others in this room, his actions could be for underhanded reasons.

"I want your respect," Hunter grates.

"I respect you, buddy. Otherwise I would've taken off with your girl a long time ago."

Sarah laughs. Long and loud. The sound is contagious. "Decker, you wouldn't know how to handle me."

"Maybe not, but I'm willing to learn." He waggles his brows.

"I'm going to fucking kill him." Hunter takes a threatening lunge forward.

Sarah grabs her fiancé's hand and entwines their fingers. "You touch him and it means we have to stay here longer explaining the bloodied mess to Torian."

Decker clucks his tongue in another taunt. "That's a good puppy, *Hunt*. We all know Torian is as forgiving as I'm—"

"Intelligent?" Hunter interrupts.

"Sophisticated?" Sarah adds.

I want to add a sarcastic contribution and say unattractive, because God knows this man is as sexy as he is comical, but instead I offer, "Socially aware?"

"Jesus." He retreats, and from the corner of my eye I see him slap a palm over his chest. "You don't understand how much your words hurt."

"My fists will hurt a lot more." Hunter cracks his knuckles.

I smother a laugh under an unconvincing cough. "I'm going to get another dr—" My sentence is cut short by a burst of noise.

Glass shatters. People scream. *Pop, pop, pops* echo from the street, and I stand frozen as gunfire peppers the night like rain. Guests scatter, running, shoving. The lights go out, bathing us in darkened madness.

Decker barrels into me, knocking me to the ground, stealing the air from my lungs. I gasp for breath and fight to break free.

"Don't move." He shields me with his body, his head low, his gaze darting around the room as he pulls a gun from beneath his suit jacket. "Hunt, you good?"

"We're good," Sarah replies.

"*Torian?*" Hunter yells.

There's no response other than women hysterically wailing and men shouting.

I struggle to get out from beneath Decker's hard body, his weight becoming heavier. I'm trapped while my siblings could be lying in a pool of blood mere feet away.

"*Cole*," I scream. "*Layla.*"

A shadow rushes toward us, my brother's face coming into view. He's panting, his gun in his hand. More pops ring out, but they're different. Maybe our return fire.

"Get her out of here." He doesn't look at me as he pulls something from his pocket and hands it to Decker. "Guard her with your life or risk losing your own."

2

DECKER

I clench the car fob in my left hand, my gun in my right, and scramble into a crouched position.

"No." Keira shakes her head. "Not without Layla."

"I already told her to run. Now get moving." Torian rushes toward the shattered windows of the restaurant, Hunter and Sarah following close behind.

"You heard the guy." I hold out a hand. "Let's get out of here."

She rolls onto her stomach and scans the room. "I can't leave without seeing Layla first."

"You can. You will. And you are. Either on your feet or over my shoulder. It's your choice, pumpkin." I grab her wrist and tug. "You don't want to be here if the shooter comes back."

She struggles to her feet in the long evening dress, the tight material restricting the movement of her legs. Once upright, she continues to scan the darkness, the streetlights from outside the only illumination. *"Layla."*

I pause, waiting for her sister's shout, but there's no reply. Only the sound of panic and hysteria as guests scramble like mice.

"Come on." This time I yank her hard, pulling her into my side and trapping her there with an arm around her waist. I drag her toward the back of the restaurant, ignoring the trail of blood on the floor.

Keira remains strong, a mere shudder of breath and wide eyes her only show of fear.

"Keep walking." I hold her against me and push through to the kitchen where women huddle in corners and hide beneath steel counters. "Get out of here. Escape out the back."

They rush to follow my command, eager for any leadership.

"You okay?" I murmur near Keira's ear, not appreciating her silence.

"Yes." One word. One syllable. No emotion.

I can't tell if she's totally badass or so tightly wound she doesn't know how to express the fucked up shit running through her head.

We make into the fresh air as the small crowd of females flee the employee parking lot in a mass of sobs and clicking heels.

It's then that Keira plants her feet and turns in my arms. "Layla wouldn't have run without me. I need to go back."

"I'm sure you're wrong. Fear does crazy things—"

"There's no more gunfire. I'm going back."

She takes a step, and I block her path. "It was a drive-by. How hard do you think it is for them to turn around and go for round two?"

She narrows her eyes on me, her pupils almost eating up all the pretty blue. "Who's to say they're not trolling the back streets trying to gun down those who escape through the alley?"

Good point. Unfortunately, not good enough to convince me to let her go.

"That's a risk we're going to have to take." I drag her to the black Porsche parked a few feet away and unlock the doors with the fob Torian gave me.

I don't even get her door open before the unmistakable wail of police sirens poisons the air.

The sound is close. Too close.

They were watching.

Fuck.

"We need to move." I yank open the passenger door and wait.

She blinks at me, her breathing labored. "Please, Decker, let me stay." She tries to wear me down with puppy dog eyes, her master manipulation working for more seconds than I care to admit.

"Get in the damn car." I pull her forward and have her huddled inside before she can pummel me with another protest. Then I'm sliding into the driver's seat, placing my gun in her lap, and starting the engine while red and blue flashes through the sky.

I don't turn on the headlights. I drive down back alleys in darkness until we're blocks away and I can risk returning to the city streets.

I have no clue where I'm going, I just drive, her constant anxiety-riddled glances out the rear window a torturous companion as adrenaline pulses through my veins.

I check the mirrors and don't find anything suspicious to worry about. "We're not being followed."

"How do you know?"

I pull to the curb and let all the vehicles in the vicinity pass. Then I take the next left down a side street. "See." I jerk my chin at the mirror. "Nobody is tailing us."

She keeps her focus on the rear window, poised to prove me wrong even after I turn left along a desolate road, then right down another.

"You okay?" I switch on the radio, letting the soft murmur ease the tension.

"Stop asking me that." She settles into her seat, her hands delicately stroking the barrel of my gun.

My gaze keeps returning to her fingers, the nails polished in a feminine light pink to match the darker color of her dress. "Do you know how to use it?"

Her movements pause, those soft hands shifting to her thighs. Her nails dig into the shimmering fabric along her legs, betraying her tightly guarded distress. She doesn't answer. Doesn't give me an inch.

"Would you prefer to talk about the weather?" I lean forward and check the night sky. "It's clear out. Not a cloud in sight. I thought they predicted rain."

Again, it doesn't seem to be the best conversation starter if her silence is anything to go by. Unfortunately, comfort isn't something I excel at. My verbal expertise is in the range of politically incorrect jokes and inappropriate comments. This close and personal shit usually gives me hives.

"I promise you everything will be all right." My placation is useless at best.

"Don't insult me, Decker. I'm not a child."

"Okay… Then let's discuss it. Who do you think is responsible for pulling the trigger?"

She turns to me, her brows tight in confusion. Those blue eyes scrutinize. Questioning. Searching.

"What?" I ask. "You don't want to talk at all?"

"No. It's not that." She shakes her head. "It's just that nobody has wanted my opinion before. I've never been asked to contribute my thoughts."

"Well, here's your chance. What do you think happened?"

She narrows her gaze, and for a brief second I think I've crossed a line. I've pushed. I've pried into the inner workings of the most notorious family in the state. Then, as quickly as her scrutiny arrived, it retreats.

She wraps her arms around her waist and returns to her silence.

"Keira?"

She sucks in a long breath. "I don't know." The response is tortured, the words pulled from a place etched in pain and suffering.

"I don't think anyone will for a while," I offer. "Whoever is playing games knows how to cover their tracks. Just like with your uncle."

Her arms fall, her hands moving back to her thighs, the nails digging deep.

"I bet you're worried about him."

"Of course." She scowls at me. "He's my uncle."

Her statement is a question on my intelligence. The Torians value family above all else. But the comment is also a deliberate deflection. She's keeping herself locked tight, the vibrancy in her eyes betraying strong emotions.

She's known as the weak one. The vulnerable, emotional Torian. Although, clearly, her strength under pressure proves she's much more of a woman than the average man could handle.

Despite her fortitude, I've wanted to save her since the first night we met—from her brother and this life—but I'm yet to determine if she wants to be saved. I'm also clueless when it comes to her moral compass.

"Sorry. Stupid question." I drive for long minutes, sticking to the speed limit, determined not to give any cop the excuse to get up close and personal. A speeding ticket is the least of my worries at the moment, but it's also a hassle I don't need. "Do you have anywhere safe we can go?"

"Home," she whispers.

"That's not happening." With her uncle down, this additional attack seems like an attempted family assassination, and I don't want her dying on my watch. "What's option B?"

She sighs, giving in to my protection without a fight. "Cole has a place." She opens the glove compartment, brushes aside a gun and numerous documents, before pulling out a blank security keycard. "I don't even know if this is the right pass to get through the gates. Mine is in my car at the restaurant."

"Well, we're not going to your house, or back to the restaurant, so it looks like we're giving the card a try."

"I assumed as much," she drawls.

I grin, enjoying her hostility a little too much. "Where are we headed?"

"Westport."

Westport? A ninety-minute drive.

"Second-guessing letting me go home yet?" she taunts.

Hell no. I don't want her going anywhere familiar. "Westport is a great idea. Once we arrive, we can call your brother and get an update."

"We can't call him sooner?" Her question is almost a plea.

"He'd have a swarm of police up his ass by now."

"What about Layla? Can I use your phone to call her? I left mine with my purse, and as you can probably guess, they're back at the restaurant, too." She blinks those long lashes at me.

"Sure." I lean to the side, pull my cell from the back pocket of my suit pants, and hand it over.

She's dialing in seconds, the ring tone a faint hint of sound.

It doesn't take long to figure out her sister is unavailable. There's no answer. Not on the first, second, or third time she calls.

"She's probably still running," I offer, hoping to calm the growing tremble in her hands. "I'm sure she'll get in contact when she can."

She gives back the cell and stares at the gun in her lap. "I don't even know where she was when the bullets hit. What if she was right near the glass? What if—"

"I'm sure you would've heard by now if something went wrong. Bad news always travels faster than good."

"That's comforting," she mutters. "Thanks."

"Just trying to be honest." I flash her a half-hearted smile. The expression isn't reciprocated. Her face is solemn. Pained. She fills me with guilt because I have no fucking clue how to help her. "Seriously, if something happened, I'd have Hunter and Sarah blowing up my phone by now. The silence is a sign the worst is over."

"Maybe."

I don't push the conversation further. I'm familiar with the adrenaline high. She probably thinks her mind is clear and sharp, when inside that head of hers would be a fucked up mess.

If gossip can be believed, her brother keeps her sheltered from family business dealings. She's supposed to be kept in the dark from the brutality and criminal activity. If those rumors are true, tonight would act as a bitch-slap of reality.

I leave her in silence to deal with her thoughts, keeping my mouth shut as we travel out of Portland. I should've been subtle in my concern over taking her home. It's obvious her life is under threat. But on the other hand, I doubt she would appreciate me coddling her.

The closer we get to Westport, the more I notice the stiffening of her posture. Her unease is growing instead of dissipating. I glance at her every few seconds. With each visual pass, I latch on to the fingers trembling more and more against the gun seated in her lap.

"Keira," I say softly, "I know you don't want me asking, but are you still doing okay?"

She doesn't respond. Her focus is glued to the darkness outside the window. She's not ignoring me. There's something more to her lack of communication. She's lost, her beautiful skin devoid of color.

"Keira?" I touch her wrist, my fingertips connecting with cold skin which sends my pulse skyrocketing. "*Christ*."

She's in shock.

I swerve off the road, her gasp hitting my ears. I kill the engine and rush from the car to round the hood and pull open her door.

"What's going on?" She turns to me, her lips parted.

Shit. Her eyes are wide, but the pupils are no longer dilated. She's present under her concerned stare. "You're pale. And cold. I thought you were tapping out on me."

She rubs her arms. "The air-conditioning is freezing in here. Cole always has it too low."

"I was calling your name..."

"I didn't hear you. I must have been lost in thought."

Fuck. I retreat and run a hand through my hair, trying to calm my breathing. I'm being a pussy. A tight, wet snatch with all this coddling bullshit.

"Decker?" Her voice is timid as she unclasps her belt.

"Don't." I shove my open palm in her direction. "Just sit the fuck down. I need to get us out of here."

She jerks back as if I swung more than my frustration at her. And yes, the pain in those baby blues makes me feel like a ripe asshole deserving of an unlubricated fuck.

"I'm sorry," I lower my voice, "I didn't mean to snap."

She refastens her belt and scowls straight ahead. "It's fine."

Fine—the most cringe-worthy syllable known to man. With one word, my crappy night becomes a whole lot crappier. "Okay... Well... There's not much further to go until Westport. Can you focus for me so you can start giving directions?"

She raises her chin, her lips tight. "I'm focused."

"Good." I gently close her door and round the hood, cursing my stupidity with each step.

Minutes ago, I thought one of us was losing our mind.

Turns out, it's not her.

3

KEIRA

The security card worked on the gate and again on the panel to unlock the front door, allowing us access to the house I once knew as a family vacation home.

It was never a holiday for my parents, though.

As I reached my teens, I realized our trips here were out of necessity, not relaxation. We only visited this house because our lives were threatened. Not due to my dad's desire to bond.

"Once you're settled, I'm going to take a walk outside to check the yard." Decker hovers over my shoulder as I disarm the alarm in the foyer with my fingerprint.

"Okay." I flick on the lights and lead the way down the hall, the familiar space filled with tarnished memories that threaten to overwhelm me.

Despite the reasons for our visits, my mom used to love it here. She would bake all day and watch movies with us all night. We'd chat and read for hours. And now she's gone, taken by a bullet through the chest, her life stripped by the insanity that still surrounds us.

I shake away the grief and focus on the change in decor as I walk down the hall, determined to pull myself together despite the nightmares nipping at my heels. The paintings are different, the floorboards replaced with elegant tile, and the color scheme lighter than the peach walls I remember.

As I lead the way into the open kitchen and living area, I'm not surprised the main room has also been updated. It's fresh and new. It's better this way. But even with the vast changes, my limbs prickle as if ghosts stroke my skin. It's unsettling. Almost panic-inducing with the way my stomach hollows.

"Are you sure nobody else knows about this place?" Decker swipes his finger over the kitchen counter, the trail leaving no mark due to the lack of dust. "I could eat my dinner off the marble."

"Cole would use an agency to arrange cleaning and gardening staff. Nobody should know who's doing the hiring and firing."

"Good." He nods. "Are you all right if I go outside to check the perimeter?"

"Yes. Please go." My response is quick. Enthusiastic. I'm desperate for space to pull myself together.

He raises a brow, seeming to take offense.

"I'm sorry." I shake my head. "I just need time alone."

His lips kick in a sad smile, the gentle affection reaching his dark eyes. "I get it. You've been through hell tonight."

"I'll be fine."

"There you go again with that word." He chuckles. "I don't think it means what you think it means."

He winks and walks for the front door, disappearing from view while I wonder if he deliberately dropped a line from a cult classic romance.

He's such an anomaly to me. A contradiction.

There's darkness and light. Aggression and charm. I've always struggled to determine the real from the fake, but tonight it's worse with my head a tangled mess of madness.

I've never been close to death. Not like this. I haven't had the misfortune of seeing my past transgressions flash before my eyes. And that wasn't the worst of it. The thought of my niece, Stella, being at the party hours before still leaves me in a cold sweat. That little girl means the world to me. There's nothing more important than her safety.

Not one damn thing.

Yet I'm responsible for putting her in harm's way.

I created the danger.

Nausea inches up my throat, my self-revulsion warring with remorse.

I stagger forward and press my hands to the polished marble counter, sucking in breath after breath. I need to find calm. This isn't the time for strategy to take a back seat. But I'm struggling to regain control.

Screams echo in my ears. The sight of petrified faces haunt me. I can still feel the shattered glass pinching into my palms and the weight of Decker's body on mine.

He'd been selfless in his efforts to protect me. Entirely without fear. Wholeheartedly negligent toward his own life.

Maybe joking about him having a death wish isn't such a joke after all.

I release the air in my lungs then fill them to capacity, repeating the ritual over and over.

Breathe in. Breathe out. Focus.

I drag my gaze around the room, trying to distract myself, but the only replacement to the recollection of gunfire are the childhood memories making my throat tighten.

Sparks of nostalgia flicker to life like a movie, the images from my younger years becoming clear and crisp. I used to sit here for breakfast. For lunch, too. My mom would braid my hair, and I'd complain about how long it would take. I can vaguely remember the subtle tug, tug, tug as she tried to tame my unruly lengths.

An uncomfortable ache nips at my ribs.

She died too young. Too beautiful.

One day she was reading bedtime stories and apologizing for the way my dad avoided his daughters. The next we were dressed in black and crushed under suffocating grief.

That same grief assails me now, stealing the oxygen from the air.

She wasn't made for this world. *Our* world. The one with deception, betrayal, and murder.

She'd never been flawed like my father. Her love had outshone his neglect. She was the mesmerizing smile through a crowd of scowls. The virtue surrounded by sin.

For that reason, I'm certain she would hate who I've become.

I'm guilty of horrible things. The skeletons in my closet are so tightly compacted I swear one more deceitful action will bring them toppling out.

"Stop it," I demand aloud.

The panic is increasing, my pounding heart struggling with the building mania.

I shove from the counter and kick off my heels to pad toward the tinted windows. The black of night stretches before me, lonely and cold.

I greet my reflection with a wince—the disheveled hair, the haunted eyes. I can barely stand to look at myself, not because my lavish makeup is betraying me, but because I'm disgusted by my actions.

My nose burns, the overwhelming tingle announcing a potent fragility that sickens me. It's pathetic. *I'm* pathetic.

I pivot on my toes, poised to run from my reflection, only to pause at the glimpse of an abnormality on my cheek. I tilt my chin and narrow my gaze on the darkened mirror. Spots cover the right side of my face, all shapes and sizes freckled along my jaw and down my neck.

I swipe them, the rough, dry patches scraping my fingertips.

My heart stops.

My throat clogs.

"Oh, God." It's blood.

I touch everywhere—my face, my shoulders, my neck. There's no tender areas. Not a single cut, or bruise, or scrape.

The spots aren't from me.

A stranger's blood marks my skin like a brand.

I wipe them with an open palm, the gentle swipe having no effect. I quicken the pace and severity, scrubbing over and over, my arm trembling with each movement.

I glance further down, glimpsing tiny stains on the strap of my dress and along the bodice. More splotches taunt me. The liquid is engrained.

"It's everywhere." My voice cracks as I use my nails, clawing at my cheek, my jaw, my neck.

My pulse grows frantic. I can't get enough air.

I can't breathe.

The room darkens, my vision blurring over everything else except those spots that become crystal clear. I tug at the bodice and struggle to reach behind me to release the zipper.

"Keira?"

A door slams. Faint footsteps reach my ears as I scrub, scrub, scrub.

"*Keira.*" A tight grip grabs my wrist.

"*Get it off,*" I scream. "I need to get it off."

I use my free hand to scratch my neck, only to have Decker swirl me around to face him.

"Let me help you." His eyes are wide, his concern only increasing my panic.

I'm shaking. My arms tremble in his hold.

Tonight was my doing. *I've* caused this. *I'm* responsible.

"It's all my fault." The admission bubbles up my throat without permission.

"No, baby. It's not." He leans closer, getting in my face. "That's the adrenaline talking."

I try to tug my wrists away, but he holds tight. He won't let me go, and there's comfort in that. There's reassurance he won't allow my demons to take over. Only there's fear, too. More hysteria with the restriction.

"Keira, this isn't your fault."

His seriousness is foreign. He's always the life of the party, no matter how much my brother despises his antics. But this... This strong, caring man breaks me, cracking my foundations.

Muscled arms engulf me, leading me away from the window and down another familiar hall. "Is the bathroom this way?"

I don't answer, just keep dragging my numb feet in the right direction as the dried blood sinks under my skin, making me itch.

He stops before the alcove with the basin, vanity, and mirror. The door to the toilet is behind us, another to the main bathroom by our side. He yanks open drawers and cupboards until he finds a cloth, then runs the material under water and squeezes out the excess.

It won't help.

It's not enough.

The stains are marrow deep, now marking my soul.

I step away, opening the door at our side to escape toward the shower. I flick on the light and lunge for the taps.

I don't wait for the water to warm. I climb inside, needing to cleanse my soul, the cold spray hitting hard. I scrub and scrub, not stopping until the rough patches turn smooth, then disappear completely.

It's still not enough.

I tear at my dress, yanking, tugging, until the heavy, sodden weight falls to my ankles.

I stand in my underwear, head bowed, the soaked mass of my hair curtaining my face like a shield as I stare blankly at the floor.

I can't be like this. I have to pull myself together. There's no alternative, but my body won't comply. I succumb to the burning in my eyes. I cry, the tears flowing silently, the sobs wracking my chest as I brace a hand against the cold tile and purge every last drop of self-loathing.

I surrender to fragility for long moments. Maybe minutes. Possibly hours.

Nothing breaks through until him... Until Decker's shoes come into view at the entrance of the shower.

"Keira..."

His voice wraps around me, making everything worse and somewhat better at the same time.

I don't know how to react. I never do with him.

I suck in a breath and straighten, swiping the hair from my cheeks.

Strong hands reach out before me, shutting off the water. I stare at those fingers, the tanned skin.

I summon the strength I need. I create it, building from the inside out. I have no choice. I can't be fragile around him.

I turn to find him holding a plush white towel, his expression tight. His eyes have lost the taint of concern. They're different. The comforting depths now portray something I don't appreciate.

"I'm not weak," I blurt.

"I know, tiger."

"Then don't look at me like that."

He frowns. "Like what?"

"Like you pity me." I step out of the shower, my limbs numb as he wraps me in the thick material. Despite my request, I can't help letting him dry me like a child.

"I can leer at your tits if it will make you feel better."

Something squeezes inside me. Not my stomach. Not my lungs. It's bigger. All encompassing. I guess it's appreciation.

Again, his infusion of humor has endeared me.

"What's option B?" I repeat his question from earlier, earning a slight tweak to his gorgeous lips.

"While you were..." He waves a hand at the shower, wordlessly referring to my psychotic break. "I did a quick search of the house and couldn't find any spare clothes." He wrings my hair, a mass of water droplets hitting the tile at my feet. "You'll have to wear my shirt." He wraps the towel around my back, holding the ends out for me to take. "Can you grab this for a minute?"

I clutch the offering in both hands, clinging tight.

He shucks his tailored jacket to the floor, then begins to unbutton his white long-sleeve shirt. I should stop him. I'm sure I could find a robe or a blanket; even a sheet would do. But I keep quiet as he exposes a chiseled chest, muscled arms, and a haunting mass of inked skin.

The art on his arm is a collage of ominous images—a woman in tears, skulls, a chessboard, skeletal trees. I commit the eerie images to memory, none more so than the beautifully written script on his left pec. Delicate text is written above his heart, my gaze skimming over some of the words—*gentle, rage, dying, light.*

"Please don't look at me like that," he drawls, each syllable dripping with cocky menace.

A breath of delirious laughter bursts from my lips.

Through all this insanity, he provides a distraction. This man… He's crazy. Ridiculously so. And I can't help the extra hard thump that hammers in my chest as I look at him. Nobody speaks to me the way he does. He's different, his anomalies always strumming my curiosity.

"I'm sorry." I clear my throat. "How would you like me to look at you?"

His mouth twitches, the hint of a smirk breaking through. "I'm just kiddin'. You can ogle all you like. In fact, if you've got some dollar bills, I can put on a show."

And just like that, my mental break is forgotten. He doesn't judge me for losing my shit. Doesn't even acknowledge it happened.

"Here." He hands over his shirt and takes the towel, diverting his gaze as I pull the material over my shoulders and button up.

His scent envelops me, the delicious cologne masculine and woodsy. It strengthens me, makes me feel stable again. I tilt my face to the side, craving more, and take a subtle inhale against the collar, dragging him deep into my lungs.

The comfort engulfing me is ridiculous, I know that. He's not a man I can trust. And still I wrap his shirt tighter, stealing all I can get, wanting the material to cling to me like a second skin.

I close my eyes for a brief second, take another deep inhale, and blink to find him staring at me. Watching. His ravenous gaze freezes me in place.

I no longer see an ounce of his pity. His humor is nowhere in sight. What bears down on me is narrowed intensity.

Ferocity.

Lust.

"Decker—" The flare of his nostrils cuts off my sentence, and I tremble, caught between responsibility and potential stupidity.

4

DECKER

She smells my shirt, and every hair on my body rises. Those wide eyes slay me, or maybe it's the perfect body I couldn't steal my gaze from moments ago.

"I'll check to see if there's any food in the cupboards." My voice is deep, the pitch an unintentional Darth Vader imitation. The only thing missing is the heavy breathing.

"Okay…" She nods. Swallows. Looks entirely flustered. "I'll be out in a minute. I need to fix my hair."

I stalk from the bathroom, snatching my suit jacket off the floor along the way, shoving my arms in the holes as I escape down the hall. I clench my fists. Clamp my teeth. I try hard to ignore the multiplication of my perverted thoughts when I usually allow those fuckers free rein.

She just survived a shooting, less than two weeks after her uncle escaped a warranted assassination attempt in the form of a hit and run. And here I am, drilling holes through my pants like I'm a perverted teen.

Seems my dick has a death wish, too.

If only Hunter could see me now. That prick would be laughing his ass off. Torian's reaction wouldn't be as funny. I'm almost positive he would hang me from the ceiling by my cock.

I palm my cell and play phone-a-friend to get my thoughts back on track. Hunter answers on the first ring.

"You safe?" he asks.

"Yeah. I think we're in the clear. We got out of Portland."

"Good. The cops are chasing their tails here. We're going to be stuck at the scene for a while."

I walk into the open living area and head for the kitchen. "What was the end tally?"

"None for none. All the bullets lodged in the roof. Nothing came close to striking distance."

"You sure?" I frown. "Keira was splattered with blood."

"That shit is everywhere because of the shattered glass. If you took a look at the scene, you'd think those stupid fucks were rolling around in it for all the mess they've left on the floor. But no, no bullet injuries."

I start opening cupboards above the counter. The first is empty. The second and third, too. Then the fourth holds canned goods—vegetables, soup, pickles. "So, whoever did this is either a really shit shot or—"

"Or it was a warning."

"For what?"

"Who knows. It could be anything. But once Torian finds out, heads will roll."

"How's he handling the drama?"

"He's an angry fuck at the moment," Hunter grates. "He's got a lot going on, and I'm sure I don't know the half of it. But one of the biggest issues is the cops. They got here too quick. Either the informant is handing out information like flyers on a street corner, or the pigs heard something was going down and decided to leave us out as bait."

My pulse rises, my anger building. "Do you think they'd leave women in the firing line and not give us a heads up?" Kids had been at that party earlier in the night. Keira's niece, for one. "I don't think the authorities would be that callous. They can't be."

Hunter scoffs. "You got a sweet spot for the men in blue all of a sudden?"

"Oh, yeah, baby. You know me." I open a fifth cupboard—the holy grail. The two shelves are filled with liquor bottles begging to be consumed. "I'd roll over in a heartbeat for a Taser and a pair of cuffs."

"You'd roll over for half a bagel and a used cigarette, asshole."

"Yeah. I guess." Although, I haven't smoked in a lifetime. Not since I started working with Hunter and my potential lifespan shortened by a fuckton. "So, what's the plan from here? What does the bossman want me to do with Keira?"

"Hold tight for a while. With her sister in the hospital along with her uncle, we're already too vulnerable."

"Her sister?" My pulse hammers.

"It's nothing serious. She got caught up in the glass. But we don't want anyone knowing another Torian has temporarily been affected."

Shit. "Keira will lose her mind." Again. "What's the damage?"

"Nothing major. A few stitches to the side of her face, and some in her arms."

Great, relaying the third-hand information is going to be super fun. "And I guess I'm supposed to babysit until this blows over?"

"Yep," Hunter quips. "Enjoy."

"Thanks." I pull a scotch bottle from the cupboard, stroke the frosted glass with reverence, then put the treasure back because there's no way I can succumb to my hearty thirst until this bullshit blows over. "Keep me updated."

"Same. I'll call you later."

I close the cupboard, disconnect the call, and place the cell in my jacket pocket. That's when I feel her. Keira's presence hovers close.

"I don't need a babysitter," she mutters.

I sigh and stare at the fifth cupboard, eyeing the door, wishing I could crawl in among the goodness. "I know." I turn to face her. "I was playing the macho card, hoping to make myself seem tougher than I really am. Did it work?"

I force myself to hold her gaze. I can't lower my attention. I fucking won't, no matter how much exposed thigh taunts me.

"I'm not joking, Decker. If you want to leave, then leave. I'm safe here."

I lean back against the counter, cross my feet at the ankles and my arms over my chest. "One minute you're ogling my body like a starved beast, the next you're kicking me to the curb? That hurts, shortie."

She rolls her eyes. "Don't even start. Who was on the phone?"

"Hunter."

"What did he say?"

I pause, pondering my answer. It would be easy to keep her in the dark, just like her brother does. Or I could earn her trust. "Not much."

Her chin hitches. "Decker, please."

The plea on those rosy lips is a test to all my senses. She's too gorgeous for her own good. Possibly the perfect weapon in her brother's arsenal, if the guy understood her potential.

My gaze lowers without permission, taking in every inch of the seductress. My shirt clings to her chest, the damp patches over her breasts making her bra visible. Then there's her legs. Those fucking tempting thighs with their perfectly tanned skin. If the material hanging off her was two inches higher, I'd be able to get another glimpse of that lace G-string.

"You were right," I admit. She hates being kept in the dark, and I'm going to brighten her surroundings a little. "Layla didn't get out before us."

Her eyes widen. Her lips part. "Is she okay?"

I nod. "She got into a fight with some shattered glass and came out second best. But it's nothing to worry about."

Her gasp splits the air, a shaky hand moving toward her mouth before she stops and drops it to her side. She gains control, reclaiming her strength, even though the fractures still show.

"Don't panic. Hunter told me she's already stitched up."

She steels herself, her shoulders straightening. "Do you promise?"

"I'm not lying. I swear." I paint an imaginary cross over my non-existent heart. "You can try calling her again if you like."

"She won't answer. Cole would have her on lockdown. No communication in or out apart from directly through him until he has the situation under control."

I bite my tongue, determined not to pit brother against sister. It's not in my best interests to fuck with Torian. "He's trying to protect you."

"From what?" She scoffs and pads toward the dining table, grabbing the back of a wooden chair in a tight grip. "Ignorance is no way to shield someone."

"Being in the dark is for the best. He deals with some pretty heavy shit."

"Believe me, I know. I watch the news. I read the papers. And as if that wasn't enough, I hear the whispers, too."

Pfft. The media knows jack shit about her brother's criminal activities.

But her cluelessness is a good thing. It means I don't have to feel guilty for the respect I have for her. The attraction, too. "Earlier, you mentioned tonight was your fault. Why?"

"I don't know." She shrugs and lowers her attention to the table. "I guess it was like you said, the adrenaline messed with my head. I kinda lost hold of reality for a minute."

"You sure?" I scrutinize her, trying to determine if she's lying or I'm paranoid. Something about her response doesn't seem genuine. "I don't want you thinking you're responsible."

"That's sweet. But I'm over it now."

"Are you lying to me, lemon drop?" I walk toward her, stopping a few feet away. "You were adamant before."

She meets my gaze, the connection between us growing potent for long moments until she shrugs. "I came up with the idea for the engagement party. I'm the reason we were all there." She gives a bitter chuckle. "I wanted us to have something nice to celebrate. Something normal."

I raise my brows, unimpressed. "That doesn't make you responsible."

"It is what it is."

"What it is," I drawl, "is some truly fucked up logic."

She sighs and rests against the dining table, her long lashes batting with gentle lethargy. "You have a way with words, Decker. You're rarely serious."

It's my turn to laugh without warmth. "This job is morbid as fuck. If I didn't have my sense of humor, I would've offed myself long ago."

Her eyes pin me, calculating, as if trying to determine if I'm capable of taking my own life. For once, I don't enjoy her attention.

"If you can't have fun with life, what's the point?" I add.

"You've said that before." Her voice is almost a whisper as she glances to the left, staring out the window.

I push from the counter, not liking her rapid descent into deep thought. "Is it time for a drink?"

"No." She shakes her head. "I might borrow your phone again, though, if that's all right. I want to call Cole."

"No problem." I grab my cell from my back pocket. "You're not going to rat on me for telling you about Layla, are you?"

"Rat on you?" She rakes her teeth over her lower lip and pushes from the table to pad toward me, her hips holding enough sway to trigger a reaction from my dick. "You expect me to cut loose the only person willing to tell me the truth? Not likely. If anything, you and I just became soul mates."

"Don't tease, gorgeous." I smirk, adding a thick layer of cocky arrogance to mask the way she's hypnotizing me. "You'll only break my heart."

"Not teasing. But I do want to call Cole to see how long you have to *babysit*" she snips, dealing the backhanded blow with effortless precision.

"Now, now. Don't get those panties in a twist. They're the only thing protecting your modesty."

She chuckles, and it brightens her face enough to increase my pulse. The light blush warming her cheeks doesn't help, either.

I can't afford to lose my focus around this woman, but I can see it happening. I can feel it, too.

She stops in front of me and takes the cell from my outstretched hand. "I'll try my best not to get you into any trouble."

"Great." I nod. Slow. Measured. Panicked. Because she sure as shit made that sound like more of a threat than a promise.

5

KEIRA

I palm Decker's cell and walk from the room, needing privacy and distance. One more than the other, although I'm not entirely sure which is more important at this point.

I dial Cole's number then bite my tongue as he barks, "What is it?"

"It's me." I keep my voice low.

"Keira? How are you? *Where* are you? I tried calling—"

"I left my cell in the restaurant because some jerk shoved me into the arms of one of his goons and demanded I leave."

"That jerk was trying to keep you safe."

I roll my eyes. "I can keep myself safe, brother."

He sighs. "I don't have time to argue with you right now. Hunter said you're out of town. Where, exactly?"

"The safe house."

"Which one?"

"There's more than one?" I accuse. "Since when?"

"*Fuck*." His frustration echoes down the line. "We'll discuss details later. Just as long as you're safe, that's all that matters."

"I am. Decker has everything under control. He's been perfect."

"Perfect?" The disapproval in his voice is loud and clear. "Is he close by?"

"In the kitchen. Do you want me to get him?"

"No, what I want you to do is be careful."

I continue down the hall, toward the far end of the house, glancing over my shoulder every few steps. "Yeah, I know. You don't have to warn me."

"He's still new. And reckless. And a motherfucking smartass. His attitude doesn't sit well with me."

"So why make him my white knight? I should've stayed with you."

"It was good timing and the perfect opportunity."

My pulse increases. "The perfect opportunity for what?"

"Keeping an eye on him. Getting inside his head."

I clench my jaw, unsure and a little disturbed at how my brother could've thought about strategy while bullets were flying and people were screaming. "He's been good to me, Cole."

"Good or cunning? Don't be naive, sis. You know he can't be trusted."

The intensity in his voice puts me on edge. "Am I in danger?"

"From him? No. I wouldn't have sent you with him if I thought he was capable of hurting you. But is he capable of hurting this family? I'm not sure. He's yet to prove his worth. And until he does, his intent will remain questionable."

"What do you expect me to do?" I ask.

"Nothing. Not yet. Just remain open to testing him if you get the chance."

"Testing him?" I hiss under my breath. "He's supposed to be on our side."

"What's supposed to be and what usually happens are two different things. You know we're both paranoid for good reason."

He's right, even though judging Decker as the enemy feels entirely wrong.

"Be smart, Keira. Be safe, too."

I nod. "I will."

I'm not going to plead Decker's case. Not yet. I'll take more time to come to my own conclusion first. To cement my assumptions. "Do you have any news on who's responsible for tonight?"

"There's nothing to go on. Not yet. But I'll find out sooner or later."

Nausea swirls in my belly. The slightest tremble works its way into my hands. Knowledge isn't always a good thing. Sometimes ignorance is most certainly bliss. Especially when knee-jerk, death-causing reactions are likely. "Don't do anything rash, okay?" I beg. "You, more than anyone, need to keep a level head."

"You know me, Kee, I'm nothing if not level."

His sarcasm is scary. I'd laugh if I didn't want to crumple.

"Look, I've gotta go." His tone turns dismissive. "It's not a great time to talk. I'll call you tomorrow."

There's a pause, and for a moment I think he's already disconnected. "Cole?"

"Yeah?"

I swallow over my drying throat. "How's Layla?"

"She's fine." His response is instant. Without thought. "She got out before you did."

My brows rise at the placating lie.

"Right..." I suck in a calming breath and let it out slowly. "Well, can you let her know I lost my phone in the restaurant? I have to use Decker's, and she's not answering my calls."

"She's probably screening and doesn't recognize the number. I'll pass on the message."

Liar. Liar. Liar.

"Thanks."

"I'll speak to you soon, Kee. Make sure you lay low until I call."

"I will." I hang up and stare out the window at the far end of the hall.

Cole is playing a dangerous game by distorting the truth in an attempt to keep me calm. All our enemies need is a weak spot. Just one. That's it. Then, *bam*, we're vulnerable.

But I get why he lied. We all have secrets. Some are made to protect those we love.

He thinks he's doing the right thing.

He doesn't want me to worry. And yet the intent has had the opposite effect.

I'm concerned as hell. About being alone with Decker. About my mental stability. About Cole reacting without thought when he finds out who's responsible for the drive-by.

I can't hold tight to the strength I usually cling to. Adrenaline has zapped my common sense.

Come on, Keira. Pull yourself together.

I tread lightly down the hall and pause in the shadows. Decker is still in the kitchen, now eating from a can of corn with a spoon. He isn't doing anything sneaky or covert. He's relaxed, his jacket gaping to expose his inked chest, his dark hair mussed and falling around his forehead. There isn't a glimmer of deception ebbing from him, but I know there shouldn't be if he's an accomplished manipulator.

Deceit is rarely obvious.

I inch into the living room, my gaze never leaving him as I stop a few feet away from the kitchen counter. "That looks appetizing."

His lips kick, his face the very definition of cocky arrogance.

"I was talking about the corn," I clarify.

"Sure you were." He tilts the can in my direction. "Want some? We don't have a lot of options where food is concerned."

"No, thanks. I don't think my stomach could handle it at the moment."

He shoves another spoonful into his mouth, his chiseled jaw working overtime. "How's your brother?"

I shrug. "He's the same ol' Cole. Nothing changes."

He pauses, his eyes narrowing. "Something's wrong."

It's not a question, it's a statement that catches me off guard. He can already sense my mood, can already decipher my expression. The realization fills me with apprehension and appreciation in equal measure.

"No. Not upset," I lie, indicating my face with a swirl of a finger. "This is a look of annoyance. He lied to me again."

"I'm sorry to hear that."

"I should be used to it by now, right? To be honest, I'm surprised it still bothers me."

He throws up a hand in a what-are-you-gonna-do gesture. "You've had a long day. Maybe you should get some rest."

"Yeah. That's the plan." After getting off the phone, I've gained a few new layers to my exhaustion. Only I'm finding it hard to walk away. Maybe I should test him.

Not to claim answers to Cole's doubt, but to prove my instincts about Decker are right. "Will you be okay finding a room of your own?"

He spoons a few more kernels of corn into his mouth. "I'll crash on the sofa if I have to."

"If you have to? You don't plan on sleeping?"

"I might doze a bit."

"Why? We're safe here, aren't we?"

"Yes, of course." He pulls out the garbage drawer and throws the can into the trash. "I'm only being cautious."

I don't want to believe him. I can't. One, because trust is a personality trait I rarely indulge in. And two, because the thought of him giving up sleep for me makes my stomach twist in knots.

"Keira, if there was something to worry about, I'd tell you." He leans forward, arms spread along the counter, gaze intent. "Go. Get some rest. We can figure out our next move in the morning."

I nod.

Despite Cole's warning, I do agree Decker is no threat to me personally. I can't picture this man hurting me. I can't see it at all. And I'm more than aware betrayal can come from a friendly face. "Good night, Decker."

"Night, kitten."

I drag my feet down the hall, while my thoughts stay with him in the kitchen. I don't want to be alone, and it's not because of his flirtation and dripping innuendo. I crave the truth. I need answers. I want them so much my neck prickles with anticipation.

I reluctantly close myself into the master bedroom and stare at the door handle for long heartbeats. I should lock it, even though I'm not scared of the gorgeous thug protecting me. It's the smart thing to do if I plan on getting even a lick of sleep... which isn't highly likely anyway.

I gently flick the lock, hoping the sound doesn't resonate down the hall, then do a visual sweep of every inch of the room before turning off the light and climbing into bed. I lie on my side, his shirt bunched at my shoulders, my nose nestled against the material.

His scent fills my lungs, and I struggle to recount a moment with him that could've held questionable intent.

He's proven himself to me tonight. He showed his loyalty by shielding my body with his own, and in every other action afterward.

But then again, he had proven himself to me all those months ago when he confronted Cole. My brother's hand had been wrapped around my neck, the squeeze light despite the rage in his eyes.

With one sentence, Decker stood up for me. He showed sincerity and promise.

Cole would've seen it as defiance. Not me, though. I appreciated the honor. The morals.

The outburst doesn't mean he's worthy of trust. But leniency? Yes.

He deserves to be given a chance.

I try to build on my convincing argument, tossing and turning for hours as I analyze every moment I've spent with Decker—the playfulness, the protection, the lingering lust he keeps tightly leashed.

And he told me the truth about Layla's injuries. That, by far, is the attribute I cling to for dear life.

But it could be a game. I know better than anyone that deception comes from those you least expect. I seriously can't let down my guard. No matter how much I want to.

Each minute that ticks by brings more madness to my exhaustion. I start to lose grip on my thoughts, and waking nightmares hover close.

The flashback of shattering glass enters my mind. The rapid gunfire. The screams. The panic.

I try to douse the flames with the memory of Decker's hard body atop mine. The frantic way he pulled over on the highway. The gentle hands that dried me after the shower.

Don't be naive, sis. You know he can't be trusted. My brother's words haunt me.

As if I didn't have enough to worry about without adding mixed feelings about Decker to the list.

I throw back the covers and slide from bed.

I stalk from the room, my feet slapping against the hall tiles as my pulse pounds in my throat. The house is bathed in shadow, the glow from the muted television the only illumination as I enter the living room.

I stop at the foot of the sofa, staring down at his sprawled body, his chest bare, his arm slung over his face, covering his eyes. He's peaceful, and trustworthy or not, he's truly magnificent to look at. For long minutes I peer down at him, stalker like and entirely unapologetic.

The woman tattooed on his bicep stares up at me, her beauty ethereal and haunting as a tear streaks down her cheek.

"Can I help you?" he mumbles.

My heart shoots to my throat at the sudden break in silence. "*Christ*. I didn't realize you were awake."

"I figured." His arm falls to his side as he blinks up at me. "What's wrong?"

I try to come up with the perfect response. One that seems entirely out of my comprehension the longer those midnight eyes take me in. "My brother doesn't trust you."

"You got out of bed to tell me that?" He frowns and sits up, leaning back against the armrest. "It's not really a secret, sunshine."

"You already know?"

"Of course I do." He pauses to ponder me for a moment, his brows knit tight. "Did he tell you that, or did you work it out on your own?"

"Does it matter?"

Slowly, he stands and moves toward me, his height becoming so much larger than it ever has been before. All that bare skin. All that hard muscle. All that delicious ink.

"Yeah, it does. I don't think it's a smart move to tell a woman her safety has been placed in the hands of someone she can't trust."

I swallow over the dryness in my throat, not wanting to admit how right he is.

"But he did tell you." His eyes narrow. "Is that why you were upset after you got off the phone?"

I lick my lips, struggling to combat the sudden detox of moisture. My throat is dry, my tongue and mouth, too.

"You have nothing to worry about, Keira. Despite your brother's opinion, I would never hurt you."

A bark of derision leaves my mouth. It's forced. Another act. I need to pretend I'm highly cautious even though my intuition wants to wave green flags like it's Saint Paddy's day.

I *do* believe he would never hurt me.

I *do* trust he has my best interest at heart. How can I not after he shielded me against bullets with his own damn body?

"If you're scared of me, I can take you to someone else." His expression is pained as he speaks. "I'll drive you wherever you want to go." He bends down and retrieves his jacket from the floor. "Just tell me where we're headed."

He's truly ready to leave.

"I don't need to go anywhere," I admit.

He eyes me with trepidation. "Are you sure?"

I swallow, lick my lower lip, and fight to keep in control. "Why doesn't he trust you?"

"Because my loyalty has always been to Hunter first and foremost. It always will be. Cole doesn't appreciate the defiance."

No, my brother wouldn't. He expects fealty, a blood oath, and your firstborn... Or something along those lines.

"Is that all?" I can't tear my gaze away, too eager to decipher every change in him. "There has to be more to it than that."

"I'm sure there's a million reasons." He shrugs. "But while he's paying me, I don't give a fuck about a single one."

His sterility isn't appreciated. I guess I'm like Cole in that regard. I want loyalty. Devotion. I need more than callous disregard when it comes to my family. "I understand."

"I'm not after your understanding, Keira. I want your trust. After everything we've been through tonight, don't I deserve that?"

"Trust is difficult."

He gives a half-hearted smile. "I guess it takes more than putting my life on the line to make you happy." He throws my callousness at me with such softly spoken words.

I don't like the accusation. I don't appreciate how empty it makes me feel.

"You don't understand," I whisper.

"Try me."

I measure my breathing, not succumbing to the need to suck in deep lungfuls of air. "Trust brings vulnerability. And I'm not allowed to be vulnerable."

"You're allowed to be whatever the hell you want. You're your own person. Don't ever forget that."

"No. I'm not. I can't be vulnerable or weak or scared."

He scoffs. "You *are* scared."

"No—"

"Yeah, you are." He cuts me off. "You're strong and stubborn and smart. But you're still fucking scared, and that's okay. You'd be stupid if you weren't."

I stare at him, drowning in the solemn sincerity in his expression. I want to believe his kindness. I'm dying to. "Cole is never scared."

"Cole is a psychopath. You're comparing apples to oranges."

I laugh despite the seriousness in his voice. "He's not psychotic. He's just…"

"Fucking crazy?" He approaches a step. "A narcissist?" The nearness increases. "Stop me if you want. I could go on for hours."

My smile lessens, the relief he's given me dying under the heavy thoughts of my brother. "You shouldn't joke about him like that. If he heard…"

"It isn't anything I wouldn't say to his face." He shrugs. "I work for him, and he has my loyalty. But that doesn't mean he gets my respect."

The brutal honesty surprises me. It also fills me with concern. "You disapprove of the way he does business?"

"It has nothing to do with business."

"Then what is it?"

He holds my gaze, his expression growing tight.

"Tell me." I inch closer, the sides of our feet brushing.

"That's a conversation for another day. You need to get some rest."

No. I'm finally getting somewhere. I can't stop now. *"Please."*

His jaw ticks. His eyes harden. "He laid hands on you. I could never respect a man who does that."

I stare blankly, entirely overwhelmed by his vehement response.

There's not merely a lack of respect between my brother and this man. There's more. So much more. And if I can believe his fierce conviction, it has nothing to do with my family's criminal activities and everything to do with his concern for me.

Guilt mixes with my turbulent emotions.

I'm the reason Cole doesn't trust him.

I'm the one who has put a target on Decker's back.

He walks by me, severing the conversation as he stalks into the kitchen, the flick of the light stealing away the shadowed intimacy. "Do you want me to get you a drink? I found the liquor cupboard earlier."

I sigh and follow after him. "I don't want alcohol. Coffee, on the other hand…"

"That's not going to happen." He pulls open a cupboard above the counter and retrieves a scotch glass. "Caffeine is a bad idea when the aim is sleep."

"Well, what I need and what I'm capable of are two different things."

He moves to another cupboard, this one lined with bottles of all shapes and sizes—rum, tequila, gin.

He pulls out a vodka bottle, cracks the lid, and pours a shocking amount into the glass.

"I hope that's not for me." I remain on the other side of the counter.

"For relaxation purposes." He shuts the cupboard then turns to me, the bottle in one hand, the glass in the other.

"Are you going to have one with me?"

He gives a subtle shake of his head. "I can't."

"Because you're babysitting?"

"No, because I don't want you to take advantage of me."

I roll my eyes. "But you've poured enough to take down a wild beast."

He smirks, the expression hitting me hard as the glass is pushed toward me. "Well, sometimes you act like one."

I scowl, even though it's hard to fight a smile when he's looking at me like that, all self-assured with mussed hair and sleepy eyes.

"When have you ever seen me in beast mode?" I mutter.

"Have you already forgotten the first night we met?" He quirks a brow. "You were as wild as it gets. I didn't know if you were going to get out of your sister's house alive."

The memory steals the tweak from my lips. My actions haunt me. "I never thanked you for standing up for me."

"I didn't expect you to. Any self-respecting man would've done the same thing."

I don't answer. I can't.

The truth is, no matter how many times my family's employees have seen Cole and me fight, nobody has ever stepped in. Not once. Not even slightly. Not until Decker.

I raise the glass and throw back a dangerous amount of vodka. The liquid burns my throat and nose, making me cough. I expect him to laugh at me. I anticipate the superior smirk to have curved those gorgeous lips.

When I raise my gaze, his brows are pinched, his eyes filled with apology.

"I'm sorry," he murmurs. "I shouldn't have brought that up."

"Don't apologize." I rub my nose to fight the lingering tingle. "It's all in the past."

He grabs the bottle and rounds the counter, turning off the light before he leads the way to the sofa. "You've forgiven him?"

I follow, this time sipping the alcohol instead of trying to drown myself in it. "He's my brother," I hedge.

He eyes me as he places the vodka on the coffee table and slumps onto the sofa. The analysis is unnerving, his stare telling me he's well aware I didn't answer his question.

He pats the space beside him, offering me a seat so close and personal my skin already tingles. I hesitate, my gaze drifting to the recliner a few feet away, then returning to the tempting position fraught with danger.

"I won't bite." He winks. "I prefer to lick."

"There you go again with the wisecracks." I take a seat at the far end of the sofa and turn to him, curling my legs beneath my bottom. "You're uncomfortable being serious, aren't you?"

He ponders the question, his expression exaggerated. "Maybe."

"I guess you already know it's endearing in a really unsettling kind of way."

He chuckles. "I can't help being irresistible. It's been a problem since birth."

We sit for a while, the silence comfortable as the glow from the television flickers over his face like a kaleidoscope.

"Have you and Cole ever been close?" He stretches his arm over the head rest, his strong hand within reach.

"Define close." I don't like this subject. It's too personal. Entirely intrusive. "You've already seen us at our worst."

"He was worried you were going to do something stupid. I don't think he knew any other way to make you listen." He speaks without emotion, as if we're discussing the weather instead of a physical assault.

"You're defending him now?"

"Fuck no. What he did was unforgivable. I'm just really shitty when it comes to consoling women."

Warmth enters my chest, the happy tingle taking its time to reach my face and pull at my lips. "Thank you."

He frowns. "For what? The shitty attempt at comfort?"

"No. I'm not talking about the conversation. I mean everything—for shielding me in the restaurant, for handling my meltdown, for literally taking the shirt off your back."

He shrugs. "The shirt looks better on you anyway."

"It does, doesn't it?"

His eyes narrow on mine the slightest bit. Then slowly his gaze lowers, trekking my body, over the material of his shirt right to the edge of my exposed thighs curled at my side.

He has the strangest way of manipulating me. Of making me relaxed and ready to verbally spar, then stealing away the fun to replace it with palpable anticipation.

I don't just watch him taking me in, I feel it. The attraction shivers down my spine. The lust coils in my belly.

"Are you ready to go to bed yet?" he murmurs.

I stiffen, unsure of the meaning behind his question.

"Alone, Keira. I think we need to cut and run before this conversation takes us somewhere we'll regret."

I agree, but the thought of the dark bedroom on the other side of the house strips me of any warm and fuzzies.

"I don't want to go back down there." I turn to the television, hoping my diverted gaze will lessen the vulnerability of my admission. "I'd like to stay here with you. If that's okay."

I see him watching me through my peripheral vision. I can't escape it. His attention wraps around me, adding to the warmth ignited by the vodka.

"If you're staying, you should at least catch some zs." He pushes to his feet, grabs a cushion from the closest recliner, then sits back down. "Here." He pats the makeshift pillow on his lap. "Lie down."

"No, I'm good. Honest." I finish the last of the vodka in one gulp and place the glass on the coffee table.

"Please, Keira. At some point tomorrow I'll have to sleep, and I need to know you're going to be able to stay awake while I'm out of it." He pats the cushion again. "Come on. Trust me."

It's not merely a case of dominating the exhausting T-word I can't seem to wrangle. There's more. So much more. And I can't share a single word of it with him.

"It's only for a few hours," he whispers. "You'll feel better once the sun comes up."

It's ridiculous how long I remain silent pretending contemplation when my mind is already made up.

"I'll just rest for a little while." I stretch out, slowly inching myself closer to press my head on the cushion.

He peers down at me, dark and intense. I can't look away. I don't want to. There are answers in those soulful eyes, and I need to hear them all.

"Sleep, sunshine."

"With you staring at me?" I purr.

He grabs a remote from the armrest and switches off the television, plunging the room into darkness. "That better?"

No, it's not. Not even close.

I can still see him. Can still feel his severity bearing down on me through the shadows, inching its way under my skin.

6

DECKER

I watch her for too damn long, attempting to get into her head. To figure her out.

Instead, I get caught up noticing the different stages of her sleep.

I see everything. Every twitch, every breath.

I become fascinated with her intricacies as the hours pass. The thick eyelashes that flutter, the ones in the middle longer than those on the outer edges. Her smooth skin, with the tiniest scar above her chin. The perfectly sculpted eyebrows. Her soft hair. The flawless braid.

She makes noises. The sweetest whimpers.

I find myself tensing, waiting for the next murmur of sound, not wanting the scrape of my own inhale to disrupt the experience.

This stupidity is commonly known as sleep deprivation.

She could be confused for someone weak and defenseless in this moment. She could… But she isn't.

I know better.

This woman is strong and smart. And so fucking beautiful it's hard not to become wrapped up in the thought of tasting her.

Fuck. I need to wake the hell up.

I've earned a modicum of her trust, and now I have to be careful how I treat it. I can't be reckless. I've gotta keep my mind on the task at hand, and I definitely have to ignore the way my shirt creeps up her thigh every time she moves.

I have to… And I'm fucking struggling.

Between the hours of five and six, I place bets on how much skin will be exposed. By the time the sun rises, I have the slightest glimpse of white lace at her hip, the sight of the skimpy material the sweetest torture against a sleep-starved man.

At eight, she starts to stir, her brow furrowing, nose scrunching.

I slide my hand from her hair and the other from her shoulder, placing one on the arm rest, the other at my side. Casual as fuck. Then I close my eyes and rest my head back, feigning unconsciousness as she shifts, wakes, then gently creeps off my lap.

I should let her walk away. She would need to decompress after greeting the day with a bird's-eye view of my crotch. But as soon as her warmth leaves me, my pulse rises and lust claws deep.

I catch her tiptoeing around the sofa, her hair a mess, her face pale.

"Did you sleep well?" I ask.

"Jesus, Decker," she gasps, her hand shooting to her throat. "Can you stop pretending you're asleep? That's the second time you've scared the crap out of me."

I grin. "Sorry."

"No, you're not." She finger combs her hair behind her ears, the long, wavy lengths fanning her shoulders. She looks different this morning, the gentleness of sleep still evident in her features.

She isn't a member of a crime-riddled family at the moment. She's a normal woman. A gorgeous woman. With my fucking shirt hanging from her thighs like a pinup model.

Her gaze scours the floor, her teeth digging into her lower lip. "You haven't seen a hair tie floating around, have you?" She waves a hand in a circular motion, indicating my crotch. "It would've fallen out while I slept."

It fell… Or someone pulled it out in an attempt to play with her hair.

"I haven't seen it." Not in a few hours, anyway. "Do you need to search?" I raise the cushion from my lap and hold my arms wide, ready for her to mount a full-scale search around my dick.

She throws her head back and laughs. "You're a troublemaker when you haven't slept, do you know that?"

She's right. I'm stirring trouble where trouble shouldn't be stirred. I can't help it. Those ocean eyes of hers are fucking with my mind, making me crazy.

I drop the cushion to the sofa and stand, the thin black tie falling out from somewhere between my legs.

"Here." I hand it over, our fingers brushing for brief seconds.

The touch is more than a scrape of skin against skin. The contact brings a jolt of awareness, her sultry mouth hypnotizing as her tongue snakes out to moisten her lower lip.

She swallows and takes the offering, her gaze holding mine for long, drawn-out seconds. The connection feels like a test. A game of chicken I have no plan to lose.

"You should leave it out," I murmur. "It looks nice."

She hesitates. Unmoving. For a second, I think she might humor me. Or maybe try to impress me. Then something shifts in her features.

Her chin rises, her eyes harden. She ties her hair back in quick, efficient movements and reclaims the control I can't seem to find. "It's too annoying to keep out."

I nod. Shrug. Act unfazed even though the slight change in her demeanor has woken me up to the reality of my thread-bare restraint.

She's not someone I can mess around with—physically or emotionally. She's not even someone I should be attracted to. There's a heap of can'ts, shouldn'ts, and what-the-fucks surrounding Keira, and it needs to stay that way.

"What are we going to do about breakfast?" She runs her hands down the material of the shirt, trying to straighten the wrinkles.

"I'm more focused on what you're going to do about clothes." Every time she moves, she gets closer and closer to showing off that lace thong.

"Why is that?" she teases, glancing down at herself. "Don't you think I look good in your shirt anymore?"

It's my turn to laugh. "Who's the troublemaker now?"

She chuckles, the flash of her easy smile making me question if she was adopted at birth. She's nothing like her brother. Nothing like her father or uncle, either.

"I actually think those few hours sleep made things worse. My head is pounding like I've got a hangover from hell." She rubs her temples. "Coffee and a deliriously unhealthy breakfast is the only thing likely to save my soul today."

"Okay." I rub my hands together. Getting out of here is a good distraction. "Let me take a quick shower to wake up, then we can hit the road."

I DRIVE out of Westport and along the highway for roughly ten miles to the closest town. It's nothing special. Just a tiny little place with enough amenities to handle what we need.

Keira is still bare-legged, dressed in nothing but my shirt, while my chest is exposed beneath my suit jacket. Not the best attire when we want to lay low, which means clothing is higher on the agenda than food.

"I'm buying you a skirt and blouse, right?" I park in front of a women's clothing store and cut the engine.

"Yes, please. Anything with an elastic waistband will help, seeing as though I can't try it on."

"Well, you can. It's your decision to hide in the car."

She glowers. "I'm wearing a men's dress shirt and nothing else."

I slide from the car then lean down to meet her gaze. "And I look like a fucking gigolo with my abs on display."

Her eyes fill with mirth. "But they're such pretty abs."

It's not a compliment. There's too much humor in her tone. It doesn't stop her words from packing a punch, though. The dreamy bat of her lashes is just another conniving taunt.

"I'll be back in a minute. Don't go anywhere." I scan the street, triple checking nobody is paying us attention. It's early on Saturday morning, and the only people around are oldies or mothers with young children. But we're still driving around the middle of nowhere in a Porsche, which means the occasional stare is unavoidable.

After a flirtatious fifteen minutes with the young blonde shop assistant, I leave the store, my hands full of shopping bags as I slide back into the sports car.

"That looks like a lot more than a skirt and blouse." Her eyes bug as I hand over the purchases.

"The woman in there had the gift of the gab. I ended up giving her your sizes, and in return she set out a heap of clothes. I wasn't going to stick around and coordinate ensembles, so I bought them all."

"And I see you earned her phone number in the process."

"You were watching me, baby doll?" I retrieve the business card the woman gave me and hand that over, too. "This is in case you have any problems with the sizes."

"Sure it is." She eyes me with derision, before opening the first bag to glance inside. "There has to be enough clothes here to last a week."

"Good." I start the engine and pull from the curb. "I'm not sure how long we're going to be hanging out together, so at least this gives you some options."

She leans down, toeing her feet into a white skirt, then dragging it up her legs to shimmy it over her ass.

It's an impressive show I pretend not to watch from the corner of my eye. "We passed a diner on the way in, is that good enough for breakfast?"

"You don't want to get a shirt first?"

Shit. My stomach rumbles in protest. "I'll have to leave the shopping spree until later. I'm too hungry."

"Thank God. I don't think I can last much longer without sustenance." She tugs the hem down her thighs, covering perfect skin before she moves her attention to the buttons of my dress shirt.

"Do you want me to pull into an alley to give you privacy?" I drag my gaze over the passing cars, willing the passengers not to pay her attention.

"It's not like you haven't seen it all before."

I may have seen it, enjoyed it, and committed it to memory, but that doesn't mean I'm comfortable with her sharing the goods with any Tom, Dick, or buck-tooth Bill in the vicinity.

"It's not me I'm worried about." The thought of someone else looking at her makes me edgy. Goddamn twitchy.

I tighten my fingers around the steering wheel and pull up to a set of traffic lights. My jaw locks while I glare at the approaching Chevy in my rear-view that stops in the lane beside us.

The male driver is young, with shaggy hair and a flannelette shirt. For a second, I think Keira is going to skip his attention. Then he lazily glances our way and does a double-take when he notices her gaping shirt as she works at unclasping the last of her buttons.

"You've got an audience." I inch forward to meet the asshole's gaze, shooting him a look so scathing a smart man would contemplate his mortality.

He doesn't take my expression for the warning it is. Instead, he grins like he's about to blow in his pants.

"Keira," I growl, "you might want to cover up until the light changes."

She ignores me. The peeping tom, too.

She doesn't care at all. Not about the perfect chest she has on display or the smooth stomach as she shimmies out of my shirt and reaches down to pull out a light pink blouse from one of the shopping bags.

My palms sweat. My pulse fucking pounds.

I don't know why I give a shit, but I do. The anger coursing through me is unwarranted and fucking toxic.

To make matters worse, she struggles to maneuver her arm into the sleeve, her cleavage gaping as she bends forward.

"Jesus Christ," I mutter.

The shaggy fucker is practically laughing at his good fortune while my skin crawls.

"I've got something else you can look at, asshole." I reach for my gun.

"Don't you dare," she warns, finally working one arm into the sleeve. "Just ignore him."

Ignore him?

Ignore him.

I can't fucking breathe through the need to kill him.

I check the lights. Still red. Then I glance around the intersection.

"For fuck's sake. What is taking so long?" Apart from Grandpa Joe driving his white van past at five miles an hour, nobody else is on the road. The universe is mocking me with this bullshit. "Fuck this."

I press my foot on the accelerator. *Hard.* The tires screech as we surge forward. At this point, a ticket is better than a murder charge.

"What the hell, Decker?" Keira scrambles to clutch her belt and the door handle for support.

"The guy beside us was practically jerking off at your strip tease," I snarl.

"And running a red light and potentially smashing my brother's car is worth stopping the five second thrill of some random stranger?"

"Fuck yes." I ease off the pedal and cut down a side-street, not willing to trust my waning restraint if Chevy Boy decides to follow. "Somehow I think your brother would approve of my actions."

"I think he'd be more likely to kill you for endangering the Porsche." She wiggles, repositioning herself in the seat as she fixes the first button, her gaze heating the side of my face. "And besides, it's *my* modesty to protect. Not his. I've got more concerning things to worry about at the moment."

"You could've figured that out before I pimp-walked through the clothing store on your behalf. Minutes ago, you were all shy and innocent, not wanting anyone to misinterpret your lack of clothing as a walk of shame. Now you've got it all hanging out, practically screaming 'have at it, boys.'"

"Are we really arguing about this?"

Yes, we fucking are, and no, it doesn't make sense. I'm acting like a jealous little bitch over Cole Torian's sister. "I'm here to protect you in whatever way necessary."

"And I appreciate that, officer, but you can cut the crap when it comes to anyone not wielding a gun."

I grind my teeth and focus on the road, wishing the asphalt would open up and swallow me whole. "It's the lack of sleep," I growl. "And I'm fucking hungry."

She snickers. "Don't worry. I get it."

No, she doesn't. She has no clue I'd love to whisk her away from this shit, like a badass Prince Charming. But I'm still not sure if she needs to be saved. Or wants to be, for that matter.

"You can pull back onto the main road. I'm done." She tugs at the front of her shirt and grins. "All censored for your approval."

"Not funny." I turn the car around and take the fastest route back to the diner.

"Come on." Her grin turns to a smirk. "You've gotta admit it's a little funny."

"Nope. Unless you want me waving my dick around in public to distract attention from you, let's agree to keep our clothes on."

She presses her lips tight, her chest vibrating with silent laughter. "Who says I'd be opposed to you taking your clothes off?"

Fuck. Me.

The last thing I need right now is more complication. Increased temptation. I still have the crystal-clear recollection of her in the shower last night.

Half-naked.

Wet.

Vulnerable.

"For the sake of your brother not killing me, I'm going to take that as a fucking cruel joke."

"Okay." Her laughter fades as she grabs a pair of black flip-flops from the bag and slips them on. "For the sake of my brother not killing you, I'll pretend I was joking."

Jesus.

I cling to the steering wheel while I drive to the diner, then park the car and reclaim my shirt. Seconds later I'm striding inside, her soft footfalls following behind me.

I don't face her until we reach the counter. Even then it's hard not to stake a claim on all the perfection that Chevy-driving asshole was trying to visually violate. "Can you order me whatever you're having, along with enough food to take home for the rest of the day?" I hand over my wallet. "I've gotta make some calls."

"Okay…" She frowns. "Sure."

"You're going to be fine on your own for five minutes, aren't you?"

"I think I can handle it." She stares up at the billboard menu. "But don't be too long. I might get bored and start stripping for tips."

I scowl, pissed off that the creative side of my brain can conjure up a visual faster than I can form a comeback.

I don't even bother replying. There's no point. The gray matter swirling around in my skull has the consistency of butter as I stalk from the building, her soft chuckle haunting my every step. I continue to the far end of the parking lot and pull out my cell, quickly switching the sim cards to make a private call I've been dreading.

"Hey, baby, I was wondering when you'd get in contact." Anissa's voice is sickeningly sweet.

"I've been busy." I glance back at the diner, too paranoid not to look over my shoulder.

"So I've heard. Where are you?"

"Doesn't matter. But I won't be back this afternoon. I can't catch up today."

There's a beat of tense silence. "This is the second time you've cancelled our plans."

"I'm sorry, it can't be helped." I'm not sorry and she knows it, but it's a part of the game we play. She acts sweet and innocent while I pretend to give a fuck.

"You're with someone." She drops the saccharine from her tone. "Who?"

"It doesn't matter."

"Bullshit," she snaps, revealing the bitch she hides beneath this pathetic act. "You know it does. Tell me."

"I've warned you before, Nissa. Don't hound me."

"And I've warned you. *Don't fuck with me.*"

I should've walked away from her months ago. I still should, if only I didn't need her, and she didn't need me, too. We've got a unique relationship based on threats and lies. Smoke and mirrors.

She isn't the drug I crave. But she's the dealer. The gatekeeper.

"Fine. It doesn't matter, anyway." She bottles her anger. "I know who you're with. It's not hard to figure out."

"Then I hope you also know you can trust me."

Her derisive laugh is barely audible over the passing traffic. "I doubt that, but I've got hope. And a backup plan if you fuck me over."

I close my eyes and pinch the bridge of my nose. Anissa is nothing if not entirely strategic. I've always been well aware of what she's capable of, and I got involved with her anyway. "I won't."

I can't.

Despite her poison, this woman is a necessity in my life.

"Good. Be smart, Decker. We're great together. The last thing you want to do is mess it up."

7

KEIRA

Breakfast arrives while Decker is still outside, on his second phone call.

I wait a few minutes, watching him, trying to decipher the meaning behind his rigid stance and straight shoulders. He hid his face from view for most of his conversations, playing with the device between calls, if the hustle in his arms was anything to go by. But even with his back to me, I can tell he's restless.

On edge.

A few clicks further along the agitated path he'd been on while I undressed in the car.

I slide to the side of the booth, preparing to go outside and rescue him from himself, when he pockets his cell and makes his way across the parking lot to come inside.

I watch his approach, noticing his anxiety dissipate the closer he gets.

He's comfortable around me.

I'm not sure if that's a good thing.

"I'm sorry I took so long," he says as he slides into the other side of the booth.

"That's okay." I push his opened wallet toward him, his license on display. "Sebastian Decker." I let his name curl around my tongue and play along with the life outlined in the identification, even though I'm well aware the men who surround me on a daily basis have fake IDs and equally fake personas. The thing is, I've never cared before. Not until now, when I itch to know Decker's truth. I crave it more than my own safety. "I never would've guessed you were a California baby."

"I wasn't. I only spent a few years there before I came to Portland." He ignores the wallet and grabs his cutlery to start attacking his meal. "Did you enjoy snooping?"

"I didn't snoop. You gave me your wallet to pay." I take a bite of toast and wait until he meets my gaze. "And I didn't think your identity was a secret."

"It's not." He pushes the wallet back toward me. "Have at it. I've got nothing to hide."

His transparency is comforting. I'm almost tempted to believe him.

"Was that Cole on the phone?"

He nods. "Yeah. I'm supposed to pass on the message that there's money in the office safe if you need it. Apparently, you should know where it is, along with the combination."

"Okay. Thank you." I didn't contemplate what goodies could be stashed in my father's office. But I should've. My head isn't screwed on, and it damn well needs to be. "Did you speak to Hunter, too?"

"No." He fills his mouth with a forkful of food, the momentary transparency suddenly clouded.

I can't fight the growing curiosity. "Who did you speak to on the second call?"

"A friend." He meets my gaze, the connection seeming forced. "I had to cancel some plans."

I'm guilty of overanalyzing, I know that, and now is no exception. I judge every aspect of his expression—the faux calm, the playful eye contact.

"You had to cancel plans with a friend from the other side of the parking lot?"

He forks more food, chews, and takes the time to contemplate his response. "It was a woman, Keira."

"Oh." My shock bubbles free. At least that explains why he didn't act on the lust I'd seen in his eyes last night. Of course he's got women clambering for a piece of him. The world wouldn't make sense if he didn't.

"Your girlfriend?" I hedge.

A slow smile spreads across his lips. A taunting grin. "A friend."

"A friend you sleep with." It's not a question. Intuition already has my mind made up.

"You're awfully inquisitive this morning, poppet."

I shrug, unwilling to deny the obvious. "We're spending a lot of time together. It's only natural we get to know each other, right?"

"If that's the case, let's talk about you for a while."

My pulse hikes at the diversion. I can't help the unease that strikes when people try to get to know me. But unease is better than jealousy. Especially when caused by someone who could be a wolf in sheep's clothing. "Okay. I can handle that."

The conversation eases into lighter territory as we eat. He asks me where I went to school—homeschooled. He attempts to guess my hobbies, my likes and dislikes.

Strangely enough, he isn't too far off the mark. He's noticed how I favor champagne over spirits, and my taste in music. He's paid me far more attention than I've paid him, and I thought I'd watched from the shadows quite well.

A lot of time passes while we talk, our plates being cleared long ago, when I finally realize the dark smudges under his eyes. He's practically the living dead, his lack of sleep becoming more obvious in his features.

"Come on, sugar tits." I slide from the booth and jerk my head toward the door. "Let's go."

"Sugar tits?" He snorts.

I grab our takeaway food from the table and lead the way outside into the morning sun. "You're always calling me stupid names. It's my turn now."

"I'd never call you sugar tits."

"How do you know you haven't already?"

"I'd remember." He unlocks the Porsche and stands at the hood, watching me as I walk to the passenger side.

"How?"

"Because I know, for a fact, I've never referenced your tits like that."

I snort out a laugh. "Because you're such a gentleman?"

"Fuck no." He stalks to the driver's door and stares at me over the roof of the car. "Because your tits are beyond description, and I'd never devalue them with an endearment like that."

My cheeks heat.

Seriously, I'm goddamn blushing at his weirdly flattering compliment. "Right..." I open my door, and he follows me as I slide inside. "I guess now is a good time to bring the conversation back to your girlfriend."

"I told you I don't have one, gummy bear." He starts the ignition and shoots me a glance. "But my imaginary girlfriend sounds like she'd be a point of contention if she existed."

I clear my throat. "I think we've gone too far down this garden path, don't you?"

He snickers. "Yeah, I guess we have."

He pulls from the parking lot and turns toward Westport.

"Aren't you going to get some new clothes first?"

"Fuck." His head flops forward in exhaustion before he focuses back on the road. "No. I can't. I'm seconds from crashing."

"I'll help. It won't take long."

"Seriously, I can't. I'm dead on my feet." He glances my way, his brows pinched as he takes me in. "Do you need to get something else before we head home?"

Yes, I do. I have to stop playing around in this fake, flirty dream-state and get my hands on a burner phone.

I need to determine my suspicions about last night's shooter, preferably before my brother does. But telling Sebastian will leave me open to scrutiny I'm not ready for.

"It's nothing that can't wait." The lie curdles in my belly.

I don't know how much time I have up my sleeve. It could be days. Hours. Any minute now, Cole could find out who's responsible, and I'm sure his reaction will only put our family in more danger.

"You sure?"

I nod despite my unease. I'll have to figure out another way. "Take us home, captain."

He shoots me a grin and drives back to the safe house.

Once we arrive, he ushers me inside through the garage entry, still playing the protector role as he carries my shopping bags inside.

"I'll only need a few hours. Wake me if you're worried about anything."

"I won't need to." I take my new clothes from him. "I'll be too busy sorting these out."

"Enjoy." He winks and strides toward the other end of the house, disappearing into one of the bedrooms.

For the next thirty minutes, I waste time taking tags off clothes, then trying them on. He bought me enough to fill a wardrobe. There are sun dresses, jeans, a cardigan, ballet flats, and that's without mentioning all the skimpy lace underwear.

He must have spent a fortune, and the debt doesn't sit well with me for numerous reasons.

For starters, he still confuses me. I can't pin him down, not his thoughts or his actions. He's too kind. Too protective. Too…

He's just too much for me to believe at the moment.

I walk into the laundry and check the cupboards for detergent, finding what I need stashed in an almost bare cupboard beside an unopened bottle of fabric softener. I shove my clothes into the washing machine, not really paying attention as I become distracted by dreamy thoughts that have no place in my life.

Sebastian isn't real.

He's another illusion.

A flawless actor.

But what if he wasn't?

I put the washing machine to work and can't help going in search of his resting place. The least I can do is wash his clothes. Well, that's the reason I give myself for tiptoeing down the hall in search of him.

I find him in the furthest room, in the same position he had on the sofa last night, his arm covering his face, his chest on display. I can't help wondering what lies beneath the cream sheet draped over his hips. Boxers? Briefs? Full-frontal nudity?

I creep forward, becoming hypnotized by the allure of the tattoos etched across muscled skin. The woman on his bicep tracks my movements, her tear-streaked cheeks squeezing at my chest.

The designs speak of damage. Heartache and pain. Brutality and beauty.

I step closer, to the side of the bed, and listen to his breathing. Deep in. Heavy out. Rhythmic. Calm. Controlled.

Even in sleep, he's fascinating. Despite the rumors and speculation, contrary to the secrets I know he keeps and the danger of the fake, fake, fake, his intrigue still holds me captive.

I tilt my head, taking in every inch of visible flesh. There are no defensive marks on his body. No wounds or scars. His skin is innocent apart from the ink defining his emotional injuries. But is his soul equally pristine?

It kills me not knowing.

He grunts, and I hold my breath. Freeze.

I wait for him to wake, but thankfully he doesn't stir.

Slowly, I inch back, lifting his clothes from the floor—the suit pants, shirt, and socks. I leave his jacket where it is, unwilling to test my novice washing skills on something that should probably be dry cleaned. Then I make my way back to the laundry and place his clothes with mine.

It seems intimate—his socks tangling with my underwear and dresses. It also seems wrong. Like I've taken this a step too far. And no, it's not just about the mingled clothing.

I'm faltering.

Sometimes this friendly, flirty act hasn't been an act at all.

It's real. There's truth in this charade.

I close the lid on the washing machine harder than I should and promise myself to leave the bitter taste of romance behind.

I change my focus to something safer—scavenging through each room of the house. I find new toothbrushes and paste in the main bathroom, and put them to use immediately. There's toilet paper, soap, deodorant, and tissues. Blankets are in the hallway cupboard. Fresh sheets and additional pillows, too.

I eat half a sandwich for lunch, but it's not because I'm hungry. I'm delaying the inevitable stroll through my father's office, which I can't put off any longer.

I drag my feet down the hall, toward the memories that are far from fond, and stop in the entry to rest my shoulder against the frame.

This room is the only part of the house untouched by renovations. No doubt it was from my father's demands. He wouldn't have wanted anyone in his personal space. He never did.

Even though he hasn't been here for a long time, his presence lingers close, grazing my skin with its rough texture. He used to sit behind that large oak desk, his frown tight, his annoyance at being interrupted always evident.

His tightly guarded love and affection only dissipated once my mother died. It's as if she took it with her—all his softness, all the care. But then again, he was never truly caring to begin with.

I suck in a deep breath and walk inside, taking in the stocked bookshelves, running my fingers over the criminal biographies and psychology texts.

I ignore the threat looming ahead and keep my gaze trained on the furniture, letting the memories creep into my mind as I approach the desk.

Cole was the only child welcomed in here. When he was little, I'm told he would sit and play in the corner while my father worked. He was always a part of the family business, even before he could contemplate what all the conversations meant.

He didn't need to become desensitized to the brutality because he grew up on the severity. It was always his world.

In contrast, Layla and I were drip fed. We didn't understand a lot of it until later. Much, much later when we had no choice but to come to terms with reality and make it work in our favor.

I reach the desk and place my hands on the shiny wood, needing the support before I raise my gaze to stare at the looming portrait of my mother.

My heart climbs into my throat as she peers down at me.

She's ethereal up there. Heavenly with her gentle smile and loving eyes. I'd do anything to get her back. Maybe then the family I was always sworn to honor wouldn't be riddled with lies and betrayal.

She could've kept us whole.

She could've protected me and my siblings.

"I miss you, Mom." I walk toward her, struggling to remain composed as I grab the heavy frame encasing her and take it off the wall. "I wish you were here."

I place her on the desk, her gaze tracking my every move as I turn and face the safe I've revealed. The dark gray metal looms before me, the keypad cold to the touch as I enter the family pin code.

The door releases, and I pull it wide to expose a stack of cash and a gun. But the item making my pulse pound is the phone laying almost camouflaged against the black velvet interior.

"Thank God."

I snatch at the device, sweet relief rushing through me as I turn it on and wait for the software to load. When the screen brightens, it shows a depleted battery with less than forty percent charge. But that's okay. I can make this work.

I pat my hand around the bottom of the safe, searching for a power cord that isn't there.

Damn it.

I'm determined to remain positive, even though forty percent won't get me far when I have to search to find the numbers I need. I keep scouring the office, checking my father's desk drawers and the empty filing cabinets. I even rush to the kitchen to scour there, too.

Nothing.

There's no way to charge the cell, which means my time is limited.

Shit.

I open an internet app and type in familiar businesses and contact names. I work frantically, jotting down notes and people of interest until the battery life is dwindled by half. I'm about to connect my first call when a ringtone breaks the silence, the sound coming from the far end of the house—Sebastian's phone.

Fucking hell.

I stare at the device in my palm, wanting and needing to use it, but I'm not willing to get caught making the necessary calls. I can't risk being overheard.

With a huff of frustration, I turn off the cell and place it back in the safe. It will have to stay there until later. Then I tiptoe down the hall toward Sebastian's room, the sound of his sleep-roughened voice tickling the hair at the back of my neck as I approach.

"What's up, Hunt?"

I stop before I reach his opened door and plaster myself against the wall, listening to the one-sided conversation.

"I was good until you woke me," he growls. "I haven't had a lick of sleep."

There's a pause. A rustle of sheets.

"Have you found any leads?" He sighs. "There's gotta be something. Who owned the car?"

I tilt my head, needing to hear every roughly mumbled word.

"Well, if it was stolen, who did they steal it from?" He huffs. "I need to get my ass back home to help you guys look. I can't do dick here when I don't have a computer."

My heart clenches. He wants to leave?

"She's good. Taking everything in stride."

My pulse increases at the change in topic, and I guess it's also from the softness in his voice when he talks about me. I want to understand him. I need to. Even more so now that he's pushing to go home.

"No. I slept on the sofa, asshole. I didn't go anywhere near her rocket pocket."

I press my lips tight and struggle not to laugh.

"Torian doesn't need to worry," he continues. "I'll protect her. As long as there's air in my lungs, Keira will be safe."

My laughter fades. Evaporates. I stare at the wall opposite me, trying not to become overwhelmed by his adamant conviction.

He's vowed to protect me.

He's vowed, even if his own life ends in the process.

Why?

The conversation continues, turning into snide banter as I become lost in the darkened forest of my thoughts.

I can't remember ever hearing someone speak about me like Sebastian just did. Yes, my brother values my safety. He demands it. But my protection in the eyes of my family is more of a strategy.

If we all stay safe, we all stay strong.

Not even my father has spoken about protecting me the way Sebastian has—*As long as there's air in my lungs.*

My chest tightens.

Again, why? I don't know if I should be comforted or concerned.

There's another rustle of sheets and the squeak of the bed frame. I panic, unsure if he's about to catch me spying.

I push from the wall and enter the doorway with a forced smile, but my expression doesn't matter. He doesn't turn to me. He sits on the edge of the mattress, hunched over, his head in his free hand, his bare feet on the carpet.

"She's here now. Do I need to pass on any messages?"

He tilts his head, meeting my gaze. His demeanor doesn't change. He barely acknowledges my presence. He still looks weary. Entirely drained. The lines of exhaustion in his features beg to be touched. Gently softened with the glide of a finger.

My palms tingle. My pulse increases as I move closer.

"Fuck off, Hunt." He lowers his focus to the floor, his tone still holding the lingering gravel of sleep. "I told you, I'm treating her like a queen. Unlike you, I know how to look after a woman."

He doesn't shift as I approach. There's not even a ripple of muscle. And there are so many muscles—back, arms, stomach, and God, his legs.

I bite my lower lip and wonder what it would be like to sink my teeth into him instead.

"Tell him I look forward to speaking to him," he drawls. "Call me if anything changes."

He lowers the cell, presses a button, then throws the device to the pillows before lifting his chin to look at me.

"Hey," he murmurs.

"Hey."

I itch to touch him.

"How's Hunter?"

He huffs out a tired breath. "Annoying, as always. But he said I might be able to take you home tomorrow if things stay quiet."

"Okay." I keep my emotions in check. Every single one of them. "Is he any closer to finding out who was responsible?"

"No, not yet."

I nod, becoming endeared by the lazy softness of him. With the raise of a hand, I could run my fingers through his hair. I could feel the heat of his skin. He's there. Right there in front of me.

He frowns. "What's going on, sweetness?"

I shrug and pretend those endearments don't hit me hard between the thighs. "You still look tired."

"It'll take a few minutes for me to wake up."

I want to be the one to wake him. I want him to trust me enough to remain tired and lethargic, too. It's a strange feeling, and I'm not sure if it's due to strategy or emotion, but it's there nonetheless, the delicious thrill curling its way around my belly.

I reach out, unable to hold back any longer, and run my fingers through the dark strands of his hair. It's my first deliberate touch. The connection made due to something other than fear or reliance. I'm sending a clear message, one I see reciprocated in his expression as he holds my gaze.

"Keira…" My name is a warning that brings a delicious thrill.

"Mmm?" I scrape my nails over his scalp.

He groans, the deep sound vibrating from his chest. "You're going to send me straight back to sleep if you keep doing that."

"Really?" I cock a brow. "That wasn't my intent."

His eyes narrow, and I hold my breath, waiting for him to call me out on my flirtation. Going down this road isn't a good idea. Not for either of us.

"What is your intent?" His gaze is sharp, reading me, trying to figure out what's going on in this messed up brain of mine.

"I don't know." I'm stuck between wants, needs, and responsibility. Morality, necessity, and danger. "But I should stop, shouldn't I?"

"Yeah." He leans his head into my touch. Not backing away. Not retreating.

I literally have him in the palm of my hand.

Power bleeds through me, coursing from the inside out. I tingle. Everywhere. My stomach flutters with the strength of a thousand butterflies. My skin burns.

"And what if I don't?" I ask. "What happens then?"

His nostrils flare, his hands tensing as they lay against the bed covers. "I think we're both well aware of what happens then, cupcake."

8

DECKER

Her nails against my skin... Her gentle, seductive words... Those eyes. *Fuck.* Those gorgeous innocent eyes.

All of it messes with my sleep-addled brain.

I'm hallucinating. Or worse, she's playing me, and I can't even decipher the deception.

"You were in here earlier." I hold her gaze, looking for a glimpse of betrayal. "Did you find what you were looking for?"

"Of course you were still awake." She chuckles, her nails still trekking a deliriously intense trail over my scalp. "I came in to get your clothes. I've already washed them. It shouldn't be long until they're dry."

I smother my surprise. "You didn't have to do that."

"I wanted to. It's the least I can do." She inches closer, her legs brushing my bent knees. "Not that I'm the best at laundry. But it's the thought that counts, right?"

I don't care about the clothes. I wouldn't give a shit if she shredded them to pieces. "Sure is."

With the way she's looking down at me, her appraisal delicate and pure, I'd settle for walking around half-naked until we have to go back to Portland.

"I also found the money Cole was talking about in the safe." Her nails rake deeper, the bite of pain an intoxicating thrill. "I can repay you for all the cash you've spent."

"I don't want your money."

"It's not my money. It's yours. I owe it to you."

"Fine," I mutter, no longer willing to be distracted from her touch. "We can sort it out later."

She smiles, slow and sweet. "You're still exhausted. Why don't you get some more sleep?"

Getting horizontal is the only thing on my mind, but sleep has nothing to do with it. I can feel her everywhere—in my blood, with each beat of my heart, in every twitch of my fingers.

I want her.

I fucking need her.

I stare into those eyes, trying to determine what's being hidden by her seduction. She entered my room for a reason, and I'm not delusional in thinking it was for sex. "What are you doing in here, Keira?"

Why is she touching me?

Tempting me.

Playing games.

She waits, taking her time to form the perfect answer. "I don't know."

"That's not like you," I keep my voice low. "You're not indecisive. You know exactly what you want. So, tell me. What are you hiding behind those ocean eyes?"

She sucks in a slow breath, her nails pausing at the back of my scalp. "I find it hard to read you. Usually, people aren't that difficult to understand. But with you I'm struggling."

My pulse rises, eager for her to continue the trail of those fingers. "Is that all this is? You're trying to read me?"

"No." She rakes her teeth over her lower lip. Sweet. Uncharacteristically virtuous. "It's more than that."

I'm struggling to read this situation myself. She's not usually like this. Close. Soft. Almost malleable. I'm seeing it more and more. First, in the shower last night, now here, in my room, while I'm half naked.

I'm tempted to grab her. To pull her close and drag her down to the mattress on top of me despite the stupidity. And there's so much fucking stupidity.

The temptation before me is enough to have me brushing aside the threat of her brother. Fuck Torian. Fuck her entire family. As long as I can fuck her, right?

Wrong.

Focus, asshole.

There's too much at stake to literally blow this now. "You should get out of here, hot stuff. You don't want this."

"I told myself the same thing." Her nails work in circles. "I keep telling myself. But here I am. And I can't seem to find the will to leave."

Her fingers move behind my ears, the scrape igniting a shiver that rushes through my chest. She treks her touch to my neck, along my jaw, and stops at my chin to nudge her knuckles into my skin and tilt my face closer to hers.

She's unpredictable.

Undeniable.

"Do you want me to fuck you, Keira?" I murmur. "Because that's what's going to happen if you don't get out of here."

She swallows and shakes her head. "No, I don't want to be fucked." She leans in and glides the delicate pad of her fingers over my growing stubble. "I want to get to know you. The kind Sebastian. The protective guy I glimpsed the first night we met."

"There's nothing kind about me, honey."

"Just charm and sarcasm, right?"

"Right."

"I don't believe you." She smiles, but the humor doesn't reach her eyes. "In fact, I think that's another reason why Cole doesn't trust you. You're too sweet. Too nice. You don't fit in."

That may have been the case years ago.

It sure as shit ain't now, though.

Life circumstances have made me the perfect player in this crime-riddled family. I'm here because I fit like a fucking glove.

I grab the back of her thighs and yank her forward, trapping her between my legs. She gasps, those baby blues flashing as she grabs my shoulders to stabilize herself.

"If you're looking for nice, you've come to the wrong guy." I grab the front of her blouse and tug her close. "If you want sweet, I'm not that guy either."

There's no room for weakness in this world. Not around her family and definitely not in the bedroom. If she expects a limp dick, she's got another thing coming.

"I just want you," she whispers. "The real you."

I tug her blouse harder, forcing her lips to mine. She whimpers as our mouths collide, and I keep tug, tug, tugging her forward until she climbs onto the bed. Onto me. She straddles my hips, her skirt creeping higher up her perfect thighs.

There's no sweetness. Not one fucking thing kind about our kiss.

I part her lips with my tongue, demanding entrance she allows too easily. There's no fight in her, only surrender. The sweetest fucking surrender I eagerly devour as she nestles on top of my crotch.

We're chest to chest, not a breath of space between us, and still she's not close enough.

I want more.

I need everything.

I shove my hand into her hair and fist the long strands. I palm her ass, guiding her into a gentle rock against my pulsing cock.

She's perfect. She's always been perfect. And having her nestled against my shaft, her lips on mine, is the sweetest fucking victory I've ever tasted.

But we're not supposed to be together.

Never were. Never should be.

If only the lust coursing between us didn't feel like divine fucking intervention brought us here.

She places her hand on my chest, lightly pushing, breaking the kiss. "Why did you save me last night?" Her panted breaths brush against my skin.

"Why?" I find it hard to concentrate when her kiss-darkened lips are a constant distraction. "Because I didn't want you to get hurt."

"But why? Why risk your life to save mine? You barely know me."

"I know you, Keira. It feels like I've known you for a long time."

She shakes her head, our noses brushing. "No, you don't. I barely know myself."

I don't buy it.

I can't.

"Then maybe it's a gut feeling I have," I hedge. "I've been infatuated with you since the first night we met. That doesn't happen for no reason."

"I'm sure there are many reasons—the thrill of the chase... The desire for something you're not supposed to have... Lust..."

I incline my head. "It could be all the above. And the list wouldn't be complete without noting how devastated I would've been to see your perfect body marked by a bullet hole." I slide my hands down her back and over her tailbone. "I've pictured a lot of things going into this ass of yours, but a bullet ain't one of them."

Her lips quirk and she rolls her eyes. "Always with the humor."

"That wasn't humor. That's the God's honest truth."

She chuckles and brushes her lips over mine. "You're not putting anything in my ass, Sebastian Decker."

"Maybe not today or tomorrow. But if we go down this path, I most definitely will, my sexy goddess."

She pulls back, scrutinizing me with a mix of concern and exhilaration. There's innocence, too.

"You've never let anyone play there before?" I squeeze her ass. Hard.

She sucks in a breath and shakes her head. "No."

My pulse pounds harder. The desire to claim her becomes a living, breathing thing inside my chest, demanding action. "You have no idea how fucking hard that makes me. I'm—"

My cell rings, cutting off my words and stealing the lust-filled mania.

Keira glances toward the pillows, then back at me, wrapping her hands around my neck, her fingers playing with the hair at my nape. "Ignore it."

"Why? Who is it?"

She leans in, reclaiming my mouth, deliberately trying to distract me.

I groan and struggle to fight temptation. "It's Cole, isn't it?"

She keeps kissing me as the trill continues.

Goddamn it.

"I can't ignore him." I pull back and meet her gaze. Unwanted clarity sinks into my veins, smothering the lust.

"Go on, then." She climbs from my lap and moves to stand beside the bed.

"Have I told you how much I despise your brother?" I snatch my cell from the pillow.

"No, but it's been implied more than once." She chuckles, yet the humor doesn't reach her eyes.

We both know this call will mark the end of whatever this thing is between us. Torian's perfect timing has stolen the buzz and brought too much fucking clarity.

"Don't go anywhere." I reach for her hand, only to have her back away.

"I'm not." But she does. She keeps retreating, placing more and more space between us.

Fuck Torian.

Fuck him and his horrible fucking timing.

I connect the call and raise the cell to my ear. "What's up?" I don't look away from her. I keep reading her expression, trying to figure out if the change in her features is from disappointment or something more.

"Nothing," he grates. "I just called for an update. Where are you?"

"Still at the safe house. In bed. Trying to get some fucking sleep."

"Cry me a river. How's Keira?"

"Good." Clearly annoyed that I answered this phone call if her pinched brows are anything to go by, but good nonetheless. "Want to talk to her?"

"She's with you?" he snarls.

"She's not riding my dick, if that's what you're asking." I keep holding her gaze, noting the narrowing of her eyes, the stiffening of her shoulders. "I was offering to go find her."

There's a pause, the seconds of silent contemplation ticking by.

"Torian, do you want me to get her or not?"

"Yes." His answer is a barely audible mutter. "But first I need to speak to you about the drive-by. Hunter seems to think you can help find the culprit."

"That depends on what you've already tried. I don't know the first thing about what's going on over there."

"Not a hell of a lot. We don't have any leads. I've got no idea who's targeting us, or why. Whoever is responsible is a coward who doesn't want to claim responsibility."

"It might not be cowardice. It could be strategic. Both incidents could even be a coincidence."

"First my uncle, now this. It's not a fucking coincidence."

No, it's not likely, but stranger things have happened. And when you have a list of enemies a mile long, it wouldn't be a stretch to get targeted by more than one at the same time. "What about the official investigation? Do you have access to that information?"

"Not currently."

His tone implies he can gain access, though. I assume all he'd have to do is grease a palm or two.

"If you think the same person is responsible," I continue, "there's more than likely going to be a point of conversion in those files. All I need to do is find it."

"What else would you need?"

"My laptop."

"Give me your home address, and I'll get someone to pick it up."

No. *Fuck no.* "I'll come and get it. I'll drive us back overnight—"

"Like hell you will. I don't want Keira in Portland yet."

"Then you need to get me a new computer because you sure as shit aren't going through my house."

He gives a derisive laugh. "Who says I haven't already?"

I say. I'd fucking know.

My home is a fortress, not necessarily impenetrable, but I get surveillance notifications whenever someone sets foot on the property. Even the neighbor's cat can't escape detection.

"Why don't you want me going through your house, Decker?" he taunts. "Have you got something to hide?"

"Apart from my granny panty fetish, not really. But you're a little too judgmental for my liking, so I think it's best to keep our relationship strictly professional."

"I'll get you a computer," Torian grates. "Is there anything else?"

"Let me think on it. I'll text you a list."

"Make it quick. I'll send Hunter out to see you tomorrow if nothing happens in the meantime."

"Yeah. Okay. Leave it with me."

"Have you found my sister yet?" he snips as if he anticipated her being at my side all along.

"Yeah. Hold on." I raise my attention and find her staring down at me. No, she's staring right through me, her eyes blank, lips parted, skin pale. "Keira?"

She blinks out of the trance and pastes on a smile. "Mmm?"

"Cole wants to speak to you." I cover the mouthpiece with my palm. "What's wrong?"

"Nothing." She approaches and holds out a hand for the device.

"You're not a good liar."

"I'm the best liar," she counters, grabbing the cell to raise it to her ear. "Cole?" She turns away from me, hiding her face from view.

She remains quiet for a while, taking short steps toward the door. She's trying to distance herself from me as she gets closer to her brother. I won't stand in her way. Not this time. In the future it might be a different story.

I push from the bed and stalk to the adjoining bathroom to rinse my face. The water doesn't help to clear my head, but it scrambles the words drifting from the next room for a few brief moments until I hear her muttered affirmations.

"Hmm... Okay... Yes... I understand."

I don't deliberately eavesdrop. Her answers are just there, the sound of her voice reaching my ears as if I was made to listen to nothing but her.

"I'm not sleeping with him," she murmurs.

I walked to the door, needing to see her, and cock my hip against the frame. She's sitting on the bed, her focus rising to meet mine.

"I don't like this," she says to him. "You're not involving me in decisions, and I need to know what's going on." She frowns, clenching her jaw. "Yes. I know. I'll speak to you soon."

She disconnects the call and cradles my phone in her hands.

I was right when I anticipated the moment between us ending. The lust I'd seen in her eyes is gone. There's no picking up where we left off.

"Your brother is an asshole," I grate.

She gives a half-hearted grin. "What did he do this time?"

"Every time you talk to him, your mood changes. I don't like the effect he has on you. I don't like the way he treats you."

She schools her expression, the emotion draining from her features to leave me staring at a blank slate. "You watch me too closely. Maybe you're seeing things that aren't even there."

"I'm seeing what's right in front of me, Keira. I'm seeing you."

She either doesn't like being seen or isn't used to being noticed. I'm not sure which.

"Do you want me to quit watching?" I push from the doorframe and pad into the room. "Would you prefer if I didn't see you at all?"

"I didn't say that."

There's still distance between us. More emotional than physical.

I want to get her back to the place we'd been before the phone call. To the hot and sweaty. To the imminent fucking.

I stop before her, our position switched from when she first entered the room. I stare down at her, reading a myriad of thoughts in those eyes. She still wants me, but not like she did before.

Cole has her questioning me. Again. And I fucking hate it.

"You regret kissing me," I mutter.

"I don't regret the kiss. I regret where we were when it happened."

"In the bedroom?" I know that's not the case, but my aim is to keep her talking. To keep elaborating.

"No." She shakes her head. "In a safe house. Surrounded by drama and obligation."

"Neither one of us were obligated to participate." I reach out, running the backs of my fingers down her cheek. "But I guess it's best if we forget how close we came to complicating things."

"Are you sure we haven't already?"

I stroke my knuckles over her smooth skin. Slow. Lazy. "It was just a kiss."

"Just a kiss?" Her brows rise. "It felt like more than that to me."

Good.

About fucking time.

"Either way, it's over." I drop my hand to my side.

She winces, and I leave her with the same sterility she's given me as I stalk to the head of the bed and reclaim my position on the mattress. I cross my legs at the ankles and put my hands behind my head, waiting for her to bite.

"Why?" she whispers.

It's always one inch forward, two yards back with her. I always have to be strategic.

She acts like a wild animal, tentatively taking the bites of nourishment I provide, then running for the hills when I try to get something in return.

All I want is her trust. That's it.

Nothing more. Nothing less.

For now, at least.

"Because if Cole found out, he'd think my interest in you was payback."

"Payback for what?" She turns to face me, cocking a bent knee onto the mattress.

She feeds on the crumbs I spread before her. She always devours the insight into my life. She craves my secrets. It's the only trick I have up my sleeve to reel her back in when she flees.

"A fucking lifetime of debt I'm supposed to owe him."

"Money?" she accuses.

I laugh, the sound caustic to my own ears. "No, not money. Cole demands more of me than that."

She climbs onto the bed and sits with her legs tucked beneath her. "Like what?"

"You name it." I shrug. "The debt changes depending on his mood."

"Why? What did you do?"

"I didn't do a damn thing." I don't restrain my anger. "Sarah took something from him. Something she deserved. And Hunter and I refused to let her take the fall."

Her expression doesn't falter. She continues to stare at me.

"You already know the story," I muse. The knowledge is written all over her face.

"Sarah told me a few things. My sister did, too. The rest I pulled together on my own." She shrugs. "But I didn't know about the debt. I didn't realize you were here against your will."

"I'm not *here* working for your brother because I enjoy his generous hospitality. But I'm *here*, in Westport, because I'd do anything to keep you safe."

She nods, the movement slow, lazy, and entirely unconvincing.

"You don't believe me."

She releases a huff of derision. "Actually, I do." She crawls toward the head of the bed and lies down beside me. "That's the problem."

"One of many." I shoot her a smirk. "If Cole finds out I took advantage of you, he'll make the drive-by look like a confetti toss."

"From what I recall, I'm the one who came to you, remember?"

"I'm not going to forget any time soon." Not about her lips or the fucking brilliant way she kept grinding against me. My dick is on a hair trigger at the mere memory. "But do you really think it matters? He's not going to give a shit who jumped who first. Either way, he's going to want to see me six feet under."

"Yet you kissed me anyway." She inches toward me, nestling into my side. "I've always said you have a death wish."

I wrap an arm around her and pull her close. "And I've always said you're nothing but trouble."

She chuckles. "I think you might be right."

She places a hand on my stomach and her cheek against my chest. We lie there, silent and comfortable, as my eyes grow heavy and her breathing deepens. I'm seconds away from slumber. I'm sure she is, too.

"Sebastian?" she murmurs.

"Yeah?"

"Is it crazy that despite what you just said, I still want to kiss you again?"

I close my eyes and grin at the ceiling. "No, sugar. It's not crazy. It just makes things fucking complicated, that's all."

9

DECKER

I wake up in a dark room, the furniture barely recognizable through the shadows. It takes a few seconds to blink away the lethargy and remember where I am—with Keira, in the safe house, secluded from the rest of the world.

I groan and reach my hands above my head to stretch my tired muscles. I expect to hear a sleepy response from her in return.

Nothing comes.

She's no longer curled into me.

"Keira?" I reach across her side of the mattress. It's empty. Cold.

I groan again, this time in annoyance. I'm losing my edge. I should've woken when she climbed out of my arms. Instead, I didn't even stir when she fled the room.

I throw back the covers and slide from the bed, grabbing my phone from between the pillows before I stalk for the hall. The house is dead. Not a breath of life to fill the emptiness.

"Keira?" My voice fractures the silence, my bare feet slapping against tile.

I enter the living room and find no sign of her. Everything is in its place—the cushions on the sofa, the television remote, the chairs at the dining table.

"Keira?" I speak louder, the edge of panic creeping into my tone.

I walk to the garage where Torian's Porsche lies in wait. Then I stalk to the laundry, and the bedrooms along the hall, my pulse increasing as I yank open doors and slam them shut again.

I make my way through every square inch of the house, not wanting to believe she's gone even though it's crystal fucking clear.

She's not here.

She's not anywhere.

Panic squeezes at my ribs, the pain building.

"*Keira?*" I hold my breath waiting for a reply.

Nothing.

Not a fucking thing.

"*Fuck.*" I run back to the bedroom to retrieve my gun from the nightstand drawer and struggle not to lose my shit.

She's gone. But how? Where?

I wouldn't have slept through someone breaking in. If she'd been attacked, I would've heard it.

Adrenaline rushes through my veins. Fear curdles in my gut.

Every inch of me pulses with the need to fight, yet I don't even know my opponent. "*Keira.*"

I sprint for the back door, needing to search the yard, and find the deadbolt already unlocked.

Ice-cold dread fills my reality. I picture her broken body. Bloodied. Bruised. Dead. It's all I can see. I can even smell it—the tainted scent of death and decay.

No.

I stumble outside, my finger poised to dial Hunter's number, when I hear something. The faintest voice. I swing around, aiming my gun on a bright glow in the back corner of the yard. A white light. The illumination of a phone.

"Keira?"

Murmured words hit my ears. The soft utterance of "I've gotta go" turning my blood to lava.

I run toward her, my weapon still drawn, my eyes squinted through the dim moonlight. "What the hell are you doing out here?" My harsh tone purges the toxic panic from my system. "Are you alone?"

She jerks back, the cell clutched in her left hand. "Yes. *Christ.* Lower the goddamn gun."

My throat threatens to close. My limbs fucking shake. My head is a pounding mess of turbulence, and I still can't come to grips with her standing before me. Whole. Entirely unscathed. And glaring back at me like *I'm* the one in the wrong.

I thought I'd lost her. I thought I'd never see her again.

"Where did you get the fucking phone?" I lower the gun and take a menacing step forward, my hands trembling with the need to grab her to make sure she's real.

"Calm down." She drops her arms to her sides. "I found it in my father's office."

"Calm down? *Calm the fuck down*? Do you know how scared I was when I couldn't find you?" My heartrate lessens, but the anger lives on. I can't get rid of it. "I've been searching the fucking house. I've been yelling your fucking name."

"I sat out in the sun all afternoon. I wanted some fresh air. Then night fell, and it was just as beaut—"

"I don't want to hear it." I grind my teeth, holding in another harsh reply that's destined only to prolong the argument. I count out the seconds. Fight against the rage. Then give up and grab the crook of her arm. "Get inside."

"Excuse me?" She yanks away from my hold. "Do you know who the hell you're talking to?"

I bark out a venomous laugh. "Oh, I know, princess. I *fucking know*. It's not like a Torian ever lets anyone forget."

Her face falls and slowly she pulls herself together, squaring her shoulders, lifting her chin. "You're overreacting."

"Tell that to the prick who put forty-seven bullets in the ceiling of your family's restaurant. No one has a clue who ordered the attack. For all you know, someone could've put a tracker on your brother's car. They could be watching you right now."

She glances over her shoulder, my words sinking in as she scans the darkness.

"It's a little late for that, don't you think?" I clench my fists. I grind my teeth. I do everything and anything to try to lessen my insanity. "It was a fucking stupid move, Keira. You should know better."

She shakes her head and stares at me in confusion. For long moments all I can hear are my panted exhales and her non-verbal judgement. It's loud. So fucking loud.

"Why are you being such an asshole?"

"I'm the asshole?" I point the barrel of the gun at my chest. "I'm the bad guy in this situation?" I throw my arms in the air and let them fall to my sides. "My apologies for caring. I'll try harder not to give a shit in the future."

I have two options—sling her over my shoulder and carry her stupid ass inside, or walk away and calm down in private.

Well, both aren't really options.

One is a desire, the other is a fucking necessity.

It takes all my effort to stalk toward the house and leave her standing on her own. But I'm not in a good enough place to walk inside without slamming the fucking door behind me.

Fuck this shit.

Fuck it.

I storm into the kitchen, slam my gun and phone onto the counter, and hunch over as I grip the cold marble in a white-knuckled grip.

I need to pull myself together. I'm overreacting. And I can't fucking deny the insanity isn't merely about Keira.

I've been here before.

I've drowned in fear.

I've suffocated under panic.

This is a warped kind of déjà vu I can't get away from quick enough. I struggle to fight the need to pummel my fist into something.

I'd fallen asleep beside her. I probably even had a smile on my face. Then I woke up in a nightmare I hadn't prepared for. I'd been on a fucking high. I'd been winning a battle I'd been losing for so damn long.

Then…this.

I shove from the counter and yank open the fridge to take out the lasagna we picked up from the diner. I remove the meal from the plastic container, reheat it, then drop my plate to clatter on the dining table as I take a seat and start feeding my face.

I ignore Keira. I pretend my focus isn't entirely on my peripheral vision which is stalking the darkness of the back yard as I fork food into my mouth. I don't even flinch as the sensor light illuminates the back deck.

She walks forward, coming to sit on a wooden lounge chair and wrapping herself in a blanket.

It's cold out there. I'd barely felt it when I stalked outside in my boxers, but her lithe body would be chilled all over. And now I feel fucking guilty because she's obviously keeping her distance from the asshole hiding out inside.

I fight the need to lecture her again. I ignore the rampant pulse demanding I go to her and purge all the bullshit clogging my veins.

I need to stay away. And I want to be close.

The opposing forces are pulling me apart.

It doesn't take long for her to come inside on her own, dragging the blanket behind her. Wordlessly, she demands all my attention even though I don't look at her. It's enough that I feel her through every beat of my pulse.

I anticipate every softly padded footstep as she approaches. I hear the delicate scrape of the blanket against the furniture as she draws near.

"I'm sorry I scared you." She stops beside me, within arm's reach.

I keep chewing, keep venting my frustration on the food I'm decimating between my teeth. It's not safe to talk. Not yet. There's still too much adrenaline eating up my marrow.

She drops the blanket to the floor and scoots onto the chair beside me, the smooth skin of her legs eating up my peripheral vision.

"When I came here with my family, I was never allowed outside," she speaks softly. "When I was little, we were given excuses—either the lawn had been sprayed with weed chemicals or a wild animal had been seen in the neighborhood. As we got older, the excuses stopped, but the rule of staying inside always remained. We were told it wasn't safe, no matter how many armed men guarded the property."

She sucks in a deep breath and lets it out slowly. "When I woke up this afternoon, the house felt different. For the first time since my mother died, this place didn't seem like a prison. And when I came into the living room and found it flowing with warmth and sunlight, I couldn't resist breaking my father's rules. I think I actually needed to break them to prove to myself I'm not living in his gilded cage anymore."

She's not helping to lower my pulse. I don't care what story she has or how many rules she wants to break.

I shove the last piece of lasagna in my mouth and push from the seat, dumping the dirty plate in the sink.

"You're going to ignore me now?"

I clutch the counter and bite back a snarl. "You accused me of being an asshole. I'm keeping my mouth shut to stop you from flinging the same insult again."

"You *were* being an asshole."

"And I'll continue to be if we keep talking about this bullshit. There's a fucking reason you weren't allowed outside, Keira."

"I know… Like I said, I'm sorry."

"You need to be more careful until we know who the enemy is." I turn to face her, one hand still clutching the kitchen counter. "Mistakes like that could get us both killed."

She winces, and the pained expression deals me another generous hand of guilt.

"I'm not trying to be an asshole," I grate. "I'm—"

"I don't have a problem with your honesty. It's how similar you sound to my father."

My muscles tense, every inch of me growing rigid. "I'll never be anything like him, or anyone else in your family, for that matter. The only thing we have in common is our need to keep you safe."

She nods, her eyes turning somber.

I want to go to her. To touch. To soothe. But that won't achieve a thing, not when my anger will turn to lust and we'll be fucking in the space of a heartbeat. "Who were you talking to on the phone?"

Her lips fall into a flat line, then seconds later she's beaming me a deceptive smile. "Friends. I wanted them to know I'm okay."

Anxiety and distraction—that's the story her features give. Lies and deceit. Fucking hell. For once, I wish I could believe her.

"Friends?" I approach, moving to stand beside her chair. "I bet they were happy to hear from you."

She nods. "Yeah, they were."

I hold out a hand. "Can I have a look at the phone?"

"Why?" Her brows knit tight. "It's almost out of battery."

"I won't take long." I keep my hand outstretched, waiting, scrutinizing.

She doesn't move, deliberately masking her expression, removing all sense of emotion to leave me staring at a blank slate. I have to remind myself she has every right not to trust me, but fuck, sometime soon I hope this tiresome game will end.

"Who were you really talking with?"

Her jaw tightens and she inches forward, about to slide from the chair.

"You weren't talking to friends, were you?" I growl.

More adrenaline floods my veins as I wonder what trouble is headed our way.

She's smarter than this.

I could've sworn she was.

She scowls. "You're being an asshole again."

"An asshole who fucking cares about you." I return her look of defiance. "You still don't get it. I'm here for you. No one but you. Why is it so hard to tell me the fucking truth?"

"Because trust doesn't come easily." She raises her voice. "I'm trying, Sebastian. I shared the story about my childhood, didn't I? I'm letting you in as fast as I can, but it takes time."

"We don't have time if you're using a traceable phone."

"It's not traceable." She scoots off the chair, her feet landing on the tile beside mine, bringing us chest to chest. "I may have done a few stupid things, but I'm not completely dense."

I keep my hands at my sides, instead of where they want to be—on her arms. I'm so fucking angry, but all I can see are those eyes. That mouth. The tongue that glides out to moisten her lower lip.

She tilts her face toward mine, the temptation getting closer.

"Did you tell anyone where we are?" I inch forward, her breath faintly brushing my skin.

"No."

My hips press into hers, my hardening cock pulsing between us. "Did you say anything that could risk your safety?"

She swallows and shakes her head. "No."

Damn it to hell. I've never been more caught up in a woman like this before. I've never been this intrigued. This enslaved.

I want her.

I need her.

I have to fucking have her.

"You should get out of here before I do something we both regret."

Her breath hitches, and those intense blue eyes flare. "Again, no."

10

DECKER

I steal her mouth. Her breath. Her kisses.

I force out my frustration with every swipe of my tongue. I let go of my anger through the tight grip of my fingers through her hair.

"Take off the blouse."

She obeys, her hands traveling down the buttons in a frantic rush. I shove the material off her shoulders, my mouth never leaving hers, and reach around her back to unclasp her bra. My palms scour her body, down her arms, along her waist, to the sides of her breasts.

I groan at the perfection and pull away to take in the sight.

"God, you drive me to madness." I slam my mouth back down on hers, my tongue delving deep.

She claws at my chest, her nails puncturing skin as I grab her waist and place her on the table. Her legs encircle my hips, her skirt rising to the apex of her thighs.

"I want you naked." I tug at her underwear, making her shuffle as I lower them over her ass.

I couldn't think before. I'd been delirious with rage. Now is no different, but the delirium is from lust. I still can't form a coherent thought. I'm lost in her. Mindless.

She grips the waistband of my boxers, shoving them down my thighs to pool on the floor. Our arms are everywhere. Touching. Tangling. Eager for more.

"There's no going back from this," I warn.

She nods, our noses brushing, lips touching.

"I mean it." I inch away to meet her gaze. "I won't be sated with a quick fuck. If this happens, you're mine and mine alone."

Her lips part on silent words.

"I won't share you, Keira. Not your heart or your mind." I reach a hand between us, sliding my fingers over her mound to her slit. She's wet. Slick and fucking dripping. "Not with anyone. I'll breathe nothing but you, and you'll know nothing but me in return. No other man will exist. Not to touch you. Or to rule over you. Not your uncle. Not your father. And certainly not your fucking brother."

I'm trying to scare her. Not a lot. Just enough to make her see what's at stake.

"Do you understand?" I growl. "When it comes to you, I'm not only after the physical. I'll demand more than you can imagine. More than you're probably willing to give."

This goes beyond sex. It's about claiming her. Bringing her to my side—to my team. Stealing her away from a callous brother and a monster of a father. She doesn't deserve the life they've given her. It's not right that she was born into the wrong family.

"Sebastian…" My name is a plea to stop.

"I want to save you, Keira." I grip her chin. "Please let me fucking save you."

Her lips press together as she blinks up at me with concern. She wants to pull away, and I can't let her. I won't.

"You don't need to live like this. You deserve better."

She shakes her head. "I don't."

"Bullshit."

"This is my world. I'm the same as my brother, Sebastian. I'm no different."

"You don't believe that." I stroke her cheek. Run my fingers along her jaw.

"I do." She brushes her lips over mine. "Maybe I'm worse."

"You're nothing like him." I run the pad of my thumb over her clit, making her jolt. "You never could be. I wouldn't be here if you were."

I press harder on her sex, making her eyes roll.

"Oh, God." She gasps. "That feels incredible."

"I can make it feel even better if you say yes to me, baby." I slide my fingertips through her slit, teasing her entrance. "Tell me you want this."

She doesn't rush to answer. She takes a moment, prolonging the anticipation that burns a hole through my chest.

"Yes." She shudders. "I want you."

A growl rumbles beneath my sternum. The victory is invigorating to the point of hysteria. She wiggles as I stroke her, a soft hum vibrating from her throat.

"Protection?" I ask.

She shakes her head. "If you're safe, we don't need it."

"You sure?" I'm clean. I trust she's the same. "I won't ask twice."

She cocks a brow. "And I won't repeat myself."

I smirk and grab her ass, yanking her to the edge of the table. There's no space between us. We're chest to chest. Hip to hip.

I grip my cock, running the head back and forth through her slickness. She groans, palming my cheek as she molds our mouths together.

There's never been a better feeling. Not physically. Not emotionally. I'm caught up in her. Tangled beyond the ability to get out unscathed.

This will change everything.

I squeeze my eyes shut, denying the thoughts any room in my mind, and thrust into her. Hard.

She squeals. I'm not convinced it's a pleasure-filled sound. She turns rigid. Her hands gripping my shoulders like a lifeline.

"Keira?" Her pussy is suctioned around me, squeezing my dick within an inch of its life. She's so damn wet. So fucking tight. "Are you okay?"

"It's been a while. That's all." She murmurs in my ear as she clings to my shoulders. "Go slow."

This woman is all about the torture. A leisurely pace is going to be hell to maintain. I grind into her. Retreating. Advancing. The gentle rhythm is a killer against my control.

In slow increments, she relaxes—her claws, her legs, her shoulders. She begins to roll her hips with my motions, undulating against me, kissing my neck, my jaw, my cheek.

She whimpers as I move. Moans.

God, the sound is fucking intoxicating.

"If you keep making noises like that, slow isn't going to be a possibility for much longer."

She chuckles. "Maybe slow is no longer necessary."

She's teasing me. Tormenting.

I don't care. I can't get enough.

She's beautiful. So fucking gorgeous. "What are you doing to me?"

I rock into her. Faster. Harder.

She doesn't protest, but those whimpers continue.

The room fills with the slush of her dripping pussy milking me. The slap of flesh on flesh. She curls a hand around my neck and arches her back, those perfect tits thrusting in my direction.

I lean over, sucking a nipple into my mouth. I nibble. I grate. I lap and lap and fucking lap until she's jolting with pleasure.

"This is crazy." Her thighs tighten. Her cunt grips like a vice. "I want to come."

"Then do it, gorgeous." I leave a trail of kisses along her chest, all the way to her neck, right below her ear. "Let go."

She shakes her head in refusal, and I know it has nothing to do with a lack of want. It's more than that. She can't let down her guard. She won't. Not entirely.

"Trust me," I demand. Or maybe I'm begging. Pleading. "Trust me enough to enjoy this."

She whimpers, not stopping the rhythmic undulation.

I can barely see straight. "Tell me what you need."

"You," she pants. "Just you."

She throws her head back, leaning one hand on the table, all that smooth, flawless skin on display from neck to pussy.

A masterpiece.

A siren.

The perfect weapon that's now in my very own arsenal. "You're a fucking dream, Keira. You're perfect. You're mine."

"Sebastian," she whimpers. "*Sebastian.*"

Her pussy contracts around my dick, her orgasm hitting with a feminine moan.

I match her rhythm, slamming home. My balls tighten. The base of my shaft, too. I'm done. It's all over.

I come, clinging to her, kissing her, my fingers gripping deep enough I'm probably leaving imperfections on her beautiful skin.

Nothing else in the world exists while I'm buried inside her. Not the past I'd kill to change. Or the temperamental present. And especially not the rocky future headed our way.

It's just us.

Me and her.

And I wish it could stay this way.

"I…" She sighs, her movements slowing. "I…"

"You?" I pull back, placing a kiss on her forehead as I retreat. "Can't finish a sentence because I rocked your fucking world?"

She grins and slumps forward, draping herself over me as she pants. "I don't know why I expected something other than cocky humor at a time like this."

I bury my face in her hair. "I'm always willing to give you all the cock-y you need."

She shoves me away, scoffing through her laughter. "I need to clean up."

I nod, but my hands refuse to give her up.

"Which means you're going to have to move so I can get to the bathroom." She beams up at me, her eyes dazzling, her face more mesmerizing than words can describe.

I keep nodding. "I will. Just not ready to let go of you yet."

The grin turns shy. Almost embarrassed.

Shit.

I'm done for.

She fucking owns me.

"You said it's been a while." I run my fingers through her hair, swiping the stray strands behind her ear as I give in to curiosity. "How long?"

Her cheeks darken with the cutest blush. "Long enough that I needed time to adjust."

Yeah, I got that part. I'd initially hurt her, and I feel like a fucking chump for doing it. But I'm still confused.

"What's with the abstinence?" It doesn't make sense. She's phenomenal. Fucking captivating. Men would fall to their knees to please her. "You don't like sex?"

She sobers, the glaze of lust blinking from her eyes. "It comes down to trust, Sebastian. Everything does." She places her palm on my chest, gently pushing. "Let me clean up."

I backtrack, allowing her to scoot from the table and hustle into the hall.

While she's gone, I pull on my boxers and knit my fingers behind the back of my head as reality jackhammers its way into my skull.

Tonight is a game changer.

This thing with Keira will affect my relationship with Hunter. With Torian. And I can't forget Anissa, too.

Everything will shift, and I can only hope it's for the best, because my life doesn't have room for any more wrong turns.

I go in search of the laundry to find my clothes, giving her a few minutes alone. I don't find anything in the washing machine, so I check the dryer, the warmth still radiating from the clothes as I pull out my dress shirt.

The material is clean, crisp, and scented like a florist as I shove my arm into the sleeve and proceed to get my hand stuck at the cuff.

"What the fuck?" I jab my arm harder, getting my fist through the restriction and deal with the same exact issue with the other arm.

She shrank my shirt.

My only fucking shirt.

The cuffs ride up my forearms, tight as sutures. And I can only clasp the bottom three buttons across my stomach.

"Perfect." I chuckle. "Fucking perfect."

Keira sure as shit wasn't joking about her lack of laundry skills.

I don't even bother grabbing my pants. They're a problem I'll have to deal with tomorrow. Instead, I scramble through the dryer and pull out something for her in the hopes the material will be just as tight and revealing.

I grab a see-through pair of panties and a silken slip of nightwear, then stalk my ass back down the hall.

When I don't find her in the living area, I divert my trek to the bathroom, and lean my shoulder against the door frame to find her facing the mirror, eyes blank, mouth lax.

She's off with the fairies, glancing into space.

"I'd stare too if I had a reflection like yours," I taunt.

Her lips quirk as she blinks to attention and turns to me. "Sure you would."

I hand over her clothes and watch as she slips them on too easily. Not a glimpse of fucking shrinkage in sight while she covers her tempting body. If anything, the black nightdress swims around her waist.

"What happened to your shirt?" She eyes me up and down.

"*You* happened." I raise my arms to show the new tight fit. "I can't even clasp the top buttons."

"You look…" She covers her mouth with a hand, but it doesn't hide the laughter in her eyes.

"Fucking ridiculous?" I ask.

She snickers. "Kinda."

"Hey. Not nice." I grab her, pulling her into me as I lean my ass against the vanity. "What are you still doing hiding in here, anyway?"

She drags her gaze from mine and plays with my collar. "Clearing my head."

"What are you thinking about this time?"

"Everything and nothing." Her fingers graze the front of my shirt, her palms splaying across my pecs. "I want to trust you, Sebastian."

Wants to—meaning she currently doesn't.

I clench my jaw, fighting frustration.

"Despite what you might think, it's not easy for me to let people in. But I'm trying." She sucks in a deep breath and lets it out in a sigh. "I haven't had sex in years. *Many* years."

I'd make a joke if it wasn't for her somber tone. An influx of trepidation fills the room, putting me on edge. "There's nothing wrong with that."

"And I've only been with two men. Three including you."

I nod and struggle not to shudder under the uncomfortable prickle at the back of my neck. "I appreciate you telling me."

"That's not all." Her eyes meet mine, the ocean blue stormy and turbulent. "My first sexual experience wasn't consensual."

11

DECKER

My blood turns to fire, the burn settling into my bones. "You were..."

She nods. "It's okay. You don't need to say it."

There's no fragility in her voice. She's strong. Far stronger than I am at hearing the admission.

I shake my head, still unable to finish my sentence. I can't even say the fucking word. All I can do is pull her closer and cling tight.

"Sebastian, really, it's all right." She hugs me back, comforting me when it should be the other way around. "It happened a long time ago."

"When?"

"I was a child. Barely fourteen."

"*Fuck.*" The curse comes out in a rasp.

How did I miss this information when I've dug into every aspect of her life?

"Don't worry. I've come to terms with my mistakes. I refuse to let it affect me anymore."

"*Your* mistakes?" I inch her away, holding her at arm's length so I can meet her gaze. "How could you blame yourself for something like this? You were a fucking kid."

"I wasn't to blame, no. But I wasn't free from fault either. I should've been more careful." She shrugs. "I trusted someone I didn't truly know."

The same way I've been pressuring her to trust me.

Jesus. Fuck.

Guilt pummels me.

I've pushed. I've manipulated. I've instigated a million different tactics to get what I want, not knowing what I was truly asking for.

"That's why I'm telling you," she adds. "Not because I want you to pity me. Or because I need to justify my short list of lovers. I want you to know why it's difficult for me to open up."

"I understand." I'm an asshole. The biggest fucking asshole. "You don't have to say another word."

I've made her feel obliged to cut herself open and bleed her secrets, all because I demanded her trust.

"Do you want to take this out into the living room?" I slide along the vanity, inching toward the door as I grab her hand. "Have you eaten dinner? You must be hungry. Let me warm up the lasagna for you."

She grips my fingers, pulling me back. "Please don't get weird on me now. I'm not fragile."

"I'm not being weird." I attempt a smile. "And I sure as hell know you're tough as nails."

"Good." She closes in, sauntering by me in her silken nightdress. "Because I'd have to tie you to a bed and torture you for days if you started treating me like glass."

"Wait. That bed torture thing is an option?" I fake the joke, hoping it comes out lighthearted when my chest weighs more than a ton.

She chuckles. "Not a good one, no."

"To you, maybe." I follow her into the hall and pretend I'm not holding onto her emotional baggage tighter than she is. I can't quit picturing what she must have gone through as I reheat her meal.

I struggle to stop the brutal thoughts of a violated young girl as she eats.

My sadistic imagination runs wild with the carnage, stretching out the silence into long uncomfortable minutes.

"You're going to have to suck it up," she mutters around a bite of lasagna. "Stop thinking about it."

"I'm not."

"*Sure.*" She rolls her eyes. "I'm not the person you're picturing, Sebastian. I haven't been weakened by it. I'm stronger."

I smile despite my doubts.

But she *is* strong.

I *do* know that.

I just hate that some low-life piece of shit forced her to be that way. "I wasn't thinking—"

"And I like sex," she adds.

I give her a half-hearted smile and lean forward, stretching my arm across the table to brush her wrist. "I learned that firsthand, remember?"

Her lips quirk. "I remember."

I try to hold onto the companionable mood. I cling and fucking cling, but it drifts, being snatched away by more tumultuous thoughts.

She sighs. "What part of this is eating away at you?"

I don't want to ask. Well, I do, but even a dumb fuck like me knows it's inappropriate.

"Just ask, Sebastian."

"Okay." I pull my arm back and sit up straight. "You said you've come to terms with what happened. And that you enjoy sex, but you've only slept with one other guy…"

Her actions don't really gel with the story.

"There are reasons for my abstinence."

"Do most of them revolve around having a psychotic brother?"

She presses her lips tight, containing a laugh. "No, not a lot. The lack of talent swimming in my family's social circles is actually the biggest reason. Then there's the risk of sleeping with someone who is only trying to get close to Cole. Along with the whole drug thing, too."

"Drug thing?"

She gives a barely-there nod. "Despite my family's association with narcotics, I don't approve of using, have never used myself, and I don't want to be with anyone who does."

"How do you know I don't fall into that category?"

She gives me a coy smile. "You're not the only one who's been paying attention."

I should be concerned. Instead, I'm turned on as all fuck. "You've been spying on me, sunshine?"

"I wouldn't call it that." She pushes from her chair and takes the dirty plate to the sink. "I've just noticed you. A lot."

I smirk.

"Don't turn all cocky on me again. I've been doing my due diligence, that's all."

I release an exaggerated sigh. "Don't treat you like glass. Don't get cocky. Don't shove my dick up your ass. Jeez, Keira, you're a bossy little thing."

Her cheeks darken, and those lips keep twitching in mirth. "I'm going to pretend you didn't say that." She walks around the kitchen and heads toward the sofa. "Come watch television with me for a while."

I oblige, even though the last thing I want to do is stare at anything other than her. The next few hours are spent on the corner of the sofa, her head on my lap, my hands in her hair, as a mindless sitcom plays on the screen.

This time I play with the delicate strands without remorse. I drag my fingers through the lengths and enjoy the calm. I could easily kid myself into believing I have a sweet and innocent woman resting against me. That we could have a normal life with a normal outlook for the future.

But none of that is true.

We're all guilty of a long list of crimes. And the reality of the situation is that I've just taken a giant leap closer to having a clip unloaded in my skull because I slept with Torian's sister.

Hopefully I'm lucky enough not to see the bullet coming.

"I know you're probably still wide awake after your fifteen-hour nap this afternoon," she sits up and turns to face me, "but I'm wrecked. I'm going to take a shower and crawl into bed. Where do you plan on sleeping?"

"On you." I grin. "Sorry, I meant in bed beside you."

"Sure you did." Her lips curve, but there's little flirtation, no excitement. The mood between us is different, her playful banter replaced with committed intent.

There's no backing out now.

We're a thing. Together. And yes, that's daunting as fuck.

"Let me tidy up out here, and I'll meet you in the bedroom soon." I kiss her temple, and we both push to our feet. "Enjoy the shower."

She pads away, leaving me to do a full interior check of the house. I test the windows and doors, making sure they're all secure before I start cleaning the dirty dishes in the sink.

What I should be doing is contacting Hunter, calling Anissa, even telling Torian about the cell Keira found to make sure it's untraceable. But I'm not ready to kill this buzz just yet.

External influences will only drag us apart. I need to establish myself in her life before that happens.

Once the kitchen is tidy, I turn off the television and the lights, take a quick detour to the main bathroom to brush my teeth, then make my way to the bedroom. The bedside lamp casts a dull glow over the master bed. The water echoes through the pipes in the adjoining bathroom.

I contemplate joining her, bathing her, salivating over the sight of her body covered in rivulets of water.

And I would, if only it didn't feel like I was pushing my luck.

I have to take this slow. Do things right. Make sure she's comfortable.

I pull back the bed covers and shuck my kiddie-sized shirt, letting it fall to the floor.

As the water turns off, I climb into bed and wait with my hands behind my head on the pillow until she walks back into the room.

"How was your shower?"

"Lonely." She gives me a pointed look before flicking off the lamp and crawling onto the other side of the mattress.

She nestles into me, allowing me to wrap my arm behind her neck as she huddles close, her warmth sinking under my skin. The smell of soap fills my lungs. The itch of temptation twitches through my fingers.

I haven't had beauty in my life for a long time. Only darkness. Hatred and punishment.

I've lived to work, and worked to live. Nothing else has mattered.

Until now.

Until Keira.

"Are you tired?" she asks.

"Not really. But it doesn't matter. I don't mind lying here with you."

She stretches her arm over my chest, her hand resting against my ribs. "What are we going to do tomorrow?"

I shrug. "Hunter will meet up with us at some point, and I need to get some clothes. If you're up to it, I think we should stock up on supplies so we don't have to leave the house again."

She nods. "Okay. That sounds good to me."

"Is there anything you want to do?"

She hugs me tighter. "I need to call Layla. But apart from that, I'm happy just to spend time with you. I want to get to know you better. I want to learn who you are."

No, she doesn't.

She only wants to get to know the playful Sebastian. The persona. If she knew the parts of me I keep hidden she wouldn't be nestled this close.

"Sebastian?"

"Mmm?"

"Thank you for everything today."

For someone entirely badass, she has a tendency of surprising me with her sweet as nectar routine. "Are you referring to me pulling a gun on you in the back yard? Or when I berated you in the car for stripping?"

She huffs out a barely audible chuckle. "I'm talking about you listening when I needed you to."

"You don't have to keep thanking me. You should know by now that I'd do anything for you."

"It's starting to sink in." She pauses, long enough to make me feel like a sappy chump. "I don't open up to many people. It was nice to have someone to confide in. It's as though a weight has been lifted."

My pulse increases.

This, right here, is everything I've been waiting for since the first night I set her in my sights. I've wanted to carry her burdens. To be her confidant.

"You feel like home, Sebastian," she whispers. "I've never felt this way before."

I tug her closer. "It's the same for me."

Her fingers circle over my skin, forming an intricate pattern. "There's something else I want you to know." Her tone holds the same ominous ring from our earlier conversation. This time I refuse to let it spook me.

"You can tell me anything."

She moves her hand to my chest, her palm resting directly above my heart. "You know how my father hasn't shown his face around here in a long time?"

"Yeah." I know. I've been watching. Everyone has. The cops, the Feds, the DEA. "He's somewhere in the Greek Islands contemplating retirement, right?"

"No."

The sharp denial piques my interest.

I focus on my breathing, making sure it doesn't betray my rampant curiosity. News on Luther Torian is a goldmine. One that many people would kill to gain access to. Including me. But unlike the secret she divulged earlier, I'm probably not the best person to spill Luther gossip to.

If she isn't comfortable with the way I taunt Cole, there's a high probability she won't appreciate me hating on her father.

"He's gone, Sebastian."

"Gone?" I let the question hang. "What does that mean?"

"He's not coming back. He's dead."

I don't react. I don't fucking move.

She isn't making any sense. A man like Luther Torian doesn't simply die without the whole world noticing.

Her world. *Our* world.

"Sebastian?"

Shit. "I don't know what to say."

I can't give her my sympathies, because I don't have any. Not a single one. Not for a sick motherfucker like her father. The feelings currently slamming into me aren't anything she would want to hear about.

She sits up, the delicate skin of her shoulders glowing red from the bedside clock. I'm not sure what the hell is going on, but something isn't right. She shouldn't be blurting out this information. Not to me. Not to anyone.

Not unless I've finally wormed my way under her beautiful skin.

"I appreciate you telling me." I reach out, strumming my fingers over her nightdress. "But why? Try as I might, you know I'm horrible at the whole comfort thing. I don't have the first clue of what to do when it comes to other people's grief."

"I don't need your comfort. I suppose I'm finally realizing that every moment we've shared has revolved around you being my warrior. It started the first night we met and hasn't stopped since. When I need protection, you're always the provider. And right now, I need that protection more than ever." She glances over her shoulder, her shadowed eyes meeting mine. "My family is in a really bad position, and Cole continues to keep me in the dark with all his plans. I don't know who else to count on."

Victory rushes through my veins. It's fucking pathetic at a time like this, but extracting her from the clutches of her psychotic family has always been my aim. At least as far as she's concerned.

And here she is doing it all on her own.

She's breaking the tight leash her brother chained around her neck.

She's starting to take drastic actions to revolt.

Praise the fucking Lord.

"Tell me what to do, Sebastian."

I fight to focus on her instead of the celebratory dance running riot in my head. "It's okay." I tug her down, reclaiming her at my side. "I'm not going to let anything happen to you. I'll keep you safe."

"Do you really believe that? Everything is such a mess at the moment."

"It will get better. I promise."

Problem is, it's going to get a whole lot worse before that rainbow beams down its pot of gold.

Once Luther's death is broadcasted to Torian's enemies, we're all in trouble—Hunter, Sarah, and every other son of a bitch who works for Cole.

There will be a fight for power. A struggle with anyone who wants to take over the multi-million-dollar drug trade in Oregon, along with the innumerable illegal contracts that bring a huge amount of money to the family.

We're all going to have a target on our backs.

A fucking bullseye.

"I don't want you to worry about it anymore, okay?" I raise my hand to her hair. "I'll figure something out. I always do."

She nods, nuzzling her nose against my ribs. "I appreciate you, Sebastian."

"I know." I also know she would quickly change her mind if she knew the extent of my gratitude over karma finally catching up with her old man.

I'd seriously dance a jig on that fucker's grave.

Luther Torian used to be a bastard of brutality. Even Hunter was scared of the son of a bitch who made Cole look like a saint.

And now he's gone. He slipped quietly into the afterlife while the rest of the world remains scared despite his lack of existence.

Well played, Torians. Well played.

I hold Keira close and battle the questions demanding to be answered. I need to know everything. Every fucking thing. When did it happen? How? Why? Who?

But I can't ask. Not yet. I need to wait until the dust settles. Drilling her for information will only make her uneasy.

So I'm forced to lie here in silence as her breathing descends into smooth, rhythmic inhales. Her head would be a heavy place right now, filled with death, destruction, and fear. Maybe it always has been. God knows how long she's had to bottle a lifetime worth of secrets.

And one day I'll have them all. It's only a matter of time and patience.

Patience—the one trait I've never had.

I roll away from her, needing distance to help lessen the hunger for answers. Only the space between us doesn't relieve my appetite. I throw back the covers, slide from bed, and grab my cell from the pocket of my shirt on the floor.

I don't know what to do.

Keeping this information bottled feels like I'm handling a nuclear bomb.

Hunter and Sarah are sitting ducks if I keep this news to myself. Anyone back in Portland is in the firing line. Including Layla and Stella. Doesn't Cole see that?

But I can't betray Keira. Not when she finally let me in. She gave me her body. Her secrets. Her trust.

Jesus Christ. I'm damned if I do and fucked sideways if I don't.

Decisions, decisions.

I clench my teeth hard enough for my jaw to ache and stalk for the back of the house. I have to do something. I can't stand here like a dumb fuck who's too chicken shit to make a decision.

I won't.

To hell with that.

I remove the cell case and retrieve the second sim hidden in the secret compartment. I shove out the back door, being hit with the cold night air as I start dialing.

I'm not going to tell anyone about Luther. Not yet. But I can take steps to make things right between me and Keira.

"Is everything okay?" Anissa says in greeting.

My pulse increases, building into a deep throb in my ears. I question what I'm about to say. What I'm about to do.

"Decker?"

"Yeah. I'm here." I wince and run a hand through my hair. "We're done, Niss. It's over."

"What? Why?" Her voice hardens. "What's going on?"

"I don't need you anymore. Don't contact me again."

12

DECKER

I'm staring at the sunrise creeping over the ceiling, hands behind my head, when Keira starts to stir beside me.

I didn't sleep, and it wasn't from lack of trying.

It took forever for me to come to terms with Luther's death. I didn't believe it. Didn't want to. Then things started to make perfect sense—the drive-by, Richard's assassination attempt, Cole's demand for Keira to be taken out of town.

Someone else already knows.

The power struggle has started.

Which is fucking great. I signed on for a lot of fucked up shit when I began working for this family, but helping them win a war isn't one of them.

Keira's long, labored breaths fade and she groans as she snuggles closer. "Good morning."

"Morning."

I need to convince her to leave. To walk the fuck away from this life. This family.

Her brother will be too busy keeping himself alive to track us down. At least to start off with. He'll have assholes from every direction attempting to kick him from his power pedestal. And by the time he does have the freedom to play hide-and-seek, we'll be long gone.

It will take months, if not years, to re-assert control, if he's even capable of holding onto it.

This is the perfect time to get out. To move on. To start over.

"How long have you been awake?" she murmurs. "You should've nudged me."

I couldn't have woken her even if I wanted to, probably not if my life depended on it. She'd been too peaceful. Too tempting with the covers below her waist, her cleavage gaping from her nightdress.

"I didn't sleep much. I guess I didn't need to after yesterday."

She sits and runs a hand through her hair. "You must be starving. Give me a few minutes to freshen up, then we can go out for breakfast."

"There's no rush. I still need to get ready and call Hunter to see when he's arriving."

I've been thinking about calling him ever since I figured out the truth. I should've gotten in contact hours ago. As soon as I heard the news of the century.

Instead, I lay here staring at the same spot on the ceiling, torturing myself at the thought of betraying Keira. It's too late now, though. My mind is made up. Telling Hunter isn't betrayal. It's taking the first step in an effort to keep her shielded from the violence about to rain down on us.

"I won't be long." She throws back the sheet and slides from the mattress, her seductive stride eating up the distance to the bathroom before she closes the door behind her.

I wait until the water turns on, then drag my ass from bed. Like last night, I walk into the back yard and connect the call in privacy.

"Now's not a great time," he greets.

"It's not great here either. But what I'm going to tell you can't wait."

"*Jesus*. Please tell me you didn't sleep with her."

"That's not why I'm calling."

"But you're not denying it either," he snarls. "*Fuck*, Deck. One day you're going to have to stop being the wild card and actually take responsibility. I swear to God, Torian will bend you over and fuck you so hard you're tasting dick for months."

"As delightful as that sounds, it's not why I called." I pinch the bridge of my nose and close my eyes. Maybe if I squeeze hard enough I'll have an aneurism and not have to deal with this shit. "Like I said, I've got news."

There's a pause, the briefest silent acknowledgement of the seriousness I'm about to share. "Go on, then," he grates. "Tell me."

"Keira and I got to talking last night, and she dropped a bomb I wasn't expecting. It's big, Hunt. Real big."

"Do you want me to play Twenty-Questions, or are you planning on spitting it the fuck out?"

I drop my arm to my side and stare across the open expanse of the yard. There's no life out here. No vibrancy. No feeling.

It could be considered beautiful with its sculpted statues and manicured gardens, but the property is devoid of warmth. Just like I've come to expect from anything the Torian name touches. Anything except the gorgeous woman waiting inside. "Luther is dead."

Silence.

Hunter doesn't respond.

Not in seconds. Not for long moments. Not even when I lower the cell to make sure the call is still connected. "Hunt?"

"I heard," he growls. "And Keira just gave you this information out of the blue?"

"Yeah. She's starting to trust me."

"Where are you?"

"Still at the safe house. We're about to head out for a bite to eat, but I'm not sure what the fuck I should do about this. You realize what it means, right? We're caught in the middle of a power struggle."

"Who have you told?"

"Nobody."

There's another pause. The silence of thick, punishing contemplation. "We can't discuss this over the phone. I'm coming to you. I'll call when I'm close."

"You're still bringing a laptop, right?"

"Yeah." There's a rustle in the background. A jangle of keys. "I picked one up yesterday."

"You didn't happen to buy a phone charger, too, did you? My cell is going to die if it doesn't get some juice soon."

"I'll bring one of my spares."

The line disconnects, leaving me with more punishing silence.

Remorse hits harder than I anticipate. And I'd expected that fucker to be punishing.

I don't know how I'm supposed to face Keira now. Do I tell her? Should I explain?

No, I can't.

She's the type to run first and ask questions later, which will only put her in more danger.

My betrayal has to remain a secret for now.

Hunter will keep his mouth shut. I don't doubt him in the slightest. And he *had* to be informed. I couldn't live with his blood on my hands. There's enough of that shit tainting my soul already.

The swish of an opening door hits my ears, and I turn to find Keira stepping onto the deck. The guilt increases with the soft smile she gives me. There's trust in those eyes, the gentle affection clawing me from the inside out.

Fuck.

She's a fucking sight, too. Her hair is braided over one shoulder. A white cardigan hangs loose on her shoulders, partially covering the top of her light blue sundress. The style is feminine. Laid back. Not a hint of filthy rich, drug-lord's daughter in sight.

"Are you ready to leave?" she asks.

"Let me take a quick shower." I head toward her, drowning in the need to drag her to some place far, far away from this bullshit. "Hunter is on his way. Hopefully he'll meet us in town while we're still eating breakfast. I don't want to hang around in public any longer than necessary."

"We can always bring the food back to the house. He could meet us here."

"No. He doesn't need to know the location of this place."

She frowns. "You'd keep that from him?"

"It's not my secret to tell." The words burn my throat. I'm pretending my white-knight armor is shining when it's tarnished as fuck.

Her eyes turn soft as she blinks back at me in unwarranted appreciation. "You're a good man, Sebastian."

Jesus.

I scoff. "Far from it, angel."

Maybe I was at one time. Back when life was simple and contracted killings were in the movies, not my weekly schedule.

"It's either jokes or deflected compliments," she muses, inching toward me to wrap her arms around my waist. "Is that a technique to hide the real you?"

I fight to keep my muscles relaxed. "Yeah. I guess." I kiss her forehead. "Deep down, I'm a sensitive guy who loves to write poetry and rescue injured wildlife."

She arches a brow.

"And knitting," I add. "I love knitting."

She nudges me in the ribs. "Great. More jokes."

I lean in and kiss her lips, tasting the mint from her toothpaste. "I'll never stop joking around when the end result is one of your smiles."

Her brow peaks higher. "Another joke?"

"No. That one was cheesy honesty." I grab her around the waist and carry her into the house, leading her to the sofa. "What's the obsession with getting in my head?"

"There's no obsession. Just curiosity."

I collapse onto the cushions and drag her down with me. I could get through a few more hours without food if it meant keeping her here. On top of me. Skin to skin. "Well, I'm curious about getting your clothes off."

She straddles my waist and runs her hands around my neck. "You know I'm starving, right?"

"I've got something that can sate your appetite."

Her lips tweak. "Your dick isn't going to stop my stomach from grumbling."

I lean into her, brushing the growing stubble along my jaw against her cheek. "Obviously, you haven't been introduced to oral."

She breaks out in a fit of laughter—eyes bright, cheeks high, skin flushed.

Pure beauty.

"I haven't been introduced, Sebastian." She draws out my name, that sultry mouth working around the syllables like a fucking wet dream. "But I know what it is."

I can picture her tongue grazing along my shaft, her saliva covering me from base to tip. I raise a hand and brush my thumb over her lower lip, tracing a path down her throat.

She will gag as she gets used to my size, her eyes will water. Her mouth, too.

I'll fucking love it.

"You're serious." She holds my gaze, all that bubbling humor vanishing as lust takes its place. "You want me to do this now?"

"No." I need to shower. Brush my teeth. Gain restraint. "I'll hold onto that fantasy for a little while longer."

I scoop her up and drop her onto the far side of the sofa, her back falling against the cushioned arm rest. "Take off your underwear."

"*What?*" She scrambles to sit up straight. "You just said—"

"I said I don't want *you* to do anything. I didn't say anything about me." I lift the bottom of her dress, taking in the sight of white lace panties. "Get them off."

"Sebastian…" Her eyes are frantic. A mix of anxious anticipation and nervous excitement.

"*Off*, Keira." Fuck it. I grab the waistband and tug them down myself. "I'm fucking starving."

I want her. The taste. The touch. The sound.

I'm dying to get between her legs.

I'm dying for the distraction, too.

She shimmies as I tug at the material, dragging them along her calves, over her ankles, to drop them to the floor.

"Spread your legs," I demand.

Her shoulders straighten. She grows rigid.

Shit. I need to go slow with her. Be fucking gentle.

I place my hands on her knees, exposing her slowly. "I'm going to taste you, Keira."

"I already got that part," she teases. "I just want to know what's taking so long."

I smirk, giving her a game-on look she won't forget in a while. I sink my face between those legs, wrapping my arms around her thighs to position her right where I need her.

She smells of soap, the fucking purity smothering the scent of arousal. But I'll make sure that doesn't last long.

I rake my teeth across her mound, grazing sensitive skin as I hold her gaze.

"I'm not going to break," she whispers.

"You wouldn't say that if you knew what I'm capable of."

My first lick is light. Gentle. I flick her clit and revel in the jolt of her hips. It's a prelude. The appetizer. I keep swiping the bundle of nerves. Back and forth. Slow and patient.

Her jolts continue, settling into a roll of hips to meet every brush of tongue, as she slides a hand through my hair. It's a request. A silent demand for more.

I don't need to be told twice.

I inch lower, my dick jolting as I part her folds and taste her arousal. There's nothing but sweet bliss. Pure euphoria.

She grips my hair, fucking wrenches it between tight fingers.

I lick harder, faster, delving deep.

She whimpers. Moans. The noise fills my ears and sinks into my soul.

I unwrap an arm from around her thigh and cup her ass, using my thumb to penetrate her. The sound of her pleasure increases. Everything does. The need. The rush.

I pulse, building a punishing rhythm as I suck on her clit. I crave her pleasure, if only to sate my guilt. I can't stand the thought of her hating me.

"Deeper," she demands, her thighs tightening around my head.

I close my eyes and fight against blowing in my pants like a fucking kid.

"Oh, God." Her back arches and that tight pussy gets even tighter as she milks my thumb with her orgasm.

Her juices cover my face, and those soft muffled moans continue to torment me in the sweetest possible way until her orgasm diminishes and she's left sated and lax.

I'm no longer going to question how the daughter of someone heinous can be so fucking perfect. She just is. That's all there is to it. I can't get her out of my head. I never could. And I'm not going to fight it anymore.

I retreat and wipe a hand over my mouth.

Her thighs are red from the graze of my stubble. Her pussy glistens, fucking beckoning me.

"Sebastian…" She stares at me, her breathing rushed, her eyes playful. "That was…"

"The start of an obsession," I finish for her. "A day won't go by without me wanting to repeat that."

She lowers her dress, covering her brilliance. "You'll have to teach me how to return the favor."

My dick jolts, the imminent orgasm still threatening to blow. "One day." When she's ready and I've got a lick of restraint to stop me from choking her with my dick. "I'm going to take a shower."

"Do you want me to join you?"

"Not today, jelly bean."

She winces, alerting me to the unintentional rejection.

I stand, my cock poking proud from beneath my boxers. "Babe, I'm so fucking turned on I'm seconds from blowing."

"And?"

"And it's not going to be pretty. If I had you right now, it would be hard and fast and rough. You don't want that. Not yet." I reach out, brushing my fingers over her flushed cheek. "I'll be back soon."

She nods. "Okay."

ONE JERK-OFF SHOWER SESSION LATER, I'm dressed in my kiddie shirt and driving out of the property gates.

Everything is different from yesterday—my relationship with Keira, my plans for the future, my perspective.

Even my concentration is shot to shit.

I turn from one street to the next, picturing the spread thighs of the woman beside me instead of focusing on traffic. She's all I see. All I feel.

It's a problem. A fucking great problem.

I can't remember ever being this attracted to a woman. This infatuated. It's exhilarating. And disturbing. I guess I should put a lid on it for a while.

I should…If only I knew how.

This thing between us is an avalanche. The freefall. The build of power. The upcoming carnage.

I let out a deep breath and flick a glance to the rear-view mirror. A white car follows us. One I hadn't noticed approaching. Great, I've driven miles without conscious thought of anything but the woman beside me.

I'm getting sloppy. Fucking careless.

I force my attention back on the road and pull myself out of auto-pilot. Today is going to be filled with tough decisions. This meeting with Hunt needs my full attention. I have to focus.

I check the rear-view again, this time finding the white car riding my ass. I narrow my gaze, my stomach hollowing as the vehicle becomes familiar. An even more familiar woman sits behind the wheel.

Fuck.

Anissa found me.

Even worse is the thought of how she did it. Did she hack my cell? Or was she always watching?

Keira touches my arm, and I jolt from the unexpected connection.

"Sebastian?" Her brows pinch in concern. "What's wrong?"

"Nothing." I bite back the growl in my voice and return my attention to the mirror. "Just concentrating on the road, that's all."

I flick my indicator, preparing to turn off the highway and into the small town. My tail follows, inching the nose of her car closer to my bumper.

She wants to cause trouble. *Big* trouble. And I'm not sure I know how to stop her.

"Is someone following us?" Keira swivels in her seat to look out the back window. "Answer me."

I grind my molars. "Yeah. We've got a tail."

A tail we won't outrun. Not easily. Or without attracting attention. I'm going to have to talk to Anissa. She's not going to leave me alone until I face her.

"What do we do? Can we outrun them?"

"No. It's okay. I know who it is."

She keeps her focus out the back window. "It's a woman."

"Yes," I mutter the confirmation.

"Is she a friend of yours?"

"No."

"Then how did she know where to find us?" Anger creeps into her voice.

"I don't fucking know, which obviously isn't good. I have to pull over." I straddle my attention between the road in front and the bitch behind as I drive into the main street of town. "I need you to stay in the car. Don't get out. Don't even look through the back window. It's best if you remain out of sight, keep your belt on, and be ready for us to leave as soon as I get back."

"Am I in danger?"

Good question. "I don't fucking know." I hold her gaze for long seconds, then return my attention to the road. "I'm not going to let anything happen to you. Just follow my instructions and you'll be fine."

I indicate. Anissa copies.

I pull to the curb. She follows.

I cut the engine, unfasten my belt, and open the door as my pulse pounds in my ears. "Remember what I said. Don't move. I need you to lay low until I get back."

She nods. "I will."

I slide from my seat, but Keira reaches across the car interior and grabs my wrist.

"Wait," she pleads. "Please be careful." Her eyes implore me more than her words, the glassy blue depths hitting me in the feels.

I fake a grin. "You know my motto—it's better to be safe than stupid."

She winces. "Don't joke at a time like this. I'm worried about you."

It's not me she needs to worry about. "I've got this under control."

I pat her hand then climb from the car, all humor vanishing as I shut the door and turn to find Anissa leaning against the side of the white SUV.

I storm ahead, waiting until I reach her hood before I snarl, "What the fuck are you doing here?"

She smiles, the curve of lips sinister. "Hey, lover. How are you?"

I scan the sidewalk, not appreciating the audience. "Why are you here?"

She crosses her feet at the ankles, her arms over her chest. "Your call was out of character. I was hoping you woke up and realized you made a mistake."

"There's no mistake. I'm done. You need to back off."

Her smile doesn't falter. "That's not how this works." She pushes from the car and closes the space between us.

I'm tempted to back away. Only because I don't want her close enough to sink her nails in. But I refuse to retreat.

"You promised to stick by me," she purrs. "You can't leave now."

I don't mistake her statement for anything other than the threat it is.

"We had a mutually beneficial agreement." I measure my tone, refusing to lose my cool. "And your part of the deal is no longer relevant. So, like I said, we're done."

"We're not done until I say we are." She leans close, whispering in my ear. "I call the shots here."

I turn my head to face her, those venomous lips bare inches from mine. "Like hell you do."

"Oh, come on. Don't be like that. Where's that sweet Decker I know? The one who always used to say my name with reverence."

My nostrils flare. "Quit playing games."

"I'm not." Her smile widens, a tiny dimple peeking out. "But make a woman happy and say my name one last time."

I glare. "Not gonna happen."

"Say it or I go over there and introduce myself to your travel companion."

Fucking bitch.

I want to hurt her. Strangle her. If I was Torian, she'd already be dead.

"Anissa," I grate.

She chuckles. "You've gotta say all of it, sweetie. My first name. My last. And don't forget the title."

My nostrils flare as I clench my fists. "You're fucking with the wrong person."

"Funny, I was thinking the same thing about you." Her smile tightens and her eyes blaze in fury. "Now address me properly."

My pulse pounds beneath tightening ribs as I utter the words that make my stomach turn. "Special Agent Anissa Fox."

Her flirty smile falls back into place. "Good boy. Now make sure you keep repeating my name in your head every time you think about backing out on our fucking agreement."

"There is no agreement," I snarl.

"Because you think Luther is dead, right? That's the only assumption I could make from your 'I don't need you anymore' comment."

I fight a fucking war inside myself, unsure whether to answer her or make more threats of my own. "It doesn't matter. I'm out."

"Oh, honey, it matters. You know it does." She inches closer, narrowing her gaze to scrutinize my expression. "Where did you get the information?"

I press my lips into a tight line, scowling out my refusal to answer.

"I thought you were smarter than that, Deck. I know very few people who would cut ties before determining fact from fiction."

"As far as I'm concerned, the news is concrete."

She raises her brows. "Yet in the last five hours, not one of my sources could confirm a damn thing."

My palms sweat with the need to do something, *anything*, to shut her up.

"You wanted to take them down," she snips. "*You* came to me for help, remember?"

"And now I've got what I wanted. Richard is out. Luther is dead. The fairytale lives on. Just as soon as you get out of my fucking face."

She narrows her eyes. "They've messed with you, haven't they? She got in your head. She worked you over."

"No." I lean close, unable to control my breathing. I'm livid. Furious. "*I worked her* over. How else do you think I got the fucking information, you conniving bitch?"

"You think this is me being a bitch?" She snickers. "Sweetie, I'm only doing my job, and to be honest, I'm just getting started."

She pulls a cell from her jeans pocket and taps the screen, opening icons and folders. "If you bail on me and Luther isn't dead, I'll make sure not only you get named as an informant, but your best buddy, too."

She holds up the device, showing me a picture of Hunter beside a guy I don't recognize. She flicks through more images, displaying different locations with various people, all of them interacting with Hunt in some way.

"The men in these pictures are undercover agents," she explains. "I spent months setting up these scenarios, ensuring we had the necessary leverage to tie him to us. All it took was a bump to the shoulder, a dropped piece of paper or a wallet. Anything at all, really, to make the shot look like an exchange of information."

I stare at the collection, my heart pounding, my blood boiling. The images are damning. Cole won't waste a second contemplating their legitimacy.

"I'm sorry, Decker, but you're too valuable to simply walk away. If you leave, I'll make sure your friend gets exposed as a traitor." She keeps flicking the screen, moving to similar pictures with Sarah. "His fiancée, too."

I see red, my vision narrowing into spiteful slits. "You're going to get innocent people killed."

"Innocent? Really? That's a stretch."

I react without thought, grabbing my gun from my waistband and stepping close as I ram it under her chin.

I shouldn't be surprised she doesn't respond in shock or fear. Instead, she keeps that smile in place like the fucking psychotic bitch I know her to be.

She's sweet to smell. Sweet to touch. And I know from experience, she's sweet to taste, too. But everything else about this woman is bitter. Tainted. Evil. She does a lot of wrong things for a person who is supposed to be on the right side of the law.

"Don't mess with me." I get in her face. "What you're doing is illegal. You can't fucking manipulate me."

"I already have." She maintains her grin. If anything, she appears empowered by my weapon.

It sickening.

"*Sebastian.*"

I wince at the sound of Keira's voice and the subsequent slam of the Porsche door.

"Let her go."

"Yeah, Decker," Anissa taunts in a whisper. "Let me go."

I step away, shoving my gun into the back of my pants. "Get back in the car, Keira."

Her footsteps rush up behind me, stopping a few feet away. "What are you doing?"

"Get back in the fucking car," I growl and glance over my shoulder to give her a warning look.

Her eyes are wild with pain and confusion. She doesn't understand what's going on, and that's a good thing. I can talk myself out of an ignorant situation. What I can't do is manipulate her once she knows the truth.

"*The car,*" I snap. "*Get back in it.*"

Her lips part on silent words.

"Yeah, bitch," Anissa adds. "This is none of your fucking business."

Keira balks, clearly daunted by a woman who would reject help when being threatened by a gun. And for the first time, I'm thankful for the agent's input. She's maintaining my cover, if only a little.

Keira steps back, once, twice. She meets my eyes, but the confusion doesn't leave her gaze. She's panicked. Traumatized.

I raise my hands in surrender. "Give me a few minutes and I'll explain."

She retreats another step and another, not acknowledging me.

Fuck. I can't hold her hand through this while Anissa watches. I need to attack the closest threat before I can set things right.

I turn back to the witch and lower my arms to my side. "Leave."

There are more footfalls. The pace fast and frantic. The sound becomes distant. Keira is running. Fleeing. It takes every ounce of my strength not to sprint after her and show Anissa just how much the enemy means to me.

"You're sleeping with her?" she asks. "Isn't that kinda messed up given your situation?"

It is. It fucking is. But I also know Keira isn't the enemy.

It's her father.

Her uncle.

And maybe Cole, too.

I know she's innocent of their crimes.

"I don't need my morality questioned by someone like you." Besides, the situation is too fucking complicated to explain. It was never supposed to go this far.

I wanted to watch their family from the outside. From my safe position working surveillance for Hunter. But then Sarah came along.

It wasn't in the plan to get sucked into the inner circles. I didn't anticipate getting forced to work for them.

"Well, then, what's it going to be? Are you going to stick to our arrangement, or do I leak these photos of your buddies?"

Keira's retreating steps haunt me.

I can't stand it.

"If you haven't blown my cover, I'll keep helping you," I seethe. "But you need to give me some fucking space so I can keep working this angle with her."

"I'll do one better." She winks. "I'll do you a favor."

I frown as she straightens to full height and glances over my shoulder in the direction Keira fled. Her face crumples, turning into an emotional montage.

I can't resist my curiosity. I glance behind me to see Keira staring at us from the building at the corner of the street.

She looks devastated. Betrayed. It takes all my determination to turn back to Anissa, only to see her palm rushing toward my face to slap me hard across the cheek.

"*Motherfucker*." I pull away from her. "What the fuck was that for?"

She backtracks, one tormented slide after another. "*You told me you loved me,*" she screams. "*You fucking cheating bastard.*"

"Jesus Christ," I mutter.

She's still playing the relationship angle, giving me an out that feels too fucking complicated for my current level of exhaustion.

"Thanks. This is very fucking helpful."

"*I hate you.*" She stumbles toward her car. "*You're dead to me.*"

"That's enough," I hiss. She's attracting too much attention.

She drops the act as she pulls her car door wide. "If I were you, I'd start chasing your girl before she has a chance to hide."

"Fuck you," I grate.

"Jealousy is better than the truth, Decker." She climbs into the vehicle and closes the door behind her, giving me one last wink as she starts the ignition.

13

KEIRA

I run along the side of the brick building, hoping I'll find an alley to lead me far from here.

I need to think.

Think. Think. Think.

What am I doing? What have I done?

Everything had been going so well, then that woman appeared and knocked me off my axis.

"*Keira,*" he shouts, his heavy footfalls sounding in the distance. "Please stop."

I cringe.

Goddamn it. What have I gotten myself into? Cole is going to kill me.

"Keira…" He's closing in on me. Eating up the distance. "Let me explain."

"Don't." I slow my stride to a power walk and continue to the back of the building. I don't find the getaway I need. There's only a head-high wire fence with no gate.

There's no escaping this. No escaping him.

I plant my feet, and he halts beside me, his shadow looming.

"It's not what you think." His hand gently glides over the low of my back. "You need to hear me out."

"I *need to?*"

"Please, Keira." He pulls me into his chest. "She means nothing to me."

I turn toward him, my game face fully intact. "Do you think I care about some other woman? Christ, Decker, you're the one who demanded commitment. Not me."

He grows a foot taller, his shoulders straightening. "Then why did you run? Why are you pissed at me?"

My pulse grows frantic the longer he stares, the rapid pounding in my chest becoming painful as he holds my gaze.

"I'm livid because you made me believe my safety was at risk when what you were really doing was putting space between your booty calls."

I make this about his job. About the commitment he's made to my brother. I refuse to let it be about anything else.

"You made me think I was in danger, when there was no threat at all." I shove out of his hold, placing space between us.

His nostrils flare as he glances away, letting out a huff of frustration. "I didn't mean for that to happen."

"In front of me?" I seethe. "Or at all?"

"At all," he grates. "She's not a woman who can be ignored. If I didn't pull over and speak to her, she would've followed until I did. She would've made a bigger scene."

"Making a scene is the least of your worries. You need to remember why you're here and who you work for. My protection isn't something you can push aside whenever your girlfriend shows up."

"Your protection?" His eyes harden as he meets my gaze. "Are you really going to keep playing this like it's a work related problem? It's clear you're jealous, and you don't need to be."

I bite back a retort that would only prove his point. "We can make this about sex if you like, Decker, the *unprotected sex* we had after you led me to believe you weren't sleeping around."

"I'm not sleeping around. And stop calling me Decker. You know my fucking name."

I'm not here to do him any favors. I can't. I'm beyond reasoning. "Is she the woman you cancelled plans with yesterday?"

"Yes," he growls. "But it doesn't change a thing—"

"Because she's only an old friend?"

"It's complicated."

"It always is." I start toward the street, needing to find another escape route.

"Come on, Keira. I understand why you're upset. Honestly, I am, too. But the last thing I want to do is hurt you." His footsteps follow. "*Please*, believe me when I say I'm sorry."

"Believing in someone is a luxury I can't afford." Case in point—our current situation.

He grabs my arm and turns me to face him, his eyes shining with sincerity. "I shouldn't have contacted her, okay? I don't want anything to do with her. Not anymore. But like I said, it's complicated."

"How complicated?" The question slips past my defenses without permission.

He doesn't respond, only holds my gaze, the clue to my answer flickering in his tight expression.

"Tell me," I demand, "before I find a phone and call Cole."

He sighs. "She isn't someone who can be denied. She always gets what she wants. One way or another."

I hate her already. Even more than I already did. "And what she wants is you?"

"Today, yes. Who knows what she'll want tomorrow." He shrugs. "But I'm not interested in her. I promise."

I should've scratched her eyes out instead of running to her aid. Only problem is, that's another point I can't ignore. "You were threatening her with a gun."

"Because she was threatening *you*. I'm not going to apologize for being possessive. I'll shut down anyone who contemplates putting you in harm's way. I've told you this a hundred times."

The words sink deep, the sincerity in his eyes sinking deeper. He's trying to weave me under his spell again.

He reaches out, stroking his thumb over my cheek. "I'll stop at nothing to keep you safe."

"And what if it's you I need to be kept safe from?"

His hand falls. "Is that how you feel?"

I don't know how to answer. Strategy or honesty. Truth or lies. "Getting involved with you was a mistake."

"Bullshit. You don't believe that."

I don't know what I believe anymore.

"Keira." He whispers my name, the syllables drowning in sorrow. "Deep down, you know this is real. What we've got isn't something that should be thrown away."

I scoff. "That's awfully poetic."

His fingers loosen around mine, his touch climbing my arm, moving along my shoulder, burning a frantic trail until he gently clasps the back of my neck. He demands my attention with the possessive hold. He commands my eyes to meet his without a single word.

I blink back at his fierce expression, my breathing growing ragged. I lick my lip. I shudder. All my responses are involuntary. When it comes to Sebastian, I guess they always are.

"It's not poetic. It's the fucking truth." His fingers stroke back and forth along my sensitive skin. "Neither one of us wanted this. But it happened. And I'm not going to let you convince me it doesn't mean anything to you. Because I know it does."

I clamp my lips tight.

I'm not going to confirm or deny.

"Keira. Please." His face is scrunched in pain. "I'm—"

His sentence is cut short by the melodic sound of his cell, the loud ring echoing through the alley.

"Shit." He lowers his hand from my neck to retrieve a phone from his pocket. "I need to answer this. It'll be Hunter."

I nod. "Go ahead."

He stares at me, the cell palmed in his hand. "Not until you tell me we're good."

The phone continues to ring, the annoying tone forever tattooed in my brain to remind me of the moment I made a decision that would either make me sink or swim.

"We're good," I whisper.

His features relax, the slightest smile tugging at his lips as he connects the call and raises it to his ear. "Hunt? Where are you?"

He wraps a hand around my waist, and I don't deny the touch. I've made my decision. I need to stick to it.

"How far away?" He backs me into the wall as he speaks, his hips pressing into mine. "Yeah. We're already here. After you take the turn off, you'll see the Porsche parked on the side of the road."

His heat sinks into me, the exposed skin of his chest tempting.

"I'll see you in a minute." He disconnects the call and places the cell into his pocket. "They're almost here."

"They?" Has my brother come to save me from making more poor decisions? Or would he pressure me to make more?

"Hunt and Sarah. We need to meet them at the car."

"Okay." I inch along the wall, only to have him stop me with a strong hand on my waist.

"Say it again," he begs. "Tell me I didn't fuck things up."

My stomach churns. There's no right answer when there's too much wrong in this situation.

"I'll get over it." I swallow and force myself to follow the path I've chosen. "We're good, Sebastian."

That smile returns a second before he steals a kiss. His lips are harsh and possessive. They claim me, taking me over, dragging me under. Then, just as quick, they're gone.

"You're killing me, you know that?" He grins. "I don't know what it is about you, but I swear you're slaying me one slow inch at a time."

Maybe I am.

Maybe he's doing the same to me.

I guess only time will tell.

"We better get going." I maneuver out from against him and lead the way. "Hunter doesn't seem like the type to appreciate waiting."

"Hunter's not the type to appreciate much of anything." He catches up to me, slinging an arm around my shoulders.

We walk to the car, and neither of us has words to fill the uncomfortable void as we pause to lean side-by-side against the hood. It's my fault. I went from zero to sixty in a heartbeat with this man. I pulled all the stops. Then had to swerve off course when that woman showed up.

Which sparks to life an important question. "How did she find us?"

He stares at the road, not a single flicker marring his expression. "My guess? She put some tracking app on my phone."

I frown. "You let her mess around with your cell?"

He keeps ogling the same spot of asphalt near his feet. "I think she's used it once or twice to make a call. Who knows what she did during that time. I'll have to ditch it and buy a burner until we get back to Portland."

My brows knit tighter. He's too calm. He doesn't understand what all this means. "Sebastian..." I don't know how to broach the consequences.

He crosses his arms over his chest. "Let it go."

I can't. Tracking him means she'd have a wealth of information. Every job he's done for my family would be traceable. Any alibi we gave him could be exposed as a lie. And the safe house... *Shit*. She would know the exact location of where we're staying, now and when my family needs to hide in the future. "You don't understand what this means."

"I know exactly what it means, Keira." His voice is barely audible. "And I know what needs to be done, too. Let me handle it."

My heart squeezes. We're both talking about the same thing. About killing a woman because of her infatuation. Nausea swirls in my gut, the sensation multiplying the longer we stand in silence.

I can't drag my gaze away from him. I watch his profile as he raises his attention to the oncoming traffic, his disposition calm despite the death that's about to lay at his feet.

He fits into my family better than I thought. His puzzle piece slides in right beside mine. I don't know if it's a good thing, or bad. Should I appreciate his familiarity or be disappointed that he's so similar to Cole?

"They're here." He pushes from the hood and stands tall as a black Chevy Suburban pulls in behind us.

I join him, greeting Hunter and Sarah with a faux smile while they climb from the car.

"I'm glad you're safe," Sarah says in greeting. If those words came from any other person, I'd expect a hug to come with it, but she's not the type. She cares to the fullest and despises shows of affection in equal measure.

On the outside, she's a total badass. Entirely dark, from her black tank, skirt, and fuck-me boots. But on the inside, I know she isn't that tough.

Then there's Hunter, who approaches with the same scowl that's been tattooed on his face from the first moment we met.

"Thanks for the concern, sweetness," Sebastian drawls. "I knew you'd miss me."

She turns her attention to him, eyeing his clothes with derision. "What's with the shirt? Did you become a stripper and forget to tell me?"

"Sure did." He grins. "Want a lap dance?"

I bristle, all the hairs on the back of my neck rising in jealousy.

"Quit the shit," Hunter scolds. "And why the fuck are you dressed like that?"

"I'm setting a new—"

"It's my fault," I admit, already sick of the playful joker. Minutes ago Sebastian had been someone else. Someone brutal and honest. The guy beside me is different, and I have no clue which personality is the fake one. "I shrunk his shirt, and we haven't had a chance to buy him any new clothes."

Hunter juts his chin in acknowledgement, then focuses on Sebastian as if I no longer exist. "We need to go somewhere and talk."

Sebastian nods. "There's a diner further up the road. We can go there."

"The women can," Hunter clarifies. "You and I are going to find someplace private."

There's a pause of silence, the beat of contemplation slipping through us all.

They're going to leave me behind. Alone. Unprotected.

I'm not overly concerned. Nobody is likely to find me out here. Except Sebastian's formidable ex. And even if she did approach me, there's a thing or two I'd like to get off my chest as far as she's concerned.

"I'm not going anywhere without Keira." Sebastian's brows pull tight. "She stays with me."

"Sarah can take over for a while. We won't be gone long. We'll take a short drive. We don't need to go far."

"Sarah?" Sebastian scoffs.

"Yeah, me." She crosses her arms over her chest. "Please be dumb enough to tell me you don't think I'm capable."

"Well, okay, seeing as though you—"

"Seriously, shut the fuck up," Hunter snaps, his viciousness making me jolt. "We need to get moving."

"No." Sebastian loses the playful expression. "I said I'm not leaving her. We can have a private conversation wherever the hell you like, but I'm keeping her in my sights."

There's an emotional standoff. One fierce man staring down another.

"You're not thinking straight," Hunter snarls through clenched teeth. "We need to talk. *In private.*"

This is never going to end. Not without a fistfight. Or worse.

Sarah meets my gaze and raises a brow in question. I know what she's asking. And I guess I should've opened my mouth sooner, but the display of overbearing protection is hard to ignore. It penetrates the drama-filled thoughts from earlier and leaves me a little more susceptible to Sebastian's charm.

"I'll be fine." I incline my head in the direction of the diner and start striding out the distance. "I can take care of myself until you get back."

"Keira, wait." Sebastian jogs after me, rounds me up to walk backward in an effort to hold my gaze. "I don't want to leave you."

"I know. But Hunter isn't giving you a choice." I paste on a smile. "Go. Do whatever you need to do. I'll be waiting for you once you get back."

He stops and grabs my arms, his eyes filling with furious concern. "I don't—"

"It's not a big deal." I place a hand over his and squeeze. "The sooner you go, the sooner you come back."

"Are you sure?" He scrutinizes me.

"She's sure." Sarah approaches my side. "Hurry up and get out of here before my man bursts an artery." She grabs my wrist and tugs. "Come on, Kee. Let's have some girl bonding time."

She leads me away, my hand falling from Sebastian's arm as he stands tall in defiance.

"I'll be right back," he mutters.

"Take your time," Sarah calls out over her shoulder. "The two of us have a lot to discuss."

I feel him watching me as I leave. The warm tingle follows my every step. When

I'm about to turn the corner, I glance over my shoulder, and there he is, still in the same spot, staring at me.

"You two hooked up, didn't you?" Sarah drops my arm. "I thought Hunter was joking when he mentioned it this morning."

"Excuse me?" My attention snaps to her. "Hunter said something?"

"He speculated that Decker couldn't keep his dick in his pants. But now it's obvious. That right there went above and beyond protection. He's hooked."

"No comment." I increase my pace. I'm not sure why.

I guess I'm trying to outrun the conversation. Or Sarah entirely. And she lets me. For the most part. She hangs back a little, allowing me to walk a few steps in front, until we reach the diner.

I push the door wide, letting her enter before me.

"There's no outrunning this conversation." She smirks as she passes. "I'll buy you a coffee so we can settle in and discuss you and Decker fucking."

She says it loud enough to draw attention. Loud enough to turn my cheeks to flame. Then struts those boots to the far wall to claim a booth.

I should leave. I seriously doubt anyone nearby is going to make me more uncomfortable then she is. Coffee be damned. Waterboarding would be more enjoyable than this.

It's no secret I don't talk sex with friends. For starters, I don't have a lot of people I can confide in, and second, I don't have a lot of sex.

Who the hell am I kidding? I have none of either.

Not until Sebastian, who seems to be trying to fulfil my needs on both.

"Are you waiting to be seated?" A waitress asks.

I cringe. "No, I'm waiting for hell to open up and swallow me whole."

She frowns.

"I'm fine," I mutter and drag my feet toward the booth.

Sarah still has the smug expression plastered on her pretty face. It brings me chills as I slide into the opposite seat.

"We're not discussing it." I place my hands on the table and look her straight in the eye. "Anything about Sebastian is off limits."

"Sebastian?" She purses her lips. "Is that his name?"

I ignore her and glance at the waitress approaching our table.

"What would you like to or—"

"A strong coffee, please. Very strong. And a bagel, too."

Sarah chuckles. "I'll have the same."

"Why don't you try decaf?" I taunt. Caffeine is the last thing this interrogator needs.

Her lips quirk in amusement as the waitress finishes writing up our order and leaves us alone.

"You're edgy. Why?" She scrutinizes me. "It's just sex, right?"

Yeah. There's nothing else going on. Not at all.

Not one damn thing.

"That's exactly right." I grab a salt shaker to keep my hands busy. "So drop it."

Her mouth continues to provoke me. "You like him." It comes out as an accusation. "I mean you *really* like him."

"The only thing I'd like at the moment is an end to this conversation."

"Why?" She relaxes back into her seat, her expression losing its humor. "What's the big deal?"

"That's exactly it, there *is* no big deal. We had sex. That's it. End of story."

"Wow." Her eyes widen. "Was he that bad?"

"*No.* He wasn't bad at all." I can't help defending him. "He was good."

"Good?" she rants. "That's not really a glowing reference."

"*Jesus.*" I throw my hands in the air. "He was mind-blowing. He rocked my world. I saw stars and unicorns, and maybe a baby llama, too. Is that better?"

She laughs. "Yeah. Better. Although the mention of farm animals is a little disturbing."

I hang my head. "You're killing me."

The laughter continues. It's uncharacteristic for her. She's not usually an overtly happy person. It must be her sadistic side coming out to play.

"So, tell me," she starts, "if you saw stars and frogs and fairies, why isn't this a big deal?"

I drag in a deep breath and hold it tight in my lungs, letting the burn distract me. "Because nothing can come of it."

"Why?"

I scoff. "Sebastian isn't the best poster boy for a healthy relationship."

"And you think Hunter and I are?"

"I…"

She has a point.

Her relationship with her fiancé seems flawless. They're perfect together. Happy. In sync. Committed. But my issues are far deeper than I let on.

"It's not that easy." Nothing about this situation is. It's messy and complicated. It's downright scary at times.

"I know." She nods. "There's your brother, who will wear Sebastian's skin like a coat. And the two of you being together will draw attention. You'll be his weakness and become a bigger target for anyone wanting to mess with the family. But he's obviously infatuated with you."

"I don't know what he is." That's the problem. He has secrets. Lots of them. And after this morning, it's clear he's hiding things that are dangerous.

"Then find out. Ask him. Or just sit back and see where this llama sex takes you."

I roll my eyes. "Do you twist Hunter's words as much as you twist mine?"

She ponders the question. "Yeah, I guess I do." She shrugs. "See, no relationship is perfect."

I smile through my contemplation. She's right. No relationship is perfect. But most aren't built entirely on lies, either.

14

DECKER

"Get in the Porsche," Hunter demands as he strides for the passenger door. "You're driving."

"Is that really necessary? Why the fuck can't we just stay here?"

He doesn't answer, just keeps pounding out the steps around the hood. He's more volatile than I anticipated, which isn't good.

I thought he'd be edgy from the news—an upcoming power struggle isn't something anyone wants to be involved in—but we can make a plan. We can get in front of this before it blows in our faces. "Do you have a destination in mind?"

"I'll give you directions."

I yank open my door, and we both slide inside.

"Head out of town." Hunter clasps his belt, and I start the ignition. "Toward Portland."

I nod and pull from the curb, the small town being left behind in the rear-view as we steamroll closer toward apprehension. "Are you going to start talking?"

"When we pull over. I don't trust this car isn't bugged."

I hold tight to the steering wheel and wonder if he's right. Not only could the authorities be listening, but it's a possibility Torian could've placed a recording device in his own car.

All those phone calls via Bluetooth, or any conversation he's held behind the wheel could be kept and used to his advantage…along with all those I've had with Keira.

Shit.

"You need to start talking." I demand. "I know something's wr—"

"Here." He focuses out his window, tapping his finger against the glass. "Pull over."

"You sure?" He's pointing toward a dilapidated barn. The structure is barely holding its own, the wooden wall planks filled with dark, rotted cracks exposing the black inside. One gust of wind and the fucker is going to fall.

"Yes. Pull into the drive and park at the gate. We can walk the rest of the way."

"You want to go inside?"

He scowls at me. "What's with you questioning me this morning? You're getting on my nerves."

"Feeling's mutual." I pull into the dirt drive and cut the engine.

Being at each other's throats isn't a great way to face this storm. We have to be a team. Focused and reliable. I need to be on his good side if there's any hope he'll help me convince Keira to run from this mess.

"Get moving. I don't want to keep the girls waiting." Hunter is out and striding for the fence before I can release my belt.

He doesn't want to keep them waiting?

I didn't want to leave them in the first fucking place.

Something is seriously eating Hunter's ass right now and it's not an A-grade hooker.

I rush from the car, slamming the door behind me. "Hey." I jog to catch up. "What's going on?"

"You tell me." He opens the gate, holding it wide until I walk through. "This morning has been a fucking disaster."

"Because Luther went to meet his maker?" I continue along the drive, rocks and dirt crunching under my shoes.

"Among other things, but we'll get to the rest later." He lags half a step behind, his heavy frame taking up the corner of my eye. "First, I want to know what Keira told you."

"It's like I said on the phone—Her dad is counting worms, and they're keeping it quiet while they prepare for the approaching shit storm."

"I still don't understand why she would tell you when nobody else has been told. Not even me."

"Is that what this is about?" I huff out a chuckle. "You're pissed because your best buddy, Torian, didn't tell you first?"

"Like I'd give a fuck about that. I just want answers. I want to know why she would blab to you."

I glance over my shoulder and waggle my brows at his fierce expression. I wouldn't have guessed it possible, but his face becomes stonier. Those eyes harden to disapproving slits. His lips flatten into a straight line.

"So, you did fuck her," he grates.

"That's such a crass term for the magic we shared."

"It must've been some monumental fuck to have her spilling her family secrets."

I shrug. "What can I say? My moves bring out the trust in people."

"Torians don't trust," he snarls. "You know that." He slows his pace, falling further behind as we reach the barn. "Who else have you told?"

"Nobody." I grab the splintered door in both hands and have to lift to get it to budge. "I called you—"

A heavy weight slams into my back, buckling my knees and shoving me into the rotted wood.

"What the—" My gun is yanked from my pants as I right myself, the barrel jabbing into my ribs.

"Get inside," Hunt mutters. *"Move."*

I freeze, the world stopping around me as I relive every move I've made in the last forty-eight hours in an attempt to pinpoint my failure. "Is that a gun in your pocket or are you—"

Pain explodes through the back of my skull, the impact coming from his knuckles or maybe the butt of the gun.

"Open the fucking door. We're not doing this out here."

"And what is this, exactly?" I murmur. "Because I'm fucking clueless."

Cold metal presses to the top of my spine. "Inside. *Now.*"

I scramble to figure out what's going on. What he knows. How I've failed. "You're being a dick, Hunt. Cut the shit and tell me what's got your panties in a twist."

"Don't try my patience, motherfucker."

Fuck.

I have no clue what's going on. No fucking idea what has turned my friend against me. I lift the door, adrenaline coursing through me.

My head throbs as I shove inside, dust billowing at my feet. I inch into the darkened interior, the nudges from Hunt prodding me forward.

Splinters of light pierce through the broken walls. Cobwebs blanket the beams along the ceiling. This place is empty, apart from the dread filling the space to capacity.

It's certainly not the nicest place to die.

I guess it's not the worst, either.

"Who do you work for?" He shoves me forward with a heavy hand between my shoulder blades.

I stumble, gaining enough space to turn and face him. "You're paranoid." I scowl at him. At my friend. My only fucking friend.

"And you're a fucking traitor." He aims the weapon at my chest, his arm strong, his resignation even stronger. I can see it in his eyes. He's capable of pulling the trigger. He's considering killing me.

"What have I told you about skipping your meds?" I raise my hands in surrender. "I don't know what's gotten into you today—"

"Who do you work for?" he demands. "Is it the fucking DEA?"

"I work for you. I've always worked for you."

His eyes flare. His jaw ticks.

He knows. He fucking knows.

How?

"Tell me what's going on." I step closer. "Whatever it is, you've got the wrong impression."

"Do I?" He raises a brow. "In the early hours of this morning, one of Torian's cop friends calls to tell him an informant has started whispering about Luther's death. Not long after, you give me the same information."

Fucking Anissa.

That bitch exposed me.

"And you're blaming me for the leak?" I scoff and lower my hands. "Fuck, man, you said it yourself, I called after the cop. Who knows who found out before I did. Keira has probably told all her friends. And then there's Layla. Or even Cole. It's obviously not a well kept secret."

"It's not a secret, you piece of shit. It's a lie."

A lie?

A fucking lie.

I school my expression, facing the news head-on as hell rains down on me.

"He isn't dead, you dumb fuck." He lunges for me, one hand grabbing my throat while the other keeps me in place with the threat of a bullet. "From what I can piece together, it was a bullshit story to flush out a rat." He tightens his grip, restricting my breath. "Keira set you up. She tested you. She fucking played you."

I raise my chin, sinking into the pain taking over my throat, letting it sharpen my thoughts. "No." I don't believe it. I won't. "She must have told someone else. I didn't breathe a word to anyone but you."

He glares his fury, his stare more lethal than any weapon. "The game is over. Quit the fucking act."

Fuck.

I'm done.

Dead.

"Hunt..." I swallow to clear the rasp from my voice. I can't believe Keira betrayed me. I can't figure out when. I don't understand how. "Let me explain."

"Fuck." He shoves me. "It's fucking true?" He retreats a step and another, the gun still trained on me. *"Jesus. Fuck."*

Guilt takes over, the toxic agony rushing my veins, pounding into every limb, through all my organs.

"Let me tell you every—"

He rushes forward, grabbing me around the waist to haul me to the ground. My head hits the dirt. All the air leaves my lungs. I grapple to get on top, but I can't bring myself to fight him. I fucking can't.

He straddles my waist, the gun still pointed, as he strikes with punishing blows. He punches my chest, my ribs, my stomach. Agony takes over my insides, the wounds more emotional than physical.

"Fight back, you dog."

I can't. I don't want to.

I deserve the punishment. I've earned the beating.

"Do you know what you've done?" He keeps his fist cocked, preparing to make another strike. "You've put my neck on the line. You've made me look like a fucking accomplice. But that's not the worst of it. You've done this to Sarah, and that's un-fucking-forgivable."

He punches my sternum, the crack of bone ringing in my ears. I don't do a thing to stop him. I won't deny him the retribution. Not for himself. And definitely not for his woman.

"I had no choice," I wheeze.

He lets out a derisive laugh. "Money or freedom? What did the DEA offer you?"

"It's not like that." I shake my head and grunt as he lands another blow. "Luther is involved in horrible shit you can't even imagine. He—"

"*Are you really going to make this about morality?*" he roars. "I'm paid to kill people. *You're* paid to help me."

"It's more than—"

He lands another blow, this one against my jaw, the smash of teeth and tongue filling my mouth with blood.

"*It's more than death?*" he bellows. "Fuck you, you traitorous little fuck. How am I going to explain this to Cole? How the fuck do I tell him you're the informant?"

Wait. What?

"He doesn't know?" I mumble through a mouth full of gore.

"Nobody fucking knows. He thinks it was another external attack to take down his family. He's pulling his hair out trying to find the culprit."

"But Keira…"

"Hasn't answered his calls. As far as I can tell, the dead-father strategy was something she thought of on her own."

"You're telling me you had no proof?" I huff out a chuckle and my ribs protest with a bite of pain. "You were working on a hunch?" My laughter becomes maniacal. Delirious. "I fucked myself over? All I had to do was keep my mouth shut."

He grabs me by the shoulders and slams my back down on the ground. "If it wasn't today, your dumb ass would've fucked up sooner or later." He climbs off me, coming to stand beside my hip. "Get on your feet."

"No." I remain one with the earth and spit the coppery taste from my mouth. "If you're in such a hurry to kill me, you can do it like a coward."

He grabs the front of my shirt, twisting the material in his fist. "I'm in no hurry. I'm happy to make this slow if you like."

"I'd prefer if you fucking listened." I prepare to play the only card I have—knowledge. "I've got years of research at my house. I've got thousands and thousands of files you're going to want to see. Let me show you what they're doing. Give me the chance to explain why I'm here."

"I don't give a shit. I'll *never* give a shit."

"Maybe not, but Sarah will. And she'll never forgive you once she finds out. Especially if my death is on your hands."

His jaw ticks.

"Come on, Luke. You don't want to kill me."

He stiffens at the sound of his real name, his fury surging.

"If you do this," I continue, "I promise you'll lose Sarah. She'll leave you as soon as she learns the truth."

His hold on my shirt tightens as he presses the barrel right between my eyes. "If it's so important, tell me."

I smirk, and my swollen lower lip protests over the movement. "You know that information is the only leverage I have."

"You're wrong." His voice softens. Slows. The defeated tone inciting fear. "You've got no leverage. You've got nothing but lies."

My friend disappears from sight, a cold-blooded killer taking his place. The barrel presses harder against my skull and I see death swirling in his eyes. My death.

He's going to pull the trigger.

He's going to end my life.

"I'm sorry," I murmur.

His eyes glaze, the depth of his breaths increasing. He's preparing himself, finding the necessary calm to do the job.

"Hunt, believe me, I'm fuckin' sorry." For the past, the present, and now, the future.

I duck to the left and slam his wrist upward, breaking the lethal trajectory of his weapon. The gun fires, the blast ringing in my ears as the bullet shoots toward the ceiling.

He swings back toward me, and I latch onto his hand, shoving it in a high arc as I lean in and strike with a double elbow slash, the menacing blow hitting the right side of his jaw, then returning against his left. His head jerks with the motions. He stumbles.

I don't let go. I swing around into him, my back to his chest as I wrench his arm over my shoulder. His elbow hyperextends. He tries to choke me as I jerk him down, once, twice, threatening to break the joint before he gives in and drops the weapon.

I keep him hostage as I kick the gun away and watch it skitter through the dust. He pummels my face with his free hand. But it's not until he gouges at my eyes that I have to drop to my haunches and set him free.

I scramble away and turn to face him nursing his elbow, his feet spread wide, knees bent, preparing for battle even though shock is written all over his face.

He's never seen me fight. He probably thought this smartass, tech head had no moves. Truth is, my skills have always been capable of rivaling his own. I didn't storm into hell armed with nothing but a computer and a cocky attitude.

I knew I'd have to fight for my life one day.

Fight or die.

"What's wrong, Hunt?" I raise my brows, letting the adrenaline take over. "You didn't anticipate me kicking your ass?"

I studied him. I know he works best when he's calm and in control. I don't plan on letting him have either.

He smirks, the curve of lips predatory and feral. "You fight like a little bitch."

"Says the man who had to lower himself to eye gouging."

"Lower myself?" He laughs. "I've been wanting to ruin your pretty boy face for a while." He inches forward, beckoning me with his left hand. "Come on. Let's finish this."

"I don't want to finish it." I steady myself, hands raised, waiting for him to strike. "I want you to walk out of here and go find my research."

"You think I don't want that?" He comes closer, almost close enough to pounce. "If this was just me and you, things would be different. But I can't protect Sarah from Torian. Not every minute of every damn day. You put me in the middle of this. And I'll do whatever it takes to protect her."

"We can leave. All three of us. We'll start over somewhere new."

"You want me to run away with you?" He snickers. "That's fuckin' sweet. But I don't run with snitches." He rushes me, coming forward with right-left-right punches.

The first blow hits my nose, then I block the next two strikes and take a hard step right at his last swing. As he moves by me, I launch my fist into the side of his face, knocking him off balance.

"Motherfucker." He rushes me again with a sloppy, uncalculated assault that I defend with a sharp side kick to the shin.

He snarls, his eyes flaring with fury. "Kicking? Seriously? Where the fuck did you learn to fight?"

"Look, man. I told you, we don't need to do this." I raise my hands in surrender. "Walk away while you still can."

"Still can?" He snickers. "Jesus, you're one cocky prick."

And that's exactly what I need to be to put him off his game. I can already feel his frustration. I can see it in his impulsive moves.

He clenches his fists and holds them in front of his chest. "This is how real men fight. With their hands."

I shrug. "Seems like all it's doing is getting your butt whooped."

I counter his circling steps, watching his every move, reading his expression. I know he'll swing first. He lacks the patience to wait me out.

"How long did you study me before you figured out a way for us to work together?" He feigns relaxation his expression doesn't back up. He's tense, tight, almost panicked.

"You came to me for help, remember? You instigated this."

He flashes his teeth in a snarl, my verbal strike inflicting injury to his ego.

In reality, it took months to find a way into his life. Then many more to train to fit the role. Hunter's weakness has always been technology—computers, hacking, online surveillance.

With a million hours' study, I became a master. I built a name for myself so quickly in the Portland criminal circles that Hunter came running to me.

He lunges, swinging a powerful blow. I dodge the punch, grab his wrist, and swing out my leg, using his own momentum to knock him off balance.

He falls to his back, and I go down with him, bending his wrist while pinning his chest with my knee.

"I'm not doing this anymore," I growl.

He swings at me with his left hand and bucks, fighting like an animal. I slice at the blows and grab the attacking arm, pinning it with force.

"Go to my house. Find the information. Then pick a side."

The look he gives me is the most brutal offense. My bruises don't mean shit. That pain will eventually fade. But I'll never forget the loathing in his eyes. I won't lose the guilt of what I've done to him.

His lip curls. "Get fuc—"

I lunge forward, head butting him right above the eyes. The impact ricochets through my skull, temporarily blinding me. But it does the trick.

It's nighty-night for the big, bad Hunter.

15

DECKER

I grab his belongings—keys, wallet, phone, gun—you name it, I've got it. Then I run for the car, hightailing it back into town.

I pull over at the start of the main street and scan the shopfronts, looking for any reinforcements who may have arrived to protect Keira.

I could keep running. I *should* keep running.

It's not like I'm capable of taking down Luther from the inside anymore. But Hunter's right. I've dragged him and Sarah into this. Torian will kill them as soon as he finds out I'm the informant. He'll consider them accomplices. At the very least, he'll hold Hunter responsible.

And as trigger-happy as my friend was moments ago, I'm not going to let them take the fall for something I've done. I don't want him punished.

But Keira…

I clench my teeth, fighting back anger. She set me up. She manipulated me with her body, making me sink head deep into her game.

It's her fault we're all in this position, and she's the one who has to fix it.

I park the Porsche behind the diner and run back to Hunter's Chevy. The Suburban will attract less attention, and I guess I get a kick out of stealing Hunt's car.

I fill the tank with gas and wash up in the bathroom, cleaning away the blood and gore the best I can.

I get supplies. I make calls. I do everything and anything possible to set my next move into action before I park in front of the diner and spy on the traitorous woman inside.

Keira and Sarah are seated against the wall. Smiling. Laughing. The only sign of apprehension comes from the way Keira continues to glance at her watch—waiting for me? Or waiting for her brother to save her?

I climb from the car, my clothes covered in dirt, and jog up the sidewalk, meeting her gaze through the window.

Her smile is instantaneous. Immediate deception. There's no glimmer of fear or panic. Then a split second later the expression flickers, flittering away as she scrutinizes my swelling face.

I shove past the glass door and meet her near the counter.

"You're hurt." Her eyes are wide, her lips parted in shock.

I keep one hand at my back, near my gun, as I lead them toward the door. "We need to leave." I'm on edge, every muscle tense, waiting for her to end the charade.

"What happened?" She rushes to follow, bathing me in fake concern. Her acting skills are in full force, which is a great sign. It means she's still playing the game. "Who did this to you?"

"They know we're here. We need to hit the road."

"They?" Her voice fractures.

Sarah comes up behind her. "Where's Hunter?"

"He's tying up loose ends."

"Loose ends?" the little liar whispers.

I ignore her, pinning my stern focus on Sarah, wordlessly telling her that's all the information I can give. "He won't be long. Be ready to leave once he gets here."

She gives a tight nod. "Is he okay?"

"He faired better than I did." I continue to the door. "We've swapped cars. Hunt has the Porsche to try to take the heat off us as we run. I'll take the Suburban."

"Why don't we go back to Portland with them?" Keira's voice is frantic. "Aren't we better to stay in a group?"

"No." I can barely stand to look at her, can hardly glance her way without wanting to wrap my hands around her neck. "We need to get off the grid."

"But—"

"Trust me," I growl.

I gain the slightest solace betraying her, manipulating her, lying straight to her beautiful face. I gain even more when she nods, seeming to come to terms with the plan.

"Okay..." Her throat works over a heavy swallow. "I trust you."

Everything inside me revolts. My pulse. My heart. My stomach takes a dive, too. Even though I know she's acting, I still can't see it. Not the slightest flicker of a charade.

She's fucking brilliant in her deception.

Entirely flawless.

I squeeze her arm in a fake show of support, then turn back to Sarah.

"I'm sorry." I hate that she'll soon see me in the same light I see Keira. She's going to hate me. Despise me. "I don't want to leave you here like this." The depth of my apology runs far below the surface. She won't understand it now, but hopefully, once I'm gone and my actions become clear, she'll make sense of it.

"It's okay. Go. Keep Keira safe."

"I will. But I fucking hate this." I'm not like the snake at her side. I don't enjoy lying to people who trust me.

"You're getting soft, Deck. And making me uncomfortable at the same time." She frowns and jerks her chin toward the door. "Hurry up and get moving."

Fucking hell. I don't want to leave her. I'm struggling to walk away. Sarah has become a major part of my life. She's a gorgeous woman. A moral woman. Lethally so. It's a good thing I'm not going to be around when she finds out what I've done.

"Don't miss me too much." I paste on a grin and lean in to kiss her temple.

She rolls her eyes as I retreat, not allowing a second of softness. "Be careful. Guard her with your life."

"I'll do everything I can." I shove open the door. "When Hunt gets here, you need to remind him to go to my house. There's stuff I need him to pick up."

I don't look back as I escape onto the sidewalk, Keira following close behind. We jog to Hunter's car and climb in. I don't spare a second as I gun the engine and pull from the curb.

She doesn't talk as we speed down the highway, her hands fidgeting in her lap. She's giving me the same act she did when we fled Portland. An exact replica of the innocent actress.

I can't blame her, seeing as though the duplicity worked so well the first time. Obviously, it's a familiar role, a default, because beneath the fragility is a calculated bitch planning her next strike.

"Do you still have that phone?" I ask.

"Yes. But it's flat. There's no battery." She fumbles in her cardigan pocket and pulls out the device. "I need to buy a charger."

"No, you don't." I lower my window and grab the cell to throw it to the wind. I watch in my mirror as it bounces and shatters along the road behind us, the destruction a comforting sight.

"*Sebastian.*" She raises from her seat to stare out the back window. "Why did you do that?"

"I don't know how they tracked us. I'm not willing to take any chances."

"What about your cell? I need to call Cole. I want to know what's going on."

"Sorry, babe. I've already ditched mine. We need to get off the grid as soon as possible."

Those fingers increase their nervous wringing. Her leg begins to jitter. "Where are we going?"

Her panic is an aphrodisiac. I can't get enough. "As far away as possible. I've already filled the tank with gas. I have no plans to pull over until we've disappeared."

"Are you sure going home isn't a better option? If people are coming after us, I'd prefer to be moving toward my family. Not away."

I glance at her and give a grin filled with pure menace. "Aren't I good enough anymore?"

I want her to bite. I *need* her to. My blood rushes with adrenaline, waiting for the finish line. But now isn't the time to let her know I'm already aware of her lies. Not when I'm behind the wheel.

"It's not that..." Her leg jolts faster. "I'm just nervous about being out in the open."

"Don't worry." I reach over, sliding my hand behind her head to squeeze the back of her neck. It takes all my strength not to grip hard. To sink my fingers into muscle and inflict pain. "Hunter and I dealt with the issue. Moving forward, I'll be more cautious. I promise nobody will find us."

Not a fucking soul.

Not until I'm ready.

My palm itches, needing to feel her pulse quicken beneath my touch. I hunger to cause more fear. Instigate more panic. Instead, she leans into my hand and briefly closes her eyes, pretending to gain comfort from the connection.

Conniving little bitch.

She's brilliant in her betrayal. Mesmerizing.

I keep my hand in place, lazily tracing silent threats into her skin while she pretends to enjoy the affection.

It's a romantic picture from the outside. A curious state of normal I would've liked to explore if this wasn't the fucking Twilight Zone.

But it is.

All of this is fake—the vulnerability, the friendship, the beauty.

"Are you okay?" she whispers, breaking the stable silence.

Out of all the questions she could've asked, this one fills me with the most anger. She should be curious about the imaginary men following us. Or how I plan to keep her safe. Or when she's going to see her family again.

Instead, she pretends to care about me. *Me*. The man she's slowly leading to execution.

"I'm tough." I shoot her a wink and place both hands back on the wheel. "It takes a hell of a lot more to get me six feet under."

"Your face is pretty beat up. You're bruised everywhere—your jaw, your cheek, your bottom lip."

I keep smiling through her nauseating charade of pity. Keep pretending, just like she does. There's a beat of silence, an awkward, fractured beat that thickens the air between us.

"Sebastian, I need to tell you something."

My lungs tighten, my ribs restricting my breathing. "I'm all ears."

The quiet returns, the moments passing with building anticipation.

I glance her way, seeing her brow furrowed as her teeth dig into her lower lip. "What is it?"

She sucks in a breath and lets it out slowly. "I lied to you."

"Oh, yeah?" My hands tighten around the steering wheel.

She nods. "This morning...When I said I didn't care about you being with that woman."

For fuck's sake. This shit is already getting old.

"I do care, Sebastian. The jealousy is eating me up."

I focus on the road, my knuckles turning white with my harsh grip.

Not only is she saying my name in that sickly sincere tone, she's playing the endearing card on top of the stacked deck of deceit.

Fuck her.

Fuck those soft eyes that seem to blink with genuine honesty. And the tempting lips making her lies easy to believe. She was born to fool me.

"I told you, she means nothing."

"I know." Her voice fractures. "And I believe you. I guess I just wanted you to know I wasn't unaffected by her. She made me realize how much I've enjoyed this time with you, despite the reasons behind being stuck together."

I grin. At her. At the lies. At the fucking absurdity of this entire situation. "I've enjoyed it, too."

I'll enjoy it even more once she knows the truth.

I turn my focus her way, needing to shoot her a smug glance she will hopefully look back on later. But I regret the glimpse immediately.

She's staring at me, her body turned my way, her cheek pressed against the head rest. That gorgeous mouth of hers is kicked at one side, her eyes gentle.

I don't understand how she can be so undeniably beautiful and entirely monstrous at the same time. The body of a goddess with the strategic mind of the devil.

"You should get some rest." I press my foot harder on the accelerator. "It's going to be another long day."

"I couldn't sleep even if I wanted to. I've got too many questions."

I bet she does.

The more answers she has, the better she can control me.

"Now isn't the time. My head is killing me." Not a lie. My brain is seriously fucking with my vision. My bottom lip is swollen and throbbing. And my ribs protest with every inhale.

"I understand. But I need to know, Sebastian. Once you've had time to decompress and think things through, I want you to tell me everything that happened while you were gone. It's important."

I nod. "We can talk tonight." We'll talk about everything. Every fucking thing she's been hiding from me. "For now, just let me concentrate on getting us somewhere safe."

HOURS GO by with nothing but the sound of asphalt beneath the tires and the crinkle of junk food wrappers as we decimate the stash of snacks I purchased at the gas station.

The further I drive, the less I see. There hasn't been a house in miles, or a street sign, for that matter, which means I'm headed in the right direction. The eerie desolation is familiar.

"I think I'm going to have to ask you to pull over again." Keira stretches her arms above her head. "My bladder is beginning to protest."

"We're almost there. Can you wait ten minutes? Maybe twenty?"

She sits up straight. "There's a town nearby? I haven't seen any sign of life for half an hour."

"There's a house up ahead. That's where we're staying."

She leans closer to her window, scanning the scenery. "You had a destination in mind all along? I thought you were aimlessly driving."

"I don't usually do anything aimlessly. And if memory serves, the house should come into view once we get over this hill."

As predicted, my brother's home appears as a small speck toward the horizon. It's all alone. A solitary building in the middle of nowhere. A hermit's dream. A kidnapped victim's nightmare.

Twenty minutes later, I turn onto the long dirt drive, a trail of dust billowing in our wake as we approach the place I chose to have our showdown.

There's no sign of life. No cars. No crops. No cattle. Not a glimmer of help in sight. Just a house and more than enough room for a scream to die on the wind.

She inches forward in her seat. "How do you know about this place?"

"From an online rental site. I've stayed here once before." I drive into the house yard, the smaller block fenced off from the mass of vacant land. A pebbled path leads to the front door, but I steer onto the grass and park by the side of the garage to hide the car from the road.

"It looks nice." She unfastens her belt and opens her door. "What are we going to do about food? And both of us are back to having no clothes."

"Don't worry. The host told me the fridge would be stocked. And I'm not seeing the lack of clothing as a bad thing." I wink at her and slide from the car, my bruised muscles aching in protest.

I'm not looking forward to checking my injuries, but my heart pounds in anticipation as the seconds tick down to the moment when I get to tell Keira she's far from safe with me.

I can't fucking wait to wipe that saccharine smile from her face. For those eyes to blink at me in fear instead of sweet manipulation.

"Is the front door unlocked?" She starts walking for the house, probably trying to reiterate the story about needing to use the bathroom, when I'd bet my life she wants to hunt for a phone.

"The key should be under the mat."

She increases her pace, disappearing inside while I open the trunk and take inventory. There's a laptop case, a new phone, and a gray duffle bag—Hunter's trusty tool kit.

I leave the computer and phone, not wanting Keira to know she has a way of communicating with the outside world, and lug the bag.

I don't see her again for ten minutes. I hear the flush of the toilet as I enter the kitchen and dump my supplies on the counter. Then her footfalls trek through the rooms, the pace frantic.

"Did the rental listing mention a landline?" she calls out. "I can't find one anywhere."

I smirk as I pull two beers from the fridge. "There's no landline. Or internet. We're on our own little island out here."

I crack a can of beer open and take a gulp as she comes to stand in the doorway.

"I need to call Cole. He'll be worried."

"Don't stress. Hunter would've told him the plan."

"What plan?" She pads forward, her feet devoid of socks. "You still haven't told me anything."

"I will. First—drink." I hold a beer out in her direction. "We've got all the time in the world to talk."

She takes the can from me, her brow furrowed. "Why do I get the feeling you're trying to avoid the conversation?"

I laugh, and the rushed movement of my chest produces a stab of pain through my ribs.

"Sebastian?" Her frown deepens and she steps closer, her concerned gaze flicking between my eyes. "Those bruises on your face aren't the extent of your injuries, are they?"

The sharp stab turns into one motherfucker of a throb, her charade weighing down on me. I'd once thought she was a phenomenal woman. I guess I still do, just not in the admirable ways I'd once assumed.

"It's okay."

She steps closer, stopping toe to toe. "No, it's not." She grips the bottom of my shirt and tries to lift, only to have the tight material restrict around my stomach. Then she sets her sights on my buttons, frantically undoing them to stare at my chest.

"*Jesus.*" She clasps a hand over her mouth and steps back. "What did they do to you?"

I don't avert my gaze from hers. My injuries aren't going anywhere. But her affection soon will—the meticulous act.

"You need a doctor," she demands.

"I've already told you, you can't get rid of me that easily. I'll be fine." I take a deep pull of alcohol and lean back against the counter.

She peers up at me, her eyes pleading. "Sebastian, please. Let me drive you to a hospital."

I hear the truth through the lies—*Let me drive you to civilization where I can find a phone.*

"We're not going anywhere."

"I'm worried about you." Her hands raise to my face, her palms cupping my cheeks and the heavy stubble beneath. "And you're scaring me. What happens if there's internal bleeding? What do I do if you pass out?"

Resentment burns through my veins. I despise her bullshit concern. I fucking loathe it. I can't even answer her without blowing what little hold I have on fury.

"Talk to me." She leans in, her hips pressed against mine.

Her expression is sickening. The position of her thigh between my legs is a blatant strategy.

I hate it.

I hate this.

And, God, I wish I hated her.

But my dick hasn't read the memo. I grow hard, my erection rubbing against her. Despite everything—mainly self-preservation and common fucking sense—my base desires run rampant.

I want to fuck her.

Fuck her over.

I lean close, my mouth a breath away from hers. "I'm not interested in talking."

Her eyes widen. Her tongue snakes out to slowly moisten her lips. "You're hurt…"

"I'm hungry," I growl, my tone letting her know my appetite has nothing to do with food.

"Sebastian…"

I wait for her to continue. To confess. To fucking open her mouth and tell me what a lying, traitorous snake she is in an attempt to stop this moving any further.

The words never come.

She eyes me, those baby blues intense as she slowly leans in, approaching me like I'm a wild animal she shouldn't want to touch. But she does touch. She brushes her mouth over mine, the connection soft and devastating. Everything inside me wages war. Control struggles with lust. Anger fights with desire. Sense battles with complete and utter lunacy.

She pulls me under her spell. Slaughtering me. Reclaiming me as her fucking puppet.

She's had me hooked since we first met.

All this time I've been her pawn.

I smash my mouth against hers, parting her lips with my tongue to delve deep. I punish her with my kiss, detesting her with every swipe of connection.

She's slow to react. I think she might pull away.

Then her hands find my chest, and she moans. Mewls. The needy sounds only increase my livid rage.

She pushes my jacket from my shoulders and rips at the buttons of my shirt. Her touch journeys over my injuries, gentle, caring. The delicate nature is a reminder to keep my head. To stay in control because she's always on top of her game.

"I can't wait to fuck you." I speak into her mouth.

Her arms circle my back, those fingers searching until she finds my gun and begins to pull it from my waistband.

"*Don't*." I snatch the weapon from her grip.

She stares at me, wide-eyed. "I only wanted to get it out of the way."

Like hell.

Does she really expect me to believe that?

Fuck.

Was she going to shoot me?

"Let me take care of it." I push the weapon along the counter, out of reach, then walk us to the other side of the kitchen, pressing her into the drawers.

"I wouldn't have fired it by accident," she murmurs. "I know my way around a gun."

"I don't doubt it. But after this morning, it's best if your fingerprints stay far away."

She recoils, her lips parting for a brief moment before she slowly nods. "I will. I promise."

I slam my mouth back on hers with punishing force as I wrench at my belt and lower my zipper. She's all over my dick in seconds, stroking, squeezing, working the length through her angel soft skin.

We're all hands and lips and tongues. Lust and deception and lies. It's a storm of manipulation. A tsunami of wrong.

Flashbacks of the last few days pummel me. Stabbing me. Punishing unlike any other assault.

We'd had a connection. An attraction. I believed she was going to be mine.

"Turn around." I can't stand the fucking sight of her. I grab her shoulders, spin her, and bend her to my will. "Let me show my innocent little baby a thing or two."

Those lies cut the deepest. All that bullshit about being sexually assaulted. There's a reason I never found that information when I dug into her life. Everything she told me was fabricated. I'm starting to believe the whole fucking shooting was staged to bring us together so she could work her deceitful magic.

She's splayed over the counter in seconds, her dress lifted above her ass, her thong shoved to her ankles.

I squeeze her thighs, making her squeal before I delve higher, skimming her traitorous pussy with my fingertips. She's wet, dripping at the thought of undermining me.

Again.

I position my cock at her entrance and slam home. The jolt jars my ribs, the pain physical as well as emotional. I stand frozen, battling self-loathing while she grinds against me.

This isn't a virtuous woman. I'd gobbled up that bullshit like a seafood buffet.

Nothing was real.

Not a damn thing.

She lied about everything, and the thought of her misleading me about contraception makes my blood turn cold. How do I know she's not trying to get pregnant in another elaborate scheme to set me up?

Jesus. The last thing I want is a child spawned from this monster. The thought of my genes matched with those of a family bathed in sins and destruction... *Fuck.*

I slam into her. Over and over.

I loathe her, yet I can't leave her alone.

I want to punish her, but I'm only torturing myself.

My dick quits. It taps out, unable to function through the mud in my head. And here I was thinking this situation couldn't get any worse.

I slow my movements, only to have her glance over her shoulder to meet my gaze with lust-filled confusion, then even worse, pity.

"Sebastian?"

I step back, my limp cock falling free of her bear trap. My self-respect falling even further.

"Fuck." I yank at my pants, zip, belt up, and prepare for battle.

"Sebastian…"

I can't play these games anymore. It's clear she's far better at pretending than I am. She's got no heart. No fucking soul.

She turns, reaching out to grab my arm. "It's okay."

"Is it?" Her touch seeps under my skin, poisoning my veins. "Do you really think this is okay? From my point of view it couldn't be worse."

"You need to rest. We shouldn't be doing this while you're hurt."

"My dick isn't playing Sleeping Beauty because of my injuries," I snarl. "Disgust is the only reason I can't keep it hard long enough to finish."

She jerks back as if I've slapped her. "Disgust? Over what?"

"*You*." I hold her gaze, letting the fear in her eyes strengthen me. "Drop the act, peaches. I know you set me up."

16

DECKER

She stiffens, her body instantly rigid, her face draining of color.

I allow her time to process. Give her the sweet, delicious seconds for my words to sink in. "Want me to give you a few minutes to strategize your way out of this one?"

She remains silent for a minute. Then two. Finally, resignation blinks into her eyes, and she begins righting her clothes. Her movements are violent, a frantic storm of yanked underwear and loose hair.

I lean against the fridge, pretending I'm calm and in control when my pulse is erratic. "How long have you known I'm the informant?"

She doesn't answer. She keeps those lips pressed tight as she straightens her dress and flips her hair out from beneath the collar of her cardigan. She's striving for anger when I can clearly see panic in her features.

"How long, Keira?"

She stalks away, and I stop her with a tight grip around her wrist, yanking her back to my side. She glares at me, her eyes filled with fury.

"*How long*?" I growl.

"Two minutes." She snatches her arm away. "You're the last person I thought capable of snitching."

I chuckle under my breath. "That's a nice story, but I don't believe you. You've known for a while. You used that sweet pussy of yours to distract me from the truth."

She winces.

"Don't worry. If I whored myself out for my family, I'd be embarrassed to admit it, too."

Her arm snaps up, flying toward my face.

I grab her wrist before she can slap me and entwine our fingers with force. "I've suffered enough injuries because of you today."

"I can't believe it was you this whole time." She pulls away, claiming disgust when she had no problem fucking me a few minutes prior. "You're the one who's been betraying my family?"

"Pretending you weren't setting me up is a waste of time."

Her gaze meets mine, vicious and stony. "I didn't know."

I clench my teeth, my patience lost. I walk into her, pushing her backward to cage her against the counter, my face a breath from hers. "Stop lying to me."

Her eyes blaze with emotion—fear, anger, heartbreak. The kaleidoscope changes so quickly I'm not sure which one she expects me to believe.

She leans back, placing an inch of space between us. "Sebastian, I didn't..." She shakes her head, her face draining of color.

"How long?" I snap.

"Get off me." She pushes at my chest, digging her fingers into ribs I'm sure are fractured.

I grunt through the pain, stumbling back, and she rushes out from beneath me. I clench my teeth and clutch the counter, trying to figure out the motives behind her continued denial.

"I'm going to grow tired of this pretty fucking quickly. I already know you lied about your father. There's no point pretending."

She maneuvers around the dining table, using it as a shield. A fucking pathetic one at best.

"That table won't save you," I drawl. "There's no phone out here. No communication devices. Not another soul for miles. Nobody even knows you're here. So I suggest you stop fighting the inevitable."

"You need to let me go." She grips the back of one of the wooden chairs. "Cole will track you down if you hurt me. He won't give up."

I laugh. "He'll have to beat Hunter to it."

"He knows?" Her brows skyrocket. "That's why he took you away to talk this morning." Slowly, her face slackens. "He never came back. What did you do to him?"

"Far less than he did to me, that's for sure." I point to my face, my ribs, and take solace in the fact she's doesn't assume Hunter is my accomplice. Yes, it might be another ploy, but I'll take whatever solace I can get at this stage.

"Is he safe?" she demands.

"He's safer than you are. Now sit down."

A rapid exhale rushes from her lips and her gaze shoots around the room—to the door leading outside, the entrance to the hall, the pictures on the wall, then finally the duffle on the counter. "What are you going to do? Kill me?"

"Let's take it one step at a time. First, I want answers. How long have you known?" I repeat. "What did I do that tipped you off?"

She shakes her head in denial.

"You're going to tell me everything, Keira. Either by choice or by force."

She becomes more frantic with the assessment of her surroundings. She takes in the chairs around her, the knives in the distant cutting block, the empty fruit bowl in the center of the table. She wants to hurt me, and I'm a sick motherfucker for the buzz of anticipation shooting through my limbs.

"Before you consider running, please understand that your position will get a lot worse once I catch you. I don't want to make use of my handy bag of goodies."

Her gaze flicks to the gray duffle again. "What's in there?"

"Hunter's tools." I grin. "Let your imagination run wild with the possibilities."

"*Stop it*," she snaps. "I know you won't hurt me."

"Either sit down or I'll come grab you and tie you in place. It's your choice. And God knows I'm itching for a reason to manhandle you." I snatch at the duffle, sliding it toward me. I yank open the zipper and pull out the cable ties, electrical tape, rope, and pliers, placing them on display along the counter. "This is the last time I ask—how long have you known?"

"I've told you," she pleads. "I didn't know."

"Then why tell me the bullshit story about your father?"

"To prove your loyalty. I thought it would be an easy way to convince Cole you're on our side. I told you a huge secret—"

"A huge fucking lie," I clarify.

"Yes." She nods. "I told you a huge lie to convince him we could trust you. I thought you were different."

"Oh, believe me, I thought you were different, too, precious. But your story doesn't make sense. You would never risk a rumor like that getting out."

"Exactly. I didn't have any doubts of your loyalty."

"Bullshit." I snatch the cable ties off the counter and stalk around the table toward her. "Do you want me to tell you what I think happened?"

She pulls out a chair, slowing my chase.

"You and Cole organized the shooting, making sure I was by your side when the bullets strategically hit the ceiling to ensure nobody got hurt. Your brother then demanded I protect you, and you led us out of town to a place where you could attempt to seduce answers out of me. Am I close?"

She keeps retreating, her position always opposite to mine.

"The breakdown in the shower was bullshit," I accuse. "Sleeping on the sofa with me was a strategy to win me over. You fucked me in an attempt to get under my skin. And that sob story about being raped was a load of fucking crap."

"No." She shakes her head, reiterating her lies.

"You and Cole planned the entire thing to confirm your suspicions, and voila, here they are." I lunge, climbing onto a chair, then the table to dash along the wood.

She screams, the sound reverberating off the walls as she sprints for the hall.

I jump to the ground, catching her from behind in two steps. I cage her arms to her sides, her ass bucking against me as I place my mouth near her ear. "Chasing you feels as good as I thought it would."

She struggles, killing my chest with the wild-beast routine while I drag her to the closest chair and force her to take a seat. I straddle her, pinning her in place as I loop one tie around her wrist and the wooden slat of the backrest, making the plastic strip cling tight. Then I do the same with her other arm, keeping her strapped to the chair.

"You son of a bitch." She kicks, bucks, and yanks at her arms.

I move off her, glancing down to admire my handiwork. "There. That's better." I tower above her to watch the show. "Throw a tantrum, by all means, but you ain't going anywhere until I have what I want."

She shouts in frustration, her chest rising and falling with heavy breaths. "*Fuck you.*"

I quirk a brow. "Been there, done that. I don't plan on being a repeat offender."

"I swear to God, Decker, Cole will make sure your body is never found."

I shrug. "I know. That's the beauty of this—I have nothing left to lose. My fate is already set. But I can make sure I take a few souls with me on my trip to hell."

Her rampant breathing increases.

"You're not the naive innocent you pretend to be." I slide onto the table in front of her and place my feet on her seat, either side of her thighs. The slightest cage to add to her restriction.

She holds my stare. "I've told you, and I'll keep telling you—I had no idea you were a lying piece of shit. The story about my father was a test. I thought you'd keep your mouth shut."

I lean forward, my elbows on my knees as I bring our faces close. I watch her for long moments, staring into those eyes, reading her expression. "Such a pretty little liar," I murmur. "I always knew you were the best weapon in your brother's arsenal."

"If you're right, then why isn't he here?" She cocks a brow in defiance. "If this was all an elaborate scheme to set you up, why am I strapped to a chair while you hold me hostage?"

She fractures my thought process. But only momentarily. "Because you didn't tell him about the lie. You deviated from the plan. Then your phone ran out of battery, and now you're stuck trying to clean up the mess."

"Even so, if I organized something with my brother, he would've had men watching us the entire time. You never would've been able to drag me out here. They would've been all over you. You know that."

I sit up straight, trying to sort the truth from the deception. What aren't I seeing? What have I missed?

"There was no plan, Sebastian. I didn't know you were the informant. I didn't even suspect you."

I run a hand over my mouth, thinking, thinking, thinking. She's manipulating me again. She's working a new strategy, and I've got no fucking clue what it is. But I have no intention of succumbing.

"Let's switch topics for a moment." I cock my head to the side, studying her. "Tell me, do you know what your uncle was doing the night he got splattered over the front of that SUV?"

Her eyes flare with awareness. With knowledge.

"You *do* know," I taunt. "I can see it on your face."

"He was at a whorehouse. So what?"

"Is that what you call it? A whorehouse?" I laugh, the sound bitter. Her ability to fuck me while deceiving me makes far more sense now. "You know, I watched you for a long time. I seriously thought I knew it all, and I'm ashamed to admit I was wrong."

I gently grab her chin, flaunting my control. "I know better now. You're just like your uncle, aren't you? You've got the same filthy perversions as the generation before you. You've been in on it the whole time."

Her skin turns ashen beneath my touch.

I'm getting closer to the truth. I can see it. Feel it.

"Answer me." My tone is a menacing threat.

"I don't know what you're talking about. My uncle was at a brothel the night he got run down. If you've heard a different story, it's news to me."

I stroke my fingers along her jaw, over her bottom lip. The more I stare, the more I notice.

Her eyes are the deepest blue, the outer edges melting into green. And those lips, those dark tempting lips, are ten times more beautiful as they tremble.

"Sebastian..."

I slide my hand to her throat, my fingertips grazing her carotid, her heavy swallow pressing into my palm. "Mmm?"

"Tell me what you think my uncle was doing."

I let a lazy smirk take over. "I don't *think*, Keira. I *know*."

"Then tell me," she whispers.

"Okay. I'll play along." I'm enjoying this part of the game. The revenge. The torture. It's the justice I've been craving for years. "Your uncle was breaking in sex slaves."

17

KEIRA

"*No.*" I push to my feet, only to be dragged back down by the ties binding my arms to the seat. "You're lying."

"Is that guilt I see in your eyes?" He clucks his tongue. "Silly me. I'd convinced myself you knew nothing about the human trafficking."

"What you see in my eyes is disgust. *For you.*" I've hated my uncle for years. Despised him. But I won't believe he's capable of this. I refuse. "You're digging for evidence. And it's not going to work. You won't turn me against my family. Especially not with far-fetched stories."

"You want proof?" He remains on the table, the sides of his feet pressing tight against my thighs. "Should I show you the names of the girls in this state who've gone missing over the last few years and how the Torian name can be linked to more than a third of them?"

My heart stops. "*All. Lies.*"

"I can tell you exactly how it happens. I know every move that's made." He leans closer. "Your uncle claims to be a bigshot movie producer, or the owner of a modeling agency, or whatever else his victim needs to reach their dreams. He fawns over his targets, making them feel special as he promises them the world. He takes them to fancy restaurants, buys them expensive clothes, then clinches the deal with an overseas trip which is supposed to mark the start of their career. That's when your daddy takes over."

My father?

My stomach revolts, twisting and turning.

My dad started a modeling agency years ago. It was a hobby, a 'bit of fun on the side,' he'd told me. I'd even designed his website with images he'd contracted from an overseas photographer. "I don't believe you."

He shrugs. "It's a little late to claim that when I'm already convinced you're involved."

"No." I shake my head. "You're wrong. About all of us."

"The case is closed on your dad and uncle, pumpkin. There's no question about it."

"Then why haven't they been arrested?" I raise a brow, trying to convince myself of their innocence.

He frowns at me as if I'm stupid. "Maybe because dear ol' dad has been hiding out in another country. And Uncle Dick is practically a part of the produce section."

"No, no, no." I keep shaking my head. "Why are you doing this? Is it for money? Is that what the authorities are giving you?"

"I didn't snitch for greed. I did it for me. For the pleasure of your demise. There's no game show prize waiting for me at the end of this. Only the thrill of seeing you all rot in prison like you deserve."

My heart clenches, the erratic beats painful. I don't understand. I don't want to.

"Come on, Keira. It's bad enough that you say you're not involved, but to pretend you didn't know, or your family is incapable, is an insult." He gives me a condescending smile. "It's not like you guys have ever been on the right side of the law."

"If I knew, I would never let that happen. Me, of all people, would never *ever*, let that happen."

"You, of all people?" His words drip with condescension.

"Yes. *Me, of all people.*"

"Oh." He rolls his eyes. "Because of your traumatic sexual past, right?"

My eyes blaze in fury. I hadn't lied about my history despite his theory of this being a game.

I'd wanted to tell him more. So much more. All my secrets had been his to own. But I'd needed to test him first. I had no choice in sharing the story about my father's death. It was the quickest way to see if he was loyal. Honest. I knew a revelation as monumental as the mighty Luther Torian's passing would either be spread in an instant, or held tight because of our connection.

I didn't want to delay my feelings for him.

I didn't want to draw out the trial.

I had to prove I was right about Sebastian, and I didn't care how that happened as long as it happened quickly.

But it turns out Cole had been right all along.

My brother's suspicions were on point, and now I can only assume the damage caused if Sebastian has circulated the lie.

I blink through the anger burning in my eyes, and a heated trail slides down my cheek. He watches the path of the lone tear, seeming mesmerized, until I swipe it away with my shoulder.

"That's fucking brilliant," he whispers in awe. "You're a seductress and the most flawless actress all rolled into one."

"Stop it." I scream and tug at my bindings.

"Are you crying because you think it will fool me? Or is it because you know you're going to get locked up for a very, very long time?" He leans close, getting in my face. "Don't worry. You're one of the pretty ones. I'm sure you'll make a good little bitch."

I hold his gaze, ignoring the blur in my vision as I force myself not to blink. "I had no clue." I lean forward, showing him I'm not scared. I'm not daunted. "I only lied to you about my father because I was falling for you. *Because I cared about you*. You're the one who betrayed me."

I don't recognize him anymore. I don't even recognize my own voice.

My vision continues to blur, but it's not just from building tears. It's from the manic hysteria I'm trying to hold in. My heart beats wildly. My chest is so heavy I can barely breathe.

I become lost down a rabbit hole of mental anguish. My demons haunt me. My history crucifies me.

I hyperventilate, my throat punishingly tight. My face is on fire. My heart, my lungs, my everything pounds and squeezes hard enough to kill me. I can't think past the horror. I can't see through the images my mind conjures of all those tortured women.

"Keira." He scowls, his face growing shadowed, the edges of my vision darkening. "*Keira*." He shakes me, pushing back a small part of the overwhelming tide of emotion. "Cut the crap. I'm not falling for your shit."

My throat clogs with revulsion. "How many—" I croak. "How many women?"

"Who knows. It's a lucrative business. Your father knows how to cover his tracks." His expression hardens. "It could be hundreds. Maybe thousands."

Bile rushes into my mouth, and I swallow to bite back the need to purge. I know what it's like to be physically manipulated, for my body to be used. I know, and it fills me with blinding...everything. Sorrow. Fury. Fear.

"They always make sure those women leave the country of their own free will. Happy and fucking eager to please. And they actually follow through with the photo shoots. But not until after they've lived it up with booze, sex, and drugs. Lots of pictures are taken of that, too. And always uploaded to social media. That's how the corrupt cops in foreign countries can tell the families back home that the women went off the rails due to addiction or poor decisions."

I suck in lungfuls of breath, trying to push through the pummeling nausea. "I'm going to be sick."

He scoffs. "Do you think I care?"

His sterility makes my anguish ten times worse. I'm not the person he thinks I am. I'm not that type of monster.

I try to stand again, only to fall back in place under the restricting ties. Heat consumes my throat and mouth. I crane my neck to the side and tilt my face away. I lean as far as my bindings allow and retch the toxic sludge in heaving waves.

"Jesus Christ." Sebastian shoves from the table.

I continue to vomit the contents of my stomach. Tears follow, streaking my cheeks, staining my soul. I don't stop until my belly is empty. Then I wipe my mouth on my shoulder and hang my head as I sob.

"Quit it," he growls.

"I didn't know." My lips tremble as I turn my face toward him. "I swear."

He glares at me. There's a wealth of hatred in those eyes, but maybe there's the slightest bit of doubt, too.

He wants to believe me. I know he does.

"Please, Sebastian. You have to trust me. I never—"

He slams a palm down on the table. "Trust you? Are you kidding? I can barely bring myself to look at you."

"You lied to me, too," I say in a rush. "But I'm not the enemy here."

"You're not the victim either," he snarls through gritted teeth.

He pushes away from the table and storms to the kitchen. He stands there for a moment, clutching the counter, silent and still.

I want to say something, anything to break him out of this anger, only the words form in disjointed sentences. I can't think straight, not with the nuclear explosion of reality devastating my mind and the heartache taking over my chest.

"You know me." I swallow to ease the taste of bile. "I know you." I heave out a breath. I frown through the overwhelming confusion. If only I could focus so everything would make sense. "Sebastian, please explain all this to me. I don't under—"

"Shut up."

I balk at his continued vehemence. "I don't know the real you, do I?" The realization comes with an icy cold chill.

The harsh reality I thought I'd been living in wasn't reality at all. *That* existence was the fairytale. *That life,* full of deception and betrayal, was nothing in comparison to the truth.

He yanks open the duffle, his movements filled with livid rage as he pulls out a utility knife.

Oh, God.

He swings back around, lifting the blade while he walks toward me.

"No." I shake my head. "Please, Sebastian, don't do this. I promise I can prove I'm not involved. Just give me a chance."

"How?"

How? Jesus. I don't know. "Let me call Cole. Let me call Layla. Or my father."

"What the fuck is a phone call going to do?" He keeps approaching, not stopping until he's in my face. His livid rage steals away the gentle man I thought I knew.

He grabs my upper arm, drawing it high, making my wrist ache as it pulls against the plastic binding.

He's going to stab me.

Kill me.

I thought at a time like this I'd fight like hell. All I want to do is get on my knees and beg. Not only for my life. I want to plead for forgiveness for not recognizing my family's sins. I need to pray for absolution.

I should've known.

I should've paid more attention.

"I don't know how to make you believe me. Tell me what to do. Tell me how to make this right."

He lowers the blade to my wrist as horror fills my veins. I can't watch the metal penetrate. I refuse to witness the start of my own death. So I stare at him instead. I focus on his dark eyes, the deep pull of his brows, those tight lips that still seem entirely beautiful despite the tight line they're now clamped in.

He's going to slice my wrists. I'm going to bleed out.

"You're not this man, Sebastian. I know you're not. And you should know I don't deserve this. I shouldn't be punished for the crimes of someone else."

He narrows his gaze on me, his lip curled in a snarl. "The only thing I know is that I'm fucking sick of you playing the victim."

He starts wiggling the blade, and I hold my breath, waiting for the pain to breach my panic.

"All those women your family stole *are the victims.*" The knife stops moving, and my arm falls free. "My *fucking sister* is the victim."

I hear static after those defining words—*my fucking sister.*

I don't pay attention as he releases my other arm. I don't feel fear or hysteria or disgust. I'm hollow. Empty.

That's why he's doing this? His sister is the reason he became a traitor to the most dangerous family in the state?

I stare up at him, a million questions waiting on immovable lips. I can't speak. I barely breathe.

He flings my other arm away and turns, heading back to the kitchen. He snatches the duffle, his gun, and his can of beer before stalking to the back door.

"Don't bother running," he snarls. "If I have to chase you again, I won't be as kind when I catch you." He grabs the door handle and pulls it wide. "Clean up your fucking mess."

18

DECKER

I sit on the back deck, the beer can now warm in my hand after hours spent staring at the setting sun. I can't go back inside, and it's not only because my brother's house is now filled with the smell of vomit.

I can't stand to look at her. I can't keep questioning the facts just because of her pleading blue-eyed gaze. So I'll continue to hide out here, drowning in doubt.

I'm not worried she'll run. I'm too fucking drained to give a shit. But even if she does, we're miles from civilization. More than a day's trek to salvation if she has hopes of escaping.

All the external doors are locked except for the one a few feet to my right. She's caged. Unless she decides to climb through a window, which I have no doubt she will. In that case, I'll hear her and have another chance for retribution once I chase her down.

I think that's the only thought keeping me upright—the possibility of sprinting after her, scaring her, punishing her.

There's no sound out here. Not even the whimsical chirp of a bird. There's only the breeze rustling through the dried grass and the heavy beat of my pulse echoing in my ears.

I never should've told her about my sister. I hate her having insight into that part of my life. But those words had burst free, demanding to be heard. After all this time, I wanted someone to know the truth.

My life changed the moment I realized Penny had been taken.

Now there's no hiding the darkness shadowing me, or the crimes I've committed to get here.

I'm not the man I once was. That happy-go-lucky fucker is gone. The naive sack of shit who lived a simple life is dead and buried. And I guess the guy I became soon will be too, but that shit won't be a metaphor.

My days are numbered. The finish line to failure is fast advancing, and I have no clue how to stop its approach.

I raise my beer and take a long pull. I don't know where to go from here. I'm not sure there's a way out, or if I'd even take it if there is. I've spent years seeking answers. Striving for revenge. I no longer know how to live any other way.

Footsteps approach from inside, and I lower my drink to listen. Her figure cuts through the yellow light beaming through the glass panes of the door. Her presence tickles the back of my fucking neck.

Don't come out here.

Don't you fucking dare.

The door opens and she slowly steps outside, walking to the railing to look out over the vast expanse of vacant land as she clings to the cuffs of her cardigan.

She remains quiet, her silence eating up the night until it feels like I've been staring at her for hours.

"How long?" she whispers.

I take another mouthful of beer and drag my gaze from her slender body. I hate the attraction that lingers when I look at her. I fucking loathe it after everything she's done.

She turns to face me, her face blotchy with the remnants of crocodile tears.

I won't be fooled. Not again.

"How long have you been trying to take down my family?"

"Why?" I glare. "What cunning plan have you concocted to use against me?"

"I want to help."

"*Help?*" I scoff. "Go back inside. You're wasting your breath talking to me."

She lowers her gaze, playing a meek, apologetic role that doesn't suit her. Not anymore.

"Then why tell me? Why am I here?"

I can't answer that. I honestly don't know.

Originally, I feared for Hunter and Sarah's safety. At least that's what I told myself, even though I know better than anyone that those two can look after themselves.

I guess I'd wanted to prove Hunter wrong.

I knew he believed Keira had set me up. But, Jesus, I'd hoped like hell he'd been smoking crack, too.

The whole drive here I hated on her, despising every fucking breath, while also wishing she'd do or say something to prove Hunt wrong. That somehow he'd been mistaken. That I hadn't been fooled into falling for her.

"I didn't tell you anything you didn't already know." I take another chug of beer to drown my pity party.

She leans back against the railing, her hands resting behind her ass. Calm. Subdued. "What do you plan on doing with me?"

"Whatever I like," I grate. "And the more you annoy me, the worse the options get. So leave me the fuck alone."

Her chin hitches. "You won't kill me, Sebastian. I know you won't. You've said it yourself, you're not like my brother, and I know that wasn't a lie."

"Do you?" I'm not entirely sure she's right. If given the chance, I'd kill her father. I'd kill her uncle as well. And despite her claims of Cole's innocence regarding women trafficking, I'm pretty sure I could fuck him up without feeling an ounce of guilt, too.

I could massacre her entire family and dance a fucking jig in their blood. I wouldn't care how I had to do it. With my bare hands. Up close or from a distance. With a knife or a bullet or a fucking frying pan.

I'm at the point where I'd pay good money to look deep into the eyes of those motherfuckers while I revel in their pleas for mercy.

"Are you seriously that confident I wouldn't bury you out here if I had proof of your involvement?"

"But you don't," she murmurs. "And you never will, because I'm not involved. Neither are Layla or Cole, and I'd bet my life on it."

I raise my brows. "You might regret that wager one day."

"I won't. I don't have the slightest doubt."

"Give it time. Earlier you were certain your uncle and father weren't involved either."

She lowers her attention to the wooden slats of the porch. "That's different. Layla is too kindhearted to even imagine doing something like this. And Cole…"

"And Cole what?" I sneer. "Is he kindhearted, too? Have you forgotten he tried to strangle you the first night we met?"

Her gaze darts to mine, her mouth parting on a confession that doesn't breach her lips.

"Go on, say it," I taunt. "Weave me another bedtime story."

She sighs, her shoulders slumping with the deep exhale. "Cole never tried to strangle me."

"Oh, yeah? Then what would you call it?"

"A ritual. An act." She keeps clinging to the cuffs of her cardigan, pulling on them like a lifeline. "Whenever someone new comes to work for my family, Cole and I put on a show to pretend we have a temperamental relationship—a weak spot that could be manipulated. It's an easy way to flush out those trying to tear us apart. But the truth is the opposite."

I frown, reliving that night in my mind. She'd been scared. Cole had been in a rage.

It was all for show.

Fuckers.

"He tells me everything, Sebastian. He has since our mother died. I know how you came to work for us. I know about the hits my brother has ordered and why. I know where our money comes from and how it's laundered. I know everything."

I throw back my beer and take a long pull, emptying the can. "So, you act like a docile puppet when you're really a coldhearted bitch. No surprise there."

Her jaw tenses. "That's not entirely true. I'm not a good person, I've never claimed to be, but I'm not guilty of what you're accusing me of. I need you to stop judging me through your anger and listen for a minute."

"I don't need to do shit." I crush the can in my fist. "Are you forgetting this is personal for me? *I know* what your family does. Quit trying to talk your way out of the facts."

"I'm not. You say you have all the proof you need on my father and uncle. And I believe you." She winces. "But you need to let me plead my case for me and my siblings. Let me prove Cole isn't involved. I think if you understand he's not capable of this, you'll realize Layla and I are innocent, too."

I throw the can toward the door and scowl at her, impatient.

"*Please.*" She chews on her lower lip. There's no seduction in the expression. Only feigned desperation. Pretend fear. "I was six when I was first sexually assaulted by someone I trusted."

"Jesus Christ." The diversion back to this conversation is enough to make my tired head spin. "I swear to God, Keira, I'll lose my shit if I have to listen to more of your lies."

Her throat works over a heavy swallow but she holds my gaze, determined. "I didn't know what was happening at first. My parents were in the kitchen. Cole was on the floor watching television right in front of me, while I sat side-by-side on the sofa with an attacker I'd grown to admire."

"Stop it," I mutter. "You're wasting your breath."

"He started complementing me," she continues as if I didn't speak. "Whispering right in my ear about how I was such a pretty little girl as his index finger ran in circles on my thigh, just below the hem of my skirt."

She's doing it again, trying to delude me with her sob stories.

It won't work.

I can't let it.

I clench my hands into fists, hating how her lies hypnotize me even though I know the truth.

"I can still remember how it felt." She lowers her attention to her feet. "The lone finger that changed to a full splayed palm which worked its way beneath my clothes. When he reached the crotch of my underwear he smiled and chuckled an apology, pretending the intimate touch had been an accident."

I run a hand over my face and clench my teeth to maintain control. How the fuck does she do it? How can she spin her web of fiction like it's the truth?

"He did it in plain sight. Mere feet from Cole. I could hear my parents talking clearly in the next room. It made me think he mustn't be doing anything wrong if he wasn't trying to hide it."

"Nice story," I mutter. "You done yet?"

She lifts her gaze to mine, but the annoyance I anticipate isn't in her expression. Her forehead is etched in pain. Her eyes are glassy and filled with exhaustion.

I despise her beauty. I hate her duplicity. Most of all, I loathe the way she makes me want to believe her.

"He did it often, Sebastian. And I was too young to understand the severity of his actions. Whenever he came around, he'd hug me tighter than anyone else. He'd pay me more attention than Layla or Cole."

Her gaze trails off, disappearing in memory. "We'd always play chasies, and when he caught me it was usually with a splayed hand across my chest or my ass. I guess I always knew he was doing something wrong, but he was kind to me. He made me feel beautiful and bought me expensive gifts. As a little girl, I guess my greed for shiny new toys outweighed the discomfort."

"Just like your dad buys for the women he sells to the highest bidder."

She cringes. "Yeah. I guess you're right. And I was brainwashed in the same way. But then the casual touches turned into something more. His appetite increased the older I got, and I didn't know how to make—"

"*Keira*," I warn, needing her to stop before I give in. "You're not going to fool me with this. I'm never going to believe you."

I spin my own lies in the hopes she'll quit this vicious cycle. My hands itch to comfort her.

Her—a cunning, heartless bitch.

She shrugs, her face filled with resignation. "When I was twelve, my dad threw a party at our house. All the adults were drinking and talking loud. I could hear them from my room upstairs because us kids had been forbidden to join the fun." Her chin trembles. "That night he came into my room and laid beside me. I could smell the alcohol on his breath as he touched himself...right there...on my bed...while I pretended to sleep."

"*Stop*," my voice fractures.

Her eyes glaze with unshed tears. "No. Not until you believe me."

I scoff. "Don't hold your breath."

She wraps one arm around her middle, hugging herself. "Like I told you, I was fourteen when he raped me. I could never lie about that. Cole is the one who saved me by storming into my room and dragging a grown man off me. My brother never left my side. He stayed with me while I cried, his own tears mingling with mine as everyone continued to party downstairs."

"Yet there's no police report," I accuse. "I've dug deep enough into your life I've practically given you an enema. And not once have I found evidence of this."

"I couldn't report it."

"Of course not," I snap. "God forbid you ever have one piece of proof to backup your bullshit."

Her eyes harden, her spite finally coming out to play. "I couldn't report it because—"

"Shut it, Keira." I shove to my feet, ready to go inside just so I can get away from her.

"I couldn't report it—"

"I said *shut the fuck up*." I descend upon her in five fierce steps to grasp her upper arm.

Her hand raises in defense, or at least I think it does, until I catch the glint of silver as it sails toward my neck. The blade pierces my skin, the bite of pain barely felt over my rising fury.

Fuck. Me.

She's done it again.

She's fucking played me.

Jesus. Fucking. Christ.

I deserve to have my throat slashed. If I get out of this, I swear to God I'll do it myself for being so fucking stupid.

"How fast can you move, Sebastian?" she hisses. "Can you disarm me before I slice through your carotid? Because like you've mentioned before, there's nobody here to save you. There's no phone. No devices. No people. You'll bleed out before I reach the main road."

Her gaze flickers between my eyes, frantic even though I estimate she's got more than a fifty-fifty chance of doing exactly what she's threatened.

"Slice deep," I snarl, "because if the cut isn't fatal, what I inflict on you will be."

She shakes her head. "I'm not doing this to hurt you. I'm doing it to earn your trust."

She sucks in a deep breath and retreats, the kitchen knife clattering to the floor as she raises her hands in surrender.

My heart beats in an erratic pulse, waiting for the punchline to her joke.

"I couldn't report the rape because my attacker would never have gone to prison, no matter what I said." She articulates the words slowly. Succinctly. "Just like you said, criminal charges don't stick to men like my uncle."

My muscles pull taut, every inch of my skin crawling. "Richard?"

"Yes." She inclines her head. "Richard."

She steps toward the back door and reaches for the knob. "I didn't lie to you about the rape, and I wasn't playing games when I broke down the night of the shooting. The only reason I told you my father died is because I wanted nothing more than to trust you. I had to prove to myself you were the guy I thought you were, especially when I was falling for you."

Jesus. She's working me like a pro. "And now you know I'm not that guy."

"Now I know you're a better person than the man I fell for." Her gaze pleads with me. "But you still don't believe me, do you?"

I clench my jaw. Unable to open my mouth.

I can't let her know she's reclaimed the upper hand.

I won't give her the satisfaction of knowing I'm hooked.

"Okay. I get it." She doesn't break our gaze, just keeps staring, keeps wordlessly pleading. "And I guess it won't make a difference if I tell you I'm responsible for putting Richard in hospital."

It takes all my strength not to jump at the information. She's feeding me exactly what I want to hear, but I can't let myself believe her.

Fuck me, I just can't.

She pauses briefly, waiting for a reply I refuse to give. Then she pulls the door wide and disappears inside, leaving me alone to deal with my increased self-loathing.

19

KEIRA

The house smells like the discarded contents of my stomach as I drag my feet inside.

I don't know what else to do other than reclaim the cleaning products from beneath the kitchen sink and start scrubbing the floor again. I crawl on hands and knees, polishing the tile when what I really need to do is scramble out of this torturous limbo.

I don't want to believe my father is capable of such destruction. I don't want to, yet, deep down, I already know the truth.

He's a monster. Not merely a criminal, but the devil himself.

In contrast, Sebastian has made himself into a vengeful angel. A hopeful savior.

Righteous.

Honorable.

Perfect.

And I betrayed him.

I scrub the floor harder, cleaning the tile like I want to cleanse my soul. My arms burn from the tension. My fingers ache with my tight grip.

Sebastian's right. I'm guilty. Even if I didn't participate. Even though I didn't have a clue. These atrocities were done by my family. My own flesh. There's no way I can free myself from blame.

I sit back on my haunches, unsure how to right all the wrongs. I can't fathom the pain I've caused with my ignorance.

I should've known.

Should've fucking known.

I push to my feet and pack away the chemicals. Then I make myself a coffee and sit down at the dining table while I wait for the masked scent of bile to die a slow death.

I sip from my mug, the liquid tasteless as I try to figure out my future when I have no control over the outcome. I'm still Sebastian's prisoner, and I don't think he has any plan to change the dynamic anytime soon. I also don't have the will to run. Or the desire.

What I want is for him to believe me. To finally trust me despite what I'm guilty of. But he doesn't come back inside to face me. Not even once my coffee has turned cold and the forced solitude makes me hollow. He leaves me to battle my demons on my own, and I can't help thinking about those that plague him.

He pretended to be Hunter's friend. His accomplice.

He faked his way into my heart. My body.

I guess I would've done the same.

If Layla had been one of the women taken... If Stella...

My lungs clench through torturous inhales. I can't fall down that mine-filled rabbit hole. All I can concentrate on is knowing I would've deceived or destroyed anyone who stood in my way of revenge.

But that doesn't make me feel any better for being the one Sebastian wants to punish. I don't like being his enemy. I want to go back to the place where he gave me kindness and protection.

His lust and adoration.

The fake fairytale.

I sigh and push from the table to pour the remaining dregs of coffee down the sink. The pungent scent of bile follows me with each step, smothering my nostrils and taunting my gag reflex.

This house needs fresh air. *Lots* of fresh air.

I walk from the kitchen and into the hall, finding the first bedroom with its queen size bed and lone bedside table. I increase my pace across the room, thankful for the distraction as I unlock the window and push the glass panel high.

The night breeze rushes through the gauze, filling my lungs with relief. I suck in a deep breath, only to have it rush back out at the sound of a slamming door.

I swing around, on alert as heavy footfalls thunder through the house.

"*Keira,*" Sebastian bellows.

I hesitate. I've waited over an hour for him to come inside and face me. To see me. The real me.

But the fury in his voice is a crystal clear indication he isn't ready to see anything other than his cemented misconceptions.

"*Keira.*"

I remain still, tracing the sound of his pounding footsteps from the dining area to the hall. I can't stand to speak to him like this. Not with raised voices and more drugging adrenaline.

My chest squeezes as he skitters to a stop in the doorway, his eyes blazing, his chest heaving.

He glances from me, to the open window, then back again. Judging. Convicting. "Trying to escape?"

I slump my shoulders while he continues to cast me as the enemy, his narrowed gaze too vicious for me to hold. "I'm trying to get rid of the smell." I turn my focus to the floor and drag my feet toward him, stopping before the doorway where he blocks my path. "Please move."

I ask for the one thing I don't want—space.

What I need is his proximity. I need him to face me. To face *this*. And, God, more than anything, I need him to believe me.

But he steps to the side, breaking me with his cold dismissal.

I can't stand his continued hatred. His loathing. I'm not the person he thinks I am and I have to fight from the pull to slap some sense into him.

Bitter resentment coils in my blood making my limbs throb as I squeeze by him and stalk further down the hall, to the next bedroom. I repeat my actions, making a beeline for the window and gripping the pane to thrust it high.

"Quit it." His menacing steps follow. "Leave them closed."

For the briefest second, I contemplate obeying him. It's only a blip in time. A breath of acquiescence before my spine grows rigid and I take hold of my anger.

I inch away from the window, leaving it open, then make toward him at his barricaded position at the door.

This time he doesn't move out of my way. He blocks my escape, his chest broad, his shoulders wide. "I said leave it closed."

"And I say we need fresh air." I hold his dark stare. "Or are you too scared you won't catch me if I run?"

He takes a predatory step in my direction, those chocolate eyes punishing through menacing slits.

My pulse spikes. A breath hitches through my lips. I backtrack, my pulse pounding in my throat as I retreat from his animosity. The toxicity of his malice coils around me, making my heart fracture.

"I'm not scared of anything," he grates.

I believe him.

He's not filled with fear. The emotion overtaking him is in stark contrast.

There's so much revulsion. A wealth of disgust and hostility. But up this close, there's more. Pain ebbs off him. I can see it now. There are fissures of misery in those eyes. Tiny glimmers of agony and torment.

Despite trying to hide it, his suffering matches my own.

It's like an awakening.

Slowly, I come to understand how the sarcasm and humor has hidden the tortured man beneath. He's pretended to be the joker, when his reality is shadowed by anguish.

"I have no reason to run." I take another retreating step toward the window.

His jaw ticks as he stalks closer. "If you knew how I felt, you would."

"Then tell me." My words fracture through parched lips. "Explain why I should be scared, because I'm not. You would never hurt me. Not physically, despite how you're trying to emotionally tear me apart."

He stops, his shoulders stiffening as if my admission has inflicted a bone-deep wound. "You've got a short memory. It wasn't long ago you thought I was going to kill you with a utility knife."

"That wasn't you. You were mindless. I never—"

"It was me," he snaps. "The real me."

"So who is the man I spent the last forty-eight hours with? Who's the guy I've known for months?"

He releases a derisive scoff. "You mean the schmuck who eagerly lapped up your attention? That guy doesn't exist."

He's lying. I refuse to believe otherwise.

I know fake people. I've been surrounded by them all my life. And the man from the safe house wasn't one of those. He was caring and kind, despite his deceptions.

"You liked me," I accuse.

He'd wanted me. That part hadn't been an act. He'd slept with me without revulsion or disgust. It wasn't until we came here—until he knew I'd lied—that he couldn't stomach touching me.

He'd thought I was innocent until I'd given Cole what he wanted by testing the man who risked his life to protect me.

"It wasn't an act for you either, was it?" I scan his eyes, searching for threads of the truth in those dark depths. "You felt the same way I did."

He doesn't move. Doesn't even blink.

Hope sparks inside me, the sweet, delicious optimism working its way through my veins until he releases a sigh of exhaustion.

"I'm fucking tired, Keira. We're going to have to postpone this delusional conversation until tomorrow."

"Why? Sleep won't change our situation. The truth will still be here no matter how tired you are."

"Sleep will bring patience, which is something I don't have with you at the moment."

I can live without his patience. What I can't endure is another minute without his honesty. "I'll make this easier for you. Just tell me why you slept with me in Westport. Was it because you wanted to, or because you thought it would get you closer to the truth?"

He stares at me. Stares right through me. There's no warmth. No kindness. No Sebastian. There's only sorrow and detachment. He's a shell of the man I once knew.

"Close the window," he mutters.

"No. Not until you answer me."

"*Close the fucking window, Keira.*"

He's trying to scare me with his vicious tone, but there's no fear left. There's only determination and the strongest sense of perseverance.

"You were attracted to me," I demand. "You *wanted me.*"

His nostrils flare. "All in the past, honey."

My insides react. Squeezing. Tingling. "What changed? Do you hate me now because I told one lie? Because I tried to protect myself with the same dedication you protected me with?"

He falls quiet, those tired eyes lazily blinking back at me with sterility.

"Answer me," I plead. "Tell me how I'm the bad person when I betrayed you once, yet you made me fall for someone who doesn't exist."

"Can you hear yourself? Are you really begging for me? You're practically on your knees for a fucking informant." His nose scrunches in disgust. "If only Daddy could see you now."

Rage shoots to the forefront. "Don't throw him in my face." I take a menacing step forward. "Don't hold me accountable for my father's actions. *I* didn't do this. *I* didn't hurt you. *I* didn't take your sister."

He winces. "No, you did something worse. You made me crave the daughter of my sister's murderer."

His admission slices through me, piercing skin, muscle, and bone. I've been waiting for this truth. It's what I wanted. I just never anticipated it would tear me apart like this. "And I fell for a man who's trying to put my father in prison. I fell for the guy who deceived my family for months, if not years. I fell for you, despite your intentions." I swallow over the ache in my throat. "And I don't regret it, Sebastian."

His hands clench at his sides.

He's going to yell at me again. He's poised to lash out.

My heart pounds in tumultuous arrhythmia, anticipating the onslaught. Every second lasts an eternity waiting for him to berate me.

But he doesn't.

His expression doesn't change. He's still harsh and unforgiving, as he retreats from his predatory stance to slump back onto the mattress and runs a hand through his hair. "Tell me about your uncle. How did he end up in the hospital?"

My chest continues its accelerated pulse. His question isn't a white flag, but it's something. The door he slammed closed on us has inched open just a little. "I paid someone."

He raises a brow in disbelief. "Why now? Why not all those years ago?"

"When I was fourteen? I wasn't capable of plotting murder back then."

"I mean when you became an adult. Why didn't you do something as soon as you were capable? When you turned twenty, or twenty-one, or any other year since. Why now and not earlier?"

"I guess I didn't want to awaken old ghosts." I return to the window and lean against the sill. "After he hurt me, he stopped coming around. I don't know if he thought I'd tell my father or if Cole would. But he kept his distance and concentrated on business instead of family. Which gave me the space I needed to move on."

"Until?"

I force down the emotions trying to bubble to the surface. I breathe in the calm I need to continue this conversation. "Until Stella turned six."

"Stella?" His eyes flash with rage. "He didn't—"

"No." I shake my head. "He's never touched her. I made sure of it. He may have groomed me at an early age, but I educated her even earlier, making sure she never spent time alone with him. That didn't stop him from thinking about it, though. I watched the way he interacted with her. How he'd make her laugh. How they'd hug. I knew what was going on in that sick mind of his."

I pause, waiting for an acceptance of my truth, praying and pleading silently for him to believe me.

"Keep going." His expression doesn't soften. He doesn't give a hint of sympathy or solidarity. "Tell me everything."

I have to be thankful for the slightest glimmer of curiosity. For the baby steps. "I knew it was only a matter of time. So I took the law into my own hands and paid for someone to take him out."

"You paid for them to kill him, and they fucked up?"

"No." I cringe. "I'm the one who fucked up. I found someone willing to do the job and paid half the arranged price up front…"

"Then?"

"Then I chickened out." I swallow over the admission.

"You changed your mind?"

"No. I still wanted him dead. But I hadn't thought about the danger I'd put everyone in. With my father spending longer and longer out of the country, I realized I couldn't risk weakening our defenses."

"I don't get it. How does making him a vegetable help the situation?"

"It doesn't. I tried to break the contract, or at least put it on hold. But apparently there's no take-backsys when it comes to arranging a hit."

One side of his mouth kicks in a half-hearted smirk.

That's all he gives me. A slight change in expression. A casual tweak of lips.

The tepid simplicity is blindingly beautiful.

His slight hint of friendship turns my insides to flame, and I'm weak-kneed for him all over again. "In hindsight, I guess I should've asked Hunter to do it."

"Why didn't you?"

"Because I knew he wouldn't do the job without permission from Cole. And my brother still has no clue I'm responsible." I stare at him, waiting for him to realize the secret I've just laid at his feet.

Nobody knows why Richard was run down.

Nobody is aware I tried to have someone in my own family slaughtered.

Nobody but the murderer I hired and now the man seated before me. The same man who could crush my heart that sits firmly in his calloused hands.

Sebastian could give this information to my siblings. The authorities. The media. I've handed him my skeletons. I've given him my whole fucking closet.

"Why couldn't you get Cole to arrange the hit in the first place?" he asks. "You said he was there for you."

"Because family doesn't kill family."

"Is that one of your father's rules?" He crosses his arms over his chest, his lips flattening into a tight line. "Your uncle raped you, Keira. The punishment fits the crime."

There he is, the protective man I know.

I may not have an understanding of who Sebastian really is, but the way he feels for me was never a lie.

"It doesn't matter." I shrug. "You never turn your back on family. You can punish them, but death is reserved for enemies, not uncles."

"Enemies like me." His eyes sparkle with mischief. His death wish lingers again. He lets out a derisive chuckle and lowers his gaze. "So, this hitman refused to let you back out of the contract, then fucked up the hit anyway?"

"No. I'm certain the change in plan was deliberate."

"Why?" He straightens, inching closer to the edge of the bed.

"He figured out who I am. Now he's trying to extort me for more than double the price and demanding I make the drop in person. I don't know what to do. I'm smart enough to realize he's going to keep extorting me no matter how much I pay, but I don't know how to make it stop. And it's not merely intimidating phone calls anymore." I bite my lip, not wanting to tell him everything, and dying to spill my guts at the same time. "He's escalated to physical threats."

His chin hitches, his eyes glazing as he becomes lost in thought, the wild contemplation written all over his face.

"The drive-by..." He scowls. "You said you were responsible. You told me you were to blame."

I don't move, don't breathe while he realizes even more of my truth.

"*Fuck*." He pushes to his feet. "You've known who it was all along—"

"No." I push from the window sill. "I'm not entirely certain. I still haven't confirmed it. I tried making some calls last night, but I didn't get any answers. I don't have his phone number. All the information is stored in my cell, which is back in Portland."

"Who is he?"

I swallow over the dryness overwhelming my throat.

"Keira?" He approaches, closing in on me. "Who did you pay?"

"I don't know. I found him on the dark web. I thought he was a nobody from out of town."

"A nobody that had the balls to shoot up one of your family's restaurants?" He gets closer. He's there. Right there. His hips brushing mine. "Give me his name."

I work my lips together, buying time, hating the disappointment bearing down on me before I admit, "I don't know."

"Jesus." Concern seeps into his eyes.

Concern for me?

"I thought I'd done everything right. I made contact. I arranged the hit. I even drove to Salem and placed the first half of the money in a locker before he knew where I was making the drop so he wouldn't be able to stake out the scene. It all went smoothly. I'd made threats, telling him I had my team watching him to ensure he didn't take off with the cash without fulfilling his part of the agreement."

"What happened when you changed your mind?"

I heave out a breath, fighting the tingle in my fingers demanding I reach out and touch him. "I contacted him online. I told him not to go ahead with the hit, but he refused to discuss the situation unless it was in person."

"You didn't, did you?"

"No." I shake my head. "I convinced him to call me on a burner number. But the verbal communication took away my power. I became flustered, and slowly, he chipped away at my anonymity. Before long, I was sure he'd figured out who I was."

"Fuck." He turns away, massaging his forehead. "That's when he realized extorting you was a far bigger cash cow than killing your uncle."

"Yes."

"This is an impressive mess you've gotten yourself into." He keeps his back to me, those strong shoulders calling for my hands.

"I know." I need his help. I want it. Crave it. "I owe him money, and Torians always pay their debts. But I can't approach him on my own." I take cautious steps toward him. I don't stop until his body is within reach. "I don't know how to fix this."

"Some shit can't be fixed."

I'm not deluded into thinking his response is aimed squarely at the hitman issue. He's referring to this mess as a whole. He's talking about us.

I place my hands on his waist, needing to reclaim our connection. "Please…"

He stiffens, every muscle rippling under my touch while I fight for words.

"Will you come with me?" My lungs seize under the agonizing request. My ears burn waiting for his response. "Can you tell me what to do to fix this?"

"You want my help?" He swings around, incredulous. All those fissures of torment and pain disappear under a renewed show of fury. "How the fuck do you expect me to fix anything now that you've put a target on my back?"

My hands fall to my sides, my fingers trembling with both adrenaline and anguish as I withdraw.

"Don't confuse my curiosity for concern, Keira." He looks me up and down, judging me again and finding me unworthy. "You've ratted me out, and it's only a matter of time before your actions put me six feet under."

I retreat at the verbal punch and watch in silence as he stalks for the door.

"Close the fucking window," he snaps. "It's time you got some rest."

"Sebast—"

"You've got five minutes to take a shower before I come back and restrain you to the bed."

20

DECKER

I snatch a t-shirt from my brother's wardrobe, then trudge to the bathroom and throw it inside the steam-filled room while Keira showers.

She doesn't protest the intrusion. Or acknowledge the clothes I've given her to wear. She doesn't even make a sound apart from the slight shift in the shower's spray before I slam the door shut.

The damn woman has me tied in knots.

This whole situation is a cluster fuck of epic proportions.

The worst part is the demanding urge to help her. It's the biggest bitch slap my intuition has ever handed me, and I don't know how to bury the impulse.

While I wait for her to finish her shower, I retrieve Hunter's handy duffle of goodies and dump it on the floor in the room where she will sleep.

A few minutes later, she returns to the room, my brother's shirt billowing at her thighs, her hair damp and hanging around her shoulders.

She entices me like no other. She always has.

The woman embroiled in more crime than a small country. The daughter of my sister's murderer. The sister to the man who will soon kill me.

She's my weakness, my downfall, and still I can't ignore the temptation of her.

"What are you doing?" she asks as I weave a cable tie through the one already looped around a wooden slat in the designer bed head.

"I'm creating shackles."

She sighs. "You don't have to do this. I'm not going anywhere."

"I know." I pull back the covers and pat the mattress. "Get in."

She glares at me, but that's the extent of her protest. She climbs on the bed and remains quiet as I secure a cable tie around her wrist, then another at her ankle.

She can't complain. I've set up the restrains in the middle of the bed. She has the ability to rest on her stomach or her back. She's not spread starfish like I could've demanded. If anything, I've been highly accommodating.

"Where are you sleeping?"

"Wherever the fuck I want." I cover her with the quilt, cutting off the sight of her laying like a BDSM pinup model. The only problem is, instead of her body slaying me with temptation, her eyes implore me with wounded emotion.

She wordlessly begs for my trust. She tears me apart with those big baby blues.

"I don't want to hear from you until sunup." I need to erect a big fucking wall between us. It's the only way I'll stay sane.

I start for the hall, flicking off the light and closing the bedroom door as I pass.

She doesn't wail on me like I expect. Not a single word leaves her lips as I pause outside the room, waiting for a theatrical reaction to make me feel like less of a prick.

I'm still waiting for a dramatic response as I shower. And again, when I pull on a clean pair of boxers from the drawers in the main bedroom.

She continues to surprise me as I climb into my brother's bed and listen to the eerie silence. I didn't expect her to take her punishment quietly. I also didn't anticipate feeling like such a sack of shit at having her tied like a prisoner in the next room. But there's no other choice.

She would run if left to free-range the house. Or worse, she would attempt to punish me for all the fun-filled choices I've made, and only end up getting hurt in the process.

It's safer to have her restrained.

Smarter.

I keep telling myself that while I fade in and out of guilt-ridden consciousness.

I wake with every subtle squeak of her mattress as the hours pass. I picture her tossing and turning. It isn't until three in the morning that those squeaks become something more.

There's rustling, grating, and the continued snarl of something hard running over tough plastic. Then the slightest footsteps and the lightest squeak of a door hinge.

I'm not surprised she freed herself. To be honest, I would've been disappointed if she hadn't made an effort to escape. What I'm not looking forward to is the retaliation. The revenge.

Yesterday, I would've eaten that shit up like prime rib. Now, I can't stop the dull ache under my sternum. The thought of continuously fighting with her makes my stomach turn.

I retrieve my gun from under my pillow and hold it frozen at my side. I keep my breathing heavy, feigning sleep, as her slim silhouette enters the doorway.

She creeps into the room, one slow step after another. I can't see her face in the darkness, but I feel her stare. She's scrutinizing my breathing, waiting for a sign to show her I'm prepared to fend off her attack.

I continue to inhale deep and exhale slow as she approaches the foot of the bed. I have no clue what I'm going to do when she reaches my side. I'll have to fend off a weapon; that much is clear. She didn't yank or tug her way out of those cable ties. There's a blade on her somewhere.

What I don't understand is why she didn't finish the job earlier when she held my jugular hostage. Did my refusal to help her with the hitman situation make her change her mind?

She doesn't continue toward my side of the mattress like I expect. Instead, she heads in the opposite direction, making my breathing falter for a second while I try to figure out why she's moving to the left of the bed.

Slowly, she raises the covers, and I scowl through the darkness as I battle confusion.

Is she going to try to suffocate me? Really?

Of all the ways to attempt homicide, this is a shitty one. I'm so goddamn disappointed in her poor excuse for a murder plot that I gently glide my grip away from the gun to free both my hands. This way I'll have the ability to shake some fucking sense into her.

Then the bed dips, and her weight nestles onto the mattress.

I hold my breath, my ears attuned to her movements, my muscles tense and poised for her strike.

But she doesn't.

Slowly, silently, she inches under the covers as if preparing for a secret slumber party.

I keep waiting for the violence to start. I stare into the shadows and bite my tongue to stop myself from asking what the hell she's doing, even though the answer is clear. She's snuggling into the bed, her back toward me, her head on the pillow.

The question is—why?

Once she's settled, she doesn't move, not one fucking inch. She just lays there. Less than a foot away.

I don't get it.

What's her plan? What's the strategy?

I remain on alert, waiting a lifetime for her to pounce.

Thirty minutes pass, and she still hasn't budged. The only thing that changes is her breathing, the inhales deep, the exhales languid.

I don't know what's more fucked up—her freeing herself of the cable ties and escaping her room, only to crawl in bed beside the man who's keeping her captive, or me for being the sick son of a bitch who relaxes under the wash of relief at having her close.

I'm one dumb fuck for ignoring the inner voice telling me she's playing me. That everything she's said and done has been one shovelful of bullshit after another. And this right here is merely another steaming load.

But it's hard. It's really fucking hard, when all I want to do is believe her.

No matter what I do, I can't convince myself she's the enemy. I struggle to see anything heinous and vindictive about her. Instead, I've battled with the obsession that comes with wanting her.

And maybe it's the lack of sleep or the emotional exhaustion, but I'm too fucking tired to fight it anymore. I'm too battered and bruised, and not from Hunter's beating. It's the months spent searching for revenge I no longer think is achievable.

I want her—the Keira I had before she stabbed me in the back.

I crave the woman who needed my protection. The one I would've taken a bullet for.

I keep staring at her shadowed form, the minutes ticking while the world stands still. Nothing changes. Not the relaxation in her body. Not the deathly silence. Nothing but my restraint.

I'm drawn to her.

My palms sweat with the need to feel her soft skin.

I can't fight the stupidity anymore. What's the point in struggling, anyway? I've got nothing left to lose. I no longer care what happens. Not about anything other than touching her. My hands have to be on her. If that gives her the opportunity to effortlessly slit my throat, then so be it.

She can kill me.

She can bathe in my blood and increase the destruction her family has rained on mine because there's nothing I can do to stop the pummeling thoughts that tell me she's innocent. That *I'm the one* who's treated her like hell and not the other way around.

I grab my gun, sliding it back under the far side of my pillow, and gently inch my way toward her. I listen for a change in her breathing. I continue to be attuned to her movements.

She doesn't flinch.

I creep closer and closer, her heat seeping into me right before skin touches skin. That's when everything stops. The gentle ebb and flow of sound ceases. She snaps rigid. I do, too.

But I don't retreat. I can't.

I nestle against her. Spooning. Her arms and thighs are bare against mine. The only thing between us is a thin cotton shirt and silken boxers as I weave my hand around her waist and drag her back into me.

She doesn't fight me. She doesn't succumb either.

Her body remains tight, while I rest my head on her pillow and place a kiss to the back of her neck.

That's all it is. A brief brush of lips against her skin, but it's everything.

The show of affection is my acquiescence. My capitulation to the devil.

She sucks in a shuddering breath, and one by one those muscles loosen. I hold her. Cling to her. I don't look forward to ever having to let her go.

"Sebastian…"

I shake my head. "Don't."

I can't face her questions. Her lies. I just need this. *Her.* For a little longer, until clarity sets in and I hate myself for succumbing all over again.

"Go to sleep." I close my eyes, squeezing them tight. "We can keep fighting in the morning."

The bullshit isn't going anywhere. No matter how much I want her—need her—it doesn't change our situation. We're enemies, and that shit will never be resolved.

. . .

I WAKE up to her shifting in my arms. It's only a faint movement, but I'm instantly alert, my eyes flashing open to the sunlight seeping through the edge of the curtains.

It's late. If the brightness of the room is any indication, it's close to midday.

I raise on one elbow, my swollen face and battered chest not appreciating the shift as I stare down at the woman in my arms. She's still resting, her eyes closed, her body soft.

I no longer fight to understand the cloying feelings threatening to overwhelm me. Instead, I savor the calm. I teach myself to enjoy the temporary peace. Because it sure as fuck won't last.

"You're awake?" she murmurs.

"Yeah." I inch away from her, not wanting to crowd her now that the bitter light of day has arrived.

"Don't go. Lay with me a little longer."

She doesn't open her eyes. She lets those words do the pleading for her. And that's all it takes—her words, her tone, the delicate sweep of those sultry lips. I wish for nothing more than to go back to the safe house where neither one of us had a clue we were deceiving each other.

I miss that ignorance.

"There's no point putting off the inevitable." I keep backing away.

"Let me pretend for a few more minutes," she begs. "I'm not ready for this to end."

She slays me. And I'm the stupid chump who can't fucking deny her. I can't deny myself either.

I let out a frustrated breath and sink back onto the mattress, reclaiming my position behind her with my arm draped around her stomach.

We're both insane.

We lie so much we can't face the truth.

"Thank you," she whispers.

I hate those words. I despise how they make me feel like more of a man for providing her with what she needs. There's nothing more unhealthy than the two of us together.

"Quit thanking me," I mutter. "We're not doing ourselves any favors by pretending."

"This isn't me pretending, Sebastian. This is me hoping you'll come to your senses and find the strength to trust me." Her hand finds mine, entwining our fingers. It's all romantic and shit. A dreamy existence in a waking nightmare.

"You said it yourself, trust doesn't come easily."

She nods. "And yet I found the will to trust you."

No, she didn't. She doesn't trust me at all.

"I know what you're thinking," she utters. "And you're wrong. I *do* trust you. I trusted you enough to risk starting a rumor that would endanger everyone I love. I hope, in time, you'll be able to look beyond your anger to see what really happened."

There is no anger. Not anymore.

All that's left is pathetic weakness and punishing betrayal—for both of us.

"Please tell me about your sister." There's a delicate edge to her tone. A fragility that rips me apart. Like she's been contemplating how to ask for hours.

My defenses shoot up. All those barriers I've honed through a dark sense of humor and a morbid death wish come out in full force.

Telling her more about Penny isn't something I should do. Yet it's everything I crave at the same time.

"What do you want to know?" I become her slave, brushing my lips over her shoulder, the scent of her clean skin filling my lungs.

"Everything." She squeezes my hand. "How old is she? What is she like? When was she taken?"

I focus on the freckles along her arm, determined not to close my eyes and face the sister who will stare back at me.

"She was…" Too young. Too sweet. Too vulnerable. "Smart."

I place a kiss on her neck and swallow over the ache in my throat. It shouldn't be this hard to talk about Penny. The last thing I want is for the world to forget her. "She always had her head buried in a book. But what she had in brains she lacked in life experience. She didn't spend a lot of time in the real world."

Keira doesn't respond. She listens, never losing grip of my fingers.

"She didn't wear make-up or dress in trendy clothes. She didn't need to. She was pretty without all the glitz. Hell, from what I remember, she didn't even pay the opposite sex much attention. Yet those high school boys were always testing my patience."

"You were a protective older brother?"

"The worst." I let out a breath of solemn laughter. "I remember this one guy who kept coming over because he wanted to hang out with her. Every time I'd tell him to get lost, but he wouldn't listen. So I slashed his bike tires and told him I'd do the same to his throat if he ever stepped foot on our property again."

She glances at me over her shoulder. "You didn't."

"I did. I didn't feel an ounce of guilt either. I knew what he was after even though she had no clue."

"I'm guessing you've never shied away from a fight." She turns toward me, those bright eyes taking in the war wounds that must be littered all over my face.

"I got into a few. But nothing that wasn't fueled by teenage hormones." I give a half-hearted smirk that quickly fades. "After I finished school, I packed up and moved out of town, just like my older brother had done a few years before. We weren't there to look out for her anymore. She had nobody to keep the assholes at bay."

"You speak about her in past tense." She pauses, the silence punishing.

"Yeah. I guess it's easier that way." My chest tightens with the coward's admission.

"Do you have any proof she's no longer alive?"

I swallow over the bile edging its way up my throat. "The Greek authorities like to think so. Her DNA at a shallow, burned out grave is enough to satisfy their investigation. But all they found was a tooth and some hair. Nothing substantial."

"So there's hope?"

"Hope?" My voice fractures. "No. I could never hope she was living through hell every day. I prefer to believe she's at peace. But until I have concrete evidence, the thought of her suffering will haunt me."

Her face crumples. "You blame yourself."

"Yes. I should've listened when she told me about the modeling contract. She'd never mentioned stepping foot in front of a camera before. Not once. It came from so far left field that I didn't ask the questions I should've. I got caught up in her excitement about traveling the world. All it would've taken was an internet search on your father's bullshit company."

"Then hold him accountable." Her voice hardens. "Don't blame yourself. It isn't healthy."

"If you haven't noticed, none of this shit is healthy. My life is as fucked as they come. And yours isn't any better."

She winces and lowers her gaze to my chest. "If I could get my hands on a phone, I could sort this out. I'll call Cole…"

I glare. "Is that what this is all about?" The bed? The proximity? The subtle manipulation? "You're not getting your hands on a fucking phone."

I shuffle backward toward the edge of the mattress, curing my stupidity. She's screwed me all over again and every goddamn time I'm surprised.

"Please don't." She grabs my arm. "I'm sorry. I shouldn't have asked for a phone. I wasn't trying to betray you or escape. I just want to keep talking. I want us to get back to the way things were."

"Back to when we were lying through our teeth? Why? What good can come from that?" I wait for a response to stop me from leaving. I honestly want her to say something to make me stay in this fantasy world. But what can possibly be said to change this situation?

There's no righting all our wrongs.

There are too fucking many.

"I want to help you." She implores me with sad eyes, her teeth nibbling into her lower lip. "Together we can make this right."

I chuckle and shove from the mattress. "Nothing can make this right. The best I can hope for is a lifelong prison sentence for your father. That's the end game. You can't unrape all those women. Nobody can reverse the pain that's already been inflicted."

She sits up, bundling the covers in her lap. "That's what I mean. I can help you get him arrested."

I wish it were that easy. In fact, I'm pretty fucking pissed it isn't. "You can't help me. My cover is already blown. But you can work with the Feds—"

She shakes her head. "I won't work with the authorities. I'll work with you. We can do this together. You can't give up now."

"I'm not giving up," I grate, hating the accusation. Fighting for my sister is all I have… *Had*… The battle is out of my hands now.

"Then what do you call it?" she asks.

I clench my teeth and ball my fists. "I call it self-fucking-preservation."

She scrambles from the bed. "My father needs to be stopped. You can't walk away now."

"Do you think I want to walk?" Fury spreads through me like wildfire. "I've got no fucking choice but to run." I can't stop my voice from rising. "You ratted me out. Hunter knows I'm the informant. And by now Cole and Sarah would too. I can't get inside information anymore. I'm useless. Everything I've worked for is gone."

Her face pales.

"The rest of my life will be spent hiding from your brother, Keira, and that's only if Hunt doesn't get to me first."

Her throat works over a heavy swallow. "I'll speak to my brother."

"Words won't change the level of my betrayal. Your brother is going to fucking kill me the first chance he gets."

"I have more power than you think. Have faith in me."

I wish I could. Seriously, I do. But my fate is set. I either hide or die.

"I'm going to take a shower." I stalk for the bathroom, needing to lock myself away from her deluded beliefs. I can't be the one to make her feel better about this, no matter how much I want to.

"Sebastian, wait."

She rushes after me, almost making the distance before I close the door on her.

"Please." She pleads through the barrier between us. "I'll figure something out. Let me talk to Cole."

I smother a derisive laugh. She'll *talk* to him—a guy with unfathomable determination when it comes to slaying his enemies. I bet that conversation goes down like a cheerleader at an after party.

I strip and climb into the shower, not bothering to wait for the water to warm before I sink under the harsh chill.

"*Please, Sebastian.*"

Christ. This woman doesn't let up.

I step under the spray and raise my swollen face to the water. The pain blocks out her pleas as I rest one hand against the tile to keep myself upright.

Talking to Cole won't change a thing. No matter what she says to try to convince him I'm innocent, he won't spare a second thought when it comes to ending my life. I've known that all along. I set out for revenge knowing I'd have little chance to make it out alive. The likelihood of getting caught was always high.

At least I have a head start to escape.

Once I freshen up, I'll pack a few of my brother's things and flee. I can cross multiple state borders before dark. And I'll keep crossing them, changing cars and IDs along the way—

A foreign noise breaks me from my plans, and I lean my head toward the glass shower screen to listen.

The door jangles. She's trying to pick the fucking lock.

I huff out a defeated breath as she breaks in. I've gotta give it to her, she's persistent as shit.

She approaches me, the sight of her taking up my peripheral vision.

"I can fix this." Her determination bears down on me from the other side of the glass. My dick isn't immune. Her tenacity is sexy as hell, no matter how hard I battle to ignore it.

I slink back under the water, keeping my head bowed, my hand against the tile.

"Sebastian…" She opens the screen. "Let me talk to Cole. I can work this out. I'll bet my life on it."

I don't respond. Well, apart from my cock that continues to thicken.

"*Sebastian*," she snaps. "Listen to me." She steps inside the shower, sliding along the wall in front of me, her shoulder grazing my splayed hand.

"What the hell are you doing?" I growl.

"You should know that I hate when you ignore me."

"Yeah, I do. But this isn't a place you want to be right now."

She sighs. "Yes, it is. We need to work this out."

"Not right now, we don't." I straighten, backing away from her. "Get out of here."

"Not until you listen to me. Cole will—"

"*No. You* listen to *me*." I narrow my stare. "Comprehending this conversation would be problematic at the best of times. But when I'm hard as a fucking rock, there's absolutely no chance. So I suggest you get out of my face."

The slightest frown knits her brows, then understanding dawns in those naive eyes. She swallows, hard, and her tongue dashes out to lick her lower lip. "I'm not leaving."

"Don't do this to me," I beg.

I don't want to fuck her again. I can't. The thought of leaving her behind is hard enough without giving in to the addiction one more time.

"I'll fix this," she whispers.

I press my forehead to hers and close my eyes. "You can't. If I stay, I'm dead."

"I'll protect you."

I let out a breath of laughter. "Yeah? And how are you going to do that?"

Her hand weaves around my neck, her nails scraping my scalp. "I'll do whatever necessary. Just like you did for me." She leans in, her nose brushing mine, the splash of warm water trickling down our faces. "I've fallen for you, Sebastian. I can't let you go."

"That's the adrenaline talking. It's the fear." It's probably a case of Stockholm Syndrome, too.

"No, it's not. I've felt this way since before the shooting." She digs those nails deeper, demanding my attention. "I'm never scared when I'm with you. I feel safe. I'm home." Her lips brush my jaw. My cheek. "I need this to work. I don't care what it takes."

What it takes could be her life. I refuse to be responsible for that.

I pull back, opening my eyes as I cup her face in both hands. "Listen. Hunter is going to come after me. And if he went through my house like I wanted him to, he's going to find this place real fucking soon."

"How? We're in the middle of nowhere."

"We're in the middle of my brother's house," I confess. "I called in a few favors and asked him to disappear for a few days."

Her eyes flare, the panic evident before being smothered with more of her determination. "Then we run. Together. We get out of here. We hide."

"You don't want to leave your family, beautiful. You couldn't live without Layla or Stella. And you told me last night how close you are to Cole."

"It will only be temporary." She brushes her mouth over mine, slaughtering me with the sexual plea. "We can figure out—"

"This isn't a negotiation." I wish I could find a way to make this work, but the truth is, her optimism has no place here. Hunter will never forgive me, and Torian will take pleasure in putting a price on my head.

It's over.

"I'm leaving here, Keira, and you're not coming with me."

21

KEIRA

I shove at his chest. "Why are you so goddamn stubborn?"

Those dark eyes turn pained. "I've already lost someone I care about. I have no plans of letting that happen again."

My stomach revolts in both anguish and anger. "That's not good enough." I get in his face, the shower's spray dousing my shirt, making the material cling to my skin. "I've lost someone, too. I know how it feels. It's the reason I won't let you go."

He gives a sad smile. "Keira..."

"*Don't*," I scold. "For once, just listen."

He sucks in a breath and straightens, placing space between us. "Fine. I'm listening."

My heart thumps in my ears. I don't know what to say to make him stay. There's only hope and want and so much need spurring me to fill the silence. "Once Cole finds out about our father, he will disown him. He knows what I went through with Richard. He would never associate our name with that type of—"

"That's not the point, buttercup. The issue here is that I'm an informant. I gave the Feds enough probable cause to wiretap your uncle's phone. It's only a matter of time before they take you all down, and I fucking helped."

"You're not the first, and you won't be the last. People have been feeding the Feds information since before I was born. It's nothing new. They rarely find anything that sticks. And when they do, we've got men on their payroll to help us out. I'm not worried."

"Can you hear yourself?" He cringes. "I fucking betrayed your family."

"You did what was necessary to fight for your sister."

"Cole won't see it that way. *You* shouldn't even see it that way."

I give him a sad smile, pouring my heartfelt affection into the expression. "What I see is someone who should be admired for their strength. You're fearless, Sebastian.

You did what was right for you and yours without worrying about the consequences."

He closes his eyes briefly, his brows pinched. "You're being delusional, princess." He pins me with a placating expression, his lips pulled into a sad smile.

"No, I'm not. If the authorities had anything on us, they would've used it by now. There's nothing they can do."

"They've already told me exactly what they're going to do. If I run out on them before they can make an arrest, those assholes are going to make Sarah and Hunt look like rats." His eyes narrow as he leans close. "And look at me, already running."

He appears entirely tortured. But I still have to ask. "Are they? Rats, I mean. Are they involved?"

"*No.*" His response is vehement. "Why do you think Hunt tried to kill me yesterday? Nobody fucking knew except the agent I've been working with. And she's going to set up Hunt and Sarah as soon as she finds out I've high-tailed it. She probably already has."

My belly does that tumbling, squeezing thing again. "If only one agent knows, then maybe that's the answer. We take her out. Problem solved."

He winces. "You need to stop fighting. This shit can't be fixed."

I won't.

I can't.

"I'm not ready to let you go."

He gives me a sad smile. "I wish there was an alternative."

I inch closer, my soaked chest leaning into his, the hard length of his cock pushing into my abdomen. His jaw ticks as he backtracks, moving to the far wall of the enclosed space.

I don't allow for any distance between us as I follow.

"You want me." I reach a hand between us and grab his length. The hiss of his breath is sweet victory. "You can't deny it."

"You're right, I can't." His eyes soften. "But fucking you isn't going to make me change my mind about risking your life. I won't be seduced into hurting you."

"Hurting me?" I falter. I almost break.

This isn't about my safety. It's about his. When it comes to my family I can look after myself.

"Yes, hurting you," he repeats. "Hunter and Cole will come after me, guns blazing. It's too dangerous for you to be anywhere near me. I should already be gone."

I want to shove some sense into him. But the sight of his bruised and battered body keeps me in check. "No."

"Yes," he growls. "I need to get as far away from you as possible."

I crumple, my insides turning to dust with his continued protection. "I'm begging you." My fragility is clear in the fracturing of my tone. My throat burns. My eyes, too. "Don't run. I don't want this to end."

He grabs the wet material of my shirt, scrunching it in tight fists. "Give it a day or two. Once you're back home with your family, this will be nothing but a bad memory."

"Like hell it will." I snuggle into him, my mouth an inch from his before dawning hits me hard in the ribs. "Is that what I'll be to you? A bad memory?"

His face pinches, his hands still clinging to my shirt. "I've wanted to save you since the first moment I laid eyes on you. I could've run that night and not worried about Cole wasting the time or effort to hunt me down. But in the back of my mind, I thought if I couldn't save Penny, the least I could do is save you."

"You *have* saved me."

He reaches a hand between us, the pad of his thumb brushing my bottom lip. "It wasn't real, remember? That defining moment for me was nothing but a lie for you. I'm not who you think I am, and you're not who I thought you were, either. You'll realize that once you've had time to think."

"I don't need time. Or space. Or whatever else you want to suggest next." I clutch his wrist, keeping his hand at my mouth. "My mind is clear. My decision is made. We may have fabricated stories that brought us together, but we're here for a reason."

"Yeah, because I tried to take on the biggest crime family in the state and failed."

"No. You're *here*." I tap my chest. My heart. "You're in here for a reason."

He cups my cheek, and those eyes fill with pity. "Keira—"

"Don't." I squeeze his wrist. "Don't you dare tell me you're still leaving."

He sighs and tugs against my hold to lower his arm to his side. "Then I don't know what you expect me to say."

"Don't say anything. Just be with me." I pull the sodden shirt over my head to bare my body to him. "Help me make this work."

His chin hitches. His eyes flare.

"I need you, Sebastian." I drag the waistband of my underwear down my thighs, letting them fall to the floor. "I know you need me, too."

He's contemplating surrender. I can taste the sweet victory on my tongue. I can see the effect temptation has on him.

"Manipulation runs deep in those veins, doesn't it, baby cakes?"

I guess I should be insulted.

I'm not.

I know it's his last ditch effort to reject me. I'm wearing him down. Convincing him of what we both need. "I can be manipulative. But that isn't what this is. What you're feeling is a connection you know you can't deny. There's a reason this seems right despite all the reasons it should be wrong."

"That's the thing—" He reaches around me and shuts off the water with harsh twists of his wrists. "This doesn't seem right at all. The way I feel for you—the way I've *always* felt for you—is a fucking disgrace to my family."

He grabs me around the waist and carries me, soaked and dripping, to the bed where he lays me down. The sheets grow damp beneath me, and my skin prickles with a harsh chill. But the worst part is the way he backs away, retreating as if he's finally found the strength to cut ties.

"I'm going to grab a bite to eat, pack some things, then get out of here. You won't be alone for long. Hunter will find you soon."

He starts for the door, and I panic.

I don't know what to do. I'm out of ideas to make him stay. "Sebastian."

He pauses, and I do something so out of character my whole body trembles as he glances over his shoulder.

I slide a hand over my waist, down my stomach to the apex of my thighs. With my heart hammering in my chest, I part my legs to him.

I'm no stranger to my own touch, but I've never considered myself a temptress. The desire to instigate sex has never been a driving force for me. Not until now, when I have no other tricks up my sleeve.

He stares, his lip slowly curling into a snarl.

I don't know if the expression is from disgusted fury or despised temptation. I don't know anything anymore…anything but want.

"Stop it," he growls.

I shake my head. "I can't."

I slide a finger along my pussy and close my eyes, moaning a little with the penetration. My pleasure is drowned under possible humiliation, but I pretend I'm swimming in lust. I work my finger in circles and cup my breast. I do all the sexy things I've seen and read about despite feeling fake the entire time.

"Keira, *stop*."

I don't listen. I continue my display, keeping my eyes squeezed shut to ward off the nerves.

"*Fuck*," he grates.

There's torment in his voice. So much anger and aggression aimed in my direction.

I'm not scared by it. He won't hurt me. I'm more concerned I'm hurting him for pushing an agenda he won't admit he wants to be a part of.

Blood rushes in my ears as I play with my clit, rubbing my thumb back and forth. I can't hear anything over my heartbeat. The loud throb echoes through me, increasing the anxiety.

I'm tempted to take a peek to see if he's watching. Maybe he already left the room. He could've walked away.

My heart pangs.

"You're killing me, shortie." His hands latch onto my ankles and drag me along the bed.

I squeal, opening my eyes to his anguished stare.

"Why are you doing this to me?" he murmurs. "Why do you keep playing games?"

I lean up on bent elbows. "There's no more games. I promise."

A myriad of emotions wash over his features—determination, uncertainty, and a glimmer of hope. They all mix together, showing me the kind soul buried behind the bruised and battered exterior.

"There's no more lies, either," I admit. "All I want is you."

I adore him. I won't even bother denying it. How can I when he challenged my father—the most powerful man I know? Sebastian stormed the castle. He made himself into a warrior and protected me every step of the way.

My dad couldn't even safeguard his wife from all the dangers he created. And he sure as hell didn't protect me from his own brother.

From birth, I've been sheltered, not shielded, and Sebastian is a breath of the freshest, purest air against that harsh reality.

He's strength and commitment and discipline.

Honor, morality, and pride.

He's far greater than someone with my track record deserves. But I guess I'm a slave to my bloodline, because despite knowing I'm undeserving, I'm not willing to give him up.

"I'm yours," I whisper. "Whether you want me or not."

His jaw ticks. "I fucking want you, Keira. I can't stop."

I sit up and drape my legs over the edge of the mattress, coming up close and personal with his bare waist. I hold his gaze as droplets trek his body, dripping from his hair to his chest, all the way down to the erection within reach.

He's a masterpiece. All that muscle. All that ink.

And now, knitting them together is all the pink and purple flesh caused from my lies.

My heart trembles beneath tightening ribs as I lean forward and place a kiss on his stomach. He peers down at me, his intensity bathing me, warming me. He fucking invigorates the hell out of me as I inch lower, dragging my lips on a slow trail until I'm nestled right next to the head of his cock.

I pause and watch him swallow deep. He has so much power over me, but right now, I can see that influence shift. I'm in control. He's at my mercy.

I tilt my head toward his sex.

He's thick and bulky. An entirely new discovery for me.

I've never done this before, and I know exactly why. I wasn't supposed to. This moment was made for Sebastian.

I lean closer, poking out my tongue to trail it along his shaft. I lick the water droplets. I taste the salty tease of him seeping from the head of his cock.

"*Jesus*," he hisses.

My tension eases, his curse uplifting in its ferocity. He fists my hair in his hands, the strands pulling tight.

I shudder, becoming a slave to his brutality. My pussy throbs. I have to squeeze my thighs tight to stem the ache. But then he steps away, and I'm petrified he's found the will to leave.

"Move back on the bed, sweetheart."

I nod, overwhelmed with relief as I comply.

He slides over me, gentle and slow, his heavy weight pressing me into the mattress. His mouth finds mine. His tongue delves deep. He kisses me like he's taking his last breath. He cups my face and grips my waist as if I'll skitter away in the wind.

He's everywhere. His hands. His mouth. His affection.

I'm royalty under his touch.

I rake my fingers into his hair and hold tight. "Promise me you won't leave."

He ignores me, nudging his hips into mine, the head of his cock parting my folds.

His stare holds all the promise I need. I see the commitment in his eyes. The pure, undeniable want for me, just like I want him.

I raise my ass off the bed, making him sink deeper. The pleasure is instantaneous. Every inch of me tingles, from my toes to my nipples, my fingers to my face.

I moan. I don't bother holding it in.

I'm not going to shy away from how he makes me feel.

I want everything he has to give, and I refuse to take it on a temporary basis. This can't stop. He can't walk away.

His hips begin to roll, the slow undulation sinking through me. We're made for each other. There's no denying how right this feels. He increases his pace, the kisses growing in intensity, the hands roaming my body seeming addicted to learning my curves.

My back arches off the bed. My hips rise to meet him.

We move in perfect harmony. Two people. One act.

Pure fate.

He's fucked me hard before, with strength and dominance. We've groaned and clawed as we sought our pleasure. That's the way I'd always thought sex would be. Rough. Hard. Punishing.

I never imagined it like this. Not with him. Not with anyone.

I never realized how soul crushing the connection could be. How one man would have the power to shatter me to my core and build me back up, piece by piece, with the heated, sweaty movements of his body.

I'm transfixed.

Enslaved.

He increases his pace, sliding into me and retreating in smooth synchronicity as he peers down at me.

I've never felt this beautiful. Entirely worshiped.

I'm overwhelmed with emotion as he whispers compliments I never would've imagined would be spoken about me. He speaks of my beauty. He murmurs his adoration.

You're gorgeous. You're perfect. You're mine.

Those words are everything.

I kiss him—his cheek, his jaw, his chin. He grazes his teeth across my neck and licks a delicate trail along my shoulder.

He tastes. Savors.

I wrap my legs around his waist, allowing him the deepest penetration. But it's also because I need to hold him. I have to cling tight. I refuse to let go.

He slides a hand between me and the mattress, cupping my ass.

Our movements increase, every thrust becoming harder, the pleasure growing more potent. I shake with the intensity, my body screaming for more.

His mouth devours my skin, the scrape of teeth and lap of tongue making me mindless.

"Sebastian..." I don't know what else to say. His name on my lips is all there is.

I'm not me anymore. I'm not singular in heart or body or soul. Everything I know has been entwined with this man. We're one. Never to be broken apart.

"I don't want this to end." I grip tighter to him and squeeze my thighs with his thrusts.

The thrill is intense. His affection becomes overwhelming.

"I wish I had the stamina to make this last all day, but you're too fucking perfect, Keira. You always have been."

I shudder, my limbs and nerves tingling until the vibrations culminate in my pussy and I fall over the edge.

I break apart, my neck arching with the euphoria as moans escape my throat. I close my eyes, clinging to this moment, savoring the bliss while Sebastian's thrusts of release match the contraction of my pussy.

Flawless. Monumental. Intense.

I'm at the highest of highs, bathed in his tenderness and swimming in endorphins when everything begins to incrementally slow.

Our movements lessen. His kisses disappear. The pleasure dims while our panted breaths fade.

The warmth I'd been blanketed in seconds earlier becomes chilled as I open my eyes to the tortured man staring back at me.

"You're everything, Keira." His words sound like a goodbye. A whispered farewell.

"Good. Then don't leave."

He winces and buries his head against my neck. He falls quiet, not even his labored inhales heard over the pounding in my ears.

I don't release my hold. I continue to cling tight, convincing myself he's going to stay right up until his body turns rigid atop mine.

His emotional withdrawal is a living, breathing thing. I feel it escaping from between us, then in a rapid burst of movement he slides off me and shoves to his feet as if I've burned him.

"Sebastian…" I wait for his rejection, for the words that will call an end to all of this and shatter me into a million pieces. I don't know how else to fight this. I've begged. I've pleaded. I've used my body like a weapon.

"Do you hear that?" He cocks his head toward the window.

My pulse spikes. "Hear what?" I remain still, trying to hear the elusive sound. "What is it?"

"Someone's here." He lunges for the pillows and pulls out his gun. "You need to hide."

I scamper from the bed and spin in an anxiety-riddled circle, not sure if I should be looking for clothes or a weapon.

"Get in the bathroom and lock the door." He stalks to the dresser and yanks out a pair of boxers, dragging them up his legs one-handed. "Don't come out until you know it's safe."

"I'm not leaving you on your own."

"Don't argue with me." He strides for the door. "You'll only get in my way."

22

DECKER

I rush down the hall, mentally preparing for battle, and peek out the glass panels of the front door.

"Who is it?" Keira's whisper travels from somewhere close.

"Peanut," I grate, "for once in your life will you listen to me and go hide."

"No." She tiptoes toward me, pulling a fresh shirt over her head as she approaches in a pair of baggy shorts that hang from her slim hips. "I need to know what's going on."

I sigh and return my focus outside. "There's a car coming up the drive."

It's a vehicle I don't recognize, but I can already identify the stocky build of the man behind the wheel.

"Who is it?"

"Hunter." He's the only person who could've figured out where I am, and he's too ego-driven to have given the information to Torian. My best buddy will want to be the victor in this situation.

She creeps up behind me, wrapping her arms around my waist. "What will he do?"

That list is too fucking long to contemplate. "Who knows."

He won't kill me in front of Keira. At least I hope not. I need to start praying that he's willing to take me back to Portland for Cole to deal with. That way, I'll have a chance to escape on route.

"Sebastian..." She clings closer, her warmth touching every part of me. "I'm scared."

"You've got nothing to worry about. He's here to take you home. It's me he's after."

"That's why I'm scared," she murmurs.

I want to believe her. God, how I want to believe her, but there's still the slightest twinge of doubt gnawing its way through my chest. "It'll be okay. Stay inside. Hide at the back of the house."

I grip the knob and turn, only to be stopped when she places her hand on mine.

"I'm not leaving you." She squeezes in front of me, her back to the door, her chest brushing against mine. "I know you doubt me. I can hear it in your voice. But I'm here, Sebastian. I'm right where I want to be."

"In the line of fire?"

"If that's what it comes down to, then yes." She spins, yanks open the door, and slides outside.

I wait for her to flee. To escape. To run to the man who pummeled my body to a pulp mere hours ago.

She doesn't.

She flicks her gaze between the black Mercedes and the house, making sure she positions herself between us both.

"Jesus Christ." She's suicidal. I follow her outside, and she continues to keep me as her shadow, mimicking each of my steps to ensure I stay behind her. "Get out of my way, tiger."

"No. I'm not going to let them hurt you."

The car inches into the yard and circles to the front of the house. It's then I notice Hunt isn't alone. His trusty sidekick, Sarah, is in the passenger seat, her face impassive as they pull to a stop.

"Move." I'm trying like hell to be patient, but having her in front of me feels beyond wrong. I want her at *my* back. I'm the one who needs to protect her.

She grabs my left hand and wraps it around her stomach, her touch comforting and soft. Then she yanks at my right, raising the gun to aim it toward her face.

"*Fucking hell.*" I pull away. "I'm not playing you as my hostage."

"*Please.*" She turns to me, her eyes pleading. "He's going to kill you."

"I can take care of myself. All you're doing is making this worse by distracting me." I drag her behind me, ignoring her scrambling, scratching protests as I shield her with my body. "Or maybe that's the plan." I inflict the emotional blow in the hopes of diverting her attention.

It works.

She stops protesting, her pain at my accusation taking over her features as she blinks those baby blues my way. "You'll never trust me again, will you?"

"How 'bout I trust that you're going to stay behind me and keep quiet while I handle this?"

She presses her lips tight.

I don't wait for another response. I swing around to face our visitors as they climb from the car, both of them scowling at me, no guns drawn.

Sarah is the first to step away from the vehicle, which is surprising. I never would've imagined Hunt would let her breathe without permission in a situation like this, let alone allow her to walk toward me.

They know I'm armed. The weapon may be rested at my side, but despite my laid-back stance, they both have to realize I'll fire shots to lay cover for an escape. And yet she approaches, her stride determined, her pinched expression increasing, while he stays at the driver's side door.

"What do we do?" Keira's question is barely audible as I stand my ground.

I don't move. Don't even flinch.

Sarah holds my gaze as she reaches the steps, and I start to wonder if she's the decoy to distract me from Hunter's kill shot.

"We went through your shit," she says in greeting.

"I figured as much. You wouldn't have found me otherwise." I clear my throat, trying to ignore the build of adrenaline. "Is my place still standing?"

She shrugs. "It's definitely not in the same state as when we arrived."

I'd probably give a shit if I had any possibility of returning home. But at the moment, I'm not convinced they'll let me make it through the day.

The thing that hurts, though, is what they would've done to all my research. All those years of searching. All those faces of innocent women. All those pictures of a sister I'll never see again.

She takes the first step, still scowling, but those harsh eyes are different. They're glazed. Glistening. Her nose scrunches as she takes another step, and another, coming to stand a foot away.

Regret hangs heavy in her expression, making me anxious as all fuck. Hunter knows I'd never hurt her. I couldn't. Maybe that's the beauty of their plan. He's letting her take me down effortlessly.

"You should've told me," she snarls. "I would've helped."

I stare at her. At the emotion building in her features, the trembling lips, the liquid building in her eyes. I feel heavy—my chest, my limbs, my soul. Everything weighs me down under her anger.

I frown. "I don't understand."

"If I would've known what they were capable of, I would've stood by you, helping every step of the way." She sniffs, her chin hitching slightly. "I would've found a way to kill everyone involved. Every single one of them, Decker."

Keira sucks in a breath, and from my peripheral vision I see her stiffen. Sarah is talking about Keira's family. Her father. Her uncle. Possibly her brother. No matter what they're capable of, those words would be hard to hear when spoken from someone you considered a friend.

"Why are you here?" I ask.

"I want to show my support."

I—singular. There's no 'we' or 'us' or mention of Hunter.

"You're not here to kick my ass for being the informant?"

The anger slowly fades into a sly grin. "Actually, I'm strangely proud of your deceptive ways. I never would've thought you were smart enough to pull this off."

"Obviously, I'm not. Look where we are."

"You had me fooled."

I'm not convinced. This has to be an act. A scheme. But God knows why they're dragging out the end game. Hunt doesn't usually like to fuck with his prey. "Thanks?"

She steps forward. "Don't mention it. Now, give me a hug, you manipulative prick. I can't believe what you've been going through without me knowing."

She casts her arms wide, and I brace for an attack.

Sarah doesn't hug.

Ever.

This woman is the spokesperson for emotional detachment, so it's more than likely she's going to stab a knife into my back. And yet, I oddly crave the connection like a motherfucker.

I've allowed very few people into my life since Penny was taken. Three, to be exact. And those trio of souls are all staring at me, each of them capable of taking me down.

"Sebastian," Keira warns.

"It's okay." I spread my arms, willing to sink or swim, as I drag Sarah into me.

I hug her, waiting for the betrayal, expecting the sharp bite of a blade. It doesn't come. She rests into me, clinging tight as I glance at Hunter over her shoulder, his glare mutated to an epic level.

"I'm going to take a wild stab in the dark and assume your fiancé doesn't have the urge to hug this out like you do."

"Don't worry about him. He's still recovering from your scuffle yesterday. He can't ditch his migraine." She retreats, her hands falling to her sides. "But he hasn't breathed a word of this to Cole. That in itself is a huge sign of support despite his unwillingness to voice it."

Support? I'm still not buying it.

There has to be a catch. A hidden motive.

"There wasn't a scuffle yesterday, Sarah. That fucking ogre tried to kill me."

She rolls her eyes. "It sounds like you've both exaggerated your side of the story." She turns her attention to Keira, her expression transforming to a snarl as her arms cross over her chest. "Did you know about the trafficking?"

I glance at Keira, getting caught up in the shock spread across her features. She's traumatized by the harsh accusation. I have to admit, I am, too.

Sarah is usually the devoted feminist, slaying the dragons that enslave other women. But right here, right now, the only thing she looks eager to slay is an undeserving woman.

"No, she didn't," I answer.

"I didn't ask you. I want to hear it from her." Sarah levels her tone without quitting the glare. "Did you know they were selling sex slaves? Were you involved?"

Keira raises her chin in defiance and opens her mouth, only to snap it shut again. I can't tell if she's about to lash out or cry. I don't want to see either.

"I said she didn't know. And if I can believe her, you can, too." I walk for the front door, despising every second my back is turned to the homicidal fucker in the yard. "Let's go inside. This is going to be a long conversation that doesn't need to happen out here."

I pull the door wide and stare at Sarah, waiting for her to comply.

She takes her sweet-ass time, not hiding her animosity for Keira when she finally strides toward me and kicks off her shoes to leave them by the door. "It will take a lot more than your word to convince me she didn't know. Especially when she's the one who set you up."

I don't bite. I can't afford to.

This outcome is far better than the bullet to the brain I expected. But the sight of Keira's emotional struggle is far more punishing.

Those ocean eyes hold me captive, the pained depths ripping me apart.

"It's okay," I mouth.

She scoffs and turns her attention to the front yard. I follow her gaze, yet again finding the ire of one grumpy motherfucker bearing down on me like I encouraged a football team to live stream a group orgy with his mom.

"He doesn't look happy," she whispers.

"He's angry at me. Not you. He'd do anything for you and yours. You know that."

"That used to be the case." She starts toward me. "Who knows how he feels now."

She continues into the house on silent footfalls while I wait outside to see what the eye-gouger will do. Apparently, standing there scowling is all he's capable of because he doesn't budge an inch.

"Hey, asshole," I call out. "Are you coming inside?"

His lip curls. "What was that? I can't hear you over how stupid you are, you dumb fuck."

I guess that's as close as I'm going to get to a temporary cease fire.

I walk inside, locking the door behind me so I'm aware of when Hunt makes his next move. He won't stay outside for long. He's stubborn, but he's also impatient. He'll want to take action sooner rather than later, and although Sarah claims to be on my side, I'm not letting my guard down.

I make my way into the kitchen and find her at the sink, filling a glass with water from the tap. "Where's Keira?"

She shrugs. "Don't know. But it's best if she keeps her distance for now."

"Lay off her. She's gone through enough."

"Why do you believe her?" She shuts off the water and gulps from her glass. "She's the one who set you up."

"I've got my reasons." And I'm too fucking loath to admit all of them revolve around intuition and attraction instead of evidence. "I've spent enough time with her to believe she's innocent."

"Forgive me if I'm not as easily convinced."

"Isn't she supposed to be your friend?"

Her eyes harden. "I've been fucked over by people far closer to me than her."

I know that. I wish I didn't, but I'm well aware of the horrors she's endured.

"Decker, we only found your information ten hours ago. I've spent every minute since reading through those pages. Even on the car ride here. I'm still coming to terms with all of this."

"And so is she. You need to hear her out."

She raises a brow. "Or maybe you need to stop letting your dick make decisions."

I clench my teeth to stop a sharp reply. I breathe. I force calm. "If she's guilty, then what about Hunter? You have to hold him accountable, too. He's close as fuck to Torian."

She narrows her gaze for a spite-filled moment, then turns away, focusing out the kitchen window.

"You know I'm right," I say into the growing silence.

"Have I said Hunter is innocent?" she snaps. "This conversation is about *her*. Not him."

I straighten with the dawning realization.

Now I understand why Hunt didn't come up the drive with a barrel pointed at my head—she didn't let him.

They're fighting.

She's taken my side when he clearly hasn't. And like the lovesick fool he is for this woman, he doesn't want to upset her by slitting my throat in front of her. Great. All he's waiting for is privacy.

"Come on, Sarah. You can't believe he's in on this."

"You said it yourself, he's close to Torian. How could he be clueless?" She grips the counter, her shoulders slumping. "He always knows everything."

"He had no clue about me." I approach, moving to stand a few feet away. "He's capable of some pretty heavy shit. But for as long as I've worked with him, he's never done anything to anyone who wasn't deserving."

"I know." She hangs her head. "I just…"

"What? You don't trust him anymore?"

She glances over her shoulder, meeting my gaze. "I've been working with them, Decker. I've been helping a family who should be burning in hell."

"Not the entire family, Sare. They're not all responsible."

She shoves from the counter in frustration. "How do you know?"

"A gut feeling."

She gives me a look of incredulity. "Like I mentioned before, I think the body part you're referring to is a little further south."

"Maybe." I shrug. "I'll admit Keira has gotten under my skin. But there's more to it than that. She's battling her own demons. And if you can't trust her, you need to trust me until she proves herself to you."

"Trust you? The informant?" She laughs. "The guy who has made a life out of lying?"

"You would've done the same."

She nods. "Yeah. I would've… And I'm sorry about your sister."

I stare out the window, unable to stand her pity.

"Our baggage kinda looks the same, doesn't it?" She cocks her hip against the counter and crosses her arms over her chest. "I understand you a lot more than I did days ago."

"Are you falling for me, sweet cheeks?" I send her a smirk that she shoots down in flames.

"Don't pull that cocky, jokester bullshit on me, Decker. I know what it's like. And I'm here if you ever need to talk."

"You mean for now," I chuckle, "in the short space of time before Hunt kills me."

She winces. "He'll calm down. Eventually."

"I doubt it. I stabbed him in the back. I know him well enough to realize there's no way back from being his enemy."

"Obviously, you don't know him at all. Because being the informant isn't the reason he wants to gut you like a fish." She grabs her glass and takes another sip. "You're not even close to understanding him, Deck."

"Okay. I'll bite." I walk to the fridge and grab myself an apple from the crisper. "What am I missing here?"

"He's pissed off because you kept him in the dark. You pretended to be his friend and made him look like a fool."

"I don't think we're talking about the same guy. This is Hunter. The son of a bitch who gives no fucks about anyone or anything, except his pride and his fealty to the all-mighty Torian."

"That's a little harsh."

"Tell that to the eyeballs he tried to gouge yesterday."

She presses her lips tight, but her humor seeps through in the curving edges of her mouth. "How many people do you think he has in his life?"

"I don't know. He knows everyone."

"Yes, he knows everyone. That's his job. But he doesn't *have* anyone. Not apart from you and me. We're all he's got. And in one surprise revelation, you halved his support network." Her face turns somber. "Despite the weird testosterone-fueled, we-have-to-act-like-schoolyard-thugs thing you two have going on, he fucking adores you."

"Adores?" I drawl. "That sounds delightfully charming."

She glowers and points a finger at her chest. "My words. Not his."

I grin, because drilling down to the seriousness of this conversation isn't something I'm comfortable with. "You should've seen how much he adored me yesterday when he had a barrel between my eyes. That shit was affectionate as hell. I really felt the love."

"You mean when he warned you about being uncovered, then let you get away?"

"Oh, no, Sare bear." He came prepared to kill me. He was on a mission to seek revenge for his almighty leader. He chose money over friendship. "Despite what he might have told you, he didn't *let me* get away at all. I had to beat the fuck out of his ogre ass. And that shit ain't easy."

She raises a brow, her condescending look making me feel like I'm simple. "He *let you* get away, Decker. I'm pretty sure, deep down, you know that more than I do."

23

KEIRA

I hide out in the main bedroom, slumped on the mattress. I'm not in here because I'm intimidated by Sarah.

It's the opposite.

I'm fearful of what I'll do to her if she turns her accusatory face my way again.

Days ago, she was my friend. Now she dares to glare at me with disgust, as if I instigated my father's entire operation.

Her goddamn righteousness boils my blood.

She's no angel. I'm well aware of the things she does. How she works side-by-side with Hunter as a loan shark, or an enforcer, or whatever else my brother requires.

And yet I'm the heinous one? Go figure.

A *tap, tap, tap* sounds to my right. I panic at the intrusion and glance at the window, finding Hunter's menacing face staring back at me from outside.

I don't move. For a moment, I'm too scared to even think.

Although Sarah is being a bitch, Hunter is a cold-blooded killer, and right now I'd prefer her hatred to his possible intent.

"Open the fucking window," he mutters.

I remain cemented in place, not willing to sign my own death certificate.

His glare turns lethal. "Now. We need to talk."

The rap sheet of crimes he's committed for my family pokes at me from the back of my mind. The assault. The murder. He's killed people for far less than what my father has done. For all I know, he's turned his back on us and claimed Sarah's high moral code.

"Keira." His tone softens despite the harsh expression, his voice barely heard through the glass barrier between us. "We don't have much time."

I swallow over and over, trying to bottle my fear as my palms begin to sweat.

My brother trusts this man with his life. I should be able to trust him to hold a non-violent conversation. Shouldn't I?

I inch to my feet and take cautious steps across the room. My hands tremble as I reach for the window.

He stares me down. Stares so emotionless and heartlessly that I'm sure I'm making a huge mistake. Yet I refuse to let fear rule me as I flick the lock.

There's no pause for contemplation. In seconds, he has the screen unhitched, the pane raised, and is preparing to climb in.

"You couldn't use the front door?"

"I'm not ready to speak to that asshole yet." He winces as he hauls himself into the room, alluding to more injuries than the stark bruising across the bridge of his nose and under his eyes.

I retreat as he stands, his bulky frame dwarfing me. I aim my path toward the door, backtracking closer and closer to escape while I wait for him to attempt to crush my bones to make his bread.

"I fucking hate this," he murmurs.

"I didn't know." My admission is blurted like a frightened little bitch.

He jerks his head in a barely-there acknowledgement. He doesn't believe me. Or doesn't care.

"When did you figure out Decker was a snitch?"

"I didn't know about that either." I take another backward step and collide with the side of the bed frame, the corner of the thick wood stabbing into my thigh. "Shit."

Hunter's brows pinch, his face changing into a mask of incredulity. "Sit down before you hurt yourself." The words are a command. Almost a threat.

I shake my head. "I'm fine."

"Sit," he grates. "Your apprehension is making me fucking uncomfortable."

"Uncomfortable?" I've known this man a long time. I even thought I'd grown to trust him despite my aversion to the weakness. And over all the years watching him, I've never seen him uncomfortable.

In a rage, yes.

Menacingly cocky, definitely.

But never uncomfortable.

"Maybe angry is a better word," he snarls. "You're acting like I'm a threat, and it's seriously pissing me off. You should know better."

"I should know better?" I work the statement around in my head, denying its vehemence. "I've just found out my father is the devil. That the man who raised me is my worst nightmare. I've known nothing my entire life, Hunter, so forgive me if I question your motives."

He winces, the silent seconds ticking by before he murmurs, "Sorry."

The apology hits deep.

He doesn't have to repeat his command to sit because my legs collapse beneath me and I slump to the bed in a heap of emotional baggage.

"Tell me about Decker." He remains in place, the pinch of his brows tight. "How did you find out?"

"He blew his own cover once we got here. He just blurted it out."

"Did he hurt you?"

"No." My response comes instantly. But it's a lie. I'm beyond hurt by Sebastian. He didn't show one sign of relief when he found out Cole is still in the dark. He found out he hadn't been outed as the informant and not once did he celebrate us having more time together.

He's resigned to leaving.

Nothing I do will change his mind.

"You're lying." His eyes narrow. "What did he do to you?"

"Nothing." I shake my head and lower my gaze, my cheeks turning to flame.

"Bullshit," he snaps. "Tell me what he did."

I keep my mouth shut, too embarrassed to admit the truth.

"I'm going to fucking kill him." He starts for the door.

"*No*. Wait." I shove to my feet and rush to block his path with a shaking body and a splayed hand. "I promise he didn't hurt me."

"Then what are you hiding?"

My fingers are insignificant against the muscles of his chest, the rampant beat of his heart like a hammer beneath my palm.

"I'm not hiding anything." I cringe when his gaze intensifies. "What you see is shame. I fell for him. I fell really hard, Hunter. And the more minutes that pass, the further I fall. I can't seem to stop."

His lip curls. I'm not sure whether it's in frustration or incredulity.

"I think we both know he's never been one of us," I admit. "He's always been an outsider. The good, while we're the bad. And there's nothing I can do to change that."

"He's no saint. Don't go making him into something he's not."

"He is to me." I drop back to the mattress. "I've never wanted to change who I am more than I do right now."

"Yeah?" He sobers and comes to sit beside me. "I get it. I feel the same way about Sarah."

"Maybe you should listen to your own advice," I mutter. "She's no saint either."

"She's still far better than I deserve."

I disagree. I've always known she was perfectly matched for this man. Now her callousness makes it even more apparent. What that woman needs is a dose of her own medicine.

The worst part is that she's currently out there, alone with Sebastian, probably turning him against me.

"What did she say to you on the porch?" he asks.

I bark out a derisive laugh. "Not much. She just told me, in a not-so-subtle way, that she thinks I'm involved."

"Ignore her. She's lashing out. That's all. She's made herself into this badass defender of the weak and innocent. So having this happen right under her nose makes her feel like a failure."

"She's not the only one who feels that way."

"I know." He shoves a hand through his hair, his frustration so palpable I can feel it throb inside my chest. "This whole situation is fucked up."

"Uh huh." I lean into him, needing to ease his burden and rest my shoulder against his. "Never in a million years would I have thought my father was capable of this."

"What about Cole?" He wraps his arm around me and pulls me into his side. "Do you think he's involved?"

My stomach twists in knots, inspiring a mass production of bile. "I've sworn black and blue he has nothing to do with this... But if you're unsure, then maybe I should be, too."

Hunter knows my brother. He's one of the very few people who does. If he's in doubt, then I'm not sure I should be confident of Cole's innocence.

"No. Ignore me. I'm questioning everything at the moment."

"Me, too."

"Especially Decker." He shoots me a glance, then focuses toward the vacant corner of the room. "I can't get over that lying little fuck."

"He's not enjoying this either. He doesn't feel good about what he's done, despite how moral it is."

"There's no place for morality around here. That's not how things work."

"And maybe that should change. This never would've happened otherwise." I stare at my fingers clenched in my lap. "I need to fix it."

There's no other choice. I don't think I can move forward with these atrocities hanging over my head.

"You need to think long and hard before you contemplate getting involved."

"No, I don't. My thoughts on this won't change." Maybe if I'd reported my uncle for his crimes when I was little, or taken it into my own hands long ago, this never would've happened. I could've stopped it all before it even started. "I won't be a spectator in this life anymore. I don't care if I die trying. I *will* make my father pay."

He turns to me, his brows pulled tight, his eyes narrowed.

I hold my breath, waiting for him to tell me I'm an ignorant, whimsical fool. Instead, he slowly nods.

"It won't be easy."

"I know."

He pushes from the mattress and holds out a hand. "We're going to need a fucking brilliant plan."

"And Sebastian needs to be involved." I grasp his offering and push to my feet, waiting for his refusal. "Is that going to be a problem?"

"Yes." His grip tightens around my fingers. His jaw ticks, too. A multitude of frustration flows off of him, making my heart tighten. "But I'll do anything for Sarah. And right now, you both have the same goal in mind."

"Will you promise not to hurt him?"

"Nope." He doesn't release my hand as he leads me to the door.

"Hunter, please. This is serious."

"As serious as a grown man kicking me in the shin?"

I frown. "Excuse me?"

"Forget it." He drags me out into the hall. "I promise to behave. For now. Is that good enough?"

I roll my eyes. "Do I have a choice?"

"Not at all."

A derisive scoff leaves my lips. "Then I guess I'll have to deal. Just as long as you realize I'll take a bullet for that man if necessary."

He winces, and I'm not sure if it's in confusion or distaste. "Let's hope it doesn't come down to that."

He guides me along the hall, the murmur of conversation drifting from the kitchen. I can hear them talking. About me. The whispers don't stop until we reach the entry to the dining room to find them sitting opposite each other at the large wooden table, the space between them scattered with snacks.

I meet Sebastian's gaze, his expression growing pained when he lowers his focus to my grip on Hunter's hand.

"We need to talk." I squeeze the fingers entwined with mine then let go.

"It looks like you two have already been doing that." Sarah scowls. "Should we be thankful you've decided to include us?"

"Cut them a break." Sebastian drags out the chair beside him and raises a brow, wordlessly offering me the seat. "The big guy was too scared to knock on the front door. We don't want to frighten him away from a conversation."

"Funny." Hunter wanders forward and rests against the wall behind Sarah, relaxed, yet the readiness of battle is evident in the clench of his fists. "I guess I was trembling in my boots at the thought of you landing another kick to my shin, you fucking pussy."

I watch the exchange, unsure whether it's friendly fire, or something more sinister. They both appear tolerant and calm despite the underlying tension.

"Are we even capable of discussing this in a civil manner?" I make toward the offered chair and sit, my oversized shirt billowing over my thighs.

"This is civil." Sebastian grabs a granola bar from the center of the table and pushes it toward me. "You need to eat."

I grab the offering, my fingers deliberately sliding over his in a show of thanks before he moves his hand away.

"Start talking." Sarah doesn't quit scowling. "What have you two been scheming behind our backs?"

I raise an unimpressed brow as I break open the food wrapper and take a bite. "There wasn't any scheming. All we discussed is how I need to make this right. I can't let my father get away with what he's done."

"*You?*" Sarah drawls. "You mean *us*, right? What could you possibly do on your own? Well, apart from slapping your daddy on the wrist and telling him he's been a naughty boy. But given his proclivities, I'm sure he'd enjoy the hell out of that."

My throat clogs with a spike of fury. My pulse thumps. Everywhere. In my ears. My head. Behind my eyes. I clench my teeth and take a deep breath before I do something that will delay any possibility of fatherly vengeance. "Someone needs to shut her up before I do it myself."

She laughs. "I'd like to see you try."

"*Sarah*," Sebastian warns. "Either leash your bitchiness or I'll kick your ass out."

"Her bitchiness?" It's my turn for derision. "Is that what we're calling her personality these days?"

"Both of you, put a sock in it." Hunter's voice is a mere grumble of authority. "We don't have time to fuck around. At the moment, Cole thinks you two are hiding because you had the fuckers from the drive-by tailing you. But that bullshit story won't hold for long."

"I agree. I need to tell him what's going on." Bottling this news isn't healthy. Being separated from my family isn't helping either. "He needs to know the truth."

"About your father?" Sarah asks.

I glare through a sharp nod.

"And where, exactly, will you tell him you got the information? How are you going to explain the knowledge without exposing Decker?"

My skin turns clammy. My brother finding out the identity of the informant isn't my biggest issue. What I don't want to face is the reality of Sebastian leaving me.

But that *is* the reality.

He's no longer going to be a part of my life. He's walking away. He already made his choice clear. "Sebastian isn't sticking around. He's—"

"Like hell I'm not," he growls. "I'm not going anywhere if you're putting yourself in danger."

My heart stops, the missing beats consuming me.

Is that all I had to do to keep him close? Risk my safety?

I bottle a laugh in my tightening chest. I should've known.

"I'll look after her." Hunter crosses his arms over his chest. "You need to cut and run. As soon as Torian finds out, you're dead. Or worse."

"Who says he needs to find out anything?" Sarah counters. "We have to keep this to ourselves for now. How do we even know he's not involved?"

"*We know*," Hunter and I say in unison.

"Fine." She huffs. "You have unwavering faith in his innocence. But you need to realize Torian is going to want to take over as soon as he finds out. When that happens, we won't have a say in the outcome. And he sure as hell won't let his sister be involved."

The truth in her words is a betraying punishment.

I don't want her to be right. Yet she is.

"I agree," Sebastian murmurs. "You've said it yourself, Keira, there's different rules when it comes to dealing with family. If he learns the truth, it's only going to make this situation more complicated. And your father will never be punished accordingly."

He's right, too.

The severe frown pulling at Hunter's brow says he agrees.

"Okay." I nod. "So I won't tell him." Despite the guilt already eating away at my stomach.

"Are you capable of keeping something this big from him?" Sarah asks.

I glare at her. "I'm not a child. I've kept things from him before."

She holds up her hands in surrender. "I wasn't being a bitch this time. I was only asking if it's something you think you're capable of. I know you two are close, even though you lead people to believe otherwise."

The thinly veiled apology means nothing to me. Not when all her knives still linger in my back.

"She's capable." Sebastian grabs my hand in my lap, our fingers twining beneath the table. "You've got no idea what she's kept from her brother."

I plotted the murder of my uncle and kept it to myself. Planning the demise of my father should be no different.

It should.

Only it already feels a million times worse.

"Keeping Cole out of this is obviously ideal, but how the fuck do we get Luther back in the country without him?" Hunter pushes from the wall and begins to pace. "No, Keira, but your old man hasn't given a shit about you for years. He's not going to drop everything and come running just because you ask him to."

I steel myself against the brutal truth—my father doesn't care. He never did. Not when I was a child. Not when I was a vulnerable teen. And definitely not now. "I know a way."

I know possibly the one and only driving force to get my father back in the country.

"Which is?" Sarah asks.

"I'll finish what I started weeks ago."

Sebastian's hand falls limp in my lap. He knows what I'm about to say, and there's no comforting hold to reassure me I'm making the right decision.

"I'm going to kill my uncle." I forge through the judgmental silence. "My father will return for the funeral. There's no way he'd miss it, despite the authorities breathing down his neck."

The quiet continues, the thickness expanding as all eyes turn to me.

"Finish what you started?" Hunter asks. "You're the one who ran down Richard?"

This time Sebastian doesn't answer the hard question for me. He straightens, his hand retreating.

"That's a story for another day." I swallow over the scratch in my throat. "Right now, we need to focus on the future, not the past."

Nobody fills the silence. The tension thickens, their judgment weighing down on me.

"You're not going anywhere near Richard," Sebastian mutters. "I'll take care of him."

No, he won't. But that's a conversation for later, too.

"What's this all about?" Sarah scrutinizes me. "Is there something else we need to know?"

"Only that I'm well aware of what my father and uncle are capable of. I'm not going to be lenient on either of them."

Her chin slowly rises, her lips parting as understanding begins to flicker to the surface.

I don't want her to delve into my past. I don't want her to even contemplate what I've been through. "We need to stop moving in circles and make a goddamn plan." I release a huff of frustration. "All any of you have done so far is poke at everything I say."

There's more silence. More judgment, too.

"What's the end game here, Keira?" Sebastian reclaims my hand, the touch gentle. "Are you talking about putting Luther in prison or..." He looks at me, our eyes meeting across an emotional battlefield.

There's a wealth of connection between us. A hidden conversation where he relays his protection and strength while I struggle not to confess my fear.

"No," I whisper. "Prison isn't an option. My father has the means to buy the best lawyers. Hell, he could grease the palms of an entire jury. Or pay a team to help him escape whatever cell they put him in." The overbearing weight of my father's power presses down on me. "He has men everywhere. There's nobody who can withstand his threats or influence."

"Which means?" Hunter asks.

I shuffle my ass back in my seat and sit at my full height. I raise my chin, straighten my shoulders, and become the warrior woman I've always considered myself to be. I think of my past. I contemplate Stella's future. I picture all those helpless, fractured women. Then I resign myself to the only outcome possible. "Death is the solution. For both of them."

Relief shadows my statement, but the underlying pain lingers.

He's my dad, and I'm planning his murder.

He was my mother's one and only love, and I vow to send him to his grave.

"First, I'll take care of my uncle." I clear my throat to dislodge the emotion roughening my words. "Then when my father returns for the funeral, we end this."

"I said I'd deal with Richard," Sebastian reaffirms. "Don't even think about going near him. I'm not letting you get caught up in that again."

"Caught up in what?" Sarah asks.

"I *want* to do this," I demand. "I *need* to be the one who ends his life. I won't fail this time."

"You won't get a chance." He pushes from the table and stalks for the fridge, grabbing four cans of beer before returning to place them among the snacks.

He's still trying to protect me, that much is clear, but I won't let him this time. Not when it comes to Richard. "I'm capable, Sebastian."

"Really?" The question is an accusation. "There's a reason you didn't go ahead with the hit in the first place. Killing someone isn't a crime you want on your conscience."

"Excuse me." I shove from my chair. "That wasn't the reason, and you know it. I told you I didn't follow through because I didn't want to make my family vulnerable."

"Hold up." Sarah flattens her hands on the table. "So, you did run Richard down?"

Sebastian's jaw ticks, his nostrils flaring. He's beautiful. An exquisite show of masculine dominance. "Do you think you'll be helping your family's situation when your dad and Richard are dead and you're in prison? You don't want to spend the rest of your life behind bars."

"And you do?" I quip.

He doesn't snap at my ridicule. Instead, he cracks a can of beer and takes a long pull. "We're not arguing over this."

"You're right." I shove my chair back into place and stalk around the table. "We're not."

"Why don't we take a break?" Sarah glances between us. Back and forth. Over and over. "We can discuss this later."

"There's no need. Richard is mine to deal with." I continue toward the back door. "I'll never forgive anyone who gets in my way."

I pull the porch door wide, escape outside, then slam the wood shut behind me. The bang reverberates through my bones, shaking my soul. The vibration spurs me to move faster, to skitter down the steps and stride toward the end of the yard.

I have to get out of here.

To go home.

More than anything, I want to speak to my siblings. I need to hear a familiar voice. A calming, strengthening voice that won't have me questioning my every breath.

I keep pounding out the distance, not stopping when I reach the waist-high fence. I climb over the metal and keep walking along the dirt car track leading around the paddock, the pebbles and stones tormenting my feet.

It doesn't take long for my anger to dissipate and for regret to take its place.

I get it. Sebastian wants to protect me. He *always* wants to protect me. It's what endeared me to him in the first place. I can't grow to hate it now. I just need to make him understand.

I have to do this.

And yes, maybe he's right. Maybe I wasn't strong enough before, and I couldn't handle a hit marring my conscience. But things have changed.

I want Richard's death on my hands.

I need to be strong enough to make him pay, not only for his recent transgressions, but those he made against me in the past.

I don't stop until I'm half a mile from the house, the early afternoon sun beating down on me as an all-consuming hollowness creeps inside my chest. I haven't felt alone since before the shooting. It's been days with Sebastian within reach and readily accessible to keep me stable.

I need to learn to function without him.

Just because he's staying by my side for now doesn't mean he can for long. Cole will learn the truth eventually. The time will come when the man I adore is wrenched from my heart.

A scuffle of noise sounds behind me, inspiring hope.

It's him. I know it is. He's here to apologize. To make things right. And I want nothing more than to run to him and claim the warmth.

I turn, my eyes gentle in anticipation for the remorse I expect to see. But he's not the person behind me. I'm bitterly disappointed at the sight of Sarah a few feet away, her feet bare, the bottom of her jeans covered in red dirt as she navigates the stones in the path toward me.

"What are you doing out here?" I mutter.

Her ankle rolls, and she rights herself with a curse. "Do you mind if I join you?"

"Do I have a choice?"

"Yes, you do. I can leave you alone if you like. But I think you'd prefer to watch me suffer through an uncomfortable apology."

Jesus Christ. Sebastian told her. The pity is right there, written all over her face.

"I don't want an apology." I start toward her, retracing my steps toward the house. I don't want anything from her. Not now. Not anymore.

"Then tell me what to do to make this better." She pauses in place and waits until I reach her side. "How do I fix this?"

"You don't. This is as good as it gets." I stride by her, and she hustles to follow.

"Despite me being a total dick, we're friends, Keira. I can make it up to you."

"That's where you're wrong. We're not friends. We never were. We couldn't have been if you were so eager to burn me at the stake."

She cringes. "I deserve that."

She deserves more. Much more.

"I'm sorry." Her words are pained. "I can't imagine what you've been through. I didn't realize. I honestly had no clue. And I hate myself for it."

"Sebastian had no right to tell you." I keep stalking away, the distance between me and the house seeming to grow further and further with each breath.

"He didn't say a word. I'm working on assumptions at this point and hoping my imagination is on overdrive."

"Your original assumptions about me were entirely off base. Why would this be any different?"

"Will you tell me?"

I try not to fracture from the regret in her voice.

She doesn't deserve my sympathy.

Goddamn it, she doesn't deserve anything from me. "I'll pass."

I lengthen my stride, increasing the pace of my escape. She doesn't try to keep up. I hear her fall back, the scuffle of rocks drifting behind as I approach the house yard.

I don't stop until my hand is on the fence.

"*Fuck.*" Her curse splits the air.

I pause and glance over my shoulder, finding her looking at something shiny poking from the bottom of her foot.

"Motherfucker." She pulls out a sharp spike of glass and throws it into the long grass beside the trail.

I bite back a reply. I shouldn't care if she's hurt. I swear I don't despite the pang beneath my ribs that demands I help.

She limps forward. One step. Two.

Damn it.

"Are you okay?" I mutter.

"Yeah. I'd call this karma."

"I guess." I shrug. "If Karma turned into a lenient little bitch."

She shoots me a grin.

It's too easy. After what she put me through, the slide back into friendship needs to be harder.

I turn away in rejection and raise my leg to climb over the fence.

"Keira, wait."

I sigh, my shoulders slumping as I reluctantly face her hobbling toward me.

"I fucked up. Big time." Her usual expression of pride-filled strength becomes a softened plea for understanding. "But I'm begging you, is there any way I can make this up to you?"

I can't hold her focus. Not when she's efficiently wearing me down with the sincerity in her expression. I lower my gaze, over the wrinkles in her shirt, then further to the rectangular bulge in her jeans pocket.

I stop. Stare.

Maybe there is something she can do.

"Is that a cell?" I look her in the eye. "Let me call Cole."

She blinks, once, twice, her lips parting on silent words.

"That's how you make this up to me, Sarah. You give me that cell in your pocket and leave me alone to call my brother."

"Decker doesn't want you contacting him yet."

"I'm well aware of what Decker wants."

She glances toward the house, her forehead wrinkled from an internal battle I can practically hear. "They're going to kill me."

"That's a small price to pay."

She sighs and presses her lips tight as she bridges the space between us in a few limped steps and hands over the device. "I hope you know what you're doing."

I don't. Not at all. "I'll figure it out." I grab the cell and continue to hold her stare. "You can go inside now."

She doesn't budge. For a few brief seconds she holds my gaze, wordlessly pleading with me to change my mind.

"Go."

She huffs out a breath and throws her leg over the fence.

I wait for her to walk across the lawn, up the stairs to the porch, then into the house. Then my fingers are frantically flying over the cell screen, dialing one of the very few numbers I've committed to memory.

Cole answers on the first ring, his panicked voice loud and clear. "Where is she? Have you found her?"

I smile. I almost sob. "Are you referring to me, brother?"

"Jesus. I've been fucking worried. What happened? Are you safe?"

I close my eyes, fighting the burn.

I want to tell him everything. All the secrets. All the lies. All the deception our father has intricately woven into our lives.

"I'm—"

A loud crack of noise draws my attention to the back of the house. Sebastian stands there, the door wildly swinging back toward him as he stares at me, wide-eyed, shoulders tense.

I swallow at the defeat I see in his features.

I'm betraying him again. I'm hurting him.

"Everything is okay, Cole."

Sebastian descends the stairs in one leap and storms toward me, his stride menacing.

"Where are you?" Cole asks. "Why the fuck haven't you called?"

My heart lodges in my throat as Sebastian uses one hand to bound over the fence, coming to an overbearing stop right in front of me.

"I'm safe," I say into the phone. "Decker is looking after me."

His chin hitches in defiance as he stands tall, the pain of my deception evident in his eyes.

"We didn't mean to worry you," I continue. "But we had to get off the grid. We had a tail."

"Who?"

"I don't know. We lost them outside Newport."

"Where are you now?"

"I don't know that either. And I think it's best if I don't say anything more over the phone."

Sebastian's chest rises and falls with harsh breaths as he remains ramrod straight. I want to reach out and touch him. I have to ease the heartache. But what I'm going to say to Cole is far more important.

"You're upset," my brother growls. "I can hear it in your voice."

"It's just good to speak to you. And I miss home. I can't wait to see Layla and Stella."

"It's more than that, Keira. Tell me what's going on."

My hand trembles as I lower the phone to press the speaker button. Sebastian needs to hear this.

"You're right." I clear my throat. "Something *is* going on."

Dark eyes turned panicked as they stare down at me. Concern is written into every inch of him—his posture, his expression. I have to ignore it all and forge forward.

"I need to tell you something."

Sebastian makes a grab for the phone.

I dodge, holding up a hand as I mouth a plea for him to wait. "*Please.*"

He bares his teeth, his nostrils flaring while he fights against trusting me.

"Cole..." I turn away, facing the sun. "I..." The words stick in my throat. Clogging. Choking.

I'm about to change everything. I'm going to flip this script on its ass, and I'm not going to know if it's the right decision until it's already too late.

I fill my lungs to capacity, the tortured breath stabbing through my lungs, bearing down on my stomach. "I love him."

Silence reigns. Nobody utters a sound at my admission.

"I know you're angry," I murmur. "And that you don't trust him. But *I* do."

"Keira—"

"I'm not finished. We've been through a lot in the past few days. I've gone to hell and back, and he's been beside me the entire time."

"That's what he's paid for," he scolds. "I told him to protect you with his life."

"And he has. Without fail."

"We can discuss this when you get back—"

"We're discussing it now." I add steel to my tone. "We've slept together, Cole. We had unprotected sex, which means there's a possibility I'm pregnant. I could be carrying his child."

I hear Sebastian's sharp inhale. Cole's vicious curse is far louder.

I battle with panic, the overwhelming force threatening to take me down.

"Tell me where you are," he demands. "I'm coming to get you."

"No, you're not. I'm staying here for now. I'll come home soon. But until I do, I need you to realize this is what I want. *He's* what I want. I won't put up with any asshole behavior once we get back."

"I swear to God, Keira. Tell me where you are."

"I'm safe," I repeat. "That's all you need to know."

24

DECKER

She doesn't wait for a reply before disconnecting the call. She doesn't wait for me to pick my jaw up off the ground either.

She stands there, her arm falling to her side, the cell hanging limp in her hand as her back continues to face me.

"Was any of that true?" My question is barely audible.

"I'm not pregnant."

The gentle utter of her admission has no effect on me. My mind is rabid. My face seeps with sweat.

"I have a hormone implant," she admits. "I lied to Cole to buy us some time." She turns to face me, an apology written in her features. "This way, even if he does learn the truth, he'll pause long enough to contemplate the repercussions of his actions."

He'll pause.

She's not pregnant.

"You lied to your brother for me?" She's delusional if she thinks the deception will change Torian's actions, but still, she lied. For me. "Why?"

"You know why."

No, I'm pretty sure I'm clueless. Whenever I think I've got an edge on this woman, she pulls the rug out from beneath me.

"It's only temporary." She wraps her arms around her stomach, hugging herself in a show of such brutal vulnerability I have to fight the need to drag her against me. "Once you leave, I can tell him there's no baby."

I nod, strangely wishing the fake story she concocted had a possibility of reality. But like she said, that lie of hers will only buy a pause in time. It won't stop Cole from gunning me down in the long run.

"What about the rest of the conversation, Tinkerbell? What else did you lie about?"

"Are you asking if I love you?"

Yeah. I am. I just can't find the fucking balls to open my mouth and say it.

She nibbles her lower lip, her brows pulling tighter by the second as she glances away. "I think I've loved you since you stuck up for me months ago. I don't think anyone could be exposed to your level of protection and care without falling hard, Sebastian."

Her words cut to my core, her admission slashing deep enough to scar. "So it's the badassery that won you over, not my sparkling personality?" I paste on a grin, hoping to suck the deep and crazy out of the conversation.

"You're no badass," she whispers. "You're the opposite—A good Samaritan with a frightening death wish, and really inappropriate timing with your smartass comments."

My grin lessens.

I can feel her fear. I can almost taste it.

"I don't have a death wish." I step forward, my feet falling hard against the dirt as she backs herself against the fence, keeping distance between us that I refuse to allow. "Not anymore." I continue to advance, not stopping until my hips cage hers in place. "I just know what I want and don't plan to stop until I get it."

"Which is retribution, right?" Her eyes turn pained. "That's all you're focused on."

"My hopes for retribution are delayed for now."

"Because I exposed you?"

"No. Because I'm focusing on something more important." I glide a hand into her hair, holding her possessively, never losing sight of those gorgeous eyes as I bring us chest to chest. "Right now, all I want is to make sure you're safe. That's all that matters to me."

"Why? You've made it clear you don't feel the same way I do."

"Jesus, Keira." I close in on her with my free hand, dragging my thumb over the softness of her lower lip. "Who says I don't feel the same?"

Her face crumples, her baby blues tortured. "You do. In your actions and your plans."

"You know this has been a fucked up mess from the start, but how can you not see that I'd kill for you? Despite knowing what your father has been doing, I put my life on the line for you. And I'll continue to do the same, because there is no way in hell I'll let you anywhere near Richard."

"This isn't about him. I'm talking about you not being excited to hear your secret is safe. Hunter didn't tell Cole. And neither did I. But you never celebrated having more time with me. You don't care."

"I fucking care." I bring us face to face. Almost nose to nose. "But I've also gotta keep it real clear in my mind that leaving is the only conclusion here. A few extra days with you is huge, but we don't get a happily ever after. No matter how badly I want to give that to you."

"You're acting as if you're already gone."

"No, I'm not. I'm just trying to keep a level head. Your safety is the most important thing here. I can't lose sight of that."

"I'm scared you're losing sight of me entirely."

I wince.

Truth is, I wish I could lose sight of her. If that was a possibility I'd already be long gone. I would've taken my beating from Hunter yesterday and headed for the hills. My inability to let go of Keira is the only reason I'm still here. "I'll never do that. Not even once I'm gone."

"I'm going to do everything in my power to change things so you don't leave," she whispers against my lips. "I'll keep lying to Cole. I'll make that agent who's blackmailing you disappear. I'll do whatever it takes, Sebastian."

"Shh." I claim her mouth, brushing my lips over hers as she slays my fucking heart. "Let me handle it. I'll work something out."

She whimpers, her tongue sweeping mine.

I wish I wasn't lying. I wish I had faith. But this hole I've dug is too deep. You don't rat on the most powerful crime family in the state and live to tell the tale.

I'm a dead man walking. I can already feel the darkness of damnation.

"Promise me," she pleads. "Don't let this be another deception."

Fuck. She knows me too well. Her insight creeps into the furthest reaches of my mind. She's a part of me, stealing my secrets and reading my soul.

I kiss her deeper. Harder. With all my fucking heart and determination.

"Sebastian..." Her hand finds my chest, the pressure growing as she tries to push me away. "Please."

The doomsday clock sounds another tick. I don't want to betray her again. Not over this.

"*Please,*" she repeats. "I need to believe this can work."

"It can." I lean harder into her, grinding against her pelvis. "We'll figure it out."

Lies. All lies. But I'd promise her the world if it meant I'd get to continue hearing those needy little moans that vibrate against my mouth.

I'd do it all.

I'd do everything.

I fall into her. I burn. Every inch of me is attuned to every move she makes.

We're one.

It's intrinsic.

Fate.

At least for now.

I drown in her until I can no longer breathe. Long enough for me to pretend I'm someone else. Somewhere else. There's no approaching detonation. I don't have to walk away. I'm not going to break her heart. It's just us. A happy couple, without a care in the fucking world.

"I want to drive back to Portland tonight," she murmurs against my lips. "I don't want to wait any longer."

I turn numb. All the pleasure evaporates, leaving me cold and bitter.

"Okay..." I pull away, meeting the determination staring back at me. "But just so you know, I haven't changed my mind about Richard. You need to let me and Hunt handle it."

The hand on my chest grows talons, her nails digging into skin. "Don't fight me on this."

"I'm not fighting you, slick. I'm keeping you safe."

Her chin hitches, a wealth of strength building in her features. "No."

That's all she says. One word. A single, adamant denial.

She slides to the side, leaving me with a look filled with more force than reason.

She doesn't understand what she's asking. There's no fucking clue behind those gorgeous blue eyes as she leaps the fence and sashays her sexy ass toward the house while I'm stuck dealing with a hard dick and a hollow chest.

I watch her climb the stairs and turn toward the porch railing, Sarah coming outside to meet her. The two of them murmur together, their heads close, their camaraderie a fucking uncomfortable sight.

The last thing Keira needs is a master manipulator at her side. They could take down hell if they teamed up. And I sure as shit don't want that happening on my watch.

I leap the fence and stride to the house. They stop chatting as I approach, the cease of their Secret Squirrel conversation raising the hair on the back of my neck.

"We haven't finished talking, Keira."

She doesn't look at me. Doesn't even budge an inch to acknowledge my comment.

"I made sandwiches," Sarah offers. "Go inside and start eating without us. We'll join you soon."

I don't tear my gaze from Keira, but she doesn't glance my way. She deliberately refuses, too busy holding the railing in a white-knuckle grip as she glares into the distance.

"Soon," I repeat in warning. "We don't have time to fuck around."

Sarah rolls her eyes. "We'll be there when we're ready."

It's a subtle fuck you, and I have no choice but to listen.

Instead of planting my feet like my ego demands, I act like a scolded puppy and slink inside to watch them from the other side of the glass-paneled door.

"Are they coming in?" Hunt mutters from his seat at the table.

I close my eyes for the briefest second, begging the holy heavens for strength while I'm stuck inside with this unforgiving motherfucker who could end our ceasefire at any moment. "Not until they've annoyed me enough to cause a hemorrhoid."

"Is Keira okay?"

I shrug. "Your guess is as good as mine."

"She looked fine a few minutes ago when you were groping her against the fence. What did you do to fuck it up?"

I clench my teeth and swing around to swipe my beer off the table, throwing back gulps like I'm dying of dehydration. Hunt's trying to make me snap, and I refuse. I'm not going to bite. Not until the alcohol numbs the bruises I already have to make way for the new ones he wants to give me.

I empty the can and retrieve another from the fridge. I waste time tidying up the mess Sarah made while creating the pile of sandwiches on the table. I fuck around, trying to play it cool while Sarah taunts me through the glass, frowning at me as she speaks.

I can't hear what she's saying, but I can tell it's filled with annoyance aimed in my direction. Revenge Barbie is getting in Keira's head, filling her with confidence and misconceptions about slaying dragons and taking over the world.

"Hunt, you better get control of your girl." I grip the counter and mentally count out my frustration. "She's starting to piss me off."

He scoffs. "Bite me. You two were best buddies when we arrived. Don't come crying to me now."

I'm still gripping the counter ten minutes later when Sarah walks inside, leaving Keira on the porch.

"What's going on?" Hunt pushes to his feet. "How is she?"

Sarah grabs one of the empty plates stacked on the table and begins grabbing sandwiches from the platter. "She's annoyed, which is entirely understandable when someone keeps treating her like a child."

I see red. My focus fucking glazes with anger. "Those are your words, not hers. She knows I'm not treating her like a fucking kid. Stop filling her head with bullshit."

"Then stop telling her what she can and can't do." She places down the plate piled with food and walks into the kitchen, bypassing my rage-filled position by the counter to open the cutlery drawer. "You'll never win this fight if you treat her like she's fragile."

I slam my palm down on the counter. "Goddamn it, she's not like you." My shoulders convulse with my labored breathing. "Killing someone will fuck with her head for the rest of her life."

"It's not your choice to make."

"It's not yours either. You've got no right to weigh in on this."

"I haven't done a damn thing. All I'm doing is listening to her vent." She retrieves a knife and slams the drawer shut.

"What the hell is that for?"

She scowls. "To cut my sandwiches. Is that okay, your highness?"

"Just as long as you're not using it to stab her in the back again."

Her lip curls as she stomps to the table. "I never stabbed her in the back, *Decker*. I said a few things I shouldn't have, but I've apologized, and she's been decent enough to forgive me. So I'm going to stay out there and chat things out while she's willing."

She holds the knife in a tight grip and picks up her filled plate. "Can I have the car keys?" She turns her focus to her fiancé. "I'm going to see if any of the clothes I packed will fit her. She can't keep wearing that oversized shirt and shorts."

"Yeah." He pulls a fob from his pocket and lobs it toward her. "If she doesn't find anything suitable, I can go for a drive."

"Thanks, babe." She turns on her heel and heads for the door, shooting me one last taunting glare before she walks outside and leads Keira from the porch.

I miss the sight of my blue-eyed goddess as soon as she's out of view.

I don't know how to fix this shit. Not the issue of her wanting to walk through hell unnecessarily. Or the gauntlet I'm going to face once her brother has my dick in a vise.

There are no easy options. No fucking path of least resistance.

There's only struggle and torment.

"Did Richard put hands on her?" Hunt murmurs.

I don't deny the mental images assailing me. I let the picture of Richard's hands on Keira take over in the hopes it will increase my understanding of her need to face him on her own.

But it doesn't.

No matter what I think, what I do, I can't stand the thought of her anywhere near him.

"Yeah." I stalk to the table and snatch a sandwich from the pile.

"How did they keep it a secret? I should've noticed."

"You weren't around back then."

"Back when?" His eyes narrow.

"When she was fourteen." I take a bite of bread and chew as I watch the avalanche of reality bear down on him.

His jaw sets. His shoulders straighten. "Fourteen?" He raises his voice. "Fucking fourteen?" He shoves back from the table, his chair clattering to the floor. "I don't fucking blame her for running him down."

"She didn't. She paid someone to do it."

He begins to pace, stalking back and forth. "Who?"

"The same asshole who shot up the restaurant."

He stops and swings around to meet my gaze, his face a mask of confusion. "She paid someone to shoot up my engagement party?"

"No. She paid someone to take out Richard, then backed out of the contract. Now the motherfucker is blackmailing her."

"Who?" he repeats. "How do I find this fucker?"

"I don't know yet. But I'll figure it out. Hopefully before Torian gets his hands around my neck." I hold his gaze, my eyes pleading. "If I don't get the chance, I need you to promise to take care of him for me."

"I'm not doing shit for you." He continues pacing. "But I'll do it for her."

"Semantics, asshole." I take another snap of sandwich, not tasting the food as I swallow.

"No, not semantics. You don't deserve a damn thing from me, you self-righteous prick."

Self-righteous?

Self-fucking-righteous?

I return to the regular broadcast of biting my tongue, my anxiety building the longer Keira remains out of view. I slump into a seat and fill my gut despite the lack of hunger.

I don't want to eat at a time like this. I doubt I'll ever regain my appetite, but fuel is a necessary commodity. Or it will be once we sort out a plan.

"What did she tell Torian?" Hunt makes a dramatic show of flinging out a chair and sinking onto it. "I assume it wasn't anything dramatic, seeing as though you ran out there and punished her by shoving your tongue down her throat."

"You fixate on my love life way too much," I taunt. "Not gettin' enough at home, big guy?"

"I get plenty," he snarls. "At least I did until you fucked up my schedule."

"A well deserved punishment for trying to gouge my eyes out, if you ask me."

"You threw the rule book out the window when you started the five-year-old shin kicking."

"Yeah? What rules are there when it comes to my sister getting raped and tortured?"

He sobers, the bitterness fading from his expression. He lowers his focus to the table, remaining quiet through the thickening discomfort.

"Keira told Torian she's pregnant," I say to break the silence.

"What?" His head snaps up. "Are you serious?"

"Unfortunately." I slide my plate to the center of the table. "She thinks it will stop him from blowing my brains out."

"Is it true?"

"No." I push from my seat and go to the kitchen. "At least that's what she says."

"You can't blame me for asking. You're not known for doing the smartest shit."

"Thanks." I pull open the fridge and ignore the fresh insult. "Want a beer?"

"Yeah."

I walk back to the table and slide a can toward him. "We need to figure out this plan before Keira gets carried away with ideas of her own vigilante justice. We can give her something basic to do. Surveillance or some shit. Something to keep her busy and feel like she's played a pivotal role."

Hunt stares at me with an annoying level of patronizing judgement.

"What?"

He shrugs. "Nothin'."

"No, it's definitely something. You're looking at me as if you know more than I do."

"I know determined women, that's all."

"You know *one* determined, psychotic woman. Keira's nothing like Sarah."

"Maybe not." He takes a large gulp of beer. "But if Richard laid hands on her, shouldn't she have the right to fuck him up on her own terms?"

"You weren't with her after the shooting. You don't know how something like this would stick with her. She'll be eaten alive with remorse, regardless of how he deserves to rot in hell."

"Or she could be eaten alive with regret if she doesn't do it herself."

No. I don't believe that would happen.

She's got a big heart. She's not capable of murder. Not with her own hands.

"Look," Hunt grates. "I agree with you. I don't think she should be anywhere near him when he takes his last breath. But I want you to think about what she's missing out on before you take the option away from her."

"I've thought about it. I don't need to fixate on it anymore."

He shrugs. "Okay, then we make sure she knows it's not a possibility."

"We?" I raise a brow. "Are Hunt and Deck back together again, kickin' it like old times?"

He glares. "Don't push your luck, motherfucker."

I chuckle but take the warning like it's a death threat.

I don't push. Not at all.

I work my ass off to keep a level conversation sprinkled with sarcastic insults and blatant contempt. Just like the good ol' days.

We mutter murderous ideas at each other while we finish the sandwiches. We work out a plan for Richard, and Luther, and also that fucker who's blackmailing her. We'll knock them off one by one. Strategically. Quietly. Without a single lead weaving its way back to us.

"Keira wants to drive back tonight." I finish off another beer and throw the can across the kitchen, scoring a three-pointer in the sink. "I'm going to give her the rest of the afternoon to cool off and talk to her about the plan in the car. Even if we leave soon, we won't arrive until late. Hopefully, she'll be too tired to argue."

"Good luck with that."

I glance toward the porch, no longer able to ignore my need to lay eyes on her. "They've been out there for a long time."

"That's because neither one of them wants to be near us."

I push from my chair and walk to the back door, not seeing a soul in sight. "They're still out front."

Sarah's plate rests on the railing, a half-eaten sandwich sitting in the sun. It's quiet. Everything is detached, devoid and bare. But funnily enough, not Hunter.

Despite his thick layers of hatred, I'm grateful for his willingness to talk. It's more than I deserve. But it doesn't stop me wanting more.

His understanding would go a long way right about now.

The briefest flicker of empathy is all I ask.

"Do you plan on finishing me off after all this is done?" I keep my focus outside, not willing to betray my feelings on the subject.

"I haven't decided."

I nod, appreciating the honesty.

"Do you think you've got the balls to kick my ass again?" he asks.

"Apparently, I didn't kick your ass. I've been told you let me win."

He huffs out a derisive laugh. "You won, asshole. I was too surprised to know what to do."

My skin prickles, my senses unfamiliar with his thinly veiled compliment. "Surprised at the betrayal? Or—"

"You being an informant is beyond surprising. That shit falls into a category above and beyond. But I had a few hours to come to terms with it before we got to that barn. What threw me off was your ability to pack a punch. I guess I don't know shit when it comes to you."

Maybe there's a glimpse of truth in what Sarah told me earlier. I guess Hunt could be a hard man filled with gooey softness after all.

"I did it for my sister."

"I know," he grates, as if deliberately trying to harden up the conversation.

"And I wouldn't change a thing. Apart from getting my ass exposed."

"You're not exposed. Not entirely. We could still find a way to get her back."

"No. It's too late." I wince through the tightening in my throat. "I found out a few weeks ago that she's gone. It was Murphy's fucking Law that Torian finally brings me into the fold, then days later I get news that they've found her DNA in a shallow grave."

That dreaded, uncomfortable silence creeps back in and makes itself at home for long seconds.

"That's tough." Hunt's words are measured. Gentle. "I'm sorry."

I frown, battling the feels like they're waging war against me. "Yeah, well, the good news is that I'm not going to have to grieve for long. You're going to take care of that shit by putting me six feet under."

"I'm not going to kill you, asshole. It's just bullshit that you didn't tell me in the first place."

"That was never an option and you know it. You're loyal to Torian. You would've gunned me down long ago."

"I was fucking loyal to you, too, you piece of shit," he seethes. "More fucking loyal than you were to me."

"And how would I have broached that conversation, *Hunt*?" I swing away from the door and glare at him. "There's no rulebook for this shit."

"We've worked together a long time. There was a lot of opportunity for you to open your fucking mouth and sing to me instead of chirping like a fucking canary to the Feds."

My lip curls as I hold in a snarl.

The judgmental prick has no idea how I've battled keeping my secrets from him. He doesn't know what I've been through.

There are a thousand possibilities that could've, should've, and would've happened with each decision I made. I had to come to terms with my actions. I can't go back and change any of them.

"What's done is done." I walk toward the table and shove my chair into place. "And I'm sick of wasting more time waiting on the girls to finish their make-up session. I'm going to go drag them back in here."

He remains in place as I leave the room and stride down the hall to the door. I scope the front yard through the glass, finding a pile of discarded clothes resting at the top of the stairs.

But I can't see them.

They're not on the porch or in the yard.

"Hunt."

Apprehension skitters down my spine. I press my head to the glass, trying to see further to the left and then the right.

That's when I notice the abnormality.

Something is missing.

Something fucking important.

"*Hunt.*" I yank the door wide and step outside.

His footsteps thump down the hall. "What?"

"Notice something absent in this pretty little picture?"

He glances around, taking in the open expanse of vacant land before his gaze settles right in the middle of the drive. "Fuck."

"Yeah. Fuck."

They've taken the car.

I barge past him to stalk down the hall. "You might want to get on the phone to that woman of yours and tell her to stop whatever the hell she thinks she's doing."

I enter my brother's room, heading straight for the wardrobe to pull out a pair of jeans and a clean shirt.

"Call her, Hunt," I yell, my words vibrating off the walls. "Get her on the fucking phone."

Once I'm dressed, I jog from the bedroom and find him in the kitchen, his cell in hand.

"She's not answering." He shoves the device in his pocket, only to have it beep with a message.

"What does it say?" I inch closer and lift my chin, trying to read the screen.

His jaw clenches. His nostrils flare.

He raises the cell to show me the text—*We thought you two needed some bonding time. We will see you back in Portland.*

"Get your shit," he growls. "We can catch them. They can't have gone far."

"Help me lock up." I rush into the kitchen and pull a plastic garbage bag from beneath the sink, filling it with snacks to last us the upcoming hours on the road.

Hunt disappears down the hall, the slam of a window pane echoing in the distance.

Minutes later, I meet him at the front door, and he shadows me as I jog around the side of the house to his car that I stole yesterday.

"*Fuck.*" Hunt stops dead in his tracks and shoves a hand through his hair. "Fucking Sarah."

I search for the trigger that set him off, my chest pounding, my limbs shaking as I find a kitchen knife protruding from the front passenger side tire. "Something gives me the distinct impression that they don't give a shit about us bonding."

"Ya think?" he drawls.

"They're going back to make a move on Richard." I break out in a cold sweat.

Keira's going to commit murder, without taking the time to create a proper plan. Without me there to help.

Jesus.

Hunter meets my gaze. "And without a spare fucking tire, we're never going to catch them in time."

25

KEIRA

The hours spent on the road, strategizing the murder of one of my family, were some of the longest I've endured.

It's not like I haven't thought about Richard's death before. I've pictured it. I've even paid a man to complete the task. But I've never discussed every intricate detail that would lead to his last breath.

Sarah spoke each word with emotional detachment. She didn't appear fazed by the brutality. It was business. Nothing more. So I mimicked her demeanor, shoving all my fear and panic deep down inside.

I want this.

I need it.

His demise has to rest on my shoulders. I don't want Sebastian to be responsible. Or Hunter. Or even Sarah.

This needs to be all me.

I'm just nervous as hell at pulling the metaphorical trigger.

What if I freeze? Or get caught?

What happens if I can't think on my feet and I make a crucial mistake?

I suck in a shuddering breath, resting my hip against the cold metal of the car as I turn my attention to the hospital looming in front of me. The dominating building is bathed in shadow, the outside lights only illuminating the lower levels and leaving the dark rectangular windows to peer down at me.

"Are you sure you want to do this?" Sarah asks. Again. For the seventy-fifth time.

I've heard the question so many times it rings in my ears. "I'm sure."

"And you don't want me going in there with you?"

I wipe a hand over the arm of the leather jacket I borrowed, making sure the capped syringes are still firmly taped to my wrist. "No. It's better if I do this on my own. Less suspicion that way."

"We can only hope." She steps closer, grabbing the fringe of the long black wig to give it a jiggle. "At least you don't look recognizable."

The different hair, the colored contacts, the fake lashes, along with the full mask of plastered make-up that accentuates my cheekbones and slims down my face, have all worked together to transform me into someone else.

Someone who will hopefully slip into the ICU without drawing attention.

"Will you call Sebastian and let him know what's going on?" My heart clenches at the thought of him racing here to stop me. He needs to know he'll never make it in time. He can't. If he does, the whole plan could blow up in my face.

She nods. "He's going to be pissed."

"I know." God, how I know. The guilt over the anger and disappointment he would be harboring claws at me, digging deep into my soul. "But he gave me no choice."

This was my decision to make. Not his.

I'll own my actions.

The consequences, too.

"Just remember to keep your cool." Sarah continues to run her fingers through the long strands of the wig. "If something goes wrong, don't panic. Most people get caught making rash decisions."

I could laugh at the absurdity. Every decision I've made in the last three days has been rash.

Every. Single. One.

I don't know how to think differently anymore. The adrenaline-filled snap decisions have become my new norm.

"And I know you don't want to think about this…" She gives me a sad smile. "But if you get up there and can't follow through, it's not the end of the world. I'm not going anywhere. I'll stay right here in the parking lot, so you can come back and ask for help at any time."

She's wrong.

I can't back out twice. I don't want to prove Sebastian right. It's not an option. I failed a lot of women for not reporting my uncle when I was a child. And I've failed them every day since.

I won't do it a moment longer.

"You've helped enough already." I inch to the side, moving out of reach. "And we both came to the conclusion that this is an easy plan. In and out, remember? Undetected and unnoticed."

"I never said easy, Keira." Her brow furrows, the concern written all over her face. "Please tell me you're not jumping into this without being emotionally prepared. I need to know you're ready."

"I'm ready," I lie. "I've been ready for years."

I'm not ready. I never will be. But there's no way in hell I'll let fear keep me from giving Richard what he deserves.

"Okay." She reaches into the car, grabs the large bouquet of flowers lying in wait, and maneuvers them out the window to hand them to me. "I'll be waiting."

"Thanks." I grab the overbearing arrangement, holding it high in the crook of my elbow and take a steadying breath to keep the nerves at bay.

Taking the first step feels like the hardest part. I have to consciously think about putting one foot in front of the other. Heel, toe. Heel, toe. I keep my head strategically low, making the blooms and colored cellophane wrap shield my face from any hidden surveillance cameras. The long hair shrouding my cheeks helps, too.

It's my heart that causes the problems. The heavy beat pulses in my throat as I stride through the sliding doors and straight into the nearest elevator.

The confined space suffocates me. I cling to the flowers like a lifeline, breathing nothing but the floral scent tattooing my nostrils.

I'll never be able to enjoy the smell again. Not without remembering this moment.

By the time I reach the ICU, I'm a sweating, shaking mess. The only thing saving me is a lifetime acting out a fake persona. I know how to exude confidence when I don't have it. I'm no stranger to playing a role.

I stroll down that hall, relaxed and laid back. My fear and overwhelming hysteria hidden. I blend, letting the bouquet shield me as I pass the nurses' station.

The closer I get to Richard's room, the more my chest aches with heavy beats. I've only been to see him once. The sight of him battered and lifeless could only keep me captive for a few minutes before I strode from this hall, and this hospital, for what I hoped would be forever.

I prayed I would never have to see him again. That divine intervention would fix this mess. Somehow. Some way.

I pinned my savior on the great unknown, and look how that turned out.

I know better now.

Nobody else can fix this.

It's me. All me.

"Excuse me, ma'am."

The voice calls from behind me, back toward the nurses' station.

I ignore it, hoping like hell the woman is speaking to someone else. I only have one more room to pass until I'm at my destination. Five more feet. A few pained breaths.

"Ma'am?"

My pulse becomes a deafening throb in my ears as rushed steps approach, freezing me in place. I don't know what to do. I can't fathom what to say. Have I been caught already? Did Sebastian make a call and warn staff about the crazy woman about to commit murder?

"I apologize for disturbing you." Her voice is closer now, almost right behind me, raising the hair on the back of my neck. "But flowers aren't allowed in the ICU."

All the air leaves my lungs in a barely audible heave. Relief washes through me, then just as fast as the relaxation arrived, it flees.

No flowers means no shield.

No shield means my face will be harder to hide.

Don't panic. I hear Sarah's voice in my mind. *Most people get caught making rash decisions.*

"I'm sorry. I didn't realize." I keep my gaze low and my back toward the nurse. "What should I do with them?"

"I can take them, if you like. We sometimes place them in other wards. I know it does little for your loved one, but it saves them from being wasted and helps to comfort other patients."

I nod and pivot toward her on the pads of my feet. I don't meet her gaze, I keep those flowers in line with my face as I hand them over. "Thank you."

I turn away and take the final steps to my uncle's room, my heart rampantly beating, while she wrestles with the bouquet.

"Are you here to see Mr. Torian?" she asks, killing me slowly.

I pause in the doorway, the darkness of the room within reach. "Yes."

There's a pause, another torturous, agonizing heartbeat.

"I'm sorry to bother you again, but we've been asked by family to take note of visitors. Only immediate relatives and pre-determined friends are allowed to visit."

The stipulation stinks of my brother. I should've known Cole would've transformed the hospital ward into a secure location.

I should've fucking known. But I didn't even think about his possible security measures.

My chest hollows.

Richard's room is here. *Right here.* And she's not going to let me step foot inside.

"Please," I whisper. "I haven't been able to see him since the accident. I promise I won't stay long."

"What's your name? You might already be on the list."

I close my eyes and send out a silent prayer. Yes, a fucking prayer…to God… to help me kill someone. The ridiculousness hits me like a violent slap across the face. "I'm not on the list. His family doesn't know about me."

My chest restricts. My limbs grow heavy. My heart thunders.

Every part of my body protests, *demanding* I flee. It takes all my strength to remain in place.

"Are you a friend? A work colleague?"

If I say I'm a colleague and she knows what my uncle does for a living, I'll never be allowed to step foot inside that room. And being a friend, who isn't close enough to make the list, seems like a long shot, too.

I need another strategy. Something to pull at her heart strings and worm my way into her trust.

I sniff and pull a handkerchief from my pocket as I delve into the haunted recesses of my mind. I retrieve memories that make my eyes burn. I pull forward images of my mother. I force myself to remember the funeral—the coffin, the flowers, the sobs from family and friends. I bathe myself in devastation and let the pain resurface, all in an effort to sell my story.

Then I glance over my shoulder and meet her gaze through drenched eyes. "I'm his mistress."

She stares at me with trepidation, her lips parting in shock. She shifts the flowers from one arm to the next, cradling them like a child in her silent contemplation.

She's older than I am. I guess in her mid-forties. Much closer to my uncle's age than I am, and I hope like hell she doesn't notice through my heavy make-up.

"Please." I blow my nose and force myself to relive the grief of years gone by. I cling tight to the horror, squeezing every inch of torment from those memories until a single tear treks down my cheek. "I only want a few minutes with him. Just in case…"

She winces, reaffirming that his situation is still dire.

"*Please.*"

She nods, retreating a step, then two. "Okay." She continues walking backward toward the nurses' station. "But don't take too long."

Gratitude overwhelms me, suffocating me with its giddy tidal wave.

"Thank you." I dab at the moisture on my cheeks and pretend it takes all my strength to drag my feet forward to face a heartbreaking goodbye. I keep my focus straight ahead, away from the bed. Then I turn and close the door behind me, shoving the handkerchief in my pocket as the darkness of the room inches its way into my marrow.

I cling to the handle for long heartbeats and give myself a mental pep talk.

I'm *not* going to fail despite the attention I've drawn.

I'm *not* going to get caught even though I can feel the noose tightening around my neck, cutting off my air.

I'm *not*. I'm *not*. I'm *not*.

I switch my mindset, moving from relief to anger. To pain.

I relive Richard's lingering stare. His compliments. The unwanted touches. I remember that night and all the things he took from me. I shove every ounce of weakness deep down to the pit of my stomach and become my father's daughter.

The criminal.

A murderer.

I become emboldened. Strong. Un-fucking-beatable. Then I turn and face my demons.

Richard lies lifeless, innumerable tubes and IVs piercing his skin and delving under the covers of the clean, crisp bed. The right side of his face is bandaged, the white stark against the fading blue and purple bruising visible on his left.

His chest rises and falls. Slow and steady.

My feet move of their own accord, bringing me closer to Satan, until I'm stopped at the foot of the bed. I peer down at him and smile at how our positions have changed.

For a long time, he was the one with horror in his belly and violence in his soul, while I lay meek and vulnerable, unable to defend myself.

I gain the briefest insight into his sick perversion as I stand there. I acknowledge the rush of power. The tingle of adrenaline. I breathe in the approaching victory and square my shoulders against the unwanted niggle of building sins.

"Hello, Uncle." My lips kick as I curl every syllable around my tongue.

The more I stare, the more invigorated I become. My breathing quickens. My nerves tingle.

"It's been a long time since we last spoke." I lean over and swipe at the wrinkles in the bedding near his feet. "I've learned a lot about you since your accident."

I watch for the slightest flicker in his features. I'd give anything to know he can hear me. To have just one sign of acknowledgement.

But I get nothing. Not even a twitch.

I sigh and glance around the room, taking in the monitoring equipment, the cards on the bedside table, the Bible.

I roll my eyes.

Whoever thought religion could save this man had delusions beyond my comprehension. Nothing can save him. Not in this life or the next.

I walk around the bed and take a seat on the chair at his side.

Death coats my skin, tickling the back of my neck. I've never felt this way before. It's a strange mix of exhilaration and trepidation.

Good and evil.

Right and wrong.

I have two options. Only two. And both revolve around the syringes taped to my wrist beneath my jacket.

The potassium chloride overdose will mimic a heart attack and end his life. There will be no injuries to investigate or sign of foul play. The only thing left behind will be an elevated level of potassium in his bloodstream—the same elevation that would be present with a legitimate heart attack.

The first option is to inject into the IV line. The results will be fast, and I'll have mere seconds before the magic begins and the monitors alert nursing staff.

The alternative is to inject into the IV bag and walk away without hearing any bells and whistles. I'd have time to escape the ward before his heart started to react.

I'd also be unsure whether I succeeded or failed. And that success is something I crave.

"I want it to be quick," I whisper. "Not because you don't deserve to suffer. It's because I want to be here when you die."

But the price of fulfilment could come at the cost of a prison sentence. And I'm not willing to let him affect my future like he has my past.

I stand and grab a pair of disposable gloves from the box on the wall. I quickly cover both hands, then unfasten the syringes from my wrists, placing one in my pocket for easy access.

My heart pounds in my throat. My tongue swells. My fingers tremble.

It's not fear.

No, that weakness is long gone.

What I feel is euphoria. A strange sense of ecstasy.

I grab the IV bag, twist the syringe onto the attachment, and hold my breath as I depress the plunger. I'm hyperaware of everything—sound, movement, thoughts—as the two liquids blend.

At any moment, the nurse could return.

I could walk from this room and be greeted by a security team.

Oh, God, what if this is a setup?

What if? What if? What if?

I gasp for air and shake away the paranoia, not willing to be taken down by my own mind as I shove the used syringe into my pocket and pull out the next.

I repeat my actions, this time pushing the plunger harder. Faster.

Once the last drop of lethal injection is administered, I stagger backward, fighting my building conscience as I shove all the evidence into my pockets.

"See you in hell, Richard." I don't recognize my own voice. It's foreign to my throbbing ears. "I hope you suffer for your sins."

I rush for the door, gripping the handle with a hand covered by my jacket sleeve. I wipe away my earlier prints in a frenzy of rabid movements and then escape the room.

There's no relief at the sight of the empty hall, only pure, delirious focus to measure my steps. I shake uncontrollably. My arms, legs, and hands quavering.

I want to run. To sprint.

My instincts beg me to flee. But I hold my pace, keeping my head low as I pull out my handkerchief and cover the lower half of my face while I pass the nurses station.

I'm almost hyperventilating when I reach the elevator. My breaths are short and shallow. Everything moves in slow motion.

Each heartbeat feels like an eternity waiting for the elevator doors to open. And when they do, my relief is so overwhelming I gasp out a breathy laugh.

It's too good to be true.

The rush of success floods my veins, the sensation ten times more exhilarating than adrenaline alone.

I escape into the confined space, no longer feeling suffocated, and smile at the graying man who enters behind me.

I'm no longer a victim.

Richard can't torment me anymore.

He can't hurt anyone else, either.

That part of my life is over, and all I want to do is rush into Sebastian's arms and start on something new.

I press the button for the ground floor, still smiling, still basking in success. Then something shatters the celebration. Something hard and unyielding that presses gently into the low of my back.

"It's a gun," the man murmurs. "Scream and you're dead."

26

DECKER

"Who, in their right mind, doesn't have a spare fucking tire?" I don't know how many times I've repeated the rhetorical question over the unending hours on the road. "It's fucking ridiculous."

Hunt had used the space where the tire should be and filled it with tactical shit—guns, ammo, knives. There was even equipment to make a fuel bomb.

"Who the hell has fertilizer on standby, yet no fucking spare tire?"

"You seriously need to shut the fuck up before I slam on the brakes and hope your thousand-year-old seatbelt fails."

The thousand-year-old seatbelt, and my brother's thousand-year-old Jeep, have seriously slowed the time it should've taken to get back to Portland. We found the beat-up pile of metal in his garage, the keys in the ignition, because even my brother is begging for someone to take this piece of crap off his hands. "Slamming on the brakes won't do shit when you're driving like a nanna."

"I've got my foot to the fucking floor," he grates. "It's the car that's lagging."

Frustration gave way to insanity three hundred miles ago, back when I gave up on trying to speak to Keira.

Sarah ignored all my attempts to get in contact. Every fucking one.

The only information we've had came half an hour ago.

One fucking phone call to cement my fears by telling us, "She's finishing this. I'll call again when it's over."

That's all she said. Two rushed sentences before Hunt snatched the phone away and took over the conversation.

"Head toward the parking lot." I scan the area surrounding the hospital. "They haven't been back in contact, so they've gotta still be here."

"They should be gone by now. It doesn't take this long."

He's right, but until we get confirmation, I'm going to assume they haven't finished the job. I'm also going to assume everything that could go wrong *did* go wrong. That panic isn't going to wear off until Keira is safe and sound in my arms.

They've rushed into this.

It's too soon.

"There." Hunt points toward the back of the half empty parking lot. "That's the car."

My stomach plummets as I turn my gaze in the direction of his finger. Sure enough, he's right. *Fuck*. What the hell could be taking so long?

"Sarah said she was waiting out here." Hunt's hands squeak as he white-knuckles the steering wheel. "Where the fuck is she?"

I lean forward as we pull into a parking space two cars away, glancing through the neighboring vehicle to find the Mercedes empty. "I've got a really shitty feeling about this."

"Well, that's a bonus." He cuts the engine and unclasps his belt. "And all that scientific research tried to tell me psychopaths don't have feelings."

"Funny." I scowl. "Are you really cracking jokes right now?"

"I can't help it." He attempts to mimic my voice, his face entirely deadpan. "I'm a funny guy."

"Fucking hilarious." I shove from the car, slamming the door behind me, before stalking to the Mercedes. I check the back seat as I pass. There's nothing in there. Not a scrap of paper or a piece of rubbish.

"Stop freaking out." Hunt comes up behind me, his gait casual. "They might have changed their plan and fled on foot."

I inch forward, checking out the front. It's clean, too. Nothing on the seats or along the dash. Nothing but the car keys dangling from the ignition.

"Jesus, Hunt." My stomach takes a nosedive. "I don't think their change of plan was deliberate."

He gets up close and peers over my shoulder.

He doesn't say a word. He doesn't have to. The sudden surge of panic ebbs off him.

I rush around the car, looking for a hint to tell me what the hell went down. "Something went wrong."

Something when terribly fucking wrong. But what?

Hunt pulls out his phone and starts dialing. Seconds later he's dialing again. Then again.

"Fuck." He massages his forehead. "Why the hell won't she answer her fucking phone?"

"Maybe because they've been caught." I pinch the bridge of my nose and ignore the bite of pain that comes from my growing headache. "Your woman pushed Keira into something she wasn't ready for, and now she's going to spend the rest of her life in prison."

"Sarah isn't stupid."

"Really?" I drop my hand to my side. "Her engagement to you says otherwise."

His eyes harden.

"You two never should've gotten involved." I focus on the sliding doors of the hospital. I will the glass panels to open and for Keira to walk out. I beg for her to appear before me. I fucking pray. "I'm going in there."

"Not yet, you won't." Hunt rests against the Mercedes. "You'll only draw attention. We need to wait a little longer."

"That's easy for you to say when Sarah's not the one committing murder."

"We're waiting," he repeats. "Suck it up and deal."

Oh, I suck it up, all right. I bottle that shit like it's gold, letting the panic and hysteria build into an uncontrollable force. Each second that ticks by feels like an hour as I pace behind the car. Any minute now, I'm certain I'll hear a police siren. Or a gunshot. Or Keira screaming for help.

The phantom sounds ring in my ears.

I scrutinize every person who approaches and leaves the hospital. I commit their clothing to memory in case I need the information later. At this point, everyone is the enemy. They all stand between me and the woman I need to protect.

"Is that..." Hunt pushes from the car, his gaze tracking the Porsche pulling into the other side of the parking lot.

"Oh, shit."

It's Torian.

I start walking, my pace increasing with every step as two men climb from the sports car. The fear and panic I had moments before is nothing in comparison to the sheer terror I feel now. "If he finds her..."

Christ, I have no idea what he'll do.

"Torian." I break into a jog. "*Hey, Torian.*"

Hunter curses behind me, his footsteps following. "What the fuck are you doing?"

"He can't find out she's here." I keep running, keep bridging the distance, not giving a shit about the consequences. "*Torian.*"

I catch his attention a few yards from the sliding doors. He stops and turns my way, not showing a hint of surprise at my appearance. What stares back at me is his usual mask of calm indifference.

I slow my pace and relax into a casual stride, inclining my head in greeting. "Hey, Mr. Boss Man." I switch my attention to the dark scowl of the tank at his side. "Luca. I haven't seen you in a while, buddy."

Luca Hart—Layla's brother-in-law. He's reckless and equally callous. He's also an ex-SEAL, and definitely not my buddy. The muscled-up fighting machine is the only guy I've met who's left the armed forces without a shred of national pride intact.

The guy hates everyone.

Especially me.

"What are you doing here?" Torian asks.

I point to my face, then lift my shirt to show my bruises as Hunter stops beside me. "I needed to get the rig checked. I think I've got a few fractured ribs."

"And you?" He turns his scrutiny to my accomplice.

"Decker needed me to hold his hand."

Torian raises a brow and nods. Slowly. There's no rush for answers, hint of panic, or twitch of hatred. Even after his conversation with Keira this afternoon, he's civil, and it's scary as fuck. "Where's my sister?"

"Don't worry, she's with Sarah."

It's the only answer that came to mind. But it's the wrong one. I don't realize my mistake until Hunter clears his throat in a subtle reprimand.

If Cole finds out what Keira is up to, Sarah will be accountable.

"Have you forgotten the instructions I gave you at the restaurant? You're responsible for her safety?" Torian smiles, wearing the expression like a threat.

"She's safe." Hunt claps me on the back. Hard. "Sarah has the situation under control."

"So he knocks her up and leaves her to fend for herself?" Luca crosses his arms over his chest and backs away an inch, scoping our surroundings like we're being watched. "He's not what I'd call father material."

I press my lips tight, half smirking, half scowling at the fucker who's throwing me under the bus. "Cool your horses about the daddy stuff. Although it's clear I'm an over-achiever, even I don't believe my swimmers are that efficient."

Luca snickers. "You're dead. You know that, right?"

"Seriously, don't go laying the blame on me." I raise my hands in surrender. "That woman is a fucking force of nature. I'd have to be blind, deaf, and dumb to turn down her advances."

"You amaze me." Torian speaks slowly. Softly. "I can't believe you'd be careless enough to use your distasteful sense of humor to disrespect my sister. You really do have a death wish, don't you?"

Beneath the calm façade, he's pissed.

If the tick under his eye is any indication, he's fucking furious.

"Look, Torian, I'm just trying to cut through the awkwardness here." I let my arms fall to my sides. "In all honesty, I care for Keira. I'd do anything for her."

He looks me up and down, his smile strong. "We'll see."

Hunter remains ramrod, his statue status letting me know he's tense as fuck. It's also a great indicator that my conversation skills are lacking.

"What are you doing here at this hour, anyway?" Hunt asks, diverting the conversation without subtlety. "Isn't it late to be making a visit?"

"Keeping a close eye on Richard. You two should come with us." He starts for the doors. "I'm sure he'd appreciate the extra company."

"Maybe some other time." Hunter steps back. "We need to get the girls."

"I'm not asking."

Shit. We don't have time for this.

I shoot a frantic glance at Hunt, and a whole heap of what-the-fuck-do-we-do silently passes between us. Keira could be running for her life while we stand here chatting. She could already be in custody.

"Hurry up." Luca jerks his chin. "Get moving."

The trill of a cell has Torian pausing inside the entrance, the sound increasing as he pulls the device from his jacket pocket and connects the call. "Yes?"

I face Hunter, my eyes wide in silent communication. *"What do we do?"* I mouth.

His shoulder hitches in the slightest shrug. *"What the fuck can we do?"*

I rub a hand over my jaw, hoping to inspire a spark of brilliance that doesn't come.

Hunt creeps closer. "He doesn't know anything at the moment. If we don't follow, he'll get suspicious."

"No." I shake my head. "He knows something—"

"He knows you're banging his sister. That's all."

There's more to it. There has to be.

"Thanks for the update." Torian's murmured words reclaim my attention. "I've already arrived. I'll see you in a minute."

He's meeting someone.

Is it Keira? Sarah?

I pivot back toward him, gaining no clues from his blank expression. "Is everything okay?"

"That's a good question." He places the cell in his suit jacket and heads toward the elevators.

My pulse pounds harder the further he walks. I'm not naive enough to think we've been dismissed. He expects us to tag along, like fucking puppies, or he'll blow a damn fuse.

Hunt obviously knows it, too, because he starts to follow. "We're leaving the first chance we get."

"Yeah," I mutter through clenched teeth. "First chance."

The elevator doors open on our approach, and all four of us enter. It isn't until the steel doors close that the confined space begins to resemble a tomb.

"That was the hospital on the phone." Torian presses the button for the ICU and levels his eyes on me. "Richard passed."

The news flash hits like a heavyweight champion, the impact bringing more fear, but also pride. Keira didn't fail. She accomplished what she set out to do, despite the stupidity.

So where the hell is she?

"What the fuck happened?" Luca asks.

"They suspect a heart attack." Torian's eyes don't lose their intensity as he waits for me to break. "But I'm sure I'll find out more information soon."

"Shit." I wince. "I'm sorry for your loss."

"Same here." Hunt shoves his hands in his pockets, all casual in his feigned surprise. "Do you want us to head out of here and start contacting the family?"

"Yeah, good idea." I nod. "We can get the process started."

"There's actually something more important you can do here." Torian turns to the elevator panel and presses the STOP button, the moving tomb jolting to a halt. "You can both cut the bullshit and tell me who killed Richard."

There's no emotion in his statement. No malice or anger. No heartbreak or grief. His voice doesn't even raise an octave, his words held inside this tiny space for no one else to hear.

"You said they suspected a heart attack." Hunter scrutinizes him. The act flawless. Believable. "Why do you think it's murder?"

"Because I received a call from hospital staff less than half an hour ago telling me Richard's mistress was paying him a visit."

A mistress? That was Keira's cover, a fucking mistress?

Jesus Christ, sweetheart. Why the hell did you do this without me?

"I have no clue who she is." I shrug. "I didn't know he had a mistress."

"Don't play dumb." Torian's eyes narrow. "The fact that you're here means you're involved. And I'll find out why later. For now, I just want to know who followed through with your manipulation."

"We didn't manipulate a fucking thing," Hunter growls. "Watch who you're accusing, because that shit can't be taken back."

There's no reply. No reaction. Apart from the few inches Torian grows as he contemplates his options.

Hunt has been his right-hand man for years. His enforcer.

Burning that bridge with unfounded allegations is a huge deal.

But it's also a huge fucking gamble pretending they're unfounded.

"Why don't we take a breather?" I raise my brows and look each man in the eye with a calm I don't feel. "It's been an eventful week. Let's not make it a stupid one."

"Says the man who slept with Keira," Luca mutters.

Hunter clears his throat, the sound vaguely close to a chuckle.

"I'm sorry, man." I meet the Navy asshole's gaze with fake sincerity. "Did I fuck your mother in a past life? Or are you threatened by me for another reason?"

"You're no threat," he sneers. "You're a fucking embarrassment. You never should've been entrusted with Keira's safety."

The throat clearing happens again. This time there's no linger of laughter. It's a warning to stand down.

A fucking warning *to me*.

I clench my jaw and bare my teeth through the jealousy. He's jonesing for Keira. And apparently, I'm supposed to let that fly. "Thanks for the constructive criticism. I'll take it on board."

"Enough." Torian glares at me, the ferocity finally deserving of a gold star. "We'll discuss this later." He slams his fist against the STOP button, making the carriage jolt back into movement. "Until then, neither one of you steps foot out of my sight."

Great.

Fucking perfect.

We ascend surrounded in tension, all four of us a breath away from reaching for a weapon. The atmosphere doesn't change when the doors open. One by one, we pile out, Torian in the lead, Luca in the back, as we walk toward the start of the silent ICU.

The lights are dim, the late hours marked with desolate halls and gentle footfalls.

A lone woman stands from behind the nurses' station as we approach and hustles to greet us in the middle of the corridor.

"Mr. Torian?" She gives a sad smile. "My name is Carly. I spoke to you earlier."

All four of us come to stand shoulder to shoulder, forming a makeshift wall before her.

"Thanks for your call." He reaches out a hand for her to shake. "I appreciate you keeping me informed."

"There's no need to thank me. I just wish I hadn't had to make contact under these circumstances."

Torian inclines his head and releases her hand. "It can't be helped. My uncle has been fighting for a long time."

"Yes." Her brows pinch, and for a heartbeat she pauses. There's no mistaking her apprehension. "That's something I need to discuss with you." She glances along the barrier of muscle surrounding her and swallows. "Maybe in private."

"Privacy isn't necessary." He indicates the three of us with a wave of his hand. "These men know better than to betray my trust."

I cringe through yet another warning.

He's nothing if not repetitive.

"My concern is the woman who was with your uncle prior to his death." The nurse wrings her hands in front of her. "Like I mentioned on the phone, she wasn't on your approved visitor list, and the timing of his passing is oddly coincidental. Normally, the death of a man in Richard's position wouldn't require a coroner's investigation, but I think it's best—"

"No." Torian shakes his head. "She had every right to see him."

"But the timing... And she admitted she wasn't known to your family. Aren't you—"

"Her presence wasn't a surprise." He gives a sad smile. "She may have thought she wasn't known, but I endeavor to make sure there are no secrets or surprises when it comes to those I care about."

It's another warning.

Another threat.

"Not even the nursing staff have escaped my scrutiny," he continues. "I know about all the employees on this ward, Carly. I'm aware of their shifts, their address, down to the details of who they live with."

She stiffens.

It's a smart move. She should definitely be on edge.

"From memory, you've got a young daughter in prep-school, isn't that right?"

"Yes. That's right." She frowns. "But, Mr. Torian, what I'm trying to articulate is that I wouldn't be doing my job properly if I didn't push for an autopsy. I think it's necessary."

"No." Torian slams down her request. "My uncle is finally at rest. I refuse to allow his peace to be disturbed."

"I understand, but—"

"He said, 'no,'" Hunter grates. "Take the hint or the consequences."

Her mouth gapes, her fear-filled gaze snapping to Hunt.

"Carly," Torian diffuses the situation by reaching for her hand, "I'd appreciate if you worked with me to ensure the wishes of my family are met. We don't need to waste hospital resources here. My uncle fought for weeks, but now he's gone." There's another placating smile. "Now I need you to do whatever necessary to ensure there's no delay in laying him to rest."

She inches back, moving out of reach. "I don't think…"

"I'm no longer asking." He doesn't change his tone. That placating smile remains in place. "There won't be an autopsy. Or any further investigation. Do you understand?"

She glances over her shoulder, searching for help that's nowhere in sight.

I almost feel sorry for her. If only Keira's innocence didn't hang in the balance.

"Your continued care for Richard will be compensated," I offer, ready and willing to pay out of my own pocket. "This situation doesn't need to get complicated."

"Yes," Hunter adds. "Take the money and keep your daughter safe."

She exhales a shuddering breath, the depth of his threat delving deep.

"Are we clear, Carly?" Torian asks.

She nods, slow at first, then more definitive. "I understand."

"Good." He turns and stalks for the elevators.

There's no farewell to the deceased uncle. No grief or emotional turmoil.

Luca and Hunt follow, while I hang back with the woman frozen in place.

"You don't want to fuck with him." I grab her arm and give a supportive squeeze. "Do what he asks, and you and your daughter will be fine."

She jerks back, her lips trembling, her eyes full of tears. "Get your hand off me."

I comply, letting my arm fall. "Just stick to the script."

I leave her to battle her demons and follow the guys down the hall then into the open elevator.

We don't talk as the doors close. The tension does enough of that for us.

But once we're trapped inside, Luca points a menacing finger in Hunter's face. "You should've kept your mouth shut. You scared her."

"That's the fucking point. And also my job, asshole."

"Not for much longer."

Hunter shoots a glance to Torian for confirmation. "Are you kidding me? You want this guy at your side over me?"

"You haven't been at my side," Torian scolds. "You've been missing for two days."

"For good reason. I don't need to give you a play-by-play of my movements. But you should know I'm doing my job regardless."

The elevator doors open at the lobby, and Torian walks out without reacting, continuing outside to the path leading toward the parking lot.

"Don't fucking walk away from me." Hunter stalks after him. "I put my life on the line for you every goddamn day."

I jog to keep up and fall into step at his side. "Let him go. We've gotta get out of here."

"What's the hurry?" Luca asks from behind us. "Have you got someplace more important to be?"

"Yeah," I mutter. "You're mom's house. She's waiting for her daily dose of D."

"Keep talking, deadshit, it's gonna get you killed."

I grind my teeth through the distance to Torian, who waits at the start of the parking lot.

"I've got places to be." I bypass him and head toward the Jeep. "I'll check in later."

"I told you before, you're not leaving my sight."

I swing around, walking backward away from him. "You also told me to protect Keira. And I can't do that while I'm here holding your hand."

"Protect her from what?" He gives me a checkmate stare. "You said she was safe with Sarah."

My steps falter. "She is. But I'm not going to leave her for longer than necessary."

"Do you even know where she is? Could you take me to her?"

I can't answer. Not with the truth that will expose her secrets, or lies that will easily be uncovered.

"Was it Keira or Sarah?" He doesn't elaborate. He doesn't need to. I already understand the question.

"I don't know what you're talking about."

He smiles, the curve of lips more threatening than a scowl could ever be. "This is your last chance. Keira or Sarah?"

I keep my mouth shut, determined not to be disloyal to her.

"It was Keira," Hunt mutters. "She took him down."

My brain explodes.

He betrayed her.

He betrayed me.

What the fuck?

Torian's mouth pulls tight. His nostrils flare. I watch every flicker in his expression as he begins to realize his sister is a murderer. "You convinced her to take action against her own family." He continues to stare at me. "Why?"

Hunter's cell tone breaks the conversation, and he jams his hand into his pocket like a madman.

"Leave it," Torian demands. "I don't want any interruptions."

"I need to answer this."

"How much do you need it?" Torian faces him. "Do you need it more than your next breath?"

Hunt bares his teeth, his shoulders tense as he pulls his hand from his pocket and lets it rest at his side.

Luca hangs on the periphery, slowly inching his way toward me, his arm behind his back and in close contact to his weapon.

"Start from the beginning." Torian approaches, cocking his head to the side, attempting to read me as the *trill, trill, trill* continues and finally dies. "Tell me exactly what you thought to achieve by brainwashing her."

"That's not how this went down." Hunter follows, all three of them approaching me like a death squad. "She did this on her own."

"I disagree. She's not the violent type."

I smother a laugh. The knife she had at my throat proves otherwise, but I'm not going to argue.

"You're after power," he accuses. "And you probably think me and Layla are the only ones left to deal with."

"You'll have to get through me first," Luca snarls at me. "And my brother, too."

"You're fucking paranoid." I drop the insult like a bomb. "Why the hell would I want to take over? I can't handle the level of psycho you've already forced onto me. Why the fuck would I want more?"

"My restaurant was targeted, my sister was discovered while in hiding. Now this." He throws an arm wide, indicating the hospital. "It's no coincidence you've been there every step of the way."

"*Your sister* has been there every step of the way." Hunter increases his pace and steps in front of him, blocking his path as the ringtone reignites. "I don't know the story like Deck does, but she's the common-fucking-denominator here. Not him. Or me."

I glare at the back of Hunter's head. I glare so fucking hard through the anger.

I know he's outing her because she's the least likely to be punished. But it still feels like he's being a bigger snitch than I've ever been.

"What story?" Torian shoves by him. "Tell me."

I keep my trap closed. I don't even open it when Luca settles behind me and the butt of his gun sails toward the back of my head.

My vision blackens with the blunt impact. My knees give out.

I stumble to the asphalt, falling at Torian's feet while ringing resounds in my ears. This time it isn't the cell phone, the trill noise having disappeared again.

He peers down at me and grips a fistful of my hair. "What has she done?"

I chuckle. "I don't know what you're talking about."

Hunt curses. It's the prelude to Torian's fist finding my jaw.

My head swings with the impact. The pain clouds my thoughts. Then the fucking phone releases its siren call again.

"He needs to answer that." I spit blood from my mouth. "It's probably Keira. You can get all the answers you need right from the source."

He has to answer the fucking phone.

I need to know she's okay.

The constant appeal for connection makes my stomach twist. You don't call three times in a row to inform someone you're safe. You call three times when your life is on the line and you need a shitload of help.

"I don't want the story from her," he drawls, releasing my hair. "I want it from you."

"*Answer the fucking phone,*" I roar.

The ringtone vanishes, and I slump into the silence.

"Eventually, I'll call her," he taunts. "But I want to hear your version first. That way I can see which puzzle pieces match."

I chuckle and hang my head, no longer capable of looking the son of a bitch in the eye. "Why? Do you think she's going to lie to you? Don't you trust your own flesh and blood?"

"If she can lie about being pregnant, I'm sure she can lie about anything."

Jesus Christ. If he's known this entire time, why didn't he greet me with the accusation? Why wasn't a gun placed to my temple the second we stepped within reach?

This asshole's poise and tactics are beyond my fucking comprehension.

"Come on, Decker, don't you recall what I told the nurse? I take a vested interest in knowing everything, which includes my sister's health. I know she's taken measures to ensure she can't conceive." He steps closer, the toes of his polished black shoes taking up my vision. "I'll ask one more time—what's the story Hunter is alluding to?"

I promised I'd protect her.

If that means I need to keep her safe from her brother, then so be it.

At the moment, he thinks she finished a job someone else started. He doesn't know her involvement in the hit and run. He has no clue what caused the restaurant drive-by.

For now, her secrets are safe, and I won't change that.

"Why don't I tell you my story instead?" I raise my chin and meet his gaze. "I think you'd be more interested in my secrets."

"Decker," Hunter warns, "stop messing around."

Torian glances between us as the cell trills again.

"Fucking hell, Decker." Hunter raises his voice over the sound. "Keira's responsible for the hit and run. She paid a guy to do the job. He's the same guy who shot up the restaurant. And he's the same reason lover boy here is panicked about her safety. She's being blackmailed."

Torian scrutinizes me, trying to find the truth through the shock. "Is that true?"

"Call. Her." I enunciate the words slowly.

This time Hunt's phone isn't the one to break the silence. Torian's ringtone rings gently from inside his jacket.

"Answer it." I move to stand, only to be shoved back down by Luca. "*Answer your fucking phone.*"

He doesn't budge. He holds my stare, asserting his authority despite the danger to his sister.

"She's in trouble," I beg. "I know she's in fucking trouble. Just answer the phone. I'll tell you everything after you speak to her."

He reaches into his suit jacket and pulls out the device, glimpsing the screen for a second before he connects the call. "Sarah?"

Sarah?

I focus on Hunt, his concern just as visible as mine is overbearing.

"Who is this?" Torian's voice turns stony. "What do you want?"

I push to my feet and swing out a heavy elbow when Luca tries to stop me. "Either shoot me, or stop riding my fucking ass," I snarl. "I don't have the patience for your shit."

"What do you want?" Torian repeats. "Touch her again and I'll—"

Again.

My heart lurches at the word.

Touch her—*again*.

Someone has hurt her. *Is* hurting her.

"Where is she?" I reach for the phone only to have Hunt grab my wrist.

"Back off," he warns. "Let him talk."

Torian turns his back to us and takes steps in the opposite direction. "Where, Drake? Tell me where she is."

Drake? There's no second guessing who this unknown asshole might be. He's the guy responsible for the blackmail. The hard look in Hunt's eye says he thinks the same thing.

"Give me the phone." I stalk after Torian. "Let me speak to him."

"Airport Way? Which warehouse?"

"Torian, give me the phone." I make another attempt for the cell, and this time nobody stops me. Not even Torian. I snatch the device from him and plaster it to my ear. "Drake? *Keira?*"

The line is dead.

"I need to go," Torian says to Luca. "Take them back to the restaurant. Keep them there until I arrive." Then he runs toward his Porsche.

He *runs*.

This is the same man who barely breaks out in a brisk walk when he's under fire. And now he's winning a two-hundred-yard dash.

I start after him, only to have a heavy weight barrel into my chest.

Luca knocks me back with a splayed arm, then aims his gun at me from the subtle position at his hip. "You heard him. You're coming with me."

"Like hell I am. I'm going after Keira."

There's a slam of a car door, the roar of an engine, then the heavy squeal of tires as Torian reverses from the parking space.

"Let me go." I get in his face, the seconds ticking by like hours.

"It's too late." Hunt grabs my arm and yanks me backward. "He's already gone. We need to take the Jeep."

"You're not going anywhere but the restaurant." Luca plants his feet. "Where's your car?"

"Didn't you hear the phone conversation?" Hunt snaps. "Torian's walking into a hostage negotiation on his own."

"You're not kidding me with this macho bullshit." He jerks the gun again. "You've got no intention of helping him, and every intention to run."

"Whoever has Keira has my woman, too. I ain't running from shit. I never do. You're the one who's being a traitor by letting Torian drive out of here, on his own, unprotected, and without a fucking plan."

Luca's expression flickers, the tight pinch of his features growing more adamant. "I can't let you go. He doesn't want you out of my sight, so that's where you'll stay."

"Then come with us," I snap.

He scowls. "You expect me to help you?"

"I expect you to do what's right for the fucking family."

He squares his chin, the waver in his expression now resembling indecision as he faces Hunt and flicks his gun in my direction. "I don't like him, let alone trust him."

Hunt shrugs. "Nobody does. It doesn't mean you pussy out of this."

"Are you kidding me?" I seethe. "We're stuck here because GI Joe has trust issues?"

He bares his teeth at me, but his weapon lowers an inch. Then another.

I don't hang around for him to holster the weapon like a Girl Scout. I run, not pausing to take a breath as I sprint toward the Jeep.

27

KEIRA

Rope burns sear my wrists. The corners of my mouth ache from the material gag. But that pain is nothing in comparison to the heavy throb in my stomach from where I was punched.

I'd willingly followed that man through the hospital. I'd had no other choice. Either I walked with him or I screamed for help, which would either end with a bullet in my skull or a police investigation that would retrace my steps to a murdered uncle.

He told me he had Sarah. That he'd seen us both in the parking lot and would be rewarded beyond measure when he took me back to Drake.

I didn't need to ask for clarity.

I was smart enough to figure out Drake was my hitman.

As soon as we were alone in a desolate hospital hall, I spoke in a rush, offering my captor bribes in exchange for my freedom. I promised large sums of money. Anonymity. Immunity. When those didn't work, I vowed retribution and scathing retaliation as he dragged me out a staff exit and led me through a soulless parking lot.

I pledged to give him a death full of so much pain and suffering that my threats must have started to sink in.

That's when he threw the punch.

He yanked me to face him and landed a blow to my stomach strong enough to cause bile to rush into my mouth.

My life went downhill from there.

He hauled me to a waiting car, the man in the backseat cradling Sarah's limp body, her face bruised, her cheek scratched. She'd put up a fight. She battled for her freedom.

All I'd done was crumple under one hit.

The realization threw me into fight mode. I kicked. I thrashed. I screamed my fucking lungs out. And then I woke here, in an empty warehouse, my arms bound to a chair as five unfamiliar faces stare down at me plus my gray-haired captor.

"Your brother will be here soon." A smirking man saunters closer to lower my gag. He's young. Around his mid-thirties. His blond hair spiked. His eyes light.

He's almost handsome. Almost beautiful.

If only I didn't recognize his voice.

"Drake." I force the name through my swollen throat. "Why are you doing this? I was going to get you the money. I still can."

The smirk increases. "Don't worry your pretty little head about it. It's all under control." He crouches before me and places a large hand high on my thigh. "And I actually prefer the theatrics. I've dreamed about this moment for weeks."

I clamp my teeth together as his palm slides back and forth. "If you don't remove your hand, my brother will make sure you have nightmares about this moment for years."

He chuckles, his fingers digging through my jeans and into skin. "You've got a sassy mouth. Be careful or I'll fill it with something you might not like."

A shudder ricochets through me, hitting every nerve. It's not a threat. This man is making a promise. But it's more than that, too.

He's dripping with confidence. Entirely fearless.

He plans to get something more than mere money from this exchange.

"You're not so tough after all, are you?" He pushes to his feet. "Don't worry, this will be over before you know it."

He returns to his posse a few feet away, and I frantically rush to scan my surroundings.

The warehouse is bigger than a small house, the large expanse entirely empty. Fluorescent bulbs dangle from the roof, six of them, to match the six windows along the left wall, the glass missing in places and stained with dirt, cobwebs, and grime in others. But no illumination shines from outside. There are no traffic lights or street lamps. Just darkness and the eerie feel of desolation.

We're not close to the city.

We're away from witnesses.

Far from help.

And it's cold in here, too. Hollow. Or maybe that's just me.

I glance over my left shoulder and find the same expanse of emptiness. All except for the pair of feminine feet right behind me. I suck in a breath and swing my head to look over the other shoulder.

Sarah lies limp on the cement floor, her body curled in a loose fetal position, her arms and legs snuggled in front of her. She doesn't move. I can barely make out the rise and fall of her chest. But it's there, the slightest increments letting me know she's still alive.

I remain still, trying not to show my attachment to this woman, while my insides wage war.

She shouldn't be here. This has nothing to do with her.

It's all me. All my fault.

The beep of a cell echoes through the open space, the touch of external life giving me the slightest hope. I drag my attention back to Drake, who now holds a cell in his hand.

"Ben said he's here. And alone." He jerks his head toward the door twenty yards away. "Liam, go out and help bring him in."

Him—my brother.

But he wouldn't have come on his own, would he?

"Kyle, you stay with the girls. The rest of you, follow me." Drake leads them across the warehouse.

"*Wait.*" The plea escapes my lips without thought. I don't know what to do, what to say. The only thing I can think of is distracting them while I buy Cole time to think through the poor decision to arrive alone. "Let me go, and I'll get you the money. I'll double what I owe."

"It's time for you to be quiet. Bottle that fear deep down inside and let it out once Torian gets in here." He winks at me. "Your tears will make this perfect."

"No, please. You need to listen."

He walks away.

"Drake, I'll get you the money."

He doesn't stop. He's not interested in me.

He only wants my brother.

My pulse kicks up a notch as Drake reaches his team at the door, a lone man slipping outside.

"Please," I murmur to the guard standing a few feet away. "It's Kyle, isn't it?"

He crosses his arms over his chest and pretends he didn't hear me.

"You need to untie my hands. Once Cole gets here, he's going to place a price on the head of everyone here. You could be the savior. Wouldn't you prefer to work for us instead?"

"Shut your mouth."

"I'm serious." I wiggle, trying to loosen my arms from the rope. "You're going to get hurt. Or worse."

I've never seen the inner workings of a hostage negotiation with my brother. I haven't heard him speak about one before, but I anticipate this interaction won't be civil. He's going to be furious—at these men *and* me.

"I said *shut up.*"

"You're making a mistake…"

Kyle starts toward me, his menacing steps a fair indication he isn't interested in my caution. The hard slap across the face clinches my assumption.

My head swings with the blow, my cheek blazing.

I blink back tears, determined not to let this asshole see me cry, even though dams build in my eyes. The show of emotion isn't from weakness. It's from pain. From fury. Rage spreads through my veins like wildfire.

I snicker out a maniacal laugh. "You'll regret that."

His arm lashes out, aiming for my neck. I tense, every muscle rigid as I wait for another blow.

Instead, he chuckles and grabs the gag to yank it back in place. "Keep quiet or I'll glue your lips shut."

I yank at my bindings. I squirm. I throw a hissy fit, my actions hopefully disguising my attempt to jolt my chair closer and closer toward Sarah.

He doesn't notice the inches I gain as he moves back to stand with his arms crossed over his chest, his sight fixated on the men at the door. He doesn't even notice I spend the next few minutes staring down at my friend lying directly at my side.

She's so pale. Entirely fragile.

Hunter is going to kill me... That's if she gets out of here safely. If not, I'm sure he'll think of a punishment much worse than death. And I'll deserve that, too.

I'd begged her to bring me back to Portland and added a dash of emotional blackmail. Then I'd increased my argument with a feminist protest.

She hadn't been able to ignore my pleas to let me slay my own demons. Despite her obvious reluctance, she concocted the plan to steal Hunter's car and beat the men back to Richard.

Now she lies lifeless at my feet, the bruising on her face swelling as it darkens.

I wordlessly beg her to wake up. To blink. To show a sign that she's still okay.

I wiggle a little more, nudging my chair leg against her knee as a deafening pop echoes through our metal cage. The gunshot makes the world stop. I don't move, don't breathe. But the shock isn't enough for me to miss the jolt of Sarah's hands.

She heard it.

She's awake beneath those closed eyes.

As men shout orders, arm themselves, and fill the warehouse with panic, I continue to watch her, waiting for another sign that doesn't come.

"Sarah," I mumble into the gag. "Please, Sarah."

She doesn't blink or flinch. There's no sign of life for long seconds. Then her pinkie finger taps against the concrete, twice, in quick succession.

That's it. That's all the acknowledgement she gives me, and it's all I need.

I suck in a deep breath and sit up straight, trying not to let fear take over. I try so damn hard to picture my brother making the shot instead of taking it. Then the sound rings out again and again, the night being blasted with gunfire.

Kyle pulls out his gun and rushes to crouch behind my chair, while the men in the distance form a wall a few feet back from the door, acting as warriors to protect Drake, who remains behind them.

"I'm coming in," Cole yells from outside.

Sweet exhilaration fills my belly, growing and expanding. It takes all my restraint not to scream out in relief when the door swings wide and he storms inside, an unfamiliar man held hostage at his chest.

"The dead guy in the parking lot is the price you pay for messing with my family," he seethes. "How many more do you want to lose?"

He's okay. He's safe.

Not even a wrinkle or stain mars his tailored suit.

But he's still alone. There's no sign of Sebastian. No Hunter.

The men retreat as he approaches, their weapons at the ready, while the barrel of a gun slides across my temple from the coward at my back.

"Don't move," Kyle whispers in my ear. "You know I'll shoot."

I do as he says, not daring to move a muscle.

"She owes me money." Drake walks backward, leading the way toward me.

"*Then you come to me.*" Cole's voice roars through the empty space. "You never approach her. You never lay a hand *on my fucking family.*"

My eyes burn as I watch.

He isn't fearful. Not even when outnumbered six to one. There's a wealth of determination ebbing from him. An undeniable lack of doubt.

But there's no doubt in Drake either. He turns his back to Cole and strides toward me with an open grin. "Your sister was a means to an end, my friend."

"I'm not your friend." Cole drags his hostage closer, the three goons following with him. "I will, however, be your executioner."

Drake laughs, the sound a strategic taunt as he swings around and pulls a gun from the back of his pants. I don't have a chance to scream. I barely feel myself blink as he fires, shooting Cole's prisoner in the stomach.

There's blood, so much blood, as the man wails and slumps to the ground.

What's worse is the look on my brother's face.

The confidence and sheer determination he had moments before is gone. I glimpse his shock, then the terror, before he hides the weakness under a mask of indifference.

Oh, God.

We're not going to make it out of here. We're all going to die. Just like the man on the floor who's coughing the life from his lungs.

"Don't look, Keira," Cole demands. "Close your fucking eyes."

No. I can't.

I've done this.

I started the chain reaction that will lead to our deaths.

"What are you going to do now, Torian?" Drake keeps his weapon raised, the barrel now pointing in Cole's direction. "You've got no hostage, and I've got a man with a gun to your sister's head."

Cole raises a brow. "Am I supposed to be impressed?"

"No, you're supposed to be scared. And you're also supposed to drop your weapon."

Cole complies, the gun falling to his feet. "You're going to have to try harder because all you're doing is digging yourself into a hole you won't get out of. No amount of owed money justifies your actions. You're all going to die for this."

"This stopped being about money a long time ago."

"You plan on taking over with these four, plus the guy hiding behind my sister?" Cole smirks and indicates the human wall protecting Drake with a wave of his hand. "My men are loyal. Whether I'm dead or alive, they won't stop until you're gunned down."

"Loyal? For starters, you came here alone. That doesn't scream loyalty to me."

Drake moves to my side, and Kyle takes the hint to step away. "Not even your own flesh and blood is devoted to your family. Didn't Keira tell you about our agreement?"

Cole doesn't respond. He stands tall, unaffected by the taunts.

"I still don't have your attention?" Drake muses. "You're right, I'll have to try harder."

His fingers tangle in my hair, gentle at first, then he yanks at the strands, forcing my head back and a shriek from my throat. "Once you're dead, I'm going to hurt her. We're *all* going to hurt her."

My neck screams in protest, the pain taking over my shoulders. It's nothing in comparison to my regret.

"And everything you do to Keira will be reciprocated tenfold. If not by me, then by my father."

"I'll deal with that if it happens." Drake releases my hair and jerks his chin at one of his thugs. "Kill him."

My heart stops. I can't breathe.

I stare at Cole, wide-eyed and frantic, as I wordlessly beg for him to tell me what to do.

"Close your eyes, Kee."

No. I shake my head over and over as my heart kicks back into action, beating so wildly it pounds in my throat.

"*Please,*" I plead into the gag. "*Please. Please. Please.*"

"Close your eyes." His words are gentle. Peaceful. "Don't remember me like this."

The man stops a foot away and aims for my brother's head.

This can't be happening. It can't.

How could one stupid decision cause me to be responsible for his death?

"Keira, *don't look.*" This time it's a demand. An order. "Shut your eyes."

I keep shaking my head. *No. No. No.* But I listen.

For one last time, I promise to obey.

Tears blaze down my cheeks as I sob into the gag, my eyes squeezed shut, my chin tucked into my chest.

Then the gunshot sounds, and I scream and scream and scream.

28

DECKER

"Nice shot."

I ignore Hunt's compliment as I continue to stare at Keira through the broken window at the far end of the warehouse.

My heart hasn't stopped racing since Luca parked the Jeep at the far end of the road. I'd jumped out of the car before the engine stopped and ran from warehouse to warehouse searching for the Porsche.

I'd been the first to see the dead guy in the parking lot. The first to reach the side of the building and determine I had seconds to save Cole's life.

I hadn't thought, hadn't planned, hadn't strategized.

I aimed the barrel of my gun through the broken window, pulled the trigger, and watched Keira as the man fell to the floor with half his skull missing.

Her eyes remain clamped shut, her screams muffled through the gag.

"Why doesn't he talk to her?" I grate. "Why doesn't he open his fucking mouth and tell her he's still alive?"

She doesn't realize her brother stands before her while one of her captors lies dead at her feet.

"I don't know." Hunter keeps his gun trained on our enemy, the men taking cover behind the ringleader, who grabs Cole around the neck and uses him as a shield. "It's probably because he thinks the next bullet has his name on it."

"It will if we don't come up with a plan," Luca mutters. "I'm not sure about you guys, but I don't have a lot of experience with hostage negotiations. How the fuck do we get all three of them out alive?"

Pop, pop, pops slash around us, the return fire pinging against the side of the warehouse.

I drop to the ground, the dirt and pebbles scratching my cheek as I face Hunt. "What are you thinking?"

"I'm thinking this son of a bitch isn't smart. He's in an empty warehouse, without any cover, with nobody keeping watch. He's got no idea what he's doing, or who he's up against, but he obviously thinks he's invincible."

"That's a dangerous combination."

He winces. "My thoughts exactly. He'll kill them without considering the consequences."

"I need to make a call." I keep my voice low, out of Luca's range. "We won't get them out on our own."

He frowns at me, his brows tightening as understanding dawns. "No. You're not making any fucking calls. We do this on our own."

"We've got no other—"

"*No.* You're not letting that cat out of the bag, do you hear me? Keep your fucking mouth shut."

It isn't a warning about being a snitch. It's a caution not to blow my cover. Despite his woman being in there, this grumpy fucker is trying to protect me.

"Hunt, they're dead if I don't."

He glares. "And you're dead if you do. Don't be a pussy and give up yet. We've still got choices."

Like hell we do. I can't see one fucking option that's going to get Keira out of there alive. Hunt's gotta know his reputation isn't going to have Drake waving a white flag. This shit is serious. One rogue bullet and Keira is dead.

"Wipe the judgmental look off your face." He shoves to his feet as the last of the bullets sound. "I've got more invested in this than your twenty-four-hour fling."

I follow, wanting to knuckle dust him for the harsh comment.

It's been more than twenty-four hours with Keira.

I've spent months consumed with thoughts of her. I've waited a lifetime to have her close. Deceit or not, I'd do anything to keep her safe.

"Don't criticize our relationship." I fall in beside his position against the wall. "You don't know shit about us."

He shoots me a look of incredulity. "Focus, asshole."

I clench my jaw and peer inside. Keira has raised her head to face the scene before her, her eyes wide as her gaze searches her surroundings for answers.

Pride fills my lungs. Through all this, she's still got hope, which is more than I can muster at this point.

"I'm here, precious. I'm not going anywhere."

Hunt scowls at me. "Are you for real right now?"

"Stop worrying about me and get a fucking grip. You're the one who excels at this tactical shit. So be fucking tactical."

"Would you two shut up?" Luca hisses as he stalks toward the side of the building. "If you haven't noticed, we're about to have company. You might want to prepare."

He's right. A man is running through the warehouse, heading for the door.

I crouch and aim my gun along the wall toward the door, where Luca is acting like wallpaper. "He needs to get out of the way."

"No, don't shoot," Hunt whispers. "Let him take care of it. The less Drake knows about us out here, the better."

"Are you sure?" I creep closer, only to have Hunt place a warning hand on my shoulder.

"Just watch."

I do as he requests, sticking to my haunches as the door opens an inch.

The barrel of a gun peeks out, and a warning shot lashes into the distance.

Luca doesn't move. He remains in the shadows, propped against the warehouse until the guy creeps forward into the darkness.

The gunman's vision must take too long to adjust from the fluorescents. He stands there, doe-eyed, batting his lashes into the night. The second the door closes behind him he's grabbed by the wrist and flipped onto his back.

Luca follows him down in a knee slide that stops near the guy's shoulders, the move seeming like a practiced dance routine. The subsequent glide of hands over the enemy's face and the break of his neck is done with such smooth efficiency it almost looks artistic.

"Holy shit." I stare in shock. "He's got skills."

"Aren't you glad you didn't try to kick his ass earlier?"

"Yeah." I nod. "Really fucking glad." I shove to my feet and stalk the warehouse interior again. "What now?"

"Now we wing it." He aims his gun inside. "The warehouse is surrounded," he yells. "Put your weapons down and you'll live to see another day."

I watch Keira, watch her so damn intently as her face brightens.

The guy in front laughs, his arm wrapping tighter around Torian's neck while the two men behind him crouch for cover.

"That's gotta be Drake." I jerk my head in the guy's direction. "I'd bet my life he's the one blackmailing Keira."

"This has gone beyond blackmail. It's an assassination. He's making a power play."

"Is that you Hunter?" Drake calls. "You're late."

"And you're sloppy," he shouts back. "There's no way you're getting out of this alive."

"Even when I've got your girl?" Drake backtracks, dragging Torian toward Sarah lying lifeless on the floor. "From my perspective, I'm the only one walking out of here a happy man."

"Who is this fucker?" Hunter rubs his knuckles over his mouth. "And why does he know more about me than I do about him?"

"Probably because you've got a fucking huge reputation." My pulse pounds at my temples. Having that psychotic asshole in close proximity to both Sarah and Keira doesn't sit well with me. I can barely breathe through the panic. "What are we doing? We can't just stand here. He's going to do something."

"I want you inside, Hunt. *Now*."

Drake shoves his boot into Sarah's ribs, but her limp body doesn't jolt from the impact. It stiffens. Spins. She launches from the cement, lashing out with a kick that has him stumbling to right himself with Torian's weight.

She swings out, jabbing at his throat, punching at his fist, only to be knocked out with a hard whack to the back of her head from the coward who had been hiding behind Keira.

Her legs buckle beneath her, her delicate frame crumpling to the floor.

"Son of a bitch." Hunter takes off, running for the door.

"*Wait*." I sprint after him. "You can't rush in there."

I grab his arm only to be shoved away.

"Fuck off, Decker. You won't stop me." He barrels forward, approaching Luca, who spreads his feet and braces for impact.

"He's right." The Navy ninja blocks the path. "You know more about this shit than I do. You need to stay out here and call the shots. If you go in there, you're dead."

"I don't care. Get out of my way."

Hunt isn't thinking. He's reacting on fear, not tact.

Fuck. Fuck. Fuck.

"Let me go instead." I maneuver around them both. My life isn't a loss. Not when I'm dead already. "I've got a plan."

"What plan?" Luca defends against another one of Hunter's attempts to barge past, whacking him in the throat. "You better not fuck this up."

Hunt jackknifes, coughing and spluttering.

"I don't have time to lay a blueprint." I continue for the door and grip the handle. "You're going to have to trust me."

I pause, not waiting for permission, but still waiting for something. Anything.

I don't know what the fuck I'm doing here. All I need is a thumbs up from Hunt to tell me I'm making the right decision. All I get is a deadly stare as he continues to cough up a lung.

"Go." Luca juts his chin at me. "I'll watch your back the best I can."

The assurance doesn't sound promising, but me and Navy boat have come a long way from his threats to murder me. All I can do is have faith as I yank the door wide and brace for the unknown.

"I'm unarmed." I slide my gun along the cement floor. "I just want to talk."

I raise my hands in the air, my pulse pounding behind my eyes while I take the first step into the light.

Adrenaline is rich in my veins, heightening my senses and clearing my mind. Problem is, I lied. I don't have a plan. All I've got is the death wish I've clung to for too damn long, and the necessity to save Keira.

Her sobs ring in my ears, her heartache increasing with every inch I approach.

I don't look at her. I can't.

Those eyes will kill me. They'll kill us all.

"Who the fuck are you?" Drake faces me, his tight neck-hold keeping Torian pointed toward the windows. "I said I wanted Hunter."

"I'm more valuable than Hunt. I'm the guy who can help you make the right decisions to get you the position of power you want."

He snickers. "You think I need your help?"

"Yes. I do." I keep my hands at shoulder height and continue my slow pace forward. "You're not going to get your happily ever after if you kill Torian."

"And why is that?"

"I'll show you." Slowly, I lower my hands as two of his goons place me in their sights. "I don't have a weapon. I'm reaching to get my cell." I slide my fingers into my pocket and retrieve the device. "If you kill anyone else, Hunter won't let you out of here alive. But if you listen to me, and nobody else gets hurt, I'll tell you how you can get exactly what you want."

"Put it away." He repositions his choke hold, making Torian stumble backward. "You can go take a seat next to the rag doll on the floor."

"Wait." I dial a number, connect the call, and show them the screen. "This is a friend of mine."

"Hang up the phone," Drake snarls. "Turn it off."

"Why don't you take it instead?" I approach another step, leaving a desolate yard of space between us as I reach the device toward him. "Here. All you need to do is listen."

Take the cell. Just inch forward and take the fucking cell.

"I'm losing patience," he seethes. "Either take a seat or a bullet. Your choice."

I raise my free hand in surrender. "Please. You're making a mistake. Killing Torian is going to piss off a lot of people."

"*You're* pissing off a lot of people." He swings his gun in my direction and pulls the trigger, the projectile skimming past my thigh. "That was a warning. The next one won't be."

"Okay. Let me do it for you." I press the speaker button and pray to hear something other than a dial tone. But I don't hear anything. Not even static. "Are you there?"

Silence reigns, the seconds ticking by while failure shadows every beat of my pulse.

"Decker?" Anissa's dubious voice breaks the quiet. "Where are you?"

A rush of breath leaves my lungs and the slightest glimmer of relief takes its place. "I need you to tell me your name. I need you to say it like you made me recite it yesterday."

Drake needs to know who she is without me prompting her. He has to believe she's telling the truth.

"Decker," she warns. "What's going on?"

"Put down the phone. Drop it. *Now.*"

"Anissa, please," I beg. "Just say it."

"*Drop the fucking phone or someone dies.*"

Another heavy breath escapes, this one full of defeat.

If only Drake would take a step forward and move into the line of fire. If only I hadn't fucked things up with Anissa and she trusted me enough to tell me what everyone needed to hear.

If only.

If. Fucking. Only.

I look past Drake and the cowards behind him, and finally meet Keira's gaze. Those ocean blues are glassy as they plead back at me. She's begging for help, and for once I can't save her. I can't do a fucking thing to protect her this time.

I'm sorry.

She can't hear my thoughts, but I pray she understands my anguish over failing her. I don't know what else to do. This is going to end in a shootout, and the odds aren't in our favor.

"Okay." I crouch, placing the cell on the cement before I straighten to my full height. Death lingers close. I can feel it. The icy chill of nothingness nips at my fingers, preparing me for the worst.

Drake returns his aim to Torian, his focus still on me. "I don't know what your game is—"

"Decker, are you still there?" The strong, feminine voice rises from the ground. "I'm here. It's Special Agent Anissa Fox of the Federal Bureau of Investigation."

"*Shut it off,*" Drake roars. "Someone shut it off."

"*Decker?*" she shouts. "Decker, answer me."

A gray-haired man runs forward, his gun aimed on me. He sweeps the cell off the ground, one hand madly working on the buttons when a single pop rings out. I feel the bullet skitter past my shoulder, the impact, throwing old man silver backward, instantly penetrating skin, then bone, then brain. He falls to the floor, the crack of skull the last thing I hear before *pop, pop, pops* slice around me.

I run. I fucking sprint while gunshots whistle from outside.

I rush toward the men crouching to take aim, bypassing the threat of their weapons as I leap for Keira.

I take her to the ground, both of us sliding into Sarah while five more shots ring out. I cover them both the best I can, straddling body parts and chair legs. It's a fucking mess as I cradle Keira's head in my hands and feel the soft hum of her sobs.

The heavy slap of a lifeless body falls behind me.

I don't know if it's Torian. I don't dare to look. The outcome is a double-edged sword when the only possibility of being with Keira is dependent on the death of her brother.

There's another shot, another clap of death hitting the cement.

Then silence.

I can't move. All I hear is ringing in my ears. All I feel is her life vibrating against my chest.

"They're down," Luca yells. "Hurry up and get out of there."

Thumping footfalls approach as I lean on one elbow and remove Keira's gag. "It's okay. It's over."

Her lips tremble, the tears still streaking her cheeks.

"It's okay. I promise." I wipe away the moisture and slam my mouth against hers, needing the split second of connection. "You're safe, buttercup. You're fucking safe."

She sobs into my mouth, her nose nuzzling mine as more tears flow.

"I've got your phone." Hunt's boots enter my line of sight and he crouches down next to Sarah. "You need to get moving."

He strokes her hair, trying to wake her, and gets a soft moan for his efforts.

She's okay. For now.

"He's right." I inch back and don't deny the euphoric twist to my stomach when Keira's eyes peer up at me with relief.

She's so fucking beautiful. Even here. Now. Surrounded by a mass of chaos.

Then her expression falters. Fractures. Her baby blues turn frantic, her skin immediately pale.

"No." She shakes her head. "*Cole, no.*"

I hear the click of a cocked gun a second before the barrel presses into the back of my skull.

"*Cole, please.*" She thrashes despite her bindings, her face a picture of grief and horror.

"It's okay." I climb off her, retreating slowly, and turn to face Torian.

This was always going to be the conclusion. If not here, then somewhere else. Somewhere soon.

"You're the snitch," he accuses.

I thought I'd be scared in the moments before my death. I anticipated hysteria. Panic. Maybe even regret. I feel none of that.

Nothing but calm now Keira is safe.

"Yeah." I hold his stare. "I'm your snitch."

"No. No. No," she wails. "Cole, stop, let me explain."

He doesn't acknowledge her pleas. I'm not sure he hears them through his anger. "For how long?"

"Back off." Hunter steps toward us, Sarah cradled in his arms. "You don't want to do this. Not here. Not now."

"Like hell I don't. I've been searching for this son of a bitch for too damn long."

"You've been searching, but it's not him." Hunter starts for the door. "He's not the fucking informant. He's covering for me. But I ain't talking shit in here. We need to leave."

"Bullshit." Torian's lip curls. "I know it's him. I've always known."

There's a wealth of conviction in his tone. An undeniable belief. It's the waver in his hand that catches me off guard and the slightest hint of uncertainty with his scrutinizing look.

He's not entirely convinced.

"You're a smart man," I mutter. "Too bad you didn't stop me a long time ago."

Hunt's not going to take the fall for me. Not even temporarily.

After everything that's happened this week, I'm too fucking tired of hiding in plain sight.

"*No.* They're both lying," Keira wails. "It was me. I worked with the Feds. It was all me, Cole. That's why you thought it was Sebastian, but could never find proof. It's because you never suspected me. You never would've imagined I'd be the one to betray you."

Torian's scrutiny increases, and his weapon lowers a click.

"Think about it." She wiggles in her toppled chair. "I killed Richard. I put us in this situation with Drake. I've lied to you about everything. It was all me."

"Keira, don't," I whisper.

The warehouse door swings open to slam against the metal wall, and Luca storms in. "Did you think I was joking?" He runs toward us. "We need to leave. I can hear sirens." He places a hand on Torian's extended arm and meets my gaze. "Everything else can wait."

A silent message passes between us. One that doesn't hold a threat of violence.

For once this Navy fucker isn't throwing me under the bus.

He might actually be trying to save me.

My fucking hero.

"What's it going to be, Torian?" I ask.

He doesn't move.

Dead bodies are scattered around us, Keira is bound to a chair that's toppled to the floor, and cops are approaching, yet he doesn't budge an inch.

"Cole. *Please*," she pleads. "You need to listen to me."

He steps closer, nuzzling the gun into my chest. "Don't even think about running." The metal presses harder, my life hanging in the balance of a hair-trigger. "I'll distract the cops. You make sure you get her out of here."

29

KEIRA

I jog beside Sebastian, twisting my wrist to bring back circulation. There's no one else in sight. No cars. No people. No life out here.

"I don't think the sirens are headed in our direction." I pant. "They're not coming for us."

"It doesn't matter." He encourages me to keep moving with a gentle hand at the curve of my back. "We don't want to hang around."

"What about the bodies? There's evidence."

"Your brother will make the necessary calls. He knows what he's doing."

I push my legs harder to keep up and glance over my shoulder to see Hunter running with Sarah in his arms. She winces with every jolt, her face pinched in pain.

My guilt becomes overwhelming. It's hard to breathe through the torment.

But it's what I deserve.

Everything that happened in the warehouse was my fault.

I put everyone's life at risk. My stupidity could've killed my brother, the man I love, and three more people I care about.

Sebastian presses harder on my back. "Keep running."

I nod and follow him around a bank of bushes to an old Jeep hidden in the darkness.

"Ride shotgun. Let Hunt lay Sarah down in the back."

He doesn't wait for me to comply. He climbs into the driver's seat, starting the ignition while I slide in the other side.

The engine splutters into action, jolting my bones over and over.

"She's a piece of work, isn't she?" Sebastian shoves the car into gear and inches us out of the shadows. "We had to drive this deathtrap back from my brother's house."

I grimace, letting the shame sauté my insides as we approach Hunter and wait for him to climb inside.

I attempt to think of ways to make up for my actions while we drive through streets bathed in moonlight. My mind becomes overwhelmed trying to fix something that seems shattered into a million pieces. Everything is a mess.

"Any requests on where we should go?" Sebastian keeps his gaze on the road, his knuckles white against the steering wheel despite his calm demeanor. "I need to know where I'm driving."

"Out of town." The words rasp from my sore throat. "You need to get as far away from Cole as possible."

The last time we had this discussion, I was fighting for him to stay. Now I want nothing more than to get out of here. To flee Portland. Escape my family. At least for a little while.

"Sarah needs medical attention." The glow of Hunter's cell beams from the back seat. "I've already texted my guy to meet us at Keira's house. It's the closest option."

"Then we have to pull over." I wiggle forward in my seat, speaking directly to Sebastian. "Hunter can take the car while we move on foot."

His fingers clench and re-clench against the wheel in his ongoing silence.

"Sebastian?"

"Put your seatbelt on." He shoots me a look of warning. "I'm not running anywhere."

"Cole isn't going to—"

"I don't want to hear it, Keira. Just let it go. I'll be fine."

Fine.

Why does nobody use that word for its intended purpose anymore?

"I don't think that means what you think it means." I repeat the phrase he spoke to me a lifetime ago. Back before the craziness. Prior to my love.

His mouth kicks at the side. It's slow. Subtle. The emotion hits me right in the chest, giving me the slightest hope for redemption.

"Please." I keep pleading. I guess I'll have to for a long time to make any sort of dint in the forgiveness I need to earn.

"We're not running." This time his statement is grated, demanding an end to the conversation.

I slink back in my seat and lean my head against the window, breathing slow through the building regret.

I'm going to lose him.

After everything we've been through, despite all the good he's done for me, this is going to end. And right now, it feels like it will kill me in the process.

Hunter's voice murmuring from the back seat doesn't help. He speaks to Sarah in hushed tones, promising to look after her, complimenting her bravery, and pleading for her forgiveness.

She whimpers through his admissions, her pain filling the car to capacity.

The intimacy is hauntingly beautiful as Sebastian veers around one corner, then another, his sterility promising something entirely different.

He doesn't want me anymore. I've burned that bridge.

And rightly so.

But I'm not ready to give up. There's still fight left in me despite the weary exhaustion.

By the time we reach my house, there's an older man waiting on my doorstep. He doesn't fit the wealthy neighborhood demographic with his loose sweatpants and dark hoodie. The only thing that suits his reputation is the doctor's bag hanging at his side, which looks entirely mismatched against his clothing.

"Have you got your keys?" Hunt opens his door and slides Sarah toward him along the back seat.

"No. I don't have anything." Not keys, a phone, or any self-respect. "Just break a window. Break them all. I don't care. All you need is the code for the alarm which is five-seven-two-nine."

He doesn't wait for more instructions. He hauls Sarah into his arms, kicks the door shut, and carries her around the front of the car to speak to the shifty doctor.

"We need to leave," I whisper. "Cole won't be far away."

Sebastian breaks my heart by cutting the engine. "I'm not running. I'm done hiding, too."

I hang my head, fighting frustration. "You wouldn't be on your own. I'd be with you. We can go together."

"You're not going anywhere. Your place is in Portland, with your family."

"If you haven't noticed, I've betrayed my entire bloodline. My place isn't here at all. It's with you." I glance his way and find him focused out the windshield. He can't even look at me anymore. "*Please.* You need to trust me."

He lets out a derisive laugh, and all I can do is squeeze my eyes shut against the pain.

"Trust isn't the issue," he murmurs. "I've always trusted you. Even when I shouldn't."

There's a jingle of keys, the opening of a door, then his slide out of the car.

I don't move, not apart from my jolt of shock when the door slams.

We need to leave. We *have* to.

There's no other option.

Cole will already be tracking us down. His temper will be in full force. Hysteria will make all his decisions for him.

My door swings wide, and a gentle hand glides over my thigh.

"They opened the house for us. Let's talk inside."

I open my eyes and stare down at the fingers splayed against my jeans. I remember all the times he's touched me—physically *and* emotionally. A wealth of craziness has been shared between us, but I've become even more rich in appreciation.

This man has become my world.

He's my everything.

Maybe Cole will understand.

"Keira, sweetheart, come on. You don't want to stay out here." He's crouched beside me, his gaze solemn. "I need to get you cleaned up."

"I don't get why you're fighting me on this. Yesterday, you were ready to run."

"We'll talk about it inside." He stands and holds out a hand.

I frown at his offering and ponder all the things that come with it—the resignation and surrender.

It means goodbye.

I swallow hard and place my fingers against his, dreading every step as he leads me into the house. He drops his hold when we reach the living room, focusing his attention on Sarah laid out along my sofa.

"Is she going to be okay?" he asks.

The doctor cradles her head in both hands, using his thumbs to press against her skull. "It's hard to tell without scans."

"No." Sarah winces. "No hospital. I'm not going back there."

"She's going to be okay." Hunt sits down on the arm rest, right near her head. "I'll make sure of it."

Sebastian nods. "Yell out if you need anything." He turns to me. "Is there some place private we can talk?"

I keep my gaze on Sarah, taking in every wince and hiss of pain.

"Keira? It's this way to your bedroom, right?"

He points a hand toward the hall, and I ignore my curiosity at how he knows the intimate details of my house. Nothing surprises me anymore.

"Yeah."

He leads the way down to the last room on the left, indicating for me to enter first before he closes the door behind us.

I drag my feet to the end of the bed, not willing to face him anymore. I don't know how to look at him and remain strong at the same time.

"How are you holding up?" he murmurs. "Has shock set in?"

"Is that a trick question?" Maybe I was wrong, maybe I can still be surprised, because he's not making any sense to me. "You know I'm frantic, Sebastian. And yes, I'm shocked as hell that you're keeping us here when Cole is on his way."

He reverts back to the silent treatment.

"Why won't you run?" I turn to face him, not holding back the frustration in my voice. "Are you waiting for an apology? Is that it? Because I'm sorry. I'm so goddamn sorry I didn't listen to you. What I did was selfish and stupid, but I didn't see that at the time. All I wanted was to be able to fight my own battles."

He focuses his attention on the bed, his gaze wandering over the beaded quilt and the mass of decorative pillows. "That's not what this is about."

"Then what is it?" I start toward him. "Tell me, and I'll do whatever needs to be done."

He closes his eyes for long seconds, then huffs out a sigh. "I don't want you to do anything, precious."

I stop before him and lean toward his line of vision until he meets my eyes. "What are you going to do when he gets here?"

"Nothing."

Nothing.

The word shudders through me, bringing an icy chill.

"I can't stop him, Keira. We both know that." He bridges the space between us and weaves his hands around my waist. His touch is everything—gentle, smooth, affectionate. "I just want to stay here while I can. No running. No hiding. No panic."

"He's going to—"

"It doesn't matter. It's out of our control."

"No, it's not." I slam my palm against his chest. "You're giving up, when we could be running. It wouldn't be forever. Only until he has the patience to listen to the full story. We can stay away until he forgives you."

"Forgives me? Really?" He snickers through a mocking smile. "You're not very good at this, pumpkin."

I shove at him. "This isn't a joke."

He's laughing at me. Laughing when so much hangs in the balance of every second that ticks by.

"Why won't you listen?" I grab his shirt, entangling my fingers in the material to tug, tug, tug some sense into him.

His humor fades, and those eyes turn somber. "Because if my minutes are numbered, I want to spend every second standing here with you... I'd just prefer it without the fighting."

"No." I shake my head and thump my fist against his chest. *"Please."*

He pulls me close, his arms a vise around me as he presses his lips to my temple. "Just enjoy what we've got."

"I'll die without you," I whisper.

"And I'll die for you. It's always been that way." He rocks me back and forth, moving us in a silent dance of farewell. "I love you. Never forget that, okay?"

I cling to him. To the words. To the warmth.

"I won't let go." My breathing begins to fracture, each breath getting shorter, sharper, until I'm hyperventilating. "I can't."

Tears fall, staining his shirt as I lean into his chest. I hold him with everything I have, and everything I'll ever be.

He found me. He saved me. He made me whole.

There's no going back from that.

A thunderous knock at the front door tears a gasp from my throat, and those arms clamp tighter.

"Shh. It's okay." He speaks into my hair. "Don't let go."

No.

No, no, no.

My limbs shake. I struggle to breathe.

I don't want this. I can't live through it.

My door handle turns, the wood inching wide to bring Hunter into view. "Do you want me to let him in?"

Sebastian nods. "Yeah."

"No." I vehemently shake my head. "Not yet."

Hunter winces, ignoring my protest as he disappears down the hall.

"Please, God, no." I yank at Sebastian's shirt. "It's not too late to get out of here."

"Don't worry." He steps back and takes hold of my wrists, his grip gentle.

"Nothing is going to happen here. He'll take me for a ride. That's when I'll find a way out. *Then* I'll run. Okay?"

He's lying. I can tell this time.

I see the dishonesty in his eyes.

It's in the grief-stricken smile.

"You can't deceive me again. You know once you get in that car there's no coming back."

And I'll never learn the truth. Cole will never tell me what really happened.

"Hey." He leans close and nuzzles his nose against mine. "Do you know what I'm more certain of?"

I shake my head. I don't want to hear it. Nothing else matters.

"That you mean the world to me," he murmurs against my lips. "You're everything, Keira."

I squeeze my eyes closed, the heated trail along my cheeks growing wider.

My knees threaten to buckle, and all I do is hold the heartache tight inside my chest.

"Hey. Come on, sugar. It'll be okay." He brushes my cheeks, resolute.

I can't fathom his level of acceptance. I never will.

"It's time." He gives me a sad smile, never breaking our gaze. "We've got company."

I shoot a frantic glance to the door and find Cole standing there, his face a mask of harsh lines and barely contained rage.

"Get out of my house," I demand. "I don't want you here."

"Is that any way to greet your brother?" The question is a threat, his words intricately laced with more than disappointment.

"I won't let you hurt him."

"I'm unarmed, aren't I?"

"You are?" I scrutinize him. Up and down.

"Yes. Thanks to Hunt." He flicks open the sides of his jacket, then does an unenthusiastic turn with his hands out in front of him. "See. No gun."

I glance back at Sebastian in confusion.

He gives me an unconvincing smile, his eyes speaking of distrust. He's waiting for the other shoe to drop, and I need to do the same.

I turn back to my brother and strengthen my shoulders to steel. "You need to let me explain."

"That's why I'm here."

"Okay… Good." I nod, my head jerking back and forth as I sniff away the last remnants of tears. "Sebastian has a good reason for what he did. Our father isn't who we think he is. He's been trafficking—"

"I know."

My heart stops. My skin crawls. "You know?"

"Yeah." He holds my gaze, unrepentant, remorseless. "He offered to cut me in on the action after Richard was admitted to hospital."

There's a wealth of heartlessness in his words. Such cold, sterile detachment.

I shake my head, unable to comprehend what I'm hearing. "No." I place a hand over my mouth, attempting to bottle the effects of his betrayal. "You've been helping him? All this time?"

"Of course not," he snarls. "*Jesus*. Don't look at me like that. I said he *offered* to cut me in, not that I accepted."

"Why would you keep this from me? We tell each other everything."

"Do we?" He cocks his head in confusion. "Like assassination attempts against family members?"

"That was one thing, Cole. And it was *my* thing. I needed to cut him out of our lives."

"And this was one thing, *Keira*. One thing I knew you couldn't handle."

"But you still knew." Sebastian's hands find my waist, his touch possessive. Protective. "And you didn't do a damn thing about it."

My brother takes a threatening step forward. "I think we're getting distracted from the real issue here, don't you? How long have you been singing to the Feds?"

Those hands on my waist tighten. "Since before you knew I existed."

Cole's brows rise as if impressed by the honesty. "Why? You had to know the consequences." He takes another step. "Something like this doesn't end well for you."

"Back off," I warn. "He had good reason. I would've done the same."

"In that case, you'll need to enlighten me, because I can't think of anything capable of justifying his actions."

I itch to blurt the information. The painful truth sits right on the tip of my tongue, waiting for permission.

But Sebastian needs to provide these answers.

He needs to... Yet he doesn't.

I turn, facing Sebastian as he glares at Cole.

"I can't say it," he murmurs. "I don't want him knowing about her."

"There's another woman?" Cole scoffs. "Keira, what have you gotten yourself into?"

"He knows." Sebastian meets my gaze. "And he didn't do a fucking thing."

The truth is a heavy weight against my heart.

Yes, Cole knows, but I have to believe there's a reason he kept quiet. He wouldn't knowingly allow for women to be tortured. He couldn't. Not when I've seen his compassion for my own torture. "Let me tell him."

"It's over." He kisses my forehead and drops his hands from my waist. "Your brother and I are going to go for a drive."

"No." I grab his wrists. "I'll tell him."

He doesn't respond, just keeps glaring his fury at my brother.

I swing around. "It was his sister. His *only baby sister*. And our father took her."

Cole acknowledges the confession with the straightening of his spine and the slight hitch of his chin. He understands family loyalty. And the heartache of loss. There's no way he can't empathize with Sebastian's situation.

"Now do you understand?" I plead. "You would've done far worse in his situation."

"Is it true?" He focuses over my shoulder, his eyes narrowed in scrutiny.

"Yes." Sebastian's hands reclaim my body, the heated palms searing my hips. "They manipulated her. Sold her. And eventually killed her."

"You're certain?"

His fingers dig into bone. "Yes. I'm fucking certain. I wouldn't be anywhere near your family if I wasn't."

I flinch, not expecting the rejection. In seconds Sebastian's arms are wrapping around me to lessen the blow.

"You know what I mean," he whispers in my ear. "I wouldn't have dared to betray your family if it wasn't for Penny."

I nod, because yes, I do understand. Venom flows through our family tree, and he isn't the type of man to shake branches.

He's here for vengeance. Not me.

We never would've found each other without his sister's death. And that hurts. It's brutal and punishing, and goddamn heartbreaking because I struggle to quit the selfishness to tell myself I'd give him up if I could change the past for Penny.

Cole nods. "I understand your situation. And can appreciate your motives. But unfortunately, it's time to deal with the consequences."

"If you can contemplate punishing him after everything he's been through, I don't want to know you anymore," I snarl. "I'm done. You can—"

"Keira," he warns.

"No. You would've done the same. *Actually,* you would've done far worse, and you know it."

"And I would've accepted my fate."

"I accept my fate." Sebastian steps around me, heading toward the door.

"No." I stagger forward to remain between them, placing a palm on Sebastian's chest to hold him back, while holding up a hand of warning to my brother. "This ends now. We've all been through enough. There are no repercussions. It's over."

"Keira." Cole's eyes soften, his expression changing to one of derision. "He paid back our family by manipulating you. You may not see it, but you became the mark."

A wave of goosebumps flows down my back, and for a split second I believe him. "No." I shake my head. "*No.*"

I shove at Sebastian's chest to keep him at bay, then face my brother head-on. "Fuck you for thinking I can be easily manipulated."

"You've lived with what Richard did for years. Then all of a sudden you can't handle history?"

I storm forward, getting in his face. "All of a sudden I couldn't handle him looking at Stella the way he looked at me. My decisions regarding our uncle have never had anything to do with Sebastian. Or me. I was keeping your niece safe."

Cole snaps taut.

"I planned to kill him well before you made Sebastian my protector. And he had no say in what I did tonight. He's the one who tried to stop me." I glare all my fury at him. "Do you hear me? *He* tried to stop me. So I'm not the weak, defenseless woman who can be easily manipulated. I'm the one who will burn your house to the ground if you dare think about hurting him ever again."

My brother remains quiet, scrutinizing me while my heart beats a staccato through my entire body.

I know that look.

He's thinking. He's actually contemplating. The anticipation for his response becomes agony.

"Did you use her to get to my family?" He glides his attention to Sebastian, his expression impassive.

"I don't know."

I glance over my shoulder, wordlessly begging Sebastian to falsify an answer. It's clear he used me. I understand that. But our truth became far stronger than those lies.

"I never planned on getting this deep," he admits. "I was ready to run the night you made me your bitch boy. Keira is the only reason I stayed."

"Because you thought you could manipulate the tumultuous relationship we portrayed?"

"No." His eyes harden. "Because I wanted to save her. From you."

"She's never needed saving," Cole grates.

"Tonight suggests otherwise. I saved her from your knee-jerk decision to walk into that warehouse without backup. *I'm* the reason she got out of there alive."

I swing back around to my brother. "He's the reason *you* got out of there alive. He risked his own safety to save us all. Doesn't that mean something?"

He doesn't answer.

"Cole, *please*, you need to let this go."

"What was your end game?" he asks. "What was the point of working with the Feds?"

"To shut down your father's operation. I wanted him behind bars."

"Bars won't hold him." Cole's lip curls. "You should've known that."

"He does now," I say in a rush. "That's why we've worked out a better plan. I want him dead, Cole."

"You're not working on a fucking thing," he snaps. "There's no *we* in this."

His eyes narrow on mine, and for the first time I see his disappointment. The emotion wasn't there when I was trapped in the warehouse, but now it stares back at me in stark clarity.

"If you have even the slightest inclination to keep this piece of shit alive, then you'll stick to the fucking sideline. You won't breathe a word of this to anyone. Not about Decker. Not about our father. And not about fucking Richard."

His words bear down on me, harsh and unrelenting. His anger is worse.

"You won't think about interfering with my plans for our father," he continues. "You won't even dare to ask to be involved. You will keep your thoughts and your relationship to yourself, and save your boy toy the pain of getting a knife in the neck. Do you hear me?"

I hear him.

I hear him too loud. Too clear.

The ultimatum repeats in my ears like a life sentence and clemency, all at once.

"Okay," I whisper.

"And if you upset her," he points a menacing finger at Sebastian, "even once, I won't kill you. You won't be that lucky. But I'll make sure you wish you were dead."

"Understood." Sebastian pulls me into his side with an arm around my waist.

We stand together, closer than we've ever been while my brother retreats toward the door.

"Wait," Sebastian calls out. "You need to know Hunt wasn't involved in this. He wasn't aware of my connections."

My brother pauses, his stance rigid.

There's no belief in his features. There's no dispute, either.

"He knew at some point."

"Two days ago," I interrupt. "When he beat Sebastian to a bloody pulp in an attempt to get answers."

Cole nods, his acceptance inconclusive, before he walks down the hall and out of view.

I remain in place, stunned. "What the hell just happened?"

"I don't know."

I stare into the hall as my mind does a rerun, trying to work out the puzzle. "Maybe he likes you after all?"

"No, pop tart." He steps into me, wrapping an arm around my neck, the other around my waist. "He doesn't like me in the slightest. He's only saving my ass to make you happy."

"Well, it worked." My chest burns, every nerve tingling beneath warmed flesh. "I'm so happy, Sebastian."

"Me, too. But what happened tonight is going to catch up with you pretty soon. The shock will be brutal."

I nod and snuggle into his chest. "I know. I can already feel it."

The memories hover on the periphery, fighting to be heard.

"You won't be alone." His hold tightens. "I've got you."

My eyes tingle with the threat of tears. I don't want to ruin this. I need our moment to remain with me a little while longer before the demons arrive. "Do you think we're capable of getting through a twenty-four-hour period without deceiving each other?"

He chuckles, the vibrations nuzzling my cheek. "God, I hope so. If you didn't pick up what your brother was putting down, I kinda need for us to get through a lot of twenty-four-hour periods if I don't want my dick blown off."

"How many do you think you can handle?"

"I'm pretty sure I don't want to lose this third leg of mine, which means you're stuck with me indefinitely."

"Why doesn't it surprise me that you're making jokes at a time like this?"

He blankets me with affection, the adoration seeping under my skin. "Because you know me, sparkles. You know me better than I know myself."

EPILOGUE
DECKER

"You're beautiful," I whisper.

No truer words have been spoken.

Keira is a vision before me in a sleek black dress, her hair loose and draped over her shoulders. She stands in front of her hallway mirror, her lashes dark, her make-up subtle. Everything about her is flawless, especially the way she smiles back at me with understated perfection.

"Thank you." She turns to me and bridges the space between us, her high heels tapping against the tile. "And you're utterly handsome."

Her arms slide under my suit jacket to hug my waist, accidentally bumping the gun lodged in the back of my pants. "Sorry. I'm still getting used to you wearing a weapon."

It's her brother's fault I've been unarmed. He demanded I hide my gun at home. To stow my only protection so the two of us could participate in a trivial game of chicken.

It was a power play. A reclaiming of his authority.

He also took away my cell and made two of his thugs shadow me.

And I understood the necessity.

I can also understand why he gave me back my freedom and my right to bear arms this morning.

"It's okay." I pull her into me and kiss her forehead. "Are you ready?"

"How can anyone be ready for something like this?"

I don't know.

Today, she lays her uncle to rest after suffering through days of turmoil pouring her secrets out to her sister. I've been with her through it all. I hugged her while her nightmares wreaked havoc and held her hand when she demanded Richard wasn't worthy of a church service.

There will only be a brief graveside vigil for a man who deserves far less.

I've stood by her through everything. I honestly haven't let this gorgeous woman leave my side. Half the time it's by choice, the other half is because she doesn't want to tempt her brother's itchy trigger finger.

But that fucker won't kill me. Not anytime soon.

Turns out, he's wrapped around his little sister's pinkie tight enough to cut circulation. Behind the charade of animosity, the two of them are thick as thieves. Cole wouldn't do anything to hurt her. So it all boils down to me treading the straight and narrow to keep this woman happy. Which is far from a hardship.

"Come on, guys," Sarah calls from the living room. "We're going to be late."

Keira stiffens in my arms, her slender body coiled tight.

"Don't worry." I grab her hand and entwine our fingers. "Life will get easier after today."

"Do you really believe that?"

"Yes." I shoot her a wink. "You know better than to think I'd lie to you."

She gives a half-hearted chuckle, and I know the apprehension in her features has nothing to do with me. The trust between us is unbreakable. Her fear comes from what she's about to face.

Not just the burial of her rapist, but the possible appearance of her father.

"We haven't heard a word from him," she whispers. "What if he doesn't show?"

"He will. You've said it before, he's not going to miss his brother's funeral."

"That's what I thought, but now I'm not so sure."

I squeeze her fingers. "It's out of our hands. Let Cole deal with it. I'm sure he's got it under control."

I lead her along the hall, only to have her pull me to a stop steps later.

"And you're okay with not being involved?"

"I'm fine."

"*Sebastian*," she warns. "Don't use that word."

I chuckle. "Okay, I'm not fine. But I'm dealing with it."

The intricacies of Cole's plan aren't at my disposal. He's kept the details a tightly held secret. Yet, this morning, he had the decency to tell me I'd have my vengeance before nightfall. That his father would be dead if today worked in our favor.

It was a murmured promise from my woman's brother.

A barely civil vow from the son of my sister's murderer.

It's all I have, and more than I need.

"Come on. If we don't get moving, we're going to miss the funeral."

THE RIDE to the cemetery is done in silence. Hunter drives, I ride shotgun, while Sarah and Keira sit in the back.

Expensive sports cars and luxurious SUVs are lined up bumper to bumper along the narrow cemetery street. We park at the front, claiming our reserved space as a member of the notorious crime family.

"There are more people than I expected." Sarah unfastens her belt and scoots forward to peer through the windshield. "A lot of cars means a lot of witnesses."

Hunter cuts the ignition and scopes the growing crowd. "Torian isn't going to make a move at the funeral."

"You know what's going down?" I shoot him a questioning glance, which is quickly deflected with a look of caution.

"Everything will be handled after we leave the cemetery." Hunt opens his door and Sarah follows, both of them keeping their distance from Torian and Layla, who wait beneath a portable gazebo, Luca and Layla's husband standing one step behind.

I remain in place, not moving until Keira's ready.

"He's not here," she murmurs. "I can't see him anywhere. What happens if he doesn't show?"

"That's out of our hands. We've both known that for days."

She winces, her disappointment killing me. "You don't regret giving up on retaliation?"

"Not at all. That shit was tearing me apart. Besides, I got the better end of the deal when I walked away with you."

She sighs and rests her head against the window as she stares across at the gravesite. "It looks like they're ready to start."

I nod. "Yeah, the evil glare your brother is giving me is a great indication."

Her halfhearted chuckle fills the car. It's all the reward I need.

It's all I'll ever want.

She sucks in a deep breath and releases it slowly. "Let's do this."

She shoves open her door, and I rush from the car to meet her.

We walk hand in hand to the crowd that parts as we approach.

"I don't know half these people," she murmurs. "How could they all have cared about Richard?"

"I don't know. Business associates, I guess. Try not to think about it."

"Business associates would make it worse."

She's right. But as always, I'm not the best at comfort. Not in situations like this.

It's hard enough dealing with the constant prickle of the hair at the back of my neck. The vibe here feels wrong.

She pulls us to a stop at the front of the crowd, next to Hunter and Sarah, our position opposite the gazebo. It's her choice not to stand near her brother and sister, and I get it. She needs to do this on her own.

Her grief is far different than theirs.

The officiant steps forward, opens a thick, leather-bound book, and begins the proceedings.

I don't listen to a word he says. I'm too busy fighting disappointment.

I honestly didn't think Luther would miss his own brother's funeral. Keira had convinced me he would attend, despite all obstacles, in the face of all adversity.

Even though I've come to terms with being stripped of any role in his demise, the thought of him not being punished sits like a lead balloon.

But he's not here.

Torian's pinched face says he's not coming, either. And he'd know.

He has airport staff in his pocket. Cops on the payroll. His own men on the streets. If he hasn't heard anything by now, he never will.

I lower my gaze to the grass around my shoes and take solace in having Keira by my side.

She's the prize despite the losing hand. The peace to soothe the torment.

She reaches out, as if hearing my thoughts, and grabs the crook of my arm. Her fingers dig deep. Tighter and tighter, to the point of pain.

I shoot her a glance, wondering what the claws are all about.

"He's here." Her announcement is barely audible, yet the anticipation rings loud as hell in my ears.

I follow the angle of her vision to see her father striding forward from the other side of the cemetery, weaving in and out of gravestones in his flawless suit and tie with matching thugs flanking him on either side.

I've never seen the guy in person. Only in family photos in the restaurant or online. But it isn't hard to recognize him. He's an older version of his son. Broad shoulders. Stern face. The guy demands respect without saying a word.

Everyone remains still as he approaches, bringing a halt to the proceedings as he greets his eldest daughter with a hug. Then Cole with a handshake.

Keira bristles at the shared affection, and I can't help doing the same.

"It's all for show," Hunter murmurs. "Torian knows what he's doing."

I have to trust his faith because I have none of my own.

Cole is supposed to be kill the man before him. His own flesh and blood. Yet, here he is playing happy families.

I cup Keira's biting hand and squeeze. "Do you want to go over and see him?"

"No. It doesn't feel right."

"I don't think there's a right way to feel about this, honey," Hunter drawls.

"I know. But I thought I'd feel remorse at the sight of him." She meets my gaze, staring back at me in confusion. "And I don't. All I see is a monster."

"There's no rulebook here. And no judgment." I wipe the stray hair away from her cheeks. "You feel whatever you need to. It's the only way you'll get through this."

She crumples, her shoulders wilting as she nestles in front of me and wraps my arms around her waist.

Luther moves to stand between his children, his granddaughter before him, the goons at his back, when Torian inclines his head at the officiant to continue.

Adrenaline eats away at my veins while fabricated good deeds are recited to a silent crowd. We're painted a story of a man who never existed. A philanthropist. A devoted uncle and cherished brother.

Over and over the lies continue, twisting my stomach and making me livid.

But I'll have my peace soon.

The sweet taste of victory is on its way.

A few sobs ring out when the coffin is lowered a foot. Stella wails. People sniff.

I don't think anyone really cares except that little girl. She's the only one naive to Richard's actions and capabilities.

My heart breaks for her. Not only did she lose an uncle, she lost a fairytale, and one day the truth will come out to reveal a reality darker than her worst nightmares.

"I'd now like to call upon anyone who would like to place petals or sand in the grave as a personal goodbye." The officiant turns to the gazebo, offering the family the first opportunity.

Luther sidesteps Stella to move forward, away from his henchmen and toward the grave. He grabs a handful of petals as he passes, every set of eyes watching his movements. He scatters the offering, his actions delicate, then kisses his clenched fist and thumps it down on the coffin.

Keira jolts with the impact, her body trembling against mine.

There's a rustle of noise behind me, and a broad, middle-aged man bumps my shoulder to break through the crowd, his enthusiasm to throw sand on a dead guy outweighing his manners.

"Watch it," I mutter.

He ignores me and continues toward the grave. "Luther Torian?"

Keira's father scowls at the intrusion, openly hostile at the man stupid enough to call his name.

The stranger doesn't falter, his stride strong as he holds out a hand. "I'm Special Agent Anthony Easton, and you're under arrest for human trafficking," he clasps Luther's palm and retrieves a pair of cuffs with his left, "and solicitation involving minors under the age of sixteen."

Gasps break out in a chorus. Then whispers and growing chatter.

Keira freezes. So do I.

All of us—Hunt, Sarah, Torian, and Layla—watch in horror as the agent takes charge of the scene.

"You have the right to remain silent."

"No." Torian stalks forward. "*Stop.*"

Keira turns to me, her eyes pleading the same denial.

If Luther goes to jail, his crimes won't end. He will hire the best lawyers. He'll pay everyone and anyone to get him out of there. Then he'll disappear.

He won't go to prison.

He won't die for his sins.

He'll be free.

"What the fuck do you think you're doing?" Torian doesn't shout, he seethes, the words holding enough venom to filter through the gathering.

The agent continues without pause. "Anything you say can and will be used against you in a court of law."

Luther's goons approach, but so do more unfamiliar men and women in the crowd, all of them pulling badges from pockets in a mass show of authority.

"Jesus," I hiss. They're everywhere. "That's the reason you didn't recognize half these people. They're all Feds."

Keira grabs my shirt, clinging to the material. "Do something. *Please.*"

Fuck. Her plea tears me apart, and there's nothing I can do.

I can't save her this time. I vowed I wouldn't get involved, and Torian knows I've kept my end of the deal. I won't lose her now. Not even at the expense of my revenge.

"We'll figure something out." Sarah places a hand on her shoulder. "This isn't the end."

The agent doesn't quit reciting the Miranda rights as he hikes Luther's hands behind his back and leads the silent man to the long line of cars.

"Everyone move," a woman shouts. "Make way."

"Anissa." Her name slips from my lips. That fucking bitch.

"Keira, you need to start making calls." Hunter hands over his phone. "Prepare your legal team."

"Why?" Her brows knit.

I lean close, placing my mouth near her ear. "This game is far from over. We both know he'll get out. And when he does, he needs to know you made every effort to protect him."

"I want to speak to Cole first." The device trembles in her hand as she stares at her brother now talking to Anissa. "What is she saying to him?"

"I don't know."

I'm not sure I want to. Not when the look on her face says she's enjoying the victory.

Keira starts toward them, and I follow close at her back, neither of us making it to Cole before Anissa saunters after the rest of her team.

"What did she say to you?" Keira demands.

"A lot of things." His lips press tight for a moment, his anger barely contained. "She has the impression we're going to be seeing a lot of each other in the future."

"She said that?" Sarah snarls from behind me. "She comes to your uncle's funeral, arrests your father, then lays more threats?"

That's Anissa—thirty percent cocky, seventy percent bitch.

"What are you going to do?" I hitch my chin at Torian. "Apart from the legal team moving into action, what's your plan?"

His jaw ticks, his narrowed eyes still focused on Anissa as she saunters to the mass of cars parked along the narrow cemetery road. "I'm going to give that woman exactly what she wants."

TORIAN

PROLOGUE
TORIAN

I'VE DONE SOME HEAVY SHIT IN MY TIME.

I've taken the lives of many and ordered the death of more.

I was barely out of my teens when I had to take down one of my own men—a guy I'd trusted—because he'd dared to touch my sister. He'd raised a hand to Layla, and in return, I'd raised a gun to his temple and didn't bat an eye when I pulled the trigger.

My father instilled that sense of protection in me. Which, I guess, makes my task today more than a little ironic.

The man who taught me everything, who shaped my prejudices and guided me through my entire life, needs to be shut down for the betrayal he's inflicted on his children.

Today, I will punish my father out of respect for all of us. And that, by far, is the heaviest shit I've ever had to deal with. Not just the thought of confronting his actions, but addressing the betrayal—his against me, and mine against him.

At one time, he was all I knew. Everything I looked up to. All I aspired to be. There was no greater man than the mighty Luther Torian.

Now, he's everything I despise and all I crave to defeat.

My only concern is the consequences.

If I had my way, I'd tap the brakes and allow myself more time to work out this plan. But stalling isn't an option after I made a promise to an irrational sister who was hell-bent on taking the task into her own hands.

I won't allow anyone else to sentence him. I don't care how big the grievance. He's mine to deal with.

My mentor. My flesh. My blood.

If anyone is going to instigate a war of loyalties among the men in my organization, it will be me. And I've never been more aware of the dangers of a possible split than I am now, standing beneath a portable gazebo, before a polished coffin, waiting for my uncle's funeral to begin, in front of a crowd filled with potential enemies.

Richard Torian was an unscrupulous bastard.

A rapist.

A pedophile.

But both he and my father have always provided an unyielding level of protection toward our family that very few people dared to breech.

Without them, my stronghold will take a major hit.

Me, my sisters, my niece—all of us will be vulnerable unless I make the right choices.

"Unkie Cole, where's Aunt Keira?" Stella drags her feet toward me, peering up with pained eyes.

"I'm sure she isn't too far away." I lean forward, palm her delicate chin, and encourage her focus to remain on mine. "How are you holding up, pumpkin?"

She nods, silently lying to me as she blinks through grief-stricken tears.

The heartache she harbors for a man who never existed cuts me to the core. She isn't aware of Richard's perversions, the ones that brought pleasure to him and agony to others. Hopefully, she never will be.

"She's doing okay." Layla grabs her daughter's shoulders and encourages the child to retreat from me. It's a subtle shun. A barely recognizable retaliation in front of a crowd filled with dark suits and darker souls. "Aren't you, sweetheart?"

I stifle a snarl while Stella nuzzles her face into her mother's stomach.

My sister isn't letting go of her grudge against me any time soon. She's made it clear she doesn't appreciate me hiding family secrets from her. Secrets that weren't mine to share. And, like every woman on the face of the earth, she's clutching the grievance as if it's a fucking lifeline.

"Lay off him, my love." Her husband, Benji, places his hands on her waist. "The situation was complicated."

"*Your* situation will be complicated if you don't make intelligent choices about where your loyalties lie." She scowls straight ahead, fixing her attention on something in the distance.

Benji's hands drop from her body, his nostrils flaring in a show of annoyance. He's not romantic or sweet. He's not weak or defenseless either, and definitely not the type to withstand female ultimatums. Especially not in front of me.

He's harsh. Aggressive. And threatening at the best of times.

When he opens his mouth to retaliate, I shoot him a look—one that orders him to be smart and keep quiet.

I know exactly where his loyalties lie. I always have. It's the reason I gave him my blessing to marry my sister.

Besides, this isn't the place to air relationship issues. God knows I've got enough shit to deal with without their egos fighting for supremacy.

"Unkie Cole?"

I sigh, this time ignoring the pull of angelic eyes as I glance across the crowd. "Yeah, little one?"

"Aunt Keira is late."

"I know. Just try to be patient for me. I promise she will be here."

Keira is definitely late, but she'll show.

That boyfriend of hers will be at her side, too, when I'd much prefer he took up residence in the free plot beside my uncle.

I haven't hidden my animosity toward Decker. In fact, I've made it clear I'd like to take the fucker swimming. While he wears cement blocks for shoes.

He's a traitor. Not to mention a smart-ass who makes me want to extract every one of his teeth. *Slowly*.

The only thing keeping him alive is his dedication to my sister.

He saved Keira's life. And, okay, he saved my ass, too.

But my generosity is wearing thin with every breath he takes.

"Want me to make some calls?" Luca asks over my shoulder. "She was riding with Hunt and Sarah."

"Give them a few more minutes." I bite back the annoyance from my voice. Luca is starting to grate on my nerves.

Fuck.

With the mess in my head, everyone is rubbing me the wrong way. I understand he's still trying to find his feet in the position of my right-hand man; he just needs to do it quicker. Before I lose my shit.

Maybe it was a mistake giving him Hunter's previous role. I demoted my longtime enforcer to prove a point about loyalty. I demand allegiance. Honesty. Reliability. Hunt had wavered on all three counts. The non-compliance wasn't something I could ignore.

Nobody fucks with me.

Not even a little bit.

But Luca will be a suitable placeholder until my point is made. He's an ex-SEAL who entered the fold due to his relationship with Benji—his brother.

I'm always willing to take on new members who vouch for others with their lives. It makes for easy leverage.

But Luca's loyalty has always been clear. He's already had the psychological manipulation implanted in him from the government, making him the perfect soldier.

He's just asking too many fucking questions when all I want is silence.

The funeral can't start without Keira. And as much as I'd prefer to put this morning in my rearview, I don't have the luxury of wishing away the minutes.

She isn't the only person missing from the festivities.

My father is yet to arrive.

Maybe he's not going to show.

I could've sworn he wouldn't miss his brother's funeral, despite the threat of the authorities breathing down his neck.

Each second that ticks by acts like a tightening vise around my chest. I haven't heard a word from him since I called to relay the details of the graveside service. Not one fucking word.

There have been no whispers of travel arrangements. Or sightings among the many people I pay for information.

As far as I'm aware, he's still in the Greek islands, pretending to kick back and soak up the scenery, when what he's really doing is tainting our family name.

Desecrating my mother's memory.

He's branded me and my sisters, associating all of us with the sex slave trade.

To anyone else, it might not seem a far stretch from the schemes I've spent years cultivating. And maybe drug distribution, money laundering, racketeering and extortion—to name a few—aren't all that distant from the brutality of women, but to me, they're fucking worlds apart.

Extortion is about exuding power and claiming money. The distribution of drugs, again, is about power and money. Everything I do holds the same values.

I never target those who are fragile and innocent.

I'm not weak.

Yet my father holds entirely different views, or so it seems. The man who I thought was beyond strength and power is nothing but a pitiful, spineless fool.

He preys on those who can't protect themselves while succumbing to perversions ninety percent of the population can keep in check.

There's no power in that. Only deficiency.

The thought of being associated with those activities makes my skin crawl.

Luca inches closer. "They're here."

I glance toward the narrow road leading through the cemetery and find Hunter's black Suburban pulling into the only remaining parking space reserved for family.

Decker rides shotgun. The women must be behind the back tinted windows.

Two doors open and Hunter and Sarah make their way toward the crowd, while my sister remains in the car, taunting my impatience.

"Want me to get them to hurry up?"

I pretend not to hear yet another one of Luca's questions and breathe deep to find some calm.

Despite my diminishing tolerance, I know Keira doesn't deserve to be rushed. She loathes Richard more than I do. She has every reason to.

My struggle is centered on something entirely different.

Something more brutal.

I fear what I will become once I condemn my father.

I grew up worlds apart from my sisters. I didn't have my mother's guidance. The kindness. The nurturing. The fucking morals that have begun to drive me bat-shit crazy. I remained tightly guided under my father's influence.

He molded me into a resilient warrior.

His spitting image.

The perfect protégé.

I learned about the drug trade while kids my age were getting beat up in middle school. There was no gentle upbringing. I shuffled through crime-scene photos like other teens flicked through *Playboy*. I was born to live in my father's footsteps. Taught to lead. To control. To conquer.

The only softness I knew was my predecessor's greatest lesson, the one that continues to ring in my ears to this very day, haunting me—*money is power, but family is everything.*

Family. Is. Everything.

Giving him what he deserves means I'm spitting in the face of the only warmth I know.

My reputation for ruthlessness will be cemented—the horrors etched in stone.

But maybe the lesson was strategic on my father's behalf.

I wouldn't be surprised if he taught me the highest value of family because he knew the day would come when I would question if he deserved his next breath.

And I am questioning it.

I'm questioning every thought. Every feeling. Every twinge of consciousness.

I guess the moral crisis is a blessing in disguise. It means I haven't reached his level of savagery.

Not yet.

"Here they come," Luca mutters.

"I can fucking see that." I don't need a blow-by-blow update. *Jesus.* I'm not blind.

Layla glares at me. "Watch your mouth in front of Stella."

I roll my eyes and hold in a sigh. Her parenting isn't a battle I'm willing to fight. We need to be strong. To be unified. I'll release my thread-bare frustration soon enough, and God help the poor motherfucker who has to deal with the nuclear detonation.

"I apologize." I grind the words through gritted teeth as Keira slides from the car.

Surprise, surprise, Decker meets her at the side of the vehicle with an outstretched hand.

That guy never ceases to piss me off.

I hate how she submits to him too easily. And maybe I envy it a little, too.

She's happy with this asshole. Despite the reasons for her being here today, beyond the weary eyes and wearier expression, she's at peace. And that solace can't be easy to find when you know your father is responsible for the death of your boyfriend's sister.

Yep. My father led Penny from the country using fake promises of a bright future in modelling.

Last I heard, her DNA was found in a mass grave.

What a great foundation for a flourishing relationship.

I drag my attention from the smitten couple who choose to stand away from our family gathered beneath the gazebo, and focus past the crowd, staring into the distance. I ignore the pound of a building headache. I block out the increased chatter from friends and strangers alike. I try to clear my head of the noise even though my mind pummels me with a million unanswered questions regarding my father's whereabouts.

Fucking hell.

He's not coming.

Which means Keira is going to crumple. Momentarily. Then bounce back even harder with a vengeance.

She will nag and nag at me to finish this. And if I don't act quick enough, she will revert to making threats to take the matter into her own hands.

I don't know what's worse—the thought of the guilt that could consume me once I deal with my own father or the fear Keira will attempt an attack before I have the chance.

I can't allow her the opportunity.

I've already failed her many times before. I won't let her be in harm's way again.

"You can start." I jerk my head toward the funeral officiant murmuring with mourners. "The last of our family has arrived."

Layla shoots me a look of concern. "You're not going to wait?"

My pulse is triggered by her panic, the frantic beats ratcheting up another notch. "There's no need. If he's not here already, he's not going to show."

The admission should bring relief. I wanted more time, right? This was what I'd been praying for. So why do I feel defeated?

The officiant steps forward, a leather-bound book clutched in his hands. He greets the crowd of people I barely recognize and speaks scripted lies, his showmanship engaging everyone in attendance as he weaves something closer to a fairy-tale than reality.

I watch Keira as the funeral drags on. I don't know how to make this right. To ease her burden. But maybe this is for the best.

I need to keep her safe. *All of us safe.*

Delaying the drama with my father will afford me the opportunity to build more loyalties. To cultivate a better plan.

As if hearing my thoughts, she freezes in place and grabs the crook of Decker's arm. She stares blankly ahead, her lips parted, her eyes wide.

She could be lost in past nightmares or predicting the horrors of the future for all I know, but I follow her gaze across the open expanse of the cemetery only to find the devil stalking toward me.

"Shit." The curse brushes past my clenched teeth.

Layla shoots me another glare, then quickly mimics my line of sight.

"Oh, God," she whispers.

My father strides toward us, passing angel statues and monuments to lives lost, his shoulders stiff beneath his expensive suit. It's been many months since I've seen him. Not enough to lessen the sense of authority he brings. Or the gut-wrenching animosity I feel.

I've never battled with such vastly conflicting emotions as I do right now.

The anger. The resentment.

The fucking brutal pain.

He used to be a storm of power and hostility, the attributes intimately entwined to make him a force to be reckoned with. At least that was what I'd thought, until he started delving in things only a weak man would entertain.

Now I see it as nothing more than a show.

A facade to hide his deficiencies.

Two men flank him, providing protection, their faces unfamiliar.

All three of them approach, inspiring a wave of whispers to break out among the mourners. The respect my father wordlessly demands is enough to make the officiant stop his fabricated remake of Richard's life and stand at attention.

Game on.

It's time for me and my sisters to fake our loyalty.

"Dad." Layla's the first to greet him, the two of them sharing an awkward embrace that is interrupted by Stella squeezing between them.

"Grandpa? I didn't think you were going to make it."

"I couldn't stay at home when I knew you needed me." He runs a hand through her hair, the action taunting my restraint. "Nothing could stop me from coming to take care of my little button."

My niece beams up at him, her grief seeming momentarily forgotten.

"Father." I hold the disgust from my tone and reach out a hand. "I'm glad you could make it."

"Thank you for taking care of everything. Even though you didn't bother to wait for me." He clasps me in a grip with unyielding strength. "We've got a lot to discuss once this is over."

His tone almost holds a threat as he steps back to settle between me and Layla, his men moving in behind him. He encourages Stella to stand at his feet with the wave of a hand, and holds the little girl's shoulders as the crowd stares.

Vengeance rushes through my veins. Anguish pounds in my chest.

"Where's Keira?" His question is low. Almost indecipherable.

"To your left." I jerk my chin in her direction and find her huddled into Decker, her suffering seeming to outweigh everyone in attendance despite her lack of grief.

What everyone doesn't realize is her tears are for the man beside me. The one she wants to see six feet under.

"She's temperamental at the moment." I don't know what else to tell him. Obviously, the truth isn't an option. "She hasn't been doing well."

He nods. "I should've come back sooner. Girls always need their father at a time like this."

I could laugh. I probably should. That way, the building resentment might have an outlet. Instead, I grit my teeth and try to ignore the men behind me, despite their proximity raising the hair on the back of my neck.

I don't trust them. I don't even trust my own flesh and blood after a lifetime trusting nothing but.

"Are you okay if we continue?" the officiant asks.

"Yes." I incline my head and the man proceeds with his elaborate fiction about Richard while I focus on pushing myself toward a resolution my sister will appreciate.

Hunter is already on standby. All I need to do is say the word and this train wreck will start rolling forward.

I'll get my father alone, confront him about the mess he's made, then look him in the fucking eye when I tell him his fate.

It's the only way. With respect and honor.

I refuse to make a sneak attack. I can't stab him in the back even though he's stabbed me in mine.

The officiant's words trail off, and I fight to understand the sudden quiet. Then the coffin lowers, the foot of space it descends enough to make Stella wail. Her grandfather comforts her by rubbing his hands down her arms. The same hands that have molested many and scarred more.

He shouldn't be touching her—shouldn't be anywhere near her innocence. The horrified look Layla gives me tells she's come to the same judgment.

"I'd now like to call upon anyone who would like to place petals or sand in the grave as a personal goodbye." The officiant meets my gaze, offering my family the first opportunity to take from his small wicker basket.

Luther sidesteps Stella to move forward, away from his guards. He grabs a handful of petals as he passes, every person in attendance watching his movements. He scatters the offering, the gentle show of mourning leaving a bitter taste in my mouth, before he kisses his clenched fist and thumps it down on the coffin.

The bang reverberates through the crowd, stealing gasps and making the people before me jump in unison. None more so than Keira.

But it's not her shock stealing my attention. It's the man behind her who jostles his way to the front of the crowd, bumping Decker's shoulder in the process.

He's either drunk or suicidal. Maybe both.

"Luther Torian?" He calls the name loudly, without remorse.

My father bristles, every inch of him tightening in what I learned at an early age to be vehemence. He scowls, not hiding his hostility.

The man doesn't quit his approach. He strides forward, holding his hand out for my father to take.

That's when it hits me.

The reality.

The trap.

Right before the man says, "I'm Special Agent Anthony Easton, and you're under arrest for human trafficking." The fucker clasps my father's palm with his right hand and retrieves a pair of cuffs with his left. "And solicitation involving minors under the age of sixteen."

A mutiny of whispered retaliation rises from the crowd, the noise building into chatter. The only quiet souls are my siblings and the people who know the severity of this situation. Not just the criminal charges, but the complication of a prison sentence.

"You have the right to remain silent."

"No." I storm forward. "*Stop.*"

This asshole isn't going to steal vengeance away from me. My father's punishment is my decision to make. If Luther is taken into custody, there's no doubt he'll escape, then disappear.

"What the fuck do you think you're doing?" I hold my anger in check, my voice coming out in a lethal calm.

The agent doesn't pause. "Anything you say can and will be used against you in a court of law."

My father's men move forward, only to stop dead at the sudden shift in the crowd. A mass of strangers nudge their way through the familiar faces, holding their FBI badges high.

Jesus. *Fuck.*

I chance a glance at Keira, finding her in panic mode, her body facing Decker, her hands wrapped in his white button-down as if begging for help.

Hunter and Sarah look at me for guidance. Luca and Benji, too.

They're all waiting for instructions. All my men are.

But what do I tell them? What the fuck do I do?

This can't end in a blood bath. Not with women and children in attendance. We can't fight our way out of this.

The agent continues reciting the Miranda rights as he hikes my father's hands behind his back. Not one word leaves the mighty Luther Torian's lips. There's no spite. Not even a glimpse of the rage I'm feeling.

Everything is locked down. Shut off.

I meet his stare and jerk my chin the slightest inch, letting him know I'm strong. Fucking defensive. He needs to think I'm on his side. That's the only play I have. The only strategy available.

"Everyone, move," a woman shouts. "Make way."

The female agent steals my attention as she spreads her arms wide and keeps my extended family at bay.

I stalk to her, my fists clenched at my sides. "What the hell do you think you're doing?" I keep my tone level. "This is a fucking funeral."

She raises a brow. "Please accept my sincerest apologies for the inconvenient timing." She flicks her attention toward my father and proceeds to ignore my existence.

Who the fuck does she think she is?

We're not a family to be messed with. Not even by the Feds.

"We've done this dance a dozen times before," I seethe. "You make an arrest. Then the charges are dropped. But this is going too fucking far. You can't come here and tear apart a place of mourning. Do you have any idea who you're messing with?"

Her lips kick into a sultry smile, exposing a viper beneath the feminine facade. "I know exactly what I'm doing, Mr. Torian. I'm putting a sick son of a bitch behind bars for a very long time. If I were you, I'd get my legal team in order. It's not just your father who's going to need it."

My pulse doesn't spike; it fucking detonates. The simmering madness I've been carrying turns into full-scale psychosis.

I see red. I hear static. I crave revenge.

"You've got some nerve, throwing your weight around, sweetheart." I scrutinize her eyes, looking deep into the hazel-green depths to try and grasp the slightest glimmer of fear. But this woman isn't scared of me. She's not even threatened. Not yet, anyway. "The FBI has nothing on me and my family. Never have. Never will."

"I wouldn't be so sure." Her grin remains in place. "In fact, I think we're going to be seeing a lot of each other in the near future." She glances away, seeming unconcerned with the threat standing right in front of her as she watches my father being hauled around headstones.

"Until next time, Mr. Torian." Briefly, those taunting eyes meet mine and she winks. "Enjoy your day."

She strides away, head high, shoulders straight, and a careless sway to her hips.

I clench my fists tighter, my nostrils flaring.

Maybe I'm closer to my father's perversions than I thought, because I want nothing more than to take her down. To watch her suffer. To make her pay.

But this woman is far from weak. There's no hint of vulnerability.

"What did she say to you?" Keira reaches my side, Decker close at her back, Sarah and Hunt following behind.

"A lot of things." I grind my teeth, still fighting for the illusive calm that's nowhere in sight. "She has the impression we're going to be seeing a lot of each other in the future."

"She said that?" Sarah snarls over Decker's shoulder. "She comes to your uncle's funeral, arrests your father, then lays more threats?"

Yes. That's exactly what she did.

With a fucking wink.

"What are you going to do?" Decker juts his chin at me. "Apart from the legal team moving into action, what's your plan?"

I return my focus to the female agent sauntering toward the mass of parked cars along the narrow cemetery road.

She poked a bear.

Fucking taunted a predator.

"I'm going to give that woman exactly what she wants."

1

TORIAN

One week later

I DRUM my fingers along the steering wheel of the rental, deliberately keeping my hands busy.

One lapse in concentration and I'll succumb. I'll pull over and slide out of this car to approach my favorite special agent on her ritual five-mile jog instead of stalking her from afar.

The temptation of being face-to-face has taunted me for days. But this morning isn't the right moment to have our reunion.

Not yet.

I need to bide my time and ignore the enticing sweat-slicked exercise gear hugging her body like a second skin.

I thought I'd be immune to her haughty sterility by now. Desensitized. Turns out, she's had the opposite effect.

I'm itching to play with her. To mess with her head, just like she's messed with mine.

Every morning, she runs circles around the city streets, each step like fuel to a fucking wet dream. Her cheeks are slicked with wisps of dark, shoulder-length hair, her skin flushed.

She pushes herself to the limit, always slaying the same path, never stopping, not even pausing for breath. She doesn't smile at people as they pass. There's no friendly hello or gentle finger wave.

Ms. Fox is the queen of hostility, keeping herself at a distance from any unnecessary human contact.

Turns out, she doesn't have a lot of friends. Not that her solo status is a surprise, with her prickly personality. The woman doesn't just have resting bitch face; it's more an expression of overly enthusiastic aggression.

There's minimal family, too.

Her mother is dead, and her ex-FBI father left the scene a while ago, with the suspicion of his crimes probably more familiar to me than they are to his own daughter.

She's all alone, which makes these secret moments of ours all the more intimate.

It's just the two of us.

Me and her.

Even though she's not aware.

The best time to watch her is early morning. At sunrise. When her clothes are flattering and her motivation is high.

She's far more alluring now than during office hours when she hides her figure behind masculine business suits.

Ninety percent of the time she insists upon dressing like a man. It's clear she's overcompensating for the lack of appendage between her thighs. The FBI is a men's club. Always has been. Probably always will be.

A woman with her lack of physical flaws would struggle to gain respect since she's a walking, talking turn-on. I think that's why she never gentles her expression. She's always harsh: either aggressive with her arrogance or spiteful with her intimidation.

There's no softness to her. It's all stiff shoulders and tight features.

But not for too much longer. I'll weaken her. Soon.

She's going to regret fucking with me.

I'll make sure of it. Take pleasure in it.

I just need to ignore the building anticipation urging me to get this show underway, and enjoy the foreplay.

It's not like I'm stupid enough to think she's oblivious to the eyes she has on her.

She's a smart woman. She's aware her actions have consequences.

Right now is the perfect example. She slows to a walk as she approaches her favorite coffee shop, her gaze trekking the street as she pushes open the glass door.

She's always searching.

She never finds what she's looking for.

I use a different car each day. Sometimes I'm on foot. Today, though, I pull to the curb at the end of her block and focus inside the cafe, watching as she takes her headphones out to place them in her pocket.

She knows someone is close. How couldn't she?

The list of criminals she's fucked over is a mile long, and I'm at the top of her list. This pretty little thing would be well aware of my history of retaliation. My reputation speaks for itself.

But is she aware I haven't outsourced the surveillance to my men?

Not entirely, anyway.

It isn't Hunter who witnesses the dimming of her apartment light every night. Luca and Decker don't trail her through her morning routine.

I do.

The last week of predatory stalking has become a favored pastime. A sport. I've grown to appreciate the shared parts of our lives.

It's even got to the point where my pulse spikes whenever I lay eyes on her. The dose of anticipation increases every damn day.

It's a fucking drug.

I live for it.

Crave it.

I'm impatient, waiting for the moment when I get to wipe her smug smile from my memory. The one she etched into my mind at my uncle's funeral. I'll replace the expression with something beautiful. Something full of fear and panic.

The shock of parted lips.

The horror of wide, shimmering eyes.

She needs to learn the dynamic here in Portland. I want to show her who holds the power. I plan to teach her that lesson over and over until her soul is crushed with the weight of her mistakes.

The Feds can't threaten me.

They have no control here. Not over my family.

They may provide a temporary inconvenience. But that's all it is. An annoyance. A mere disruption to a flawless system.

"You're mine, Ms. Fox."

I continue with the *tap, tap, tap* of my fingers, the beat growing faster to match my pulse. My fun for the day is going to end soon. I can feel the seconds ticking down.

When my cell rings from the passenger seat, I glare through the annoyance, never taking my gaze from Anissa as she hands payment to the cashier.

I already know who's responsible for the intrusion. Hunter. It always is at this time of morning.

I snatch the device and connect the call. "What is it?"

"Are you ready for me to take over?"

I withhold my instinctive response.

I could spend all day staring at this woman, daydreaming about the moment I get to speak to her again. The threats I'll promise. The taunts I'll make. But exposing my obsession is a weak move. I need to remain focused.

My father is still in custody. And Keira is a constant thorn in my side, her lack of faith in me growing every day.

"Yeah," I mutter. "Soon. Where are you?"

"In a rental on the other side of the street. A woman in red is just about to walk by me."

I drag my focus from the café to the sidewalk, finding the lady in red, then Hunt behind the wheel of a beat-up blue minivan.

"Nice wheels."

"Thanks," he grates. "I'm switching it up to stay off the radar."

"Where's your babysitter?" I return my attention to the shopfront and ignore the way my chest tightens when my gaze locks onto my target.

Hunt knows I'm referring to his fiancée. What I hope he doesn't realize is my attempt to waste time as I steal a few more precious moments with my prey.

"Sarah decided to bow out of the surveillance gig for a few days. There's not enough action to keep her happy."

"Interesting." I watch as my mark smiles at the barista, grabs her coffee, and hustles from the cafe. There's no bagel this morning. Or maybe she buys a croissant. I never know what she carries in her paper bag. "You better make sure you've got Sarah on a tight leash. If she starts whispering in Keira's ear I'll—"

"She's not doing a damn thing to Keira. I've got her under control."

"About time."

"Speaking of time. Have you heard any news on your father's court appearance? Do we have a date?"

Anissa approaches the street and looks both ways. Like always, I stiffen, wondering, waiting to see if she'll find me sitting here.

I'm like a fucking junkie in need of a fix.

But she doesn't discover my hiding place. She doesn't even come close as she starts to cut through the light traffic to get to her apartment on the other side of the street.

"I'll have more information today. Don't worry; you'll be the first to hear."

"The first?" Hunt pauses, and I can already sense the direction of his thoughts. "What happened to your new lapdog?"

"My new one?" His annoyance at Luca's promotion has been a constant point of contention. He doesn't appreciate being second best, which was the entire point of the exercise. "Are you implying you were the previous lapdog?"

"I've never been your bitch," he growls. "Never will be. Unlike Luca, I've got a fucking backbone. But you know as well as I do that I'm the best person to have at your side."

"He does his job. I have no complaints. And I'm pretty sure you were one of his cheerleaders when he got you and Sarah out of that warehouse alive." I cut the ignition and slump back in my seat. "You, on the other hand, fucking betrayed me."

"Jesus Christ," he mutters. "Not this shit again."

"It will continue to be this shit until I quit questioning your loyalty."

Anissa reaches the door of her apartment building and stops before the security panel to enter her three-digit code. I can't help reciting the numbers in my head as her finger works across the buttons. *One-four-eight.* Her deceased mother's birthday.

It was too fucking easy for Decker to get the information. A heat-sensor camera focused on the keypad was all it took. The additional pinhole device he planted between the brickwork was overkill. But I've taken advantage of the screen time it provides.

I watch her more often than I care to admit, trying to read what's going on behind those hard eyes.

Like every morning this week, she disappears inside with another cautionary glance over her shoulder. And like every morning this week, I ignore my disappointment at her not finding me.

In another forty-five minutes, she'll be back, showered, dressed, and wearing one of those fucking suits I've grown to hate. But I won't be here. I need to return to the family restaurant and concentrate on the things that matter.

Things like my father's fucking court case, and the shipment of blow that came in ten bricks short.

"Just let me do my fucking job," Hunt growls.

"Unfortunately, I can't. Trust is important. I hope this is a lesson you won't forget."

Like Keira, he recently showed his allegiance to someone other than me. Information was withheld. Friendship came before the family.

That shit is never acceptable. And he should know; he was the one who previously punished those who betrayed me.

"Don't even fucking start," he snarls. "We've gone over this. I've told you. I've explained. So either man the fuck up and let it go. Or tell me to cut and run, and I'll walk out of here and never look back. I'm sick of being treated like an ex you want to bang when it's convenient, but can't stand the sight of every other second of the day."

"Nice analogy," I drawl. "Fits perfectly."

He mutters a string of curses under his breath. And yeah, I get it. He's pissed at me. He's pissed at himself.

That's the price he has to pay for making mistakes.

If I let it slide without penalty, any motherfucker will think he can run rings around me. Hunt's just lucky very few people know about his blunder.

"Look, we're as good as we're going to get for now." I glance up at Anissa's window on the fifth floor, hoping to catch another glimpse. "Luca will remain at my side. But I have plans for you. Ones I can't entrust with anyone else."

"What plans?"

"We'll speak later."

I won't discuss the necessity for a recruitment drive, even on a burner. Not when I've been paranoid enough to switch phones every other day.

We have to boost our numbers. Expand our presence. Increase our power. All outstanding favors need to be claimed. Anyone with even a glimpse of loyalty has to be enlisted into my outer circles to keep my family safe.

And Hunt is the guy I want on the job. He sees through the bullshit, sometimes better than I do. And when my focus is shot to shit, it's a smart move to let him do what he does best.

"Fine. I'll meet you back at the restaurant this afternoon." There's another pause. "You can leave now. I've got her covered."

I don't appreciate the nudge. Or the reminder he's going to be taking over my part in this game.

I hate anyone else's involvement. If I had my way, I'd be the only player. I want full responsibility.

Unfortunately, my empire won't run itself.

"I'll leave when I'm ready," I mutter.

Which doesn't feel like it's going to be anytime soon.

I disconnect the call and throw the cell to the passenger seat.

My hands return to the steering wheel, my fingers tapping out an agitated rhythm, but it's the devil on my shoulder causing the burn in my chest.

I've denied the impulse to mess with her for longer than I thought possible. I've fought and fought the nagging urge even though anticipation has had me by the balls.

I don't think fighting will be enough today.

I need something more. The slightest hint of her apprehension. The sweetest taste of her fear.

I'm going to have to succumb.

Just a little.

As much as I don't want to buckle, it's time to start toying with my prey.

2

ANISSA

You run like a gazelle. I should know—I'm someone who loves to hunt.

I sprint out the last of my five-mile run. It isn't difficult. Spurring my legs to move faster despite the fatigue is easy when I'm being followed.

I've known for almost two weeks. Since before the flowers started to arrive with their taunting notes.

Being aware of my tail before they deliberately announced their existence wasn't because my watchers are novices. In fact, it's the opposite.

I've never seen them. It's the raised hair on the back of my neck making their presence known. Pure instinct.

I'd anticipated the retaliation after my outburst at the funeral. I hadn't been able to bite my tongue. For once, I lacked my usual restraint because victory had been too invigorating not to bask in its glory.

One failed investigation after another had led to Luther's arrest. Finally, we'd taken him into custody, and I'd struggled to curb my need to gloat.

It then proved impossible when his son, the formidable Cole Torian, had tried to talk his way out of the situation using intimidation and threats. That dark, soulless gaze had been fixed on me. Conniving. Vindictive. He'd wanted to squash me like a bug, and in that moment, I decided I'd prefer him to see me as more of a lion than a cockroach.

I'd stared the devil in the eye, and without any subtlety, I kinda told him to go fuck himself, adding a provoking wink for good measure.

Euphoria had shot through me, the thrill entirely worth the death sentence his expression had promised. At least, that was what I'd thought at the time.

Now, I'm not so sure.

Your body is a masterpiece, but your screams will be my symphony.

The deliveries keep coming. Every day for the last five days. Roses, lilies, carnations, irises. Yesterday, tulips.

After the first bouquet, I didn't accept another offering. I refused the blooms and only took the cards. Those tiny envelopes, with their delightful messages from my secret admirer, are all the evidence I need.

I just have to find a way to tie them to a source.

Problem is, I'm not entirely sure who the sender is. The florist won't help without a warrant, and the list of potential candidates is mighty long. Even narrowing my search to the latest investigation leaves me with more options than I'd like—Luther, Cole, and Decker. I've also made threats toward Hunter and Sarah, so those two can't be ignored.

Any one of them would want revenge. It's merely a case of who's willing to claim it.

The advantage is in their court, especially when I haven't mentioned the constant tail to my supervisor.

I can't.

I kept the heated exchange with Cole from my report, too.

My presence in this department has been a point of contention since my father left his badge behind to join the dark side. Without a word, he disappeared, removing every penny from his bank account to start a new life among the crime rings he'd spent the majority of his adult life trying to disband.

Now he's dead to me. As far as I'm concerned, I lost both parents the night my mother died, but the taint of his actions still linger.

Nobody here trusts me. Well, I don't trust that they trust me. Not really. They don't have my back, and I don't fucking care. I've always worked on my own anyway.

It's their judgment that kills me. They think I'm a traitor, too. They expect that I'm a hair-trigger away from packing my bags and switching to a life of crime.

It didn't fucking help when my only informant inside the Torian organization chose to take the same path as my father. Apparently, I'm a magnet for turncoats.

Or, if I listen to the taunting whispers inside the bureau, I'm a recruiter for the other side.

A fucking leper.

So keeping my slip-up from the funeral to myself is important. And I refuse to let anyone think I'm weak and in need of surveillance. I can handle these threats on my own.

Do you dream of me? Because I dream about what I'm going to do to you.

My anger leaves no room for fear.

Instead, I work harder, sprinting faster, pushing myself further until I reach the café doors in a panting, sweating mess.

I suck gulps of air into my lungs as I wipe the dampness from my face and succumb to the uncomfortable shiver at the back of my neck.

I glance over my shoulder and scan the sidewalk.

They're here. Somewhere. They, he or her.

It doesn't matter that I can't see the culprit. There's only a street filled with parked cars and what appears to be innocent pedestrians pacing along the cement, but they're here. I can feel it.

The mornings and evenings are the worst. I don't know why. I don't think I want to know. It's bad enough that my entire body gets blanketed in goose bumps whenever I leave my apartment to exercise, and then again when I return home from work.

Their presence shadows the start and end of every day.

But it can't last forever. Whoever it is will grow tired before I become scared.

Not long now, little fox. Not long at all.

I push open the café door and walk inside, determined to put their existence to the back of my mind.

Today is about celebration. Luther Torian is making a court appearance, and I get to witness the magnificence. Nothing can drag me down from the heightened anticipation of seeing him in cuffs. His suffering will make my hardships worthwhile.

The barista meets my gaze as I approach, her subtle nod a confirmation of my order. She's run off her feet. Like always. The line of customers are banked up like a traffic jam.

There's a reason I come here to join the weary queue, and it has nothing to do with the convenience of the café being directly across the street from my apartment and everything to do with the strong coffee and creamy aftertaste.

"The usual?" the cashier asks over the hiss of steam from the machine making the heavenly liquid.

"Yeah. Thanks." I shove a hand into the gauze pocket in the side of my leggings, my fingers grazing the crinkled bills as a skitter of awareness shoots up my spine.

A figure moves to stand close. The large frame right by my side.

"Allow me," a man offers.

I freeze, watching as a hand reaches out, offering payment, the material of a tailored suit jacket entering my peripheral vision.

I know the voice. I've heard it ring in my ears. Whisper into my dreams. Murmur through my nightmares.

It's the friendly tone that's unfamiliar. The deep, smooth words drift over my skin, making the hairs on the back of my neck dance.

"No. Thanks." I scoot my money along the counter. "I've got this."

I don't look at him. I won't risk letting him hear my thoughts.

"I insist." He inches his fingers farther, creating a race toward the cashier that I'm loath to participate in.

"Again, *thanks*," I grate, "but the Bureau frowns upon agents accepting gifts from criminals." I speak loud enough for my accusation to be heard by the line of people waiting for their morning solace.

It's another taunt. A mistake. One I'm too pathetic to resist.

I glare at the cashier, silently demanding she take my money while I wait for Cole Torian to retaliate.

Instead, he chuckles, the thickly rich sound sinking into me along with the woodsy scent of his expensive cologne. "I've got a clean record, Niss. So there's no need to fear."

He lets the sentence linger. The last word hovers in the air between us like a threat before he gently nudges in front of me and places his cash directly in the hand of the slack-jawed woman I seriously want to slap.

I should turn around and walk out. I should… But my addiction to caffeine and the allure of withstanding his intimidation becomes a living, breathing thing inside me as I stalk to the serving station to await my order.

I continue my refusal to make eye contact. I won't give him the satisfaction of my attention, not when I'm unsure if my emotions are masked.

"Why are you walking away?" He follows behind me, stopping on the fringes of my personal space. "You said we were going to be seeing a lot of each other. Then you didn't call. You didn't text. I'm beginning to think you led me on."

My pulse spikes and I pivot to face him. "Don't—"

I snap my mouth shut at the grin he beams at me. The provoking, manipulative curve of lips.

"Don't what?" His deep blue eyes glisten, his enjoyment crystal clear.

My heart rate becomes a crescendo, the growing beats transforming into a throbbing pound in my ears.

He's playing with me. Toying. And it's all my fault.

I started this game. I whacked the hornet nest and thought I could get away with it. But I'm not going to be terrorized. Not now. Not ever.

I'm immune to his charm. I don't see the beauty in him, not like all the women around me seem to.

Those dark eyes are threatening, not mesmerizing. The thick eyelashes. The chocolate hair. The richly tanned skin with enough stubble to increase his masculinity. It all means nothing.

Nothing.

He's packaged strategically. To lure his prey.

And I won't be enticed toward that web.

"Mr. Torian." I raise my voice above polite conversation in an attempt to gain an audience. "I don't think it's appropriate for you to be speaking to me seeing as though your actions are constantly under FBI scrutiny."

His shoulder lifts in a faint shrug. "You've got nothing to worry—"

"And don't you have more important things to do this morning?" I speak over the top of him, one brow cocked. "I thought you'd be making your way to court. Your father's case is going to make headlines. It's definitely an event I won't miss."

Those dark ocean eyes remain on mine. The smile holds in place. But something waivers. There's the slightest change in him to make the charming expression turn forced.

Good.

I've struck a chord.

If he doesn't leave, I'll strike many more.

"I understand the hostility." He reaches out an arm and checks his watch. "And yes, I assume my father is being transported to the courthouse as we speak. That's why I'm here. I'd like to offer a truce."

"A truce?" The question escapes my lips without my permission.

"Yes." He loses the grin and quits the playboy act to stare at me with a solemn facade. "I want to clear my name and any misconceptions you might have. I don't want to be associated with my father's crimes."

"Misconceptions?"

The cashier slides my coffee and an apricot Danish encased in a paper bag across the collection counter and murmurs my name.

"I don't have any misconceptions." I step forward to claim my bag and travel cup, then indulge in a sip. "Only cold, hard facts. I know exactly what type of man you are. There's no need to waste your breath."

He follows me, stepping close and lowering his voice. "You may not agree with the way I do business, but I'm not anything like my father."

"The way you do business?" I keep repeating him. I can't help it. His insanity is worth hearing more than once. "That's a delusional way of describing what you do."

"I'm nothing but a ruthless businessman."

"Ruthless, with stalking tendencies, right?"

The accusation isn't a stab in the dark. He came here looking for me, which means he already knew my routine.

"I wouldn't call this stalking." He flashes me a flawless grin. "I asked a colleague or two about your habits, and they led me here. I don't think there's anything wrong with that, do you?"

I wave a hand in the direction of his face. "Intimidation, threats, lies, and now flirtation? You really do have a remarkable set of skills. But none of them will work on me. I suggest you quit while you're ahead."

I start for the doors, his footsteps following close behind.

"You've got the wrong idea. I just want to talk."

Despite the calm tone, there's a wealth of authority in his voice. He's used to being obeyed. He's perfected the art of coercion.

"I'll tell you whatever you want to know." He maneuvers around me, cutting me off before I reach the door. "What do you have to lose?"

"My integrity." I stop, not wanting to barrel into him. I'm sure his heat is enough to scar. "My self-respect."

"You don't know me." Again, he's calm. Collected. He's entirely locked down, but there's the slightest hint of panic in his eyes.

He needs this.

Why?

"I don't want to know you," I drawl.

He raises his chin as if offended. "I understand that. But you want to know the facts, right? You want to learn the truth."

I scrutinize him, trying to understand his hidden motives. He's not making sense. Cole Torian doesn't beg. He never shows weakness.

Something must be amiss in his magical world of criminal activity to have him scrambling for my attention.

The possibilities eat away at my curiosity. That hyper-sensitive skin at the back of my neck regains its tingle.

"I've already told you I've got places to be this morning." I focus outside, trying to fight the wicked web he's weaved. "I can give you five minutes. Nothing more."

"That works for me."

He takes the lead, moving away from the door. But I can't follow. My feet are cemented in place, the instinct to flee scratching at my skin.

I should call this in. Or request assistance. Even a silent witness.

Then again, it's just a conversation. No other agent would show anything but excitement at this opportunity. Unless they had a tarnished reputation.

"Anissa?" His voice brushes my ear, the material of his suit grazing my arm. "We can take the empty table next to the window."

"Yeah. Okay." I nod, my mind made up, and push past him to lead the way toward the front corner of the cafe, the glass window providing an unrestricted view of the sidewalk.

I take the far seat and place my paper bag on the table, my back to the wall while his remains exposed to the room.

"I assume you won't protest the need to record this conversation." I pull my cell from the Velcro strap stretched across my bicep and place it between us.

"Not at all."

I expected a refusal. This man is definitely full of surprises today.

"Good." I place my coffee down and swipe through the cell screen until I find the voice recorder. "You can get started whenever you're ready."

He eyes me, those navy depths examining me closely. "You're going to fight this friendship every step of the way, aren't you?"

I don't bite. I refuse.

He's trying to get me to admit to a non-existent relationship, one that will worsen my position within the Bureau, and I won't let it happen.

He won't gain the upper hand here.

I sigh. "What's this about, Cole? What's the game?"

"There's no game." He leans back in his chair, the picture of relaxation. "I just want to make both our lives easier. You keep trying to pin me for crimes I haven't committed. You even planted an informant to gain evidence that doesn't exist. What will it take to make this stop?"

I press my lips tight, feigning contemplation while I push aside the unwanted reminder of my defective narc. "I don't know, maybe when you quit breaking the law we can all get along."

"Then why do I get the distinct impression you won't be satisfied until you see me behind bars?"

"Maybe that's what you deserve."

He cocks his head. "Because you think I'm guilty of the same atrocities as my father."

I sigh. "I think we're getting sidetracked here. My opinion doesn't count. The evidence is all that matters."

"And there is no evidence. You'll never tie me to my father's crimes."

"Is that because you're smarter at covering your tracks?"

His eyes narrow. His irritation quick to ignite. "No, it's because I was never involved." His tone is vehement, the words dripping with conviction.

I could almost believe him. *Almost.* If I were high and insanely stupid.

Unfortunately for him, I'm neither.

"Even if you didn't participate, there's no way you wouldn't have been aware of what Richard and Luther were doing. And the fact you stood by while women were manipulated, escorted from the country, then sold as sex slaves, makes you an accomplice."

"There." He points a finger at the table. "That right there is an unfounded misconception."

"For now," I drawl. "It's only a matter of time before misconceptions become facts."

His jaw tics, his building anger entirely delicious. "I'm a businessman, Niss. A successful entrepreneur. I don't have the time or inclination to keep up-to-date with my father's activities."

"I don't think entrepreneurship extends to the drug trade. Do you?"

His nostrils flare. "That's yet another unfounded accusation."

"That part of your reputation is far from unfounded." I take a sip of coffee, trying to disguise my annoyance. "Do you think we're not aware of how you run your business? You set up your lower ranks to take the fall. That's all part of the deal. You pay them beyond their wildest dreams, but the drawcard is the possibility of prison time if the shit hits the fan. Isn't that what happened to Trenton White and Samuel Puglisi? One of your deals went bad, and they took the hit. But hey, I guess you should be commended for looking after their wives and children while they rot in a cell."

Cole sighs, and reaches out his arm, taking another look at his watch.

I should be doing the same. The court case will start in roughly ninety minutes. Just enough time for me to shower, dress, and get my ass across town.

"Regretting your decision already?" I muse. "Did my insight hit a little too close to the mark? Or have you had enough of this delightful conversation already?"

"I see this as less of a conversation and more of a trial." He crosses his arms, making the collared shirt beneath his jacket cling tight to his chest. "When you're ready to stop the accusations and have a civilized discussion, please let me know."

"Don't reach for the sympathy card, Cole. Not with all the horrors your family have inflicted."

I take a gulp of java, throwing it back like a shot.

Fuck him.

Seriously, fuck this manipulative prick for thinking he can gain any understanding from me.

He won't change my opinion. I'll never see him as anything other than a waste of possibilities.

It's obvious he's attractive. His intelligence isn't in question either. A stupid man could never have risen in power, expanding his family's grasp further and tighter, without a glimpse of brilliance.

But he could've been so much more. An academic. A doctor. A politician. Even an entrepreneur who made millions from something legitimate instead of criminal.

"I'm not after sympathy, Nissa."

That's another thing I despise. The deliberately taunting way he takes liberties with my name. Nobody calls me Niss. Or Nissa. I've only ever been Anissa. Or Fox.

"Good." I hold his gaze and smile. "Because you'll never get it."

My cell vibrates on the table, the incoming call from my supervisor. "I need to take this."

Cole sits forward. "By all means, answer the call, but I'm not going to wait around." He pushes his chair back, poised to stand. "Either you talk to me, or him."

Him. Taggert.

I'm not surprised he recognized the name on my screen.

"You're not making it a hard decision when you haven't told me anything of value." I raise a brow, waiting as my cell continues to trill. "I'm still not sure why you're wasting my time."

"It wouldn't be a waste, Nissie, if you asked questions instead of running your mouth."

Nissie.

Fucking. Nissie.

This asshole has crawled under my skin like a plague of parasites. Problem is, I've already succumbed. I'm here, ready and waiting. And if I leave without a thread of valuable insight, I'll look an even bigger fool.

"Fine." I reject the call. "You claim you didn't know what your father was doing. How is that possible?"

He stills, not only in his movements, but in his expression.

He's considering lying to me.

Not a smart move when my patience is threadbare.

"I confess." He raises his hands in surrender. "I *was* aware."

My heart stills in shock and I glance down at my cell. *Fuck.* The recording stopped when the call came through.

Fuck. Fuck. *Fuck.*

"You didn't get that on the record?" he taunts. "What a shame."

I breathe through the anger, not letting him get to me. "How long before?"

"Since Richard went to hospital." He glances at his watch again, seeming bored with the topic. "My father offered me the lucrative position my uncle held within their organization. Apparently, there's a lot of money in sex trafficking."

I don't appreciate the candor. The complete and utter lack of empathy.

"Have some respect," I seethe. "A lot of those women were raped and murdered for sport. I don't know how you can look yourself in the mirror with their torture on your conscience."

"I knew about it, but I wasn't involved. Never have been and never will be."

"How noble of you." My sarcasm is profound. I could win an Academy Award for the performance. I could also have a stroke from the potency of my rage. "Do you really expect praise just because you didn't take a golden handshake from the scum of the earth? Those women continued to suffer until me and my colleagues could pull together enough evidence to arrest your father."

His eyes narrow, the intense depths turning spiteful. "Are you that naive to think his arrest helped their situation?" He scoffs. "You've got no idea what you've done by putting him behind bars."

"Then tell me."

There are still a million leads to follow in Luther's case. A myriad of tangled threads to unravel before we determine how many women he abducted. And we're not getting anywhere with his father's refusal to answer questions.

"Tell me what we've done," I repeat.

The trill of my cell breaks the moment, stealing away the glimmer of insight I'm dying to hear. I lower my gaze to read *Taggert* across the screen again. *Shit.* He's going to be pissed I've ignored him, but I'm finally getting somewhere. The smoke and mirrors are subsiding to reveal the truth I need.

"Please continue." I reject the call and return my gaze to Cole's. "What's changed now that Luther is behind bars?"

Yet again he's looking at his watch, his patience seeming to grow thin. "Forget it. You're needed elsewhere and I've got places to be."

"No, it's fine. I'll return the call once we're finished."

Another cell tone interrupts us, but this time it isn't mine.

"Excuse me." Cole reaches into his jacket and pulls out his phone. "Unfortunately, I'm going to have to take this."

He pushes to his feet, placing distance between me and the information I need when he connects the call. "Yeah?"

He listens for long moments, his brow furrowed. "Okay. I understand. I'll see you soon."

He lowers the device, presses the screen to end the call, and places the cell back inside his jacket. "I'm sorry. I need to leave."

"What?" I push to my feet. "You're the one who wanted this. Not me."

"Again, I apologize. It can't be helped." He gives me a sad smile, one that drips with satire. "Maybe we can reschedule."

Reschedule?

This asshole has been stalking me, invading every inch of my privacy. And now he has the balls to fuck with me?

"Or maybe not," he drawls. "Either way, don't be a stranger." He winks, and the gesture is so familiar I want to stab myself for doing it to him at the funeral.

He lured me here, provoking me, and I fell for it.

He starts for the door, dismissing me as if I don't exist.

"What the hell was this, Cole?" I stalk after him. "Did you come here just to waste a few minutes of my day? Because I can assure you, it takes more than that to piss me off."

"This hasn't been a waste." He keeps walking, only to stop suddenly before me. "Actually, before I leave, there's one thing I've been meaning to ask you."

I glare, my fury rising because I don't understand his motive. He's inspired a wealth of questions inside me only to deny me at the last second, and now he wants me to play nice?

He turns to face me, his brows tight as if he's deep in thought. "Why do you insist on wearing those masculine pantsuits to work when the little black dress in the back of your closet would look ten times better?"

My stomach drops. It completely bottoms out.

Everything inside me hollows as I quickly realize this meeting wasn't about misconceptions; it was purely about payback. His presence is entirely based on a threat.

He stares, waiting for a reply I can't give. I *won't* give.

I'm not going to release a breath of panic, or utter a word of fear. Not even when I picture him in my apartment. In my fucking closet.

"Forget it." His eyes dance with mirth. His mouth kicks at one side. "I can see I've touched a nerve. But it's definitely something you should think about. You've got great legs; you should show them off."

I fight to keep my mouth shut, my shoulders strong, and my restraint locked tight.

I won't falter.

I won't show fear.

"Enjoy your day, little fox."

3

ANISSA

I hustle from the café, my hands shaking as I cross the street and escape into the tainted sanctuary of my apartment building.

The tremble isn't from fear.

Oh, no. I refuse to let him get to me that way.

What I feel is fury. Spite. And a huge desire for retaliation.

I ride the elevator to the fifth floor and quickly rush to open my apartment. I'm already running late, which I'm sure was Cole's plan, but I refuse to miss Luther's day in court, even when the desire to figure out how Cole got into my home is gnawing at me.

I run down the hall to my kitchen, slam my cell on the counter, then strip, leaving my sweat-soaked clothes strewn all over the floor. Then it's a mad dash to the bathroom, where I stop on the threshold at the sound of my cell.

"Damn it." I rush back to the kitchen and read the screen. *Taggert*. "Shit."

One missed call is acceptable. Two means I'm in trouble, but three is a clear sign I'm about to get my ass whipped.

I swipe to connect and raise the phone to my ear. "I'm running late," I start before he can get an accusatory word in. "There was a slight change in plan."

"What kind of change?" he growls.

I contemplate keeping the truth to myself. If I could slide this under the rug along with everything else, my life would be less complicated. Unfortunately, I've hidden too much to keep track of. "I ran into Cole Torian. He sought me out and wanted to talk."

Silence greets my admission. Cold, judgmental silence.

"I took the opportunity to try and get some information out of him."

"And did you?" His tone is lethal, laced with anger and not even a hint of curiosity.

"I'm not sure. I'll need to do some research. For all I know, he was wasting my time in a vain attempt to intimidate me."

"And let me guess; you were there on your own."

"Yes, but—"

"Get to the office," he snarls.

"Sir, let me explain."

"Get to the office. *Now*."

I squeeze my eyes shut and clench my free hand into a fist. "But I planned on going to Luther's—"

The line disconnects and I'm left to despise his increased animosity toward me.

I've been a target for Taggert's anger for too damn long, and this shit is growing old. Fast. He has no right to judge me for my father's actions. I've done nothing wrong.

Nothing but let a smart-mouthed informant slip through my fingers.

I slam my cell down on the counter and stalk to the bathroom. This time, I don't even contemplate a much needed shower. I bathe Irish-style, dousing my sweat in a truckload of deodorant, before I dress in one of Cole's favorite pantsuits and head for the door.

I don't even do my hair or spare a few minutes for makeup.

If Taggert wants to see a dragon, I'll give him one.

I REACH the Bureau less than twenty minutes later and walk into my department on the third floor to find a frenzy of scrambling colleagues. Agents rush to answer phone calls. Assistants hustle to get coffee. And I start to second guess my decision to use the quiet car ride to mellow myself out instead of listening to the radio.

Something has happened.

Something that has put me in the firing line.

I cut through the war zone, increasing my pace through the middle of the partitioned desk spaces until I reach Taggert's office at the end of the building.

He's already glaring at me as I approach, his face flushed.

"Good morning," I mutter in greeting. It's a far stretch from sarcasm, but he wouldn't have missed my contempt.

"Close the door behind you."

I ignore the instinct to panic and do as he requests, closing us into the confined space and coming to stand between the two leather chairs situated before his desk. "What's going on?"

"You tell me." He leans forward, placing his elbows on the desk to steeple his fingers. "I want to know where the fuck your head's at."

"I'm sorry, but I missed the news flash. I don't know what's going on."

"Then tell me what you do know. What happened between you and Cole Torian?" he asks, as if my actions are a dirty little secret. Like I've committed a cardinal sin.

"He approached me after my run. He wanted to talk. He paid for my coffee, despite my firm refusal. End of story. I thought it would be a great opportunity to get information."

"And did you?" he drawls. "Did you actually get any information, Fox?"

"I already told you. I need to do some digging first."

He huffs out a derisive laugh. "Let me save you the time. Whatever he told you was bullshit."

"You don't know that." He couldn't. He doesn't have a clue about the basis of our conversation. "He said he—"

"He used you." The derision remains in his voice, growing thicker with each passing syllable. "He played you."

I stiffen, not appreciating the accusation even though I already know it's true.

"He was trying to keep you busy."

"He was?" My pulse grows frantic. My heart squeezes. "For what reason?"

"His father's transport van was ambushed on the way to the court house."

I don't react. I won't flinch despite the words that act like a physical blow.

"You were Cole's fucking alibi."

I raise my chin, taking the punishment as it pummels me from the inside out. "How?" My voice cracks, exposing my proximity to breaking point. "How could that happen?"

"We're still working on it. All I know is that the driver is dead and another guard has been rushed to hospital."

Nausea thickens at the back of my throat, the bitter taste growing stronger. I lower my gaze, no longer able to look him in the eye. "And Luther? What about him?"

"Gone."

I press my lips shut, fighting the need to scream. My head grows heavy, my arms and legs, too. I'm weighed down by failure. But the shame is heavier, threatening to suffocate me.

I'd known Cole had deliberately sought me out. I'd never assumed it was a coincidence. I'd just had no clue how badly he wanted to screw me over.

He'd wanted my degradation. My complete and utter humiliation.

And now he has it.

"I'll find him," I vow. "I'll get Luther back."

I have to. There's no other choice. My reputation was on its last legs before today; now it's completely shattered. I need to be the one who makes this right.

"No." Taggert's rejection hits hard. "You're going to do the opposite. I need you to take some time off."

"You're suspending me?" My gaze snaps to his. "No. Please." I take a step forward. "Don't do this."

"It's not a suspension. It's time off. You haven't taken a break in over a year."

"Forced leave is as good as a suspension. All it does is save you the paperwork."

He gives me a brittle smile. "And I thank you for it."

I keep shaking my head. Keep refusing.

No. No. No.

This is bullshit.

"It's only until Monday. You need the week to get your head on straight because it's clear you can't think to save your life at the moment."

"I don't need—"

"It's not up for discussion." He lowers his hands to the desk and pushes to his feet. "Monday. No sooner. Do you hear me?"

I grind my molars harder and harder until my jaw aches in protest.

Fuck him. Fuck Cole. Fuck the whole Torian family along with the Bureau.

I've lived and breathed their justice all my life. I knew I would be an FBI agent from the first time my dad showed me his badge with an insane amount of pride. This is my home. My existence. And it's imploding around me.

I swing around and stalk to the door, yanking it wide. The slam of the flimsy wood is my only response, the resounding bang drawing the attention of the entire department. My fellow agents stop and stare, not bothering to hide their judgment, although I'm pretty sure they don't even know what I've done. Not yet. At least, not this time.

Their intolerance is engrained.

I continue my trek toward the elevator, holding my head high despite the disgrace. How the hell am I going to face them on Monday? The distance will only make the situation worse. I'd prefer to deal with their animosity now. To answer all the questions before they have time to fester.

"You okay?" Luther Torian's arresting agent jogs to catch up with me, squeezing close to my side along the narrow walkway.

Anthony Easton is the closest thing I have to a… I don't know what to call him. He's not a friend. But he's not an asshole either.

"No." I keep pounding out the distance across the building, not willing to lose my shit in front of an audience.

"What's going on?" He follows me past the open cubicles. His heavy footfalls match mine. "Is Taggert riding your ass again?"

"Nope, not riding it. He's setting it loose."

"What?" He grabs my arm, forcing me to stop as he steps in front of me. "What does that mean?"

The concern in his expression is a trigger to the growing storm inside me. I feel my restraint slipping. One more nudge and I'll go over the edge.

"It's nothing. Don't worry. I'm just going to take the week off. That's all."

"But you don't take time off." His brow furrows. "Tell me what happened. Is he blaming you for this morning because he thinks we would've had foresight if your informant hadn't bailed?"

"Oh, God." I scrub a hand down my face. "I hadn't even thought of that."

This is too much. I can't fucking take it.

I shove past him, the remaining distance to the elevator covered in a blur.

"What the fuck is going on, Fox?" Anthony continues to follow. "Just tell me what he thinks you did."

"It's not what he thinks," I mutter. "I'm actually guilty this time."

"Of what?"

I don't want to say it. But the truth will come out while I'm gone, and I'd prefer if it wasn't explained with Taggert bias. "Cole approached me this morning. He said he wanted to talk, when what he really wanted to do was use me as an alibi for his father's escape. He's taunting me. Deliberately messing with my life."

"Oh, shit."

"Yeah, oh shit." I slam my hand against the elevator call button. "I'm not even on desk duty. Taggert wants me out of here until Monday."

He cringes. "Maybe that's for the best. You know how nasty some of these pricks can get."

"And you think me not being here will change that? It's only going to delay the inevitable and leave me out of the search for Luther." A search that I need to be a part of, goddammit.

"Forget the search. We'll catch him before the day's out. You need to concentrate on holding that temper of yours in check."

I glare at him. I keep glaring until the elevator doors open and I step inside. "I'll see you on Monday."

He moves between the doors and spreads his legs to hold them at bay. "Don't let this get to you."

I roll my eyes. That ship has well and truly set sail.

"And keep your head up," he continues. "If you can, enjoy the break while you have it. I can't remember the last time you took a vacation."

That's because I don't take them. The last thing I need are long stretches of inactivity where I'm at the mercy of my thoughts.

"Bye, Easton." I rest against the back of the enclosed space, waiting for him to move.

"Yeah, okay." He retreats. "I'll keep you updated."

It's on the tip of my tongue to tell him not to bother but the truth is, I'm dying inside knowing I won't have access to every detail of this case. "I'd appreciate it."

He juts his chin in response as the doors close between us, and all I'm left with is the walk of shame from the building.

Every step across the parking lot is filled with thoughts of retaliation. I know it's not normal for a federal agent to seek revenge. And it certainly isn't healthy. The problem is, it's what I crave, and the one thing I need to distance myself from.

These types of thoughts are for criminals. Ones like Cole Torian who take the law into their own hands.

That's never been me.

Despite my father's blood running through my veins, I'd never stoop to his level. The FBI motto is carved into my soul—fidelity, bravery, and integrity.

My fidelity is unbreakable. My bravery is in abundance. And my integrity is entirely intact.

But those attributes don't stop me from fantasizing about going entirely postal on Cole's ass. I could fucking kill that smug son of a bitch.

I stalk across the parking lot to climb into my car, grip the steering wheel, and scream. I release my rage in a mass of ear-splitting decibels. I shriek until my throat sears in protest. Then my anger escalates because I have no way to let it out.

The Torian family has been a thorn in my side for too long. Too damn long to take a back seat now. Luther is out there. He could be anywhere. With anyone. About to do anything to sate his perverted nature.

And I can't do a goddamn thing about it.

I start the ignition and slam my foot down on the accelerator, letting the rev of the engine match the roar of my heart. I'm going to take that asshole down.

I'll drag each and every one of those motherfuckers under—Cole. Hunter. The Torian sisters and the Hart brothers. I don't care if Layla's daughter gets placed in foster care. Her life will be all the better for it.

I'll destroy their family, like they destroyed so many. And I'll keep a fucking smile on my face as I do it.

I shove the car into reverse, escape the parking space, and squeal my tires out into the Portland traffic.

Is Taggert going to be pissed at my lack of control? Hell, yeah.

Do I give a flying fuck? Not a single one.

I head out of the city toward the open road, weaving in and out of traffic like a speed racer. I drive and drive and fucking drive, praying that a traffic cop will pull me over and give me an outlet for my rage. But, just like with everything else today, I don't get what I want.

Nobody approaches me. The cars I pass barely pay me attention.

I drive for more than fifty miles, and all my heart rate does is climb. There's no calm to be found. No relief. I'm still fuming when I turn the car around and retrace the miles back into Portland.

I can't stop seeing Cole's face. That provoking wink plays on a continuous loop in my mind.

I don't know what to do. There's nothing I *can* do. So I give in to temptation and head for Hillsboro Airport. I slow as I pass the wire fence to make sure cops are lying in wait for a mastermind criminal who is likely to charter a private plane out of here.

Local authorities are already on the scene. Sniffer dogs, too.

The show of force settles my nerves a little. But not enough to discourage me from taking the forty-minute drive to Troutdale Airport to do the same surveillance.

Once I find more police and unmarked cars on the scene, I crumple. I pull to the curb and slump over the steering wheel, totally and utterly disgusted in myself.

I can't do this.

I need to... *shit*. I don't know what I need, and I don't think I'm going to find the answer anytime soon.

I lean back in my seat and keep clinging to the wheel, hoping and praying something will relieve the tightened ache inside my chest. Then I pull back onto the road and try to maintain a relaxed commute.

I take a left, then a right, then a left, driving aimlessly while my pulse finally begins to quit the marathon pace. I weave through Portland. Back and forth. Side to side. I pass playgrounds and schools. Churches and sporting fields.

I don't pay attention to where I'm going. Not for a long time. Not until I find myself on a familiar street, with an even more familiar building coming up on my left.

The harmonious heart rate I worked toward starts to pound a deeper beat. A faster tempo. Slowly, I inch past the extravagant Torian family restaurant, my gaze firmly affixed to the people inside.

Couples eat. Families dine. Waitresses stroll around with trays of drinks and plates of food.

They're all naive. Ignorant to the criminal pockets they're filling.

It's disgusting.

It shouldn't be legal.

These people should know who they're giving their money to. The crimes they're supporting. The evil they're encouraging.

My stomach churns with the need to do something. My insides turn and tumble, demanding more of me than I'm supposed to give.

More and more and more until I'm forced to pull over and take action.

4

ANISSA

I cut the ignition despite the guilty nudge from my self-preservation that tells me not to. I open my door and climb out even though my throat tightens in protest. And I stalk down the sidewalk, undeterred by my reflection in the neighboring buildings that clearly point out I look like Medusa after a five-week bender.

Before I know it, my palms are splayed on the glass door of the Torian restaurant and I'm pushing my way inside.

Heads turn in my direction, the curious stares of strangers kicking my insanity back a notch.

I'm making a mistake.

I shouldn't be here. But neither should these people.

"Table for one?" A suit-clad young man approaches me, his smile more of a troubled grimace.

This guy knows crazy when he sees it, and I'm sure he's getting an eyeful looking at me.

"No... Thanks." I glance around the lavish restaurant, hating the sparkling cutlery and immaculate tablecloths. It's too pure. "I'll take a seat at the bar."

I start toward the place in question.

One drink and I'll leave. I'll douse my roller-coaster blood pressure with a taste of liquor and be on my way.

"Excuse me, miss." He rushes after me. "I'm sorry, but we only provide table service. There's no seating at the bar."

I stop dead in my tracks and try to ignore the irritating tic plucking the skin at the top of my left cheek. This poor schmuck is going to be the innocent bystander who receives the heavy weight of my wrath if he doesn't back off.

"Miss?" he repeats. "Let me seat you at a table."

"I don't want a table."

I won't be another nameless, faceless customer.

I turn to face him, pulling my badge from the inside pocket of my suit jacket. "FBI." I force a fake smile. "I'm going to take a seat at the bar."

He straightens, his back turning ramrod. "Okay... Sure." He nods, over and over. "Go ahead."

"Thank you." I keep my lips gently curved. I'm sure it exudes goodwill and peace to all as I eye those in the vicinity who think I'm the latest live-stream entertainment. "I appreciate the hospitality."

I continue to the back corner, to the beautifully crafted wooden bar with its shelves lined with expensive bottles of liquor. But the host was right; there's not a damn stool in sight. Not even one.

I slide my badge along the counter and make eye contact with the slick-haired bartender cutting up limes, letting him know I'm taking all the liberties my badge will afford me. "A mimosa, please."

He pauses his task to wipe his hand on his black slacks. "You realize we—"

"Don't do bar service? Yeah. I get it." I tap my badge. "Today, you're making an exception."

He quirks a brow, annoyed or maybe slightly impressed, as he grabs a bottle of champagne from the fridge beneath the bar and begins making my drink.

"We don't see a lot of your type around here." He adds orange juice to my glass and then slides it over.

"My type? You mean federal agents?"

"No." He grins. "I mean disheveled women who start drinking—" He checks his watch. "—before noon."

Before noon? Okay, so time hasn't slid by as fast as I thought, but they're already doing lunch service which means it can't be far off. "I'm getting in before the rush."

I grab my drink and turn to rest my back against the counter while I take the first sip. The bubbles explode on my tongue, the sugary sweetness a welcomed reprieve against my sore throat.

I contemplate addressing the room in a come-to-Jesus speech about the dangers of drugs and how supporting local crime only increases their reach. I think of how I'll shock them into losing their appetites as my delicate sips turn into large gulps.

I'm throwing back the last drops of alcoholic goodness when the bartender takes residence in my peripheral vision and asks, "Another?"

"Yeah." Fuck it. Why should I leave? "Keep 'em coming."

I'm not doing anything wrong by being here. The restaurant won't be on Cole's radar when he has his father's escape to occupy him. He's probably out living it up with his psychotic family. Drinking their own alcoholic beverages in celebration instead of commiseration.

Good for him.

Cole won this round fair and square. He poked and prodded until he gained my attention. Then he made a complete and utter fool out of me for giving him even a slight second of my day.

He'd insisted on talking to me. He wasn't going to take no for an answer.

First, he attempted to charm his way in, then he teased my curiosity with his uncharacteristic behavior. He didn't give up, his determination entirely subtle in the moment, but fucking obvious in hindsight.

Goddammit.

How many times had he glanced at his watch? On alert. Waiting.

He was counting down the minutes until his father was out of custody so he could cut and run.

He could've used any public place for his alibi. Anywhere with surveillance and a constant stream of witnesses would've worked.

Instead, he'd deliberately sought me out, kept me distracted, and ensured I didn't answer my phone.

Fucking asshole.

I gulp at my second mimosa, downing the contents like a shot as a waitress walks in my direction, her gaze deliberately skirting mine. She continues by me with a guilty look on her face and stops at the opening of the bar to wave the bartender toward her.

She pulls him close and whispers in his ear, her eyes darting in my direction every few seconds.

Subtle. Real fucking subtle.

The bartender doesn't react, his face not giving a hint to their conversation apart from telling me it's all about little ol' me. He nods. Whispers. Nods again. Then the woman walks away, her face downcast.

Interesting.

I slow my consumption, taking smaller sips, and watch the guy go back to his chore of chopping limes. Something has changed. Something that could be entirely based on my paranoia. Or maybe not.

He's stiff in the shoulders. His cuts are slower. His face is deliberately blank.

I glance around the restaurant, my gaze latching onto the host at the door. His eyes widen when I catch him staring at me, then he quickly looks away. I frown, and focus on the nearest employee. A waitress. She places a plate of food down in front of a customer, but her attention is on me. At least until we lock eyes then, just like the guy at the door, she quickly averts her gaze.

Even more interesting.

I take another sip as I continue my scrutiny and lock eye after eye, only to have every staff member show fear at the connection.

"Can I have another, please?" I place the flute on the bar, my fingers resting on the stem.

"Are you sure?" The bartender's brows are pulled tight in a wince. "Why don't you take a breather and I'll go out back and find you a stool?"

I cock my head, studying him. "I don't need a breather. And I'm okay without a stool."

He scrubs his hands on his pants again and clears his throat. "Look, ma'am, I'm sorry, but I've been told I can't serve you another drink."

I continue to analyze the slight change to his expression. The discomfort. The uncertainty. But it's my own curiosity taking precedence. "I'm not drunk. Why am I being refused service?"

"I... Um..." He glances toward the swinging doors leading to the kitchen. "I'm not sure. I'm just told the order came from management."

I don't react.

Instead, I think.

I put two and two together and pretend the addition hasn't resulted in a lotto win.

"Is Cole here?" I keep my tone light. Calm. I don't show an ounce of the exhilaration currently flooding my veins at the thought of the smug piece of shit hiding out in the building somewhere.

"I..." He scrubs his hands against his pants for a third time. "Let me get you that stool." He starts for the end of the bar. "I won't be long."

He walks away, taking long strides across the open expanse of the restaurant to disappear behind the swinging doors.

I lock down my emotions, determined not to jump to crazy conclusions while my limbs tingle, and the slightest buzz begins to take over my head.

Normally, Cole would be back there somewhere. Not in the kitchen. He would be in the surrounding rooms he uses as offices to run his operation. But not today. It's stupid to think he'd be anywhere in the vicinity while his father is being hunted.

No, that smug piece of shit would be somewhere strategic.

He's smart. Really smart.

That's why I've always been drawn to this case. The Torian family aren't simple. They know what they're doing and have a brilliant method to their madness.

But what if he is?

What if Cole is here? Watching me? Laughing at me?

He would think I was weak and pathetic for succumbing to my anger. And he'd be right.

I *am* weak.

I *am* pathetic.

I'm also a little psychotic, just like him, but my psychosis remains on the right side of the law. I'm crazy with the need to take him down. I'd do anything. *Give* anything.

I grip the bar and dig my fingertips into the wood as I stare at my reflection behind the wall of mirrors partially covered by glass. I look like hell. My eyes are wild, my cheeks rosy. And my hair. *Jesus*. The chin-length strands are a tangled mess that would probably seem trendy if I had a speck of makeup on to help me appear slightly respectable.

I'm the living, breathing definition of what Cole has made me—distraught.

Tormented.

I really should go.

"I'm told you need a stool."

The briefest snippet of a horror re-run brushes my ears. That voice. The provoking lilt. The arrogant tone.

I remain still despite the threat at my back and the mass of wasps swarming in my stomach.

"Where is he?" I whisper.

"Where is who?" Cole drawls.

I close my eyes, succumbing to the comfort of darkness for a few seconds before I turn to face the picture of arrogance standing right before me in his perfect suit.

"I would've thought you were far too proud to play dumb, Mr. Torian." My voice climbs, letting those in the vicinity hear our conversation. "Is he here? Do you have him hiding out back?"

He inches closer, leaning into me so we're almost chest to chest. His cologne regains its hold in the air around me, the woodsy scent settling into my lungs. "As much as you seem to be enjoying yourself at my bar, why don't you follow me and take a look for yourself? We can talk in private. Just the two of us."

The words are intimate. Almost like a lover's promise.

"Just you and me?" I mimic his sultry tone, refusing to retreat even though he's deliberately smothering my personal space. "Without witnesses or anyone to hold you accountable for what you might try to do to me?"

He chuckles, the warmth of his breath brushing my cheek, triggering an ambush of goose bumps to skitter across the back of my neck. "A woman like you wouldn't be able to fathom the type of things I want to do."

He's toying with me again. Playing the master manipulator. Attempting to inspire fear.

"I'm not scared of you."

"No." He inclines his head in agreement, his mouth kicking at one side. "I'm well aware you shiver for different reasons."

I glare, my lips parting, about to spew my bottled hatred.

"You didn't come here to make a scene, Niss." He enunciates the nickname with deliberate affection, dangling it like a noose. "You came here to my restaurant, despite the risks involved, because we have unfinished business you want to resolve. So let's resolve it."

He turns and strides away, heading toward the swinging kitchen doors.

I'm sure the attention of every person in a one-mile radius is on him, taking in the perfect fit of his tailored suit, the styled hair, the thick, broad shoulders.

He doesn't wait to see if I follow. He knows I will. This asshole is well aware he's got the upper hand, and it needs to stop. But how? He'll only gain more power if I walk away.

I'm left with no choice. I have to give chase.

I stalk after him, catching up at the kitchen door he holds open for me. The bartender stands inside, his eyes curious.

"Thanks for the drinks," I mutter. "You can put them on Cole's tab."

Torian chuckles, the thickly rich sound another taunt to slap away my attempt to anger him. He leads me through the spotless kitchen, the staff staring at me with intrigue.

Their attention is reassuring. He can't pay everyone for their silence. Someone in here has to cling to a moral or two. So if I wind up in a ditch in the early hours of the morning, Cole won't get away with it.

"This way." He holds open another door with a dimly lit hall on the other side. This time I take the lead, not letting the darkened shadows spook me.

"Keep going until you reach the last door on the right."

I glance over my shoulder. "And what if I want to check these other rooms?"

"Have at it. But I think you're smart enough to know there's nothing illegal on this premises."

Another taunt. More softly spoken ridicule.

God, I detest this man.

I continue to the end of the hall and pause, waiting.

"After you." He indicates the door with the wave of a hand, his gaze narrowed as if daring me to continue.

I don't play into his intimidation. I refuse to whimper in fear.

In fact, I scoff, practically laughing in the face of it, and step closer to the door.

I grab that handle, twist, and shove inside, a woman on a mission, only to stop dead at the wall of muscle that greets me.

The three men put an immediate halt on their murmured conversation, their menacing faces turning to take me in, their relaxed expressions morphing to incredulity as recognition hits.

"Don't stop now, little fox," Cole whispers in my ear. "Make yourself at home."

5

TORIAN

My men glare at the female intrusion, their hatred palpable, their shock evident. I can only assume they don't understand why I'd willingly lead an FBI agent into our sanctuary without a warrant.

I'm not too clear on the tactic myself.

It's part of the fun, I guess. Leading the prey behind enemy lines.

"What the fuck is she doing here?" Decker snarls.

Her chin hikes. That's all she does. It's her only sign of defense.

And it's nowhere near enough to sate my thirst.

"Back off. She's with me." I walk around her, placing distance between us in the hope it will increase her apprehension. "We'll finish our conversation later. I've got confidential things to discuss with my favorite special agent."

"Are you kidding?" Luca asks. "You can't be left alone with her."

"He's right." Hunt questions my sanity with the tight pinch of his brows. "You need a witness. Who knows what shit she'll try to pin on you."

"Don't worry. This is a friendly visit." I tilt my chin toward the door, wordlessly telling him to get moving. "Isn't it, Niss?"

She ignores me, her attention remaining on the men a few feet away.

One in particular.

Decker.

"Leave us," I reiterate, adding steel to my tone.

Two of my trio know better than to push my patience, and reluctantly head toward the door. The third always has the opposite reaction, so it's no fucking surprise when Decker remains in place.

"She can't be trusted," he seethes.

"Thanks for the concern. But I'll take it from here."

"This is bullshit." He clenches his fists at his sides, Hunter and Luca waiting for him at the door. "She'll throw you under a bus the first chance she gets." A wealth of hatred ebbs from him, his hostility barely leashed.

She doesn't react. Not in concern, anyway. If anything, she relaxes into the animosity, her shoulders losing their tight edge. "And here I was thinking you've been pining over me like I've been pining for you."

His upper lip curls as he takes an aggressive step forward, and this time, I don't warn him to back down.

I watch their interaction play out, transfixed, my gaze glued to every flicker in her expression.

She intrigues me, and I'm not entirely sure why. Maybe it's the absence of self-preservation. Or how she lacks the fragility I'm used to from women. Either way, her oddly captivating personality has my attention.

I observe the gentle increase in her breathing. The twitch of her fingers against the hem of her suit jacket. Nothing goes by unnoticed, not even the slight curve to her lips.

But still, there's no fucking fear, and the famine is killing me.

She thrives on this—the fight, the aggression. Anger seems to be her favored emotion. Her happy place.

"Leave," I repeat. "I can take care of myself."

Decker's upper lip continues to curl. "Watch her." He backtracks, pointing a menacing finger in her direction. "This bitch has claws."

"And I remember you enjoying them not too long ago," she purrs.

They've slept together?

Of course they have.

Decker has the uncanny ability to taint everything I crave. And yes, the games I want to play with her are near the top of that list.

"Out," I snap. "Now."

He swings around, storms for the door, and nudges past Hunter. They leave in a group, the latch clicking shut behind them.

For a few moments, the room is quiet. The air is filled with something thick and thrilling.

"Take a seat." I continue toward my desk, my pace slow, before I turn to sit my ass against the polished wood.

"I'd prefer to stand." She takes in her surroundings, her gaze trekking over the bookshelves and expensive artwork.

She's more controlled than I thought. Or more stupid.

The jury's still out on that one.

But her fearlessness is magnificent. I could watch her battle intimidation every day of the week and never grow tired.

"That's an admirable group of men you've got there," she murmurs. "Not only threatening an FBI agent, but a woman. Is that something they're trained to do during the induction process?"

I snicker. I gather it's the response she wanted because there's no way she could make me angry. Not again.

"No, those skills are engrained. I doubt they're teachable. But I should probably look into it for future recruitment, right?" I cross my legs at the ankles, exuding relaxation. "Especially when the level of bullying from your people is continuously increasing."

"Your people." She scoffs, her brows rising as she continues her examination of my private space. "I don't think you can consider it bullying when you spend every waking minute breaking the law. Most people would refer to it as justice."

"Good to know."

She sucks in a deep breath, as if bored, and lets it out on a sigh. She's playing the game, too. Trying to appear disinterested while in the lion's den.

"Why are you here, Anissa?"

"Why?" Her tone drips with sarcasm. "I don't know. I guess I thought it was a lovely day for a visit." She turns to face me, her fake tranquility vanishing with the narrowing of her gaze. "Why don't you save us both a lot of time and just tell me where Luther is?"

I grin, my expression having the opposite effect on hers.

Those eyes turn hostile. Her jaw tics.

"You're such a tight ball of hostility, aren't you?" I journey my gaze over her body, taking the liberty to let my attention linger on the parts I like most.

I wonder if she'd mind me hiring her a personal shopper. These suits of hers really are pathetic. Sexy, yet pathetic. What hot-blooded woman doesn't want to show a bit of leg? Especially with the set of pins she has hiding under that stiff material.

"Tell me, little fox, do you drink to drown your sorrows?"

She doesn't reply.

Silence reigns for long, drawn-out seconds.

I raise my gaze over the hips hugged in navy, along the white blouse showing the faintest outline of a lace bra beneath, past the tight line of her lips, to her cold, calculating squint.

"Did I hit a point of contention?" I smirk. "Have I already driven you to the bottle?"

Her mouth curves. "You couldn't drive me to do anything. You don't scare me, despite how hard you try."

"Understood." I nod. "So I assume you won't mind me reporting this incident as harassment."

"By all means." Her chin hitches, the action a beaming tell. "Go ahead. I'm not going to stop you."

"You don't even want to try? I'm sure we could come to a mutually beneficial agreement to make up for you badgering my staff."

Her eyes dance, and the renewed kick to her lips gives me the slightest glimpse of a dimple in her right cheek. "It's already clear your obsession with power is an overcompensation for something you lack. And I've been dissatisfied too many times to struggle my way through a pity fuck. So by all means, report me. But I assure you, I can do whatever the hell I like. I haven't broken any rules."

She keeps throwing cheap insults at me, and I seriously think she expects me to react.

It's disappointing.

Truly.

She needs to be aware of my control.

"Interesting." I uncross my legs and grab the desk at my sides. "I thought there were strict rules within the Bureau. I didn't know you could do whatever you liked. It sounds like the perfect job. Maybe I should become an agent."

She releases a breathy laugh and heads toward the only window in the room, flicking the curtain aside to peer across the staff parking lot. "I'm sure you already have enough people inside those walls doing the dirty work for you."

I nod, slow and subtle. "Maybe you're right."

Again, her chin hitches. There's no other sign of her fury, just the damn chin that demands my tight hold.

"I suppose I should thank you for the flowers," she murmurs. "That's the polite thing to do, isn't it?"

"Flowers?" I push from my desk and stroll around to sit in the office chair behind it. "I have absolutely no idea what you're talking about."

She sighs, not buying my bullshit, and steps away from the window. "This was a mistake."

"Of course it was. You never should've tried to take me on, especially not at my uncle's funeral."

"I didn't try to take you on," she snaps. "Your father came out of hiding for the first time in months. I couldn't have cared less if he was celebrating the birth of a grandchild, or lying on his death bed. He's a vile waste of oxygen who needs to be behind bars. And anyone who disagrees should be there with him."

I raise my arms in front of me, holding out my wrists. "Then lock me up, honey, because I strongly disagree."

She bares her teeth, and the vicious snarl she releases does things to me that defy logic.

This is what I wanted. The brilliant rage. The blinding beauty. It wipes away the memory of the provoking smirk she inflicted upon me and replaces the expression with something I'll cling to for a damn long time.

All I need now is her fear.

"One day I will, asshole." She stalks for the door. "I bet my life on it."

"Oh, no, this isn't over." Far from it. I shove from my chair and take two quick strides to step in front of her, blocking her path before she reaches her escape. "We're not done."

Her eyes flare as she stops. "Move."

"No. You came here because you want something from me. What is it?"

"I already told you," she growls. "I wanted to know where you're hiding him, but obviously you're not going to do the world a favor and fill me in."

"Bullshit." I lean closer, getting right in her face. "You came here for something else. You were trying to turn the tables. To get back at me for humiliating you earlier.

You came storming in here with your over-cocked attitude and attempted to intimidate my customers."

"Like hell I did. I came here because a man died today. And another is fighting for his life." She throws her arms wide. "Hell, for all I know, he may already be dead. And for once, I wanted to see the affect the brutality had on you. *For once,* I wanted to know if you were anything but a heartless piece of shit."

"You expect my remorse when I'm not responsible?"

A jilted breath brushes past her lips, half laugh, half hatred. "You approached me at the exact moment it happened. You kept me busy the entire time." She holds my gaze, her cheeks turning a dark shade of pink. "You're guilty, Cole Torian. And suspension or not, I'm going to take you down."

Suspension?

I pull back to scrutinize her. I take in all the features I haven't had enough time to appreciate. Her short, sleek hair, the black strands cut at different lengths to give a loose, messy vibe. But it's those eyes, the same ones that slayed me this morning, that keep me engaged now. They're a captivating color—a mix between hazel and green.

"Stop looking at me like that, and get out of my fucking way." She sidesteps, waiting for me to move.

"I can't. I thought I knew everything there was to know, but now I'm baffled."

She huffs. "Move."

I lean back against the door, my head cocked, my brows furrowed. "This morning I was certain nothing could be more of a turn-on than your unjustified arrogance. But here you are, entirely defeated, humiliated, and flushed with rage, and I've gotta say, I think I made the wrong assumption. Nothing is more attractive than you at your lowest."

Her face transforms into a mask of shock. Then utter rage.

My pulse kicks in anticipation. In pure, undiluted pleasure.

She's going to break. To fucking explode. And I can't wait for the detonation.

Each second that passes makes my heart beat faster, my limbs pulse harder.

Do it, little fox. Let me have your worst.

"You—" She snaps her mouth shut and sucks a deep breath through her nose, gaining restraint.

"Me, what, Nissie?"

Her jaw works overtime, those beautiful lips pressed tight. But still, she clambers for control, scrambling for dear life. "*Move.*"

"We're not done."

"No?" Her eyes narrow. "What's left to say? Do you want to throw some more threats around? Maybe remind me how much you like hunting?"

I frown. "I do enjoy hunting. How did you know?"

The rage continues to bubble, the heat in her cheeks growing despite her attempts to chill. "Move, or I'll use whatever force necessary."

"And add to the harassment case already hovering over your head?"

Her hands shake. And her face—God, her face makes her seem like a bull about to slay a pen of matadors. This woman is lit and about to blow.

She lunges for the nearest bookshelf and grabs a novel, throwing the projectile at my head. The heavy weight misses by half a foot, its only achievement a weighty thunk against the wood.

"Jesus," I scoff. "I hope you're more accurate with your gun."

"Do you want to find out?"

I laugh.

I think I do. I have a strange urge to be in her line of fire, as I push her closer toward the edge. She'll have the lethal weapon, but I'll be the one in control, calling the shots.

"I can't wait to snap those cuffs around your wrists." Those green eyes turn manic, her smile crazed. "I'm going to take pleasure in nailing you to the wall."

"By all means." I crook a finger at her. "Have at it. I've often thought about nailing you myself."

She grabs book after book, throwing one after another until I score a spine in the gut and another on the thigh. She's deliberately aiming low. Trying not to leave the damning evidence of a bruise. Or maybe just aiming for my cock.

But why not reach for her gun? Suspension or not, why isn't she phoning this in?

My threat of reporting her must be far more terrorizing than I'd thought.

How perfect.

This feisty little thing might be on the verge of losing her badge.

"Okay. Okay. Let's call a truce." I hold up my hands in surrender. I won this round; I don't need to beat a dead horse. "You can't blame me for levelling the score. You picked this fight. Not me."

She turns rigid, her eyes flaring again, only this time it's in horror. Pain. "This is you levelling the score?"

"Yes. We both enjoy winning. There's nothing wrong with that." I itch to swipe the hair from her cheeks. To frighten her with a gentle touch. "We're even. For now."

"Even?" Her voice is raw. "You killed an officer and another may already have died. But now we're even for my few taunting words?"

She doesn't give herself credit. She did more than taunt me with a few words.

I haven't come close to losing my calm in public since I was a teenager, yet this woman inspired madness and incredible instability in me. I could've raged at that funeral—not because of the injustice or the unfortunate timing, but because of Anissa. Because of her perfect provocation.

She's unaware of her power, which, for me, is a good thing.

"I've told you, I had no involvement in my father's escape." I lower my arms to my sides. "But if you'd like me to send a floral arrangement to the deceased's family, I'll happily oblige."

"How do you sleep at night?" She reaches for another projectile, this time retrieving a small clay statue.

To anyone else, it would be considered a novelty item. An inexpensive trinket.

To me, it's more.

The woman and child figurine was given to me by my mother. It's the only weakness I allow inside these walls.

"I'm not sure what you expect from me, Niss." I move away from the door, no longer willing to antagonize her when she holds a fragile treasure in her shaking hands. "I actually came to you this morning with information. The FBI has made mistakes regarding my father's arrest. Mistakes that those women will pay for."

"Is that another threat?" She slams the figurine down on the shelf and storms toward the exit. "Because I'm goddamn sick of your threats, Cole."

"It's no threat." I hold her gaze, staring deep into the tumultuous sea of her eyes, hoping to tempt her into staying. "It's a peace offering. I'm happy to tell you everything I know. Maybe over dinner? Tonight?"

She snatches at the door handle. "Sell the story to some other sucker. I'm not that gullible."

"Wait. What makes you think you've got me perfectly pegged?"

"Let's call it months of meticulous investigation." She draws out the words like a queen talking to a servant. It's fucking brilliant.

"There are two sides to every story."

"Right." She swings open the door. "And you're the poor defenseless drug lord who deserves a break?"

"Maybe. You won't know unless you give me the chance to plead my case." I shrug. "Who knows if some random fact might hold the key to capturing my father all over again?"

She glowers. "I'm not taking the bait."

"That's a shame." I flash a smirk even though I'm disappointed our encounter is coming to an end. I didn't expect this meeting to be as long, or as spicy. It's above and beyond my expectations, and I'll miss the theatrics once she's gone. "But the offer still stands. Feel free to contact me whenever you're ready to work on leaving this animosity behind us. I assume the Bureau has my cell number on file."

She chokes out a breathy laugh and gives a roll of those beautiful emerald eyes before she makes for the hall. "Goodbye, Cole."

6

ANISSA

I tried to stay away.

That night, I fought anger and determination as I paced my bedroom. I battled against the passion to provide justice and the need to obey Taggert. I also struggled under the heavy weight of shame.

But I remained inside those four apartment walls. I didn't leave. I stayed out of the investigation despite the instinct to act.

The only connection I had to their world were the news broadcasts reminding me of my failures.

Nobody had a lead on Luther.

He'd disappeared. *Poof.* Gone. Right into thin air.

My fellow FBI agents were on the case, along with local law enforcement, airport security, and sniffer dogs, just to name a few. Everyone was entrusted to help find him.

Everyone except me.

The next morning, I wasn't going to wallow. I wouldn't let him beat me into depression. Moving forward was my only option.

I woke at the usual time, jogged the same five miles, not diverting a single foot off my regular path. And every step I took felt wrong. My thoughts weren't even right. Everything that filled my head had been about Cole. The ridicule. The manipulation.

I pushed myself to run through all the pummeling memories, spurring my legs faster.

I wouldn't stop my exercise routine on his account.

I refused.

Yet the streets I crossed and the people I passed seemed different.

I no longer had the tingle at the back of my neck. My senses weren't hyper-alert. The feeling of being hunted had vanished.

By the time I reached the café, I knew why my intuition was off-kilter.

I was alone.

Nobody followed me. There was no need to watch me anymore. No unexpected visitors waited to buy me a coffee. The flowers with their threatening notes had stopped, too. And why wouldn't they?

Cole had won.

He'd set a goal and claimed victory.

The reprieve should've been a blessing and a leap in the right direction for my safety. So why did it compound my failure?

Instead of rejoicing with goddamn relief because a psychotic fuck had grown tired of me, I became consumed with isolation. Slammed with abandonment issues.

The overwhelming sense of solitude didn't make sense.

The grief from my mother's death returned. The anger over my father's betrayal cut deeper. And the reminder I had no job to escape to made me entirely unhinged.

That day, I'd been a fucking mess.

But again, the next morning, I refused to wallow.

I ran my five miles, hoping against hope for the skin to crawl at the back of my neck. I prayed for the skitter of awareness. For the brush of my sixth sense.

Nothing came.

I had no connection to the case and no outlet for my spiraling mind.

Easton didn't call to give me updates like he'd promised. There were no e-mails or texts or carrier pigeons. Everyone and everything had turned against me, leaving me secluded.

I couldn't hack it.

I kept that routine for three days—three full days when I battled to contain my hysteria. But I couldn't do it for a fourth.

Friday morning started with a pre-dawn escape to Cole's exclusive neighborhood. It was only meant to be a drive-by—a brief insight to reassure my frustration that the good guys were keeping him under control with constant surveillance.

Instead, I found nothing.

No cars. No cops. No fellow agents struggling through an early-morning stakeout.

Nobody watched the son of the escaped sex trafficker, and I couldn't understand why.

I parked on the nearest side street, close enough to the corner to have a slightly restricted view of the ostentatious mansion purchased with dirty drug money.

He wasn't inside. He couldn't be. Cole Torian was somewhere else, enjoying his victory while the good guys watched from their secret hiding spots.

I told myself over and over, until the garage door rose and his glistening black Porsche drove out.

And that's how I came to be sitting here, out the front of a local nightclub fifteen hours later, watching Cole escort a sophisticated, young brunette inside.

I'm not proud I disobeyed Taggert's orders to shadow a suspect. But do I regret it?

Hell, no.

I didn't see one agent today. Not at Cole's restaurant. Not when he returned home at dinner. Nobody is riding his ass and it doesn't make sense.

For the fifteenth time, I palm my cell and click through to Easton's contact details. I've attempted to dial his number every hour, almost on the hour. Pride has been the only leash holding me back.

I don't want to beg for information. Being ostracized is bad enough without having to grovel for insight, but I can't remain isolated a moment longer.

I press "connect" and the dull ringtone filters into my ear. Each subtle vibration of the cell feels like a siren announcing my weakness. It nestles deep, tearing apart my self-esteem.

The final click of the connection makes me hold my breath.

"You shouldn't be calling me," he mutters in greeting.

I close my eyes, taking the kick to my teeth without a flinch. "And I wouldn't be if you'd kept your promise to feed me information."

He sighs, the sound long and loud. "I couldn't. Taggert made it clear you're not to be contacted. He's pissed. *Really* pissed. Nobody is willing to mess with him right now."

I run a hand over my face, attempting to scrub away the remorse. The last thing I should be doing is dragging Easton down with me. I'm well aware of the risk I'm placing on his job, yet here I am, unable to disconnect the call.

"I did try." Guilt laces his tone. "Despite the warning, I came to see you today, but you weren't home."

"Really?" The news is the slightest balm on my battered ego. "I've been out."

"Where?"

"Just out."

There's a long-drawn breath of silence. "I don't want to know, do I?"

I sigh and slink farther down in the driver's seat. "It's better if you don't."

"Dammit, Fox. What the hell are you doing?"

"Nothing." I grind my teeth through the need to defend myself. I ball my fists, and still, the frustration escalates. "Nobody is watching him. *Why* is nobody watching him?"

"Jesus fucking Christ, you're going to get your ass kicked. If Taggert finds out—"

"He's not going to find out. And I'm not doing anything wrong. In fact, I'm the only one doing my job. Why the hell doesn't anyone have eyes on him?"

"Because he didn't have anything to do with the escape. Not only was he with you at the time, but we've listened to all the phone recordings while Luther was incarcerated. They never discussed any plans. Neither one of them even alluded to what was happening. And Cole never stepped foot in that jail."

"That doesn't mean a damn thing, and you know it."

"All Cole's men have airtight alibis. Their stories check out."

So either someone is feeding them the right story to tell, or the FBI are dropping the ball. Hell, it sounds like they're not even taking the fucking field.

"Still doesn't mean a damn thing." I turn my attention to the nightclub, the slow-moving line out front growing by the minute. Maybe I need to go in there and make my presence known. I can't let Cole think his family is winning. He should be scared. Intimidated.

"Look, I shouldn't be telling you this," Easton admits, "but we've been warned. Someone went over Taggert's head and told the department to back off unless we have a lead. And we don't."

Mother.

Fucker.

"You should've told me that in the first place," I grate. "It makes more fucking sense."

"You're a loose cannon when it comes to these people. And I get it. I'm frustrated, too. But you only have to wait until Monday. It's three days. So let me shield you from this shit until then."

Three days.

Three fucking days where I'll go insane without more insight.

"No, please." I wince through the plea. "You need to tell me something. Anything. I don't care what it is. I just need an update to tide me over."

"Fox…"

"Come on. How long have we worked together? Doesn't that count for something?"

"You know I've got your back. That's why I've kept my mouth shut. You're going to get in some deep shit if you keep poking your nose around this investigation. The stakes are building too high, and anything that distracts Taggert from the case is going to send him postal."

My pulse kicks up a notch. "So something else has happened. Something that isn't public knowledge."

"Fox," he warns.

I sit up and frantically try to force my brain to find leverage. *"Please. Please. Please."* God, the begging makes me feel dirty. Fucking filthy. "I can help. You know I can. Nobody knows this family better than I do."

"Jesus," he hisses. "You must be desperate."

"You have no idea." I hold my breath through the growing silence, and my leg jolts, out of control. I'm shaking, my need for a fix uncontrollable.

"More women have gone missing," he mutters.

I slump as the information sinks in.

"Young, attractive women from stable families," he continues. "These aren't runaways or girls likely to get caught up in trouble. We're leaning toward abduction. And all of them have happened since Luther escaped."

My throat goes dry, and the memories of past crime scenes come back to haunt me.

I've been inside homes used for the exchange of sex slaves. I've witnessed mass graves filled with the remnants of tangled female bodies.

These women could be next, and what's worse is the suffering they might endure before they finally receive the peace that comes with death.

"It could be a coincidence," he murmurs. "You know how these things go. It wouldn't be a shock if this turned out to be entirely unrelated."

"But you don't think so?"

"No. I think Luther is sending a message."

One that announces to the world he's above the law and shouldn't be fucked with. A duplicate message to the one Cole has already given me.

"How many?" My heart beats rapidly in my throat as seconds pass. "How many women, Easton?"

"Two. Every day. For the last three days. Wednesday, Thursday, Friday. All of them from Portland. Whoever is responsible isn't even spreading them out across the state."

My heart drops at the additional stab to my ego. I've been wasting away the hours while these women get abducted, and still, Taggert doesn't want me involved.

"What about today?" My thoughts snap to the woman who accompanied Cole inside the club. The beautiful brunette. "Have there been any additional reports?"

"Just one. We're waiting on a second. I don't think the pattern will change anytime soon."

Seven women.

With more likely to fall victim.

I can't sit on my hands any longer. Nobody should.

"I need to help." I'll take Cole up on his offer. I can sit down with him and use my own manipulative magic to get inside information. I won't need much. The slightest slip could lead to their downfall. One tiny straw to instigate an avalanche. "I *can* help."

"Don't even think about it. It's not worth it. If Taggert finds out, you're gone. Not only from the department, but maybe from the Bureau entirely. He's gunning to take you down. Don't give him the opportunity."

"It's been days. Am I meant to sit on my ass and wait while more women are taken?"

"No, you're meant to detach from the situation and rely on us to do the work. You're not the only agent in Portland. We've got this."

I scoff. I'll believe in their abilities when they're focused on something other than their hatred for me.

"Promise me, Fox. Tell me you're not going to do anything crazy."

I keep my mouth shut. My teeth are snapped tight. I don't want to make a vow I can't keep.

"Fox, fucking swear it or I'll come find you. I'm not joking."

"It's not that easy."

The Torians have been a part of my life since I was on the cusp of my teenage years. I still remember the night when Cole's mother died from a gunshot wound. I remember, because my father cried that night. He'd walked through the front door, his eyes red and glistening, then slumped into my mother's arms.

I wasn't told why.

As a child, I wasn't told much of anything, especially about my father's position within the FBI. I had to figure it out from the newspapers. The following day, I'd seen his photo on the front page, his solemn face encapsulated for the world to see as he helped investigate a young woman gunned down before her time.

I've hated them since then. They're a vile family whose actions are gruesome enough to make an unshakable man like my father tear up.

But I can't let my cravings for justice blind me to the warnings from Taggert. I have to be cautious. Smart.

Easton's right, no matter how much I want to deny it.

"Don't be a fucking moron," he snarls.

"Fine. I swear it." I slam my palm against the steering wheel and glare toward the front of the club. "I'll speak to you later."

I don't wait for him to respond. I disconnect the call and throw my cell to the passenger seat.

I know he's only trying to look out for me, but there are so many other things I'm aware of too. For example, I'm blindingly aware Cole is involved in every deceitful action attributed to his family. I'm also mindful of his influence and reach. And it's crystal fucking clear he has no plans to change his criminal ways.

I don't care if there's no evidence of his involvement in Luther's escape.

He participated.

I can feel the potency of his treachery in my blood. Can taste it with every breath.

There has to be an evidence trail.

He can't keep everyone quiet forever. More witnesses have to come forward. DNA had to be left at the scene. It's only a matter of searching harder, for longer.

I turn on the radio to distract myself from the maddening loop of frustration and focus on the front of the club for hours.

I don't leave. Not when my eyes grow tired or my butt goes numb. I have nowhere else to go apart from an empty apartment filled with reminders of my failure.

I'm still sitting there at three in the morning when a familiar man walks out the front doors and farewells the bouncer with a hand clasp and a pat on the back.

After all this time, Cole remains crisp. Entirely impeccable.

I don't know how the asshole does it. He never appears anything other than immaculate. The hair. The style.

He's a flawless illusion. Perfect on the outside with a charred soul hidden beneath.

The only thing missing is a woman at his side.

He's alone.

The gorgeous brunette isn't with him, and I doubt she would've rejected his advances. He isn't the type of man anyone denies. And I find it hard to believe he chose to end the night on his own.

So where is she?

My palms sweat as my mind runs wild with possibilities.

Is the club a cover? Is she trapped somewhere inside, her screams muted by loud music? Was his companion the next victim?

He walks for his car in the reserved space a few feet from the entrance of the club and slides into the driver's seat. We both start our ignition in unison.

I promised not to do anything crazy, but following him home doesn't break that vow.

I hang back, waiting until he's almost out of view before I tag along for the ride.

As expected, he drives more cautious than normal. He navigates toward his suburb, sticking to the speed limit like a good little boy, which only makes me more suspicious.

Why would he pretend he's driving Miss Daisy unless he didn't want to draw attention to himself and the abduction he just instigated?

Three a.m. delirium has me convinced he did something to that woman. And even if he didn't, I refuse to let him curl up in bed thinking he's getting away with his crimes.

Something has to be done.

But what?

I creep my car closer as we approach his street, giving up the pretense of an early morning drive to make it clear he's being followed.

He doesn't react. There's no increase in speed or diversion to put me off his trail.

I can still picture him behind that wheel, all smug and self-assured, acting entirely untouchable.

It drives me fucking crazy.

It drives me so fucking crazy I break my promise and plant my foot on the accelerator.

I zoom along his desolate street, overtaking him to pull to a stop in front of his driveway. I block his entrance and storm out of my car, frustration and resentment seeping from my pores.

His window lowers as I turn toward him, the sight before me more daunting in its appeal than I remember. He's gorgeous. Perfect teeth. Smooth skin. Healthy tan. So much masculine stubble along that incredible jaw line.

God, I want to break this motherfucker. I want to break him more than words can express.

"What a pleasant surprise," he purrs. "To what do I owe the pleasure?"

He's all sophisticated charm and oozing chivalry. The heavy flirtation doesn't skip my attention either, but two can play that game.

"Having a good night?" I close my door and start toward him.

"It's definitely shaping up to be memorable." His mouth kicks in a wicked grin. "I've been waiting for you to face me again."

I gasp in fake concern. "I hope you haven't been holding your breath."

"Only since I spied you out the front of my house this morning."

Shit.

I ignore the heavy pulse in my chest and saunter toward the Porsche. "Well, here we are. Reunited at last."

"And ready for round two?" he muses. "Or is this round three?"

I answer the provocation with a breath of a laugh. "Did you have a good night? I assume the date didn't go well."

"Date?"

I reach his door and grip the window ledge to peer down at him. "You took a woman to the club. Two of you went in. Only one came out." I watch for a flicker in his expression, hoping for a clue that never comes. "I was wondering if she was your next victim."

"Victim? You speak as if women aren't begging to get in my bed." He snickers. "And that woman in particular wasn't one of them. Her name's Beth, and she's a bartender. I gave her a ride for her birthday, because she wants to have a few drinks after the doors close. I'm sure she's still in the VIP lounge if you feel inclined to stalk her, too."

What I feel inclined to do is shove that cocky attitude down his throat.

His self-assurance makes it hard not to believe his story. There's not a single hint of guilt or apprehension.

"You know, you never cease to surprise me, little fox."

"Yeah?" I add sugar to my tone. "Why is that? Did you think I'd give up after our last encounter? Are you really delusional enough to believe you intimidate me?"

"Not at all." The smirk reaches his eyes, the deep blue glistening as a dimple becomes visible in his left cheek. "What surprises me is that your jealousy is ten times sexier than your anger."

Jealousy?

Not even if hell froze over, buddy.

He's baiting me. Tap, tap, tapping at my grated nerves.

I won't bite.

"Do you know what I find really sexy?" I ask. "The thought of slapping a set of cuffs on you and watching you rot in prison."

"Don't tease, gorgeous. You've got no idea how hard it makes me."

I struggle to hold my smile when all I want to do is snarl. The mental pictures of his erection aren't easily ignored with my frazzled brain.

He makes fire burn in the pit of my stomach, the flames growing, licking higher with every second his arrogant expression remains fixed in my direction.

He's a sociopath.

An emotionless, narcissistic predator.

"You're incredible." So undeniably, unbelievably remarkable. Like a rotting corpse desecrating the purity of heaven.

"I like to think so," he drawls. "But tell me why you agree."

I crouch, leaning down until I'm at eye level. "With the amount of suspicion piling up behind you from the new flood of missing women, I would've thought you'd be cautious." It's a bluff. A rather large one, considering I'm the only agent paying him attention. "But not you. You keep swinging around that ego of yours like it's a footlong dick."

His features tighten, the smirk more of a gnashing of teeth, the stare edging toward a scowl.

I've struck a nerve.

Good.

"What missing women?" He asks the question on a breathy sigh, as if he's suddenly grown tired of my company when he'd delighted in it moments earlier. "What crime are you trying to pin on me now?"

Surprise, surprise. Feigned ignorance. I can't say it's a favored facet of this man, but it's better than when he's antagonistic.

"I'm sure it's nothing." I wave away the comment, taking his smug, superior attitude and running with it. "What's a few cases of abduction among friends?"

His jaw tightens. His nostrils flare.

"Did you come here for a reason, Ms. Fox? I mean, other than adding to the harassment case you continue to build. Are you searching for a nightcap? I think a good fucking is exactly what you need to distract you from making more false accusations."

"Tempting." I nod. "Seriously, tempting. But not tonight. I actually came here because I need to apologize for my behavior. The last time we spoke, you offered an olive branch and I threw it back in your face. I was hoping the offer might still be open."

The tightness fades from his features, and he settles back into his comfortable role of arrogant asshole. "Dinner?"

"Yes, dinner." I nibble my lower lip, pure and innocent. "You said you wanted to clear up any misconceptions I have and to also enlighten me on your father's disappearance."

He inclines his head. "I remember. I promised to tell you everything I know about his escape."

"So, is the offer still open?"

He shrugs. "That depends on what I get in return."

I gasp in fake outrage. I even clutch at my chest for dramatic effect. "Do you mean to tell me the pleasure of my company isn't enough of an incentive?"

"Possibly." He ponders the question, or maybe he ponders the situation in general, those eyes taking me in, seeing everything. His gaze rakes my body, narrow with speculation. Down my chest, over my hips, and farther, to my thighs. "What happens if I want something more substantial?"

"Like?" I'm not signing my own death certificate. I might be slightly crazed with dedication. I'm not fucking stupid.

"Leave it to me. But don't worry, I'll make my terms known before you're asked to sign in blood." He flashes a bright-white smile. "Would tonight suit?"

"Tonight is perfect." I stand and retreat a step to counter the overwhelming rush of triumph. He doesn't know what he's getting himself into.

In fact, from his pretentious expression, it looks as though he considers himself the victor.

No way in hell.

All I need is a clue. Just one.

It doesn't matter if he strings together a conversation full of lies. I'll figure out the pattern. I'll find what he's hiding. All I have to do is keep him engaged and control my temper.

"Then it's a date," he drawls. "I'll send a car to pick you up at seven."

Again, I refuse to bite at the taunt. He can play his games.

I'm sure they'll be his downfall.

"I'll be ready." I continue walking backward toward my car, keeping him in my sights while he chuckles and raises his tinted window.

It's not until I'm behind the driver's seat, inching down the road, my vision stalking the rearview, that I realize I'm tingling with adrenaline. That's when the apprehension kicks in. Not because meeting with him will be dangerous, but because it suddenly feels like this is a game to me, too.

7

ANISSA

Unease accompanies me the entire way home, the dull throb pulsing through my veins.

This isn't me—the taunting. The facade.

Okay, maybe that's a lie.

Just a tiny one.

When working with informants, I need to be able to bend them to my will. It takes a certain level of manipulation to convince them to talk when they don't want to. And yes, it becomes a game of mastery.

But I never indulge criminals.

Especially not antagonistic pricks like Cole.

I'm giving him exactly what he wants—my attention.

I can't win without engaging in battle. The situation is a double-edged sword that requires a foolproof strategy.

I can't get him out of my head. Not once I reach my apartment, and definitely not while I'm in the shower, attempting to scrub my skin of his effects.

When I turn off the lights and climb into bed, he's all I see. Every time I close my eyes, he's staring back at me with that devilish smile. The satanic smirk. All I hear is the deep purr of his voice. It whispers in my ear, making the hair on my arms stand on end.

I'm still awake when the sun rises. I don't pass out until after the busy rush of peak-hour traffic fills my head to distract me from the nagging thoughts of a predator.

It's quieter when I wake, the bedside clock glowing red to announce it's two in the afternoon. But that's good. It means I have less time to worry about the risky choices I've made and all those I'll be forced to make in the near future.

Every time I think about Taggert, I distract myself with exercise. I punish myself with sit-ups or squats. I even lower myself to the pain of burpees. I let the burn take away the thought process, because I can't change my mind.

I'm doing the right thing.

I know I am. Despite breaking a promise to Easton.

I don't lose sight of my goal, not through the slow afternoon hours when I try to strategize. And not when my pulse beats faster as the time of reckoning approaches.

I dress simple. Black slacks, white blouse, and two-inch heels, with a faint hint of makeup to mask the sleep deprivation.

For the briefest second, I'm tempted to put on a business suit, until I force myself to realize the appeal is based on nothing but a cheap thrill.

I'm as eager to antagonize him as he is with me. It has to stop. At least on my behalf.

This is serious. I can't keep walking into every trap he lays before me. The lives of so many women are at stake. Not just the nine who have been reported missing over the last five days. It's also all those who remain in the clutches of Luther's sex-trafficking syndicate.

When seven o'clock draws near, I catch the elevator downstairs, my cell in my pocket, my purse and keys in hand.

I don't wear a wire. I don't even contemplate going behind Cole's back to record our encounter.

I'm sure he's smart enough to have contingencies in place to scramble any signal. And if he doesn't, then he has no intention of spilling secrets. My aim is to trick him into revealing the truth. Taunt and torment.

I push through the glass lobby door and step outside, finding the streetlight beaming down to highlight a nightmare.

Double-parked right in front of the building is a sleek, black limousine drawing the attention of people passing by like a stripper handing out hundred-dollar bills.

This isn't the car Cole sent. It can't be.

Neither one of us want to be seen together. The prince of the underworld and a special agent with the FBI. Whispers of an alliance wouldn't be good for either of us.

I glance down the street, then back in the opposite direction, searching for another option as the driver climbs from the limo.

"Ms. Fox?"

I ignore the call as my irritation climbs to new heights.

Should I flee inside to escape being seen? Should I give up because I didn't anticipate yet another game?

"Ms. Fox?"

Shit.

Why the hell am I surprised?

I suck in a deep breath and stand tall, meeting the driver's gaze. "Yes?"

He smiles, the expression filled with gentle kindness. Obviously, he's not a seasoned asshole like his employer.

"It's nice to meet you." He swings an arm in the direction of the back door. "Are you ready to leave?"

No.

Hell fucking no. But do I have a choice?

Wherever my tormentor is, I bet he's laughing his ass off.

"I'm ready." I'm not going to let the prick win this early.

I make my way toward the limo, pause when the driver opens the door, and then slide straight inside. I'm closed into the shadows within seconds, immediately finding the significant space occupied by another soul.

Cole sits on the leather seat running the length of the vehicle, his expression filled with smug satisfaction as he swirls a finger of scotch in the glass resting atop his palm.

"Good evening." I measure my breathing, not willing to show I'm off balance. It's too early for him to be getting to me. "Thanks for the ride. I didn't think you'd go to this much trouble in an effort to impress me."

"Then you must doubt your allure." He takes a drink, the action highlighting the rough tease of stubble along his jaw. "You look nice."

I ignore the compliment as the vehicle begins to move, the slow glide either marking the start of another mistake or the beginning of my victory.

"Would you like to join me in a drink?" He indicates the stocked bar with a tilt of his scotch. "I took the liberty of pouring you a glass of Beluga. I vaguely recall vodka being your poison of choice."

It's not a vague recollection. Or a guess.

It's a fucking statement of knowledge.

I'm sure he's learned everything there is to know about me. I just don't want to contemplate how.

"That's right." I drag my gaze toward the lone glass sitting in front of expensive bottles of liquor, the ice swimming amongst a sea of clear liquid. "But I'm not in the mood to drink right now. Maybe later."

There's another tweak to those lips. "You can pour your own, if that's what you're worried about."

I mimic his expression. Smug. Self-assured. Fucking confident. "I'm not worried."

I'm almost certain he has no plans to kill me. This is nothing more than a show of power. He's succumbing to the weakness of messing with me, which can only work in my favor.

He's a slave to these games.

It's only a matter of time before he makes a mistake.

"Good." He licks his lower lip. "My aim for tonight is to build trust between us."

"That sounds nice."

He continues to eye me over the rim of his glass, drinking in slow sips.

His attention is consuming. It's almost tangible. The potency of his gaze wraps around me, slightly restricting.

He isn't distracted by the passing traffic or the blare of a nearby horn. He keeps watching me. Reading me. He coils his presence around me so tightly, without a single word, that I grow discomforted by the silence.

"Where are we going?" I turn my attention to the window and focus on the passing buildings. He will surprise me with the location. He'll either take me to a place in full view of the public eye. Or somewhere entirely remote. Because he thinks both locations will daunt me.

And he's right.

I don't want anyone seeing us together. If my actions get back to Taggert, I can kiss goodbye all new information on any case revolving around the Torians. I'll be locked out, if I don't lose my job entirely.

The only problem is, being away from civilization provides yet another risk.

"Cole?" I keep my attention on the other side of the tinted windows as we cross the Willamette River and merge onto the I-85. "Where are we going?"

"It isn't far. And we won't be alone. There will be witnesses to ensure your safety."

His attempt at reassurance doesn't hit its mark. I'm not going to let him lull me into a false sense of security.

"I remember at one point you said I could choose the time and location."

"Yes. I did." The flirtation leaves his voice. "But the situation has changed. Things are more complicated now."

"They are?" I turn to him, his eyes immediately meeting mine as I frown in feigned confusion. "How so?"

He keeps staring at me, keeps attempting to read what I try to hide. The taunting expression has vanished and what greets me now is nothingness. No seduction. No arrogance. He's reined it all in.

"We've had our fun, Anissa. Now it's time to get down to business."

My brows raise at the change in gears. "You mean you're ready to tell me about your father's escape?"

His detox from humor doesn't shift. Nothing but hard severity stares back at me. "I'm going to be up-front and explain, with all honesty, that I have no valuable information to give you in relation to that matter. I wasn't included in his plans."

Bullshit.

Bull. Shit.

I don't fucking believe him. I never will. Not on this.

I keep my frustration under wraps, unwilling to divert from my plan. Cool, calm, charismatic. That's the way it's gotta be. I'm determined to match his demeanor every step of the way. He can set the tone, but it won't stop me from laying the trap.

"Then why am I here?" I ask.

He takes another drink and returns to swirling the liquid inside the glass. "Because we both want the same thing."

My mind works overtime while I attempt to work out his meaning.

Is he thinking what I think he's thinking? Does he believe his flirtation is enough to seduce an FBI agent?

Oh, hell no.

"If you're talking about—" I shudder at the mere thought.

If he has the misconception that my panties are melting because of his bad-boy reputation, he's going to get a rude awakening. I'd prefer to commando roll from this moving vehicle and aim for the tires of the next oncoming truck than have sex with him.

"No, I'm not talking about fucking." A half-hearted grin breaks his seriousness. "But if it's at the forefront of your mind, maybe we should get it out of the way."

I scoff.

Well, it's more of a sputter.

He is *not* going to get the better of me. I'm not going to break character. "What do we both want, Cole?"

Cool, calm, charismatic.

Those three words will be imprinted on my brain before the end of the night.

His grin kicks up again, the flicker slight before it fades to nothingness. He breaks the potent fix of our stare and focuses out the window, detaching from the conversation.

Usually, he's fully engaged. Yet, tonight he seems distracted.

He's such an accomplished actor I'm not sure what to believe.

He keeps building the tension to the point where it crackles in the space between us before a sudden detox. There's always so much push and pull. A tedious game of tug-of-war I keep succumbing to.

He lets out a huff of exhaustion. "Neither one of us wants to see another abduction."

It takes all my control not to drop the civil act and loudly voice a call of bullshit right in his deceptive face. With this man, I swear I could call it over and over, but it wouldn't stop the lies falling from his lips. Everything he says is fiction. I wouldn't be surprised if he wasn't aware of reality anymore.

"Are you referring to the women you knew nothing about a few hours ago?" I contemplate taking the drink he offered. Safety be damned. I'm going to need it to get through a meal if I'm already struggling in the limo ride.

"Yes. I've since been informed."

For a moment, I hear static. There's no traffic. Not even the subtle crunch of asphalt. Only annoyance as he uses those women as a ploy.

"You want to help?" My question holds a hint of incredulity, the friendly charade temporarily faltering. I can't help mentally inching toward his trap. I know it's there. He's baiting me, and it's tempting to take a hearty bite.

"You judge me too harshly," he mutters. "I'm not the man you think I am."

Doubtful.

Very doubtful.

"I didn't know anything about the abductions until you mentioned it." He fixes me with narrowed eyes. "Apparently, I've been more distracted than I thought."

"Now all of a sudden you're informed?"

"That's right." He nods. "My sources have given me substantial information that I'm happy to pass on. But now that I think about it, I'm not sure it will do you any good seeing as though you're on leave." He delivers the provocation with a straight face, even though I'm sure he's delighting in my situation.

"How many days until you can return to the office, Ms. Fox?"

"I'm sure you already know, Mr. Torian."

His breathy chuckle brushes my senses, tattooing my ears. But it's the allure of intel that sends my pulse higher.

I focus on settling my eagerness and strive to hear the deception. The manipulation. I try so fucking hard to work out his next trick, when all I want is a clue to help those women.

"You're right." He finishes the liquid in his glass. "It seems I've spent more time being informed about you than anything else."

"Should I be flattered?"

He shrugs. "I'm confused to be honest. Who would've thought an aggressive FBI agent would be so entertaining?"

"Maybe it's your inability to break me that holds the allure. You've probably never met a woman you couldn't walk over."

"Anything can be broken. But I didn't agree to tonight to continue our fun-filled arguments. I'm here for my own reasons."

"Which are?"

Those deep eyes slowly turn back to the window, and for a moment, I wonder if he's striving for sympathy.

"I don't appreciate being labelled a sex trafficker. I don't appreciate that word being used in conjunction with my family at all. I need the judgment to stop."

The statement is more bait.

More taunting, tempting, teasing bait.

I can't bite.

I couldn't care less about his reputation. It's the convincing reasoning that holds my interest. If he would've claimed to care about the welfare of those women, I would've known he was lying.

Now, I'm not so sure.

"I'm capable of many things, Cole, but I don't think changing your reputation is one of them."

"You wouldn't have to. If I share this insight with you, an arrest will be made. I only need you to withhold any ties it has to my family."

I can't do that.

I won't.

But I'm willing to lie to get what I want.

"Okay…" Hope grows wings inside my chest, the gentle flutters increasing the need for oxygen. "Go ahead. I'm listening."

"Not in here. We need to discuss this somewhere neutral and out of listening distance from anyone likely to eavesdrop."

Seclusion. That's what he's aiming for. "Are you saying your own driver can't be trusted?"

"It's not him I'm worried about. I don't believe you're careless enough to meet me without backup, and you should know I'm the same. We need somewhere we can both feel comfortable to speak openly."

His assumption about my carelessness is incorrect. I've gone above and beyond stupidity by meeting Cole without informing anyone. I wasn't going to shoot an e-mail to Taggert. And I didn't want Easton to know I broke my promise.

I'm here entirely on my own, using his presumptions to keep me safe, along with a tracker app on my cell that sends half-hourly location coordinates to my work e-mail. But that security net isn't going to be helpful until after someone realizes I'm missing. I'll already be in a ditch somewhere, my body decomposing by the time anyone thinks to ask for permission to check my inbox.

"You want to get me alone," I muse. "You have to understand how careless it would be if I agreed." I scrutinize him, using everything I've learned over the years in an attempt to find the truth. I need to determine reality from fiction, deceit from fact. "And I'm also confused at why you would come to me for help. It's no secret I'm not your biggest fan."

"For starters, you came to me."

Okay, so he's got me there.

"But the main reason is because of the animosity you wave around like a red flag in front of a bull. You're my toughest critic. I prefer to tackle the hardest tasks instead of wasting time building up to it."

I may be his toughest critic, but I'm also the type of gal who doesn't budge an inch when a man has proven to be untrustworthy. Yet, here I am, falling under his spell.

I want to believe him. The need burns inside my stomach, growing hungrier by the second.

And why wouldn't I?

Obtaining answers about the abducted women goes above and beyond my objective for this meeting. Yes, I'd been aiming to get information to find his father, or take down Cole, but helping those women is far more important.

"So where's this secluded, neutral place you have in mind?" I rub a hand along the back of my neck, easing the prickle of goose bumps. "How far away is it?"

His lips part, but then the limousine pulls to a stop.

He doesn't answer my question. Instead, his mouth thins into a tight line as he juts his chin toward the window, instructing me to take a look.

My chest tightens before I even bother to comply. It's the change in the air between us that unsettles me. Intuition has my nerves hyper-sensitive as I glance outside and become overwhelmed with a heavy sense of dread.

Stretched out before me is a private airport with a jet waiting on the other side of the fence, our names practically written all over it.

8

TORIAN

She keeps staring out the window, the increasing rise and fall of her chest the only indication of her unease.

Manipulating her is a beautiful thing. Molding and shaping this woman's perception is growing beyond an addiction. It's an obsession.

Only this time, there's some truth beneath the deception.

She surprised me with the news of the missing women. I hadn't been aware of the problem. Nobody had fucking told me. Which meant I initially thought it was a provocation.

Unfortunately, I learned otherwise when my informants corroborated the news.

The tally of abductions continues to climb, along with the suspicion my father is responsible. Which only makes me fucking furious because the stigma always attaches itself to me.

"This information will help us both." I speak softly, not wanting to spook her any more than necessary. "If I'm not mistaken, you need something to get back in the good books with your boss."

Her eyes narrow into spiteful slits as she loses her hold on this playful act we've got going.

"I'm not trying to bait you." Not right now, anyway. "I'm only laying out the facts before you attempt to shut me down. For once, we have to work together." I murmur the admission because saying it with conviction is a struggle.

I've never turned to the authorities for help.

Never wanted to. Or needed to.

Even now, it sickens me.

But the truth is, I do need her. The necessity has gone beyond entertainment.

"No." She shakes her head, the refusal barely audible. "I'm not getting on that thing with you."

My optimism takes a hit, the injury striking hard.

I hadn't expected her to skip across the tarmac and rush up the stairs to enter the aircraft. I'd anticipated rejection. I'd predicted it. But my confidence in convincing her had been stronger when she wasn't sitting across from me, her shoulders straight with conviction.

"It's a safe environment." I don't move an inch. I'm not going to scare her into running. "If we're airborne, neither of us have to worry about being followed. I won't have to question whether or not your FBI buddies are tailing us, and you don't need to be concerned about being ambushed by my men. This is the smartest, safest move."

I pause, waiting for a response that doesn't come. She just keeps staring out the window, while her expression turns stoic.

"If I'm going to give you incriminating information, I'm going to do it in a controlled environment, with all my bases covered."

"How incriminating?" she murmurs.

"Incriminating enough to go to the expense and effort of hiring a private jet."

She nibbles her lower lip, raking those teeth deep enough I'm sure I'll see blood.

I'm fully aware her companionable attitude tonight is all for show. She's a tight bundle of aggression under the friendly act. Nothing has changed between us, at least not from her side of the battlefield.

"It's not my jet." I'll keep gently prodding until I get the response I need. "I don't know the pilot, and he doesn't have any loyalty to me."

"It's neutral ground," she drawls. "Just without the ground part."

"You'll be safe, Anissa. I promise."

"It's not about safety."

Like hell it isn't.

She's on the cusp of fear, yet not quite close enough to sate my hunger. She refuses to show weakness, and I can relate to the aversion. I rarely allow anyone access to my underbelly.

Her strength is admirable though. Or it would be if I wasn't so fucking eager to witness her crumple.

"Then why are you stalling?" I ask.

She winces and sinks those teeth farther into her lip.

"Nissa?" I keep waiting for an answer, my patience waning. "If you're not scared of me, what's stopping this from happening?"

Her gaze snaps to mine. "You like thinking I'm scared of you, don't you? It's a thrill. Taunting me is your favorite game."

"*Was* my favorite game," I correct. "We're moving on, remember?"

"Yeah," she mutters. "I remember."

"I'll be clear and admit this is an exercise where we're using each other. Pure and simple. I have information to help those women, and you have the ability to steer evidence away from me and my sisters. That's all this is. Don't make it out to be anything sinister."

Her tongue swipes over the flesh she's been torturing and it drives me to madness. "Where would we go?"

"Wherever you like, as long as it's not here—Seattle, LA, San Fran. I can arrange a driver to meet us at the airport when—"

"No. We don't land." She sits up straight. "We take off, discuss whatever needs to be discussed, then we return."

I incline my head, the heat of adrenaline spurring to life inside my veins. "We can do that."

She narrows her gaze and seems to attempt to siphon my trickery with the sheer force of her evil eye. She's looking for an excuse to deny me. *Any* excuse.

But I can see now that her stubborn determination will get her on the tarmac. She'll climb aboard the aircraft thanks to her sheer dedication to the task of taking down my father. And yes, me as well.

"If you fuck with—"

"What is your obsession with us fucking?" I give a lazy smirk. "It's crazy how often sex is on your mind."

"Don't. Even." She snarls the words with vehemence. It's incredibly provocative even though I'm sure she's completely unaware.

The constant ferocity of her denials makes my dick twitch.

"I won't." I vow an end to the flirtation with a definitive cross of a finger over my chest. "We've both had our fun and made our hostility clear. Now it's time to set that aside and move on."

She sighs and focuses back out the window. "I can't believe I'm even contemplating this."

Contemplate, little vixen. Then hurry up and make a fucking decision.

"I assure you, I want these women found as much as you do." I slide along the bench seat and open the door. "I can step outside to give you privacy if you'd like to call someone and let them know where you're going to be."

There's another huff of laughter. "Don't bother."

I guess she suspects the limo is bugged. And she's right. I'm curious to know who she would contact. I'd love to find out who her go-to person is—the one soul she relies upon now her mother is dead and her father is in hiding.

That nugget of information hadn't been something Decker could source with his expensive surveillance equipment. Not when she's such a solitary person.

She doesn't go out with friends, makes little to no personal calls, and doesn't live it up on her days off.

"Are you sure? This will be your last opportunity to contact someone. I want to make sure all devices are locked in the cockpit while we're onboard."

She meets my gaze with a forced smile. "It's fine. I'll make sure I speak to company staff, along with the pilot before we leave. I won't agree to take off unless I feel comfortable."

I incline my head and climb outside, holding the door wide for her to follow. "That sounds like a good idea."

She keeps those shoulders tight and her back stiff as we enter the small charter building to go through the security process. She hands over her gun, our belongings are scanned, and we're escorted through a metal detector. There's no protest when a pat down is requested. There's also nothing inappropriate found on her person, easing my concerns of her wearing a wire.

I wait patiently as she grills staff on their association with me.

How do you know Mr. Torian?

How often does he fly with you?

The security officer answers her with subtle annoyance—no, he doesn't know me. And he can't recall ever seeing me before.

Or so he says.

We're almost on our way, about to reach the glass sliding doors leading to the tarmac, when she stops and turns back toward the room.

"Is everything okay?" I lean close, whispering the question near her ear. "You're not having second thoughts, are you?"

"I passed second thoughts a long time ago. This goes well beyond that."

"Is there anything I can do to reassure you?" It's surprising how easy the offer to comfort her flows from my lips. This act is so enjoyable, I guess it has become engrained.

"No." She eyes everyone in sight, as if instructing them to remember what she looks like.

It's disappointing.

She should know by now that I could cover up our time together if I wanted. There's rarely anything money can't buy, and with the help of the police in my pocket, I'm almost untouchable.

It also makes life easier when the staff here know and trust me. This company is mine, after all. My name might not be on the documentation, but I sure as hell own it.

I have legitimate businesses everywhere. Gas stations. Freight carriers. Pharmacies. All of which remain under the radar from law enforcement.

There's minimal association between me and the people at the helm of these companies to maintain my anonymity. They give me their assurance they will work honestly, while they trust me to commit to my vow that they will never see the bright light of day again if they even think to fuck me over.

Profit for conformity.

That's all it is. I help them work toward a comfortable future, and they allow me to gain necessary information and untraceable supplies.

The authorities have no clue of the hold I have on this city. Not the slightest glimpse.

My influence is woven through every brick, along every street and sidewalk.

I *am* this city, despite my current need to get away.

"Why don't you make that call? It might settle your nerves." I place my hand at the low of her back and watch her stiffen further.

"I'm not nervous." She swings around and steps out of reach in her approach to the door. "And I don't need to make a call. I'm already covered."

I strongly disagree.

I found Benji's car edging its way into the private airport parking lot as we walked into the building, but I didn't see any other vehicle. Either the Feds are better at hiding than my own men, or she isn't covered as well as she thinks.

"Let's do this." She leads the way toward the jet, not stopping until she reaches the staircase.

"After you." I wave a hand, indicating for her to proceed. "Go speak to the pilot. Inspect the cabin. Do whatever's necessary to make yourself feel comfortable before we take flight."

"I will." She narrows her eyes. "Just remember, climbing onboard doesn't mean I've agreed to go with you."

"I'm well aware."

She takes the first step, her hips holding a gentle sway as she ascends before me.

I don't follow for a few minutes, giving her space to talk privately with the flight team before I make my way to the liquor cabinet in the main cabin.

I don't use the opened bottles. I reach for the Macallan in the back and pour myself a generous glass of fifty-five-year-old scotch.

I'm seated in one of the cream leather chairs when she walks toward me, then directly past to disappear into the bathroom. She bangs and clatters around in there, making me smirk as she no doubt searches for another reason not to trust me.

She won't find anything in there, and I'm pretty sure she already knows it.

The dramatic display is her not-so-subtle way of showing me I'll have to work hard if I expect her to believe a word I say. From the looks of the co-pilot retrieving the staircase and locking us in, it seems she's already given the all-clear for take-off.

I continue drinking, paying her no attention when she returns like a whirlwind, skittering her way around the cabin to lift seat cushions and look behind the television.

"What are you searching for exactly?" I ask.

"Nothing." She doesn't stop her inspection.

"Then why don't you join me for a drink?" I raise my glass in toast. "There's a fully stocked bar. Help yourself."

She pivots toward me, her arms crossed over her chest, plumping her breasts beneath the sheer blouse. I don't pretend not to notice. In fact, I make it known those tits of hers are fucking mesmerizing for so long she rolls her eyes and slaps her arms back down to her sides.

"For once, I think you're right. I doubt I'm capable of getting through a conversation with you without the help of a slight buzz." She makes for the liquor, retrieves a glass, and pours herself at least a double from an opened vodka bottle sitting in the display. "Cheers." She tilts the glass as if toasting the cabinet itself, then throws back a gulp.

Yet again, this woman surprises me.

"Top up your glass before you take a seat. It won't be long before we're in the air."

The cabin jolts on cue, the aircraft slowly moving forward.

"Great." She throws back another gulp, pours more liquor, then approaches to take the seat opposite me, the toes of our shoes barely inches apart.

"Your phone?" I ask. "I'd like to put it in the cockpit."

"I already gave it to the pilot." She holds my stare, taunting me to call her bluff.

I don't bother. Telling her I needed the cell stowed was more of a strategy to forewarn her I would be in control in this environment. And she agreed regardless.

The device itself was never an issue.

"I also told him our flight plans." She places her glass in the cup holder and clasps her belt. "He didn't seem to think doing circle work around the Portland area would be an issue."

"Efficient." I give her a slow grin. "I like it."

She ignores my subtle flirtation, choosing to stare out the window.

She isn't unaffected though. I'm wearing her down—slowly digging my claws beneath her smooth skin.

"Good evening, folks," the pilot announces over the speakers. "Please take your seat and buckle up. It shouldn't be long until we're cleared for take-off."

I follow orders and hide my annoyance at the interruption. I'm finally gaining momentum. I can't risk her having the time to change her mind.

"Do you enjoy flying?" I watch the tarmac roll, the daylight completely faded to night.

"Usually, yes. But I have a feeling the private jet experience will be slightly different."

This one definitely will be.

I have no idea when we'll land, and the thought of returning to Portland isn't something worthy of inspiring excitement. This place doesn't feel like home anymore. Instead, it resembles a war zone.

Keira keeps riding my ass. Layla continues to fight with her husband. Stella doesn't understand why she can't speak to her grandfather.

Our family is in turmoil, and I'd like nothing more than to be a thousand miles away.

The tether tying us together has vanished. We're separate entities instead of one unit, and I'm the poor sucker who needs to pull everyone back into place.

Me, and the woman seated directly in front of me.

Her left hand grips the armrest as the aircraft accelerates, the entire cabin shaking. She doesn't look scared. But she's not comfortable either.

"Is the vodka to your approval?"

She keeps her focus on the world outside, her chest rising and falling with slow breaths. "Yes. It's beyond my pay grade, if that's what you're asking."

"No. That's not what I was asking. I only wanted to make sure you were enjoying yourself."

"I'm having a wonderful time." Her sarcastic tone implies otherwise. "We should do this more often."

I can't help a grin.

I fucking can't.

Her suffering is cathartic. Pure and utter bliss.

"Why don't we? We could make this a weekly ritual. You can share the inside scoop on the Bureau and I'd vow to listen to you more intently than any other man has ever listened in your entire life. Just you and me—"

"Give it a rest." There's laughter in her voice as she rolls her eyes. "You're entirely shameless, aren't you?"

No. Not at all.

The shame I harbor is marrow deep, eating me from the inside out. "I think you mean I'm entirely charming."

"Actually, entirely self-centered is a better fit." She purses her lips, claiming victory, and this time I'll let her have it. The little wins are all she's going to get. "I suggest we get to the point before this slides out of hand. Talk to me about your father."

The jet's acceleration increases, faster and faster. The speed, the approaching victory, along with the unfiltered defiance staring back at me has my cock pulsing.

It's ridiculous.

She's an enemy. One who likes to remind me of the vast differences in our morality. And still, the appreciation I feel in this moment thrums through my veins.

"It's barely eight. What's the rush?"

She cringes, and the air that leaves her lungs is forced out, as if she's in pain. "Come on, Cole. I know you like games, but I can't sit here and pretend to play along when the lives of women hang in the balance."

"I can't share information without trust, Nissa. We need to get to know each other first."

Her fingers clench tighter around the armrest. "I thought you already knew everything about me. What could I possibly share to earn your trust?"

"It's not information as such. It's whether or not you'll give me the truth when I need it."

She takes another sip of vodka, growing unsettled.

She's struggling not to show weakness, and I'd admire her strength if I wasn't so hungry to witness her buckle.

"Okay. Fine. Let's get this over and done with."

I incline my head. "Good. You can start off by telling me how many men you've slept with."

Her face snaps tight with incredulity. "I'm not playing those sorts of games with you."

"It's not a game. Like I said, it's about trust. And don't discount the fact that you can learn a lot about a woman by the number of men she's allowed into her bed."

"Like what?" she growls.

I chuckle, in my fucking element with the appearance of her feisty attitude. "Like if she's a risk-taker or high-strung."

"You're telling me a woman who doesn't have a long list of lovers is high-strung?" She scoffs. "That's probably the most narrow-minded thing I've ever heard. A low tally could simply mean the few men she's slept with didn't know her ass from her clit, so she didn't bother wasting any more time."

I wonder if that's her. If she's a woman with a low tally because the men she's slept with didn't have a clue how to inspire her pleasure.

"True," I admit. "But a healthy number speaks of trust toward the opposite sex."

She laughs this time, and the humor almost reaches her eyes. "Again, I disagree. It could simply mean a woman is confident she can protect herself. Among other reasons." She rolls her eyes again. "You can't claim to need that information to get to know me, Cole. Some women pay no thought to the men they sleep with, while others examine everything. You can't pigeon-hole me from these questions. It's ridiculous."

She's right. I only wanted to hear her talk about sex. To lighten the mood. To mess with her head a little more.

"Okay, then, I'll ask another. What is—"

"Oh, no, buddy. You had your turn. It's my go now."

Perfect. I'm dying to hear what she wants to know. Out of all the questions she could ask, what draws her attention the most?

"Tell me about the first crime you ever committed."

I expected the hostility. I actually anticipated more, but I straighten, feigning offence as the jet evens out. "I assume this is off the record."

"Of course." There's a quirk to her lips. "This is about trust, remember?"

An ache forms beneath my sternum. I'm not sure if it's caused by her arrogance, the curve of her lips, or the way her gaze makes her appear fully invested. Her features are no longer mismatched. I've learned she can fake a smile like nobody's business, but those eyes never lie.

"Okay." I nod and take a gulp of scotch. "I stole from my local church."

"Wow. When you commit a crime you really start at the top, don't you?"

"It sure seemed like it at the time. I think I was eight. Maybe nine. And the piece of chalk I pocketed felt as if I'd lifted a million dollars."

Her face falls into a glower. "That's hardly a crime, Cole."

"But it's the truth. Which is more than I can say for you with your non-answer."

She snickers and quickly hides the response behind a sip of vodka.

She makes it hard not to stare. It's not often that she laughs or smiles. Not without derision or spite.

This right here is something I've never seen before. Maybe something even more enjoyable than the misery I've been searching for. To have an FBI agent comfortable in my presence is quite an achievement.

"You can now unfasten your seatbelts and move around the cabin," the pilot announces. "It should be a steady flight for quite some time."

The interruption acts as a trigger to reality. Her face falls, the glimpse of happiness replaced with detachment.

"Do you want a top up before we continue?" I unclasp my belt and tilt my glass in her direction.

"I shouldn't." She scrutinizes me, the flicker of indecision working over her features as she glances from me to her vodka then back again.

"You shouldn't or you don't want to?"

"Does it make a difference?"

"Yes, of course it does." I stand and peer down at her. "If you don't want to, that's fine. But if you're not drinking because you feel there's a certain way we need to interact, or you're scared, or on edge—"

"I'm not scared. Or on edge." Her chin hikes, her ego coming into play entirely on cue. "And no matter how many times you question me about it, my feelings aren't going to change. I'm not scared of you."

"Then I can only assume attraction is stopping you from sharing another drink with me." I start toward the liquor cabinet and grab my scotch from the back. "Are you worried you'll succumb to my charm?"

"I'm more worried about leprosy."

She always has a comeback. Her necessity to have the last word is obvious. But those words draw a reaction out of me every time, either enjoyment or competition. I'm always impatient to hear how she'll respond next.

I grab my drink and the bottle of vodka before I return to my seat.

"Are you sure you don't want another?" I hold out the temptation, knowing full well she craves the alcoholic buzz. "Not even a little bit?"

She huffs out a breath and raises her glass. "Fine. Give me a top up, just don't pour too much."

I nod, placing my drink down in the cup holder to give her my full attention. Our eyes hold as I open the bottle, and she doesn't stop me when I pour a generous dose.

"That should keep you occupied for a while."

"I'm sure it will." She gives a gentle smile in thanks. Again, I know it's fake. She despises me under those heavy layers of goodwill.

"Have I earned your trust yet?" she murmurs. "Can we finally address why we're both here?"

This is the tricky part.

The pivotal point.

I break eye contact and retrace my steps, placing the vodka back in the cabinet.

"The trust isn't only for my benefit, Nissa. I need you to feel the same way about me, too. Otherwise what's the point in sharing information you won't believe?"

"Why wouldn't I believe it?" She narrows her gaze. "I think we've come as far as we're going to get today with our faith in each other. We've been civil for, what?" She glances at her watch. "More than an hour now. I think that says a lot."

"I guess it does."

She sits forward in her seat, moving closer. "So, tell me, why don't you think I'll believe you?"

"Because the information isn't going to be what you want to hear."

She bristles and slumps back in her chair. "You're going to try and convince me your father isn't involved."

"Yes."

"Then you're right." Her voice grows bitter. "I don't believe you. Just like I don't believe you had nothing to do with his escape."

I chuckle, but the enjoyment is forced. I'm growing tired of this. "I guess this means we've returned to square one."

"This isn't a joke." She throws back a gulp of vodka, the slightest tremble taking over her hand. "And I'm sick of your goddamn games. You need to tell me something. Anything."

"I just did." I keep my tone measured. Level. "What can I do when you're determined not to believe me?"

"You can start by telling me anything with a glimpse of truth to it. Tell me something I can believe," she begs. "Something true."

Her pleas are music to my ears, sweet and powerless.

"How 'bout I come clean and tell you my comment about the little black dress in your closet was nothing more than a calculated guess?"

She stiffens, her lips pressing into a tight line of disbelief.

"What woman doesn't own one of those dresses?" I smirk. "And I made an assumption about your preference for vodka. I haven't invaded your privacy as much as I wanted you to believe."

She keeps eying me, no doubt pondering my honesty, her tongue snaking out to quickly moisten her lower lip.

"But I did send you those flowers," I admit, "and I enjoyed coming up with the notes. I even watched you myself. Every morning on your run, and every night when you returned home. The rest of the time, my men kept an eye on you."

She swallows, her delicate throat working overtime. "I appreciate the honesty."

I want to laugh. I've divulged my secrets, along with incriminating information, and all I'm getting is appreciation? "You're a hard woman to please, Ms. Fox."

"And you're a hard man to trust, Mr. Torian."

Being hard is definitely becoming an issue. The more time I spend with this viperous enemy, the more she holds my attention.

"But I will trust you," she lies, her voice breathy with the rush of anticipation. "Now, please, tell me what you know."

9

ANISSA

Cole holds my gaze, his eyes intense. "The person responsible is trying to impress my father."

All my instincts tell me to shoot him down in flames. To deny every single word he says. But I can't.

Game or not, manipulation or sincere confession, I have to remain open to the possibility he's telling the truth.

I force myself to be patient—cool, calm, and collected—and sip my drink as the aircraft pivots to the left.

This situation is going to be difficult to explain to Taggert. Not only did I disobey his orders, but I kinda spat all over them when I boarded this exquisite jet and began doing circle work above the Portland skyline.

All I can do is hope the information provides enough evidence to take down a highly sought-after criminal. Maybe then my disobedience might be excusable, or at least ignorable.

"How do you know?" I take another sip, letting the burn of vodka energize me.

"Information isn't hard to obtain when you know where to look." He shrugs. "Unlike the authorities, people actually want to talk to me."

"You mean they're threatened to spill their guts, otherwise you'll do it for them. Literally."

He raises a brow, gently scolding. "For a smart woman, you have a very narrow-minded view of right and wrong."

"How can it be considered narrow when the majority of the population holds the same view? You're the one making up your own rules."

His eyes consider me with patience while he swirls his glass. "When I ask for information, I give a reward in exchange. Not just occasionally. Always. People want to help me. Yet, in your case, you threaten and intimidate for what you need, and still continue to call yourself the right side of the law."

He's delusional.

A gorgeously charming slip of reality.

"You may reward your informants, but those people know there will be hell to pay if they don't talk."

"Not true." He gives a subtle shake of his head. "I'm not the monster you think I am."

"No, I'm sure you're far worse."

"I'm a businessman, Anissa. And I do my job well. I can only assume you're one of those people who believes money is the devil."

Not money, just you. "That's not the case. But I do think there are more important things in life."

"Like?"

"That's a long list." I'm getting distracted. I'm not usually prone to straying from a conversation, especially not when evidence is involved. "Can we stay on topic, please?"

"Humor me. Tell me one or two things more important than money."

I pause. For some reason, I know I shouldn't blurt out an answer. This isn't merely chatter to him. He's trying to learn more about me. To understand who I am.

I take another sip and ponder my response through a brain that begins to feel sluggish. "Family, for starters."

He nods. "I can agree with that."

A funny, twisting feeling takes over my stomach.

His relaxed sincerity is getting to me. When compared to his antagonistic flirtation and his unpalatable games, he now seems entirely endearing.

Even though I loath to admit it, he's not a terrible conversationalist.

"I'd have to say family are at the top of all my lists," he adds. "Nothing is more important."

"I already knew as much." The Torians are famous for many things, but criminal activity and family honor are their calling cards.

I think that's the main reason my father became heavily invested in the death of Cole's mother. I'd never seen him affected emotionally like he had been that day. I'd assumed he was living in fear of the street war predicted by the newspapers, even though the scaremongering had proven unnecessary.

The bloodshed had been strategic.

Specific.

Contained.

Every victim could be tied to Denise's death. Nobody else had been hurt on either side of the battlefield.

Not the Torian men. Their enemies. Or the police.

Well, not that the hospitals had reported.

The Torian protection umbrella stretches past blood, covering all those loyal to the family.

I guess it's kinda like God promising the bliss of Heaven to anyone who vows their life to him. And when it comes to Cole, the god complex entirely fits. I've never met anyone with a more holier-than-thou attitude, even when it's clear he has no morals.

"What's so funny?" He cocks his head to the side, scrutinizing me. "What brought on that amazing smile?"

Shit.

I raise my glass, hiding my mouth behind another sip of alcohol.

I'm losing track of why I'm here. We're talking about dirty money, threatening civilians, and abductions, yet my mind keeps wandering. What's worse is that I haven't had to keep a constant leash on my animosity.

I've been civil without having to act.

There's no venom from either of us. No anger or annoyance.

For a short space of time, even though I've been well aware of who I'm speaking to, I fell under the spell of his charisma.

What the hell is wrong with me?

"It's nothing." I shake my head and a sudden case of vertigo sends me reeling. For a moment, I have to fight to blink back clarity. "Holy shit."

I'm drunk. Already.

This isn't right.

I stare at my glass, trying to recount how much liquor I've consumed.

"Are you okay?" Cole's tone is dire as he leans forward and brushes a hand over my knee. "You do realize the oxygen up here messes with the alcohol. That vodka will hit you a lot quicker than normal."

"Yeah."

I watch his fingers, entranced. They're large. Strong.

Big, solid hands capable of many, many bad things. Yet there's comfort in his touch.

This man, with his threats and lies and dripping innuendo, is capable of softness.

Fuck. I need to sober up.

"I guess I forgot." I squeeze my eyes shut and the vertigo disappears with the darkness.

What I'm left with is an overwhelming sense of stupidity.

I tried to drown my annoyance and trepidation with vodka, and yippee, it worked, but now I'm dizzy drunk without even being buzzed.

"Do you want me to get you a bottle of water?"

The kindness in his voice doesn't sit right. It's too nice. Too uncharacteristic.

This isn't the Cole Torian I know. Well, it's not the man I've researched. He's meant to be callous and spiteful. Just like the man I verbally sparred with in his restaurant.

"Water would be great. Thanks."

I hear the squeak of his chair, the soft pad of footsteps, and the gentle suction of a fridge door opening and closing.

Goddammit, I need to pull my shit together. This isn't professional. I've found a cash cow of information, and I'm kicking it in the teeth.

Not that it's deliberate. I can usually hold my liquor. One or two drinks a night is my daily sedative to help me get to sleep. And here I am, floundering like a teenager on their first bender.

I massage my forehead, trying again to figure out my intake.

I threw back a generous amount initially, needing an immediate hit to lessen all the emotions. Then Cole topped me up with the same amount, which is still half full.

That makes... What? Two standard drinks in quick succession? Maybe three?

"Here." Coldness presses against my upper arm, the chill from the bottle seeping through my blouse.

"Thanks." I meet his gaze as I grab the offering. "I'm sure I'll be okay in a minute. I guess it's the oxygen thing. Or a lack of food. I haven't eaten much today."

"Then it isn't a good idea to keep circling the skies." His brow remains pinched. "Why don't we land and get a bite to eat? We've only got snacks onboard."

"No. I'm fine. Honestly." I crack the lid and drink the water, wiping my hand over my mouth when I finish. "Where were we?"

I need to concentrate on why I'm here.

This isn't an exercise in growing numb to Cole's monstrous influence. He's still a heinous criminal.

He leans back in his seat, eyeing me with fatherly worry. It's annoying.

It's fake, Anissa.

Fake. Fake. Fake.

"Do you have a name for this person who's trying to impress your father?" I take another gulp and another, impatiently waiting for the water to wash away the liquor's effects. "Do you have any proof?"

"I have everything you need. I even have an address of where he's keeping his victims."

"What?" The question bursts free, sounding more like an accusation. "You know where they are, yet we're up here talking instead of taking action? Why didn't you phone it in to the authorities?"

"I need to know you will hold up your end of the deal first."

"My end?" My vision blurs, his face growing cloudy.

I'm drunk. Seriously smashed.

It's fucking embarrassing.

I chug more water, hoping it will clear the confusion, but my sight doesn't improve.

"I need you to clear the stigma around my name. I'm not involved in this, and neither is my father. That needs to be noted and the information shared. I don't want this sex-trafficking bullshit associated with me a moment longer."

I frown. "But your father is guilty."

I unclasp my belt in a vain attempt to help ease the overwhelming discomfort. I feel wrong. My limbs are heavy. My head's a foggy mess. I can barely hold on to the topic of conversation. It keeps slipping away, like sand through my fingers.

"We need to land. I have to call this in." I place the bottle down beside me and push from my seat, intent on walking to the cockpit, when the jet takes a nosedive.

I lunge for the headrest, clinging tight with the sudden descent.

I struggle to battle the swirl and fight from passing out. But when I glance at Cole, he looks at me as if I'm insane. He's not gripping the armrests or staring in panic. From what I can see through the blur, he's relaxed. Calm. In control.

The jet isn't spinning.

It's me.

All me.

I fight against the darkness and make myself concentrate. I pull together the only thoughts I can cling to—the alcohol, the sudden insanity.

This shouldn't be happening.

I squint through muddled vision and stare at Cole.

"What did you do?" I whisper the accusation as I struggle to make out his features.

Lazy assurance blinks back at me, his gentle expression transforming into a smug grin that robs me of any comfort.

"*You,*" I seethe. "You drugged me."

Oh, God.

I cling tighter to the seat as he stands, his nearness increasing the rapid sway of my head.

I fight to understand. I struggle and snatch for clarity yet I can't grasp hold. Everything is a riddle. A convoluted game.

I poured the first drink. I watched him like a hawk with the second.

He didn't slip anything into my glass. I know he didn't.

I fucking *know.*

"It's okay." He grasps my wrist.

I slap at him, trying to bat away the contact, and fail miserably.

Every move I make takes the effort of a marathon. My co-ordination is off. I struggle to lift my arms, move my legs, keep any type of focus.

"You son of a bitch." I turn toward the cockpit and stumble forward. "Help me… Help."

"It's too late for that."

No. No. *No.*

I shake my head and it increases the turmoil. I sway with the movement. Stumble some more.

Holy shit, I'm in trouble.

I should be scared. I should be fucking petrified. Instead, I'm consumed with blinding rage.

I continue to fight against his hold, unable to see, barely able to think. "Don't touch me."

My voice grows hollow, barely recognizable. I'm not sure I even have the energy to yell.

I bump into things. I hit my knee, my thigh, while Cole's grip remains gentle on my arm.

There's no vision at all now, only the rampant thump of my heart in my ears and so much anger.

"Sit back down, Nissa." His words haunt me, echoing over my pulse. "Don't make this any harder than it needs to be."

I fling out a hand, and it connects with something solid.

Muscle.

Tightness wraps around my wrists and I'm dragged, pulled against something warm.

I attempt to fight. In my mind, I'm battling the enemy with all my might, but in reality, I'm not sure I even move.

I can't.

My head droops against his chest. I can smell him. Can scent the dizzying masculinity of his cologne. "Fuck you."

"Shh." His breath caresses my cheek. "Give in, little fox." His arms wrap around me, holding me close. "Stop fighting."

"No," I mumble, my lips numb. "You're going to..."

The words don't come. I hear them, think them, but they don't leave my mind. They're stuck in the growing darkness, clambering to break free.

I want him to know how much he will regret this.

He's going to pay... But the heaviness... The encroaching shadows.

I collapse, falling into his hold, succumbing to obscurity.

"It's okay," he murmurs in my ear. "I've got you."

10

ANISSA

I wake in comfort. The softness of a delicate pillow cradles my cheek, the gentle press of silk sheets brushing my neck.

I jerk upright, opening my eyes to an immaculate room brightened by the sunshine pouring in behind thick, elegant curtains.

I don't know this place. I've never seen any of the furniture before. Not the polished, dark wood dresser. Or the carved antique chair in the corner.

But more unnerving than the unfamiliar setting is the uncomfortable dawning I've lost at least eight hours of my life if the brightness of the sun is any indication.

I remember Cole picking me up in a limo, taking me to the airport, and then being on a private jet. We were civil. He offered to help find the missing women.

No. He had information to assist in saving them.

Important information.

Then... I struggle to remember what comes next.

I'd been drinking. I'd poured myself a glass of vodka. Then Cole gave me one more.

There's no way I would've consumed enough to make me pass out. I've *never* passed out.

That asshole must have slipped me a roofie.

I throw back the covers, and the rush of movement makes my wrists protest. They ache. Throb. I glance down to see red streaks marking my skin, the damage peeking out from beneath the cuffs of my blouse.

My stomach lurches at the thought of what was done to me. The possibilities batter my mind. I rush from the bed, my feet hitting plush carpet.

My shoes... I've got no shoes.

Thank fuck my clothes are still intact. But someone took my goddamn shoes.

Cole.

Why?

Why the hell would he drug me and bring me back to his house? Why the hell would he do any of this?

I pace as I frantically contemplate. I need to settle myself before I storm from the room to face him.

He didn't hurt me. Not apart from the marks on my wrists.

Maybe he didn't drug me either.

Maybe... *Fuck.*

The possibilities are endless, and my wild imagination isn't helping.

I inhale deep, measuring my breath. I'm not going to hyperventilate over this. Not yet. There's no reason to panic until I know what happened.

Doesn't mean I shouldn't protect myself.

I crouch, reaching for the ankle holster hiding my pepper spray. I'm not surprised to find it isn't there. There's only more tenderness to match my wrists.

"Cole, what the hell have you done?" The question whispers from my parched lips.

I must have been bound, hog-tied, while left fully dressed and without any indication of sexual violation.

He then made sure I was comfortable. My binds were removed. I was placed in an expensive bed. In an extravagant room.

The evidence is contradictory. Hog-tied and comforted. Drugged yet nurtured.

The pounding beneath my skull doesn't make the puzzle any easier to figure out.

Maybe he realized he made a mistake. He could've been worried about my safety.

Did he want to keep an eye on me?

I can't help trying to convince myself of the placations. But that's exactly what they are. I'm grasping for the best-case scenario.

Worst-case?

I shudder, my chest hollowing.

Am I victim number ten?

I glance around, taking more notice of my surroundings. This isn't a prison cell. It's an elegantly furnished bedroom, oozing sophistication.

It isn't a place that promotes confinement.

There's a window, for heaven's sake. And yes, Cole's house is big, but it isn't a palace with walls too high to scale down.

If I wanted, I'm sure I could open the window and escape to the lawn below. Then all I'd have to do is walk to the nearest house to ask for assistance.

Easy.

I'm certain there's a simple explanation for all of this. I'll be laughing over my wild imagination as soon as the dust settles.

I bridge the distance to the window and pull aside the curtain. The material grates along a metal track, causing a growl of noise to spike my apprehension. But it's the view that ignites panic.

I see water. An open expanse of deep blue that doesn't resemble anything close to the Willamette River.

This is the ocean. Lots and lots of ocean as far as the eye can see.

"Holy shit." I gasp.

The view doesn't resemble anything close to the beaches along the Oregon coast. There's no sand. Only rock. And the shore is close to the house. This doesn't look like any place I've visited before.

Everything inside me hollows—my stomach, my chest, my lungs. Confusion and hysteria battle for supremacy through a rapidly pounding heart.

I grasp the pane and pull, opening the window a crack.

Fresh air engulfs me, the warm breeze hotter than the cooler Portland weather. But the temperature shouldn't be my focus. I have to remind myself the window opened.

It fucking opened.

I'm not a prisoner. My thoughts return to this being a simple misunderstanding… With burns on my wrists.

I start toward the door, my steps slow as I pull myself together.

I'm not going to show fear. Nothing has changed. I'll remain cool, calm, and charismatic… *Yeah, because that worked so fucking well for me last night.*

I grasp the door handle, the brass twisted in an elegant style, and slowly lower the lever. I don't make a noise as I pull the obstruction open a crack and listen for clues.

At first, there's nothing—only the rustle of breeze in the distance. The gentle *whoosh* of air is comforting, portraying freedom.

I inch the door wider and peek outside, finding a dimly lit hall, the runner along the carpet plush and, yet again, elegant. To the right, large, ornate paintings are spaced along the walls. Some sort of Roman warrior statue stands atop a pedestal, staring back at me from the very far end.

To the left, there's more hall, much, much more, with a break in the middle leading into a light-filled area.

A clatter sounds in the distance. The noise associated with a kitchen. Then there's a clink of cutlery.

Food.

My stomach rumbles in optimism.

I pull the door wide and tiptoe from the room, creeping my way toward the opening in the hall. My wrists and ankles throb with each twinge of movement. My heart thunders, each step bringing a harder beat.

The further I trek, the brighter the light seeps in, the louder the breeze gets, the more definitive those food-prep noises become.

There's no hint of danger, only the prickle at the back of my neck making my nerves sensitive to everything around me.

I pause before the opening of the hall, pressed tight against the wall while I remain in the shadows. For long heartbeats, I stay frozen, breathing deep, preparing myself for the worst before I glance around the corner and find Cole in an immaculate kitchen.

He's standing before a cooktop in the middle of an island counter, a stainless canopy rangehood above his head as he grips a frying pan with one hand and a spatula in another.

The sight is almost comical. Entirely bizarre.

He's different—almost unrecognizable in a short-sleeved collared shirt, his dark hair damp and casually mussed.

It's the first time I've seen him without a suit. He seems almost naked in comparison, his arms holding more muscle than I would've imagined. If I'd ever imagined them. Which I haven't.

"You hungry?" He doesn't take his attention from the pan, and my pulse rate increases with the thought of someone else being here with us.

A threat.

An accomplice to my abduction.

"I've been waiting for you to wake up," he continues. "I hope you like eggs."

I don't move.

"Anissa?" He glances in my direction, and I plaster myself back against the wall.

Shit.

I'm unprepared.

I don't know what to do. What to say. I have no idea how to react, but I refuse to appear weak.

"You must be starving." His voice is entirely casual.

Fuck.

I can't stand here forever. The lack of movement is more telling of my vulnerability than words could ever be.

I suck in a deep breath and bounce my butt off the wall, striding out into the open space. "What time is it?"

Sheer curtains billow in front of an open glass door leading outside. I see the faint outline of deck chairs, a beach umbrella, maybe even the corner of a pool. But nothing beyond. No hint or clue as to my location.

He flips something in the pan, the accompanying sizzle crackling in my ears. "That depends." His tone is ominous.

No, I'm wrong. It's not his tone. It's his words. They almost resemble a threat.

"What time is it?" I repeat with a bite of impatience.

"Like I said, that depends." He flicks his gaze toward me, giving me a glimpse of lazy contact before he returns his attention to the food. "Are you referring to Pacific time or Eastern European?"

Eastern European?

I chuckle even though my stomach free falls, his taunt hitting its mark. "Why would I want to know Eastern European, Cole? Where are we?"

"The Greek islands." He offers the insight without faltering. Just blurts that shit as if it doesn't have the ability to inspire a heart attack.

I swallow over the desert claiming my throat. "Quit playing games. I didn't have a passport. I wasn't even conscious. You're not going to get me to believe we're in another country."

He raises his brows and holds my gaze. Waiting.

There's nothing smug about his expression. It's not taunting or impatient.

I guess it's curious.

Why is it curious?

I glance toward the billowing curtains again and try harder to make out the background beyond the pool loungers.

He wants me to go outside. He expects me to panic and rush toward clarity, only to laugh in my face when I realize we're somewhere close to home. Maybe Astoria or Cannon Beach. A few hours' drive from familiarity.

The need for answers kills me, the tendrils of possibility coiling around my chest to squeeze tight. I can't help giving him what he wants.

I start for the glass doors, slow and gradual, hoping to keep my self-respect intact.

"You don't want to have breakfast first?"

There's another sizzle from the pan but I ignore it, along with the question as I reach the curtains and pull them aside. The double glass doors are open, allowing me to step outside onto the warm cement tile.

An outdoor oasis spreads before me. A crystal-clear pool. Manicured waist-high hedges. A spa.

This place resembles some sort of mini resort. It's a multi-million-dollar property with another view of the ocean from this side of the building.

I walk around the pool, heading toward a path between the hedges that leads somewhere outside this hellish paradise.

The air is different here. Crisper. Cleaner. The salt of the ocean lingers with every breath. It doesn't feel like I'm Stateside. Or that could be Cole working his way into my head to trigger my paranoia.

He keeps manipulating me, messing with my thoughts.

I increase my pace, finding a stone path leading through long, wild grass. The expanse of land opens up before me, an unfettered view of ocean across 180 degrees.

I break into a jog, following the trail toward a pier. My feet hit the wooden planks hard in my rush to the very end. My body is a mix of numb limbs and throbbing arrhythmia as I turn in a full circle to find more water. It's everywhere. In every direction, apart from the restricted view behind the stunning beach house.

What the hell have you done, Cole?

I shove my hands through my hair, trying to rack my brain for a possible name to my location. We could be on the tip of the coast somewhere. A secluded hideaway exclusive to the rich and famous.

I stalk from the pier, bypassing the path to jump along the rocky shore. I pass shrubs and more wild grass in my search for humanity. I lunge over crevasses carved out by the tide. I push my legs harder, accelerating into a jog. All that does is help me see more water.

There's nothing else out here.

No land. No escape. No options.

I pivot and sprint in the opposite direction, cutting through vegetation, my feet punished by prickles and stones until I reach the perfectly manicured grass of the yard. I dash around the pool to take another path on the far side, leading in the opposite direction, only to be devastated by the sight.

More water.

We're surrounded.

The ground beneath my feet is nothing but a tiny island.

More are scattered in the distance, with a large expanse of land stretching along the horizon. Any chance of escape too far away.

Escape isn't within my grasp.

Even if I had assurance the water wasn't littered with hungry sharks, I could never swim that far. There's no hope of paddling to safety.

No hope for anything.

My breathing comes short and sharp. Each exhale is a shudder.

I'm stuck here. On an island. With a murderous criminal.

I drag my feet to the shore and crumple, slumping onto the rock to stare blankly across a building nightmare.

This feels like an alternate reality. I stepped onto that jet and my life changed. It fractured.

All because I couldn't keep my nose out of it.

I had to go after Cole. I had to succumb to that nagging twinge deep down inside me. For what? What had I hoped to achieve? Why didn't I stay away?

I undo the buttons on the wrist cuffs of my blouse and inspect my skin in the bright light of day. They're burns. Potential rope marks. I twist my arms back and forth, cursing Cole for every inch of damaged flesh.

This isn't right. I don't understand his angle. How can he benefit from holding me hostage?

I lower the cuffs back in place and begin undoing the buttons down the front of my blouse, determine to inspect every inch of my skin for possible violations. My stomach is clear, without a blemish, but I have to do a double-take when I tilt my head to look at the side of my waist.

My skin bears a bruise, the area circular, under an inch in diameter. I crane my neck for a better look, and hold my breath at the sight of a puncture mark.

Oh, God.

Bile goes into mass production in my stomach. Nausea takes over.

Did he bother to use a clean needle?

My breathing becomes ragged. My arms tremble.

There's no way he's going to get away with this.

Once he takes me home, he'll be charged with a string of offences. I'll take pleasure in outlining all the crimes he's made against me.

A prison sentence is inevitable. I'll make sure of it… Unless he doesn't plan on taking me home at all.

I give way to the buckle of my legs and descend to the rocky shore, sitting my ass down to pull my knees to my chest.

Could he seriously be contemplating keeping me here? Killing me?

My death wouldn't achieve anything, except maybe mild satisfaction on his behalf. And even if he successfully disposed of my body, there's no way he wouldn't be linked to my disappearance.

I battle confusion, my head growing heavy the more my speculation builds.

I can't make sense of his actions. No matter what way I look at this, his motives seem careless and unplanned. If he wanted to kill me, he could've achieved his goal easier in Portland. He has an enforcer on staff to handle those situations. They've perfected the art of getting away with murder.

So why bring me here? What is his objective?

I don't know how long I sit there, wallowing in impending doom with the sun directly overhead to sizzle my skin when I hear an abnormal buzzing, burring sound.

I snap my gaze to the left, a speedboat catching my eye in the distance.

It's approaching.

I'm on my feet in seconds, my heart racing as I flail my arms in an attempt to draw attention. The hope of savior brings time to a grinding halt. The progression takes forever, the boat barely seeming to move despite its generous size.

It's definitely not small, and the closer it gets the more luxurious it appears. A rail borders the elongated front with enough room for a tanning area, while the back and upper deck, have more free space than my apartment.

Much more than a speedboat, it's a knight in sea-sprayed armor.

I continue to wave my arms, swinging them wildly while I jump, jump, jump.

The boat progresses closer and closer, spurring my hope higher and higher, until it pivots within half a mile of the shore, heading somewhere behind my private island hell.

"*Where are you going?*" I scream.

I collapse back onto the rock, listening to the burr of the boat as it fades, then abruptly stops.

One minute the sound is there, then it's gone. I tilt my head, wondering if my mind is playing tricks on me.

No. It's not.

The boat must have diverted to the pier.

I scramble onto my feet and sprint, heading back along the path I came. Through the yard, alongside the pool, and down the other trail. I silently pray as I pant out the distance, hoping and wishing for a quick salvation.

And there it is, my savior, docked at the very far end of the pier.

I glance over my shoulder as I run, cautious of my captor trying to stop me, but he's nowhere in sight.

Hopefully the sizzling of the frying pan is too loud for that motherfucker to hear me speed out of here. And if I'm really lucky, he'll choke on whatever breakfast he's slaved over.

This time, when my feet hit the wooden planks, my heart soars.

Two men are aboard the fancy boat. They're both in the back, one bent over, tending to something at his feet. The other smiles at me as I approach, the laugh lines of a man well into his fifties filling me with relief.

"*Kali mere, omorfo thyma.*" He waves at me in greeting.

I stupidly wave back, momentarily stunned because I don't know a lick of Greek. Not one single word.

"I need help." I pause, waiting for a glimpse of understanding.

His smile grows wider, the bright white of his teeth in heavy contrast to the dark tan of his skin.

"I have to get to the mainland. Do you have a phone?"

I have to tell someone my location. Nobody knows where I am.

Nobody even knows I was docile enough to meet up with Cole.

"Cell phone," I repeat as I stop beside the boat. "Tel-uh-fohn?"

The man continues to smile. No, he's almost laughing.

I frown, not appreciating his humor over my lack of communication when my captor could come after me at any minute. "Ih-mur-juhn-see."

"He's not going to help you."

I turn my attention to the man bent over two large duffels.

His voice is pure American English. Not a hint of an accent.

He straightens, lifting one of the bags onto his shoulder. Our eyes meet and familiarity brings an icy chill to my bones.

Luca Hart.

One of Cole's men.

His lips are set in a tight line, his brow pulled tight. "I suggest you go back inside." He lugs the duffel onto the pier, then does the same with the second. "You're not going anywhere today."

"I need help," the old man mocks in a high-pitched, almost unrecognizable accent. "Ih-mur-juhn-see. Ih-mur-juhn-see." He releases a belly laugh, the noise ricocheting through my head and turning my cheeks to flame.

I retreat a step, then another.

I've been furious before. Recently, I've been caught in one red-hot rage after another. But what I feel right now goes beyond that.

It's fire and ferocity. Venom and vengeance.

This man is taking joy from my life-threatening situation.

He wants my fear, and I sure as fuck won't give it to him.

"Thanks for the ride." Luca climbs from the boat and drags one of the duffels from the pier over his shoulder. He jolts with the weight, and I force myself not to think of what could be hidden inside.

"Anhjoy." The old predator grins.

Enjoy? Fucking asshole.

"Yeah... Thanks." Luca nudges past me and stalks toward the house, not sparing me a second glance.

They're cocky as hell, with no concern over my possible escape.

They think I'm stuck here, but I refuse to believe it.

The statistics on survival for abducted victims is low once they're taken to a new location. It's imperative I find a way off this island. Cole has all the power here.

I need to demand assistance.

This old wrinkled fuck isn't going to get away with leering, laughing, and loading me with his caustic vibes.

"I need help," I repeat, this time with a venomous tone as I approach the boat. "You need to give me your phone."

I move to climb aboard, swinging one leg over the side of the vessel to place my foot on a padded bench seat beneath. "And take me to the mainland."

I chance another glance over my shoulder, making sure Luca isn't rushing back to stop me, before raising my other leg.

The unmistakable click of a cocking gun makes me freeze.

My heart stutters and I struggle not to become a victim of hysteria when I tilt my face to find a barrel aimed right between my eyes.

"Off," he grunts. "Off my boat."

I raise my hands slowly. "Please lower your weapon."

"Off." He jerks the gun toward the pier. "Off. Off."

"Okay. I'm getting off." I measure my movements, backtracking gradual and steady. I can feel the aim between my eyes. The pressure heavy.

I watch him, watch the gun, watch anything and everything in the hopes the scrutiny will save me.

One foot reaches the pier, closely followed by the other.

Even without the threat of me being on the vessel, the man keeps me in his sights and sidesteps until he's under the shade of the cabin, directly in front of the steering wheel.

There's no smile anymore. No taunting laugh or infuriating leer.

But there's annoyance.

He's angry I spoiled his fun.

"I'm an American citizen," I repeat. "I work for—"

My words are cut off by the roar of the boat's engine. Then he's taking off, speeding away in a mass of swirling whitewash and taking any hope of escape with him.

I stand there for so long, watching him drive out of view. Then longer, until I'm unable to hear another sign of life. Or freedom.

The anger doesn't dissipate. It builds, growing alongside my frustration.

My life can't be in danger. It can't be, despite the gun that threatened to blow my brains out moments ago. Cole isn't a stupid man. Thinking he can kill me and get away with it is ludicrous.

Yet, he's brought me here against my will, exposing himself to a whole new level of crime.

The staff at the airport saw us together.

The pilots. The limo driver.

Someone will talk.

Someone *has* to talk.

My pulse grows frantic, beating out of control.

Cole and his family have gotten away with a multitude of offences. He's a walking, talking bucket list of unpunished criminal activity.

God, if his father can escape incarceration for sex trafficking and solicitation, what's to stop Cole from covering up the disappearance of a disgraced FBI agent?

"Fuck." I swallow over the horrid taste at the back of my throat and clasp my hands behind my head.

I need to think.

Think. Think. Think.

This is just another taunting game.

He'll try to pretend I agreed to this impromptu vacation. Maybe he even has a video of me, drugged and disorderly, slurring through an agreement to accompany him here.

He would've covered his ass somehow, which means this is only temporary.

Once he's had his fill of entertainment, I'll be worthless.

Meaningless.

My hands fall to my sides, and my focus shifts to the lone duffel still sitting on the wooden planks before me. I sink to my haunches, determined to find something useful—a weapon, a phone, I'd settle for matches to set this island ablaze—as I pull the zipper.

Material comes into view as I yank the opening wide. Material I begin to recognize as I scrounge around inside.

These are my clothes. My blouses. My jeans. My fucking underwear. Along with a large clip-lock bag containing my hair and toothbrushes, hair-ties, and moisturizer. Almost anything and everything that lived on the top of my bathroom vanity.

They've been in my apartment, scavenging through my belongings.

Cole thought of everything. This wasn't a spur-of-the-moment plan. He must have had each step and contingency in place. Maybe even from the moment he met me in the coffee shop.

He anticipated my retaliation. He knew I'd come after him when he made me his alibi. He created the perfect opportunity to offer me information in exchange for another meeting. He predicted I'd take him up on his offer. He fucking read me like a book.

I became distracted by my need for justice and never noticed the moves he made toward a far bigger game.

"Fucking hell." I wipe a hand over my face and drag my feet back down the pier.

I don't bother with the duffel. I leave it where it lays. Luca might expect me to haul my own luggage inside, but they'll both get a surprise when they realize I have no intention of going back inside at all.

If they want entertainment, they won't get it from me.

There will be no begging for freedom or bending to their will.

If Cole Torian wants to continue to make a fool out of me, he will need to come find me first.

11

TORIAN

Luca eyes me from the sofa, his stare holding a hint of judgment. "How long are you going to keep her outside? There's no fresh water out there, and she's been in the sun all day."

"Keep her?" I continue to cut the fruit housekeeping stocked in the fridge. "The only thing keeping her outside is her stubborn pride."

"You sure she's not scared?"

I scoff. "That woman wouldn't feel fear if it bit her on the ass."

"And you're not worried she'll do something stupid?"

"Not at all. What's she going to do? Build a raft and paddle her way off the island?"

He holds up his hands in surrender. "It's just getting dark, that's all."

I'm well aware.

I've waited all day to speak to her. I've deliberately given her space. I wanted her to have time to think. I also needed my own breathing room.

This morning didn't go to plan.

Luca was meant to be here before she woke up. I wanted the island contained. Free from the possibility of escape.

The confrontation with the boat driver shouldn't have happened.

It was neither predicted nor appreciated.

I'd walked outside to check on her after Luca updated me on the situation, only to find a gun pointed at her head. Her life whittled down to the hair trigger of a simple ferry man.

It took all my restraint to watch the interaction play out, my hands clenched at my sides, my jaw wired shut.

Common sense demands nobody would dare kill a woman of mine, captive or not, but common fucking sense seems to be in short supply these days.

"In half an hour, it's going to be pitch black out there," Luca adds. "And if you do finally decide to search her out, it's going to be the prime opportunity for a woman like that to do a surprise shank attack."

A woman like that—determined, vindictive, strong.

"I'm well aware." I finish slicing the watermelon and place it on a plate beside nectarines, grapes, and cherries, then grab a bottle of water from the fridge. She's spent too long without food and water. And with or without Luca's prodding, I had every intention of going out to face her as soon as I'd finished preparing her something to eat.

I palm the filled plate and place the bottle under my arm, then start for the open doors.

"You're going?" he asks.

I don't answer. Luca's unhealthy obsession with preparation needs to be worn down. He doesn't always have to know what I'm doing.

He sits up straight. "If you're not back in an hour, I'll come rescue you."

"Don't bother. If she outsmarts me, she deserves to get away with it."

He doesn't respond, neither confirming or denying the instruction.

It's so he can claim ignorance later if he does have to rush to my aid.

His loyalty has recently stretched far beyond anything given from my other men, even though everyone in my employ is impeccably devoted. I think he's been waiting for something to focus on since his discharge from the SEALs, and thankfully, me and my family became his distraction. He's becoming an asset. A dedicated soldier.

I walk outside, around the pool area, right up to the manicured hedge used as a makeshift boundary to the yard, and scope out the desolate island.

There's no sign of life.

She's not on the pier or along the shore as far as the eye can see. She could be on the other side of the house, but I doubt it.

I'll bet her hiding place is among the only group of trees straight ahead. I wouldn't be surprised if she'd monkey-d her way up one of them, determined to stay out of reach.

I slip through a break in the hedge and walk through tall grass, the long strands whipping at my jeans in the breeze. The wide trunks and billowing branches provide a secluded canopy out here—the perfect shelter. Or an ideal base camp for war.

I'm a few feet from the boundary of trees when I hear a nearby rustle of undergrowth. *Bingo.* She's here. And hopefully not about to swing from a vine to ruin the fruit platter I spent way too long creating.

"I come in peace." I hold the plate up with one hand and the bottle of water high in the other.

More rustling sounds, then the snap of a twig.

"I've got food." I take another step and another. "You need to eat."

There's no response. I guess I don't expect one. Not if it isn't violent.

I reach the first tree and peer around to see what's hidden inside the circular canopy. I don't react at the sight of her standing with her back to one of the trunks, her body in a fighting stance, a sharpened stick clutched in her fist.

I don't allow myself the luxury of an opinion. I'm not going to fixate on the tangled mess of her short, dark hair. Or the gentle glow of her skin that says she's spent too much time in the sun.

I'm not going to acknowledge how impressed I am at the pile of makeshift weapons at her feet, the sharpened branches resting into a subtle pyramid. And I'm definitely not going to be annoyed by her constant need to fight.

I'm nothing.

I can't mess with her anymore. Things have changed.

"Drop the weapon, little fox. The chances of you succeeding are slim to none. But the likelihood I'll retaliate is one-hundred percent."

"Slim to none?" She quirks a brow. "I can deal with those odds."

I clamp my lips shut, determined not to grin, and throw the bottle of water at her feet. "Drink."

She scoffs. "And be drugged again? No, thank you."

"There's no drugs. It's time to move forward."

She doesn't budge, remaining in her battle position, slowly twisting her stabbing stick between the fingers of her right hand.

"Okay. I see you're reluctant to trust." I hold up my free hand, solemnly vowing my surrender. "That's understandable. But why don't you sit for a while and give me the chance to explain?"

"If you think I'll believe your words will ever hold any truth, you're delusional. Have you heard the story of the boy who cried wolf?"

"Yes, I'm familiar."

"Then you'll also be familiar with what happens to that little fucker." Her words are vicious, snapped between fierce lips. "And do you know what else, Cole?"

I keep my mouth under control, fucking determined not to smirk. There's something invigorating about her. Something in her violent energy that makes me burn. "What, Nissa?"

"He deserved it. And you will, too."

"When I get eaten by a wolf?"

"You are the wolf," she grates. "But you'll get what you deserve. I have no doubt."

I raise my brows, impressed at yet another new level to her anger. She's a feisty little thing. "Are you finished with the fairy-tales?"

"Fuck you."

I can't help it. A grin breaks free. "I'll take that as confirmation."

I glance around, searching for a place to sit—a rock, a ledge, something—because I have a strange feeling we're going to be stuck in a verbal sparring match for quite some time. "Don't go postal on me, but I'm going to come a little closer to put this plate down near your feet. I'd prefer if you didn't try to stab me in the jugular."

"I'd prefer if you crawled into a hole and died." She shrugs. "I don't think either of us are going to get what we want."

I chuckle. It can't be helped. "You're always filled with spirit, aren't you, Niss?"

"And you're always filled with sh—"

"Okay. Enough." I raise my voice, demanding control. "You need to eat." I take a step forward.

"Don't bother." She holds her weapon higher. "I'm not going to consume anything you've prepared. I've already learned from that mistake."

"Then you'll die from a lack of sustenance. Is your stubborn pride really that strong?"

"Stubborn pride?" She huffs out a derisive laugh. "It's called self-fucking-preservation. You got me suspended, broke into my house, and went through my belongings—my fucking underwear. You then plied me with a date-rape concoction. Kidnapped me. Injected me with drugs and—"

"There were no drugs or date-rape concoctions." I inch a step forward. "Only sedatives."

"I have track marks," she snarls.

"You have an injection site from a liquid sedative. I needed to make sure you remained asleep while we transported you."

"Bullshit."

"No, not bullshit. Do you seriously feel like you've had a narcotic hit?"

"How would I know? I'm not a user like you." She keeps the stick clenched in her hand and her stance strong.

"You'd know. Most drug highs usually demand an adverse payment. All those good feelings are reimbursed in the aftermath when you feel like hell."

"I certainly don't feel peachy, Cole."

I won't laugh again. I can't. I'm almost certain she will take the lousy odds and attempt a stabbing spree. "They were only sedatives. Nothing more sinister."

"That doesn't make what you've done any better. I'd been drinking. Everyone knows sedatives and liquor don't mix. What if I was allergic? Or had a reaction? Despite you being oblivious to the severity of what you've done, I could've died."

"That would've been unfortunate." I attempt another step, not taking my gaze off her, having the perfect view of her expression-filled face as a new layer of rage seems to set in. "I wouldn't have let anything happen to you, Nissa."

I crouch and place the plate a few feet from the pile of sticks. She eyes the offering and swallows hard.

It's clear she's starving. I'm sure she's suffering from thirst, too.

"What if I eat first?" I shouldn't care about her struggle. Not when it's now self-inflicted. All she needs to do is take a piece of fucking fruit. "You tell me what I should eat, and I'll eat it."

"How 'bout a bag of dicks?"

I grin. The constant snap, snap, snap of her remarks is a beautiful thing. "How 'bout a grape instead?" I reach for the plate and pop the fruit into my mouth. "And a cherry?" I steal another piece, chewing the juicy morsel before spitting the seed near her bare feet. "Anything else?"

She continues to inspect the plate, her tongue nervously snaking out to swipe her lower lip. "The watermelon."

Good. Those two words are a lifeline to civility.

I obey, grabbing a chunk from the top of the pile.

"No. Not that one." She points her stick to the opposite side of the plate. "Take one from the bottom."

I incline my head, happy to oblige, and finish the watermelon piece in two bites. "Believe me now?"

She doesn't answer as I withdraw, but she does creep forward to grab the plate, placing the stick under her arm for safekeeping. The cautious retreat back toward the tree is done in silence, her gaze never leaving mine.

"You don't need to keep glaring at me, sweetheart. You've made it crystal clear you're pissed off."

She sits on the ground, her bare feet covered in dirt. "Pissed off doesn't come close, *pumpkin*."

She grabs a slice of nectarine and cautiously inspects it, her focus returning to my face as she raises the food to her mouth.

I continue to place space between us while the fruit inches closer to those lips, the slow motion fucking with my mind, increasing my pulse. I never would've thought healthy eating could be this intriguing, but here I am, transfixed as she takes her first bite.

The slightest glimpse of bliss crosses her features in the roll of her eyes, the closing of her lids. I wait for a moan, for a needy groan of satisfaction. I can already hear it. Right there, on the tip of her tongue.

"Don't forget the water," I remind her.

Those luminous green eyes snap open. "Leave me alone."

"I wish I could." I glance to the ground, finding a relatively short expanse of grass, then sit my ass down. "Unfortunately, we're just getting started."

She doesn't respond with interest. Not even intrigue. I doubt she has any intent to listen to what I have to say, but she'll soon learn she has no choice. I can't let her go unless she believes my story. And she won't believe my story unless she's willing to listen.

"Nissa..." Where do I start? *How* do I start?

What she said last night was true. I've never interacted with a woman I couldn't walk over. Hunter's fiancée, Sarah, is the closest I've come to finding a female with balls, but she can still be tamed.

Everyone can be leashed.

Yet, this woman is different. So fucking different I struggle to predict what she'll do next. Or understand how I should manage her. She doesn't have clear indicators. At least not to me.

That's why I'm not going to bother beating around the metaphorical bush.

"The only insight I had into my father's escape came from his legal team," I start. "And I use the word 'insight' loosely."

"You're wasting your breath. I've gone beyond the point of being able to listen to you."

"I was told to keep myself busy in a public place before the court case."

She lets out a derisive huff. "And that didn't tip you off?"

"I made assumptions. But I didn't know."

"You knew enough to be held accountable for not informing the authorities." She pops a cherry into her mouth, her expression filled with superiority. "You may not have pulled the trigger that killed the guard, but you're guilty just the same."

I grind my teeth at her judgment.

I think this is the only time she gets to me. *Really* gets to me. When she looks down at my life, I see red. Until her, nobody has come close to making me feel inferior, and I want nothing more than to prove her wrong in whatever way possible.

She thinks she's better than me. That her way of thinking exceeds mine. That her form of justice is superior.

Like fuck.

She has no right to climb aboard her high horse.

"I said I didn't know the details. I never said I didn't want him free."

"And finally, the truth comes out," she drawls. "It's what I've known all along."

"You don't know shit." I force my mouth shut, clamping my teeth tight to stop another outburst.

For long moments, she taunts me with the raise of a haughty brow, popping one grape after another while I stew under her bigotry.

"I know you attack the lovely state of Oregon with your drugs."

And here we go with the illicit-substance debate. It's one of my favorites.

"The drug trade isn't an attack on anyone. It's an addiction not unlike caffeine or nicotine. The only difference is you consider it illegal."

"It *is* illegal. And heroine is nothing like coffee or cigarettes. Hard drugs kill people. They ruin families and create more violence and crime. You're literally poisoning the masses."

"And what about the poison you indulged in last night? You had no problem throwing back that Beluga. Alcohol also kills people, destroys families, and inspires violence. But because it's legal, you've got no problem with it. There's no logic to your rules."

Her nostrils flare. "There's a big difference."

"No, there's not." I've honestly never understood the distinction. "They both take away control from the user, act as a toxin against the body, and cause addiction."

She shakes her head, her jaw working overtime. "If you ever had to make the devastating discovery of a dead coke-head's frozen body on the streets, or had to watch a baby struggle through an addiction her mother gave her in the womb, your opinion wouldn't be the same."

She glares at me for a second, then lets out a bitter laugh. "What am I thinking? You're Cole Torian; you wouldn't give a shit about a homeless person, let alone a newborn. You've got no heart."

Maybe she's right.

Maybe I don't.

To me, the thought of the underprivileged valuing drugs above food, shelter, or health is fucking infuriating. They have no control. No sense. It's pathetic. And the mothers who shoot up while carrying a child should be sterilized.

But their actions have nothing to do with me. Never have.

"I provide a product. I don't force people to buy it. I can't be held responsible when a woman decides her next fix is more important than her fetus. And I certainly don't give a fuck when the homeless choose one more hit over a warm bed and a free meal from a shelter. It's their choice."

"There aren't enough shelters—"

"Don't fucking argue about things you know nothing about. I fund a local shelter, Ms. Fox. I get their reports and feedback. I know exactly how many people turn up in need of a bed and a warm meal, yet they arrive high as a fucking kite when they know it's against the rules. Then it's society's fault for not looking after them. They blame everyone but themselves. I don't create these fucking problems, Nissa. The users do."

"You taunt the weak. If your product wasn't available, they wouldn't succumb."

"You think the problem will disappear if I do?" I ask. Her comment is disappointing. Entirely naive and almost pitiful to hear. "All that will achieve is a war between rivals wanting to claim the position my family has held for generations. That's when your precious crime rate would skyrocket. Drive-bys would be an hourly occurrence. The streets would be bathed in blood until someone claimed power. But the problem would never disappear. Drugs are a necessary evil, whether you like it or not."

I let the information sink in.

She may detest the way I do business, but my crimes keep the peace. That's why I have willing police in my pockets. That's why the authorities help me, despite my illegal actions.

"*I'm* a necessary evil, little fox. And if you take the time to think about it, without society's blinders, you'll realize I'm right."

She shakes her head and slumps back against the tree. "Not going to happen."

"Then you're not only narrow-minded, you're a fool."

"And you're not only delusional, you're narcissistic." She crosses her arms over her chest, plumping her breasts beneath the blouse. "I bet the next thing you'll do is try to convince me you've done nothing wrong by abducting me. You haven't broken any laws. You haven't violated my freedom or safety. You're entirely innocent and free from blame."

I divert my gaze to the setting sun between the trees, unwilling to let her any further under my skin. We'll soon be in darkness. Nothing but the black of night and a wealth of hatred. As if our current situation wasn't already a volatile concoction.

"Again," I murmur, "it was a necessary evil."

Silence descends.

She doesn't reply. There's no curiosity. No apparent impulse to learn more.

"I understand you're not willing to give me a chance because you're clouded by misconceptions and preconceived notions. You're caught up in the regulations of a naïve society."

"I'm not willing to give you a chance? Really?" Her words are barely above a whisper. "Do you hear yourself?"

I return my gaze to her face, the shadows of approaching night creeping over her features.

"I agreed to have coffee with you. I boarded a jet even though the dangers were blindingly clear." She eyes the water bottle at her feet, suspicion and need pulling at her features. "I went with you, despite everything you'd previously done to me. I've given you chance after chance—"

"You're not kidding anyone," I growl. "You didn't want to meet with me to give me a chance. You were only hoping for the opportunity to take me down."

She grins, the curve of her lips sinister. "And now I have it. Because of this, you're going to be locked up, right alongside your father, for a damn long time."

This loop of hatred is unending. Tiring. I guess I have a limit when it comes to bitchy bad-assery, and she's reached it. I'm also growing annoyed at her stubborn nature. She's preoccupied with thirst, her gaze continuously straying to the bottle mere inches from her feet. Yet she won't fucking take it.

"Just drink the water, for Christ's sake." I scrub a hand down my face in an attempt to wipe away the frustration.

"And wake up tomorrow in another foreign country with my arms shredded from rope burns?"

"Shredded?" My attention snaps to the wrists covered by her white blouse. "Show me."

"Go to hell." She scowls, disbelieving my concern even though the emotion nips at my heels.

She hadn't been bound for my pleasure. The binds were necessary. Vital. There hadn't been a choice.

"I didn't mean for you to get hurt." A nagging pulse starts under my sternum, the throb digging deep.

Physical torture isn't a part of this. Yes, there's been mental manipulation and psychological fuckery. But that doesn't mean hurting her was in the plan.

"Only sedated and abducted," she drawls.

I ignore the barb, determined to pull this conversation back on track. "If you can't trust the unbroken seal on the bottle, then we can finish this inside where you have access to running tap water. Or do you think I would've drugged our entire water supply just to play games?"

"I wouldn't put it past you." She reaches for the bottle and cracks the lid. "I guess I don't have anything left to lose. You've already violated me in every way imaginable."

Hardly.

I could've done far worse, especially if I had my father's proclivities. "In the end, I'm sure you'll appreciate what I'm trying to achieve, despite the way I had to go about it."

"No, I won't." She drinks, taking large gulps before swiping a hand over her mouth. Then she returns her attention to the fruit, taking small bites of watermelon.

She's not going to let up with the attitude.

After all the scheming and plotting, I'm beginning to think my plan won't work. I've made a mistake. She won't listen.

"Better?" I ask.

She sighs. "Just say whatever you have to say, Cole. I'm growing tired of this."

Me, too.

Jesus Christ. Me fucking too.

"There's no point." I push to my feet. "You're not ready to hear me."

Maybe she never will be. Which puts us both in a difficult position.

"Look, I'm sorry things have turned out this way." I brush the dirt and leaves from my ass. "But for you to get home safely, we need to be able to work together. You have to forget the circumstances surrounding your arrival and concentrate on *why* this is necessary."

I pause, giving her the opportunity to continue the conversation. To reach out for a fucking olive branch. Instead, she remains quiet, glaring into the approaching night.

"Fine. I guess you've made your choice." I start for the edge of the tree canopy, each step a conscious reminder of how flawed my patience has become. "I'm going back to the house where there's plenty to eat and drink. If I were you, I wouldn't stay out here long. If the bugs don't get you, the wildlife will."

12

ANISSA

I don't say a word as he strides away.

I remain seated, stuck in sullen silence as the sunlight fades and darkness rapidly descends. The shadows grow taller, wider, as the gentle lap of the ocean becomes louder.

I'm entirely lost.

Physically and mentally.

I'm angry at myself. At Cole. And Luca. Not to mention that old fucking asshole on the boat.

But the aggression toward my captor is tainted with curiosity.

There was something different about him tonight. A change in demeanor I'm not familiar with.

He needs me for something. What? I'm not sure.

I clung too tight to my pride to ask. Or even listen.

I refused to surrender. I still don't want to budge an inch. Now, I'm stuck in ignorance.

It doesn't take long for the smell of a home-cooked meal to fill the air, brushing away the scent of salt and replacing it with enough herbs and spices to make my mouth salivate.

The fruit wasn't enough. It barely touched the sides of my hunger, and my throat remains dry with no more water to soothe the ache.

I'm growing cold. I'm dirty as hell. My feet throb. And I'm tired—the type of weary tiredness that starts in the bones and works its way out.

Yet, I can't will myself to get up and walk into that house with my tail between my legs. I don't want to go crawling back to him, even after his deluded attempt to make peace.

I'm always at war with him, regardless of the topic or the location. It's fight, fight, fight, and I'm not sure I know how to act any different.

Work together?

I scoff every time I contemplate the comedic partnership.

I can't work with him. I wouldn't even know how. Not when he's manipulated and fooled me enough times to eviscerate my self-respect.

The problem is, he brought me here for a reason. He wouldn't risk his freedom for a game. He couldn't. He acts invincible, but believing he can get away with the abduction of an FBI agent is insane.

He must need me for something.

And I'm certain I won't leave this island until he gets what he wants.

I close my eyes and rerun our conversation in my mind.

He was emotional. More prone to anger than his usual state of being calm and in control. He'd also seemed genuinely surprised and disturbed at the mention of my injuries.

I didn't mean for you to get hurt.

I can't believe his kindness at the moment. There's only speculation.

He tied me up. Drugged me. Took me from the US, without my consent or a passport.

But since waking in a foreign country, I guess I could agree he hasn't hurt me.

He didn't lock me in the bedroom. There weren't any restraints keeping me captive. He left me alone all day, not chasing me down or demanding anything from me. He gave me space, and later, food and water. He also arranged for my clothes to be brought here.

I can only conclude he wants my comfort.

I just wish I knew why.

The grass rustles in the breeze while I continue to speculate, the cool chill sinking into my arms. The temperature only drops with the passing hours.

At one point, I think I hear my name called in the distance. The temptation of a warm bed almost has me responding. But I remain in place, dozing against the trunk of the tree until the rustle of grass grows, the sound loud enough to bring me back to consciousness.

This time it's a contained noise. Not caused by the breeze. It's specific. To my right. Approaching.

"Cole?"

I sit up straight, the star-filled night subtly illuminating the darkness.

"Luca?"

My heartbeat increases, not quite loud enough to silence the *rustle, rustle, rustle*.

"I know you're there." I raise my voice and slowly inch to my feet, grabbing one of my sharpened sticks from the pile. "I can hear you."

There's no response. Not in words or in continued sound.

Everything falls quiet. There's only the lap of the ocean and my pounding pulse thundering in my ears.

"Is this another game? Am I meant to be scared?"

If so, he might be succeeding.

My imagination runs wild wondering what he's trying to achieve this time. Am I expected to run? Is this one of those games where rich fuckers pay to hunt people down?

A twig breaks to my left. A crunch of grass follows.

I twist toward the noise and scan the horizon for a silhouette.

Someone is out here.

I'm not alone.

"Cole?" I hold my stance, frozen, barely breathing. I stay there for long minutes, becoming one with the night. "I've got a weapon."

I cling tight to the stick, my palm growing slick with sweat. There's another rustle. A crunch. A snap.

Air congeals in my lungs, making it hard to breathe.

"I'm—"

Something slides over my foot. Heavy and smooth.

I scream, not even thinking before I break into a run and escape the circle of trees. Pain slices through my bare feet. I step on pebbles, rocks, prickles, and still I keep running. I stumble over unlevelled ground, tumbling to the grass, the stick stabbing the dirt with the heavy weight of my shoulder falling on top of it.

I cry out, the impact sending an explosion of pain to slice through my collarbone and down my arm.

"Jesus. *Fuck.*" I drop the stick and roll onto my back. I clutch at my shoulder, my fingers gliding over dry material, not blood, despite feeling like I've been shot.

There's another rustle, a snap, and I'm on my feet again, ignoring the injury to continue sprinting toward the house. My vision through the darkness vanishes as I focus on those bright lights, but I don't care.

I keep running toward the only refuge available.

Air pants from my lungs as I push myself faster, bumping into the hedge, before my sore shoulder collides with something solid and unyielding. I twirl with the impact. I probably perform a perfect pirouette before starting another rapid descent toward the ground, only to be stopped by strong hands gripping my arms to pull me upright.

"Cole?"

In this moment, I don't feel any anger. Or fear. Or resentment.

I've been running toward safety—toward *him*—and I can't deny the overwhelming rush of relief.

"No, not Cole."

Luca.

His deep voice brings an icy chill.

I yank my arms from his grasp, wincing at the throb in my shoulder, and stumble backward, my feet connecting with soothing tile.

"Calm down," he warns. "You're safe."

I continue retreating, not believing him. "Where's Cole?"

He steps toward me, his profile gaining more definition as my eyes adjust. He's wearing a thread-bare tank and boxers, exposing inch after inch of muscle, which seems like a threat to my safety. "Inside. Asleep."

It doesn't feel right that the man who abducted me now suddenly seems like my only solace. In fact, it feels downright pathetic, but there's no one else. *Nothing* else.

All I have to cling to is the brief glimpse of Cole's kindness and his solemn promise that he has no intention of hurting me.

"Are you okay?" Luca's voice softens. "I heard you scream."

My cheeks heat.

I'd thought I was under attack, when it's more likely I've scared the hell out of whatever creatures call this island home.

"Anissa?" His shadowed hand reaches out.

"Stop." Whatever he's trying to achieve—my trust, my comfort—he's not going to succeed.

"Okay." His arm falls to his side. "Are you ready to come into the house? There's leftover dinner in the fridge."

Through the heavy rush of adrenaline and the rapid heartbeat, my stomach still has the ability to grumble at the thought of food.

God, I'm starving.

"Come on." He turns, leading the way toward the house.

I don't want to follow. I shouldn't.

My head tells me to go back into the darkness and learn to live with the wildlife, while my aching limbs, tired bones, and hollow stomach encourage my feet to inch forward.

I can't stay strong without food. I need fresh water, otherwise my health will deteriorate quickly.

He walks through the open glass doors, the sheer curtain gently billowing around him as I tag a few feet behind.

I'm blinded by the lighting. Every lamp has been switched on. Every overhead glistening halogen beams down with a warm glow. Did they leave them on for me?

"What do you want to eat?" Luca starts toward the kitchen. "There's leftover tacos. Or fruit. Chocolate. Cake. You name it."

"No." My mouth would salivate over week-old bread at the moment. But sustenance needs to wait. "I want to see Cole first."

If he's asleep, he needs to wake to the sight of me. I have to see his instinctual emotion, the sleep-roughened truth, before he can hide it behind lies.

Luca nods and diverts his path, continuing toward the start of the hall I'd walked down earlier. I hustle to keep up, my feet beginning to protest, my shoulder incessant with its dull throb.

He flicks on another light, and this time I'm prepared. My sight rapidly adjusts and I can see the large length of space stretched out before me, the overbearing art lining the walls.

I'm led right to the very end, to a lone closed door.

"He's in here?" I stop a few feet away, still needing space.

"Yeah. Just knock to wake him."

I ignore the instruction and snatch at the handle, pushing the door wide.

Light invades the darkened room, highlighting a monstrous four-poster bed and an equally monstrous man snapping upright from beneath the covers. Shirtless.

I'm stunned.

Speechless.

A mass of chest, stomach, and arm muscles are on display. Thick muscles I never would've expected hidden beneath those expensive suits he always wears.

I knew his mind was lethal, but the strength laid out before me proves his body is, too. All this time I thought he liked to flaunt his strength when the reality now seems far different. He's hidden his capabilities. At least his physical ones.

I don't wait for him to invite me in.

I stalk forward, reaching the bottom corner of the bed before he's had time to blink away sleep. He's an entirely different man with his hair mussed and eyes squinted. I could be fooled into thinking he has vulnerabilities when I see him like this.

"Why am I here?" I grip the elegantly carved wooden pole holding up the canopy. "I need to know the point of all this?"

He quickly wins the battle to wake up, the docile expression transforming to a frown as his attention treks over my face. My blouse. My arms.

There's no anger or spite in his features. His animosity isn't evident. All that stares back at me is concern.

"What's going on?" he demands. "What happened?"

"Nothing—"

"I heard her scream," Luca interrupts from the door. "She came running toward the house in a panic. I tried to get her to eat, but she wanted to see you first."

I clench my teeth against the pathetic truth, and tell myself their opinion doesn't matter. They can believe what they like about me. I'll happily prove them wrong.

In fact, it's better if they start to think I'm weak.

"Thanks," Cole directs toward Luca, but his eyes never stray from mine. "Go to bed. I can handle this from here."

There's no reply. Not in words. The light pad of retreating footsteps are the only response, the sound quickly fading to leave us alone in silence.

"Go to the kitchen." He swings his legs to the side of the bed and grabs the covers, poised to fling them away. "I'll meet you there in a minute."

I don't move. I'm not willing to let him out of my sight. If he's going to grab a weapon, I want to know where he retrieves it from. I'm done with being clueless. "I'll wait."

"Suit yourself." He throws back the quilt and shoves to his feet, exposing an entirely naked ass.

"Holy shit." I avert my gaze as heat not only floods my cheeks, but my entire body. "You could've warned me."

"I did. Forgive me for being subtle."

There isn't a damn thing subtle about that sculpted body.

Not a damn thing.

Every inch of him is toned. Calves. Thighs. Hips.

He pulls on a pair of jeans, the thrust and tug of legs and arms visible in my periphery. "Let's get you some food." He strides for the door and treks his hands through his hair, regaining some of his air of perfection.

"I want answers first." I tag along after him. "Food can wait."

"You can have both at the same time."

He flicks off the hall light as we enter the main room, and stalks straight for the fridge. He pulls out container after container, placing them on the island counter, before returning to grab a jug of water and a bottle of juice. "Help yourself."

I lift the offerings, glancing inside the plastic tubs to inspect the contents while he grabs a plate and a glass from a nearby cupboard to sit them in front of me.

"Juice or water?" He places a hand on both jugs, waiting.

It still doesn't feel right to accept anything from him. Even a simple glass of OJ seems like a bribe, but I can't be stubborn a moment longer.

"Water."

He lifts the jug and begins to pour as if he's entirely at home. "You were outside a long time. I thought you would've succumbed earlier when you needed to make use of the facilities."

I glare. "I made do." I had to resort to squatting against a tree and using leaves instead of toilet paper.

He doesn't laugh, but I see the mirth in his eyes.

Asshole.

I reach for the closest container and prepare to open the taco mince, only to wince at the protest from my shoulder. It throbs with the movement, letting me know a wicked bruise will be waiting for me if I ever get the chance to look at myself in a mirror again.

"You're hurt." Cole dumps the jug on the counter and stalks around the island toward me. "What happened?"

"Nothing." I backtrack, staying out of reach until he stops.

"Anissa." I'm not sure if my name is a plea or a warning as he wipes a rough hand through his hair. He's the picture of exhausted frustration. "Tell me what happened. If you're hurt, I can arrange for a doctor to see you."

A doctor?

Hope distracts me from the pain.

I analyze his tone, his features, his…everything. Is the kindness a ploy? A tactic?

"I tripped and landed awkwardly. I strained or pulled a muscle in my shoulder."

"Show me," he demands.

"Like hell."

He might be eager to flaunt his nudity, but that shit isn't mutual.

"I'm not asking for a lap dance. I only want to take a look at your shoulder." Annoyance seeps into those ocean eyes, and I kiss goodbye to the thought of a doctor's visit.

"It's nothing." Nothing that will have me stripping in front of him, anyway. "Can you please just let me eat?"

His jaw tics, and he takes a few steps back to snatch the container from the counter.

"I'll do it for you." He pops the lid and places the taco mince in the microwave, the spiced scent filling the air in seconds and sending my stomach into an unending loop of somersaults.

"I won't be able to eat all that," I admit.

"Eat what you can. I'm not concerned about waste."

He's not concerned about anything. Not wasted food, or the expense of a private jet, or abduction. Life is void of problems for him. And he's definitely not in a hurry to talk, seeing as though he remains quiet while he retrieves tortillas from a cupboard, then opens more containers filled with diced tomatoes and thinly sliced lettuce.

I climb onto a stool hidden beneath the counter, my need for answers temporarily diverted by the heavenly aroma of food.

When he slides the heated mince toward me, I try my best not to show how starving I am by making the slowest taco in living history.

I have no doubt he can see right through me, especially when my hand shakes as I spoon the tomato onto the tortilla. It's a foregone conclusion when I take my first bite and bliss explodes on my tongue, dragging a moan from the deepest depths of my gratitude.

It feels like I haven't eaten in weeks. Every mouthful is euphoric. And all the while, Cole watches me, his attention rarely leaving my face.

"I'm ready to listen." I take a sip of water to clear my throat. "I was frustrated earlier, but now I'm willing to hear what you have to say."

"Once you finish eating." His focus turns to my mouth. My lips.

It's daunting. Far more disconcerting than when he raises his voice or plays his conniving games.

I'm under his control, a slave to his whims, and with all that power he's going to sit there at whatever hellish hour this is, and watch me down a taco or two?

"Please, Cole." I'm not too proud to beg when his attention makes goose bumps erupt over my skin. He's unsettling me. Unnerving.

"Have one more," he demands.

I sigh and finish the first taco in two more bites, then quickly make a second. "You enjoy watching people eat?" I ask and take another mouthful.

He moves to lean back against the main kitchen counter with a shrug. "I enjoy watching *you* eat. It's comforting after being concerned about you all day."

I don't scoff, despite wanting to. I don't roll my eyes either.

I keep eating. Bite after bite until my plate is bare. "I'm done," I murmur. "Please start talking. I won't argue with you this time."

"You had every reason to argue with me, Nissa. I won't expect anything less now, and I shouldn't have expected anything less earlier."

"But you did?" I scrutinize him. "You expected me to react differently?"

"I thought you'd wake up ready to fight," he admits. "I anticipated things to be heated for a few hours. Maybe you'd throw a lamp or a few plates. But I didn't expect you to run. And I sure as shit didn't think you'd have a gun pointed at your head before dinner."

I stiffen, and my shoulder pinches in protest. "You saw that?"

His eyes narrow, as if sensing my pain. "I caught the final moments between you and the boat driver before he took off. Trust me, having him threaten you wasn't in my plan."

He's remorseful. At least, that's what he wants me to believe.

"So what *was* your plan?" I hold his gaze, relying on his expression to lead the way, not his words. I watch his breathing, how often he swallows. I take note of everything, because he's already fooled me so many times before.

All I see is discomfort.

Awkward frustration.

He sucks in a deep breath, expanding his chest then letting the air out on a sigh. "It's a long story. Are you sure you don't want to get some sleep first?"

"All I want is to go home. I'm willing to live without sleep and discuss whatever needs to be discussed until that can happen."

His chin tilts, raising the slightest inch. Without him knowing, he's made it crystal clear this conversation isn't going to be my ticket home.

"Just tell me." I slide from the stool and grab my dirty plate to round the counter. "Start from the very beginning if you have to."

"Like I told you before, I didn't know the details of my father's escape. I've had very little contact with him. But I'd been warned to keep myself busy. To remain in the public eye. Seeking you out to be my alibi was out of spite, not only for the way you spoke to me at my uncle's funeral, but because you fucked up so many of my plans by making the arrest."

He pauses, seeming to doubt whether I can handle what he's about to say next.

He shouldn't.

After everything he's put me through, words could barely faze me at this point.

"Keep going." I place the dripping plate on the sink and return to my stool, ignoring the close-up view of all the threatening muscles. "I'm listening."

"What you and your FBI buddies don't realize is that there's no place for my father's actions within my organization. I don't condone his behavior. In fact, me and my siblings are furious. We hadn't been aware of what he was doing—"

"You knew before the funeral." It's not a question, and not a statement either. "I refuse to believe you were oblivious."

"You're right." He inclines his head. "I'd been informed a few weeks prior. But there hadn't been enough time to decide what to do."

"You knew for weeks and didn't do anything?" It should've taken hours to act. Mere minutes. "Seconds is all I would've spared to pick up the phone and make a call to the authorities."

His jaw tics. "Let me make this clear, Anissa. I have no intention of letting my father get away with his crimes, especially when they tarnish my family name, but all the authorities have done is fuck this up. The FBI has made one mistake after another. Their growing level of incompetence is the reason I'm fucking thankful he's now free."

My chest expands in anger, my blood running hot. I fight against the need to defend myself and my colleagues. Not only that, I'm beyond skeptical at his claim to want justice against his father.

His family has never shown a glimpse of morality. And even if I could skirt reality for a moment and become a believer, it's equally ridiculous for Cole to think he has the right to take the law into his own hands.

"And you think you can do a better job than we have?" The faintest hint of incredulity taints my voice. "I'm sorry, Cole, I'm trying really hard to be patient, but what you're suggesting is delusional."

"You want to talk about delusions?" He slides from the stool and stands, gripping the counter in both hands. "How 'bout we start with the Feds who locked up a sex trafficker with no thought to the women he had imprisoned?"

"We imprisoned him *because* of those women. He can't hurt anyone when he's behind bars."

"Bullshit. You put them in more danger when you arrested him."

I snap upright. "How? They're free. They've been returned to their families."

He laughs. It's a bitter, resentful sound that unsettles me.

"The information you passed on to Greek authorities led to the freedom of six victims, right? *Six.*" He clucks his tongue. "Do you really think a man like my father had such a small grasp?"

No, I didn't.

We didn't.

The FBI knows there are more victims out there. It's only a matter of time before we find them. And even with their location unknown, it was better to arrest Luther while we searched for more evidence than to build a case while he continued to terrorize.

"Tell me what you know," I plead. "How did we put women in more danger?"

"You're smart." He meets my gaze, his eyes begging me to figure it out on my own. "What do you think criminals do when they discover the authorities are onto them?"

He leans back against the fridge, crossing his arms over his chest. "You say he couldn't hurt anyone while he was behind bars, but did you consider what the men working for him would do when they figured out you were closing in on the scheme? Or did you kid yourself into thinking he worked alone?"

My throat dries.

I see spite in his eyes. The torment of harsh truths.

It sinks into me, tainting all chance of hope.

"Come on, Nissa. Take a guess at what a lowlife criminal would do with the evidence."

"I don't know." I don't want to give oxygen to the possibilities. Not when my mind has fixated on the worst possible outcome.

"But you could anticipate a reaction, right? You would've thought about what his men would've done."

I don't answer.

With any arrest, there are possible repercussions. Sometimes it's inevitable. We have to weigh the odds and hope for the best.

"What do you think happens to sex slaves when the men imprisoning them think the Feds are closing in?" He pushes from the counter and stalks forward to rest his elbows on the island counter, getting closer to eye level. "What does any criminal do with evidence when they think they're about to get caught?"

I shake my head, not letting him push my buttons. "Stop it."

I refuse to play along to yet another game.

"That's right, little fox." His lips curve into a feral smile. "Finally, the truth is starting to wiggle its way through your naive concept of justice." He mutters the words, his anger simmering below the surface. "If my father's men had a location which they thought caused suspicion, it would've been burned to the ground. They would've killed those they couldn't hide. Somewhere out there is a mass grave full of tortured women, and it's the FBI's fault."

"No." I keep shaking my head. "If a mass of imprisoned women were murdered, we would've heard about it."

"Are you trying to tell me the Greek police have been eagerly gushing to help you? If I took a guess, I'd say they've fought against your investigation every step of the way, letting you know it's their jurisdiction, not yours. Thus the basis of them only finding six victims—the bare minimum to get you assholes off their back."

I'm loath to admit the truth. Not because being wrong is an issue, but because him being right means women have died.

He gives a sad smile, as if understanding my suffering. "The police were never going to rat on one of their biggest sources of income. Your interference only helped to line their pockets with more money."

My stomach twists in knots, the tacos preparing to make a comeback. "Do you have proof?" My voice is weak. Fractured. "Is there evidence women were murdered?"

"I don't need evidence to know they would've been disposed of. Just like I didn't need evidence to know my father would escape. It's logical. It's human nature in my world."

I'm beginning to believe his continued references to this alternate society are necessary. Maybe he does live in a reality completely different to mine. One where people can talk about murder and rape without any emotional attachment.

"That's not human nature," I whisper. "It's psychotic."

"Yes, it is."

"Are all the people in your world psychopaths?" It's a legitimate question, not an attempt at humor.

Regardless, he laughs. "I think that depends on your definition. It's clear you've judged me to fit the—"

"I didn't say that." I may have thought it more times than I can remember, but I've never truly wanted to believe this man was devoid of emotion.

And I can't now, not when my life is in his hands.

"You didn't need to." He sobers, turning his focus away to stare toward the living room. "You're very good at showing your criticism with a single look."

"Your name has been mentioned with suspicion around the deaths of many men. You're not innocent in all of this. Drug dealers. Businessmen. Police officers. Even government officials."

"Men," he snarls. "*Guilty* men. Those who have stolen from me. Or tried to stab me in the back. Not innocent fucking women, Nissa." He spits the nickname as if it's poison. "What about my commitment to my sisters? What about my devotion to protecting them? And my niece…" He winces. "A fucking niece who I would give my life for. How can I be psychotic when my family are my life?"

"Your father shares the same family. Those sisters are his daughters. Your niece is his only grandchild. I'm sure he'd lay down his life to protect them, too; it doesn't make him any less of a monster."

His lip curls and I'm caught on the edge of anticipation, waiting for him to defend himself.

I want him to.

Each time he exposes me to a remorseful side, I relax a little. I don't fear for my safety as much.

I need more of that reassurance.

God, how I need it.

"You don't have a response?" I ask. "Aren't you going to tell me I'm wrong?"

"You're so fucking wrong," he snarls. "But I'm sick of defending my reputation. It's pointless and entirely unnecessary when I didn't bring you here to gain your respect."

"Then why am I here? Why did you risk life behind bars?"

His nostrils flare. "Because you're going to be my proof of following through on a promise."

The skin at my nape prickles. I'm not sure what he means, but I'm certain it's not something I want to be a part of. "Am I meant to guess or are you going to clarify?"

"I made a vow to deal with my father—to punish him for what he's done. And you're going to assure those I've promised that I handled the situation accordingly."

There's so much anger in his tone. A ton of vehemence. A wealth of hate.

I swallow over the retreat of moisture in my throat.

Determination stares back at me with eyes so deep and blue.

I don't want to ask. I don't think I want to know.

"Nissa, I brought you here so you could see me shutting down my father's operation." He looks away and sucks in a deep breath, letting it out on a frustrated exhale. "I brought you here to witness his murder."

13

TORIAN

She doesn't react.

There's no disbelief, or humor, and yet again, not a glimpse of fear.

The only change comes with the slight decrease in color to her face. Her sun-ravaged skin grows pale, her ruby lips a million times darker in contrast as she swallows.

"You don't need to respond. All I want is for you to remain open to the conversation."

"Open," she repeats on a faint murmur.

She's overwhelmed with shock, or disbelief, her green eyes glazing in confusion.

I push from the counter, needing distance. "I brought you here, despite our differences, because this will give us what we both want. I will have a reliable witness. And in return, you get the justice you crave."

She shakes her head, her brows pinched. "Your justice. Not mine. This goes against everything I believe in. And even if I thought you were telling the truth, which I don't, I wouldn't be able to support your plan. This is fucking ridiculous."

"I don't need your support. Or your interaction. I only need your presence."

She lowers her gaze, her head still repeating the back and forth motion. "This is a game. It's not real."

"It's not a game—"

"You've said that before." Her head snaps up, her eyes fierce with spite. "You've told me no more games. No more lies. No more bullshit. But it never fucking stops."

"I fucked up," I admit. "I succumbed to the need to retaliate one too many times. Taunting you became my only stability after my father's arrest. So tell me what I need to do to earn your trust."

"Trust? Are you kidding?" She straightens, showing conviction. "It makes no sense."

"It makes perfect sense. I need to prove my father is dead. And you—"

"Bullshit, Cole. I'm not here to be a witness. I don't believe it for a second. You could get Luca to do that. Hell, you could get the asshole from the boat. Or a local. Anyone can be your damn witness. Or you could take a fucking photo, for Christ's sake. Or a souvenir." She lets out a maniacal bark of a laugh. "Why not chop off your dad's ear as proof?"

"I won't allow evidence to leave the crime scene." I mutter the words, slow and lethargic, trying to counter the fast pace of her rambling. "Not even a photo. The information will be shared without the horrors of body pieces or traumatic photos as proof."

"How kind of you." She shakes her head, over and over, her eyes narrowed on me. "I still don't believe this isn't some kind of trick."

I sigh, my fury and frustration mingling. "Nissa, the information can't come from one of my men. Their word means nothing when everyone already knows they would say or do anything for me. The same goes for those who could be paid off or intimidated. But an FBI agent with integrity, unwavering morals, and no fear of me? Now that's the perfect candidate to tell the truth, don't you think?"

"An FBI agent who would have no choice but to arrest you if you went ahead with this."

Her response is disappointing. I feel the hit to my chest like a physical blow.

I'd hoped she would see this as a victory. Not another opportunity to be antagonistic. "You can't. We're in Greece. You have no authority here."

"I'm well aware, but I could make a citizen's arrest until police arrive."

"The same police who've worked with my father for years?" I raise a brow. "That will either get you killed or sent to work in the same sex slums that have lined their pockets for years. Either way, you'll disappear and never set foot in the States again. They're the enemy here. Not me."

"You're both the enemy." She scoffs. "This is crazy."

"Maybe. But it's necessary. I didn't want to go down this path, but there's no other option."

"This isn't an option at all, Cole. And to be honest, if it's true, it sounds like a show of utter weakness. Who are you doing this for? What associate has enough power over you to convince you to kill your own father?"

I flinch. I can't help it. The comment on my weakness hits a target she didn't know existed. "You don't need to concern yourself with my reasons."

She holds my stare, the groove of her brow digging deeper. She's starting to believe me. Understanding dawns in her features, the anger turning to concern.

"You're serious," she murmurs. "You actually want me to witness your father's murder."

I leave her in silence, letting her come to terms with the truth.

"This is crazy." She shakes her head. "It still makes no sense when there's the much better alternative to get him back behind bars. If you work with the authorities—"

"Don't even start." I clench a fist at my side. "Have you listened to a word I've said?"

"I've listened to every insane word that's come out of your mouth. I've listened even though I'm here as your prisoner. But that isn't going to stop me from telling you this is wrong. And what you expect from me is completely delusional. I won't help you. I won't confirm anything. I can't."

I smirk, the expression so fucking tight, because looking at her in animosity is far better than exposing my fear of failure. "It isn't wrong. You're the one who's misguided. The authorities are worthless. There won't be any justice at all, unless I'm the one who claims it."

She stares, almost glares, her self-assurance growing with my conviction.

We remain in the battle for visual supremacy for long moments, those big eyes focused on mine, her ruby lips pursed.

She'll crack.

She has to, because I won't.

"Okay. Fine." She throws up her hands. "Let's talk this through. Hypothetically."

I incline my head. "Hypothetically."

Her eyes roll as she huffs. "Your plan is to kill your father while I watch. Then I can spread the good word about your deeds like you're the Wizard of fucking Oz. But what happens to those women? You said the FBI endangered those left behind by arresting Luther. What will happen to them once he's dead?"

"His death will inspire chaos. The men left behind will fight for power. They'll slaughter one another in their attempt to climb to the top. Local residents will be affected. Then the media will get involved, and police will be forced to act, in return freeing those women."

"You're working on assumptions and speculation?" she accuses.

"If things don't fall apart naturally, I'll call in reinforcements to shut it down. I'm not going to let this continue. Not under my name."

She stares at me. Stares right through me. "This is insanity."

"No. It's the only fucking option. And nobody but a trusted few need to know. Once you relay the truth of what I've done to those necessary, you can pretend you were never here."

Her eyes snap back to reality. "You think I'm capable of hiding this? For you?"

"Not for me, Nissa. For those women. For justice against my father. The consequences for being a snitch aren't worth trying to take me down for a good deed."

Her eyes flair with the threat. Air leaves her lungs on a heave and she looks away, her anger seeming to bubble.

"You'll never get him back behind bars." I lower my voice, trying to provide a calming buffer to the tumultuous battle in her eyes. "He's already fled the US. And even if you have some incredible stroke of luck and convince someone here to arrest him, he's never going to talk. He won't tell you where the rest of the women are. But he'll open up to me. He'll spill his secrets."

Her gaze snaps to mine. Speculative. Hopeful. "You'll get that information?"

"I can."

The muscles in her jaw tense. "Don't try to trick me with a strategic word choice. Tell me. Right now. If I do this for you, will you get that information for me?"

My pulse kicks with her determination. Despite her being a pain in my ass, her dedication is inspiring. "Yes."

Her chin hitches.

She's hooked, even though she doesn't want to be.

"Then you'll slaughter him?" Her tone holds a new level of criticism, the dose thick and brutal. "Your own father. In cold blood."

Fuck her. Seriously, fuck her misguided naivety.

Nobody can judge me for my plans more than I've already judged myself.

At one point, Luther Torian was all I had.

He kept my mind active after my mother's death. He taught me to be strong for the sisters who buckled under the weight of their emotions. He showed me how to clasp revenge in both fists with patience and efficiency.

He was my mentor.

Now, he's my adversary.

"This isn't a bad deed, Anissa. I'm not planning a terrorist attack or instigating nuclear war. All I'm doing is taking down a criminal. A rapist. A murderer. The same man who escaped your custody and claimed more victims while under your watch."

It isn't a hard concept to grasp. To me, it's common fucking sense. The more I have to convince her, the stronger I am in my own convictions.

"I have to think." She frowns, the battle for understanding reclaiming her features. "I need time."

"We don't have any. My father would already have heard about my arrival." I start toward her. "He'll wait a day, maybe two, to make sure I wasn't followed, then he's going to come out here. You need to be onboard with the plan before he shows up."

"You should've thought about that before you deceived me a thousand times." She walks around the island counter, placing more distance between us. "I need time. Otherwise, I'll give you a flat refusal now and deal with the consequences."

"You don't want that." It's a slight threat. The barest nudge toward a better resolution. "You can't tell me you'd prefer my father to walk away unscathed instead of receiving the lethal punishment he deserves. You know what he's done. There's no—"

"Don't guilt me into making this decision. You're threatening my career. You're trying to destroy my morals. I can't simply sit back and watch you break the law."

"But you're happy to sit back and let those women continue to suffer? That's some fucked up logic, Nissa."

"Go to hell." She hits me with a scathing glare. "You know they're more important to me than anything else." She swings around and stalks for the hall. "But I said I need time, and that's what I'm going to get."

Christ, she's stubborn.

So fucking stubborn.

"He's going to turn up unannounced. You need to be prepared."

"No." Her stride doesn't falter as she speaks over her shoulder. "What I need is clarity, because at the moment, my head is filled with static. Either leave me alone until I can think straight or take no as my answer."

My limbs grow tense. Every nerve and muscle pulls tight. "I can give you a few hours."

"You'll give me as long as I need." She turns to face down the hall, and disappears from site.

I listen to her fading footsteps, then hear a door open and close, shutting me out entirely.

Nobody has ever dared to disrespect me the way this woman does. Male. Female. Fed or criminal. She's fucking delusional with her self-assurance, and I can't help respecting her for it.

I fucking hate it, but I still respect it.

No more negotiation will happen tonight. No matter how necessary it is to my success.

"Fuck." I pace the kitchen, running my hands through my hair. "*Fuck.*"

I swipe at the counter, sending containers flying, the destruction smashing to the floor. Glass scatters. Food splatters. A huge fucking mess is laid bare at my feet, and it's more psychological than physical.

I can't let her get to me.

Anger is a weakness. A deficiency. I'm above the emotion, yet Anissa siphons it from me without effort.

She fucks with my head. Messes with my decisions. She shouldn't even be here. Dragging her along was an act of irrationality—of fucking instability. If I thought she wouldn't have me in cuffs at the next available opportunity, maybe I'd admit defeat and send her home... Maybe.

Then again, her defiance is like a drug.

I can't stop craving another hit despite the dangers.

I grip the counter, my hands clenched against the marble until my breathing slows and my pulse settles. There's power in action, not reaction.

I need to get back to basics.

Think. Strategize. Plan.

"I gather your chat didn't go well."

I cringe at the sound of Luca's voice and keep my hands clasped against the counter. I don't have the patience to speak to anyone right now. There's no calm to be found.

His footsteps approach. "Get some sleep. She'll be less scared in the morning."

"She doesn't get scared," I seethe. Or weak. Or vulnerable. Or any other emotion you'd fucking expect from a woman abducted from her own country.

"Then she'll be less of a bitch." He passes behind me, moving toward the destruction on the floor. "Go get some sleep. I'll clean up the mess."

He lowers to his haunches and reaches for a shard of glass, then another, stacking them in his palm.

"Get going." He doesn't bother to look at me as he speaks. "You need the rest more than I do."

My blood boils with his placating attitude. The coddling. Who the fuck does he think he is?

No, it's me. I'm running off the rails.

I dig my fingertips harder against the marble and clench my teeth.

She's eating away at my temper to the point where my patience is non-existent.

I wouldn't have thought I'd need more space when I'm secluded in the middle of nowhere, but even a remote island feels suffocating with the cloying churn of my mind.

I shove from the counter and stalk for the hall. I don't slow until I reach her door, then I listen for a moment, hearing the grate of a zipper and the pad of soft footfalls.

She's not throwing furniture or screaming in anger. Her control is better than mine, which only makes my blood burn hotter as I stalk away.

I don't stop myself from slamming my bedroom door before I punish myself with a long, cold shower.

Sleep isn't an option. There's no use when I'm wound up. Instead, I grab my Mac and slide into bed, logging into the surveillance app to pull the feed from her room into view.

There're two angles, one from the front-left corner, another from the back right. I can see every square inch of space, and she's not in any of it.

The instinct to panic is overwhelming and entirely unjustified.

She can't escape.

All the windows are alarmed. There's no boat. I worked hard to lock away any sharp objects. All the knives and razors, along with the cleaning products, are stored in a safe place.

If she's going to attempt to kill me, she'll need to do it with a lamp, or a fucking bedside table.

I continue to remind myself of the precautions, but my apprehension doesn't ease. My pulse rate only increases, pounding through my temples.

I'm seconds from sliding out of bed to go in search of her when the adjoining bathroom door opens on the screen before me, and she walks into view, tousling her wet hair with a towel, while another is wrapped around her body.

All my panic stops.

Everything does.

My thoughts. My pulse. My breath.

Her skin shines with moisture. Her cheeks are flushed. She looks different. Unguarded. Fucking tempting.

She crouches before the duffel on the floor, dropping the towel from her hair beside her before she shifts through clothes to pull out underwear, then a gray shirt and shorts. Pajamas. But she does it all with her left hand, while the right arm remains tucked against her chest.

That sore shoulder of hers is more than a pulled muscle.

She's hurt, and I don't appreciate not knowing the extent of her injuries.

I squint, trying to get a better view of the skin around her right collarbone. The pixilation doesn't give a pristine image; it's slightly blurred up close, and yet I can still see the darker tinge to the flesh on her shoulder.

"Pulled muscle, my ass."

She stands, throwing the clothes to the bed, then reclaiming the underwear.

I know what comes next, and I don't bother to look away. I don't spare a thought for her privacy as she drops the second towel, exposing a flawless body. Smooth legs. Flat stomach. Pert, delectable tits with dark, beaded nipples.

She leans over and toes her feet into the white, silken panties, shimmying them all the way up those toned thighs to cover the trim patch of hair at her mound.

Next she grabs the gray shirt, pulling the material over her head. Then the short shorts that she yanks on to settle over her hips.

Either she hasn't discovered the pinhole cameras hidden within her room, or this unrestricted show is deliberate. A taunt. Does she expect me to be the pervert who watches her undress? Does she assume I'm a deviant like my father?

Fuck her.

My surveillance is entirely cautionary.

I need to be aware of her location at all times. I have to keep a close eye on her.

It's fucking necessary.

It's... "*Fuck.*"

I slam the Mac closed and shove it to the far side of the mattress as I slink farther down the bed.

My father is the pervert. The deviant. Not me.

So why the hell am I walking in his footsteps with fucking brilliant precision?

I understand him in this moment. I get his perversions because even now, with the threat of becoming him a heavy weight over my conscience, I still have to fight not to take another look.

I'm being driven by weakness. Haunted by temptation. I've become what I despise and it's all her fault.

Anissa has me coiled tight. She drives my thoughts out of control. She makes me question everything.

I'm beginning to wonder if she's been a part of my game, or if I've been participating in hers. Is she winning this round? Has she claimed control?

Decker warned me about this. He told me she was a snake. A viper. A fucking bitch.

She's sneaky. Manipulative. Smart.

But not smarter than me. Or stronger.

I haven't lost this battle.

Not yet.

I DON'T HEAR from her for the rest of the night. There's only the faint fall of Luca's footsteps down the hall, then nothing until I wake mid-morning from a broken sleep and find her door still closed.

I force myself not to pause and listen. Instead, I make a beeline for coffee and find the kitchen spotless.

Luca cleaned the glass from the floor and the splatter from the cupboards. It's as if I never lost my temper, despite the memory of the weakness nagging at me.

I sit outside for hours, reclined on a pool lounger while I get to work replying to e-mails from my legitimate businesses. It's close to lunch when my cell rings and Hunter's name stares back at me from across the screen.

"What is it?" I ask in greeting.

"Rumor has it you went on a date with our least-favorite FBI agent the other night."

"And?" The animosity that faded overnight begins to rear its ugly head. I don't fucking get it. One mention of Anissa and I'm ready to break skulls.

"I want to know if I should be shutting down the claims or letting them fly. I don't give a shit where you shove your dick; all I need to know is if you want the crazy news public."

"I'm not shoving my dick anywhere." My nostrils flare with renewed aggression. I shouldn't need to justify myself. "If anyone dares to comment, let them know I'm working her over. I'm bringing her to our team."

"That's a tough feat if we're talking about the same woman Decker has been bitching about."

"Are there any other opinions you'd like to share before I hang up?"

"Well, seeing as though you asked," he growls, "I'd appreciate being told where the fuck you are. You don't usually disappear without letting me know the details."

He doesn't need the information, and I shouldn't bother telling him. But my mouth opens, and the taunting admission grates between my teeth. "Greece."

Silence follows my answer, the tense void building with the passing seconds.

"Torian—"

"Don't start," I warn. "I don't want to hear it."

"Too bad," he snarls. "Why the fuck aren't I there with you? You need me."

I let out a scoff. "I've learned that your presence isn't as fundamental as I once thought."

"Fuck you." Anger drips from his tone. "Are you seriously going to do this without me? Is that chump Luca there instead?"

"Focus on recruitment," I demand. "You've got more important work to do in Portland."

"Fuck—"

I disconnect the call, the provocation not filling me with the enjoyment I'd anticipated. There's only building frustration.

Hunter knows exactly why I'm here. My inner circle has been waiting for me to make this move for a while now. He'll also be aware it's a better plan to attack my father in Greece. I'll make dad disappear in private. Only my faithful few have to know.

I place the cell back in my jeans pocket and navigate my Mac to the surveillance feed from Anissa's room.

She's awake, seated on the floor, her back against the wall, her head in her hands. She isn't crying. Her shoulders don't shake. But her turmoil is clear. She still hasn't come to terms with her situation. Who knows if she ever will.

I let the sight of her sink into me, becoming more mesmerized with each passing minute.

I note everything. The messy light wave to her short hair. The loose-fitting red top that covers her shoulder injury from view.

She's wearing tight, black pants, cut off below the knee. Those active-wear type things that make me think she plans on exercising.

Running.

From me.

The thought creates a dull throb behind my sternum. I don't know whether it's inspired by pleasure or disappointment. Fighting with her is such a contradiction. I enjoy every minute, and hate it all the same. I want her anger, yet there's frustration and fucking guilt there, too.

We're not so different.

We both cling to strong values. We're governed by strict rules. We would fight to the death for what we hold dear.

We just happen to believe in completely opposing views.

"Boss." Luca walks from the open doorway looking like shit in nothing but navy shorts. "I gather you spoke to Hunt."

"About ten minutes ago. Why?"

"He called." He wipes a hand down his sleep-roughened face, then scratches his fingers across stubble almost growing into a beard. "He isn't too happy about me being here."

"He needs to get used to taking on a different role." I focus back on the computer and find Anissa's head resting against the wall, her emotionless face on display as she stares blankly across the room.

Luca slumps onto the lounger beside me. "That's pretty much what I said."

I frown, not taking my gaze off my captive as I try to read what's going on in that mind of hers. "You told him that?"

"I told him to fuck off." He shrugs. "It's pretty much the same thing. Have you spoken to your FBI agent this morning?"

My FBI agent.

The question is a trigger.

Everything is a fucking trigger.

"No," I grate. "She hasn't been out of her room."

"Does she know why she's here?" He stretches out along the lounger, his hands behind his head.

I slowly close the Mac screen, biding my time to ease into a conversation I don't want to participate in. "She knows enough. The finer details aren't her concern."

"Are you sure? She seems the type to want transparency. Especially when she sees you as nothing more than a criminal."

"I *am* a criminal."

"Yeah, you are, but she might attempt to trust you if she's given more details than a vague reference to her being a witness."

He listened to my conversation with her last night?

I'm not surprised. I expect him to have his finger on the pulse while we're here. It's his job. I just don't appreciate knowing he's been a fly on the wall when I'm alone with her. "You could hear us from your room?"

"Bits and pieces. I lipread some."

"You've been on the surveillance feed." It's not a question, only a necessary purge of information that smashes to the forefront of my mind.

"I set my phone to receive movement notifications. Every time she rolled in her sleep, I made sure to check she wasn't making her way into the hall to cause trouble."

"And what about before that? When she was awake?" I stare at him, my heartbeat throbbing down my neck, pounding in my ears. "And this morning? Were you watching then, too?"

Did he watch her get dressed? Has he seen her naked?

Jesus fuck.

I want to hurt him.

With or without his answer, I itch to punch my knuckles through his face.

"By the time I finished in the kitchen last night, she was in bed with the light off." He holds my gaze, his expression locked tight, as if sensing my desire to commit murder. "The same goes for this morning. She was asleep the whole time I checked on her. And once I got the notification you were moving around the house, I crashed, figuring you could keep watch on your own."

His answer eases the rage seeping through my marrow. Slightly.

Is this jealousy?

Am I fucking jealous over the enemy?

"What's going on with you?" His brows pull tight as he slides his arms down to his sides. "Is she getting in your head?"

Getting? No. She's already burrowed all the way in, grinding against every nerve.

But I'm sick of his questions. I'm fucking tired of people thinking I need to justify my actions.

"Stay off the feed." I keep my voice neutral. Level. Calm as fucking Larry. "Leave me in charge of it."

"That's no problem at all." He doesn't stop with the scrutiny. "But are you okay? This is some pretty heavy shit you have to deal—"

"Fuck off with the pep talk. I don't need it."

Movement nudges my peripheral vision, and I tilt my gaze to see Anissa standing in the open doorway leading outside, her stare pinning me in place.

Dark hair frames her cheeks, and the sunburned skin she earned yesterday has turned to a healthy tan, making those green eyes all the more luminous.

I don't speak.

I don't move.

I don't do anything capable of making her feel like I'm flaunting my control over her, despite wanting to do exactly that.

She steps onto the tile, still favoring one arm, which she holds closer to her side than the other as she walks forward.

"How did you drug me?" She stops at the end of the lounger to look down her nose at me.

Her question is multifaceted. I can see it in her eyes.

She wants to know if I'm capable of the truth. If I can be honest and refrain from messing with her head.

"I watched you," she murmurs. "You didn't put anything in my glass. I made sure of it. So was it something I touched or inhaled? You said you didn't know I drank vodka."

"I didn't know." I place the Mac on the ground and swivel my legs off the lounger, needing to tilt my head to meet her gaze. "Like I already told you, I guessed. That's why I had all the bottles on the plane spiked. Except mine. I took a chance that you wouldn't want to share my scotch."

"And if I did?"

"I would've found another way." I let a slow grin curve my lips. "Maybe I would've convinced you to come here without needing medicinal assistance."

"And you would've crashed and burned. There's no way I would've come here willingly." She crosses her arms over her chest, attempting to shut me out.

I claim her need to ward me away as a small victory. A glimpse to her unease.

"I was joking." I push to my feet. "The drugs were my only preparation."

"Premeditation," she clarifies.

"Tomato, tamato. I prefer to steer clear of terms used in a court—"

"What about the women?" She raises her voice, cutting me off. "The abduction victims back in Portland. Did you lie about them, too? Were you responsible for their disappearance?"

I sigh, yet again disappointed at her stubborn need to continuously burn me at the stake. The hours apart have only given her more ammunition.

"No, Nissa. I wasn't responsible. An ex-con from Seattle had those women. Like I said, he was trying to impress my father in an attempt to be brought into the fold."

"*Had* the women?" She latches onto the word, her eyes narrowing. "Where are they now?"

"Nothing gets by you, does it?"

"Answer the question," she demands.

I snicker, only because it will piss her off even more.

Does it help with our situation? No.

Will it delay the necessary resolution? Yes.

But can I help it?

I'm not even going to pretend I have any control over my mouth when she's around. I don't know how to quit taunting her.

"You want us to work together." She throws the words at me like an accusation. "You say I can't go home unless I help you. Well, you need to help me first. Help me fucking understand."

I glare, her fiery temperament invigorating me more than I'd like to admit.

"They're safe," I mutter. "I'd already made arrangements to secure their release before we left Portland."

She stands a little taller, her breasts plumped above the shelf of her arms. "Prove it."

Impatience becomes a living, breathing force inside my veins. I want to deny her. To shove my authority down her throat. But that won't work in my favor.

"I'm going to leave you two alone." Luca pushes to his feet. "I'll be inside."

"No." She raises her voice. "Stay."

His gaze flicks to me, requesting a response.

"It's okay." I shrug, faking a level of calm I'm far from feeling. "If she wants you here, you stay."

I pull my cell from the back pocket of my jeans and scroll through my contacts to find Hunter's number. I connect the call and place the sound on loud speaker. "I'm not sure if he's going to be in the mood to talk."

The call doesn't last one full ring before Hunter is growling down the line. "Did your bitch boy rat on me?"

"He may have mentioned you reaching out," I drawl.

"Well, if you're going to ride me for telling him what he needs to hear, I guess it's my turn to hang up."

"Quit the theatrics. I need you to tell me what went down last night with Sayker."

There's a pause. A silent heartbeat.

"Just the CliffsNotes." I lock eyes with Anissa and raise my brows to ask if the short version is enough.

She swallows. Nods.

"Was there something wrong with my first recount?" Hunt asks.

"No. I was distracted and can't remember everything. Just repeat what happened."

"We found the women in a house in Centennial. They were hidden in the basement. Bound, gagged, and scared as fuck. Their captor was dealt with. The women were freed. End of story. Unless you want me to give you the blow-by-blow of my lovely lady and her newfound skills with a paring knife."

"Save your lady stories for another time. You've told me all I need to know." I disconnect the call and return the device to my pocket. "Is the information to your approval?"

She glances between me and Luca, back and forth, over and over before shaking her head. "It's only words. There's no proof."

"It's on the news." Luca pulls a cell from his shorts pocket, then types and scrolls over the screen. "Here, I'll show you."

I bristle when he hands her the device. As far as I'm concerned, that phone could lead to her escape. He shouldn't be willingly handing it over. Or I'm just pissed he thought of it first. That he's the one convincing her when I failed.

She focuses on the screen, swiping down every few seconds. "It says the perpetrator hasn't been found."

"He has. By us." I cross my arms over my chest. "We dealt with him our way."

"Your way?" She looks up at me through thick lashes. "You mean he's dead."

I don't answer. If she wants to continuously judge me as ruthless, so be it. It's not an unworthy title. It just happens to be incorrect this time.

"No. He's not dead." Luca holds out a hand to reclaim the device. "But he won't think about hurting women again."

She returns to the visual tennis match, glancing between us, her gaze searching for more answers.

"He's not dead," I repeat. "Be satisfied with the information. It's better for everyone involved if you don't know more."

She deflates, her shoulders and chest falling in defeat before she walks back into the house without a backward glance.

Luca watches her leave, his focus remaining on the door after she disappears behind the sheer curtains. For a man who doesn't give a shit about anything but work, he sure likes to pay her attention.

"You need to give her more information," he murmurs. "She doesn't believe one word you tell her." He turns to me, his face stern. "Whatever this tactic is, it's not working, and we're running out of time. If Luther turns up and she's not—"

"Back the fuck off," I warn. "I didn't bring you here as a strategist. Or a fucking therapist. Now move." He blocks my way from between the two loungers.

"Okay, but—"

"Don't fucking *but* me." I take a menacing step forward and get in his face. "Lay off or find yourself on the next flight out of here."

He straightens, not listening to the threat. "You're spiraling out of control. I don't know what the fuck is going on with you and her, but this isn't you."

A rush of blood floods my head, the surge of rage intense and entirely overwhelming.

I shove him, making him back up a step. The guy is bigger than me. Broader. An inch taller. More muscles.

I don't give a fuck.

I push again, and this time he begins to move a second before my hands connect with his chest, preempting the strike.

"I don't know why you're looking for a fight," he continues to back up, moving out of the way. "But you're not going to find it with me."

I snicker. "You're scared?"

"Torian, I'm a fucking SEAL. You don't stand a chance."

"You *were* a fucking SEAL. You were dishonorably discharged, asshole."

His mouth snaps shut. His jaw clenches.

The show of barely restrained anger acts like adrenaline in my veins. It eases the unrelenting pressure. It gets her out of my brain for the briefest seconds, providing a slight reprieve.

"I respect you," he seethes. "And I've vowed to work by your side, not under your fists."

I continue stalking forward, praying for him to take the first swing. I'm not a fighter. Never have been. Not physically. But for once, I need the distraction. I want the pain and brutality. "You're a fucking pussy."

"No." He stops dead, his eyes narrowed. "I've got self-fucking-control, and usually you do, too. Hit the weights room instead."

I shove him again. Hard.

I need an outlet. I have to find a way to get Anissa out of my system.

"Hit the fucking weights room, Torian." He puffs out his chest, waiting for another shove. "Do you want to be like this when your father shows? Is that what you're looking for? An excuse to fuck this up?"

Everything stops. My thoughts. My pulse.

The chase for numbing adrenaline becomes a brutal war.

It wouldn't be the first time I'd made a mistake when it came to my father.

It's my fault he was arrested at the funeral in the first place.

I should've realized my FBI informant was hiding information from me. I should've known they had enough evidence to make an arrest.

"Is that what you're trying to do?" Luca's brows pinch with stern inquisition. "You're looking for a way out? You know you don't have to do this. Not now. We can go home, wait it out, and come back when you're ready"

"Shut your fucking mouth."

He's judging me. Finding me lacking. Just like she does.

I'm not incapable of taking care of business. And that's all this is. Business. A righting of wrongs.

My father was once an asset, and now he's a liability. I can't look at this any other way.

"Get out of my face." I take another step, our chests almost brushing as I scowl. "And stay out of my fucking head or you'll find yourself in a worse position than Sayker."

14

ANISSA

I linger a few feet from the sheer curtain, my pulse heavy in my throat as I wait for war to break out beside the pool.

I should be searching for a weapon. A phone. An escape plan.

Instead, I'm transfixed by the ferocity on display.

I've never seen Cole this way. He's out of control. Spiraling, just like Luca said.

But it's more than that.

The volatility presents like vulnerability. It's raw. Brutal and honest. And God, I wish I wasn't bearing witness, because now I'm finally beginning to believe this situation isn't based on a string of intricately woven lies.

Cole plans to kill his father. And I'm here to watch the bloodbath.

He takes another step, the two men toe to toe. "Get out of my face. And stay out of my fucking head."

Luca stares down his boss. "I'm trying to help."

My ribs grow tight, my unease narrowing on the possibility of Cole desperately wanting a way out. Is he trapped in this situation? Has he made me a victim because he's one as well?

I glare, despising the tiny flicker of empathy working its way into my bloodstream. These men aren't entitled to anything other than my dedication to bring them to justice. They deserve four cement walls and a lengthy sentence, not my contemplation of their hardships.

"Help by doing your fucking job. Be prepared for when my father arrives. That's all you're here for."

Cole maneuvers around Luca, clipping his shoulder as he stalks toward the house. Toward *me*.

Shit.

I turn and run, fleeing the living area on the tips of my toes to race down the hall and into my room. I inch the door closed with exquisite patience, the handle making the tiniest click as it latches.

I shudder out a relieved breath, only to question my response seconds later.

Why am I hiding? I'm not scared of Cole. And now is the perfect time to poke him for more information. To push him toward the edge of honesty.

But I guess honesty isn't a necessity. Not when getting out of here is far more important.

I sigh and lean back against the door as the loud *boom, boom, boom* of his footfalls approach. He doesn't stop. Doesn't even pause. Those pounding steps continue down the hall until a door slams, the loud crack of noise plunging the house into silence.

I should be happy he's unravelling. If he's losing control it means he's more likely to make a mistake. And mistakes will allow me to gain the upper-hand.

The tailspin is great news. If only his volatility didn't unnerve me.

There was desperation in his eyes. A sense of him being cornered prey. Did he know I was watching? Is this yet another layer to his sophisticated plot?

My stomach twists, and this time it has nothing to do with rabid hunger. I can't figure out his motives. And without understanding, I'm lost.

The only option I can think of is to convince him I'm on his side. I don't know how else to approach this. Not when he sees me as an antagonist instead of a victim.

Taking on his warped sense of reality may be the key. I'm never going to change his corrupt foundations. But I can learn to understand them in an attempt to use it against him.

The door slams again and I hold my breath, waiting as those thunderous footsteps storm back down the hall in the opposite direction before I slide to the floor in a heap.

The silence returns.

I don't hear another sound apart from the heavy beat of my heart for what feels like an hour. There's no clock in here. I don't have any association with time apart from knowing mine is running out.

I need to work on a plan—to manipulate Cole, to get away from Luca, to escape this fucking island. But none of my thoughts have substance. Everything returns to Cole's anger. Its severity. His uncharacteristic show of emotion.

If the display was real, I want to know whether it's an everyday occurrence for those close to him, or something entirely out of the ordinary. Is this situation tearing him apart? Was the dominant display an outlet for the pain he's hiding?

"You're a fucking idiot." I bang my head gently against the door, hoping the soft brain massage will kick me out of my stupidity.

It doesn't.

I can't stop seeing him when I close my eyes. I even shove to my feet, stalk to the bed, and slump onto the mattress in the hopes a new position will bring a new outlook, but that doesn't work either.

I curl into the fetal position as I scrutinize Cole's face in my mind, when a gentle knock at the door sends me snapping upright.

I'm not ready to speak to him.

I don't know how to play his game yet, let alone win. And I sure as hell don't know how to stop clinging to the hope that he's just as vulnerable as I am.

"Anissa?" The knock raps again.

It isn't Cole, and I'm even less interested in talking to the man who stood by while a maniacal old Greek mocked me.

"Yes?" I slide my legs off the bed and sit up straight.

The handle clicks, the door opening slightly.

Luca's stern face comes into view. "You need to eat. I've made sandwiches."

I hold back a response, not succumbing to the ravenous way my insides tingle at the offer.

He left me on the pier yesterday. Alone. With a man filled with giddy excitement at the thought of blowing my brains out.

For reasons that don't hold a wealth of rationality, I find Luca's actions more despicable than Cole's. I'm well aware my prejudice doesn't make sense. And regardless of my own insight, I can't change my perception.

Cole has antagonized me for weeks. He's torn my life apart and sabotaged my career. But I'm not scared of him.

In contrast, Luca frightens me. He's an unknown entity. A threat.

"I'm not going to hold your hand." His expression hardens. "If you want them, they're in the kitchen. If not, it makes no difference to me."

He snaps the door shut, the noise reverberating around the room. I stare, dumbfounded, as I wonder if the sandwiches are meant as a peace offering.

Am I supposed to be grateful? Does he expect me to fall to my knees in thanks?

I scoff, mind-blown at his audacity, while I contemplate whether or not to play nice. Not only do I desperately crave food, I need answers, too, and Luca may be able to give me both. He's as deep in this mess as Cole. I won't leave either of them off a criminal report. So if he's just as likely to fry for his actions, but less invested in the family betrayal, maybe he's a better target for my questions.

I walk across the room and pull open the door to an empty hall. "Luca?"

"Kitchen."

I make my way into the open living area and find him leaning over the island counter eating one of those highly anticipated peace-offering sandwiches.

God, they look good.

All I can see is white bread, but damn, they're like clouds of heaven as he wraps his lips around them and takes a bite.

I inch toward him, moving to the opposite side of the island counter.

"Help yourself." He slides a clean plate toward me and I willingly take it, offering a look of civility in thanks. "I'll make more if necessary."

Next, he pushes over the tray of stacked sandwiches with a mass of the same type of filling—lettuce, tomato, carrot.

"Ham salad," he offers. "That's as good as it gets when I'm left in charge of meal prep."

I nod, letting his kindness sink in. "I'm not fussy. But I am starving." My mouth salivates as I grab one of the sandwich halves.

Then I'm forced to pause.

The inundating moisture evaporates, leaving my tongue dry and parched. I eye the offering dubiously and wonder if my impatience to fill my stomach is leading me into another trap.

"They're safe." He grabs the other half of the sandwich and takes a large bite, holding my gaze as he chews.

It's another offer of goodwill. A display of obvious assurance.

Maybe too obvious.

My insides gurgle, begging, pleading for something to fill the empty space, drugs be damned.

"Just being cautious." I throw that caution to the wind and bite into the puffy, soft clouds of bread-induced heaven. Flavors burst across my tongue like they're the most expensive delicacy.

He doesn't quit watching while I eat, downing the half in a few quick bites. The scrutiny is different to what I've come to expect from his boss. More cynical. Less provoking.

"Better?" he asks.

My nod is subtle. Even though the hunger pangs have slightly dissipated, I'm not going to gush with gratitude.

"Cole said you ran into some trouble with the boat driver yesterday."

I stiffen.

"That's my fault," he continues. "Leaving you alone with him wasn't a smart move."

"What was the alternative?"

He shrugs. "I should've waited with you until he left."

Staying on the pier may have stopped a gun being pointed at my head, but the conclusion would've remained the same. I'm still stuck here. Held captive.

"Cole wants you to feel safe. The sooner you realize you're not a prisoner, the easier this will be."

I grab another sandwich, not buying his line. "I'm not a prisoner, yet I can't leave. That doesn't make a lick of sense."

"Sometimes people need to be encouraged to make the right decisions. Would you have come here if you were asked? Would you have believed Cole if he trusted you with the truth?"

I don't have the truth. I don't have anything but confusion.

"The answer is no." He stares me down as he takes another bite, his jaw working overtime. "Don't even pretend otherwise. You might not agree with his tactics, but sometimes catching bees with honey takes a lot longer than—"

"Drugs and abduction?"

His jaw tics with the accusation, his stare remaining fierce as I blink innocently at him. I'm no stranger to antagonism. I know the ropes. Hell, I've been provoking tight-lipped narcs for years, but not once did I feel compelled to obtain what I needed illegally. I may have threatened something underhanded a time or two, doesn't mean I ever followed through.

"Where is he anyway?" I divert the conversation toward something that doesn't include judging me.

"Cole?"

No, Spiderman, asshole. "Yes, Cole."

"Why do you want to know?"

"I heard you two arguing by the pool." I take another bite and another, letting the silence build. "It seemed intense."

"And?"

"I was hoping for an explanation. I've never seen him out of control. It's not like him to be aggressive. It's uncharacteristic, isn't it?"

"Uncharacteristic?" Luca raises a brow and dusts his hands over his crumb-riddled plate. "You barely know him."

I want to refute his opinion. After what feels like a lifetime learning the ins and outs of the Torian family, the denial sits on the tip of my tongue, held back only to maintain our thinly veiled civility.

"Maybe not." I shrug. "But you know him, and you said it yourself: he wasn't acting like his normal self. He was spiraling. What does that mean?"

"What do you think it means?" His eyes narrow, scathing in their appraisal. "He told you what he's here to do. Did you expect him to carry out the job with a smile on his face and a fucking bounce in his step?"

"For starters, I expected this all to be a lie—another game—but I guess when I did contemplate the possibility, I imagined Cole committing the crime with his usual calm calculation."

Why wouldn't I?

He's always been a righteous villain.

"He isn't playing around. Torian is determined, and nothing will sway him once his mind is made up." He pushes from the counter and opens a cupboard behind him, grabbing two glasses. "Juice? Water? Soda?"

"Water. Thanks." The appreciation is grated. My pride takes a hit at having to thank an accomplice to my abduction. "If Cole is so sure of himself, why is he spiraling?"

He fills the glasses from the jug in the fridge, then turns back to slide one across the counter toward me. "I don't know about you, but where I'm from, killing your father isn't something most folks do for fun."

"I understand—"

He holds up a hand. "No, you don't. And if you have more questions, ask him. Not me."

"I would, but he's not the easiest person to speak to."

His features tighten, his lips pinching. "Neither am I."

Maybe this wasn't a peace offering after all.

"Can you at least tell me why I'm here?" I swallow over the last vestiges of ham salad in my mouth and the vile taste of the plea. "What he told me doesn't make sense. If I witness a crime, I'm obligated to report it. I can't let it slide, no matter which way Cole tries to twist the situation. It's cold-blooded, premeditated murder."

"Ask him." His tone hardens.

"Please." I've lowered myself to begging, and it fucking hurts. "You told him he needs to give me more information. What else is there to know?"

He grabs another sandwich half and glares at me as he takes a bite.

"Why do I need to be a witness? Why can't he use some other form of evidence? A photo? A recording? An account from someone else?"

He continues to work his jaw, his mouth pressed into a tight line. He can't possibly have to chew for as long as he does. I suspect he's buying time. Weighing his options.

"Luca?"

"Maybe you don't need to be a witness." He grins, his entire demeanor changing. "Maybe that's not why you're here at all."

My heart kicks up a notch. "It's not? Then why?"

"I don't know. It could be the same reason you kept going after him back in Portland even though you'd been instructed to stay out of the investigation. Neither one of you seem able to leave each other alone."

The accusation stabs right through me. It's severe. Harsh. And entirely off base. "The FBI has worked for years trying to get Luther behind bars. Of course I was going to find it hard to walk away from the investigation when Cole used me as an alibi."

"Turning up at the restaurant had nothing to do with investigating." He takes a drink, eyeing me over the rim of his glass before resting it back on the counter. "Just admit your interest in him goes beyond his criminal reputation."

I ignore the rise of my pulse. It's beneath me to rebuff the claim.

"Your cheeks are turning pink." He smirks. "Don't bite your tongue on my account. I'd love to hear your denial."

"Your understanding of the situation is embarrassing. I was only doing my job."

"Since when does your job include jetsetting with the infamous Cole Torian? Without backup?" His brows rise. "Should I be taking a refresher on the FBI handbook so I can stop confusing an unhealthy obsession with official Bureau protocol?"

Obsessed?

No way. I'm focused. Determined.

"Where is he?" I slide from the stool, squaring my shoulders, then wince at the bite of pain that comes with the movement. My fall last night left me with tense, swollen muscles and a bruise dark enough to rival the night sky. But the last thing I should do is announce the weakness. "I need to see him."

He grins. "He's letting off steam in the weights room."

"Can you point me in the right direction?"

He jerks his head backward. "Down the far end of the hall. Last room. But I wouldn't suggest going after him until he's cooled down."

"I appreciate the concern," I drawl, "but you can shove your suggestions up your ass."

I walk toward the hall opening and take a right this time, heading into uncharted territory. There're more paintings down this way. More rooms, too.

I hear a clang as I approach the glass door at the very end. Then another. Weights colliding with metal. The impact sounds heavy, harsh, as if he's doing the complete opposite of cooling down.

I stop at the frosted glass and listen. The slightest sense of unease skims across my chest, the sensation igniting a mass of goosebumps.

I'm not sure if I'm about to prove Luca right.

Going in search of Cole could be misconstrued as obsession instead of investigation. And I have to admit, the man acts like a thorn under my skin. From the moment we spoke at his uncle's funeral, I've had an increasing thirst to learn more about him. To get under his skin. To understand the world through his eyes.

That doesn't mean I'm obsessed.

I press my hands against the frosted glass and push inside.

Cole is on the bench press, dressed in a white tank and black sport shorts as he locks the impressive weight back into the cradle before shoving to his feet.

He doesn't look at me, doesn't even acknowledge my existence as he stalks to the pull-up bar to start hauling himself up and down, a masculine display on repeat.

I drag my gaze from his sweat-slicked skin, showing a similar lack of interest as I scope out the room, his breathy sounds of exertion taunting me.

There's a mass of equipment in here. A treadmill. Rower. Medicine balls. Elliptical trainer. Spin bike. The list goes on and on. There even looks to be a wooden door leading to a sauna in the far corner.

I keep my focus on that door, watching Cole from the corner of my eye until he drops to the floor. I use the break in exercise to gain his attention, raising my brows at him in a silent question.

I don't know what I'm asking exactly. I don't know much of anything as he grips the hem of his tank, raising the material to wipe the sweat from his face. He exposes all those muscles normally hidden from view.

All the perfected strength.

All the beauty tainted by his personality.

"What do you want, Nissa?" Aggression coats his tone. There's no calm. No calculation. His voice is filled with barely contained rage.

"I want to talk."

He scoffs out a laugh. "We've needed to talk for twenty-four hours. What's the rush now?"

Yet again, I'm stuck on what to say—truth or lies, deception or brutal honesty. Which path will get me out of this maze?

"You're spiraling. I need to know what that means for me."

Those eyes narrow as he grips the pull-up bar, his fingers cinched tight. "You've been talking to Luca."

"I overheard you two arguing by the pool. You were upset."

"Upset?" He lifts his chin over the bar, then again and again, his arm muscles bending and flexing with the exertion. "I'm sorry my response to planning my father's death isn't to your approval."

He's wrong.

The response isn't unwanted. If anything, his reaction is what I've been searching for. Knowing he's not emotionless gives me hope for my future. "If you don't want to go through with this, why are you?"

He drops back to the ground, his chest rapidly rising and falling with aggressive breaths. "What's the point in explaining? You won't understand. Not when all you want to do is look down on me from your fucking high horse."

I jut my chin, unable to remain still at the insult. "Make me understand."

He laughs again, the sound bitter. "You have rose-tinted glasses, Niss. You think the justice system is this perfect utopia that punishes the bad and protects the good."

"No, I don't. I know there are faults."

"Then why do you fucking defend it? Why are you on the front lines, claiming victims?"

"Victims? You're—" I snap my mouth shut, biting back the remark. I silently count to ten, calming myself. "I put away criminals. I make the community safe."

"Like hell you do. You put away petty crims. Low-level scum. You imprison the fools who are too powerless to buy their freedom. Occasionally, you'll bag someone who can cause real damage, but it's rare, because anyone like me knows your system is flawed. Lawyers manipulate juries. Judges and authorities can be bought or threatened. Evidence is tampered with. There's nothing that can't be swept under the rug. I could sit here for hours and name people who have walked free from the harshest crimes because they have money and influence, yet you call it a justice system. And those who remain behind bars are nothing but a burden on society. Do you know how many people are currently incarcerated, Ms. Fox? Do you know the amount of taxpayer dollars spent every year to let rapists and murderers live? Because I sure as hell do."

He's smart. And informed.

His knowledge isn't a surprise. But the unwanted twinge of respect itching behind my sternum is.

The fact he pays attention means he's thought about the effect of his actions on the community. There's logic to his system. It may be severely unhinged logic, but it's there nonetheless.

"We need rules, Cole. Society would implode without them."

"Society is already imploding," he snaps. "And your system is to blame. At least where I'm concerned, I ensure those who break the rules are a burden to no one but themselves. My punishments are swift and impact nobody but the culprit."

"That's a lie." I step forward. "Your physical punishments impact hospitals. Nursing staff. Doctors. They change the lives of friends and relatives of those you find guilty. It incites more aggression and violence."

"It inspires loyalty and fear, which breeds compliance." He stalks to the padded bench press and positions himself beneath the weighted bar. "Imprisonment has a major psychological impact that goes hand in hand with the huge expense. How can you not see how it fails society?" He pushes out five repetitions, grunting with the lift and fall of the heavy weight.

"Okay, I'll admit our system is flawed. But you're looking at the situation entirely one-sided. Following the law is far better than an eye for an eye." I take another step, not sure if I'm inching closer toward conflict or common ground.

If I wanted, I could hurt him.

Kill him.

Right here. Right now.

All I'd need to do is grab that bar and press down with all my weight.

Simple.

Easy.

"Why is it better?" He struggles through more repetition, sweat beading his face, veins bulging in his neck. He clinks the heavy weight into the cradle, then lets his arms fall to his sides. "Give me one good reason."

"I could give you hundreds."

He glares. "I'm only looking for one."

I get it. He's lived with this mindset all his life. He doesn't understand my reasoning. He probably never will. He's been brainwashed by his upbringing.

"For starters, by my society's rules, nobody is ever placed in your position. Not one person has ever had to kill their own father in the name of justice."

"I can deal with my situation." He reclaims the bar and pumps the iron, harder, faster, punishing himself.

"Are you sure?" I continue forward, one step, two. I creep closer toward risky possibilities as the weight rises and falls, those arms trembling under the pressure. "Can you honestly say you feel comfortable killing your dad?"

He falls quiet, nothing but the aggressive pant of his breaths falling between us.

"There's more to this, Cole. And I need to know what it is. I have to know why I'm really here."

"I've already told you," he seethes.

"*No.*" I add steel to my tone. He's lying. *Always* lying. God, it drives me insane. "You haven't told me anything. Having me here as a witness isn't smart. And you're a smart man. There has to be another reason."

His jaw clenches, his movements becoming hostile, combative and unrhythmic.

"Tell me why the hell I'm here." I raise my voice. "*Tell me.*"

He doesn't respond. Doesn't even acknowledge my demand.

Fucking hell. I'm going to lose my shit.

My temples throb. My chest pounds. Adrenaline floods my system, and I move so far beyond frustration I have to clench my hands at my sides to fight a scream.

"It's time for you to get out of here," he mutters. "We can talk later."

"No." Goddammit. I can't be kept from the information a moment longer. I refuse to bend to his will.

He's fucked me over, time and time again.

He's taunted me. Threatened my career. Spat in the face of my privacy. Disregarded my safety.

Enough is enough.

I lunge forward, hiking my leg over the bench to straddle his waist and claim the weighted bar. I press down hard, his dark blue eyes meeting mine as I threaten to crush the life from him. "Tell me."

His gaze narrows to tiny slits. His lip curls in a vicious snarl.

I don't know what I'm doing other than living by impulse. I climbed aboard him without a strategy or common sense. I'm not even sure of my aim.

I want answers. I want freedom. And apparently, autopilot is pushing me toward murder in an attempt to achieve both.

If I go ahead with this, it won't be a quick death. Or a quiet one. His face will turn red. He'll gasp and splutter.

Fuck. What the hell am I doing?

Even if I could stomach killing this man, I'd then have to deal with Luca. And find a way off this island.

What I've instigated is completely irrational.

Entire lunacy.

I'm about to raise a white flag and retreat when he quits fighting. His arms drop. He lets go of the bar, leaving me to struggle with the heavy load.

My injured shoulder screams in protest, the pain slicing down my muscles. "What are you doing?" My voice trembles as I lose strength, the bar lowering with my struggle, the agony increasing. I can't hold on.

"Don't stop now." He stares up at me, his face an emotionless mask. "You want me dead? Then kill me. This is the perfect opportunity. My arms are fatigued. I can't fight back."

I shuffle my feet, trying to stabilize myself as I straddle him. I throw all my strength into the lift and cry out when my shoulder screams with another painful revolt. "Cole, I can't carry this much longer. My arm…"

He doesn't offer assistance.

"*Cole.* Please." The agony shooting down my bicep is excruciating. Red-hot and blinding. "I didn't mean—"

I didn't mean what? To threaten him? To attempt murder?

He'll punish me. He'll use this as an excuse to retaliate.

Jesus Christ, what the fuck have I done?

The bar continues to lower as I succumb to the pain. My curled fingers brush his hard chest, the bar pressing into him. Soon, I'll lose all my strength. The bar will roll. The weight will suffocate him.

A million thoughts run through my head, each and every one of them revolving around this man's death and how I'd give anything for it not to happen.

I fight harder and still I fail.

"*Luca,*" I scream. "*Help.*"

Cole's eyes harden.

In a flash, he raises his arms, shoving at the bar, the heavy weight lifting like a feather to clang into the cradle. I jerk back, yet again surprised by another form of his manipulation as he snaps upright. I slither down his body with a hollow sense of shame and come to sit in his lap, face-to-face, chest-to-chest.

"Pure stupidity," he seethes, his hatred engulfing me. "I've abducted you, drugged and tied you, yet you can't even come close to finishing me off. That's disappointing, little fox. Where's your self-preservation?"

My heart trembles behind tightening ribs.

I'm lost.

In those eyes.

In his vehemence.

In complete and utter confusion.

I still see his vulnerability. It's there. *Right* there. Beaming back at me with furrowed brows.

"Want to know why you couldn't follow through?" His voice loses the bitter edge and gains a taint of condescension. "It's because you know I won't hurt you. There's no fear because I'm no threat."

He's right.

I don't fear him. Not physically.

Not even when I'm held down on his lap, his ferocity staring back at me.

"You know I'm right," he growls. "You can claim to be a victim all you like, but you're here willingly."

I shake my head, sickened by his logic. "You *have* hurt me. Look at my wrists. And there's a track mark on my side, too. I don't even know if you used a sterile needle."

Something flashes behind those eyes. Regret? Disappointment?

I wait for an apology. I even hope for a viable explanation for his actions when the door swings open and Luca rushes in.

His eyes turn judgmental at the sight before him. "What's—"

"Get out," Cole yells. "*Now.*"

Luca complies in a heartbeat, leaving us alone, with me straddling the lap of a man who looks back at me as if I'm a disappointment.

I swallow, trying to fight the complete detox of moisture from my tongue, and lick my lower lip. The dryness only increases as Cole watches the action, his attention focused on my mouth.

The *thump, thump, thump* of my heart is a constant reminder I'm alive, but I'm entirely numb. Completely devoid of a suitable reaction to the rainbow of insanity tearing my insides apart.

There's anger and hostility. Frustration and exhaustion.

And something else, too. Something that builds the longer he looks at me this way. Something I don't even want to define.

"You've never been scared of me." His hand raises from my waist, the touch trailing to my neck, his fingers wrapping around my throat. "Not even when I set out to claim your fear."

I tremble, the quake building in intensity.

There's no pain from his hold. It's light—so light it almost seems to be made with pleasurable intent.

My pulse pounds wildly beneath his palm, my rampant heartbeat increasing to the point it's deafening. I can't stop my quickening breaths, the short, shallow pants rasping from my lips.

I don't like this feeling. It's unnatural. It's in complete contrast to self-preservation. Something is wrong with me.

He's threatening my life, his strength capable of crushing my windpipe, and I'm not trembling because of fear.

I'm... *God*, I don't know what I am, but it definitely isn't scared.

Maybe it's shame. Or a different taste of humiliation.

"You want to know why you're here?" he murmurs. "You want to know why you were my first and only choice to bear witness?"

I swallow again. I can't gain any moisture to speak. I can only nod in subtle acknowledgement.

His gaze holds mine, his stare sinking deep into my heart. Then the calm stops in an abrupt blink. His face hardens; his upper lip curls.

Finally, a tingle of caution niggles its way from the bottom of my spine, the awareness increasing the higher it climbs.

"I brought you here because I knew you'd argue your case, claiming you, with your infamous virtue, were right, and me, with my merciless reputation, are wrong. And I fucking knew all it would do is convince me I was making the right choice." His hand falls, his grip moving to my hips where he lifts and drags me off of him to stand beside the bench press. "I brought you here, Nissa, because I refuse to let myself fail with such a judgmental bitch keeping score."

15

TORIAN

I stalk away from the bench press, turning my back to her as I adjust my cock.

She's plotting to kill me, and here I am, rearranging the dick tenting my fucking shorts. If that's not psychotic I don't know what is.

But at least it's clear now. All the shit I've worried about has come to fruition.

My father's perverted afflictions must have been working their subliminal bullshit toward me for years. I've always been his perfect protégé—Luther's mini-me with bigger plans and even bigger ideas. And I naively thought his teachings had been limited to business.

Turns out he handed down the fetishes, too.

Sexualized brutality is new to me. Harming women has never brought a thrill.

Until now.

Maybe this is how the fucked-up shit starts. The twisted kinks are triggered by an event.

A woman.

This woman.

Bringing her here was fucking reckless. Indulgent. But the reasons I've told her aren't a lie.

I need someone reliable to relay the information of my father's death, because those who don't believe I'm capable will be hard to convince.

Luca's account won't hold merit. The word of anyone loyal to me, or easily bribed, is worthless.

But Anissa isn't either of those.

I didn't fabricate the truth about her being here to ensure my success either. Every time she looks at me with her narrow-eyed judgment, I grow more determined.

She's here to push me. Provoke me.

Her bitchy, self-righteous superiority will ensure I finish this thing with my father despite the guilt hovering close.

There's more though.

So much more it feels like she's the linchpin to this entire fucking operation for no justifiable reason. I'm propelled forward because of her. Not my sister's need for closure. And definitely not due to my father's nameless, faceless victims.

Anissa messes with my head to the point where I'm beating back a goddamn erection at the thought of her trying to choke me with a weights bar. I'm crazed with the need to get her back on top of me. Those wide eyes staring down at mine. That bated breath brushing my mouth.

And that fucking pussy. Nothing has ever felt better than her heat against my stomach.

"Cole?"

Gentle pressure leans into my shoulder blade. A hand. *Her* hand.

"What?" I jerk away.

"Did you hear what I said?"

I shake my arms, and it's not because of the building lactic acid. I need to get these toxic thoughts out of my system. I have to figure out where the fuck I went wrong and if there's any possibility of going back.

I'm not a weak son of a bitch who takes pleasure in hurting women. I'm not my father. I don't need to strong-arm the vulnerable to make myself feel powerful. Not for a fucking second.

"Sorry," I snarl. "I have other things on my mind. I guess when someone tries to kill you, it's hard to focus." I turn to face her and shouldn't be surprised when she straightens those shoulders and raises her chin.

"I didn't try to kill you. I just…"

"Just attempted to crush my throat, then pussied out at the last second."

She blinks at me, those eyes wider than usual, her lips slightly parted. She wants to reject my claim, but she can't.

This woman contemplated ending my life.

Maybe I would've let her, too.

Maybe I should've.

"Cole, please, I want to believe you, but your logic is hard to justify." She keeps staring. Pleading. "You know I'm loyal to my job. There's no way I could keep my mouth shut about this."

She's right.

There's no logic. No rationale. No sense. There's only impulse and instinct when it comes to her.

"If you report this, you won't live long enough to testify. Never forget that." I flash my teeth in a feral smile. "You should also realize I'm my father's son. So maybe think twice before you straddle my dick next time."

She recoils, her mouth agape.

Good.

The shock should keep her at bay.

"Come on." I stride across the room. "I'll show you where you need to be when he arrives."

I shove open the gym door, holding it wide until she enters the hall.

"You'll be in my room." I continue toward the other end of the house, her footsteps following behind me.

"Why your room?"

"You'll see in a minute." I don't stop until we reach my door, then push it open for her to proceed before me.

She stares, dubious, but walks ahead to pause near the bed. "Now what?"

"The walk-in robe." I jerk my head to the door at my left.

She sighs and does as instructed, sliding the opening wide.

"Pull the hanging shirts to the side."

"Which ones?" she drawls. "There's a whole heap."

I follow her into the cramped space, making sure to keep as much distance between us as possible. For my dick's sake. "Start in the middle."

She separates the hung clothing, the clink of hangers skittering along the rail as she exposes the door behind with a keypad lock on the wall beside it. She glances at me over her shoulder. "What's this?"

"A panic room."

A different kind of concern crosses her features, more speculation than worry.

"The code is eight-nine-seven-one. And only the two of us know those digits."

She keeps staring.

"Go on." I encourage her with a wave of my hand. "Eight-nine-seven-one. Pin it in."

She turns her focus back to the door and keys in the numbers, then the door panel slides across as she hits Enter.

"There's a light switch inside, on the right wall."

She reaches out, running her fingers along the inside of the frame to illuminate the panic room in artificial light. She inches forward, assessing the interior as she turns in a circle.

I remain in the middle of the wardrobe, not wanting to tempt myself with her close proximity. I already know what she'll find in there—a wall of six blank screens, each capable of exposing a real-life feed of any main room inside the sprawling mansion.

There's also a mini bathroom and a disabled communications station. At one time, anyone hiding in here could call for help. But I can't trust her with that option. Not yet.

"You'll stay in there." I lean back against the shelves. "You'll have access to the video and audio feed."

"How?" She pokes her head back out the door. "Can you show me?"

I contemplate denying her. I try to convince myself it's a fucking bad idea to insert myself into the small space beside her. But seconds later, I'm in there, almost shoulder to shoulder with this beguiling woman as I turn on the switch to illuminate the six monitors displaying the pool, yard, kitchen, living room, and my bedroom, along with two different angles of the hall.

"Are these the only rooms under surveillance?"

"No." I keep my focus on those screens, ignoring her as she turns to face me.

"Are there cameras in every room?"

"Apart from the bathrooms, yes. Every bedroom. Every square inch of livable space."

"How convenient." The words are grated, her anger crackling to life in the air between us. "I guess you've spent a lot of time in here."

A smirk slowly spreads my lips. Her anger is invigorating. Always has been. I bet it always will be. "Don't flatter yourself."

Her shoulders relax, her relief evident even from the corner of my eye.

"I don't need to be in the panic room. I get the video feed on my cell." I pull the device from my pocket, unlock the screen, and show her the view of her bedroom.

Her posture stiffens, snapping tight in a heartbeat.

She mutters something. A curse. A promise, maybe.

Again, I'm invigorated. Euphoric at the ease of angering her, and equally disgusted in myself at enjoying her reaction.

"The cell feed doesn't allow for audio. But you'll have access to it in here." I reach for the narrow counter and pull out a keyboard to tap in the necessary button combination. Brief flickers of noise filter through from the speakers in the corners of the room. The sound of Luca clearing his throat. The clink and clatter of plates as he piles them into the dishwasher. "You'll hear whatever my father has to say when the time comes. You'll bear witness to it all in the safety of this room."

I can already picture what she's going to see.

He'll greet me with a handshake, his designer suit flawless, his hair groomed and perfectly cut. He'll compliment me on something, then follow it up with a harsh insult. The kindness before the storm. It's how he's always been. With me. With my sisters. Reward then reprimand.

We'll talk about family. Money. Negotiations. And those women.

"Anything overheard is to be kept in the strictest confidence. I have friends in the FBI, so I'll know if you sing."

I think that's another part of this game. I like her being a threat. A constant devil on my shoulder. Once this thing with my father is over, the ball will be in her court. It will be up to Anissa if we play another round.

"You've made the threat clear, Cole. You don't need to keep repeating it."

"You sure? I have to admit, it's slightly enjoyable reminding you."

She sighs, remaining silent while her gaze is trained on the screens for long seconds. "How do you plan to…?" The end of her sentence hangs between us, her voice barely audible. Soft.

I know exactly what she's asking. It's the same question I've asked myself time and time again.

I have options when it comes to killing my father. Multiple alternatives. But the problem stems from the honor we've built our lives upon. Just because I don't abide by Anissa's justice system doesn't mean my world doesn't have a code of our own. One that demands respect.

Stabbing my father in the back is one thing. Killing him in cowardice is quite another.

I need to finish this face-to-face. Eye-to-eye. His power and authority command a full-frontal attack. An end-game of strategy, not a battle for strength.

"You don't need to know the finer details."

"All you want me to do is watch? I don't need to be involved?"

"Bearing witness is all that's necessary. For obvious reasons, it's best if he's kept in the dark where you're concerned."

She sucks in a deep breath and turns to face me, a mere foot of space between us. "Has he made contact?"

"No. But he won't be too far away. He could arrive at any minute. Either today or tomorrow. I doubt it will be much later."

"And what if he sees me? What if he arrives unnoticed and I'm found?"

"We'll hear the boat."

Worry breaks across her features. "What if we don't?"

"We'll hear it."

"But—"

"We'll hear him coming, Nissa. I promise you. That's why none of the televisions have been turned on. There's no music or noise to distract from what might be coming."

"What about when we're sleeping?"

She seems to inch closer with her apprehension. Or the space around us shrinks. Everything closes in. There's only her. Only me. And a fucking dick that won't stop with its incessant twitch.

"Trust me. I'll keep you safe. I know my father. The last thing people like us want to do is surprise assholes with trigger-happy fingers in the middle of the night. He'll make sure I'm aware he's on his way."

She nods, the movement almost imperceptible as she stares at me. Stares so deep I feel it in my bones.

Could she finally be letting down her guard? Is this fierce, spiteful woman succumbing to my charm?

I step back, giving myself a reprieve from the sweet scent of her shampoo. Or maybe it's her soap.

"Remind me why you're doing this. What's the aim?" she asks. "I understand why any normal person would want to stop your father but..."

"Just not someone like me?" I finish for her.

"You've built a crime-riddled empire. Why draw a line at sex offenses?"

"There's always a line. This just happens to be mine."

It's clear she doesn't understand why a heartless motherfucker like me would want to distance himself from a wealthy business opportunity.

This woman is a world away from having me pegged.

She has no fucking clue.

"I'm struggling to believe why your father's actions are such a hardship for you. Death and destruction shadow you, Cole. You seem to crave the horrors that stalk most people's nightmares."

I ignore the truth and focus on the words she makes seem erotic—death, destruction, craving. Her fake purity sprinkles the evil with naive innocence. But she's not entirely free from sin herself. There're darker sides to this woman, and I'd love to expose them.

"I have many cravings," I admit. "Some I think you'd enjoy."

My mouth is running away with me. Saying things better left unsaid.

I can no longer deny my attraction. Both physically and mentally.

I want this woman. Her body. Her mind.

She needs to be beneath me. At my mercy.

"Is that a poor attempt at deflection?" She raises a brow. "I know there's more to this. Killing your father will have long-lasting repercussions. Your family allies will be torn. Nobody will trust you. You're risking everything. Why?"

"To most, my father won't be murdered; he'll simply disappear. It's not like he hasn't done it before."

"You still haven't answered why. You're deflecting again. You're trying to hide."

Her strike hits its mark.

A fucking bull's-eye.

"Cole?" She looks at me. Really fucking looks at me. Like she's a sympathetic shrink and I'm her unhinged patient. "I want to believe you're doing this for the right reasons."

"I'm killing a man, Niss. My own father. In cold blood. If I were you, I wouldn't spend sleepless nights searching for whimsical reasons. Just focus on the benefits his death will bring." I turn, needing to get away from her. "I'm hungry. We're done here."

She grabs my arm, her fingers sliding over the sweat still clinging to my skin.

I don't need to stop. Her hold is inconsequential. But my feet remain immobile. Unmoving.

"Please."

She kills me with her plea.

This could be a ploy, a fucking FBI tactic. And it's working.

Her feigned need for understanding tears at me. Claws. I want to tell her everything. To shed the shame coating me like a second skin. To yell it right into her pretty face. To admit the remorse that has eaten away at me since I was a fucking kid.

I should do it. I should fucking succumb, exposing the depths of my own internal destruction for her to pick and prod.

"Quit the gentle act." I swing around and take a menacing step toward her. "We both know you don't have a tender bone in your body."

She inches back, bumping her ass into the counter as I continue to approach, looming over her, glaring. I attempt to siphon her misleading goodwill with a physical threat and I succeed.

Her expression changes, the gentleness seeping away until all I witness is interest.

Anticipation.

It might be my father's fucking perverted influence, but I see hunger staring back at me. Somehow this response is ten times worse.

I'm a breath away from taking her on this counter. From pulling apart those tight leggings and plunging deep inside her.

She swallows and licks her lower lip. "Tell me the real reasons." Her voice is filled with expectation. Delirium. She's dying for a taste of me.

I'm dying to give it to her.

It would be incredibly easy to lose a wealth of frustration in her body. The mindlessness would be cathartic. But incredibly fucking stupid.

"Why do you need me to convince you?" I grate. "Why even bother trying? We both know everyone lies. You, more than anyone, know those closest to us can lie the easiest."

Shock splits across her face, the sudden change in expression announcing she understands the subtle dig at her father.

"You will never know me, Nissa." I sink into those green eyes. I drown in them. "You will never understand me. All you can do is come to terms with what I've told you, and make peace with what's to come. It's either this way or nothing."

Her focus is intense. Confounding. Her breaths shudder between perfect lips.

Her attention sweeps over me. Through me. She pokes at secrets I wasn't aware I had.

"And nothing isn't an option?" she asks.

I scowl at her. "You still think his freedom would be better?"

"I'm not asking for me. I want to make sure you know what you're doing. You can't come back from something like this."

I scoff out a snicker, denying her concern. "I know what I'm doing. Don't worry your pretty little head about me."

She wraps her arms around her stomach.

I want to unravel those arms and place her hands on her hips. To return her to a strong, commanding warrior woman because this fragile demeanor has a mirror effect. Her gentleness makes me powerless.

Defenseless.

She swallows, clears her throat, and raises her chin a smidge. "My concern is based on the aftermath. You'll change after this. Nobody can kill their own parent and not lose themselves. I'm concerned this will inspire more violence. And in return, more crime."

I bite out a bitter laugh. I should've known. She has no concern for me. This was only part of her attempt to achieve the perfect crime-free Utopia. "You think you know me well enough to predict how I'll react?"

How can she when I have no clue myself?

I could be consumed with relief once my father is gone. Happy as fuck.

"No, I guess I don't know you well," she admits. "I doubt I know you at all. But I'd like to believe you're not capable of this."

The gentle disapproval strikes hard, punishing me with its subtlety. Her thorns are sinking farther, burying deeper.

"Then you're going to be bitterly disappointed, Nissa, because this is already a foregone conclusion. I'll pull the trigger without hesitation, and I won't look back."

16

ANISSA

I believe him now.

When he talks about his plan, I hear the truth in his words. I acknowledge the determination driving him to take drastic action. I see his conviction.

There's something deeper, too.

I feel his animosity for Luther, and it resembles the emotions I harbor toward my own father so closely I struggle to fight against the common ground.

What I lack is an understanding of how he can follow through with the crime.

I can't imagine contemplating the murder of my own flesh and blood. Not cold and premeditated. Not even if my father's actions meant the punishment was justified. I could never pull that trigger. And I'm not sure I should feel comfortable in the company of someone who can.

But I do.

There's no fear beating behind my ribs. No shock or devastation.

I want to detest Cole's plan, but I'm beginning to believe he's making the right decision.

If Luther has local police protecting him, I can't see a way to bring him down. Not efficiently. Or legally. And every minute ticking by is sixty seconds of torture for those women held captive.

This situation is a moral dilemma for me on innumerable levels. A crisis I'm sure Cole designed with pinpoint precision.

"Okay," I murmur. "I'll do it. I'll watch. I'll tell your connections whatever necessary as long as you can vow the information will never get back to the Bureau. I won't have this hanging over my head for the rest of my life."

The tightness coiled around him loosens. His shoulders relax. Those muscled arms lose their ferocity.

"That's not all." I hold his gaze and show my conviction with the hitch of my chin.

"After I've held up my end of the bargain, we're done with this. There're no more games. No more tormenting or provoking. The stalking has to stop. The flowers and cards, too. We go our separate ways and never speak to each other again. I won't spend my days trying to take you down, and you won't spend yours trying to make my life a living hell."

I need to distance myself from him as much as possible. To flee the confusion his presence brings.

"You want to take back your promise?" His eyes taunt me. The curl of his lips, too. "You were the one who vowed we would spend more time together."

"Quit the games, Cole. I mean it." I clutch the counter at my sides and stare him down, feigning strength I don't have. "I can't do this if I think you're still toying with me."

For long moments he eyes me, stroking my unease with his devilish gaze.

"I agree to your terms." He steps close, leaning into me as he murmurs, "Being done with you will be a pleasure."

His response doesn't fill me with the relief I'd anticipated.

In fact, the tightening pressure nudging into my chest almost feels like rejection.

"Good." I swallow and freeze in place as his attention locks onto my throat.

The lingering effects of his touch still plague me. The tingle remains from where those fingers wrapped around my neck.

I suppress a shudder. I refuse to give in to the adrenaline sabotaging my system, making me react in uncharacteristic ways.

"I'm going back to my room." I walk out of the small space, determined not to slink away from his bulky frame when our shoulders brush. "Let me know when I need to be at your beck and call."

I take another step, only to be halted by his tight grip on my sore arm.

"You're not up to something, are you?" He narrows his gaze. "Is this sudden agreement a ploy?"

I contemplate provoking him again. The impulse is engrained.

Instead, I bite my tongue, staring deep into those dark ocean eyes. "It's no ploy, Cole." I yank my arm away and wince at the bite of pain lashing my shoulder. "I'm well aware my life is in your hands."

His jaw tics. Anger spikes in his expression.

I fall into confusion, wondering what I've done to antagonize him this time when his gaze lowers to my shoulder.

"Show me your injury."

The sudden change in topic has my mind spinning.

"Show me," he demands.

I shake my head and take a backward step.

He counters, lashing out, slinging an arm around my waist to drag me into him.

I'm close. So fucking close. I'm plastered against his muscles, his frustration bearing down on me.

Time. Fucking. Stops.

He doesn't move. Neither do I.

I'm caught up in those eyes. His scent. His hold.

I'm in the arms of my enemy, and I'm trembling for reasons that bear no resemblance to fear.

"I'm not going to show you, Cole."

"I thought you would've learned by now I'm not a man who appreciates being denied."

My knees threaten to buckle. My heart feels ready to explode.

Am I imagining the innuendo? Have I lost all grasp on reality?

"Here." I snatch at the short sleeve of my T-shirt and tug it down my arm, exposing my shoulder through the stretched neckhole. "It's a bruise. Now can I go?"

His gaze narrows on the exposed skin. His nostrils flare.

The tight hold around my waist doesn't loosen. I'm still stuck against his body. Pressed into a wall of hard muscle.

"Just a bruise," he repeats. "You don't need pain meds? Or a sling?"

"I don't need a damn thing from you."

Well, apart from maybe a phone, a boat ride off this hell hole, a plane ticket home, and a way to circumvent customs without my fucking passport.

The intensity fades from his features. A brutal smile curves his lips. "Not a damn thing?" he repeats with humor in his voice. "I'll remember that."

It's a threat—one that inspires a shiver I'm sure he can feel.

He releases me and I stumble forward into him, before I right myself and lunge back. My flailing triggers the soft rumble of his laughter.

I ignore the infuriating sound as I turn and stride from the walk-in robe.

I drag my feet into his bedroom, escape into the hall, and then into the sanctuary of my own room.

I reclaim my favored position, back against the wall, ass on the carpet, this time right next to the door I leave open.

He doesn't follow.

I'm left to suffer through a mental rerun of our encounter for long, painful minutes, my breathing rampant until he eventually strides past my room, freshly showered and wearing an impeccable suit.

Maybe I should do the same.

Washing away his touch might clear my head because as it stands, his gentle grip still haunts my skin. But I don't have the energy to move. I'm exhausted in mind and body. So I sit, listening to the world as time ticks by.

I hear everything—the lapping of the ocean. The whispers of the breeze through the living room curtains. The shuffle of feet and clink of crockery.

The thing I hear most is his voice.

He speaks to Luca, striking a conversation that ignores the tension they'd previously had between them. He doesn't mention me. There's no bite of hostility. Not an ounce of the discomfort consuming me.

He discusses inconsequential things. Business back home. The possibility of Hunter's wedding. A planned renovation to his restaurant.

I ignore the words as his rough, deep timbre hums in my ears.

I listen to him for hours wondering where the hell my despised hatred for this man has gone. He doesn't change the volume of his voice. Not when his phone rings and he speaks to his sister, lying to her about his location.

He doesn't change his tone as the day draws to a close and he continues his civil conversation with Luca. He doesn't even quieten his voice when he starts to discuss his father's upcoming arrival and how Luther won't be alone. There will be bodyguards.

More casualties.

I'm sure Cole knows I'm in listening distance. I'm positive he's checked the video feed on his phone to see I'm positioned close to the door, hanging off his every word.

And still he doesn't hide anything from me.

He doesn't whisper or step outside to hold the discussion away from prying ears.

"I'll greet them on the pier and make sure your father's men stay on the boat." Luca doesn't lower his voice either. "That way you can do your thing while I do mine."

I tilt my ear toward the open door, latching onto a more detailed part of their plan.

"And what about her?" Luca asks. "What will she do?"

My pulse increases.

"Don't worry. She will be safe."

There's a pause, a longer than necessary delay where I have the unfortunate opportunity to wonder if they're having some sort of silent communication.

Is it a scheme? Another trick?

Of course it is. Luca has no "worry" for me. He doesn't care about my safety.

"And once this is over?" he adds. "Will she be safe then, too?"

I hold my breath, the captured air burning in my lungs.

"That's up to her."

Me. I can be safe if I hold up my end of the bargain.

I need to watch a murder and follow his protocol afterward.

The former seems far easier than the latter.

I've seen a wealth of violence in my life and the act of murder isn't what daunts me. It's the morality. But the more I think about Cole's reasoning, the more I believe he has a point.

It's becoming a struggle to straddle the righteous high-wire. Maybe I shouldn't have stepped foot on it at all when innocents are still being tortured.

I'm sure other agents wouldn't hesitate to push for a speedy resolution. If the choice came down to Luther's freedom or his death, my fellow Feds might easily choose death without pausing for contemplation.

The murder of a criminal would've already happened. The cover-up would be taking place.

Unfortunately, I don't have that luxury.

When my father diverted off the path of justice, it ensured I'd have to watch every decision I made for the rest of my life. I don't have the freedom to make even slightly dishonorable choices. Every thought I have needs to be on the right side of the law.

I can't falter.

I shouldn't even waiver.

Which, I guess, means my conflict isn't entirely based on right and wrong. I'm looking at this problem and seeing how it will affect my reputation—my career—not the women held captive.

My stomach churns at the realization.

"Shit." I hang my head in my hands, my elbows rested against my knees.

I don't give a fuck about Luther. Nobody should.

And what is the alternative? A crapload of money spent on a manhunt for someone who would then cost the government more money when he was holed up in prison for the rest of his life.

I should be out there, helping to plot a foolproof plan instead of fighting this. My skills could be put to use to ensure nothing goes wrong.

But then I'd have the issue of aiding and abetting.

"Goddammit." I massage my forehead and battle my conscience. I drown in the tumultuous waves of my internal struggle while the sound of food preparation starts in the kitchen.

I hear the fridge open and close. Drawers, too. Then footsteps.

Cole enters my peripheral vision, his frame bearing down on me as he stops in the doorway, his suit-covered shoulder leaning against the frame.

"Would you like to help me prepare dinner?"

I raise a brow, unimpressed. But it's not only the invitation to be his kitchen bitch that pokes at me. It's everything else: the laziness in his stance. The relaxation. The calm. "You want me to be your slave?"

"I thought you'd appreciate being involved so you didn't have to worry about any secret ingredients."

My cheeks heat.

He's offering me a kindness, of sorts.

"There's no pressure, Nissa. I have no hidden motives."

There're always hidden motives.

Always.

"I'll leave the decision with you." He pushes from the frame, his presence escaping my periphery as he walks away.

It's not that I don't want to ensure he's not slipping something into my next meal. My hesitation revolves around my lack of hatred for this easily hate-able man.

I've lost my animosity. Fevered bitterness no longer boils my blood. All the venom is gone.

Nothing consumes me. Nothing but frustration.

I want to return to hating him. I want to be sucked dry of my knowledge so I can float back to ignorance.

But it's too late. We have something in common: our hatred for our fathers. And I can't stop my thoughts from wandering to admiration when I think of the struggle he's willing to endure to set things right.

We're striving toward a common goal and it feels wrong. Wrong, but so damn right. And entirely necessary.

I push from the floor and ignore the bipolar reactions of my inner voice while I walk down the hall and into the open living room.

Cole is in the kitchen.

Luca is stretched out on the couch, his head poking up to watch me. "You okay?"

His concern hits me like an assault.

"Super," I drawl, making my way into the kitchen. I position myself on the opposite side of the island counter to Cole as he pulls out a frying pan from the drawers beneath, the sound of it colliding with the stove clattering off the walls.

Luca pushes from the couch and walks for the glass doors leading into the fading sunlight. He's leaving me alone with Cole. Alone with confusion.

"Where's he going?" My voice is an agitated mess.

"Outside to make sure we don't miss anything while I'm cooking."

That doesn't ease my concerns as I watch Luca push aside the sheer curtain and disappear outside.

"Have you heard from Luther yet?"

"No." He peels an onion, then begins to dice, his large, tanned hands working in proficient strokes. Perfectly timed. Evenly spaced.

"You're eying the knife like a treasure." He drops the blade to the chopping board and discards his suit jacket, placing it on the kitchen counter behind him. "Have you had a change of heart about killing me?"

I raise my gaze to his, not showing an ounce of how far from the truth he is. "Why don't you hand it over and we can find out?"

He smiles, the expression transforming his face into that of a playful playboy. He's not threatened by me. Not even a little. "Maybe later. After the risotto."

He reclaims the weapon and continues making a dish I've never attempted before. Not that his superior culinary skills are surprising. There isn't much point being a master chef when I'm only serving a table for one.

I watch him in silence, taking in the mastery as he combines ingredients, melting butter, frying the diced onion and some garlic. He does everything with perfect confidence and synchronicity. He heats rice, prepares shrimp from the fridge, stirs broth in the pan.

He's at home in the kitchen.

He seems almost normal.

Human.

Right now, Cole is an everyday guy, cooking an everyday meal, in an everyday environment.

There's no deception, no deceit, no horror.

All his atrocities are hidden. Shielded from view.

When it comes to adding the wine, he raises the bottle in my direction. "Would you like a glass?"

"Are you kidding?" I glare.

"Too soon?" His lips lift in that taunting kick he's perfected.

"Yeah. Too soon."

Asshole.

I roll my eyes and swivel my stool, diverting my attention to the glass doors, the daylight no longer in existence.

I want Luca to return. Having no buffer between me and Cole's attempts at humor is starting to get to me. I don't want to see him as a man. He needs to remain a criminal. A murderer. But with each passing second, I'm becoming more and more settled.

"After you kill your father, how long do I have to wait before I can go home?"

The rhythmic stirring of the pan doesn't stop; neither does the sound of him adding broth.

"As soon as I can accommodate it."

I turn back to him, raising a brow. "I want specifics, with your word being your bond and all that."

"I'm well aware of your urgency to get away from me." There's a gentleness to his voice. Understanding. I don't like it. "But the aftermath is unpredictable. There's the issue of cleaning up and disposing of evidence. Not to mention getting out of here with all our lives intact."

I ignore his attempt to scare me into submission. "Are we talking hours? Days? Weeks?"

He meets my gaze and holds it. "If I can't get you out of here within twenty-four hours, something has gone wrong, and the least of my concerns will be breaking any promises I've made to you."

Okay, so maybe I'm slightly daunted with the continued mention of danger. It's one thing to stare down the barrel of a life-threatening situation with a gun in-hand and a partner at my side. It's quite another to do it unarmed with the enemy as my only shield. "And how will you dispose of evidence?"

He sighs. "Is it too much to ask for us to enjoy dinner without talking shop?" He reaches behind him, pulling a spoon from the drawer on the far counter. "Here, try this." He scoops up a tiny serve of risotto and reaches over the counter toward me.

I stare at the offering, then him, not trusting either.

"Scared?" he asks.

He's baiting me. I know he is.

My assumption is confirmed when I snatch the spoon and take a taste, bringing his laughter to life.

I gave him exactly what he wanted—retaliation—but I don't care. Not when deliciousness consumes my mouth.

The risotto is good. Really good.

"Do you approve?" He watches me, waiting for praise I'm loath to give.

I take my time, finishing the food slowly before I swallow. "It's…"

"Delicious? Perfect? The best thing you've ever tasted?" He dusts his hands, then wipes them on a tea towel. "You know it's not a sin to pay me a compliment."

"How can you be sure?" I hand back the spoon. "What I was actually going to say is 'surprising.'"

"I own a chain of award-winning restaurants, and you're surprised I can cook?" The look he gives me is condescending.

"Okay, so I made an inaccurate assessment. Sue me."

"Don't worry. It's not your first."

I bite my tongue, unwilling to continue the verbal tennis match.

Maybe I have made false judgments. But so has he. I'm not the righteous bitch who's always peering down from her high horse.

"How long until you're done?" I push from my stool, needing more space than the few feet of distance the island counter provides.

"Minutes, if not seconds." He pours the last of the broth into the pan and stirs. "Could you do me a favor and get the plates?"

I pretend reluctance isn't eating me from the inside out. I don't want to help him any more than I already am. But they're only plates. And I have to eat.

I make my way to the far wall of cupboards, opening one, then another, and another.

"Here." He closes in behind me, the gentle brush of his presence making me stiffen as he opens the cupboard beside my thigh.

He's there and gone in seconds. Close then far in a brutal case of nerve-tingling whiplash.

"Do you need anything else?" I grab the damn plates and dump them on the counter beside him.

"What kind of scope do I have with my answer? Because that's a loaded question coming from a Fed to someone about to commit murder."

I grind my teeth. I won't let him keep poking me.

I can't.

"Your scope is minimal. I'm talking about cutlery or salt and pepper."

"They're already on the table."

I glance at the eight-seater table near the window with its three place settings close together at one end. Nope. No way. I'm not going to spend unnecessary time with his sly grin haunting my periphery while he watches me salivate over the meal he's made.

"I'll eat in my room."

I'm not being antagonistic or petulant. I *need* space.

It's imperative.

I have to get away from all the confusion.

"Okay." He takes a risotto-filled plate to the oven, opens the door and uses tongs to place shrimp on top. "Here you go."

He holds out the plate and I grasp it, latching on like it's a prize when in reality, it's a temporary escape plan. But he doesn't let go. He holds tight, wordlessly demanding me to meet his gaze.

I don't want to comply. Not when I know cocky arrogance will greet me.

Only the standoff is worse.

He remains close. Silent. Entirely menacing with his calm patience until I raise my gaze and come face-to-face with concern.

"Are you okay?" His brow furrows. His lips thin. "You're tense."

Again, his confidence grates on me. His worry is even worse. He's not asking if I'm tense. He's already made the claim as if he can read me like a book.

"Sure am," I drawl. "Being here is better than Disneyland."

His lips twitch, and I tug on the plate before he hits me with a full-blown grin. Then it's straight to the cutlery drawer for a fork before I'm striding away, into my now dark room.

I leave the lights off, preferring the comfort of the moonlight through the window to soothe me as I eat on the bed.

Each swallow of risotto is an agonizing chore. I detest every time I have to refill my spoon, because the flavor is thoroughly delicious—the shrimp even better—and I don't want to acknowledge Cole is responsible for the brilliance.

I practically lick the plate clean, then glare at it with disgust as I place it on the nightstand.

Why does he have to be entirely normal in some moments and a monster in others? Why can't he pick a path and stick to it?

It hasn't skipped my attention he's never mentioned his concern for the women held captive. His motivation is based on reputation. To remove the perverted taint on his name from his father's actions.

I'm only here because his word can't be trusted, not even with his business associates, drug lords, or whoever else I'm meant to inform about Luther's death.

The world knows he's a liar.

A manipulator.

And I just downed a plateful of his cooking while daydreaming he was my personal chef.

I groan with the guilt and stretch out on the bed, my head on the pillow, with a perfect view of the stars.

I can't remember the last time I simply laid back and watched the night sky. It would've been a lifetime ago, when memories of my past didn't haunt me through the quiet.

Still moments overwhelm me, because the nothingness quickly fills with pain. After all these years, I can't forgive my father. His actions were the catalyst to the end of my happiness.

We'd been the perfect family—me, Mom, and Dad.

Then he changed.

It was as if a switch flipped and my level-headed, smart, caring father turned into a paranoid, possessive stranger who refused to discuss his personality change. The man I'd admired and shaped my future career around became a shell of who I thought he was.

So I found an apartment with some friends and moved out.

My mom soon followed, stating it was better to live with her sister in a rundown house with no money than to stay with a man she no longer recognized.

The separation only made my father worse.

He hounded me to move back home. Phone calls. Text messages. He even showed up at my apartment on a weekly basis.

I held out hope of things changing once I made it into the Bureau. I told myself I'd be able to understand him and the pressures of his position. But by the time I got my badge, he was gone.

Disappeared.

All he left behind were the whispers of him turning to a life of crime, and the one damning photo taken by an anonymous source of my father participating in a money exchange with a well-known Idaho criminal.

The reason for the transaction is still up for speculation.

Everyone has a theory. Some claim it was a drug deal. Others say it was payment for classified information. Nobody knew which way the cash went—from my father to the criminal or vice versa.

I was among many who tried to figure it out.

I spent months trying to clear his name. Each day it grew harder to maintain the workload when he didn't make contact. His trail died with a one-way ticket to Spain.

Not long after, my mother died, too.

Car accident. Heavy impact. Dead at the scene.

I'd been orphaned in the blink of an eye, although, technically my father is still alive.

He makes his presence known every now and then. Sometimes there are unsigned postcards or packages delivered from overseas. And I know he's responsible for the flowers on my mother's grave.

"Nissa?"

I jolt from the memories and rub my nose, wiping away the tingle.

"Are you still down here?" Cole's footsteps approach along the hall.

I close my eyes and remain still. I don't speak, don't even twitch, as he enters the room.

"Nissa?" he whispers.

The bed jolts. I don't know if he's seated on the far edge of the mattress or leaned against it. He's close enough for his aftershave to sink into my lungs.

"I know you're not asleep. I've watched you do the real thing for long enough to know the difference."

I don't bite. I keep my inhales measured. Deep.

The mattress jolts again. More footsteps follow, the pad of his feet coming around to my side of the bed. "You may not want to believe me, but we're on the same side. At least temporarily."

I suck in a longer breath and exhale with a whimper, bringing out my A-game acting skills.

He chuckles, friendly and masculine as hell. It's the most frightening sound I've ever heard because it seems genuine.

"Okay," he drawls. "Have it your way. I just want you to rest assured I'm going to get you home safely."

The plate scrapes across the nightstand, his footfalls recede, and I'm left alone to refute his claim.

There's no resting assured. There's no ability to rest at all.

I lie there through the sound of the kitchen clean-up and his soft conversation with

Luca as the night carries on without me. I'm still lying there, plagued with thoughts of him, when they both retreat to their rooms. And I'm still thinking of him when sleep finally drags me under.

NIGHTMARES WAKE ME. I launch upright, gasping for breath.

The panic-infused dreams were of Cole.

He'd been shielding me from an unseen enemy, one arm wrapped around my shoulder as he fired his gun into the darkness. The betraying feel of his overwhelming protection continues to haunt me as I blink to consciousness and measure my inhales, trying to calm my pulse.

The sound of the gunshot still hums in my ears. The vibration continuous.

No, it's a rumble. A growl.

And it grows. Getting louder.

Shit.

It's not recollection. It's a fucking boat.

I scramble from the bed and rush into the hall. I reach Cole's door, the light from the other side glowing against the carpet.

"Knock. Make sure he's awake."

I gasp and turn to see Luca standing in the open doorway behind me, pulling a shirt over his head.

"It's time." He jerks his chin at me, telling me to hurry up. "Luther's here."

I'm not ready.

I need a weapon. My gun. I'm entirely vulnerable without it.

He disappears into his darkened room, leaving me to rely on autopilot. My hand rises to Cole's door, my knuckles rapping against the wood before I know what I'm doing. I knock. Hard. Over and over. My staccato pulse matches the rhythm of my banging.

There's no response, only the increased volume of the rumble from the approaching boat.

I grasp the handle and push inside, not sure what to expect, but it isn't an empty room. The bedside lamp is on, the room bathed in light, and he's nowhere in sight.

"Cole?" I take a step, swallowing my apprehension. "*Cole?*"

"I'm here." He stalks from the walk-in robe, suit pants the only thing covering his perfect body as he tugs on a collared shirt. "Don't worry, I got a call twenty minutes ago. I'm ready for him."

"You didn't think to wake me?" I'm shaking, fucking trembling from adrenaline.

"I didn't wake you because I didn't want this to happen." He flicks his hand in my direction. "You don't need to panic; we've got time."

"I'm not panicking." I'm not. This is…different.

He shoots me a look of disbelief and walks to the bed, grabbing the suit jacket spread out on the mattress.

"I'm unarmed," I offer in explanation. "I'm vulnerable. If something goes wrong—"

"Nothing will go wrong." He tugs his shirt collar into place, looking entirely suave while he does it. "By this time tomorrow, you'll be on your way home, relaxing in a private jet with a glass of unspiked Beluga while you reminisce on how I completed a task the Bureau failed for years."

My pulse spikes, my face heating from anger and frustration. "And what about you?" I step closer. "Will you be celebrating? Are you entirely immune to what's about to happen?"

His eyes harden. His jaw tics. "You know I'm not."

Do I?

I'd give anything to believe hell is raining down on his shoulders right now, but it's hard when he carries himself so well. He looks as if he's preparing for a day of business, just like any other.

"Scamper into the panic room, little fox, and don't open the door until I come get you."

I stare into those eyes, the ones now devoid of emotion.

He's deflecting. Again. Trying to hide behind animosity.

Has he done this the whole time? Does he poke at me when he's trying to deflect from something important—his fear or regret?

The realization is like a lightbulb bursting in the dull shadows of my mind.

"I won't ask again." He storms for the hall.

Shit.

I've fractured his calm.

He had his game face on, and was ready and waiting for action, until I came in and fucked it up. I've added to his burden and gained a dose of guilt to go with it.

"Cole, wait."

He pauses, not looking over his shoulder.

I don't want to say anything else. I should leave this how it is in the hope I don't make a bigger mess. But my life is in his hands. And the lives of so many other women, too.

"What?" he growls.

"I'm sorry." The apology mumbles past my lips. It's pathetic, and probably entirely unbelievable, but at least it's out there, clearing my conscience. "I hope everything goes to plan."

17

TORIAN

Her apology makes me stiffen. The wish for good luck just pisses me off.

"Get in the panic room." I stalk for the hall, not looking back. Those pleading eyes and pained voice are putting me off my game.

I yank the bedroom door shut behind me and stand there, my hand clutching the handle as I rest my head against the thick wood.

Where the fuck is the conniving agent with the easily provoked spite? It's like she switched a dial and had the good fortune of finding the exact channel likely to bring me down.

Or was it tact instead of luck?

"You ready?" Luca's voice carries to me from the opening to the living room.

"Yeah." I stalk toward him. "I just need my gun."

He holds out the weapon as I approach, his face stark. I'm well aware he's on edge. He doesn't think I'm capable of killing my own father, and that's okay. He can doubt me all he fucking likes. As long as he's got my back.

I grasp the gun, check the clip, and shove it down the back of my waistband, covering it with my jacket while I continue into the bright light of the open living area.

"It sounds like they're almost here." He follows at my side, staying close.

"Go greet him and make sure everyone else remains on the boat." I keep my tone level, well aware I've got eyes and ears on me now. My audience screams loud through the silence, Anissa's scrutiny shadowing me through the pinhole camera on the far wall.

"I'll have outside under control." He starts for the glass doors. "I've got everything I need. I'll just wait for your signal."

"Good."

He leaves me alone, giving me the necessary space to regroup, yet all I think about is her. I'm caught trying to determine if her actions in my bedroom were a charade or if I've messed with her head enough to make her soft.

I approach the sofa, gliding my hands over the cushioned headrest as I stare at the tiny black dot of a camera disguised in the frame of a local artist's painting.

That woman isn't soft. But she's fucking smart. Brilliant.

I made the mistake of telling her I needed her antagonism—that fucking high horse—to get through this, so she gave me vulnerability and concern instead.

A grin pulls at my lips. The conniving bitch knew exactly what she was doing and the tactic worked. Good for her. Unless it leads me to show my hand with my father; then we're all as good as worm bait.

I focus on the camouflaged dot, sending a silent message to my adversary.

You're not in my head, little fox.

I'm focused.

Locked fucking tight.

This isn't my first rodeo. Switching off emotion comes easily. Why wouldn't it, when I spent my entire childhood being punished whenever my poker face failed?

The labored beat in my chest is adrenaline-based. There's no guilt or time to second guess. I'm done with that.

After tonight, my sisters can gain closure. My family will be safe. The tarnish of someone else's sins won't mark my name. Everything will ease.

Only the nightmares will linger.

I shove from the sofa and walk into the kitchen, turning on the coffee machine. I strengthen my conviction while I wait for the java to pour.

I recall the photos I'd been given by a private investigator. The haunted eyes of women used as objects by men without souls. I've seen one of those haunted faces up close. I've witnessed the sterility staring back at me from someone I love.

That's why my father's actions sicken me to my core.

This is personal. Not business.

This depravity goes against everything he taught me—strength can never be derived from the weak. You only gain power from destroying the strong.

My father should loathe his own actions. Instead, I'm led to believe he thrives on them.

It's a disease. One without a cure.

Death is the only option.

The coffee machine kicks in, the gentle gurgle filling the room as the glass door slides open behind me.

I concentrate on my breathing. My expression. My posture. Luther will scrutinize all of the above. I make sure my mask is perfectly in place, then I turn and hide my surprise at seeing Luca walk inside.

He's not meant to return. His place is on the pier. With my father's guards.

He had one job, and he's already fucked up.

I lock down my annoyance. "Forget something?"

His tight expression says it all.

There's been a change in plan. Something has happened.

I don't react. Don't falter.

I remain coiled. Prepared.

He moves to the side of the doorway, holding back the curtain, and from the darkness my father steps inside, the strong, sure stride of my family's patriarch heading toward me, his smile holding an air of superiority.

There's no fear in his features. Not a hint of concern to explain Luca's presence. Only the thinning hair of a man too old to be causing so many problems, and laugh lines that seem all the more sinister now I know his happiness has been siphoned from the suffering of women.

"It's good to see you, son."

I return his smile and walk toward him. "You, too."

"Although, it would've been better if you didn't look so weary. I gather I caused you a few headaches while I was in the States."

"Nothing I couldn't handle." I hide a frantic search for answers under a calm facade. I scrutinize him head to toe. I analyze his tone. His gait.

But it becomes clear he's not the cause of Luca's unease.

It's not Luther at all.

The gentle pad of feet in his wake are the issue.

The tiny, barely heard steps are torture to my ears.

I quieten my speculation. I refuse to react.

Then a small boy inches out from Luther's shadow and wide eyes blink up at me. The face of innocence threatens to destroy me and send this whole plan crashing to hell. I stare, angered beyond belief while I pretend the world hasn't opened up beneath me in an attempt to swallow me whole.

"I smell coffee." My father stops before me and thrusts out a hand to shake.

It takes all my effort to drag my attention from the child and clasp the offering.

"I'll make you a mug." Luca walks around us, his narrowed gaze pinning me, giving a warning, as he heads toward the coffee machine. "Do you both want one?"

My game face must be slipping.

"Yes. Coffee." I incline my head and release my father's hand.

Now, more than ever, I need to focus, but the child reclaims my attention, his tiny arms wrapping around Luther's thigh for protection. Those eyes. That bone structure. The dark hair.

It's like looking into a mirror from my past. My own reflection stares back at me.

"What have I told you about meeting people?" my father warns.

The boy hangs his head, wisps of mussed hair shrouding the purity of his face. "Never show fear."

Bile churns in my gut, growing toxic.

The gentle innocence in his voice assaults me. It fucking rips me open and tears me to shreds. But the heightened level of my father's betrayal is what slays me.

The boy isn't an infant. He has to be older than five.

Fucking *five*.

Five years of lies. Innumerable months of a secret life lived apart from me and my sisters.

"It looks like somebody has some explaining to do." I meet my father's gaze. "Care to tell me why you brought a kid out here in the middle of the night?"

He winces.

I know what comes next. I've wondered if this day would ever come. My father has been escaping to Greece for years. He's been living another life overseas. Evidently, with another family.

"Here." Luca returns, holding two steaming mugs of coffee. "I'm going to head back outside to keep Robert and Chris company."

He hands over my father's mug, then meets my gaze as he hands me mine. A silent question is asked. He's waiting for insight. Instruction. He doesn't know where to go from here, and I need him to know nothing has fucking changed.

"Good idea." I give Luca a taunting grin. "Get back to work."

There's a pause, the tiniest second where my words sink in, then he nods. "Shout out if you need me."

He returns outside, the whoosh of the clasping glass door confining me in a situation fast escalating out of my control.

I need to reclaim the wheel. I'm not going to nosedive.

This asshole won't get the better of me.

"I've wanted to tell you for a while," he speaks in his usual tone, as if our conversation doesn't require a change in pitch to mark the seriousness. "The time never seemed right."

He sidesteps and places a hand on the child's shoulder, encouraging the boy forward. "Cole, this is Tobias. Your half-brother."

The confirmation hits me hard, but I lock it down.

I anticipated the explanation the moment I stared into the boy's tiny face. I knew this was coming. I won't let the words strike me with the force of a sucker punch.

"A brother?" I hold everything in check—my calm, my confidence, my fucking temper. My sisters will be beside themselves when they hear the news, but I can't think of them now.

"Hello, Tobias." I force myself to crouch, meeting purity at eye level.

He inches backward. Afraid. Of me.

His recoil is brutal.

"Tobias," my father warns. "What have I told you?"

The boy swallows, his shoulders drooping. "Never show fear."

"Exactly. Now what do you say?"

The kid hesitates, his mouth working like a fish before he finally finds his voice. "It's a pleasure to meet you."

My rage coagulates. My father is the most menacing prick to walk the earth, and yet he's the one who needs to convince my brother to fake a happy introduction.

"The pleasure is all mine." I grin, trying to ease the apprehension staring back at me. "But you must be tired. Does your dad usually wake you during the middle of the night to meet strangers?"

I glance up at Luther, no longer able to face one of his sins.

"Coming out at this hour was a safety precaution. We won't stay long. We can catch up more tomorrow."

I straighten, pushing to my feet, and ignore the spill of coffee escaping the lip of my mug.

"I understand." I swing out an arm, indicating the sofa. "Tell me everything. I want to hear all there is to know about this new brother of mine."

Luther leads the way into the living area, taking the farthest position on the three-seater while I take a seat on the opposite side.

"I learned a long time ago that I'd never be able to fully return to the US," he continues, ignoring Tobias as the boy shuffles onto the cushions, snuggling into his side.

I ignore the kid, too. I have to.

As far as I'm concerned, he doesn't exist.

If I want to succeed, I have to pretend my half-brother is nothing more than a physical deformity that needs to be disregarded for the sake of good manners.

"I had to start over in Greece, which wasn't easy. Being alone, without you and your sisters, was difficult."

"So you found yourself a new family?" I don't let anything other than curiosity mark my words. There's no wounded pride or bitter resentment. I push down all the animosity.

"Of sorts, yes. My business dealings kept me occupied enough, but I needed more."

What he needed was a victim. A mindless slave. Someone to look up to him and take in every lie as if the information were heaven-sent.

"You have your empire in Portland." He wraps his arm around Tobias. "And I needed someone to take over the family business I created in Greece."

That's comforting.

He had another child for the sole benefit of continuing the trade of sex slaves. This little boy was born to torture. How fucking delightful.

The bile pulsing up my throat no longer registers over the hatred coursing through me. I'm done with my father. I'm entirely finished with his manipulations. My continued civility is only for the benefit of gaining information.

"And his mother?" I take a sip of coffee. Slow. Measured.

"She was a complication neither one of us needed."

In other words, she's dead.

Just another victim.

I raise my brows. "You look after him on your own?"

"No." He chuckles. "My harem takes good care of the motherly duties. He's only with me for the business side of things."

I can't help joining in on the laughter. At the absurdity. At the fucking conceited way he boasts his depravity.

"But there's no need for you to feel threatened," he adds. "Not by Tobias, or the new family I'm creating. Nothing between you and I has changed."

I smile through the insults. "I assure you, I'm not threatened in the slightest. I'm just glad to hear you're safe. I wasn't sure what to think when you escaped without giving me any notice of your plan." I throw another one of his betrayals into the air, curious to see how he will hit it back at me.

"That was a tough decision." He cradles his coffee, raising it to his face and the aroma deep into his lungs. "I wanted to keep you as far away from the scrutiny as possible. I can handle my own mess."

I nod. "I know. But don't ever worry about what I can and can't handle. The authorities are the last of my concerns. They won't touch me."

"I used to think the same thing. Unfortunately, alliances change."

"Your business model changed," I correct. I won't let him sit here, blaming his arrest on the shift of treaties when he was the one who threw himself under the bus. He's responsible for his issues. Him and him alone. "There's a limit to police generosity, and you crossed it when you began abducting women from the country."

There's a beat of silence. A shift in his expression.

His lips tighten. His eyes narrow.

"Is that judgment I hear in your voice?" He cocks his head to the side. "I should've known. You made your lack of support clear when you declined my offer to join this part of the family business. What happened to the bloodthirsty entrepreneur I created?"

It's another insult. One that's hard to ignore.

I bite down my ever-growing rage and release the slightest scoff. "My concern is over your safety. It always has been. Drug distribution is different to trafficking women. You need to grease a lot more palms, otherwise you're going to wind up back behind bars."

"The only reason I was there in the first place was because of Richard. If he hadn't died, I never would've returned to Portland."

Never.

Would've.

Returned.

Not to see me. Or his daughters. Or his granddaughter.

He cut ties without us even knowing.

"But, son," He leans back, resting one arm along the head rest, exuding supremacy. "The benefits to my recent adventures go above and beyond anything the drug trade could provide. I'm living a new way of life. I'm a fucking king over here. Men want to be me. Women beg to sleep with me. Nothing could be better."

"Women beg to sleep with you?" I hide my skepticism behind another sip of coffee.

"They spread their legs eagerly." He smirks. "Because the alternative is far worse. My women can either take turns fucking me once or twice a day in an opulent setting, or I can send them back to work with the rest of the slaves where they will be brutalized once or twice an hour."

On instinct, I glance at the kid.

It pains me to find no surprise or confusion in his features. The topic of conversation isn't out of the ordinary. And I guess that shouldn't shock me. If his upbringing is at all like mine, he's probably heard his father talk uncensored about brutal crimes since the moment he was born.

"Don't worry about him." Luther ruffles my brother's hair. "He's not new to this. He's actually just like you when you were little—enthusiastic and excited to learn everything his papa has to teach."

Bless the naivety of Torian children.

"Speaking of teaching," I drawl. "How are you laying low here? Where do you keep these women without drawing attention?"

He shrugs. "They're moved often. If you change your mind and decide to come onboard, you won't need to worry about things like that. We're entirely covered."

It's my turn to kick back, leaning against the armrest while I eye him in contemplation. "What sort of money are we talking?"

"Are you thinking about changing your mind on my offer?" His brows raise, along with the curve of his lips. "You would love it, son. I know you've always had money, but the pussy and power are addictive."

He's ignorant if he doesn't think I've always had all three.

"I've been contemplating the pros and cons." I suck in a deep breath and let it out on a tired sigh. "I'm not entirely convinced the risk is worth the complication."

His smile grows. I can almost see a fucking twinkle in his eye. "I knew you'd come to your senses sooner or later. You've always been a chip off the old block."

"That's never been in doubt."

"I wasn't so sure," he muses. "For a while, I thought you may have become a disappointment. And I'll be honest, it concerned me. We've always been a family business. We work together, and you not having my back was an insult."

"It was an insult to have this business running under my nose for years without telling me," I counter.

"That was your conflict?" His face brightens. He's just found the pot at the end of the rainbow. "I thought you had moral issues. I actually feared you'd turned soft."

"I'm neither soft nor moral," I drawl.

"Well, regardless, the secrecy was your uncle's decision. You two rarely saw eye to eye, and because it was his brainchild, he insisted we keep it to ourselves."

The mention of Richard always makes my hackles rise, but to learn he's the reason I was kept in the dark is a fucking sucker punch. Even after death, that piece of shit has proven he can fuck with my life.

"That's all in the past now." I let the coffee soothe me, the hot liquid beating back the rage.

"Along with my disappointment." We drink in unison. Slow sip after slow sip. "When I got word of your arrival, I couldn't deny my pride for you returned."

"I've always been one flight away; all you needed to do was reach out." Maybe if he'd tried, this shit never would've happened. I could've got in his head before Richard. I would've diverted the taint to our family name, not letting it start in the first place.

"I'm not referring to your visit. I'm talking about the prize you brought along with you."

I stiffen.

The skin at the back of my neck prickles.

I hold myself in check, barely able to control the threadbare wisps of my anger at his knowledge of Anissa.

It's not that I didn't anticipate the capabilities of his spies. I knew my arrival was under surveillance. I just didn't anticipate how strongly I would want to protect her.

"A woman bound and sedated." He smirks. "You have no idea how pleased that makes me."

I snicker, because how else should I respond to a pride-filled moment surrounding the abduction of an unwilling victim?

"Where is she?"

I hold my smile in place. I nail that motherfucker down, not letting it budge an inch. "In my bed. Passed out."

I face him the way he's always taught me to face a challenge—without emotion or investment.

Anissa is nothing.

Not a woman. Or an asset. Or a fucking addiction.

My concern for her doesn't exist.

"Passed out?" He clucks his tongue, his eyes dancing with excitement. "Keeping them conscious and fighting is the best part."

I laugh and contemplate pulling the gun from my waistband.

The thirst for bloodshed beats through my veins. The desire to claim retribution for all his transgressions is a pulse throbbing through every organ, pummeling every limb.

But that kid.

That fucking kid is still here, staring up at me, taking in the horrors like a vacuum.

"Her enthusiasm to escape has grown tiring." I finish the last of my coffee and place the mug on the table. "Sometimes I need a break."

"Now your weariness makes more sense."

"I assure you, it's all been in good fun."

He chuckles again, and the pride I see in his face sickens me. He's never looked at me this way. Judgment has always accompanied his praise. Bitterness has come hand in hand with each of his compliments.

Until now.

He's finally seeing me as a worthy son to his inheritance when all I want to do is spit in the face of what he has to offer.

"I assume you've made preparations for when you grow tired of her."

I incline my head. "Yes. She's going to take a long walk off a short pier."

"Good idea." He nudges Tobias in the ribs. "People disappear easily out here, don't they, son?"

The kid nods, the movement wrought with hesitation.

It's fucking draining to watch the boy. He's this innocent sponge being filled with brutality. At what point will the damage become permanent?

I can't take my eyes off him as my father fills the passing minutes with whimsical stories about the women he's conquered. The beauties from Spain who were barely in their teens. And those from the US who are always harder to break because they're used to a life of freedom and unending human rights.

I sprinkle the conversation with my approval, convincing him I'm impressed while the need for revenge builds behind my ribs.

"And how are your sisters?" he asks. "I've told Tobias about them. Stella, too. I'm hoping you'll convince them all to come visit us soon."

"Of course." I don't comment on the ease with which he switches from the topic of rape to settle on his daughters and granddaughter. I don't let him know every breath he takes makes me grind my teeth harder. "All you need to do is tell me a suitable date and I'll have them on the jet."

He nods, seeming appeased, while Tobias yawns.

"Your boy needs sleep." I jerk my head in the kid's direction. "Do you want to set him up in one of the spare rooms?"

"No. I never planned to stay long. I should get him back to bed." Luther pushes to his feet and Tobias follows, dragging his weary frame upward to stick to his father's side. "We can catch up properly tomorrow."

"Okay." I stand and follow them both into the open space away from the sofa.

It's time to act.

Now or never.

Everything slows to the precious seconds between each thunderous pound of my pulse. The sound echoes in my ears, becoming a driving force. All I need to do is move the kid out of the way.

"You can come for a tour of the house." My father turns to face me. "And I can take you to one of the functions I host on a regular basis. You can see my business in action." He pauses, a grin spreading from ear to ear. "Bring your toy. She might enjoy the learning experience."

"I think she'd disagree," I grate. "The little bitch is hard enough to handle already."

"Like I said, that's the best part." He steps forward, holding out his hand. "I'll teach you a trick or two."

"And I'll appreciate the insight." I reach for him, holding his gaze as our palms clasp.

We won't connect again.

This will be the last shake.

The final goodbye.

I sink into the moment, letting the taint of his atrocities build my conviction. I recount all the betrayal he tried to hide, all the lies he used to cover the bullshit he caused.

Then it's over, his grip falling from mine to make way for progress.

I turn my focus to Tobias and crouch. "Goodbye, little brother." I hold out my hand, needing him to make the connection so I can drag him out of the firing line.

Instead, he shrinks into himself. Those tiny arms cling tight to my father's leg. His wide, petrified eyes start their own attack, beating into me with force, slamming my conscience.

I'm sure he knows what I'm about to do. Call it a sixth sense or sibling intuition, but this terrified child is looking back at me with so much fucking fear I can barely think through the building guilt.

"Come on, little man." I use all my strength to add humor to my tone. "You don't want to shake your brother's hand?"

I detest the sound of my own voice. I fucking hate it. I'm trying to coax a kid into a nightmare. My own fucking brother.

"*Tobias,*" Luther snaps.

The kid jumps.

"No." I hold up a hand. "Don't push him."

Don't. Fucking. Push.

Goddammit.

Those eyes tell me he's already been through enough. Not just today, but every day since his birth. I can't add to his trauma. I fucking can't.

Not tonight.

"Is everything okay, Cole?"

I clench my teeth at my father's question. Every inch of me revolts in repulsion, not at him, but at myself. I've become a plague on my family.

A pathetic curse.

A fucking failure.

"I'm sorry." I can't stop the words from grating as I hang my head. "I guess the shock of having a brother has finally hit me."

"Don't apologize." Luther steps forward, clasps my shoulder, and gives a squeeze. His comfort is the worst punishment I've ever endured. It's hell on earth. Fucking purgatory. "Family is everything, son."

18

ANISSA

I stare at the screen in confusion, my chest restricting.

I've second guessed myself so many times since Luther arrived that the reaction is a living, breathing thing behind my ribs. It's all there is. All I know.

I'd expected a vicious bloodbath. The carnage over and done with before I could think to make a protest.

I didn't anticipate my conscience having time to run havoc.

But it has.

It still does.

I stood here, leaned toward the screen showing the perfect view of the child in the living room, my hands gripping the counter, my throat closing over. Some of their conversation didn't make it to my ears. Their voices were too low or my heartbeat pounded too loud.

But the tones were coated in civility.

Everything was calm.

A planned family reunion.

I can't tell truth from fiction. Fact from deviously deceptive lie.

Cole is such a skilled manipulator I'm unsure if he's playing his father, or still continuing to play me. He'd barely reacted to the news of his half-brother. He took in Tobias's introduction as if it were a weather report for a city he never planned to visit.

There was no emotion. Very little interest. At least from my view on the pixilated screen.

I can only tell myself he must have known about the boy's existence prior. Tobias has to be what Cole referred to when he said there was more to Luther than the information in the FBI database.

Then he shared coffee with the man and talked shop. He sat there, enjoying a fucking beverage when he was meant to be claiming a life.

I remained riveted and horrified while they held an uncensored conversation in front of an innocent child. And the poor boy listened. Unmoving. Barely blinking. His tiny body nestled close beside Satan himself.

Cole only added to my confusion when he crouched to shake the boy's hand, then hung his head, claiming to be overwhelmed. Through the entire encounter, I wasn't able to get a read on him. There was no rage or intent to punish for me to bank my hopes on.

He acted as if he was going to join his father's business, not take it down. But was it an act?

The only words ringing true are those I should fear. The ones outlining me as a plaything.

A toy.

She's going to take a long walk off a short pier.

Like hell I will.

I watch with building dread as Cole stands and Luther escorts the child toward the glass doors.

I wait for something to happen. And wait. And wait.

All Cole does is stiffen while the sheer curtains are pulled aside and his father and brother disappear outside.

It's over.

There's no bloodshed. No victory or horror.

Cole has no plan to kill his father. Maybe he never did. And with the child's arrival, I'm not sure if I should be relieved or traumatized.

I don't know what the hell any of this means, and the questions only multiply when Cole reaches behind his back and pulls the gun from his waistband.

I swear his hand trembles as he begins to pace, raising the gun to tap, tap, tap the side of the barrel against his temple in an agitated rhythm.

His movements become hostile. The mask of calm disappears, making way for an expression of pure fury. The lack of emotion I've witnessed for long minutes changes with the force of a tsunami.

He's purging. Succumbing. Letting down his guard.

Then he stalks for the doors, slamming the glass panel aside and escaping out of view.

"Goddammit." I reach for the keyboard and tap buttons to cycle through the camera angles. I need to get eyes on him, but there's nothing. No more images of anyone.

Time stands still as I wait for gunfire to erupt.

The small room becomes a cell, keeping me from reality.

Pressure bears down on me. Pure panic builds.

What's going to happen to that little boy?

I switch off the screens with a hard slam of my palm against the wall switch and enter the pin-code to open the panic room door. The barrier to the world glides open in the silence and I step forward, waiting in the entry, each second without sound acting as painful torture until a boat engine roars to life in the distance.

My mind runs wild with speculation.

Is Luther dead? Did I miss the sound of a kill shot?

The purr of the boat grows distant, the rumble lessening when the familiar thump of footsteps enters my ears. The slam of a cupboard follows. The smash of glass. Then more pounding footfalls.

I was told to remain in here until Cole came to get me, but that's an impossibility. I can't stand by a moment longer.

I tiptoe from the walk-in robe, through the bedroom, and slowly down the hall. Nobody is waiting for me as I peek my head around the wall to see into the living room. The glass doors remain open, the curtains billowing in the breeze.

My steps are cautious as I start toward the glass and slip outside onto the tiled pool area.

The boat is now a far-off grumble in the night. A rumbling purr. That's all there is.

I can't hear Cole or Luca.

Not the child or his monster of a father.

I increase my pace around the pool, but the snap of a twig makes me stop in my tracks. I swing around, fists clenched, poised, and ready to fight.

Luca steps out from the darkness beside the house, his face stony. "Get back inside."

"What happened?"

"Get your ass back inside."

I lower my hands and my voice. "Are they still here?"

"No. But you need to leave Cole alone." He starts toward me, his posture threatening.

"No. I want answers."

"And you'll get them. Later. For now, you have to give him space."

That's not good enough. I don't have the patience to wait any longer.

I've done everything they asked of me. I hid in that room. I witnessed what I was led to believe would be a victory for the greater good. And now I want to know if the bad guys won, whether that includes Cole or not.

"Where is he?"

"Leave him alone," he barks. "You're not going to get what you want from him."

I disagree.

I'm sick of being a puppet. A *toy*.

I glance toward the trail leading to the pier, then back at Luca.

His expression tightens, letting me know what I need is down that path. All that remains here is irritation and impatience.

I can't take it anymore—the games, the psychological warfare. I need to know what's going on, consequences be damned.

I start for the path, Luca's frustrated snarl haunting my escape. "Don't say I didn't warn you."

My determination increases with each step into shrouded darkness. The house lights don't touch this part of the island. I'm well aware I'm walking toward a gun-toting criminal. But I don't stop.

As the trees and shrubs clear, I see the pier with Cole sitting at the far end, the moonlight gleaming down on his dark suit.

I continue toward him, measuring my approach, slowing just a little. "Is this the short pier I'm going to take a long walk off?"

"Not now, Nissa." His tone is brutal. Raw. "Go back to the house."

He grabs a liquor bottle from between his thighs and takes a long pull. When he lowers the bottle, his shoulders slump along with it. He places the liquor back between his thighs and hangs his head, making short wisps of hair frame the side of his face.

This isn't the fearless man I watched on the television screens.

This guy is something else.

Someone else.

"Yes, I failed, if that's what you're waiting to hear." He takes another drink and follows it up with a rough swipe of his hand over his mouth.

His devastation seeps into me, touching every nerve.

"I couldn't do a damn thing," he snaps. "Not with that kid staring up at me. God knows he's going to need a lifetime worth of therapy without having to witness his father's murder."

Puzzle pieces fall in place, but not enough to create a clear picture. "You didn't expect the child?"

He bites out a bitter laugh. "I didn't expect his existence, let alone his arrival."

My stomach clenches. I'm pretty sure the reflex is instigated from pity.

It doesn't stop me from despising the instinctual reaction and becoming a slave to it in the same breath. I'm torn apart. My sympathy and self-preservation collide.

"You made the right choice." The comfort is whispered from my lips. "You'll get another chance to deal with your father."

He raises the bottle, the pull of liquid long and dangerous.

I inch forward, reach the end of the pier, and sit a foot away. A wall of darkness surrounds me, both visually and emotionally. There's no hope. No confidence. Only black. "But drowning your sorrows isn't going to help."

"Like hell it won't."

"I'm serious." I reach for the bottle, spreading my hand around the glass. "It's just a minor setback."

"Finding out I have a brother is a minor setback?" He glances at me, his eyes stark, the inky depths gripping in their intensity as he tries to reclaim the liquid solace.

"The shock will wear off." I tug the bottle, pulling it from his grip. "The least you can do is share."

I take a large gulp of my own and wince as the scotch burns my throat, searing everything in its path.

He doesn't watch my struggle. Instead, he returns his stare to the water, letting me leisurely drink my fill until liquor warms my belly.

"How could I not have known?" His question is murmured. Barely spoken. "I had no fucking idea. All this time."

"I think people rely too heavily on the bond of blood," I whisper.

His uncharacteristic show of vulnerability gets to me. This criminal Goliath is on his knees, and I struggle to react the way an FBI agent should. "Some expect it will excuse any behavior. That despite betrayal and deception, all will be forgiven because they're family."

That's the only reason I can give for my father's actions. He must have thought I would let his criminal activity slide because we share DNA.

He thought wrong.

"Maybe you're right," he murmurs. "For once."

I smile, seeing the thin layer of his humor through the pain.

"Just when I think he can't stoop any lower." He shakes his head. "*Christ*. He has a new fucking family and didn't even think to tell the one he already had." He shoots me a look. "That kid had to be at least five or six, right?"

"I'm not sure. Kids aren't my schtick. But he did seem awfully young."

"Young, but too fucking old to have been hidden this long."

I wince. "Betrayal is always worse when it comes from someone you trust."

He bites out a bitter laugh. "I wish I could say this is the worst thing he's ever done, but we both know that's a lie."

"This is different. The crimes he's previously committed are against other people. I understand how hard it must be to have something aimed at you this time."

"Like I said," he mutters, "this isn't the first."

The conversation dies on the breeze. He doesn't offer more insight, and I don't push for an explanation.

We remain there, silent, as we share the bottle of liquor until footsteps approach from behind.

"How are things going out here?" Luca walks down toward us, stopping behind me. "I gather you forgot my invitation to the party." The words are somber, half-hearted banter to skirt all the doom and gloom.

"There's no party here." Cole holds up the bottle. "Only fucking resentment and a wealth of complication."

"We'll figure it out." Luca sits on the side of the pier closest to me and dangles his legs over the edge. "Have you got any idea what you want to do from here?"

"No. But I'll be taking Luther up on his offer to meet tomorrow. Any insight is good insight."

"We," Luca clarifies, handing back the bottle. "You're not going anywhere on your own."

I don't move my attention from the water. I act unfazed by the change in schedule. "Where does that leave me?"

"On the jet, headed for home." Cole's response comes without pause.

"Excuse me?" I stiffen, caught in shock.

Hours ago, I would've been excited at the prospect of freedom. Now, I'm not so sure.

"I thought I had to be here." I turn to face him. "What happened to me being a witness?"

"Things changed."

"Like what?" Luca asks.

Cole throws back the scotch, his gulp audible, before he lowers it with a sigh. "He knows she's here."

That part isn't a surprise. I already heard Luther talk about me. What I didn't hear was a problem.

"We covered our asses on arrival," Luca adds. "I thought we bound and sedated her for this exact reason—to stifle Luther's suspicion."

"That was the reason?" I narrow my gaze on Cole. "My traumatic introduction to the Greek Islands was done out of strategy?"

Not a blatant show of Cole's power? Not for his sadistic pleasure?

"God forbid you ever think I do something for your safety," he mutters. "If you willingly walked off the jet and word got back to my father, he wouldn't have stopped until he found out every last thing about you. You needed to look like a random victim."

"So why didn't you tell me this to begin with?" I grab the scotch from him, the dark liquid reaching the middle of the bottle. "You made me believe you did it for fun."

"No, I didn't." He snatches the liquor before I can raise it to my mouth. "I made it clear I didn't mean to hurt you. You chose not to listen."

With a few brief sentences I'm cast back to my arrival, seeing everything through different eyes.

"You heard the way he spoke about you. He doesn't consider you a threat. He thinks of you as a toy, which isn't something I considered. It means if he ever gets his hands on you, he won't want to kill you; he'll want to play."

Luca huffs out a defeated breath. "If she goes home, who's going to tell your sisters about Luther?"

Yet again, I'm confused.

"Tell your sisters what about Luther?"

Cole mutters under his breath, the words indecipherable as he pushes to his feet. "I'm done with this shit. We can talk about it tomorrow." He stalks for the path leading to the house, taking the bottle with him.

"What is he talking about?" I rush to my feet, my head swirling with the sudden movement.

"Fucking hell." Luca pivots, grabbing my thighs in a vain attempt to stabilize me. "How much have you had to drink?"

"Less than Cole." I shove at his shoulders and struggle to get my bearings. "What do you mean about his sisters? What do they have to be told?"

His face hardens. "You heard him. We'll talk about it tomorrow."

"No. We'll talk about it now. I'm sick of fighting and clawing to get any sort of clarity. I want the truth."

Luca crosses his arms over his chest. His mouth clamps tight. He's preparing to play hard ball.

"Luca, please." My tone is far from pleading. I can't hide my frustration. "I thought I was here to be a witness for anyone who believes Cole isn't capable of succeeding with Luther."

"You are." He speaks through clenched teeth.

"Then what does this have to do with his sisters?"

He crosses his arms over his chest. Unmoving. Barely blinking.

"Fine. I'll ask Cole." I move to walk around him only to have him jump to his feet in front of me, blocking my path.

"No, you won't."

"Watch me." I elbow his ribs, making him sidestep, then prepare myself for retaliation.

Nothing happens. He just stands there, glaring at me.

I nudge him again, trying to create enough room to get by him, but this time he doesn't stumble.

"I could do this all night." He holds up his arms. "I don't even have to use my hands."

I laugh. "What about your balls? Do you need to use them?"

I grab his shoulders and raise my knee, pretending to mount a full-scale attack on his dick. When he twists away to counter the move, I slip by him and sprint down the pier.

"Fucking hell, Anissa."

I make it onto the pebbled path and glance over my shoulder, finding him still standing on the wooden planks, not bothering to give chase.

He's watching me, arms at his sides, his face shadowed but not enough to hide his frustration. "Don't be stupid. He's drunk as fuck. That never works in anyone's favor."

I don't care.

I turn away and stumble along the rest of the path.

Truth be told, the scotch may have affected me in a not-so-subtle way, too. The liquor has cleared the deafening static from my head. I can process now. At least a little easier than before.

I don't like what I'm thinking though.

I don't want these things in my head to be real.

Not if it means Cole isn't the nasty piece of work I've always known him to be.

I make my way to the house, step inside, and flick the billowing curtain out of the way. "Cole?"

He's nowhere in sight. Not in the living area or the kitchen.

I slide the glass door shut, then lock it, buying myself some time before Luca follows.

"Cole?"

Again, no answer.

I stalk down the hall, toward his closed bedroom door, and fling it open.

He's walking from the robe to the bed in nothing but black boxer briefs with that bottle still in his hand, only a few inches of liquid floating at the bottom.

The scotch doesn't seem to have worked its magic on his brilliance. He's still a vision of masculinity. All muscles and strength.

"Do you have a problem with knocking?" He clatters the bottle down on the bedside table, glaring his anger my way.

"Do you have a problem with wearing clothes?"

"I'm going to bed." He grabs the covers, pulling them back. "Unless you plan on joining me, get out."

"I'll leave as soon as you confirm I'm here for no other reason than to inform your sisters about Luther's death."

His jaw tics. His knuckles clench tight in the bedding.

"Holy shit." I stare at him, seeing the powerful man with fresh eyes.

I'm not here to recount a murder to business associates or criminal masterminds. I'm here to let his sisters down gently.

"Why didn't you just tell me instead of dragging me through hell?"

"One, because you wouldn't have believed me. Two, I needed to sedate you in case my father's spies were watching, and you never would've given consent." He grins, the expression entirely sinister. "And three, it was more fun this way."

"You made me believe I was here to tell your drug connections."

"Bullshit." He throws down the covers and stalks toward me. "Don't go blaming me for your misconceptions. You and your high horse made those assumptions all on your own."

He's a wall of superiority. Tense muscles. Tight expression. Hard eyes.

He's almost scary, yet so entirely strong and unyielding I can't help admiring his conviction.

"So I've been wrong about you all this time?" My question is the slightest taunt. "I misconceived you as a murderous, conniving criminal when really you're, what? A saint? I don't get it. I don't get *you*. One minute, you're taking pleasure in manipulating me; the next, you claim you won't hurt me. It's clear you're hiding. I just don't know what you're hiding from."

"I'm not hiding shit." He doesn't stop his approach, not until we're toe to toe, almost chest to chest. "Your problem is that you can't fit me into one of your perfect little boxes. You want to label me as right or wrong, good or bad, moral or fucking corrupt, when all those tags apply at any given time."

He glares at me, the level of judgment sinking deep. "I don't follow your legal system, but I'm true, without fault, to the values of my world. I'm not heartless or merciless. I may not give a flying fuck about strangers, but I would die for my family and anyone in my inner circle."

He's so close, a mere whisper of space between us. His breath brushes my lips, the hint of scotch sinking into my lungs.

"I didn't tell you about my sisters because shielding them from outsiders is what I do. It's all I've ever done. I keep them safe. I maintain their privacy."

"Do they know what's happening?" I swallow over my drying throat as his intensity wraps around me. Tight. I'm almost suffocated. "I heard you on the phone to Keira. You lied about being in Greece."

He takes another step and I'm forced to backtrack, bumping into the door, making it swing shut behind me.

"She knows what will eventually happen." He scoffs out a laugh. "In fact, she wants Luther dead more than I do. That's why she can't know when it's going to happen. I don't want her or Decker involved."

Decker.

The reminder of the man who lost a sister to Luther's perversions washes over me like a bucket of ice-cold reality.

"Did you ever find out more information on Penelope?"

"You've asked enough of me tonight." His lip curls, the progression slow and vindictive. "I'm done with the subtle interrogation. And don't think, for one second, I've forgotten you tried your best to get us all killed tonight."

"Excuse me?" I take another backward step, my ass bumping into the door. "What the hell did I do?"

"I noticed how you tried to sabotage my plan, little fox. Do you really think I believed all your soft, emotional bullshit when the boat arrived?"

My cheeks heat, the shame from my needy outburst taking over my face.

"I told you I brought you here to inspire determination." He raises his arms, placing his hands on either side of my head, caging me in. "You knew your spite was my motivator. So you flipped the script, thinking I'd falter with the batting of your lashes. But I'll tell you right now, I'm not that fucking weak."

I don't answer.

I'm embarrassed to admit my emotional display wasn't a scheme. There was no sabotage. None at all.

"You're not the agent I thought you were." He leans closer, the glaze of intoxication making those dark eyes seem questioning. "The spiteful Anissa Fox isn't as tactical as she thinks."

"That wasn't a tactic." I tilt my chin higher, my shame and frustration colliding. "I've almost always told you the truth."

He laughs. "Almost always?"

"It's better than what you've given me. You can blame me for misconceptions all you like, but we both know you've deliberately tried to steer my thoughts in one direction. You've wanted me to fear you all along."

"If I wanted your fear bad enough, I'd have it."

A shiver skitters through me. It's not born from apprehension or panic. It's something different. Something I desperately have to ignore.

"I knew how important tonight was. I wasn't stupid enough to play games." The admission doesn't lessen the tingle searing through my veins. "I told you I'd do whatever you needed me to do, and I'm still committed to that promise."

He raises a brow, looking down his nose at me like I've done to him a million times over.

"I'm not lying. I agreed this was the best option for Luther, and I don't want to leave until it's done."

"Too bad." His jaw hardens. "You'll be on the jet at sunup."

His refusal acts like a match to a mountain of kindling. The tingle I'd been consumed with turns to vibrations. Heart palpitations. I'm sick of him throwing his weight around. It's fucking exhausting.

"No, I won't." I straighten my shoulders, giving him an up-close-and-personal view of my defiance. There's so much tightly coiled fury in his features and all it does is fuel me, making me buzz. "I'm not going anywhere until this is over. Not unless you plan on drugging me again."

"You'll do exactly what I want, when I want. Now get your drunk ass to bed."

My blood boils. I try to bottle it, to keep it deep down inside, but the spite bursts from me. "Yours or mine?"

His brows shoot skyward. I'm sure mine do the same.

It's the alcohol talking. The liquor puts words in my mouth. Emotions in my veins. And despite the danger, the temporary shock written all over his face is worth it.

"Cute." He eyes me, reading me, the glaze of intoxication bearing down like a threat. "Real fucking cute."

His gaze drops to my mouth, making my lips burn under the attention. "You're playing with fire. If I were you, I wouldn't push boundaries when you don't know what's on the other side."

"What are you going to do? Take a page out of your father's book?"

His nostrils flare and his hand shoots up, grasping my throat.

History repeats itself. The feral stare. The blinding fury. And yet again, that hold is gentle. Non-threatening.

"Who's to say I won't? Like father, like son, right?" His breaths come in heaves, his chest rising and falling with the aggression. "You don't understand me, little fox. We both know I could destroy you."

I've pushed too far. I've made a mistake. I know this. I know it just as well as I know day follows night. And still, I want more.

It's as if self-preservation no longer exists. Common sense has evaporated.

"You could, but you won't." I raise my chin in defiance. "I don't know if you wish you were more like your father, or if you're glad you're not. But it's clear you're hurt by what he's done. I didn't notice it while he was here because your poker face is crazy-brilliant. But I noticed after. I saw your pain. I still see it now."

His aggression falters. His eyes flare with sorrow before quickly falling back under the shroud of anger.

"Leave. Get out of my fucking room, and don't disturb me again." He doesn't move. Doesn't allow me the escape he demands.

He confuses me, telling my head one thing while my churning insides announce something else entirely.

Neither reaction makes sense.

"I don't want to leave," I admit. "I want to see this through."

I'm not sure if I'm still talking about his father. About those women. About victory for the greater good.

"It isn't safe." He doesn't break our gaze, not even when his expression falls, exposing a mass of regret. He releases his hold on my neck, his fingers grazing my shoulder, my hip, for an instant of pure friction.

It's the liquor.

The buzz.

I can't help it. My body reacts without my consent.

Before I can think about the consequences, my hand rises to his face, my touch brushing the light stubble along his jaw.

He flinches, but doesn't pull away. He remains close, one hand pressed against the door, one foot between mine.

"You're drunk." He snatches my wrist, holding it in place. "You'll regret this in the morning."

"I already regret it now. That doesn't mean I can stop." I raise my other hand, gliding my fingers gently along the softness of his cheekbone, all the way down to the side of his mouth.

I don't know what's wrong with me. But it's clear something is loco-fucking-batshit in this head of mine because this devil of a man seems entirely redeemable.

I see the turmoil in his eyes, the battle waging war beneath his impenetrable exterior. I feel his conflict. His agony. I understand all the good he's tried to do through an entirely bad situation.

"Who are you?" I whisper.

"You know who I am." His grip tightens. "Don't let the alcohol cloud your judgment."

He's right. I do know. And the alcohol is.

I know both facts as if they're tattooed across my chest, and yet my heart overrules them, twisting and turning in the need for more.

More insight.

More connection.

More sizzle.

"How do you live like this? How do you do what you do?" I sound like Dr. Seuss, the words rolling off my tongue with the tiniest of slurs. "Explain it to me."

"Tomorrow."

"No." I drag my thumb along the exquisite softness of his lower lip. "Now."

"*Niss.*" My nickname is a warning. "I've had more to drink than you. I'm not playing games when I say my hesitation won't last forever."

Heat takes over my stomach and descends, pooling in a place that should be entirely off-limits to this man's effect.

I struggle against my body's reaction. I mentally fight for stability. But the battle is too hard. *Everything* is too hard when I've never seen anything more beautiful. More stark and brutal and gorgeous.

My heart pounds behind my sternum, the beat carrying heavily to my ears. It's intuition and madness. Passion and impulse. Insanity and picture-perfect clarity.

I glide my hand over his chin, down to his neck to grasp his throat. My hold is like his has always been. Gentle. Soft. The only difference is mine doesn't elicit a reaction.

I grip tighter, harder, my fingers becoming a vise with each passing second, until I finally get what I want—a deep swallow beneath my palm.

He's not unaffected by me.

Whatever I'm feeling, he feels it, too.

"You don't want to do this." His words haunt me, the warning a kindness.

"Johnnie Walker tells me I do." My mind is consumed with those lips. My heart pounds with the thrill of just one taste.

He grins, the expression subtle, yet mocking. "Since when does Johnnie Walker cost eight hundred dollars a bottle?"

"You've got expensive taste." I can barely hear my own voice. It's breathy. A whisper.

"Exquisite." He releases my wrist. His hand moves to the sensitive skin below my ear, his thumb trailing back and forth along my carotid. "I have exquisite taste, Nissa."

My nerves catch on fire, sizzling, blazing.

"Are you trying to make yourself believe I'm a good guy?" He leans into me, hip to hip, his thigh between my thighs. "Do you want me to pretend, too?"

Everything is hard. His arms. His chest. His cock.

The thick length of his erection presses into my abdomen, making it difficult to breathe. My nipples bead. Every inch of my skin tingles. A flicker of fireworks skims along my senses.

"I don't know." I can already predict the aftermath. The mistake I'm about to make will haunt me forever, yet in this moment I'm willing to pay the price.

I can't deny myself.

I lean in, my mouth a breath away from his. A mere gasp. Then I steal the gentlest touch of connection.

It's the most delicate dance of pleasure. His lips are kind, placating, all the gentleness at odds with his ferocity.

I taste the scotch on his tongue. I drown in the flavor.

A hazardous thrill shoots through me. The temptation sinks into my marrow.

I kiss him harder, dropping both hands to his hips to grip the waistband of his underwear, and drag him tighter against me.

I grow dizzy with adrenaline. Enslaved by bliss.

I tingle everywhere—arms, legs, pussy. There isn't an inch of my skin unaffected by this man. At least until he pulls back, his eyes narrowed to spiteful slits.

"You've had your fun," he growls. "Now it's time to stop pretending you're not making a dangerous fucking mistake."

19

TORIAN

I inch back, getting a front-row seat to the indignant flare of her eyes.

She has no idea of the trouble she's getting into.

How deep the water is.

How easy it would be to drown.

She cocks her head, her expression bathed in liquor-induced ignorance. "*Dangerous* mistake?"

I would've bet good money on her scampering away. Even when I held back on the reins, not kissing her the way an indignant woman deserves to be kissed. But I could've sworn the hard press of my dick would've woken her up to where this is going to go if she doesn't run.

"You heard right," I growl. "This isn't high school. I don't fool around then walk away."

"And I do?" She pushes at me, punctuating her statement.

I clench my teeth, trying hard not to show how much I fucking love her bite.

Her animosity fuels me. Invigorates. Every inch of my skin is alive, waiting for her touch. Every nerve is raw and exposed.

"Stop provoking me." She shoves again and I backtrack with the spike of my pulse. "Stop messing with my head."

I want to beg her to do the same. To stop pushing buttons. Poking demons.

"You're fucking insane," I grate. "You've got no idea what you're doing."

She shoots me a grin. A fucking taunt of a smile likely to trigger the strongest of men. "Don't I?" She shoves again. And again. And again.

I take retreating steps with her aggression, for *her* safety. For *her* protection. "Nissa," I growl.

She slams those palms into my chest, her sultry lips curving. My own burn in response, demanding another taste of her sweetness.

I plant my feet. "Do you really want to play, little fox?"

She shoves again.

This time, I don't budge.

I straighten my shoulders, square my jaw. I look straight down my nose at her, glaring.

She inches closer, sliding up to me. Hip to hip. Chest to chest.

I clench my fists, gnash my molars. I breathe slowly, try to force a sense of calm, but that shit is nowhere to be found.

"I think," she murmurs, "maybe you're the one who's scared about the danger of fucking with me."

Her spite. Her confidence. Her fucking instability. All of it works against me, building the force I've barely contained behind my threadbare restraint.

"Last warning," I snarl.

She chuckles, the alluring scotch scent of her breath brushing my skin. "How many warnings do you need to give before you understand I'm not going anywhere?"

I snap.

It's mental and physical.

Feral and uncivilized.

I grab her around the waist and storm forward, shoving her against the closed door. Her back hits with a thwack, her entire body jolting. I hold her off the ground with the hard press of my hips and reclaim that delicate fucking neck of hers in my grip.

She shudders, her glossy lips parting, preparing to speak.

"Shut the fuck up." I smash my mouth against hers, drawing a gasp from her throat, a whimper from her chest.

I kiss her hard, fast, punishing us both with the ferocity. I release all my frustration into her body, nudging my cock against her, digging my fingers into her skin.

It's fucking brutal, made all the worse when she matches my severity, her hands grasping my shoulders, her nails digging deep. She wraps her legs around me, clinging tight, grinding the heat of her pussy directly over my dick.

She's a temptress.

A taste of heaven.

Or maybe an injection of hell.

Who the fuck knows?

All I'm aware of is the craving for more.

I hold her tighter, grind harder, breathing in her needy whimpers and moans.

"You're going to regret pushing me." I drag my teeth over her lower lip and pull back to stare at her. "I'll make sure of it."

"Maybe you're the one who's going to regret abducting me."

"Too late," I growl. "I already do."

She raises a brow. It's all the fucking defiance I need.

I haul her over my shoulder to carry her to the bed, then flop her unceremoniously on the mattress.

She looks up at me. Without regret. Without fucking fear.

"Clothes off," I demand.

Her sultry mouth opens and those eyes tell me she's poised to deliver disobedience I have no desire to hear.

I reach out, grab her ankles, and pull her closer, giving myself access to those tight pants. I yank them down, pulling them off.

Her chest rises and falls in quick succession. Her tongue darts out to moisten her lower lip.

I reach for her again, this time dragging her loose top over her stomach, her chest, her head.

It's not until I'm throwing the material to the floor that I realize she's cradling her fucking shoulder, holding her arm tight against her body as if I've caused her pain.

Fuck.

An apology clogs my throat. Choking. Suffocating.

I fucking ignore it.

I ignore everything apart from the body I'm about to dominate.

She's all smooth curves and flawless skin, her tits firmly cupped in a black-with-gold-trim bra. I've seen it before—the gorgeousness, the slim figure—and having an up-close view only makes me more determined to have her.

With rough hands, I grab the waistband of her matching lace underwear, yank the flimsy material down her thighs, and throw them aimlessly behind me. Then I stare, riddled with lust, at the trim patch of hair between her thighs leading to a perfectly smooth pussy.

She glistens.

Her core is fucking ripe and ready for me.

"Tell me to stop." I shove her knees apart, exposing more of her pretty pink brilliance. "Tell me you've made a mistake."

She stares me down, her teeth digging into her lower lip, her cheeks flushed.

"Tell me." I drop to my knees, wrap my arms around her legs, and make her squeal as I haul her to the edge of the mattress.

She's wet for me, dripping, her body reacting on instinct instead of her conceited fucking morality.

"No." She shakes her head. "I won't."

I lean down, pressing my mouth to the inside of her knee. "Why? You know it's true."

She shudders, her skin breaking out in goose bumps. "I think I want to see if your arrogance is justified."

"I'll take pleasure in proving it to you."

I palm her foot, adding pressure to her sole to gently lift her leg and guide it over my shoulder. I do the same with the other, making her my puppet.

My dirty little doll.

I never would've thought she was capable of compliance. I always imagined she'd be a handful in bed. An untamed tiger who fought and scratched her way to release. But this submissive side is intriguing.

I inch my head forward, my path marked by teeth scrapes and teasing kisses along the inside of her thighs.

She jolts. Shivers. Whimpers.

She's putty in my hands, entirely malleable to my touch.

This is usually where my interest wanes. Where I realize the hard-to-get challenge is no longer producing adrenaline.

Orgasms aren't my goal. The game is. The back and forth. The seduction. It's rare for a woman to hold my interest once she submits to the inevitable.

But this time it's different.

She's different.

I'm still wired. I'm fucking buzzing, my dick hard, my balls tight. Right here, staring down the barrel of her smooth thighs, I'm more challenged than I've ever been. More driven to prove my arrogance is fucking justified.

I slide my hands along the outside of her legs, slow, like I've got the patience of a monk on valium. I inch closer and closer to her pussy, the heat of her a dizzying temptation, but I won't fall victim to a quick conclusion.

I want to draw this out. Make her suffer in the sweetest possible way.

I reach the highest point on the inside of her thighs and nuzzle my nose against the burning skin. I lick, and suck, and devour, earning the quickening of her breathing without paying her pussy any fucking attention.

I ignore the temptation I want most. I pretend the glistening slit doesn't exist as I nip and graze my teeth along her bare flesh.

Her legs squeeze tight. Her hips buck and twist, demanding more. But I slow in response. I make my kisses long, drawn-out gifts, switching back and forth from one side of her cunt to the other.

"Oh, God," she moans.

I smirk, deliberately grazing her with my rough stubble. "You're calling out to the wrong team, little fox. It's the devil who brings pleasure."

She whimpers and claws her fingers into the bed coverings. "Stop teasing me."

"Not so fast. I need you to beg for what you want."

"Excuse me?" She stiffens, every muscle pulling taut. "What did you say?"

"Beg," I repeat.

She lifts onto one elbow, blinking away the lust-filled gaze to stare and stare and fucking stare some more. She's weighing her pride against the pleasure she knows I can give. Measuring the worth of a mind-blowing orgasm against her ego.

"Beg. Me." I enunciate the demand slowly, letting it sink right down into that antagonistic mind of hers.

She glares, her jaw ticking, her cheeks darkening.

My pulse increases while she makes me wait and wonder if she'll deny us both. Is her pride so deeply ingrained she's willing to stop this chemistry of madness? Fuck, I hope not.

Her lips part, her tongue snaking out to moisten the darkened flesh. "Please, Cole," she grates. "Stop being a pussy tease and make me come."

I snicker even though my dick is harder than stone and pulsing to the point of pain. "Not good enough. I want you to lose the death stare and beg me according to my worth. I won't give you another chance."

The ultimatum was an afterthought. An insane, fucking idiotic addition.

If she denies me, I can't walk away. I've just given her the perfect opportunity to turn the tables. I've set myself up to lose. To *her*.

The slightest hint of panic raises the hair on the back of my neck. I'm teetering on failure. With the right response she'll know exactly how much hold she has on me. But I won't give up yet.

I swipe my tongue down her core, just once, just enough to get a delicious taste and make a growl rumble in my throat.

She jolts, her lashes flaring with the spike in pleasure.

I won't be defeated.

I can't be.

She shudders out a shaky breath. "Please, Cole. You're killing me." Her throat works over an awkward swallow. "I want you to make me come… I *need* you to."

I gift her another teasing swipe. "More."

Her back arches, her head falling to the mattress. "I've never felt this way… and I… I'll never feel this way again. I know I won't."

"More," I demand.

"*Please*, it won't take much. I'm already close… And God, you feel so good… I hate it, and I don't know how you're doing it, but you make me feel so… Fucking… Good." Her nails find my shoulders, piercing skin. "I've never wanted anything like this before."

Victory suffuses me, pulsing through every vein, searing every nerve. She's never wanted anyone like she wants me. Has never experienced pleasure the way I can give it to her.

Little fox, you ain't seen nothin' yet.

I cover her clit with my mouth and suck. I lap and flick and tease the bundle of nerves while she moans and grinds into me. And still, it's not enough.

Her mindlessness needs to be bone-deep. Soul-shattering. I want to break her in the best possible way.

I devour her as I glide a hand between the bed and her ass, shimmying it in unison with her gyrations until my thumb finds her pussy. I slide back and forth along the bottom of her entrance, soaking the tip of my digit, making her squirm while my fingers nuzzle into her crack, applying pressure to her puckered hole.

I sink into her, her walls pulsing around my thumb.

She pants, her breaths heavy heaves of greed.

"Cole." She fucks my hand, eagerly seeking release.

She's ready. So fucking close.

I want to deny her. To drag this moment out forever, but *fuck*, my cock is killing me, the pre-cum sliding down my length in a silent cry for relief.

I pulse harder with my thumb, breech her ass with a lone finger, and clamp my lips around her clit.

She gasps. Jerks. Pulls taut.

Then that perfect pussy flutters, her orgasm spasming as her thighs nail me in place. She moans over and over, the sound a symphony to my ego. A fucking victory.

I don't stop until she begins to loosen and those convulsions of her core slow to a long grind.

Then nothing.

She doesn't move. Doesn't speak.

It's as if her bad decisions have finally caught up with her and she thinks going mute will save the day.

No way in hell will I let that happen.

She's going to own this mistake. Remember it. Dwell on the brilliance of succumbing to me.

I stand, wiping the heel of my palm over my mouth. "Now we can both agree my arrogance is justified."

She collapses onto the bed, her eyes closed, her lips quirked in a delirious, infectious smile. She fucking beams with afterglow. But still, she doesn't respond.

"Have I finally worked out the way to silence that snappy mouth of yours?"

She chuckles.

It's beautiful.

The sound.

The sight.

Anissa, on any given day, is gorgeous. But happy Anissa—playful, orgasm-high, Anissa—is fucking mesmerizing.

She leans up on her good elbow, her stomach and tits still bouncing with mirth. "Nothing silences this mouth."

I raise a brow. "Nothing?"

"Nothing."

I shuck my boxer briefs, letting my cock spring free.

Her laughter ceases as she eyes me. I don't anticipate my reaction.

Her hunger unravels me even though I know it's not really her behind those curious eyes. The interest is driven by liquor, yet it's equally hard to deny.

I climb onto the bed, over her, caging her body beneath mine. The stutter returns to her breathing. Her teeth reclaim her lower lip.

"Take off the bra."

She complies, arching an arm behind her back and wincing as she pivots the other side of her body harder into the mattress.

"Your shoulder..." I grind my teeth, not wanting to care and not being able to stop at the same time. "It fucking hurts, doesn't it?"

"Sometimes." Her bra loosens and those supple tits fall free. "But you're a good distraction."

I want to drag my lips over the lightly bruised skin. Nuzzle the swelling. Soothe the ache.

Instead, I grab her hips and rise onto my knees, aligning her pussy with my cock. "I would've thought by now that I'd become more than that."

"You're many things, Cole. A distraction is just one of them."

She piques my interest, all the while making my dick twitch.

"Tell me what else I am to you, little fox." I tug her farther along my thighs, then hold her in place with one hand while I guide my cock to her entrance. "Tell me everything."

She contemplates me, her breathing becoming ragged. "You're the son of Satan."

"Is that so?"

"And you're cunning." She holds my gaze, hypnotizing me with all the pretty green. "I also think you're incredibly smart. I just wish I understood your thirst for power."

There is no thirst, and I want to tell her why. I'm fucking drawn to explain my position was a birthright, not something I wished for. Nobody gets to step down from this throne. Not unless it's in a body bag.

In my world, I can only move forward.

"It's a hunger like no other." I end the conversation with a hard thrust into her heat. There's no protection. No fucking insurance policy to guard either of us against an STD or parenthood. And I don't give a damn. She's smart enough to be clean and covered. At least I hope so.

I revel in the way her back arches, her breasts reaching toward me. She's tight, her walls choking my dick in the best possible way as she releases a feminine whimper.

I can't stop myself from leaning forward, resting on one hand to hover over her. I need to get closer. Being inside her isn't enough. I want her touch. Her mouth. Her thoughts. Her future.

Fuck.

I look away, unable to remain staring into those mind-reading eyes as I continue gliding into her. Back and forth. Over and over.

"What is it?" She cups my cheek with a delicate palm.

The connection is so fucking soft. So fucking brutal.

I hate her gentleness.

I fucking loathe the way she weakens me.

"Nothing." I swoop down, stealing her mouth and a gasp along with it.

I pound my frustration into her. I buck hard. I fucking slam deep. And the brilliant woman matches me, wrapping her legs around my hips, scratching the shit out of my back.

I've never been this intoxicated, and it's not the liquor taking over my senses. It's her. A fucking Fed.

The reminder should make my balls shrivel. Instead, it brings a thrill. The world disappears through my compulsion to claim her.

I want to own her. Control her. And I itch to make her feel the same way. To bring her down with this mindless addiction.

"Waging war against you was the best decision I ever made." I drag my lips over her sweat-slicked skin.

"You fight dirty." She grinds into my thrusts, our rhythm perfectly synched. "How the hell are you doing this to me?"

I kiss her neck. I bite. I earn myself another gasp.

"I'm close again." She clings tighter, her pussy clamping like a vise. "So close already."

"That's because you were born to submit to me."

She shudders. "Don't be an asshole. I'm not submitting to anything."

"Then maybe you love slumming it on the wrong side of the tracks." I nuzzle her ear. "Do you enjoy the thrill of being fucked by a murderer?"

Her nails dig deeper into my back. "Stop it."

Her protest is in contrast to the truth of her body. There's no pause in her movements. The tightness of her legs doesn't ease.

"Admit it." I pull back, grasp her chin, and force her gaze to mine. Exotic green blinks back at me, dazed and delirious.

She's incredibly beautiful. There's never been a more alluring woman. Not in my bed or my consciousness. There's only her.

At this point, it feels like there will only ever be her.

"Tell me the truth, little fox." I kiss those lips, brushing my tongue over hers. "Tell me you're dying to have a criminal come inside you."

She shivers with a breathy exhale. Then those pretty eyes roll and her neck arches. She unravels, milking my dick with another orgasm.

For a brief second, I contemplate dragging this out, hoping to get her tally to three before I follow along with her, but her whimpers undo me. Her allure has me thrusting harder, pumping faster.

Pressure builds in my balls, the release hitting hard.

I force my mouth on hers, tasting her cries, each one of her breaths becoming mine as I lose myself. Over and over I come, and even then my mind doesn't stray from her.

There's only the need to mark her. To claim her as my own.

That's when the uppercut of unease hits me.

The clarity.

All this time I demanded she admit the mistake of fucking me. But as she lies beneath me, her eyes closing, her lips pulled in a smile, I realize I'm the one who messed up.

There was no error on her behalf.

Anissa Fox would never sleep with me out of weakness or drunken stupidity.

Hell no.

Not in a million years.

The Fed I know would've done it out of strategy. Pure manipulation. She aimed to achieve something by fucking me, and my obsession was the end result.

Shit.

I rest my forehead against her shoulder, letting her deception sink deeper than her nails, while my dick continues to jerk inside her.

Did she just win?

Did I just become mind-fucked by someone who will stop at nothing to place me behind bars?

20

TORIAN

I stew on my precarious position all night.

It's clear she made a bad judgment call by sleeping with me.

She made it twice more during the early hours of the morning, when I succumbed to the need to have her again.

But I, by far, made the biggest mistake in letting her win this latest game of ours.

She played me with her body. Seduced me with her beauty. Brought me to my knees with her lack of inhibitions. Over and over.

I kept telling myself I'd grow bored if I tasted her again… Kissed her in one more place… Fucked her repeatedly. But here I stand beside the bed, showered, dressed, and still sporting a dick that can't be tamed. At least not by me.

Currently, my favorite bodily asset is leashed by the sleeping beauty who lies before me, the thin sheet molding to the curves of her breasts and the gentle groove of her hip.

She has a hold on me. A tight grasp she's woven intricately since the first day we met.

On cue, she whimpers and tilts her head into the pillow, her dark hair fanning over one eye as the sleepy sound continues to burrow up from her throat.

She'll be awake soon, and I'm too busy battling a raging hangover to deal with whatever attitude the new day brings.

From our brief early morning fuckfest conversation, I know she remains adamant on staying, and even though I gave her a lust-filled promise of agreement, I still haven't made up my mind.

Breaking a promise to an outsider has never been difficult. I can turn on a dime for those who haven't proven their loyalty. But the truth is, I want her to stay.

Not for her benefit. Or the women she wants to help.

I need her here. For me.

To feed my growing addiction.

Despite the safety risks associated with my father's knowledge of her existence, and the myriad of complications fucking her has brought to the table, I'm not willing to let her go.

She wiggles, about to wake, which encourages me to move. I start for the door, not having the patience or restraint to listen to her fake excuses for fucking me when we both know it all came down to strategy.

I ignore the swish of sheets and another waking moan. I don't stop until I grasp the handle to the hall.

"Why didn't you wake me?" Her voice is husky. Sleep-riddled. "What time is it?"

I should keep my attention straight ahead, directly on the painted wood, on the only barrier keeping me from distancing myself. But I succumb, like I always do with her, and glance over my shoulder.

She's perched on one elbow, her dreamy gaze hitting me, her long lashes batting softly as her hand clutches the sheet to her chest.

She's a sight to behold. A vision.

One I need to wipe from my mind.

I plunge the lever, and open the door a crack. "I thought I'd do you a favor and leave you to make your walk of shame without an audience."

She groans and flops back on the bed, covering her face with a flailed arm. "The sex was inevitable, Cole. It's the scotch I regret."

I bristle. Tense. "Inevitable? That's interesting. I wouldn't have predicted an admission of guilt."

"Guilt?" Her arm falls, those eyes narrowing on mine. "What are you accusing me of now?"

I bare my teeth in a sinister smile. "The sordid scheme to try and take me down with the use of your body." I release the door handle and pivot to face her head-on. "How you planned on getting in my head by getting in my bed."

Her lips part on silent words, her look of pained defiance almost believable.

"Too bad I saw right through you. But I thoroughly enjoyed your attempt." My smile increases. "More than once."

She scoffs and diverts her attention, lowering her gaze to the bed. For a moment she seems lost in angered shock before she mutters, "Fucking idiot," under her breath.

"Don't be too hard on yourself. Ambitious is a more fitting term. Not many people would try to manipulate me with sex. Especially when it's one of my favorite tactics." I wink, just to piss her off. "If you're going to play a player, you probably shouldn't pit your novice skills against a master."

"No, Cole, *you're* the fucking idiot." She pushes up on both elbows, awkwardly keeping the sheet to her chest with one hand even though her modesty left the building hours ago. "This," she indicates the bed with a wave of her free hand, "wasn't a tactic. I can admit I'm manipulative, but I'm not a fucking whore."

For a second, I believe her.

I see the anguish in her eyes and take it at face value, but it doesn't stop me from looking at her with smug superiority to put her off her game like she's put me off mine.

She rolls her eyes and sighs. "What time is it?"

"Almost one."

"And you're leaving?" She drags her attention over me, taking in the business suit and polished shoes. "You're going to see your father?"

"Soon."

She slides from the bed, yanking the sheet from the mattress as she goes, the lengthy material trailing behind her like a sordid wedding dress. "And what about me?"

"You're packing your things."

"You're sending me home?"

Yes. No.

Fuck. I want both.

"That depends." I draw out the words as she continues closer, her sleep-roughened hair tempting me to guide the strands back into place.

"On what?"

"On your admission of guilt. Tell me the truth about why you spent the night in my bed. Explain the reasons for sleeping with the enemy."

"Why bother? You've already made up your mind."

Because I need to hear her lies.

I itch to believe them.

"There's no harm in trying." I succumb to the need to touch her hair, delicately gliding it behind her ear. "Spin me a web of fiction, little fox. Make me believe you're not a whore."

A delicate shade of pink enters her cheeks. "You're an asshole."

I incline my head. "That's always been crystal clear."

"Yeah, I guess you're right. I don't know what possessed me to forget." Her eyes soften with uncharacteristic sadness. "But I still don't want to leave. I need to see this through. Don't you think I'm owed that much after everything you've put me through?"

I owe her nothing.

Not a damn thing.

"If you want something from me, Nissa, I'm afraid I'm going to have to ask for something in return."

She balks, clutching the sheet tighter. "What now?"

I hold her gaze and force a smirk. She's different this morning. Not brimming with confidence like I'd expected. I thought she'd boast her victory, when in reality she's exuding failure.

"Drop the sheet," I demand.

She blinks at me, unmoving. "That's what you want in return?"

I'm as shocked as she is. I hadn't planned on making demands. It's her fault for throwing me off balance.

"I'm a simple man. With simple requests." All I want is a subtle humiliation, which is nowhere near the level she inflicted upon me last night.

"And if I drop the sheet, I get to stay?"

I incline my head, my pulse ramping with impatience for her to submit. "Temporarily, yes."

The muscles in her jaw flicker. The narrowing of her eyes is barely seen. Regardless of both, I can feel her animosity. It pulses from her in waves as she straightens her shoulders and drops the long length of material to the floor.

I brace myself for the burst of enjoyment at her humiliation.

I wait, and wait, and fucking wait, my gaze holding hers, but the taste of victory doesn't come. Instead, I'm the one who battles shame.

My actions resemble something my father would dictate.

A pathetic perversion.

Pure weakness.

The only thing stopping self-loathing from coating me like a second skin is how I refrain from lowering my attention. I don't add a visual violation to my pitiful demand. Instead, I stand there for long moments, silently cursing a conscience that is at its loudest around her, as I stare into those spite-filled eyes.

She's tainting me. Turning me into a fool.

"Get dressed," I growl. "You can stay until Luca and I return to the island."

She crosses her arms over her chest, the plump of her breasts taunting my peripheral vision. "You wanted me at my most vulnerable so you could reject me? Is that it?" She scoffs and shakes her head. "You're such a prick."

Yes, I'm a fucking prick.

I'm far worse, too. Especially when she continuously pokes my volatility.

"A fucking sociopath," she spits.

I clench my fists. "And what does that make you? You're the one who fucked me to claim victory."

"I didn't *fuck you* for anything other than pleasure. You're the one who keeps continuing these mind games when I stopped long ago. I've had enough, Cole." Her voice waivers. "I can't take this anymore."

I can't accept her accusation, not when she's the most recent contributor. I'm not the one who's lying here. If I'm a sociopath, I've certainly got likeminded company.

I step into her, my shoes bare inches from trampling her delicate toes.

"You're wrong," I snarl. "I'm the one who stopped the mind games."

She throws up her hands. "You just—"

"*I just tried to fucking test myself,*" I roar, the sound ricocheting through the room. "I wanted you naked because I was trying to prove I could fucking resist you. But if I lower my gaze, it will only confirm I can't."

She rears back as if I struck her.

I guess I did.

I hit her with a dose of painfully regretful truth.

"Get dressed," I repeat. "And make sure you're ready to leave once we return."

She doesn't respond, not other than the swipe of her tongue against her lower lip, which is made with blatant apprehension, not seduction.

Good.

She should be apprehensive because I've never been this unstable.

I storm for the door, forcing my attention back to where it needs to be—on my father. On the necessity to make him pay.

"Cole?"

Fuck. I pause, and this time I don't make the mistake of looking back. "What?"

"I can't resist you either." Her voice is a whisper. "You could've asked me to do a lot more than drop the sheet and I would've complied."

The admission stiffens my dick. "I know. Last night you made it clear you'll go to great lengths to stay."

I stalk into the hall and pound out the distance to the living room, ignoring how badly I want to believe her.

She almost has me convinced last night wasn't a ploy. My entire consciousness is contemplating the possibility of her malleable body being beneath mine purely for pleasure, not manipulative profit.

And that, in itself, makes her fucking dangerous.

The amount of power I've given her is insane.

"Trouble in paradise?" Luca sits forward on the recliner, elbows on his thighs, head in his hands. He stares at me as I walk farther into the room, his scathing expression telling me exactly where his thoughts are.

"Don't say another word," I warn.

"I shouldn't have to," he mutters, "but I will. You're not doing something fucking stupid like falling for her, are you?"

I answer him with a glare.

"Good." He rests back in his chair. "I thought you might have forgotten she works informants for a living. It's her job to screw people over to make an arrest."

"Your lack of faith is insulting." I continue toward the kitchen in search of something to numb the hangover. "You're also getting really close to overstepping your place in life."

"I'm watching your back. That's what I'm here for. The way you two were eying each other on the pier last night set off a whole heap of warning bells. The subsequent fucking only cemented my concern."

I grip the counter and hang my head. "I hope, for your sake, you stayed off the video feed."

"Rest assured, your lily-white ass isn't something I want to see. The acoustics were more than enough, fuck you very much." He shoves to his feet. "It's a big house and all, but I don't think you realize how easily sound travels through the rooms."

"You were the last thing on my mind." I yank open a drawer, then another, and another until I find a plastic bottle of pain relief. "And don't you dare judge me for fucking her when the alternative was to drink myself into a coma."

"It's after lunch, so it seems like you did both."

I open the pill bottle, throw three capsules in my mouth, then use my hand to cup water from the tap to swallow them back. When I straighten he's still appraising me, his gaze digging deep.

"But neither choice is any of my business. All I'm saying is that you're giving her more ammo to put you behind bars."

I stiffen, hearing an accusation of rape in his tone. "It was fucking consensual."

"I know. Believe me, I heard her consent. Continuously. For too damn long. But it's not going to stop her from fucking us over once she gets back to Portland."

"No, I won't." She inches from the hall, wearing nothing but my suit jacket cinched around her middle by her arms. My guess is that she grabbed the closest item of clothing before leaving the room in a rush to snoop. "I believe in what you're trying to do. And if you're successful, all the good you've done will outweigh the bad."

"You truly believe that?" Luca shoots her a look of scorn. "Your abduction, being sedated and hog-tied, having a gun pointed at your head? All that shit will be wiped off the slate?"

"I built my life around a career that brings monsters to justice. Who am I if I'm willing for Luther to remain free just because he can't be punished by the authorities? It's better for him to be dead since you've made it clear there's no other alternative."

I don't pay her any attention. I watch Luca instead. I notice how he straightens, his brow furrowed in dawning belief.

He believes her.

It's not only me she has wrapped around her little finger.

"There's something else I need to say," she continues. "Cole, you wanted me to admit last night was a mistake, and you're right. It was."

Fuck.

My hangover increases tenfold. My brain pounds. My gut churns. I keep my focus on Luca and jerk my chin at him. "Have you eaten?"

He nods.

"Then give us a minute." I won't let her air our dirty laundry in front of an audience. Not if it's another attempt to create humiliation. "I'm going to make some coffee, then I'll be ready to leave. Call a boat to come pick us up."

"Amar is already on standby. He won't take long to get here." He sends a skeptical glance at Anissa, then focuses back on me. "I'll wait for you on the pier."

I dismiss the instinct to demand a different driver. I don't want the old fucking Greek anywhere near here, but I also don't have the luxury of showing any more weakness toward the feminine snake in the room. I have to keep my mouth shut as Luca makes his way outside, sliding the glass door closed behind him.

"Continue," I drawl, meeting Anissa's gaze.

She cringes, a whole heap of discomfort marring her features. "Yesterday, I was convinced your plan was the right thing to do. Any alternative the authorities could provide would be too risky and time consuming. Let alone the money associated with that type of operation when the Greek police would block US officials at every turn."

"Get to the point." I drop the pills back to the drawer and slam it shut.

"The point is that nothing has changed. I'm still convinced. And I still think this is the only way to take him down."

"And your mistake last night? What does that have to do with all this?"

She remains silent for a moment, her forehead creased with concern. "The mistake is that I became a distraction. I've complicated things."

I trek my attention over her body, down along the expanse of thigh exposed beneath the jacket. "If that's your concern, maybe you should think about putting more clothes on."

"Stop it. I'm not messing around." Her eyes plead with me. "I was worried for you before your father turned up last night, and that was when I thought you were prepared and ready for what had to be done. Now, your head isn't in the game. You're too angry with me to possibly think straight, and that's scaring the hell out of me."

She doesn't look scared. After all this time I've spent craving her fear, she doesn't look anything other than a little anxious.

"Is this another tactic?" I lean against the kitchen counter, relaxed, hiding all the anger she's created. "Is there a strategy to this pity party?"

"No. This is me trying to tell you I care." Her voice grows in strength. "I'm fucking worried about you."

She attempts to stare me down, to illicit a reaction I won't give.

Eventually, she gives up, wiping her hands down her face, letting the jacket sweep open and expose a wealth of creamy skin.

My dick instantly grows hard.

A smart man would think the erotic show was right on cue for another perfect distraction. And I'm definitely a smart man. Most days.

"You don't need to worry, little fox. I'm not going to make a move. It's too dangerous to take action on his turf. I'm meeting up with Luther for nothing more than information."

I turn away and grab a mug from the cupboard to place it under the automatic coffee machine.

"Cole?"

I hear her approach. The soft pad of footfalls heightens my senses.

I don't look at her. I can't anymore.

She's too stunning to deny.

"I need you to believe last night wasn't a strategy."

I shake my head. I refuse to have this conversation. Not again. With every word she undoes me, turning me into a pathetic slave. But the question leaves me anyway. "Then what was it?"

"I don't know," she murmurs. "I guess it was a result of the intense situation. Or the alcohol. Or chemistry. Maybe it was a combination of all three. But it wasn't a trick or a betrayal. I'd sooner slit my wrists than fake an orgasm for you, or any man."

"I never said you faked it. I fucking felt your pussy melt for me." I tilt my head, glancing at her from the corner of my eye.

"Well, I don't whore myself out either. I slept with you because, at the time, I wanted to."

At the time.

I scoff, hating her need to insert the unnecessary proviso. "Thanks for clarifying."

I want to demand she revoke the defensive part of her admission. I itch to make her admit she fucked me because she needed to—*had* to—because she couldn't get through the fucking night without my dick.

But continuing this conversation will only send me into a tailspin. I'm already fucking nosediving.

Instead, I start the coffee machine and detour to the pantry, pulling the door wide to retrieve a box from the highest shelf. I remove one of the burner phones stashed there and shove the box back in place before shutting the door. "Here."

I walk toward her and lob the cell in her direction.

She catches it in both hands, then stares at the device in confusion. "What's this?"

"A phone. People use it to communicate."

She scowls. "I meant, why are you giving it to me?"

I shrug, downplaying how monumental this mistake could be. "You'll need it in case of an emergency."

If Luca and I run into trouble and don't make it back, she'll be stuck here. At least temporarily, until my father remembers the toy he can play with. Leaving her open to that situation isn't an option, even with the risk of her stabbing me in the back.

"But what if I call home?"

"Then I guess we all pay the price. You included."

Her brows pull tight as she runs her fingers over the cell. "Is *this* another game? Are you testing me?"

"*No*," I growl. "No more fucking games, Nissa. Okay? I'm done. And you are, too."

She straightens, seeming to gain some sort of strength from my animosity. "Then I don't want it." She storms forward and shoves the cell against my chest. "You need to take it back because I'll be tempted to use it."

"Then that's a battle you're going to have to fight." I push her wrist down, moving her arm away. "If you're as invested in this as you say you are, you shouldn't have a problem keeping your mouth shut. I'm only giving it to you in case I don't come back."

Her eyes widen. "Is that a possibility?"

I breathe in her concern. It sinks under my fucking skin.

No woman has ever looked at me like that. Like every blink is etched in the phantom pain of never seeing me again.

"It's unlikely. The cell is only a precaution. The last thing I want to do is die today and have your abduction stain my reputation for eternity."

She shakes her head. "I'd never admit that's what happened."

Fuck. She's killing me.

Fucking. Killing. Me.

"But I appreciate the safety net." She lowers her head and shoves the device into the jacket pocket. "Thank you."

Fuck the coffee.

Fuck waiting here within reach of her.

"I need to go." I sidestep, slapping a hand against the coffee machine to turn it off. "I'll see you later."

Her head snaps up. "You're leaving? The boat's not even here."

"Yeah, but you were right." I soften my voice, trying to bite back all the frustration. "You've become a distraction."

She cringes, her face filling with apology. "I'm—"

"Don't." I wrap my arm around her neck, pulling her into me. "Be ready to leave when I get back." I place a kiss at her temple, holding the connection longer than necessary. "Stay safe."

21

TORIAN

I spend each minute of the ride to the Naxos port trying not to glare at the back of Amar's head. I can still smell Anissa, can still feel my mouth against her temple, and this fucker dared to greet me with a smile after the disrespect he paid her.

The only thing stopping me from ripping out his throat is Luca's judgmental stare.

The scrutinizing SEAL can see right through me, and his focus isn't on the distraction of a man who threatened something belonging to me. Luca knows I'm mindfucked by the Fed.

He goddamn knows.

It takes all my hangover-depleted energy to focus on ignoring thoughts of her. Even then my subconscious refuses to stray from Anissa more than momentarily.

I want to get back to the island. She's too exposed out there on her own.

"What's the plan today?" Luca keeps his voice low, no doubt making sure we're not overheard.

"Information. That's all. We're not making a move. It's too risky."

Amar guides the boat alongside the jetty and cuts the engine.

I don't hang around to give the asshole a tip. I'm shoving to my feet and jumping onto the walkway before the gangway is put in place.

"Because the Fed will be a loose end on the island?" Luca jogs to catch up with me. "I don't know why you didn't send her packing like you promised."

"She has nothing to do with this. The risk of attacking from here is based on my father's protection. He's going to be covered from all angles." My statement is confirmed when I see Luther waiting on the rocky shore, two men flanking him. "His home has always been his fortress. And those two guards are merely the tip of the iceberg."

"They're the guys from last night—Chris and Robert." Luca remains at my side, matching me step for step. "They were also at your uncle's funeral."

"Yeah. I remember. What sort of vibe did you get from them?"

"A whole heap of arrogance with an added dose of fuck-off."

"Meaning?"

"They didn't see me as an equal. I was nothing. And I have a feeling they'll regard you with the same contempt."

"I'd like to see them try." I straighten my lapels and stride ahead to greet my father with a handshake. "Morning."

"Afternoon," he corrects, his smile forced. "I thought you would've made contact earlier."

"Blame the liquor." I laugh off his annoyance and clap him on the shoulder. "We had a big night celebrating my brother's existence. I didn't crawl from bed until lunch."

"Well, I'm glad to hear you enjoyed yourself, even if it was at the detriment of those who waited around for you to call."

Comfort and criticism. He's nothing if not predictable.

"Now that you're finally here, I'd like you to meet Robert and Chris." He waves a hand, indicating his goons. "I owe everything to them."

"Everything?" I offer my hand to the guy on the left—the steroid-infused mammoth. He doesn't have a flaccid vein in his body. Everything bulges with an over-abundance of testosterone. "Chris, is it? You look familiar."

"Robert," he grates, his ice-blue eyes emotionless as he grips my hand harder than necessary. "You would've seen me in Portland at the graveside service."

"And you didn't think to introduce yourself when my father was arrested?" I step away, turning my attention to Chris. "I assume you two are the ones responsible for the escape."

"That was us." The leaner of the two grins at me, like he's earned himself an Olympic medal. "We needed to lay low. We didn't know who we could trust."

We shake, the act dismissive on his side. He's not threatened by my presence.

Bad move.

"In future," I sneer, "you can rest assured Luther's son is trustworthy."

"Sons," Robert clarifies. "Don't forget you're not the only one."

Bitter irritation throbs through my chest, making it almost impossible not to glare as I drop Chris's hand. "Don't correct me. Not unless you want a lesson in manners."

"They're protective. That's all." My father defuses the growing tension with a soothing tone. "And they did a great job in Portland. You should be grateful I have such an exceptional team."

"So the dead prison guard was part of the plan?" Luca's tone drips with sarcasm. "That's hardcore."

I fight a grin and ignore the chastising glare my father shoots me. If he expects me to make a reprimand he's going to be waiting a hell of a while. "How many of you ran the job? Witness accounts are conflicting. Some said two. Others mentioned four."

"It was only the two of us." Robert matches my smirk with his own. "That's all your father has ever needed while we've been on the job."

"You're confident. I like it. Although, you wouldn't hear my team running their mouth if they allowed me to get arrested in the first place."

"And maybe we wouldn't have needed to bring your father home at all if you'd protected Richard properly."

My hackles rise, my hands clenching into fists. "What did you say?"

"That's enough," my father warns. "Let's get back to the house. Robert, you can get started on the project I mentioned earlier. We can meet up later."

I dig my fingers into my palms, itching to take this further into hostile territory.

"Come on." Luther strides for the row of cars parked a few yards from the end of the jetty. "We've got a lot to discuss."

I shoot a scowl at Luca, letting him know I'm far from appreciative of the warm welcome and follow after my father. "Robert isn't joining us?"

"I'd prefer not to cram five of us in the car. He can catch up later."

"What a shame," Luca drawls. "He seems like a stand-up guy."

"He's a worthy asset." Luther pulls a car fob from his suit jacket and unlocks a polished sedan, then throws the fob to Chris. "Speaking of worthy assets, I thought you were going to bring your toy along?"

The hairs rise on the back of my neck. Every nerve stands at attention. "She's not worth the frustration. I'm growing tired of her struggle."

"That's a shame. It's been a while since I enjoyed the thrill of breaking in a newbie." He opens the rear driver's side door. "Luca, you can sit in the front with Chris while I talk with my son in the back."

I follow my father's lead as we climb into the luxury car and make our way onto the narrow streets.

Luther fills the drive with idle chitchat. We discuss my sisters and niece. For a few brief moments, we skim over Richard's funeral and the upkeep of the burial plot. Then the conversation switches to my half-brother and the twinkle in Luther's eye irks me in a way I can't describe.

It isn't jealousy. My father could have a million sons and I wouldn't give a shit.

It's the way Tobias was created as an asset which has me questioning God's existence.

The boy was conceived in brutality and baptized in sin. No child should have to carry those mental scars.

"You should spend some time with him while you're here." Luther meets my gaze. "The two of you are likely to work together in the future."

"Not too soon I hope. Give the kid a chance to grow up."

He laughs. "The boy is smart, and despite being shy, he's strong. It won't be long and he'll be making me retire."

"Then I look forward to getting to know him." I bite back a curse.

That child keeps creating problems, and the complications will only grow once he's an orphan.

It's not like I'm parental material.

I won't be looking after him. But he's also family, which means one of my sisters will have to mother him—her rapist father's illegitimate, parent-less kid.

Jesus Christ.

I push back the building mental struggle and force myself to focus on the here and now. On the immaculate view. Everything here is pristine and picture-perfect. It's the company that taints it all.

I don't want to speak to my father anymore. I'm not sure I can keep opening my mouth without spewing hatred.

The pressure only builds when I consider how easy it would be to end his life right now. All it would take is a quick slide of hand into my jacket to retrieve my gun. A turn of my wrist. Then two quick squeezes of the trigger.

Luther, then Chris.

Dead.

I could do it, too. I *would* do it if I knew where Robert had gone.

If I had to place a bet, I'd say he's tailing us around every corner, providing a hidden safety net. The backup wouldn't help my slain father, but I'm sure the steroid junkie would cause enough trouble to stop me from reaching Anissa.

I wouldn't be able to get us all to the jet before reinforcements caught up to us. And even if I did, the aftermath would be riddled with complications.

The whole idea of making a move in Greece is so my father can go missing. The isolated island provides a buffer to dispose of evidence, and it also means there'll be no witnesses.

Luther would've sunk to the bottom of the ocean by now if I'd followed through last night. The three of them would've become fish food. One minute, they're building a thriving empire. The next, I'm taking over and shutting it down.

"Cole?"

"Hmm?" The car slows as I turn back to my father. "What is it?"

"Chris asked for your gun."

The driver holds his hand over his shoulder, waiting. "All weapons need to be surrendered before you enter the property. We don't allow visitors to be armed."

"Visitors? Since when is your son a visitor?"

"It's necessary." My father winces out an unspoken apology. "We had problems a year ago with one of my girls. She stole a gun from a guest and created unnecessary bloodshed. We've taken strict precautions ever since."

I don't like it. I fucking hate the idea. And the stiff posture of Luca in the front seat announces he feels the same way.

"Maybe we should go somewhere else then." I swirl my finger in the air, motioning for Chris to turn the vehicle around. "Find a cafe or a restaurant."

"Don't be ridiculous. We're almost home. And no son of mine is going to come all this way and not see where I live. I'm sure you can survive without your weapons for a few hours."

Can I? I'm not so sure.

"Cole?" Luther frowns at me. "What's gotten into you? Since when don't you trust your own flesh and blood?"

I scoff out a laugh. "Since you demanded to take my gun."

He continues to frown, his scrutiny increasing. It's only a matter of time before he realizes my uncertainty is a reflection of myself, not him.

"Okay, okay." I reach into my jacket and pull my weapon from the holster. "Look after her."

I slap the warm metal in Chris's hand and watch as Luca does the same. Both weapons are placed in the glove compartment.

When the car moves again, it's only a few yards along the road until we pull up before wrought-iron gates, the overbearing barrier guarded by a lone man with a rifle.

"Welcome to my home away from home." Luther nods his appreciation at the guard as we're allowed entry, passing security cameras and a head-high brick wall. "This is my personal paradise."

The gardens are lush. The lawns manicured. The trees blooming with flowers. All of it is a perfect frame for the massive white building coming into view as we round the curving pebbled drive.

Tobias stands at the top of the few stairs leading to the large double doors of the mansion, his innocent face pale. The poor kid seems awkward in his dress pants and collared shirt, the formal attire daunting his tiny frame.

"There's my boy." My father releases his belt, and the car pulls to a stop. "Come on. I'll show you around."

We climb out, all four of us walking toward the house, my father and Chris in front, Luca eyeing me with trepidation as we walk behind to meet the kid at the top step.

"Hey, little man." I crouch on one knee, not bothering to offer my hand when I can already see the anxiety in his features. "It's nice to see you again."

He nods, the movement jerky until he settles in against my father's side. He gains strength from Luther. Protection.

I used to feel the same.

"The two of you are strikingly similar," my father drawls. "Both worrying unnecessarily. It's a useless waste of time. I have men walking the perimeter twenty-four/seven. You've got nothing to worry about while you're here."

"I trust you." I shove to my feet. "But I'm beginning to question whether these women are worth the hassle."

"Believe me, they are." He shoos Tobias with a wave of his hand. "Go get them. Tell them we have guests."

"Yes, *Baba*." Tobias backtracks with a nod and slips between the front doors, his running footsteps echoing from inside.

We follow, my father leading us down a wide hall, through an opulent living room, past a sparkling kitchen, then outside to a stunning pool area with an unfettered view of the ocean.

"Chris, get one of the women to arrange something to eat." My father looks at his right-hand man. "I think we could all do with a drink, too."

The guy jerks his head and makes his way back inside, leaving me and Luca to pretend to take in the atmosphere while we scope the security.

"Well?" My father descends onto a cushioned outdoor chair and retrieves a remote from the coffee table in front of him. With the press of a button an overhead fan starts to spin, releasing a cooling white mist. "What do you think?"

"You've done well for yourself." It's the best compliment I can offer. I'm tired of the lies and fake placations. Every breath Luther takes is a taunt to my failure, not only last night, but years ago. "How long have you lived here?"

"A while. At least since Tobias was born. Chris and Robert used to run the household and look after the women when I was still travelling back and forth from the States."

"Look after them?" I take a seat opposite him.

"Yes. A certain level of routine needs to be maintained, otherwise the slaves slip into bad habits."

Luca takes the seat beside me. "Meaning they're serviced on a regular basis to stop them fighting back after a long stretch of relative freedom?"

"Correct. Although, I do enjoy a good fight." Luther grins. "But Robert and Chris also made sure the women saw to Tobias's education and welfare. He's home schooled, and it's a fine line between them treating him like their own son, and having him realize they're assets, not maternal figures."

"Well, from what I've seen, you've raised a good kid." Luca kicks back in his chair, a picture of relaxed calm.

"He's exceptional. With Cole, I had his mother to contend with in the early years. She made me soften the truth of the family business until she thought he was old enough to handle reality. With Tobias, I haven't had those restrictions. And it's made a world of difference."

"I wouldn't disregard the importance of balance." I spread my arms wide, indicating his riches. "No matter how much money you have, it won't be enough to pay for the therapy the kid will need if you expose him to too much too soon."

"Children are resilient. And most important, they're easily molded. You'd be surprised what he can withstand."

No, I wouldn't.

My imagination has already run wild with what the poor kid has had to endure.

"But what about you, son?" Luther asks. "Have you put any thought into expanding the family name?"

"Children?" I laugh. And keep laughing. "I wouldn't hold your breath for more grandbabies. Not from me, anyway."

"What about Layla or Keira?"

I shake my head, not willing to get his hopes up for more minions to work under his control. "Not in the foreseeable future."

"I disagree." Luca clears his throat. "Keira and Seb go at it like rabbits."

I look at him. Smile. Blink.

None of it is kind.

Not when he's discussing my sister's sex life.

"Who's Seb?" My father sits straighter. "Do I know him?"

"No. His name is Sebastian." I continue to stare my annoyance at Luca, as if the aggression has the power to force his mouth closed. "He's a tech guy who's been working on the fringes for a while. He's valuable. Knows his shit. And has saved my ass on more occasions than I'd like to admit."

"But?"

That's a good question.

I've held tight to my animosity for so long the reasons don't hold much weight anymore. He *is* a valued part of my team. His skills with a computer are beyond my comprehension. And he can handle a gun better than most.

Then there's his devotion to family. I learned the hard way he'd go to war for the sake of those he loves.

"I'm protective," I admit. "And she's been through a lot. I couldn't stand to see her suffer again."

I sprinkle history into the conversation as a test.

My father may not be aware of what Keira has been through recently, but that's not what I'm referring to. I want to trigger the past. Her childhood. Once and for all, I need to know if he's aware of what his failure as a parent did to her.

"Their relationship is serious?" His brows rise. "That's surprising. I've never seen her with a man before apart from the guy at Richard's funeral."

I want to tell him he's responsible for her abstinence. That her mistreatment as a child is to blame. It won't help, though. His predictable dismissal would only increase my thirst for blood.

"They're joined at the hip," Luca adds. "There's no separating them."

Numerous sets of footsteps approach, breaking our conversation. Tobias leads three women toward us, all of them trailing behind him in a line.

They're victims—my father's slaves—who walk forward, their faces deadpan as if they've done this strut of shame a hundred times before.

"Here they are." Luther encourages them forward with a jerk of his head. "My gorgeous beauties, I'd like you to meet my special guests."

The line stops. The women turn to face us, almost military like, while Tobias remains in the lead, his focus on my father, waiting, wanting recognition.

"Who do we have here?" Luca inches forward with a sly grin, his act unsettling.

There's no reaction from the victims. They remain in formation, staring straight ahead over our heads at the white brick wall behind.

They're attractive. Seemingly healthy. Impeccably dressed. Their hair is styled, their clothing immaculate. Even their makeup is on point.

There's no sign of the brutality they endure. Not one hint of the horrors they've faced.

"This is Nina." Luther points at the blonde on the left with her pursed lips and narrowed gaze. She's wearing a casual sundress, her hair loose around her shoulders, her skin sun-kissed with a healthy tan.

"Then Abigail and Chloe." The two brunettes are similar in appearance. Both slim. Attractive. Fashionable.

They're trophies. Not just slaves, but pretty decorations to promote my father's deviance.

"You've got a nice collection." Luca eyes the women with appreciation.

"This isn't the entirety of my stable. Lilly is resting. And I assume the apple of my eye is arranging drinks."

Tobias nods. "She's getting food, too."

"Five women?" I raise my brows. "I'm impressed by your stamina."

"I'm like a fine wine, boy." He spreads his arms along the backrest of his seat. "I only get better with age. Isn't that right, ladies?"

They voice a chorus of murmured agreement, the "yes", "of course", and "definitely" a drone of sound.

"That's not very convincing, my loves." He pushes from the chair, his approach causing them to stand taller. Straighter.

"You're remarkable, Luther," the blonde says in a rush.

"And very generous," the one next to her adds with conviction.

"We're lucky to have you." Chloe practically pleads with her eyes.

"That's more like it." He walks around them, the lazy stroll predatory. "I'm going to check on our drinks and take a quick bathroom break." He leans in to grasp the blonde on the ass. "Get moving, ladies. It's time to stop distracting the men."

He ushers them into the house, sliding the door shut behind him.

"Your dad is a piece of work," Luca mutters under his breath.

"Keep your opinions to yourself." I shoot him a warning glare. We have no idea who's listening. This place could be bugged down to the foundations for all we know. "If you can't stomach your job, go wait in the car."

He snaps his gaze away, his teeth clenched, his nostrils flaring.

"This is business." I keep my voice low, still playing the game in case I'm overheard. "Consider it a learning opportunity."

In other words, dig deep and gain information. Make this bullshit worthwhile.

He juts his chin in acknowledgement, his jaw ticking with each passing second.

"Why don't you go for—"

The whoosh of the sliding door cuts off my words. The tap of heels puts me back on edge.

I force myself to lazily sink back into the chair as a new woman walks forward with a wooden tray. She's like the others, slim, beautiful, with a braid of long dark hair resting over her left shoulder.

She meets my gaze briefly, her dark brown eyes striking me with a sense of déjà vu.

I give up on the lazy posture and sit straight, trying to get a better view of her downcast face.

I've seen her before. I'm sure I have.

She places the tray on the coffee table before us, the loose dress gaping at her chest as she bends to pick up two of the three glasses, each filled with a finger of scotch. She hands the first to Luca, her attention remaining on the floor.

When it's my turn, I reach out, about to retrieve the drink but stop before making contact, letting my fingers hover close. "Aren't you going to introduce yourself?"

She stills, her long lashes fluttering as she blinks.

There's no other outward reaction. No sign of distress, apart from the way her throat works over a tormented swallow.

"I'm Cole," I offer. "Luther's son."

She stiffens, her chocolate eyes hollow as they meet mine.

I'm not offered a greeting. Not in words. But the underlying "fuck you" in her tight expression speaks loud.

"Have we met?" I drag my attention over every inch of her, trying to find a birthmark or tattoo that might spark more familiarity. "I'm sure I've seen you before."

"You're mistaken." She shoves the glass into my hand and backtracks with the sound of the nearby opening door.

"Ahh, there she is." My old man sidles up to her, wrapping an arm around her waist to pull her close.

She doesn't stiffen or bristle. She follows the movement, flowing with the motion like water in a stream.

"I see you've already met my pretty penny." Luther's fingers tangle in her dress, deep and possessive. "I shouldn't have favorites, but it's no secret this woman has claimed all my attention."

"I can see why." I keep racking my brain, trying to pinpoint the familiarity. "Is there a reason why I feel like we've already met?"

My father seems to consider my question, glancing between us, back and forth. "I don't know. Maybe you've seen her on the television. Penny's not from Oregon. But the news of her disappearance may have crossed state lines."

"Penny?" Luca repeats. "That's her name?"

Hell opens up before me, threatening to swallow me whole.

If this woman is who I think she is, she's meant to be dead, her body dumped in a mass grave, her teeth and hair found among the remains of other sex slaves.

"Is something wrong?" My father grabs the last remaining glass of scotch from the tray and reclaims his seat. "Have you two met before?"

"No." I take a sip of liquor, gripping the glass like a motherfucking lifeline and still, the rage intensifies. "She must have a familiar face. That's all."

"I'm not sure about her face, but she has a truly unforgettable mouth." He laughs, the sound crawling over my skin like lice. "Don't you, baby girl?"

She smiles, the expression forced as she retreats.

"Where are you going?" He pats his lap. "Come here."

Penny eyes me, Luca, then my father before daring to approach with cautious steps. She considers every one of us a threat. My guess is that she's been exposed to group violations in the past.

"Come on." Luther reaches out, grabs her wrist, and yanks her onto his lap. "There's no need to be shy." He places his hand on her thigh, dragging it higher, beneath the hem of her yellow dress.

Every inch of skin he touches acts like a red-hot poker to my rage.

I want to hurt him. Torture him. I could rip his heart out with my bare hands.

Because if I don't, Decker, who I suspect is her brother, definitely will.

"I don't mean to cock block, but is that food still on the way?" Luca's words brush along the edge of my consciousness, barely breaching my growing instability.

"I'm starving," he adds, his gaze finding mine. "And you haven't even eaten today."

He's trying to pull me back. To drag me away from the tight grip of insanity.

But my father's hand keeps creeping higher and higher, on a path to violation right in front of my fucking eyes.

"Yes. Food." Luther slaps the inside of Penny's thigh then shoves her off his lap. "We need to feed our guests."

Penny stumbles to right herself, then hustles to escape inside.

"I didn't mean to spoil your fun." Luca gulps down the rest of his alcohol. "But, God, I'm hungry. I've been awake since dawn, while hangover Harry slept like a log." He jerks his chin at me. "Then he crawls out of bed and demands to leave before I can eat lunch."

He's picking up the slack. Succeeding where I'm failing.

I'm losing the battle to remain composed.

"I'm not hungover. But I am intrigued." I let the sentence fall, and take a generous gulp of liquor to help me finish. "These women of yours, are they for sale? Or hire?"

There's a tweak to his lips. A sly, overly arrogant tilt. "Yes. The women I'll show you tonight are all available for whatever you want."

"No. I'm talking about the women here. The ones I've already seen."

"My personal harem?" He frowns. "You're interested in sleeping with *my* women?"

"Maybe." I hedge my bets, but I'm not sure what for. There doesn't seem to be a level of deviance he finds unsettling.

"There's no maybes from me." Luca places his glass back on the tray. "I'm definitely interested. I'd part ways with a lot of money for just a taste."

My father snickers. "Sorry, lads. I don't give up my toys until I'm good and ready."

"You're telling me no amount of money would tempt you to hand one of them over?" Luca rubs his hands together. "I thought you were in this business for the riches."

We're getting nowhere. Fast.

"I don't think his reluctance has anything to do with money. I'd take a guess the old man is worried he'll be quickly forgotten if a newer model takes one of his toys for a spin." I smirk. "Ain't that right, old goat?"

He narrows his eyes on me, taking the provocation and raising it with a conniving curve of lips. "For interest's sake, who do you have your eye on?"

I take another sip of liquid, letting the burn take over my tongue. "The jewel in your crown, of course. What's the point of the game if I can't have your best and brightest?"

"Is that what this is? A game?" He crosses his arms over his chest, the liquid jostling in his glass. "If so, maybe your amateur skills would be best suited for someone with a little less bite. Penny's a fighter. You wouldn't be able to handle her."

"He might not," Luca adds, "but I could. I've got more patience than your son."

"Really?" He drinks down his scotch and wipes a hand over his mouth. "Then how about you go speak to her so Cole and I can finally talk business?"

My pulse kicks at the small victory.

"It's more of a tease, if anything," he continues. "But if you're eager to get close to her, by all means, try your hand. Just don't blame me when she bites."

"And when I seduce her out of those panties? What then?"

"Then you back away slowly," I drawl. "Before my father gets a hold of you."

"Yes, sir." Luca pushes to his feet, grinning from ear to ear. "Consider me forewarned."

I watch him leave, taking the jovial vibe with him.

Tension settles between me and the man I once idolized. It coils tight, wrapping around my chest until I can't stomach looking at the son of a bitch who has become unrecognizable.

"What's this Penny thing all about?" Luther lowers his voice. "It's not like you to push for something that's not yours."

"We're having a bit of fun. That's all." I glance away, out past the pool toward the ocean-filled horizon. Anissa is out there somewhere. Alone. Hopefully packing her bags so I can get her as far away from this monstrous fuck as soon as possible.

"I know you, Cole. I'm well aware there's something more at play."

I turn back to face him, not bowing down to the judgment in his eyes. "I'll admit this isn't what I expected."

"You've changed your mind about the business opportunity?"

"No. That's not what this is about." I lay the bait, dragging it out slowly. "It's been a long time since Mom died. Seeing you enjoy yourself with a stream of women isn't fucking easy."

"I'm…" His expression loses the annoyed edge. "I didn't think this would affect you after all these years."

"It shouldn't. I'm not a kid anymore."

"But you're still my son."

I hold his gaze through the fake family moment. I don't let that motherfucker go while he's trapped in my sights. Every second immersed in this bullshit is more time for Luca to talk to the girl. "Don't spare it another thought. Just be aware Keira and Layla will take it harder than me. They were closer to Mom."

"I agree. And I apologize for blindsiding you for a second time." He pushes to his feet and straightens his jacket. "On that note, I think it's best if we get out of here."

"No. That isn't necessary."

"It's for the best. I can take you to the location for tonight's event." He waves at me to get off the sofa. "If we leave now, we'll have at least half an hour of privacy until the assets arrive to prepare."

Fuck his assets.

Fuck his location.

Fuck his ability to take another unhindered breath.

Luca needs time with Penny. Time that is quickly running out.

"Don't be ridiculous." I spread an arm along the backrest of the chair. "It's better to get over the shock now. There's no point running from it."

"I insist." He starts for the house. "We will have less interruptions this way. I don't want any more distractions while we discuss business. And let's not forget that woman of yours. We need to discuss her, too."

The mention of Anissa has me blinking back rage. "She's not worth mentioning."

"Really?" He continues to the house, forcing me to push to my feet and stalk after him. He doesn't pause until he reaches the door to wait for me. "I think your toy may have a vital role in establishing a new partnership between father and son."

"What kind of vital role?"

He glances over his shoulder, and paranoia leads me to believe he's testing me. His lazy scrutiny digs deep, searching for secrets to expose.

"*Stop.*" The feminine scream carries from inside. From Penny. "*Stop.*"

I don't have time to think before my father shoves the door aside and stalks forward. I follow close behind, reaching for a gun that isn't there.

"What's going on?" he bellows.

Penny stands in the corner of the kitchen, the counter clutched behind her as Luca holds up his hands in surrender from the other side of the room.

He looks guilty as fuck, the red stain of a slap mark on his cheek turning the taste in my mouth sour.

"Someone better start talking," I seethe. "My patience is growing fucking thin."

"He didn't do anything." The innocent voice of my brother comes from the doorway on the far side of the kitchen, his head poking around the frame from the hall.

"You saw what happened?" my father asks.

"I was snooping." Tobias takes a tentative step into the room. "I know I shouldn't, but Penny sounded upset and I was worried."

"And?" I grind my teeth to lessen the aggression in my tone. "What happened?"

"Nothing." He shakes his head. "The man was being nice and Penny was…" He glances at her with guilt, then quickly looks away, hanging his head.

"What, son?" Luther approaches him, placing strong hands on tiny shoulders. "What was she doing?"

The boy keeps his head lowered. "She was being mean."

Luther stiffens and stands to his full height. "You dare to make a guest of mine unwelcome?" He swings around, approaching her, making her cower.

She turns her face away, her arms wrapping around her stomach. "I'm sorry. I don't know what came over me."

"Fucking stupidity, that's what." He looms over her, his fists clenched at his sides. "Do you need to go back to basic training? Maybe I should send you to the farm so you can be reminded how well you're treated here."

"Please." She drops to her knees and grips his trousers. "I didn't mean it. I apologize."

I can't step in. Whatever the fuck she's done, I can't save her. I can't show my cards until I'm ready to shoot my way out of here. And I can't fucking do that without a goddamn gun.

"It's my fault." Luca's voice is calm. There's no hint of panic. "I got carried away. I tried to make small talk, and when I mentioned her past, I think she took it as a taunt."

Luther grips her chin, forcing her tear-soaked eyes to meet his as he raises a hand. "You need to be punished for your disobedience."

"Dad," I warn. "I'm growing tired of the adolescent distractions from these women. Can't we get the fuck out of here already?"

I pray he hears the insult. The subtle stab at his pride is the only thing capable of lowering his hand. Yet the threatening position of his arm doesn't lower.

"Fine. We'll leave." I start toward Tobias, offering my palm for a high-five he barely taps. "Until next time, little man."

I walk by him and into the hall, Luca following behind.

I only make it a few yards before he grabs my arm.

"I can't leave." His voice is low, his eyes wild, his nostrils flared. "He's going to hurt her."

"This isn't the most opportune time to fall victim to your conscience," I snarl under my breath.

His admission is dangerous. Fucking reckless. If we're overheard—if my loyalties are questioned—I'll make it out of here because I'm blood. He won't.

"Just keep walking. My father will follow."

"And if he doesn't?"

I shrug off his hold. "We just keep walking. We have no other choice."

22

ANISSA

I sit on the living room floor, my back against the sofa, my legs outstretched before me as I cradle the cell in my hand.

I never should've agreed to take the device. Not when I knew the temptation would eat me from the inside out.

I've battled indecision since the moment Cole walked from the house, and it isn't because I want to be rescued. I'm past that. What I require is grounding.

I slept with Cole Torian. A criminal. And not just any criminal, a high-functioning, incredibly successful, lawless entrepreneur.

There's no sense. No regret. No guilt.

I'm trying to encourage thoughts of disgust and shame when the only thing consuming me are memories of shock and goddamn bliss.

It's insanity.

Nobody in their right mind would look back on what happened last night and crave more.

But those lips.

The reverence.

He was another man. One who brushed his mouth over my injured shoulder with such exquisite adoration it still brings an enjoyable shiver to my skin.

I can't quit sinking my nose into the collar of his suit jacket to breathe his scent deep into my lungs. Each inhalation is a hit that fills me with warmth. With sizzling flashbacks.

I'd snatched his jacket from the dresser because it was the first thing within reach when I rushed from the bed to snoop on the conversation in the living room.

Now I can't bring myself to take it off.

Not when the Cole from last night wasn't the heartless mastermind I'd grown to despise. They're two contrary people—entirely different souls trapped in the same body.

And the split personalities aren't the only reason I should dial home.

Common sense demands I contact the Bureau. It's necessary on multiple levels. I can't be entirely sure of my timeline since boarding the jet, but I'm confident I'm meant to be back at the office by now.

Easton will wonder where I am. Taggert will take my no-show as a silent resignation. And both are likely to mount a full-scale search for answers.

I don't want to lead them here. Not when I'm certain Cole will finish Luther more efficiently than any organization ever could. He already has the means and the determination. If it weren't for that poor little boy, I'm sure this nightmare would already be over.

So now, I don't know what to do.

The more I contemplate reaching for the outside world, the more affirmative reasons compound. But thinking about betraying Cole makes my stomach hollow.

I can't even bring myself to stop seeing him whenever I close my eyes. He's always there, staring right back at me with his smug gorgeousness.

Taggart was right not to trust me. He knew one day I'd act exactly like my traitorous father. Maybe everyone in my department could see my weakness better than I could.

I unlock the phone, the *click* sound filling me with guilt.

I focus on the square call icon until my vision blurs. I keep staring until it's Cole that stares back at me.

"Goddammit." I relock the screen and shove the cell along the carpet, sliding it out of reach.

Betraying him doesn't feel right.

Being loyal to him brings the same discomfort.

"What the hell have you done to me?" I thump my back against the sofa, hoping the jolt will lead me in the right direction. I keep rocking into the cushions, the *thud, thud, thud* oddly soothing until the sound is accompanied by a far-off rumble.

I pause.

Listen.

It's a boat.

"Shit." The only thing that noise has ever brought is trouble.

I shove to my feet and glance toward the hall. I should get dressed, but I'd prefer to assess the risks before spending precious moments worrying about clothes.

I rush for the glass door.

Cole hasn't been gone for more than an hour. I'm not sure if that means the meeting didn't go as planned. Or something fell into place.

My pulse increases at the possibility of his success. A subtle kiss of excitement settles into my stomach before I think better of celebrating murder.

I pull the door wide, listening to the growl of the boat approaching, getting closer and closer with every passing second.

He told me to be ready in case something happened, but I'm not. My belongings aren't packed. I haven't showered. I'm still naked beneath the suit jacket.

I thought I'd have more time.

I walk outside, the beat of my pulse building. I break into a jog around the pool and continue down the gravel path, my pace increasing the more I convince myself Cole has come back to get me.

I'm halfway down the path when I see the boat. The same speedboat from the first day I arrived.

Any hint of optimism flees at the memory of the gun pointed in my face.

My steps falter.

My heart stops.

I can't see who's onboard, and I didn't have the foresight to check what boat escorted the men from the island earlier. Maybe the threatening old man is their chauffeur. Or maybe he knows I'm alone and has returned to have his fun with me.

I slow, creeping forward, shielding myself behind bushes and trees.

I keep approaching the pier, not stopping until I've reached the last waist-high shrub, then I wait as my shadowed guests pull up a few yards away.

The engine is cut and the boat bobs into place while I scrutinize the shaded area underneath the upper-deck canopy, trying to make out the two silhouettes.

I'm not sure if it's Luca. The height of one person is similar to his. Big. Bulky.

I contemplate calling out. But what should I say?

If it's Cole, I want to run to him. To find out what happened to have him returning so soon. And if it's not, it's imperative I prepare for the worst. I need to know if I should be scrambling for the protection of the house before any danger approaches.

I stand, wrapping the jacket tight around me with one arm while I raise a hand to my brow, shielding the sun from my eyes to gain a better look.

An unfamiliar man steps out from beneath the shelter, his gaze fixed on me. He climbs onto the pier, tall, broad, and sporting an entirely blank expression. I've never seen such an emotionless face promote such pure hostility before. The man hurls bad juju without so much as a sneer.

I swallow, lick the dryness from my lips, and tell myself my fear is unsubstantiated. He could be here to help. This man, with his ice-cold stare, could have been sent by Cole.

"Hello?" I squint into the sun. "Who are you?"

"The name's Robert," he grunts. "You need to come with me."

"What? Why?" I backtrack, breathing through the panic.

"Ih-mur-juhn-see." The old Greek slides into view on the back of the boat, his smile wide. "Ih-mur-juhn-see. Ih-mur-juhn-see."

Fuck.

I quit fighting fear.

I turn.

Run.

Sprint.

My hair flicks in my eyes. My lungs burn from exertion. But I don't stop, don't even pause as pebbles bite into my feet and heat lashes my throat.

I head for the house, hoping it will be my savior.

I can grab the cell, call Cole, and shield myself in the panic room until he arrives.

Oh, God, how long will it take for him to get to me?

The thunder of faster footfalls follows me, the frightening sound increasing as I reach the pool.

I sense his darkness. His cruel intent. I don't want to know what this man hides beneath the blank expression.

I push myself harder, throwing myself at the glass door to yank it open. I'm inside, about to slam the barrier between us and lock him out when his arm launches through the closing space and snatches my wrist.

My heart lurches. My breathing stops.

I stare deep into those soulless eyes as I twist and tug, finally scrambling from his grip. But there's no time to close the door. It's too late. He's shoving my only protection wide to stalk inside, his shoulders broad and menacing.

I swing away and dash ahead, determined to make it to the panic room.

I don't even reach the hall.

He yanks me backward by my hair. Pain slices through my skull as he spins me around, slamming my face into the back of the sofa. My cheek breaches the cushioning and collides with the hard wood beneath, the impact buckling my knees to send me toppling to the floor.

Everything vanishes. Thought. Feelings. Consciousness.

Then it all comes rushing back in a tangled mess of panic and agony as my tormentor continues to drag me by my hair.

I kick, punch, and launch my elbows in every direction. I fight, fight, fight, never pausing. Not for a second. Not even when his hand latches onto my neck and squeezes.

The hold is nothing like Cole's.

This man's touch isn't a pleasurable grip. His fingertips dig deep, his strength tightening to restrict my breath.

I claw at his hands, scratching and flailing while fire burns a trail down my throat.

I let my legs fall out from beneath me, becoming a dead weight in the hopes he will drop me.

He doesn't.

He holds me like a rag doll, choking, suffocating while I scramble to regain my footing and ease the pressure.

"I could do this all day, bitch. But we've got somewhere to be."

I try to scream and only produce a squeak.

I need air.

I need help.

I need Cole.

"Do you want to come willingly or are you going to let me have more fun?" His gaze treks my body, over the exposed skin beneath the gaping jacket.

I struggle for air, gulping with no relief.

Darkness edges into the corners of my vision as my toes grasp for grounding. Everything moves incredibly fast and eerily slow at the same time.

I'm disoriented. Dazed.

I don't realize I'm dropping to the floor until my ass hits the hard tile and my palms slap against the soothing cold. I fall into a mass of tangled limbs, gasping, heaving, gulping. My chest rises and falls as I clamber to reclaim oxygen.

"Get up," he demands.

I don't know how.

"I said, get the fuck up." He kicks me, his booted foot launching into my ribs. The pain spreads through my lungs, bringing a dose of adrenaline-filled clarity.

He doesn't have a foreign accent. He's American.

"Who are you?" My voice is a weak rasp. "Do you work for Cole?"

"Cole?" He scoffs. "That man has no power over me. My orders come from someone with far more influence. Someone who is going to make Cole look like a puppy in comparison."

Luther?

Oh, God.

"What do you want with me?"

He grabs a fistful of my hair, dragging me to my feet. "I want you to get your ass on the fucking boat and quit wasting my time." He shoves me toward the glass doors, following a foot behind. "Keep moving."

I won't go. I can't bring myself to willingly follow.

If I get on that boat, I'm dead. Never to be found.

I make another attempt at escape, not thinking, just running. I spin, lunge, and sprint faster than I've ever sprinted before.

"Fucking bitch." He chases me, his booming footfalls tattooing my mind.

I aim for the hall, the archway within reach when he barrels into me from behind, launching me forward.

I can't divert my trajectory.

I can't stop the impact.

My head hits the wall. Hard.

Then blackness takes me away.

23

TORIAN

I lean against the hood of my father's car, Luca next to me, both of us waiting.

It's been five minutes since we walked outside, the time passing like an eternity as I glare at the front doors of the mansion.

"I'm going back in." Luca pushes from the car.

"No." I keep my focus on those doors, despising every second Luther remains inside. "It's fucking stupid to attempt saving her when we still don't know who she is, and it's obvious Luther isn't going to kill his prized possession."

"Sometimes death isn't the worst punishment," he snarls.

I know.

I fucking know.

But going in there to retaliate when our guns remain locked in the car will endanger the other women, too. Along with Tobias.

"She's survived this long." I shove from the hood and move to stand in front of him. "She's strong. A little while longer won't change her position."

He glares at me—glares right through me—until the sound of the front door opening has us both pivoting to watch my father and Chris walk outside.

"Sorry for the delay. I got stuck on a call." My father doesn't show an ounce of concern as he stalks for the car, and we all claim our previous positions in the vehicle.

We don't talk about what happened. The only reminder is Luca's hatred, which thickens in the air around us.

We're at the end of the street when Luther breaks the silence and starts telling me about the profound success of his business. He throws figures at me. Large numbers. Impressive stats.

I play along, acting interested in his scheme, pretending I'm considering taking a piece of the pie, while the hunger for retribution builds in my blood.

"My success has been built on trust. I'm known for my discretion. That's why the majority of my income is repeat business." He pivots his body to face me. "When I host parties, I don't just mingle among my clients. I participate. Not only for my own gratification, but to reassure my paying customers their actions aren't going to come with consequences."

I frown, feigning confusion when his perversions are crystal clear. "You openly indulge in the activities so everyone in attendance knows you're confident nobody will get caught?"

The strategy is business savvy. If only he didn't enjoy every vile fucking minute of it.

"It's more than that. They see me enjoying myself and understand they're among like-minded people. They're free from judgment." He waves a hand toward his window, indicating the pristine waters. "Solicitation is legal here. Pussy is easy to buy. But that's not what men are looking for. They want power and the ability to express their God-given instincts. These women provide that opportunity. Without restriction."

"None at all?" I raise a brow. "I'm assuming some of them have extravagant taste."

"Almost all of them do. There's a preference for young girls among the newer clients. And those who've been around longer tend to be sadists. Some even pay for the luxury of necrophilia."

"And you provide whatever they want?"

"There hasn't been a request I've denied."

I focus on the road, the quiet seeping under my skin. My father holds no shame for his actions. He doesn't care how Luca is now privy to his perversions. But I do. I despise the thought of anyone knowing what this man has done. What my own flesh and blood delights in. "I bet you've earned quite a reputation."

"True." His face breaks out in smug satisfaction. "I like to experience my clients desires firsthand. So whenever there's a new request, I always try it for myself."

I keep my focus out the window. I do everything in my power not to let my expression waiver. I play pretend like a fucking pro, holding my need for revenge so fucking tight all my muscles ache in protest.

I try not to picture his crimes, and fail.

I'm consumed with revulsion.

His sins are a disgusting taint on my mother's memory. So much so that the grief feels like I'm losing her all over again.

"Which brings me back to the conversation I brought up at the house." Luther relaxes into his seat. "Before we dive any deeper into discussions of a partnership, I want to see you with this shiny new toy of yours. I need to make sure you're fit for this lifestyle."

"See me with her?" I can't hold back the disgust from my voice.

"My clients need to trust you. They'll want confirmation you're one of them."

I clench my teeth, my fists, my muscles.

"It's not an issue, is it?" He eyes me with impatience. "We can sort this out today."

"That's not going to happen." My refusal holds too much anger. I can't rein it in.

"What's the harm?"

"The harm?" I grasp for a fucking tactic, scrambling to deflect this bullshit whatever way possible. "As far as I'm concerned, this is a business opportunity. One that shouldn't depend on the way I treat my toys."

"Normally, I would agree." His ageing face tightens with a myriad of wrinkles. "But my recent arrest is a blatant example of why I need likeminded people on my team. I can't risk trusting those who don't believe in my vision."

His vision? Of what? Female slavery?

He's lost his fucking mind.

"You don't trust me?" I seethe. "I didn't need to be a fucking addict to help you run the multi-million-dollar drug empire. Why the hell would you put restrictions on me now? Is this a test? Or maybe an attempt to push me away so you don't feel guilty distancing yourself even more from a family you no longer care about?" I throw the verbal punch as hard as I can, hoping to deflect attention away from Anissa. "Admit you're cutting us off. Have the balls to fucking say your adult children are out of the—"

"Stop being dramatic." He scowls, his lips pinching.

I can't stop. There's no peace to be found in this war zone. All I can do is glare at my father, wondering who the hell he's become.

"My answer is no." I hold his gaze, staring him down. "I don't have to earn your trust or prove myself. If a lifetime of servitude isn't enough, you can drive us straight to the fucking jetty and we'll be on our merry way."

He doesn't respond. Not in words.

Instead, he turns his judgmental focus out the window as Chris continues along narrow streets lined with more expensive houses.

I seethe in silence, my frustration and concern growing the longer I remain in the shrinking space.

My father won't give up. Not easily. He never does.

He'll want another round of negotiations. He won't stop until he gets his prize, which means I have to get Anissa back to the States before he grows tired of asking and transitions into taking.

I should call her and make arrangements for her immediate return home. The pilots are on standby. I can get a boat to pick her up. Hunt could meet her when she lands. He would escort her to my house, where she would stay until I have the opportunity to mold her story into what I need it to be to appease her fellow agents.

The lack of control is the only thing stopping me.

I want to see her board the jet. I don't like the thought of her travelling on her own.

"We're almost there." My father taps on his window, pointing farther along the street to another gated property. "We can discuss this inside."

"No, we're done with this discussion." I mark my line in the sand. "I'm too hungover for this shit. Either tell me to leave or quit with the domineering bullshit."

He smiles at me, the expression far from comforting. "You're right. We'll find another way to prove your loyalty to my clients."

He pulls a cell from his jacket pocket and makes a quick call, telling the person on the other end of the line we've arrived.

The car inches closer, the gates opening on our approach.

The property is a minor-scale version of the place we just left—manicured gardens, oozing extravagance. The only thing lacking is the heightened security. I don't see any cameras and there are no rifle-toting assholes walking the perimeter.

"The women live here?" Luca's scopes our surroundings, checking every angle. "Spreading their legs has to be a small price to pay for all this luxury, right?"

"No. It's cheaper to house the women offsite." My father releases his seat belt. "This place is rented by the night. We're always switching up locations, both with where the assets are held and where we hold our parties."

Chris pulls in behind another expensive SUV and cuts the engine.

"Do we get our guns back now?" I ask. "You said there aren't any women here yet."

"No, but there will be." My father opens his door. "It's best to leave the weapons where they are."

I breathe through my anger. I fucking seethe through each breath as he climbs from the vehicle, Chris following straight after. They head for the house, waiting for us at the front door.

"I don't like this." Luca glances over his shoulder at me. "Something's not right. We should call for a car and get out of here."

I agree. If only the threat of Luther's motives weren't raising the hairs on the back of my neck. I have a feeling running with our tail between our legs might be more dangerous. "Give me half an hour. I need to work out what he's up to."

We get out of the car, the doors being locked seconds after, and make our way to my father's side.

"Everything okay?" His question is probably meant to be filled with concern, but all I hear is suspicion. He's closing in on me. Taking stock of my reactions.

"Other than having the hangover from hell, I'm fine." I approach the front door and pull it wide. "I still haven't eaten. I think I'm going to have to call an early end to this clusterfuck of a meeting and come back tomorrow."

"Don't be ridiculous. The caterers should have already stocked the fridge for tonight. There's plenty to eat in here." My father steps into the house and continues down the hall.

Great.

Fucking great.

Chris passes me as I continue to hold the door.

Then Luca approaches, his silent "what the fuck" loud and clear. He's lost his patience. He lost everything back at the house with the pretty Penny.

I pull the door shut behind us and follow along the hall, heading toward Chris's laughter. A ruckus of conversation builds with each step, but it's not my father and Chris. The other end of the discussion comes from someone else. Another man.

"Is that Robert?" Luca shoots me a glance.

I cock my head to confirm his suspicions.

I guess the asshole wasn't tailing us after all.

"We need to leave," Luca mutters under his breath. "This feels like a trap."

I know it does. Unease crawls over my skin, heightening my awareness.

The laughter continues, the mumbled conversation indecipherable.

"Head back outside," I tell him. "I'll meet you there."

Luca doesn't move. He keeps watching down the hall, waiting, until the sound of a feminine whimper breeches the boisterous amusement.

"Did you hear that?" He stiffens.

"Yeah, I fucking heard it." I jerk my head in the opposite direction. "Go. I'll meet you outside."

The whimper turns to a cry.

"I don't have the restraint for this shit." He clenches his fists. "I'm ready to—"

"Stop," the woman begs. *"Don't."*

That voice. That tone.

Anissa.

I run, leaving Luca in my wake as I make it to the end of the hall to find her standing in the middle of the open living room, Robert's hand clenched around her suit-covered arm.

"What's going on?" I roar.

All eyes turn to me—my father, his men. Worst of all, Nissa.

At one time, I craved her mental torment. I wanted nothing more than to see her undiluted fear. And here it is, the horror intricately laced into her beautiful features, and the sight sickens me.

Her terror threatens to bring me to my knees.

"I said, what the fuck is going on?" I wrench my gaze from her and glare at my father as Luca closes in by my side. "What the fuck do you think you're doing?"

"Calm down." Luther gives me a dismissive glance.

"*Calm down*? You fucking stole from me." I storm forward. "That asshole has two seconds to get his hands off my property before I—"

"Before you what?" Chris blocks my path. "What are you going to do?"

I cock my fist and launch.

I don't think. I don't contemplate.

I send my knuckles into that motherfucker's nose, dropping him to the ground as I heave through panted breaths.

"That's what I'm going to do, asshole." I straighten my suit, trying to rein in the crazy. "If you dare to question me one more time my reaction won't be as kind."

"Cole," my father warns. "Control your temper."

How can I when Robert's continued laughter threatens to send me postal? The son of a bitch still doesn't see me as a threat as he slowly releases his hold on Anissa, his chest vibrating with barely contained laughter.

"You *stole* from me," I repeat.

Luther sighs. "We didn't steal anything. I told you I hoped this woman would help to cement our business agreement. That's the only reason I asked Robert to retrieve her. I didn't anticipate you making a childish refusal to prove yourself."

"That's because he's not like us." Chris spits blood onto the tile and glares as he climbs back to his feet. "It's an act."

"Jesus fucking Christ," Luca mutters over my shoulder. "What's he gotta do? Rape her in front of you?"

Chris pinches his bloodied nose. "Why the hell not? What's stopping him?"

Anissa gasps, the sound of fear almost strong enough to steal my attention. But I won't look at her again. I can't. I'll show my fucking hand if I stare into those eyes. They'll see she's my weakness, if they're not already aware.

"I'm not a fucking dog eager to perform." I work my fingers at my sides, preparing to make another strike. "That sounds more like your style."

"It definitely is." Robert waggles his brows and reaches out, running his hand through her hair. "So let me fuck her instead. You can watch."

My breaths come short and shallow. Every second his fingers touch her opens the floodgates to my rage.

"I'm done with this. We're leaving." I wave a hand at Luca, instructing him to escort Anissa. I still can't look at her. The image in my head is punishing enough. "We're going to take the car. You can pick it up at the port." I turn for the hall, ready to flee like the dog I claimed not to be.

"See? I told you he was a traitor," Chris drawls. "He set you up in Portland. He knew the Feds were making a move. Who's to say he didn't have Richard killed, too?"

Fuck.

I freeze in place.

Today wasn't about a business proposal.

My father is questioning my loyalty. He's testing me—and not my perversions. His sights are set on my obedience.

"You think I betrayed you?" I turn around. "How dare—"

"*Enough.*" Luther straightens to his full height, becoming the threatening tyrant from my childhood. "All I asked for was a show of allegiance. A fucking sign of your commitment to the family business, and you gave me nothing. All I get from you, Cole, are the whispers from people who say you've turned on me."

"Whispers?" I raise my voice. "There are always fucking whispers. You know that as well as I do."

I'm being buried, the heavy weight of dirt compacting on top of me.

I don't know how to find safety. Not for me. Not for Luca. And fuck, definitely not for Anissa.

I have to give my father what he wants—a sign.

A fucking show.

"True." He inclines his head. "But whispers backed up by your refusal only make me question who you've become in my absence."

"You want proof?" I throw my arms wide. "I'll give you fucking proof."

Luca curses under his breath as I storm for Anissa, hating myself with each inch I approach.

I no longer fight my punishment. I can't. I deserve to look into those petrified eyes, the ones that also contain defiance, and a fuckload of hatred.

She clenches her fists at her sides. Her chin hitches in a worthless show of strength.

She's still so fucking strong, staring me down, questioning my motives. There's no hint of her thinking I'll be her savior. There's only loathing and desolation beaming back at me.

I've reclaimed the villain status in her story, and that's okay. I'll pay whatever price necessary to keep air in her lungs.

"I'll show you the hits she's taken at the price of my enjoyment." I stop in front of her and steel myself, straightening my shoulders, tightening my jaw.

I pretend she's nothing.

Not my woman.

Not the air I breathe.

"Here's your fucking proof." I shove the jacket from her shoulders, pushing it from her body to fall to the floor.

But the evidence staring back at me isn't something I inflicted.

The myriad of blacks and blues marring her once milky skin aren't my doing. I didn't create the mottled bruise covering her ribs. Or the scratches along her legs. And not once was my hold against her throat worthy of creating the red marks that perfectly form the imprint of a hand.

The fading proof of rope burns on her wrists are nothing in comparison to the brutality before me.

"Well?" Chris asks. "What are you waiting for? Move out of the fucking way so we can see."

I sneer, sheer menace pulling at my lips as I meet her gaze and wordlessly promise retribution. But the woman staring back at me doesn't resemble the same person from seconds ago.

Those eyes are now glazed, her tears barely bottled.

Her lips tremble. She pleads for help without a word, and all I want to do is slay the fucking world to make this right.

"It looks like I've been outdone." I suck in a breath and force myself to turn away from her. "Here I was thinking I could show you my handiwork, but it's obvious your dog has ruined my masterpiece."

I grab Anissa's wrist and yank her forward, exposing her.

"Holy fuck." Luca's curse doesn't sink in. Nothing breeches my internal battle.

I want their blood.

I want their pain.

I want anything and everything that will strip me of the fucking guilt tearing me from the inside out.

"He laid hands on her." I glare at my father. "What would you do if someone tainted your pretty Penny like this?"

He presses his lips tight, not buying into my anger.

"Answer me," I demand. "Tell me how this is acceptable."

"My concern is *your* actions. Not his."

I'm still losing, the dirt compacting harder to bury me alive.

Anissa's breaths become audible, the tiny pants of panic undoing me.

I'd die to tell her how strong she is. To remind her of the shit she's already lived through. To show her what she looks like through my eyes.

Instead, I step away from her—away from the numbing hitch accompanying her inhales—and approach Luther. A throb builds behind my sternum. It's common sense trying to alert me to an impending mistake, but I have no other choice.

"Do you want to know why I refused to jump through your hoops today?" I get right in his face. "Do you want me to explain why I'm above all this unnecessary bullshit?"

"A legitimate reason is all I'm waiting for, son."

I scoff out a laugh and shake my head. "It's because I've already done a lifetime worth of parlor tricks. And I know how to fucking pre-empt them. I came here looking to join your partnership after already providing my evidence. Dragging this bitch here, abducting her, drugging her, and using her fucking body is my testament."

"We do that shit on the daily," Chris mutters. "It's nothing special."

I hold my father's gaze and swallow over the tightening vise around my chest. "She doesn't look familiar to you?"

Anissa gasps.

She knows where I'm going with this. She understands the risks.

"Should she?" Luther glances behind me, his brow furrowed as he takes her in. "I don't recognize her at all."

"That's a pity. Maybe none of this shit would've happened if you did."

He returns his attention to me, his eyes narrowing. "Who is she?"

"Special Agent Anissa Fox, William Fox's daughter, and one of the arresting agents from Richard's funeral."

"You brought a fucking Fed into the heart of our operation?" Robert asks. "Are you fucking insane?"

"We brought her to an undisclosed island, you fucking piece of shit." Luca stalks toward him. "You assholes are the ones who brought her here."

I ignore the build of their animosity as I continue to stare at my father. I can't read him. I don't know which way he'll swing.

I can only hope—and fucking pray—I've anticipated the correct reaction.

"You're not going to respond?" I growl. "You don't think I knew I'd need to prove my worth to you when I've spent every day of my life doing the same damn thing?"

I backtrack, returning to Anissa's side as my father watches in avid fascination.

"I knew you'd want some type of proof." I grab her wrist and force her to do a spin, flaunting my control. "So I went above and beyond. I put all your men to shame by abducting an FBI agent—a woman who helped to put you behind bars, for fuck's sake."

Nissa yanks her arm from my grip, and I pretend her rejection doesn't stab me through the fucking chest. Out of all the people I'm trying to convince of my sincerity, she isn't one of them.

"You put a lot of thought into this." Luther continues to eye her as he steps forward, reaching out to touch.

"Don't even think about placing hands on her." I block his path. "You don't deserve to play in my league."

He doesn't react. The seconds tick by in painful increments. Then finally, with excruciating lethargy, his lips lift into a grin. "Touché."

"If that's an apology, it's a fucking pathetic one." I glance down at the jacket on the floor, then jut my chin at her. "Put it back on."

"I won't apologize." My father's voice remains strong.

He doesn't need to tell me. I already know from a lifetime of experience.

"But I will admit I'm impressed. I never would've crossed the line to work off William's debt through his daughter."

"I didn't cross anything. The line no longer existed once she helped put you in jail."

He nods. "Again, I'm impressed."

"It's a little late for that." I wait for Anissa to shrug into my overbearing jacket, then grab her wrist. She fights again, trying to yank herself from my grip, slowly killing me in the process. "You can keep your business to yourself. I no longer want a part of it."

"Don't take my actions personally." My father placates me with one of those chastising parental looks. "You know as well as I do it's not smart to ignore rumors."

"Maybe that's true if you're not questioning your own flesh and blood. But you've gone too far this time, old man. You betrayed me. You stole from me. And you let that piece of shit brutalize my property. As far as I'm concerned nothing but a seriously impressive act of apology will undo the damage you've done." I hold out a hand, palm up. "Now, give me the fucking keys to your car. We'll drive ourselves out of here."

24

ANISSA

I'M A HEARTBEAT AWAY FROM HYSTERIA. THE DELIRIUM LOOMS CLOSE, RAMPING UP MY pulse as I wait for either side to crumple.

Cole and his father stare each other down. And Luther's men are just as hostile with their unshakable glares.

Tension crackles in every direction and all I can do is wait for a spark to ignite the situation into a raging inferno.

"The keys," Cole demands.

Luther raises his chin, his nostrils flaring with a deep inhale until finally, he inclines his head. "Chris, hand them over."

Hope builds wings inside my chest, lessening the craziness and smothering my internal screams for revenge.

I want them to pay for what they've done. Someone needs to answer for my injuries. For my humiliation and potent fear.

"*Chris*," Luther warns. "The keys."

The henchman bares his teeth. "If I hand them over, they'll have access to their guns."

What? A sob thickens in my throat. Cole is unarmed? He announced my FBI status without a safety net?

"It's not hard to see where the rumors are coming from." Luca shakes his head. "These assholes would make anyone paranoid."

"These assholes are the ones betraying my father," Cole adds. "Not me."

"This has gotten out of hand." Luther attempts to placate the room by raising his hands in surrender. "Walking away on bad terms won't do either of us any good."

"Then it's up to you to make this right. Fix it."

"How?" Luther grates. "What do you expect me to do?"

Cole laughs, the low grumble vibrating through my chest. His gorgeousness is lost under brutality. The harshness of his features resembles those of the devil. He's a menacing, furious predator.

"I expect you to do what's necessary. What *he* deserves. What you would insist if the situation was reversed."

Nobody breeches the void of silence. Not for long seconds as concerned glances are shared between Chris and Robert.

"Your men don't know their place," Cole continues. "Either show them the error of their ways or consider this the dissolution of our relationship."

Again, Luther remains quiet. He doesn't even change his expression.

It's Luca who breaks the gridlock by stalking to Chris. "Keys. *Now.*"

The unfamiliar man complies, slapping the car fob into Luca's palm. "Safe travels, motherfucker."

"Until we meet again, asshole." Luca turns and stalks for Cole. "Are you ready?"

"Yeah. Let's get the fuck out of here." My protector focuses on his father, his mouth breaking into a sardonic smile. "Make your decision, old man. But realize if Robert is left standing, you're as good as dead to me."

He walks for the hall, dragging me along with him, my feet fumbling as if they're painted on.

"Son—"

"Don't fucking 'son' me." Cole doesn't stop our progression across the room. "Make your choice. I won't wait forever."

Each step we take adds a layer of vulnerability to my precarious position. I don't appreciate having my back to the enemy—not when there's no protection other than the threats of the vigilant defender at my side.

We're all out of our depth. None more so than me.

"Keep moving," he mutters. "Hurry up."

We reach the shadowed hall and I glance over my shoulder to see Luca following right behind.

His focus is intense. Pained.

He pities me. The emotion is potent enough to make my skin crawl.

Fuck those monsters. Fuck them and the ease with which they broke me.

I didn't stand a chance.

Not when I was stranded on an island without a weapon or a chance of escape. I was an easy target, and it's all Cole's fault.

I yank my hand from his grip, earning another dose of pity, this time from the man himself. Those dark eyes hit me even harder than Luca's did, smothering me with their guilt.

"Robert..." Luther's ominous tone carries toward us. "You were out of line."

"Quick." Cole places a hand on my lower back, providing gentle pressure. "We need to get out of here."

The panic returns. The fear and lack of control collide with enough force to have me running for the door.

"You can't be serious." Robert's words are filled with incredulity. "The bitch put up a fight."

The bitch.

Me.

He continues to argue how I deserved what I got, his voice growing animated, his fury escalating.

My own volatile emotions build. Rage curdles among the self-pity and panic. I want to hurt him like he hurt me. To see the horror in his eyes and the shake in his limbs.

"Luther, what the hell are you doing?" Robert raises his voice. "What the fu—"

A bang bursts around me, the noise attacking my ears and reverberating off the walls.

I scream.

And scream.

And scream.

The mania I've been fighting finally takes over.

I lose all grasp on reality. I can't see. Can't hear. Can't think.

A hand clasps over my mouth. An arm is wrapped around my waist.

I'm lifted off the ground and dragged outside into the sunlight while Luca storms ahead, leading the way to a black SUV parked on the pebbled drive.

Cole murmurs in my ear. He says words I don't understand. Soothes me with things that don't make sense until Luca pulls open the back door of the vehicle and I'm guided inside.

The moment Cole releases me, I crumple. I miss his protection as soon as it's gone. I'm exposed and weak without him.

The seconds he takes to climb into the front passenger seat seem like a lifetime spent on the frontlines of a world war.

"What's the plan?" Luca sinks behind the wheel. "What are we doing?"

"You're going to start the fucking car and get us out of here." Cole opens the glove compartment and retrieves two guns, handing one to Luca before placing his own beneath his jacket.

"There's only two of them now. We could take them. We could end—"

"No." Cole slams the glove compartment shut. "Not with her here. I won't risk it."

I want to sob at his conviction. But I won't. I refuse to remain in this weakened state. I'm not a spineless damsel.

What I need to do is tell them I'm okay. I have to side with Luca and make it clear this has to end now. But the words won't form.

"Drive," Cole demands. *"Now."*

My heart lurches as the engine ticks over. Relief tingles its way through my belly with the slow inch of the car creeping forward. The acceleration increases. Going, going.

Then stops.

Luca taps the brakes, his muttered expletive filling the car interior.

I'm hit with another dose of sickening adrenaline, my gaze darting everywhere to seek answers until my focus finds the mini bus pulling into the drive, each window filled with a new nightmare.

Pained eyes stare down at us, the pale faces of female passengers filling me with an emotion far beyond description. There have to be more than twenty women on that bus. Twenty sex slaves, their haunted features tattooing my mind.

They pass slowly as I stare into the dull blue eyes of a woman who can't be older than eighteen. There's concern in her features—concern for me—when I'm the one leaving hell as she's about to enter.

"Move," Cole growls. "Get us to the port."

I shake my head, needing to deny the instruction, but my voice is lost in a deep and consuming void. There's nothing inside me. No conviction. No determination.

I close my eyes as the car rolls forward and all I see is that woman. That *girl*.

She's going to go through far more than the trauma I endured. The things they will do to her… The horrors…

"Stop," my voice is croaky, barely recognizable. Not that my attempt to speak matters. I'm ignored. Nothing changes in the tense interior of the car. Pebbles continue to grate under the slowly turning tires. The engine purrs without pause.

"Cole," I rasp, inching forward in my seat. "We need to go back."

"We can't." His tone is frosty, so damn cold as Luca accelerates onto the road.

Guilt makes me tremble—my arms, my hands, my feet.

How can I escape to find sanctuary when other women are about to endure far worse?

It's not right.

It's beyond redemption.

"We can't leave them behind." I grab Cole's shoulder, demanding attention. "*Please*."

"It's okay." Luca meets my gaze in the rearview. "We'll help them once you're safe. But we need to get you away from here first."

"No." I shake my head. "I can't. Please, Cole."

He doesn't respond. The car doesn't slow.

"Fine." I slide to the door, grab the handle, and shove, flinging the heavy weight wide.

"Jesus. *Fuck*." Luca slams on the brakes, the wheels screeching with the sudden impact.

I don't wait for them to deny me again. Once the car stops, I scramble outside and start running in the direction we came, ignoring the ache from every inch of my brutalized body.

I'll make it back to that house. I don't know what I'll do once I get there, but I'll do something. Anything.

I'll find a phone. I'll contact the embassy.

Rushed footsteps approach behind me. Strong arms engulf my waist. I'm lifted, hauled off the ground and into a hard body.

The restriction is suffocating.

"Don't." I thrash. I beat at the familiar arms enslaving me.

"We can't go back, Niss." Cole's voice brushes my ear, the apologetic tone tearing me to pieces. "You need to listen to me."

"We can't leave them." I kick. I fight.

"You don't think this is fucking killing me, too?" His hold tightens, squeezing me to his chest. "But we can't help them right now. If we go in there guns blazing, we're only going to get them killed."

"No."

No. No. *No.*

I deny him even though logic stabs through me, the truth in his words too brutal to handle.

My eyes burn. Tears consume my vision. I'd rather die than be responsible for their continued torture.

"I'll make this right." He lowers me to the ground and grabs my arms, turning me to face him. "Believe me, Nissa." He continues to hold me, not letting go. "I'll make them fucking pay."

I clench my fists and thump his chest. I fight against myself. I battle the injustice one punch at a time.

"It's okay." He pulls me close, cradling the back of my neck. "We're going to help them. You just need to trust me. But right now, we have to go. I don't want anyone seeing you."

"I don't know how to leave them behind."

"You can." His hands slide away, leaving me empty as he steps back. "And you will. Trust me enough to believe I'll get them out of there."

"Today?"

He winces. "No, but eventually. I need to get you Stateside first. We'll go back to the island, grab our things, then head home where I can work out a better plan with Hunt and Decker."

"That will take days. If not weeks."

"There's no other choice." He grabs my hand and leads me to the car. "Not unless you want to risk some of them dying in a shootout, and that's not something Luca needs on his conscience."

"What about yours?"

A lone brow rises. "You think I've got a conscience?"

"I know you do."

"Then I guess mine has taken enough of a beating today to last a lifetime." He directs me into the back of the car, this time following in beside me. He holds me close against his side as he slams the door shut, then barks an order to get us to the boat.

I can't switch my brain off as we speed through the narrow, winding streets. My stomach roils with shame at every corner. Guilt accompanies every breath. And the worst part is the relief. Every mile we move away from Luther makes me stronger.

It helps when Cole huddles me close, his arm never losing its protective hold as he bundles me against his side.

Yes, in the heat of the moment I blamed him for today, but I'm the one who fought to stay. I begged not to be sent home. I wanted to be here. And I can't pretend I didn't know the risks.

I relax into him, running my hand over his shirt-covered stomach, my fingers brushing his holstered gun.

He stiffens and remains taut.

He doesn't trust me. I guess he has no reason to.

But I trust him.

He could've left me with Luther instead of risking every future opportunity to take his father down. He didn't have to fight for me. He did some crazy shit in an effort to help me escape.

"Your dad could've demanded my death when you announced I was with the FBI."

He strokes my hair, his fingers tangling in the knotted strands. "I know."

The confirmation makes my stomach turn. "You weren't worried?"

"I was fucking petrified."

I close my eyes and wince through the pain in my ribs as I sink farther into his warmth. "He's not going to let you keep a walking, talking liability. At some point, he will want to make sure I'm silenced."

Cole doesn't answer. He doesn't do anything apart from drag his fingers through my hair.

"Cole?" I push back from his chest to look at him, but he doesn't meet my gaze. "He's going to come after me, isn't he?"

"He can try. I won't let him anywhere near you."

The adrenaline rollercoaster reaches another peak. My pulse intensifies. My throat tightens.

"Don't worry." He shoots me a half-hearted grin, his gorgeousness not doing anything to appease my churning insides. "He's going to take stock of what happened today and realize he fucked up. If he has anything planned for you, he won't set the balls rolling until we're long gone."

"Are you sure?"

He drags me back into his side and plants a kiss on my forehead. "You're safe, little fox. I promise I'll get you home in one piece."

25

TORIAN

She lets me guide her from the car and onto the jetty, the jacket huddled close around her chest.

I keep a hand on the low of her back, the touch soft but just as easily construed as threatening if any of my father's vultures are watching. We need to maintain the pretense of her being my captive, which shouldn't be hard when she's as edgy as a beaten snake.

"Are we riding with Amar?" Luca shadows Anissa from the other side. "His boat is still docked."

I nod. "I want the quickest option."

If he didn't have a duffel full of suspect items like bleach, explosives, and wireless detonators back at the house, maybe we could cut and run without this additional trip. Unfortunately, I know how thorough my father will be once I'm gone.

His men will snoop and I don't want to give them more ammo to build their suspicions. Returning to finish this will be hard enough already.

"*Shit.*" Nissa stubs her toe on an unlevelled board and stumbles forward, her jacket billowing open.

"I've got you." I grab her with both arms and haul her upright, positioning myself in front of her to cover her exposed body. "We're almost there." I hike a thumb over my shoulder toward the boat a few yards ahead. "It won't be long, and we'll be out of here."

She cinches the clothing back around her waist and glances in the direction I pointed, her eyes widening.

"That's the boat?" Her gaze cuts to mine, her pupils dilated.

"What's wrong?"

"I can't go on that thing." She jostles her arms from my grip and steps back. "Not again."

Again?

A rumble of a storm builds inside me, dark and thunderous.

"That's how you got here?" I keep my voice low. "You came on Amar's boat?"

She returns her focus over my shoulder, her skin losing the slight tinge of color she only just started to regain as she stares for long moments.

"Anissa?" Luca steps in beside me, facing her head on. "You need to tell us if it was him."

"I don't know who Amar is. But if he's an old Greek piece of shit who delights in the suffering of women, then yes, that's him." She sucks in a deep shuddering breath. "He drove Robert out to get me."

I'll slaughter him.

I'll slit the motherfucker's throat and watch the shark frenzy when I throw him overboard.

"I'll find us another boat." Luca turns in a slow circle, searching our surroundings. "We can—"

"No." I lean toward her until her gaze meets mine. "We're taking Amar's boat."

She blinks at me, confusion and fear accompanying every bat of her lashes.

"It's okay." I return my hand to her back, gently coaxing her forward. "We're going to use this as an opportunity."

"For what?" She frowns. "I don't want to go anywhere near him."

"We're going to get you some closure."

"Let's be honest," Luca drawls. "Revenge is a more accurate description."

Her eyes flare. Her lips part. She stands there for long moments, seeming lost in an internal struggle that keeps the blood drained from her face. All her features become brighter against her ivory skin. Those green irises are more luminous. Her lips are deep red and fucking inviting.

"No." She hugs her arms around her waist. "I can't."

"Can't?" A vicious bite laces my words. That asshole is just as responsible for her injuries as Robert. They both deserve death. "Why not?"

"We need to leave it to the authorities." She raises her chin, her determination returning. "I won't be a part of this."

I itch to shake some sense into her. To grasp her shoulders and rattle that deluded brain of hers.

But she's so fucking fragile.

The woman is glass. One sudden move and she'll shatter.

"What are the local cops going to do?" Luca grates. "And how the fuck do you think you're going to get anywhere near a station to make a statement? If Luther sees you—"

"This is the way we do things." I cut him off, not wanting her spooked by any more threats about my father. "This is our justice system."

She stares back at me with pleading eyes, her internal struggle loud and clear.

Our lack of similarities has never been more apparent. We're worlds apart. Polar opposites.

I've always refused to be shoved into one of her perfectly judged boxes, but when it comes down to it, she's the good and I'm the bad.

She's the light to my dark.

And no matter how much I wish I could give her common ground to cling to, I can't turn my back on giving Amar at least a taste of what he deserves.

She shakes her head. "This isn't me. I won't be responsible. I can't."

"You don't need to do anything." I lean closer so it's just the two of us. "This is my score to settle."

I know she's battling demons. Fighting her nightmares. All while she stands there blinking back at me.

"He's going to be punished regardless," Luca murmurs. "At least if you're here the retaliation will be restrained."

That's true.

If she wasn't with me I'd take my time torturing him. He'd lose fingers and toes. Maybe even his tongue. And he'd deserve it. But I can't do that now. Not with her judgment and disapproval smothering me.

I won't add to her torment.

"What will you do?" Her question is an accusation. "How far will you take this?"

After everything she's been through, she still sees me as the bad guy. It's who I am to her. It's who I'll always be.

A fucking villain.

"How 'bout I go easy on him? Just for you." I don't wait for an answer. My admission of leniency is bad enough without coddling her any more. I grab the crook of her arm and lead her forward, my gaze turning to Luca. "Go ahead and tell him we want to leave. Make sure he knows we're in a hurry."

"I'm on it." He jogs ahead.

"Cole…" Anissa grows taut beneath my touch, the tension growing tighter the closer we get. "I can't do this. I feel…" She splays a hand over her jacket-covered stomach. "It's wrong… I shouldn't… My job…"

"Sorry, little fox. I'm not giving you a choice. He needs to pay."

She stares at me. Stares and stares and fucking stares as she drags her feet as slowly as possible. "I…"

"What? Get it out of your system."

She sighs. "Do you enjoy it? Are you hungry for it?"

Again, she's making me into a monster when all I want to be is her savior. She refuses to understand how the justice system needs to be different in the underworld. We dance to a different rhythm. Sing to our own fucking tune.

"I know you like to believe I'm the devil, Niss, but taking action is a fucking necessity, not the highlight of my day." It's a lie. One I hope she doesn't see for the blatant mistruth it is.

Hurting Amar will be the pinnacle of my week after what he did. My fucking year.

"That's not what I was implying." She winces. "Revenge can cloud your judgment and—"

"I'm not clouded. Not in the slightest. Nobody steals from me, Nissa. Not if they want to live to tell the tale."

We approach the boat where Amar stands behind the wheel, revving the engine to life.

I feel the moment she sights him. Her body revolts. Her breathing quickens.

"You're safe." I glide my hand to her wrist. "He's not going to do anything to you."

"It's not me I'm worried about. I'm just…" She sighs. "I'm strung out on adrenaline and can't think straight."

"Keep quiet, and you'll be fine."

"I know. I won't say another word." She lowers her gaze as I drag her onto the boat. The closer we get to her tormentor, the more she huddles into herself, bowing her head. It's fucking torture to watch her suffer from his toxic presence.

I don't want her to wilt. Not for anyone.

"Mr. Torian," Amar greets me with a grin. "Did you enjoy your visit?"

"Unfortunately, there were complications." I glare, making it clear I'm in no mood to talk. "Just hurry up and get us back to the island."

"Of course." He nods and returns his attention to the wheel to start reversing the boat from the jetty.

I make a show of dragging Anissa to the bench seat and sit her down beside Luca. Once seated, she doesn't raise her focus above waist height. She places her hands in her lap and plays with the quicks on her nails, rubbing them back, over and over.

I stand before her, my feet between hers, our legs brushing. It's strange how much I need the contact. Even the slightest connection reminds me she's okay. And the farther we move into open water, the more I realize she isn't entirely vulnerable.

She sits a little straighter with each passing minute. Her expression grows fierce. She becomes emboldened before my eyes, her lips setting in a thin line, her forehead creasing. And those hands stop fidgeting and turn into clenched fists.

She's gains strength with the isolation, her focus raising to meet mine. "Have you changed your mind?"

"Soon." I curb the need to soothe the growing bruise on her cheek with a delicate brush of my hand. "It won't be long now."

I kid myself into thinking she's growing disappointed with my delay. That she's ditched the cloak of integrity and wants to dabble in the ways of my world.

But my mind isn't creative enough to imagine her as anything less than entirely ethical. She's too virtuous. I doubt she'll ever change, no matter how much I want her to.

"Stay with her." I glance at Luca. "Make sure she's all right."

He nods. "What's the plan?"

I shrug, despite already knowing my actions are going to be mild. I can't stand the thought of her having more confirmation of my satanic status. She despises who I am enough without more evidence to fuel her judgment. "Just watch her, okay?"

"I will."

I step away, her heat vanishing in an instant as I make my way to the helm and mimic Amar's stare across the open expanse of deep blue water. "Do me a favor and kill the engine."

There's a beat of silence. A tense pause.

"Excuse me, Mr. Tor—"

"Kill the fucking engine."

He stiffens, his knuckles turning white with his tightened grip against the wheel. "Sure. No problem." He eases back on the throttle, slowing our movement, then turns off the ignition. "Is something wrong?"

"That's exactly what I hope to find out." I turn to face him, leaning my hip against the cockpit as we bob in open waters. "Is it true you returned to my island this morning and assisted in robbing me?"

He has a "holy shit" moment. One of those brief eye-widening, lip-parting shows of shock which is quickly hidden behind fake confidence.

"No. I drive the boat. Nothing else. I don't steal from you."

"You escorted a thief to and from the island where he committed the crime, making you an accomplice."

"No. I did not know." He holds up his hands. "I thought you sent him. I thought he work for you, Mr. Torian."

I raise a brow. "Really?"

"Yes. *Yes.*" He nods rapidly. "That man, he works for your family. Your father. I thought you send him."

"You thought I sent one of my father's men to retrieve something I could've easily brought on my own? Is that the lie you're going with?"

His eyes bug. "It's no lie. I promise you. No lie at all."

"Do you know what I do to liars?"

"I'm no liar. I swear to you. I would never—"

"How was the woman taken from the island, Amar? Did she willingly walk onto the boat? Was she forced? Was she hurt?"

Panic starts to set in. His hands fidget. His gaze darts to Luca who stares with intent, appraising the situation from his position beside Nissa.

"Answer me," I growl. "Tell me what happened."

"She was sleeping. The man carried her."

"Sleeping?" I chuckle through the rage. "In broad daylight? You must have thought she was a heavy sleeper."

He doesn't respond, not apart from the agitated twitch of his fingers at his sides.

"And what about the other day? What excuse do you have for threatening my property by holding a gun to the woman's head?"

I realize the mistake of my question as soon as the words are out. I've encouraged his attention to stray to Nissa, his gaze narrowing on her.

"Eyes on me." I lash out, grabbing him by the throat, my fingers squeezing tight. "Don't even fucking breathe in her direction if you want to live to see another day."

Her gasp brushes my ears in yet another sign of our differences. Her disgust must be building, yet I revel in the retaliation. The frantic beat of his pulse beneath my fingers is cathartic. Fucking thrilling.

"I mean no disrespect." He clasps his hands in prayer. "Please. I made a mistake."

"You made many." I dig my fingers deeper. "You threatened something of mine. Held a gun to her head. Then you had the audacity to return and help someone steal her from me."

"I was only—"

"*Stealing from me*," I snarl.

He shakes his head. "No. No, sir. I would never—"

"But you did. You drove a thief to my island and stood by, watching him commit the crime. Then you gave him safe passage to Naxos." I inch closer and breathe in the fear ebbing off him. "Do you know what he did to her? Did you know he hit her? Hurt her? Choked her? Now she's damaged goods, Amar."

"I did not know." He bobs those praying hands between us. "I swear I did not know."

I release his throat and watch him stumble backward. "You're not a stupid man. You knew exactly what you were participating in."

He returns his attention to Anissa, his deeply tanned skin growing pale.

"I said, don't fucking look at her." I snatch my gun from the holster and shove it against his forehead.

I itch to pull the trigger. I fucking throb with the need to end his life.

The only thing stopping me is her.

Fucking Anissa and her goddamn morality that hovers over me like a toxic cloud.

"*Please*." Amar lowers to his knees before me, his head bowed. "I have children. Grandchildren. They rely on me."

I keep the barrel aimed on his skull and my mind set on revenge.

I can't let him walk away. He doesn't get to hurt her and then escape unscathed.

"I understand." I suck in a calming breath. "I have people who rely on me, too. Their income is dependent on my success, and that success is dependent on my power. My entire empire would crumple, affecting all those in my employ, if people thought they could get away with disrespecting me."

"I beg of you, have mercy." His eyes glaze, the hint of tears almost sickening me. "I have a daughter. She has three sons. Growing boys. I help them every day. I give them—"

"*Enough*." I can't deal with his sob story. The pathetic weakness only increases my loathing. "You can relax, old man. I'm not going to kill you. You're only going for a swim."

"A swim?"

"That's right." I holster my gun and wave a hand for him to stand. "You steal from me. I steal from you. And this boat seems like the perfect payment."

"Oh, no." He begins to sob. "Please, no."

"Hurry up, Amar." Luca walks toward us. "We don't have time for your crocodile tears."

"No, I won't go. I'll drown. This is murder."

I reclaim my gun, my patience entirely lost, and place the barrel on his temple. "No, this will be murder."

"*Get up.*" Anissa's scream splits the ocean silence as she pushes to her feet. "Swim, you heartless piece of shit."

"Anissa." Luca is the one to warn her of the precarious position she's putting herself in.

I don't say a word.

I keep my mouth shut because the storm of strength she exudes isn't something I'm willing to stifle.

"Get on your feet and fucking swim," she snaps.

Amar looks at me, then Anissa, and back again. But this time, it isn't in fear. His eyes are scrutinizing. Calculating.

"You heard the lady." I jerk my gun skyward. "On your feet. Now."

Finally, he complies, moving like a ninety-year-old as he climbs to his feet instead of the active man he's always been. "You would sentence a grandfather to death for doing his job?"

"I would slit your throat in a heartbeat for far less." I grab his arm and drag him starboard. "You should be grateful I'm being lenient."

"Let me take it from here." Luca joins me, grabbing Amar by the back of the shirt to encourage him to straddle the side of the boat.

"But my shoes. My clothes. Please, let me take them off." The old man attempts to kick off one of his loafers.

"No. Leave them on." I exude sympathy with a feigned smile. "I'm a fair man, Amar. I only want the boat. I wouldn't dare to take anything else from you. Not your clothes or your wallet. Not even your cell. You need to make sure you take it all with you."

He shakes his head, over and over.

I incline mine. "Enjoy the swim."

Luca gives him another shove, sending the man tumbling into the water with a rewarding splash. He bobs in the deep blue and struggles to remain afloat as he kicks off his shoes and maneuvers out of the clothes weighing him down.

Anissa watches every second, her arms crossed over her chest, her face a mix of anger and guilt.

"Want me to get us out of here?" Luca asks.

"Yeah. We don't have time to watch the show."

"I agree. She made her position all the more precarious by throwing her weight around. If Amar makes it ashore and word gets back to Luther that—"

"That I value a toy over the asshole who stole from me?" I shove my gun back inside my jacket. "I'm not afraid to admit her worth is more than Amar's."

"Right," he mutters.

He makes for the cockpit and turns on the ignition while I remain in place, my attention glued to Anissa as she stares at the slow-moving swimmer.

"You spoke up for his benefit, didn't you?" I move toward her, drawn closer by her internal struggle. "Your demands were an attempt to save his life."

"I don't know."

"You're too soft, Anissa."

It's that remarkable softness that has me settling in behind her to wrap my arms around her waist. I let her compassion ease my rage, my thirst for blood dissipating with her warmth.

She gives a slight shake of her head. "That wasn't softness."

"I wasn't going to execute him. I told you I'd be lenient and I was. The old man escaped without a single scratch."

She doesn't respond. She barely breathes as the boat accelerates, gliding over the water's surface to gently rock us back and forward.

"For a second, I thought you were enjoying the power trip."

"Maybe I did." She turns into me, her arms still clinging tight around her waist while she rests her head on my shoulder. "I don't know what I'm feeling anymore. Everything is so heavy."

"You should sit down. The adrenaline is wearing off."

She nods but doesn't move.

"Come on." I slide my hand over her arm and lead her back to her seat. "Sit."

She slumps onto the padded bench and stares up at me. "Will he make it back to shore?"

"Do you want him to?"

She hangs her head.

The show of guilt pummels me. There's no place for it. Not here. Not after what he did. But I need to remember she's not like me. She set up camp on the opposite side of the law and has no plan to cross enemy lines.

"He was born and raised in the Greek islands, Nis." I run a hand through her hair, gently soothing her. "He lives and breathes this ocean. I'm sure he'll be fine." I glide my touch over her jaw to her chin, raising her face to meet my gaze. "Is that what you wanted me to say?"

"I don't know." Her eyes implore me. "Nothing makes sense anymore."

"Your guilt is unjustified."

She shakes her head. "You don't understand."

"I may not be prone to the emotion. But I'm not immune, either. I've made mistakes that haunt me."

"Over what?"

"It doesn't matter." I stroke her jaw, succumbing to her tenderness.

"I don't need details, Cole, I just want a distraction. Tell me a story. Tell me about *you*."

"I don't think you need more ammunition to hate me, do you?"

She winces, her beautiful face changing into a mask of pain. "I don't hate you. I don't think I even understand you. I still don't know why you're doing any of this—fighting your father, taking down a money-making operation—it doesn't make—"

"Because when I was a kid I caught a man raping someone I cared about."

Her expression slackens. "I'm sorry. I didn't mean to pry."

"But you want to understand, right? So let me tell you."

I shouldn't elaborate. It's nothing but pathetic weakness encouraging me to spill my secrets. A blatant desire for her understanding.

"I walked in on the situation too late and had to drag the man off her. But that's where my help stopped. Instead of taking matters into my own hands, I told my father and hoped he would deal with the perpetrator."

"He didn't?"

"At the time, I thought he had. The sick bastard who hurt her disappeared from my life for a while. I knew he was still around, but he wasn't part of the organization like he once was."

"He worked for your family?"

"He *was* family. They all are. Everyone who makes their way into our circle is one of us. Luca. Hunter. Sarah. Even Decker. They may not have the same blood in their veins, but their loyalty makes their bond even stronger."

"What happened to the girl?" She blinks up at me, her eyes holding sympathy I don't deserve.

"I kept watch over her for a long time. I made sure she was doing okay. But it wasn't enough. I told myself she was moving on with her life when in reality she was bottling her anger, letting it fester for years until it became too much and she took revenge into her own hands."

She pulls back, her concern making way for shock.

"I should've dealt with him as soon as it happened. If I'd had the balls to take care of the situation back then, my father wouldn't have found a like-minded deviant. Then maybe they never would've built this empire together."

"Wait?" She frowns "They built it together? But I thought your father and uncle…"

I let the information sink in. The depravity, too.

"Jesus, Cole. It was Richard who raped her?"

"My lineage doesn't leave much hope for me, does it?"

A heave of breath leaves her lips as she sinks her head against my stomach and curls her arms around me. She hugs me tight, as if she's trying to keep the vulnerability wrapped around me, not letting an ounce of the weakness escape.

I return my touch to her hair, stroking the delicate strands. "I'm the cause of all this. One moment of weakness inspired more women to be violated."

"You said you were a kid."

"In body, not in mind. Just like Tobias, the reality of this life has been my constant since I was born. I was raised as an adult. I should've acted like one."

She clings tighter, as if her hold can save my soul. "You're being too hard on your—"

"Don't," I warn. "Don't say another word."

The punishment I live with is nothing in comparison to what I deserve. I let revenge slip through my fingers, and not a day goes by when I don't wish I'd acted differently. Just like I'll probably grow to despise letting Amar free. Because of her. All due to the instability she encourages.

"I'm sorry." Her voice is barely heard over the splash of waves against the hull.

I wish I didn't hear her at all.

"You feel sorry for *me* now?" I chuckle. "Minutes ago you were disgusted by what I wanted to do to Amar."

"I wasn't disgusted." She raises her head, resting her chin on my chest to stare up at me. "And no, I don't feel sorry for you. I'm sorry for the boy who grew up without a mother to soften him and only had a father whose influence never should've been inflicted upon a child."

"Save your pity, little fox. I'm not a kid anymore. I may have spared Amar's life but that was temporary, and only for your sake. Once Luca and I return to Greece without you, the old man will be dead."

Her eyes flare. Her lips part.

I wait for her to yell at me. To demand Amar's life be spared.

But she doesn't say the words. She knows there's no hope of us seeing eye to eye. Not on this.

We will never share common ground. Will never hold similar values.

Will always be at odds with each other.

The slowing of the boat is a welcome reprieve, the island up ahead announcing an end to our conversation.

"Don't worry. This will all be behind you soon." I keep stroking her hair. I commit the texture to memory because I'm well aware these niceties won't return to Portland with us. "You can pretend it never existed."

The engine dies, the forward momentum decreasing as the vessel bobs in the water.

Luca ropes the boat to a pillar, then jumps out onto the pier. "I'm going to start packing. Do you need me to do anything else?"

"No." This time when I meet his gaze, there's no judgment. No disapproval. Only focused determination. "We'll be inside in a minute."

He nods and stalks away, his walk turning into a jog as he reaches the gravel path.

"We should get organized. I need to get in contact with the pilot so we can be placed on the flight schedule asap."

She glances away, her tongue gently sneaking out and moistening her lower lip. But she doesn't move. She remains nestled in front of me, her breathing gentle, her skin soft below my fingers.

"Come on. We've got time for you to have a shower or soak in the bath. It might do you the world of good."

The longer we remain on our own, the more the urge to kiss her drags me under.

The need for possession, the desire to claim, it all builds in my veins.

I tug her to her feet and grow tempted to haul her into my arms. I could carry her inside. She deserves to be held.

"Wait." She drags her hand away. "What happens once we get back to Portland?"

"I don't know yet." I start for the side of the boat, but she doesn't follow.

"I need to know, Cole. Will we be enemies once we get back? Will all this change?"

All this—the lust, the mindlessness. Without the adrenaline to spur the madness, maybe things will be different for her. But I won't leave unscathed.

No matter where I go or who I'm with, Anissa will remain with me. She's fucked with my head. Burrowed deep. She's a chronic illness I'll never overcome.

"Tell me what you're thinking." She inches up to me, placing her hands on my chest. "Because all I can think about right now is being with you."

"That's survival mode kickin' in, sweetheart. You'll get over it."

"Will I?" She leans close, her palms sliding up to my neck. "What if I don't?"

"Then that will make two of us." I press my lips to hers, unable to deny myself.

If she needs a temporary distraction I'll give it to her.

If she needs an outlet, I'm here for that, too.

I grip her hips and grind into her, parting her lips with my tongue. I'm already hard as stone, my lust on a hair-trigger.

I fucking want her.

Now. Tomorrow. Next week.

I want inside her body. In her mind. I itch to claim everything. All the thoughts. All the nightmares.

This woman was made to be mine, my needy little fox.

If only our values weren't worlds apart.

"I need you," she whispers into my mouth, her hands gliding back down to the buttons of my shirt.

"I need you, too." I grip her wrists and pull back. "But we're not doing this here. Not today."

"Why?"

"The first time we fucked, you were drunk. The next time won't be because you're scared and free falling with an adrenaline detox. Tomorrow will be even more of a bitch slap of reality if you do."

"That's not true."

"It's not?" I step back. "You're telling me on any given day back in Portland, you would've fucked me? Why? Because I'm such a nice guy?" I raise a brow, waiting for a denial she can't give. "Admit it, Niss. This is fucked up."

"I don't care."

"Maybe not now, but you will. When you're walking back into the Bureau, wearing one of those ugly-ass pantsuits like it's your shield of morality, you're going to think of this moment and hate yourself."

Her throat works over a heavy swallow, her strength dissipating with the movement. "I still don't care."

"Well, I do. You can hate me for a lot of things, but fucking won't be one of them."

She glances away. Sighs.

Believe me, I hate my restraint more than she does.

But it's her fault. She's rubbing off on me after all, her virtues tainting what could've been the perfect conclusion to a disastrous day.

"Come on." I grab her fingers. "Let's go."

"Wait."

I pause, recognizing a shift in her mood. "What is it this time, sweetheart?"

"I need something from you... Two things, actually."

I turn, finding the lust gone from her features and a glimpse of the determined agent taking its place. "I'm listening."

"For starters, don't ever call me sweetheart again. I'd finally gotten used to the Niss, Nissa, and Nissie that I originally despised, but calling me sweetheart only points out how fragile you think I've become."

"I don't think—"

She holds up a hand and the return of her stubbornness is a relief. No doubt it will soon become a pain in my ass, but for now, it brings me pride.

"Whatever you say, little fox."

She nods in appreciation, her hand falling back to her side. "Now I need you to tell me what you know about my father."

26

TORIAN

I knew this moment would arrive since William Fox was brought up in conversation.

What I didn't anticipate is my compulsion to lie to her.

"Luther said something about you working off my father's debt through me. What does that mean?" She blinks up at me through thick lashes. "And why didn't you say something earlier? All this time my family has owed you money, and you never said a word."

"You owe me nothing. Women and children are never dragged into the mistakes of men."

"What mistakes? What did he do?"

I contemplate hiding the truth. I could even drip feed the information over the passing days. Or weeks. Maybe even months. The ability to hold the insight hostage, ensuring she always has a reason to remain close, isn't beneath me.

"We can discuss your father once we're in the air. We'll have hours without interruption."

"No. I can't wait. After everything that's happened today, I just need…something. I don't care if it's bad news, or information I don't want to hear. I just have to know." She pleads with her eyes, unravelling me one bad habit at a time. "Cole, please."

I waiver between a cruel plan and blatant truth.

I question my motives and the possible benefits.

"I already know he was dirty." She waves off the comment as if its meaningless. "Days after he disappeared, a photo was handed in to the Bureau. It showed him involved in a money exchange with a known criminal. So you're not telling me anything new. I just want to understand the specifics."

There's strength in her tone. Backbone. But she can't hide the pain in her eyes.

I see the emotion clearly. My pretty little fox still wants to believe in a father she doesn't think exists.

"This photo convinced you he was dirty?"

"The photo convinced the entire Bureau. Colleagues he'd worked with for years gave up on him in a heartbeat."

"You didn't answer my question."

She holds my gaze while indecision flickers in her expression. She's considering lying to me. Falsifying the truth to save face.

"You don't want to admit it, do you?" I answer for her. "Despite what everyone says, you're still trying to cling to the man you looked up to as a child."

I understand the compulsion. I've been there myself.

"Just tell me." She refuses to open up to me, keeping herself locked tight. "Confirm it once and for all."

"That he was dirty?" I shake my head. "I can't. Because he wasn't. Not in my opinion."

Her teeth dig into her lower lip, the depth deep enough to cause pain. "Tell me what you know. And don't placate me. I can handle the truth."

"Do you really think I'm the placating type?" I raise a brow, almost insulted by the accusation.

"No. I guess not." She places her hands on my hips, her warmth sinking into me. "Your skills are more focused on manipulation."

The sucker punch hits me without warning. It's another reminder of the vast differences that will always separate us.

"Your dad was in trouble." I hold her focus. "He pissed off some bloodthirsty people and his life was on the line."

I wait for a reaction. Agreement or surprise.

I get neither.

She's locked tight, keeping me from the battle waging war behind those eyes.

"He came to my father asking for help. He had no other option."

"How is that possible? If it was a safety issue, why didn't he go to the Bureau? He would've been offered protective custody."

"He did. And he was."

"Then why the hell would he approach your father?" She hurls the question at me like an accusation. Like a fucking insult. She's climbing aboard her high horse again, sitting tall to look down on me and mine.

"Maybe because your holier-than-thou Bureau only offered *him* protection. As the story goes, they wouldn't budget the expense of protecting you and your mother. Not when you weren't living together. They either didn't believe the severity of the threat, or they didn't fucking care."

She shakes her head, the grooves in her forehead digging deep. "That wouldn't happen."

"You prefer to think your father switched sides than to question your beloved FBI?" I scoff. "Come on, little fox. Don't be naive. They don't give a shit about you.

They never have. You're just another badge—easily replaceable and not worthy of financial support."

"Naive or not, your story doesn't add up. You haven't explained why he would go to your father for help. Or why he was seen giving money to someone your family isn't even tied to."

"I have all the answers you need, but I don't think you're ready to hear them." I grab her hands and lower them to her sides. "We'll finish this later. Go have a long shower. You'll think clearly afterward."

I make for the side of the boat and climb onto the pier.

"No. *Please.*" She scrambles after me, pulling on my jacket. "Just tell me."

"I'm not going to waste my breath when you don't trust me." There's still a wealth of hostility coiled inside her. Her judgment and scrutiny are quick to pounce. "You're committed to seeing everything in black and white. Right and wrong. Good and bad. I can't help you when you're not prepared to listen."

Her fingers cling tighter to my jacket, tugging. "Because it doesn't make sense."

"It makes perfect sense."

"No." She shakes her head. "He could've told me. He could've gone to a security firm—"

"He didn't come to us looking for protection, Nissa."

She stiffens. "The guy my father paid was a hitman?"

"Yes." I palm her cheek and witness the devastation seeping into her soul. "My father respected yours. Apparently, the way your dad conducted himself during the investigation of my mother's death meant he was worthy of help. But that didn't mean Luther wanted to touch a job contracted by a straight-laced agent. Instead, he put in a good word with a reputable contractor. Which wouldn't have been a problem if your dad didn't take off before paying the remainder of his debt."

"He didn't pay?"

"He ghosted as soon as the contracts were fulfilled, which meant my father felt liable for the betrayal and paid the amount owing."

"Why would my father do that? He had to know it would put me and my mother in more danger." She turns rigid, her eyes widening, mouth gaping. "My mother..." She steps back, staring at me in horror. "She was killed in a car accident. The driver fled—"

"Don't go there," I warn. "Whatever happened to her had nothing to do with us. I didn't even know she was dead or that you were a Fed until after Richard's funeral. You weren't on our radar. When it comes to retaliation, women and children are off-limits. They always have been."

"You're kidding, right?" She takes another retreating step, approaching the side of the pier. "Your family has amassed a colony of innocent victims—women and children alike—and you expect me to believe me and my mother were let off scot-free?"

I clench my teeth as she accuses my family of more crimes.

"Are you done?" I glare. "Or is there more blame you'd like to lay at my feet?"

She crosses her arms over her chest, shutting me out.

"Fine." I start walking. "I guess we're done here."

I make it to the end of the wooden planks, the lap of the ocean against rocks the only sound.

"*Wait.*" She rushes toward me. "I know you're not to blame."

"No, you don't. You hold me accountable for my father's actions. Which is fucking ironic when you refuse to be Amar's judge, jury, and executioner even though he dragged you to hell and back." I continue forward, stalking my way along the path. "Yet when it comes to me, there's no hesitation to bang the fucking gavel."

"And I should know better." She moves in front of me, walking backward to keep up. "I've lived with the same scrutiny since my father disappeared."

"Then why do you do it?" I snarl. "Why the fuck do you keep blaming me for what Luther's done?"

She stops, forcing me to do the same. The answer lingers in her eyes. She knows exactly why; she just doesn't want to tell me.

"Fucking say it, Nissa. Why hold back now?"

"Because I want you to be guilty," she admits. "I want a reason to hate you, because then I wouldn't feel the way I do."

"What way?" I snap. "How the fuck do you feel?"

She lowers her gaze.

"How do you feel?" I grab her chin, demanding her attention. "Tell me."

"Confused," she rasps. "I feel completely and utterly confused."

"About me being guilty?" I glare. "Nissa, I'm no knight in shining armor. That's a foregone fucking conclusion. You know that. But I stand apart from my father. I'm not him."

"I'm not talking about Luther." She winces and yanks away from my hold. "I'm confused about how I feel for you. About how I feel when I'm around you."

Fuck.

That's not where I thought this conversation was headed.

Not even close.

She wipes her hands down her face with a sigh. "I shouldn't have said that. See, I'm not thinking straight."

"This type of situation doesn't breed clarity."

"Just tell me one more time. Help me understand what my father did."

I shouldn't. I already regret what I've told her, and tearing open old wounds is the last thing she needs. But again, I can't fucking deny her. "Your father hired a hitman to protect you and your mother. He never worked for my family, Niss. And I'm sure he wouldn't have taken the path he did if the Bureau would've given him the help he needed. But all he did was try to keep you safe. He just didn't have the money to pay for what was done, because that shit don't come cheap."

A weary sigh escapes her. "Okay." She nods, coming to terms with the information while she sweeps the bombshell of her feelings about me under a metaphorical rug. "Thank you."

I keep my distance, not wanting to trigger any more mind-numbing conversation.

I'm done. Fucking drained.

"You need to get ready." I tilt my chin toward the house. "Take a shower. Pack your things. And grab some pain relief for the plane."

Tylenol won't help the heartache, but she's going to need something once the adrenaline clears her system and all that remains is the agony of her injuries.

"Are you coming?"

"Soon." I pull my cell from my jacket pocket. "I need to call the pilot to set the ball rolling."

She nods, seeming entirely defeated. If her expression was a torture technique, I'd spill all my secrets to make her misery stop.

"Go." I jerk my head again. "I'll come and get you when it's time to leave."

"Okay." She continues toward the house, her bare feet crunching on the path.

Relief doesn't come once she's out of sight.

The toxicity in my veins only increases.

For once, I feel like the monster she accuses me of being. The weight behind my convictions grows weak. She's fucking poisoning me.

"Jesus Christ." I swipe a hand through my hair.

I can't have her.

This woman isn't capable of being the docile puppet I need at my side. I don't have time for complications. Or issues of integrity. All I want from a partner is a place to shove my dick, and Anissa is above and beyond that.

Above and fucking beyond.

I keep a hand fisted in my hair as I dial the pilot's number. I clench my teeth as the call is left to ring on a continuous loop until the message service cuts in.

I disconnect and try again, and again, my lack of patience growing with each beat of my pulse.

"Mr. Torian, I'm sorry I missed your—"

"Meet me at the airport as soon as possible. We're leaving. I only need to pack my things and we'll be on our way."

"Sir..."

I close my eyes at the hesitation in his voice. "Thirty minutes, Jefferson. I swear to God, if there's a holdup, heads will roll."

There's a pause.

A blatant issue.

"What is it?" I growl. "How long is it going to take to get us in the air?"

"I'm sorry, sir. It's going to be a while. I'm about to land in Portland. I need to touchdown and refuel. I'm at least fourteen hours away, and that's if I fly straight back."

"You're in Portland?" I clench the cell in my grip. "Why, for the love of fucking God, would you go back there?"

"Your sister, sir. I was told to pick her up. She said you approved the plans."

27

ANISSA

I slowly peel Cole's jacket from my body as if it's a layer of skin. Every muscle aches, each movement making me want to whimper in protest.

The vulnerability accompanying my nudity doesn't help either.

The reminder of being stripped bare to stand before an audience of rapists makes my limbs break out in a toxic shiver. Then there's the evidence of the trauma staring back at me from the mirror, proving how defenseless I'd been.

Reds, purples, and pinks line my neck. My shoulder is puffy and swollen. I'm pale, my cheek bruised, my eyes lifeless.

I'd given Cole the impression I hadn't wanted him to hurt Amar, but that's only because the truth had scared me.

I'd wanted that man punished.

Tortured.

Killed.

I'd craved the sight of his blood. The sound of his screams. The taste of his panic. I didn't experience an ounce of reluctance due to morality.

My pleas were due to fear. Anger etched itself through every one of my nerves, the compulsion for revenge potent enough to frighten the hell out of me.

I still fear it now.

I'm scared of becoming Cole. Of succumbing to this need for revenge that feels more natural than a set of handcuffs, a lengthy court process, and wasted time behind bars.

I'd wanted Amar's humiliation.

My scream for him to swim only came out because I couldn't let the darkness win.

I would've watched his execution without an ounce of disgust, and I would've lost my soul in the process. Instead, I got a taste of what I wanted and disguised it as a reprieve.

Cole still thinks I'm this perfectly intact agent, when death without conviction is all I want for any bastard who makes women feel the way I do—hopeless, helpless, and entirely at the mercy of mad men.

I step into the open shower, turn on the water, and wait for ribbons of steam to inch their delicate fingers toward me.

I breathe in the warmth, dragging the moisture deep into my lungs. The heat needs to fill the hollow space carved into my soul. It has to make me whole again. But it doesn't.

After long minutes I'm still empty. Still broken.

I step under the spray and hope the peppering water will wash away the dirt and grime. Only there's so much filth left behind.

I'm not sure I'll ever be clean.

All the toxins are still there. Coating me. Smothering the light to fill me with darkness.

I can't imagine losing this sickening demand for retaliation. It's as if my body thinks the damage will be healed if I return the evil gift I was given.

I want justice, and for once, I understand that will never come from somewhere that provides shelter, amenities, and three solid meals a day. My perpetrators can't be sentenced and have an end date to their suffering when I don't know if mine will ever stop.

"Oh, God." I close my eyes and raise my face to the heavens.

I'm not this person. I don't want to succumb to the poison.

I *can't*.

I slump against the tiled wall and slide to the floor, every muscle aching in protest.

Water dances over my feet as I bend my knees, hugging my legs to my chest, and bow my head. The falling shower rains over my hair, creating a curtain to shield my face from the world—a world where I turned my back on my own father.

If I'd been the virtuous woman I claimed to be, I would've fought harder to seek the truth about him. I wouldn't have stopped when humiliation seemed like the only option waiting for me on the other side of my investigation.

I should've fought.

I should've clawed.

I should've screamed in the face of all those who took me in with judgmental eyes because they thought the blood flowing through my veins was tainted with criminal genes.

It was the system who failed me. Not the man I should've believed in.

The Bureau betrayed me. Not my father.

My stomach churns, the guilt having a building effect. Heat licks at my eyes, the sting of building tears increasing my anger.

This isn't me either. I'm not a crier.

I'm not weak.

To prove it to myself, I let the onslaught of childhood memories I'd previously disowned come rushing back. I relive the precious moments, allowing the grief to burn inside me.

I remember all those birthdays when he was the first person waiting for me when I left my bedroom. I hear him singing as he cooked dinner, his voice a deep, calming timbre. And I recall the moment that started it all—the day he attended the scene of Cole's mother's murder.

I can imagine my father paying Luther respect for his loss despite them being on opposite sides of the law. He always had a heavy sense of integrity. He wanted to help, not hurt.

He was a good man.

I guess he still is.

I'm the one who's defecting. Failing. And sweating like a pig with all this hot water.

I sit up, the skin on my toes now wrinkled after I disappeared into a black hole of thoughts for too damn long.

Stark eyes meet mine from across the bathroom. My avenging angel sits perched on the elegant white tub, his shoulders drooped in defeat, his lips set in a thin line.

He fills me with conflict. He always has. But I can't deny the connection. The pull.

I'm drawn to him. It's like the cliched moth to a flame. It's so much more than that, too.

He suffuses me with strengthening breaths. With new curious life.

He also punishes and destroys.

He makes me feel whole and empty. Right and wrong. Invigorated and eviscerated all at the same time, with every varying sensation in between.

He showed me the sliding scale of gray when I'd been used to seeing black and white for so long. He's encouraged me to think outside the constraints of what I've been taught. To question everything. To challenge anything.

Now the Anissa I once was is becoming a stranger.

"Do you feel any better?" His eyes turn sympathetic, his comfort attempting to fill the hollow ache inside.

I nod, unwilling to speak and expose any more weakness.

"Good. Are you hungry?"

There's something different about him. Something wary.

His knuckles are white as he clutches the tub on either side of his thighs. His defeat is etched into the very fiber of his being.

"What's wrong?" My voice croaks. "Has something happened?"

"There's been a change of plan. We're not going to leave just yet."

Adrenaline injects itself back among my mix of melancholy and self-loathing. I brace myself to stand, only to have him halt me with the raise of his hands.

"Sit. There's nothing to worry about. Everything is fine. There's been a holdup with the jet. Keira called it back to Portland, but it's returning now."

My breathing increases, the tendrils of steam filling my lungs to the point of suffocation.

"It's okay." He pushes to his feet, discards his suit jacket, and toes off his shoes and socks to walk into the shower. "You're safe." His frame towers above me as water soaks the cuffs of his pants. "It's a slight delay; that's all. We'll leave in the morning."

"Can't we take another jet? Or fly commercial? We can't stay here."

"We'll be fine." He gives a sad smile. A placating, condescending curve of lips. "There's nothing to worry about."

"That's not the impression you gave on the boat. You wanted us out of here as soon as possible."

"Then things changed."

He continues to appease me with a calm facade. I don't buy it. I know our safety is at risk if we remain in Greece.

"Tell me."

He lets out a breath of a laugh. "It's a delay. That's all."

"So why can't we find an alternative?"

Silence.

He doesn't appease me anymore. He just ignores me as those dark blue irises drag me in.

"Cole?"

His jaw tenses. "Because you don't have a passport."

Oh.

I let the information sink deep, the ropes of claustrophobia pulling tight.

I'm the one keeping us captive. Luca and Cole could leave, but I'd have to stay.

"It's okay." He steps closer, his protection bearing down on me as he glides a hand through the soaked mess of my hair. "Like I said before, Luther will take his time stewing over what happened. We'll still be long gone before he decides to make any sort of move to reconcile his actions."

"What if he doesn't want to reconcile? What if he looks into the day we left the States and finds out I came willingly?"

"Then he'll have evidence I used the same tactics he does when abducting women." His touch lowers to my cheek, his thumb wiping away the water droplets. "It's always been his strategy to entice women abroad with offers they can't refuse. I did the exact same."

Yes, he did. He lured me with the promise of justice, and now the concept seems laughable. But none of that dissolves the threat.

"I need a weapon." My voice breaks, my words raspy and weak. "I want a gun."

His thumb continues to stroke my cheek, his comfort sinking marrow-deep. "A gun won't help—"

"Cole, please." I place my hand over his and rise to my feet, standing naked before him. "If I'd had a way to defend myself earlier, I never would've been attacked."

"No, you never would've been attacked if I'd put you on the jet like I promised." He steps closer, the shower spray beating down on his shirt and clinging to his skin. "I don't know how you did it, but you found a way to make me buckle to your demands. That hasn't happened to me before. And it can never happen again. From now on, I'll do what's necessary to protect you, despite your protests."

"I don't want to be protected. I need to be able to look after myself."

"I know. I've figured you out enough to see you don't like relying on anyone.

Not a partner, or friends, or relatives." His hands find my hips, his palms sliding over my waist to my back and pulling me close. "My little fox is a solitary predator."

All my pain and fear dismantles under his touch. The heat from the shower becomes nothing against the burn of his contact.

"I'll get you a gun." He glides his hands lower, cups my ass, and drags me forward, stomach to stomach. "I'll unlock the knives and chemicals, and anything else I tried to keep away from you, too. I'll make sure you feel safe."

There's no room for relief. The hard length of his cock against my abdomen becomes my only focus.

He wants me. Despite his earlier refusal, he needs the connection as much as I do.

"I thought we weren't doing this," I whisper.

"Doing what?"

I close my eyes and shake away the doubt.

I'm not the only one consumed by attraction. I can't be. "You want me, Cole, even though you denied me earlier."

"I denied us both. And that was when I only had to pack our things and get you on the jet. Now we're stuck here, I'm not going to pretend I don't want you when it's all I can think about."

"But what about your speech on this being panic-driven, and a repeat of our first drunken disaster?"

He leans closer, his lips a breath away. "I never said it was a drunken disaster." He lifts me, carrying me backward until the kiss of cool tile brings relief to my smoldering skin. "And you should know my morality is flimsy at best. Those excuses were for you, not me."

He grazes his stubble against my cheek as he speaks into my ear. "They're still valid, though. You fucked me once because you were drunk. And this time, the lust is due to survival instinct. It's up to you whether you succumb."

I already have.

I need him.

Not out of spite or retribution. Not even due to pure lust.

I want him because I've never experienced hunger for common ground with such ravenous ferocity as I do right now. I've never felt this mindless connection for someone and wanted it deepened. I haven't craved understanding—for a man to know all the intricate details of the good, the bad, and the ugly—as much as I do with Cole.

I want more.

I want *everything*.

The yearning is emotional as well as physical.

"I'm not succumbing." I cling to his shoulders and wrap my legs around his waist. "I'm taking what I need."

He pulls back, grinning. "There's my wicked little fox." He grinds into me, the hard steel of his cock igniting tingles through my core. "How the fuck did we end up on opposite teams?"

"Because you picked the wrong side." I glide my hands to the buttons of his shirt, undoing them with restrained patience.

One... Two... Three.

I run my fingers over the mass of exposed muscles.

Four... Five... Six.

I slide the material from his shoulders to fall into a sodden heap on the tile. He lets me look my fill, my fingers learning the grooves of his muscles, my nails scraping the softness of his skin.

He's so gorgeous.

Utterly perfect.

Attraction intoxicates me. I'm consumed with a thickening pulse of anticipation, the beats growing longer, the vibration humming through my limbs.

"Why are we doing this?" I meet his gaze and search for answers I may never find.

"I explained before. For you, this is survival instinct."

He's wrong.

Survival instinct wouldn't have me scrambling to glimpse the future in the hopes we might be together. Survival instinct would be focused on the here and now. Not on my fears of this possibly being our last time together.

"And you?" I whisper over the ache in my throat. "Why are you doing this?"

He holds me steady with his hips and weaves those large hands down my sides, his thumbs brushing the curve of my breasts, then lower, all the way to the inside of my thighs.

"Because I can." He inches those thumbs closer to my sex, inspiring tingles. "And because I have no choice." He parts my folds, the slide exquisite in its softness. "You've become the only drug I crave."

I feel the same way.

It's all I feel.

"Then let's make the most of the chaos." I reach for his belt and fumble with the clasp.

"Here." He grabs my wrists and places them on his shoulders. "Let me do it."

He glides his hands to my hips and steps back, helping me to stand before he makes quick work of his belt and zipper. I can't drag my gaze away as he shoves his pants and underwear to the floor, allowing his cock to escape the confinement.

Every inch of him is hard, none more so than the brag-worthy length pointing between us. He's thick, the veins bulging along his shaft making me salivate.

I want him inside me. I want to have him filling me.

But first I need to taste him.

I fall to my knees, the shower's spray caressing my back as I run my hands around his hips to clasp his ass.

"Niss."

I ignore his attempt at a protest and give his length a tentative swipe with my tongue.

"Shit."

I press my lips to his shaft and smile, loving the sound of his struggle.

His thighs clench with every lick I tease along his cock. A sharp breath escapes him with every swipe across his sensitive head.

I never considered how euphoric it would be to turn such a powerful man into a panting mess. But I'm drunk on his pleasure, my bruises no longer existing, my emotional scars fading to a distant memory.

I clasp my mouth around him, working the intrusion to the back of my throat. I glide back and forth, over and over, one hand still clasping his ass, while I bring the other to grip the base of his cock.

"Fuck." His fingers find my hair and the harsh grip, along with the deep growl from his chest, makes my pussy tingle. "If you keep doing that I'll never let you go."

I close my eyes, wishing it was a possibility even though the thought is entirely foolish.

I suck harder, beating back reality. I twirl intricate patterns with my tongue. I rub my palm along his shaft and sink my nails into his ass.

"Niss." Those fingers dig into my scalp, the pain such a thrilling sensation that my arms break out in goose bumps.

"You need to stop, little fox."

I don't want to.

This needs to last forever. His protection has to remain coiled around me for longer. His strength is a guiding force through this crazy mess of my unrecognizable life.

I don't want to be alone. I can't return to a hollow existence.

"Hey." He steps back, clasping the base of his cock in a tight hold. "What's going on?" He grips my chin, dragging my face upward until I'm enslaved at the sight of those worried eyes. "Tell me what you're thinking."

I'm lost.

I'm scared.

And he's the only one who makes me feel powerful.

"I want you." I close my eyes, fighting the building burn in my vision. "That's all."

He hauls me to my feet, dragging me into his arms to place me back against the wall. "You've got me."

I hold him tight around the neck, circling his hips with my trembling legs. I cling to him, burying my face in his shoulder, my lips against his skin.

"You're better than this, Niss." He pulls back until we're face to face. "You're not weak."

"I know."

"Then snap out of it." He wraps an arm around my shoulder to grip my hair, yanking my head back, exposing my throat. "You're a fucking warrior. And if I hadn't left you vulnerable today, you would've brought Robert and Amar to their knees."

"I know."

"Good," he growls. "Then show me that bitch who likes to wear my balls as a fucking necklace."

A laugh forms in my stomach, not quite big enough to make a sound. "When have I ever worn your balls as a neckless?"

"Since the moment we met." He steals my mouth, attempting to punish me with passion.

Our lips dance. Our tongues tangle.

My nipples ache with the need for more. My pussy pulses, demanding to be filled.

"Don't make me wait," I beg. "Give me what I need."

"Always." He grips his dick from between my thighs and drags the head of his shaft through my slickness.

It's the faintest touch. A mere slide of friction.

I want to combust.

"Cole." I grow impatient, scratching my nails into his shoulder.

"Now, now, Niss. You're a fox, not a fucking cat." He thrusts into me, his cock sinking deep.

I gasp with the harsh jolt, my injuries protesting the ferocity. My ribs burn, the agony sinking into my lungs.

"I hurt you." He stops. He doesn't budge an inch.

"I don't care." I dig my nails into his shoulders. "If you don't keep moving, I'll return the favor."

"There she is." He smirks. "There's my snarky little witch."

I leverage myself against the wall, seeking selfish relief. I grind into him, over and over, while he remains still, peering down at me with devilish eyes. "Give me what I want."

"Or what? You're just going to use me like a piece of meat?" He quirks a brow. "Is that how it's going to be?"

"Maybe."

"I'm not complaining. Just asking." The tilt of his lips increases, the curve incredibly wicked. "I could watch you fucking me like this every damn day for the rest of my life."

I stifle my shock, masking it with a whimper.

He didn't mean what he said. It was a heat-of-the-moment compliment. Of sorts. But the possibility of unending days with this man leaves me breathless.

"What's wrong?" He begins to move, his hips rocking back and forth in teasing thrusts. "Are you tempted by the dark side?"

"No," I lie. "But you could always come to the light."

"You make it sound like a death sentence." He cups the back of my head, keeping his movements smooth as they grow in force. "I could change a lot of things to keep you at my side, but who I am isn't one of them."

"You don't even know who you are. You're not as bad as you claim to be."

"Don't kid yourself. I know exactly who I am." He brushes his lips over my cheek, the caress moving close to my ear. "I know what I want. What I'm capable of. What I'll do if anyone dares to touch me and mine."

He bites my shoulder, then sucks to soothe the sting, over and over, branding my skin with his marks.

"I'd kill for you, little fox." He reclaims my mouth, holding my jaw tight to trap me in place. "I'd die for you."

I shudder.

They're mindless promises in the heat of passion. Exquisite lies. And I believe them regardless.

His devotion becomes a fraudulent truth. His intensity tethers me to my waning strength.

"You could be my queen." He drags his teeth along my neck to my earlobe. "I'd be your fucking slave."

"No." I shake my head, denying his deception. That messed up reality could never exist. There's no future where we're on the same team. Where we wake every morning under the same roof.

There's no possibility of dreamy domestic bliss.

"You're tempted." He nuzzles my cheek. "I know you don't want this to end."

I deny the fantasy any more room in my thoughts. "What I want is for you to make me come."

"I can give you that, too."

He grinds harder, his hand leaving my face to slip between my thighs. He sweeps the pad of his thumb over my clit, and I buck with the resulting frenzy of sensation.

He applies more pressure, eliciting more pleasure, all the while thrusting his cock into me so slowly my walls clamp down around him.

"I want to fuck you so damn hard," he admits.

"Do it."

He presses his forehead to mine. "No. Not today."

There might not be another opportunity. This is all we have. It might be all that's left.

"Do it." I buck into him, making him sink to the hilt.

"*Not. Today,*" he growls. "Fucking you hard is a promise I'll leave for another occasion."

My whimper is the only protest I can give.

I'm close, bliss tingling the tips of my nerves. I jerk my hips harder, making him groan and increasing my own madness. He pumps faster, his thumb pressing harder.

I shake my head, not ready for this to end, but entirely at the mercy of a body that is coasting forward without my approval.

"Clamp your pussy tight, little fox," he murmurs in my ear. "Milk my cock."

I come undone, my back arching, my core fluttering.

I cling to him, our rhythm perfectly synchronized, our panted breaths a mimicked symphony as he moans into my cheek.

The rough grate of his voice grows louder, deeper as we orgasm, the slap of flesh on flesh filling the space around us until eventually, it slows.

We both recede from the bliss together, our bodies slicked with sweat.

"I love how you obey me." His tone holds a hint of humor. "We should do this more often."

I scoff out a derisive laugh. "Let me down."

"Not yet. I'm not finished with you."

I crumple, my head sinking back against the tile, my hands falling to my sides as exhaustion takes over.

He carries me from the shower, our bodies still joined when he places me on the basin counter.

"Be my queen." He issues the command on a whispered breath. I don't doubt his sincerity. "Take over the world with me."

"No." I would give anything to accept his offer. Anything but my soul. And that's the price I'd have to pay.

He chuckles, the sound sinister. *Dark.* Entirely Cole. "It was worth a try." He steals my mouth with a contrasting kiss so heavenly and soft my heart bleeds for more. "Are you sore?"

"You're not that big." I push him away, needing to separate myself from the gentleness threatening to make me weak again.

"That's not what I've been told." He smirks.

"And I bet those compliments came from mafia bunnies striving to be Mrs. Cole Torian."

"Point taken." He opens a cabinet under the counter and retrieves a washcloth to give to me. "Unfortunately, I don't like bunnies. Turns out I prefer ball busters."

"For such a monster, you really are a shameless flirt."

"Guilty as charged." He steps close again, grasping my neck to give me a quick kiss before he walks his naked ass to the door and pulls it wide. "Do you want me to get you some clothes?"

"Yes. Thanks. That would be—"

"*Torian.*" Luca's shout carries into the room.

Cole stiffens, his hand shooting up to warn me to remain in place. "What is it?" he calls back.

"You need to come see this."

28

TORIAN

"Stay in the bathroom." I tug on pants and yank up the zip. "If something happens, get in the panic room."

She nods and scoots from the counter to wrap a towel around her phenomenal body.

I stalk down the hall, not sure what I should expect when I enter the living room, but it sure as hell isn't Luca in the kitchen making sandwiches.

"I need to see this?" I stop at the counter and glare at the food. "You called me out here for ham fucking salad?"

"No." He meets my gaze with mirrored annoyance while he places two sandwich halves on a tray. "Does she look familiar to you?" He dusts his hands on his jeans and slides his cell across the counter to me.

A picture of a brunette stares back from the screen, her dimples deep, pure innocence beaming from her bright smile.

It's the woman from today. My father's slave.

"It's her." Luca grabs the chopping board and throws it at the sink, food scraps and crumbs flying everywhere. "Penelope fucking Decker."

"What about Penny?" Anissa's voice travels from behind me. "What's going on?"

Her padded footsteps approach until she stands at my side, wearing nothing but a fucking towel as she glances down at the cell screen. "That's Sebastian's sister. What are you doing with her picture?"

Luca snatches leftover vegetables from the counter, making his anger evident as he yanks open the fridge door and shoves them inside.

"Cole?" Anissa murmurs. "Has new evidence been found?"

Big green eyes implore me from my periphery as I keep staring at Penny. I can't drag my gaze away from what she used to be—before my father. Before horror tainted her features.

"Has her body been located?"

Luca scoffs out a laugh. "Yeah, you could say that."

"Where?" She glances between us, her scrutiny frantic. "Who found her?"

"We did. She was at my father's house this morning." I shove from the counter, needing space to think.

This situation is impossible. I have to get Nissa out of here when there's no jet. And I can't leave Decker's sister at my father's mercy. I can't betray Keira like that.

I've kept her boyfriend in my inner circle for a reason. He's valuable. He's got enviable loyalty toward family. He's a fucking asset no matter how much I want to deny it. And the worst part is the unwavering devotion he's given my sister.

The two of them will marry. It's a foregone conclusion.

Fuck.

I grind my teeth, unsure how I'm going to stop Luther from tainting Keira's future any more than he already has.

"Cole?" Anissa approaches slowly, her hair dripping water onto her shoulders. "Are you saying she's still alive?"

"Yes. She's still alive. Still being tortured. Still living hell on earth because of my fucking father."

"But she's alive." Her eyes brighten. "That means there's hope."

"Hope for what? A future for her with every mental issue under the sun? And that's if we can get her out."

My father won't give her up willingly. The only way to free her is to instigate war.

"Luther was meant to disappear." I stalk to the window to focus on the long expanse of nothingness. "That way, our allies don't have to pick sides. There's no retaliation. No fucking death and destruction. It was meant to be a simple disappearance."

"It doesn't have to be you," she murmurs. "I could make a call. You can let the authorities—"

"Don't even start that shit with me." I swing back around, glaring at her. "I'll let her die before I involve the fucking Feds."

She straightens, taking the insult with a deep breath. "Then what do we do?"

"*We* do nothing. You're going to get on the jet as soon as it arrives, and in between now and then, I'm going to figure out a way to fix this fucking mess."

Luca carries his tray of sandwiches to the table, dropping the plate to clatter against the wood. "I need a drink."

"No alcohol," I demand. "We have to stay alert."

Anissa starts for the kitchen. "I'll make coffee."

"No." I follow after her. "I'll do it. You need to get some clothes on."

She sucks in another one of those I-want-to-stab-you breaths and pads her bare feet from the room, leaving me to bite back anger, frustration, and fucking guilt.

"Since when did she start feeling comfortable enough to make suggestions?" Luca walks into the kitchen, pulling three mugs from the corner cupboard.

"She wants to help." I start the coffee machine, snatching one of the mugs to place it under the nozzle. "We both know the Feds will never be involved."

"Do we?"

I pause and grip the counter. I don't need to be questioned. Not now. "If you've got something to say, spit it the fuck out. I don't have time for you to pussyfoot around shit."

"I'm just wondering if you're going to switch sides."

My pulse quickens, my annoyance becoming a bubbling threat in my chest. "For your sake, I'm going to pretend I didn't hear that." I turn to him, cocking my hip against the cupboard. "And if we're going to start questioning motives, why don't you start by explaining what the hell you did to cause Decker's sister to risk her life by slapping you? Did the thought of an easy lay become too tempting?"

"Fuck you."

I raise a brow. "It's fun being insulted by idiotic questions, isn't it? If you don't know me by now, you should fucking leave." I jerk my chin toward the door. "God knows I've been doing this shit a hell of a lot longer than you."

The muscles along his jaw flex. "I tried to let her know I was there to help. But that isn't fucking easy when I couldn't say anything incriminating. I didn't know who was listening, and as it was, your little snitch of a brother overheard every word."

"What did you say to make her lash out?" I open drawers, pulling out medicine bottles, popping two Advil while I search for something to help Anissa's recovery.

"I don't know. I was speaking in fucking riddles. The only information I could think to use were references to her life back home with Decker. Clearly, she didn't like the reminder."

"That's all it took?"

"That's all it fucking took. I mentioned her brother, and she went from meek kitten to crouching tiger in seconds."

"So even if we do make a move to break her out, she's not going to trust either of us?"

He shrugs, his jaw still tight. "I don't know."

Christ.

The coffee gurgles into the first mug while I prepare a caffeine-free alternative for Anissa. It's going to be hard enough for her to sleep tonight with the nightmares waiting to take over.

Once all three mugs are filled, I slide Luca's along the counter toward him. "Here. Go have something to eat. We need to be on top of our game."

"I thought there was nothing to worry about?" Anissa returns to the living room, her hair towel-ruffled, her loose tank and sports shorts crinkled. "You said Luther wouldn't make a move so soon."

I lied.

I fucking bluffed my ass off hoping she would breathe a little easier.

"You think he's going to come out here, don't you?" She continues to the table and takes a sandwich from the tray. "What will he do?"

"The likelihood of him coming here before morning is slim." Luca takes the hit, stealing her attention. "That doesn't mean we won't prepare for every possible situation."

I grab the remaining mugs and take them to the table, sliding hers in front of her and holding tight until she meets my gaze. "You need to eat, then get some rest. Don't worry about anything other than letting your injuries heal."

"And what about Penny? I can't forget she's here." She takes small bites of sandwich, chewing slowly. "I've known about her disappearance for a long time. I was one of the first to hear about the DNA the Greek police found at a mass grave. I saw her teeth. There were clumps of her hair. I was invested in her case, Cole."

"I'm invested, too," I growl. "I'm well aware she's likely to become Keira's sister-in-law. As far as I'm concerned, she's family. But that doesn't mean I'm going to ignore the risks. I'll get her out when the time is right."

"Then you need to call Sebastian." She takes a sip from her mug. "He needs to know."

I huff out a tiny fraction of my overbearing frustration and take a seat beside her. "*Eat.*"

"Why do you even care about Decker?" Luca scowls at her. "He hates you."

"He has reason to hate me. But it doesn't mean I want his sister to remain a prisoner. Everything he's ever done has been for her."

"He'll find out soon enough," I grate. "Until then, I don't need any more distractions."

She sucks in a deep breath and takes another sip, her nose scrunching with the gulp. "What type of coffee is this?"

Great. Just what I fucking need—a woman who can sniff out an imposter.

"Yours is decaf," I admit.

She gives me a look of incredulity. "Why?"

"You don't need to be wired. You need rest."

"I think I can make up my own mind." She shoves to her feet. "Thank you very much."

An ache forms under my sternum. I'm close to snapping. So fucking close.

I place a hand over her mug before she can think to throw the contents down the sink. "Sit."

Tension crackles to life between us, our adamant pride colliding.

"I'm not a dog to be ordered around, Cole."

I incline my head. "But you also haven't shown the necessary loyalty to hold a seat at this table, yet here you are, gaining insight into topics you shouldn't be privy to."

"So you're telling me I need to drink decaf if I want to remain at this table?" She scoffs. "That's ridiculous."

"No. I'm reminding you I'll do whatever it takes to protect you, and if that includes making you rest when you're determined not to let your wounds heal, then so be it." I slide my hand back to my mug. "Now sit. And drink the fucking coffee."

She remains in place.

My stubborn little fox is loath to succumb and too determined to walk away from the information loop.

"We're going to continue with the schedule as normal." I meet Luca's gaze and pretend she's not seething beside me. "Once the jet arrives, we'll go back to Portland to regroup."

"We're going to leave Penny here?" He shakes his head. "Are you kidding? What would you do if that was Keira, and Decker made the call to leave her behind?"

I'd kill him.

I'd fucking gut the bastard and leave his corpse to rot in the sun.

But we're not talking about Keira.

If there's any hint I've killed my father, the ensuing unrest would cause havoc. I wouldn't be trusted. Rumors are fine. There's always gossip and speculation, but proof is an entirely different matter.

I can't be seen attacking Luther.

I can only play into his disappearance and dismantle his operation afterward.

"All it would take is a phone call to the Bureau and we'd have help within hours." Anissa slumps into her seat and takes a juvenile slurp of her coffee, the sound a conniving taunt. "If you weren't so stubborn you'd realize it's a viable option."

I'm not going to argue with her again. I'm done.

We're all tired. None more so than her.

I keep my mouth shut as we all fall into uncomfortable silence.

Luca slinks low in his chair and stares into space. Anissa does the same as she alternates between taking bites of a sandwich and less-provoking gulps of coffee.

No matter how hard I try, I can't see a way out. Not without risking everything.

"You can't call Luther and work out some sort of deal?" Luca keeps his focus across the room. "Is there anything he would trade for the girl?"

"No. You heard him; Penny is his prized possession. He's not going to give her up."

"What about me?" Anissa places her empty mug on the table. "Would he trade her for an FBI agent?"

Both of them look to me for a confirmation I'd never fucking give. "No."

"You didn't even consider the possibility." She pleads for understanding with the long bat of her lashes. "I'm sure there'd have to be some interest if you continued to work the angle of using me to pay off my father's debt."

"Are you insane?"

I know she's tired. Her exhaustion is clear in the dark bags forming under her eyes and the loose slump of her shoulders. But even if she was on her death bed, she would have to realize I'd never use her. Not like that.

"But what if we didn't actually do the exchange?" Luca sits forward. "It's a way to bring him out here, on our turf, so we can end this the way we planned."

I bare my teeth. "Don't make me repeat myself."

Anissa sighs and Luca collapses back into his seat, the silence returning as the sun slowly sets to bathe the room in darkness.

We sit in the shadows for too damn long, the quiet stretching until Anissa pushes from her chair to turn on the light. She drags her feet, her face ashen.

I puff out a breath of frustration. "You need to get some rest."

"Yeah." Luca frowns at her. "You look like shit."

"Thanks." She returns to her seat, leaning on an elbow to cradle her face. "That's what every woman wants to hear."

"He's right." I stack our plates and grab her mug to take them to the sink. "Your body needs to heal."

"I'm fine. Just tired, that's all."

"It wasn't a suggestion." I walk back to the table and pull out her chair. "Come on. I'll walk you to bed."

"I can sleep once we've decided on a plan."

"You're not deciding anything." I tilt her chair forward, forcing her to stand. "I'm the one who will figure out what's going to happen." I hold out a hand which she refuses to take.

"I don't need a chaperone." She walks for the hall, her posture slouched.

"Fucking hell." I scrub both hands down my face, then meet Luca's unimpressed stare. "I'll be back in a minute."

He nods. "I'm going to make more coffee."

I stalk after her, catching up as she reaches her door. "Sleep in my bed."

"No, thank you." She grabs the handle and plunges the lever.

"My bed, Nissa." I close in behind her, wrapping an arm around her waist before she can escape inside.

She stiffens, growing inches with her annoyance.

"I won't apologize for protecting you," I murmur in her ear. "You need time to recover." I press into her, breathing in her anger. "And you'll do it in my bed. Either now, or when I carry you there later."

She shudders, her entire body responding to me. "Don't be an asshole."

"I'll be whatever I have to be. Just for you, sweetie."

She turns into my chest, her eyes narrowed to spiteful slits. "You know I hate when you call me that."

"Then let me take you to my room, and I won't have to resort to any more dirty tactics."

"I'm too tired for this, Cole." She wiggles from my embrace, wincing with the movement. "I just want to crash."

"That's okay." I scoop her into my arms and expect a protest that doesn't come.

Instead, she sighs and nestles into me, her head falling onto my shoulder. She's not merely exhausted. She's barely able to function.

"I should've taken you to a doctor." I walk us to my room, kicking the door wide with my foot.

"I feel okay. I just can't keep my eyes open."

I settle her on the bed and turn on the lamp to pull the covers out from beneath her. "Things will be better in the morning."

It's a lie. We both know it. And I'm thankful she's too tired to call me on it.

She nestles onto her side, her blinks becoming longer and longer.

"Before you pass out, I've got something for you." I retreat to the walk-in robe and open the safe hidden behind the same wall of clothes concealing the entry to the panic room. After a four-digit pin-code entry, I retrieve a pistol from the stash of weapons and make my way back to her.

"Here." I hand over the gun.

She sits up, blinking away some of the lethargy. "You're letting me have this?"

"You said you wanted one."

"Yeah. I just didn't think you'd allow it." She nibbles her lower lip, trekking her attention over the weapon as she tilts it back and forth. "Which is kind of a shame, because I was hating you just fine until now."

"You didn't give me much choice. It turns out I don't like you hating me all that much."

"Then maybe you should stop being a dick."

I grin. "I wouldn't hold your breath." I reach for the weapon and release the clip to show her the bullets. "It's fully loaded. So be fucking careful, okay? No pulling it out when something hard rubs up against you later."

She rolls her eyes and slinks under the sheet, sliding the pistol under her pillow. "You better believe I will."

"You wouldn't do that to me. You love my cock too much."

"With my current level of annoyance, I'd shoot you in a heartbeat."

I chuckle and lean forward to steal a kiss.

She grumbles for a brief second but those sultry lips still part beneath mine. "Get out of here."

"I'm going." I backtrack. "But I'll be back later."

I walk for the door, the rustle of sheets following me.

"Cole?"

I stop in the hall and glance over my shoulder. The sight of her in my bed is too fucking natural. Like she's meant to be there. "Hmm?"

"No matter how much I think about it, I still can't picture you killing your own father. I don't want to believe you can do it."

There's that inescapable divide again. The one thing standing between us.

"Who knows? Maybe I can't."

Her brows pull tight. "Are you questioning yourself? Are you thinking you can't go through with it?"

"I'm thinking only time will tell. Now get some rest." I trudge into the living room, trying to ignore how things will change between us once I take Luther down.

She'll see me differently. Worse than ever before. And there's nothing I can do about it.

"How'd you do?" Luca asks from the table.

"She passed out before her head hit the pillow." I reclaim my seat and latch onto the freshly topped mug of coffee.

"Did she figure out you sedated her?"

"Not yet." I grab a sandwich and sink my teeth into the stale bread. "But I'm sure she will."

He copies what I do. Bite for bite. Drink for drink. "You like her, don't you?"

"Jesus Christ." I contemplate lying. Or denying an answer. Both would work as well as pleading the fifth. "She's an indulgence."

"Is that all?"

I ignore him and take a larger bite, filling my mouth to capacity.

"You let Amar jump from the boat without so much as a fucking bruise when I've heard you make an execution order for far less."

I take another bite. "Would you have preferred if I made you an accomplice to murder right in front of a Fed?"

"You were going to do it with Luther. Why was Amar different, apart from Anissa making it clear she didn't want you to kill him?" He leans back in his chair, relaxed. "You drugged her. Abducted her. Made unending demands of her. Yet you're worried murder is crossing the line? That excuse is bullshit, and a clear attempt to hide the fact she has your balls tightly grasped in her fist."

"I'd be careful where you take this conversation. My patience is threadbare."

"I never said it was a bad thing," he mutters. "Only something I hope you're conscious of."

I'm fucking conscious. Her hold over me hasn't left the forefront of my mind since she came into my life.

"Do you think it was a smart move to sedate her considering the looming threat?"

I sedated her *because* of the threat. "I gather I'm not the only one who thinks Luther isn't done with us."

"You made demands of him today. Whether he's your father or not, I think he's going to want to do something to save face."

"Well, whether he does or doesn't, it's best for her if she sleeps through it. If he comes here, I'll put her in the panic room."

"And if we're gunned down and unable to save her?"

"Then I'm going to hope like hell nobody finds where she is until Hunt and Decker arrive."

Luca straightens and leans forward, his elbows pressed to the table. "They're on their way?"

"I assume so. The pilot said my sister made travel arrangements for herself and three others. It doesn't take a genius to figure out Hunt and Decker are behind the jet's disappearance."

"It couldn't be Layla and Benji?"

"They wouldn't risk bringing Stella here, and Keira is the only person they trust to look after their kid. It has to be Deck, Hunt, and Sarah."

"Which will bring even more issues."

"Yep." If Decker shows up here, I'll have to tell him about Penny. Then all hell will break loose, and we'll have a madman on our hands—someone unlikely to think rationally about danger when his sights will be set on rescuing his sister.

"But," Luca continues, "with seven of us able to work together, maybe we could finish this."

"If we don't get ambushed between now and then."

"Yeah." He sighs. "That's a big if."

He's more adamant of the danger than I am, which doesn't sit well with me.

I'd like to think I know my father better than anyone. Only problem is, my head is now clouded with worry for my FBI agent.

"Why don't you go get some sleep?" He yawns and stretches his neck from side to side. "Rest while you can."

"There's no way I can switch off right now. You go." I jerk my chin at him. "I'll take first watch."

"You sure?"

"Yeah." I deserve to spend more time thinking about what I dragged Anissa into. I need to let that shit percolate as long as possible to get a full dose of punishment.

"Call out when you want to switch." He pushes from the table and walks across the room, leaving me alone with my regret.

"Luca." I focus on him as he reaches the hall. "Before you go, tell me why you think Luther is likely to come out here. Do you anticipate he'll want to make amends or will he want to drag me over the coals for calling him out on his bullshit?"

"I think it's neither." His expression becomes bleak. "If he comes out here, my bet is that it's for Anissa."

Dread slithers its insidious fingers down my spine. "Why?"

"Because she intrigued him enough to get one of his men to take her away from you. Then you went and told him she was a Fed, and the daughter of someone who owed him a stack of money. And whether it was from liking her as a person or a possession, you made it fucking clear you would guard her with your life."

Then I made demands for him to punish the prick who dared to touch her.

I encouraged Luther's interest with every single one of my reactions.

Fuck.

"Honestly, Cole, if Luther comes out here, I'm not worried about us. My concern will only be for her."

29

TORIAN

I didn't sleep.

Caffeine, the threat of my father, and the fact I stayed in bed until lunch had me powering through until the early morning hours.

I spend my time trying to ignore what has to be done—I have to say goodbye to Nissa.

She needs to return to Portland while I stay to finish what I started, and secure Penny's freedom along the way.

Problem is, I don't want to say goodbye.

For starters, Anissa needs to be watched. For her protection as well as mine.

Secondly, I'm not ready to let her go.

I need more time to… I don't know. I just need more time.

But I don't have any. The sun is about to rise, meaning the jet should be here soon.

"Why the hell didn't you wake me?" Luca slinks into the living room in jeans and a T-shirt, squinting as he scratches the top of his head with the butt of his gun.

"I had no chance of sleeping. I thought you might as well get the rest."

"What about Anissa? Is she still knocked out?"

"Yeah. I've checked on her a few times, but the sedatives are working wonders." I push from the dining table and head for the kitchen. "Coffee?"

"Fuck, yes. Make it strong." He slides onto a stool at the island counter, placing his gun in front of him. "Any word from Luther?"

"Nope. I'm starting to think I'm going to have to figure out a plan to get him back here."

His brows tighten. "So, we're staying?"

"Yeah."

"And Anissa?"

I grab two mugs from the dishwasher and start the coffee machine. "I'm sending her home."

He doesn't respond.

I don't look to him for answers. I don't need his opinion. I don't want the questioning stare he gives me when I slide his steaming mug of java across the counter.

"I've already packed her things. They're in a duffel at the door. All I have to do is get her to the airport."

"When are we doing that?"

"Soon." I check my watch. "I called the pilot for an update a few hours ago. They shouldn't be too far away. But once I finish my coffee I'll call again to confirm."

"What's the plan after that?" He palms his mug and takes a sip. "Did you decide what to do about Penny?"

I pretend not to notice his invested interest.

One conversation and a slap across the face, and the guy is fully absorbed in her rescue.

"Once Hunt and Deck arrive, we'll chat it out together. Like you said, if it were my sister, I'd kill anyone who didn't put their life on the line to save her. So, for the sake of Keira and her bad taste in men, I'm going to have an open discussion about the options."

"That's more than fair."

"And if Decker can't keep a cool head, I'll contain him however necessary. But at least I'll have given him the choice."

He nods. "I wouldn't expect anything less."

Good, because that's the extent of my generosity.

Decker will be a fucking nightmare once he finds out his sister is alive, but I can admit he deserves to know.

"On second thought, I'm going to make the call now and speak to Hunt." I push from the cupboards. "It will be better if one of them isn't blindsided."

I snatch my cell from the counter and walk outside into the barely dawning light, not wanting to wake Anissa.

Like yesterday, my call isn't answered. I'm left to listen to the ongoing dial tone.

I try again and this time something else accompanies the ringing.

There's a faint hint of added noise. A hum.

I disconnect the call and hold still, listening to the whir of sound in the distance.

It's almost negligible. But it's there. Approaching.

I stalk back to the door and shove my head inside. "Luc, come out here for a sec."

He slides from his stool and strides toward me. "What is it?"

"Listen."

He cocks his head. "Do you think it's a boat?"

"I'm sure it is."

"Keira?"

"I doubt it." Something uncomfortable builds in my chest. A bad feeling. Maybe I'm being paranoid. Or trying to delay sending Anissa home. But I don't think so. I shouldn't have tried to convince myself the passing hours were my first stroke of good luck. Luther always knows when to turn up at the worst possible moment.

"It could be a fishing boat, but I'll check it out." Luca jogs for the path, fast disappearing behind the vegetation.

I remain in place, contemplating whether to go after him.

I should wake Anissa. And I also shouldn't leave Luc on the jetty without protection. It didn't skip my attention he ran off without his fucking gun.

"Shit." I slide my hand inside my jacket and touch my pistol for confirmation before I stalk for the path, striding out the distance as the noise approaches.

It isn't hard to find the boat with its bright light illuminating the inky black water. I don't divert my attention as I walk onto the pier, trying to determine who's onboard.

"For confirmation, if this is Luther we're ending this, right?" Luca turns to me. "And if it's Keira, we're taking Anissa straight to the airport?"

"Exactly."

He nods. "Can you see who's behind the wheel?"

"I can't see a damn thing." The slight glow from the approaching sunrise isn't enough to dilute the headlight. The back of the boat remains hidden in differing shades of darkness.

"*Look.*" He shoots me a grin. "There's a woman. Port-side."

I squint, seeing the silhouette of a slim figure. Seconds later, I make out the long hair billowing in the breeze.

My bad vibe intensifies. The reality of saying goodbye to my little fox hits me with full force. This fun-filled adventure with her is over. Once she gets to Portland, I'll be nothing but a bad memory.

"Go wake her." I jerk my head toward the house. "Tell Anissa she's got two minutes to get down here because she's getting on this boat as soon as it stops."

"You got it."

"And next time, don't go anywhere without your fucking gun."

His brows snap tight. "Shit. I—"

"Never again," I warn.

He nods and jogs for the house as I turn toward the approaching boat.

This is it. The end. The moment where I stop tormenting someone who turned out to be more than I expected.

More bright.

More determined and admirable.

More fucking woman.

I never should've brought her here. My excuses for the abduction were messed up to begin with, when in reality, I think I only dragged her here because of my addiction.

I spent so long following her it became impossible to stop.

But I risked her safety. I stole her freedom. And I deserve to fry for her injuries.

Maybe she'll ensure I do.

I move to the end of the pier, preparing to help moor the boat in place opposite Amar's when the outline of the woman's silhouette becomes crisp.

Her frame is thinner than I thought. The free-flowing hair is longer.

I don't drag my attention away. I don't even blink as her features come into view—the shadowed face of misery, the eyes narrowed with spite.

It's not Keira.

Shit.

It's Penny, with Tobias nestled against her hip.

"Luca," I shout toward the house. *"Luc, it's not her."*

I can't hear a response over the approaching roar of the boat.

I'm stuck.

Fuck.

I won't run and show my surprise. I refuse to let my father think he has the upper hand. All I can do is straighten my shoulders and face him head-on as Chris cuts the engine and the vessel bobs into place.

"What are you doing here?" I cross my arms over my chest, strategically nestling my fingers close to my holstered gun.

"Morning, son." My father holds out his palm to help Penny from the boat, her loose black blouse waving in the slight breeze. "We need to talk."

"And if I'm not interested?" Obviously, I am. Despite my concern over Luca dragging Anissa back into the thick of this, I'm done waiting.

This shit ends now.

"I've already lost a brother." Luther continues his gentlemanly act, helping the kid disembark. "I can't live through losing a son."

I give a bitter laugh.

That's not why he's here.

Luca was right.

I showed my hand yesterday. I let this asshole know how important Nissa is to me, and after I made light of taking Penny from him, it's clear he wants to prove how easy it is to take what's mine.

He needs to reassert his power.

"We're unarmed." He steps onto the jetty and flicks open his jacket, exposing shadows beneath. "Feel free to pat us down if you like."

Now he's adding a game of chicken, daring me to refuse the offer.

"Thanks." I bet he thinks my pride will get in the way of checking him for weapons. At one time, it would've. But I can't be self-serving anymore. I refuse to let Anissa get hurt again.

I walk toward him, a smile stretching my lips as I skim my touch over his arms, waist, back, and legs. I check everywhere and come up empty.

He's clean.

Confusingly vulnerable.

"I've never known you to go anywhere unarmed, old man."

He inclines his head. "And Chris is as well. It's a show of good faith. I'm here to apologize."

"I'll believe that once I check him, too." I motion for Chris to get off the boat and then follow the same routine, checking his arms, waist, back, and legs.

He snickers as I pat his ankles. "While you're on your knees..."

I rage against my pride. I fucking battle self-control when all I want to do is slit this asshole's throat.

"Don't start," my father growls. "Cole, an apology isn't the only reason I'm here. We need to have an important conversation that should've happened a long time ago."

I stand and take a backward step, placing necessary space between us. "If you came to talk, why did you bring a woman and child as a shield?"

"A shield?" He balks. "Do I need one against my own son? Because I brought her here as a peace offering. The woman is yours."

He pushes Penny toward me, her spine snapping ramrod as she stumbles forward.

No. This isn't right.

There's an ulterior motive to his submission.

He must have found out why I want her, and now he's dangling success in front of me.

"You're handing her over?" I scrutinize the woman's face, seeing the undiluted panic in her eyes. She's filled with fear. More so than yesterday. I don't know if that means she's truly panicked over being handed over, or if there's a bigger picture sparking her horror.

Either way, I guess it doesn't matter.

They're unarmed and I'm sick of second-guessing his intent. I reach into my jacket, no longer willing to play a role.

"Cole, I need you to listen. There's something I have to tell you. It involves you and your sisters."

I pause, my fingers brushing the grip of my pistol.

He's triggered the only thing capable of making me hesitate. The only fucking thing.

"What about my sisters?" I return my hand to my side, granting him a temporary reprieve.

"Can we at least sit inside? The boy is tired."

I scoff. "Probably because you brought him out here when he should be in bed."

"Well, I couldn't sleep after yesterday, and there's something on my mind that can't wait."

"Fine." He might think he's manipulating me, but being inside works in my favor. I'll have an extra gun on my side. Two if I count Nissa's. "Go ahead." I indicate for them to start walking.

"Penny." Luther does the same, instructing her to lead the way. "You first, my sweet."

She complies, holding out a hand for Tobias to join her.

Chris continues a step behind, then my father starts his progression, stopping a few feet later to glance at me over his shoulder. "Are you coming?"

"Of course. I wouldn't miss this for the world." I lag back, not getting within arm's reach for the duration of our friendly stroll.

Chris remains quiet. Penny maintains her stiff posture, while the kid is skittish, anxiously clinging to her hand. None of them act any different than I would expect. Tobias is always a few breaths short of a panic attack, and the woman has every reason to be rigid.

There's nothing out of the ordinary. No hint of betrayal as Penny reaches the glass sliding door and stops to await instruction.

"Go." Luther shoos her forward. "Get inside."

"Wait." I claim control, deliberately throwing my weight around. "You, the woman, and the kid can go inside, but your dog isn't welcome."

My father bristles, a few heartbeats passing before he nods. "Whatever you say."

I don't understand the compliance. I refuse to believe yesterday triggered the respect I've always struggled to earn. He shouldn't feel comfortable being separated from his thug-for-hire. Not unless he truly is here to talk.

"I guess I'll stay here then." Chris steps out of my way. "Just so you can feel like more of a man for keeping me outside."

I clap him on the shoulder as I pass. "If I were you, I wouldn't forget your best buddy ate lead yesterday because of me."

"Don't worry. I'll never forget."

"Good." I follow everyone inside, locking the door behind me and sliding the sheer curtain across to block his view.

Luther has already claimed the recliner, while Penny stands tall at his side. It's Tobias who shocks me with his perched position in the middle of the sofa.

He eyes me, as if waiting for company.

"The boy's no longer glued to your side?" I ask.

Luther shrugs. "We heard you're leaving. I guess he wants to make the most of the moments you have together."

I'm about to call bullshit when Luca walks into the room, his face a mask of indifference.

"What's going on?" He eyes me casually, not showing a hint of panic.

"I'm not sure yet. But apparently, my father comes in peace."

He doesn't react, neither in belief or concern. I'm not given a hint to his mindset or what was happening inside the house before our visitors arrived.

"Is my little fox still sleeping?" I need to know what he's done with her. Is she safe?

He holds my focus for long moments. "She's back to the same tricks as she was on her first night here."

Her first night? When she hid outside?

Shit. Did I lock her out with Chris?

"Is there anything I need to be concerned about?"

He pauses. Shrugs. "No."

The response took too long.

He's worried.

"Go check on her," my father encourages. "By Amar's account, she took quite a beating yesterday. She probably shouldn't be left alone."

"You spoke to him?" My face heats, the anger quick to infuse my veins. I approach the sofa, taking a seat beside Tobias to look my father in the eye. "How is my old friend doing?"

"I received a call from him last night. He mentioned you might be enjoying his boat."

"I'm surprised that fucker survived the swim." I stretch my arms along the back of the headrest, flaunting my lack of concern.

"A boat of tourists picked him up. But I appreciate your leniency. I would've understood if you took harsher measures."

No, he wouldn't. For reasons unknown, he's telling me everything I want to hear.

Luther has no protection. No weapons. Nothing.

I'm in control, yet he's entirely calm.

"Tell me why you're here," I grate.

"First, why don't you let Luca make use of my peace offering so we can talk in private?"

The woman sucks in a breath.

"What's he talking about?" Luca approaches, stopping beside my armrest. "What peace offering?"

"I'm handing Penny over as a symbol of my apology. Why don't you take her to one of the bedrooms and get her accustomed to a new way of life under my son's reign?"

Luca glances at me with a raised brow.

"Go." I wave him away. "Enjoy yourself."

Penny doesn't move. Neither does Luca.

"*Go*," I bark. "Teach her what she needs to know."

Her lips tighten, pure spite entering her features.

"Remember what will happen if you don't behave." Luther slaps her on the ass. "Now make me proud."

She grows an inch, her shoulders rigid. "Of course." She maneuvers around the coffee table and waits for Luca to join her before they continue to the hall.

"Right." I rub my hands together. "It's just us now. You can quit the act."

His mouth lifts at one side. "You've always lacked trust."

"I learned from the best." I lean back, stretching my arm along the headrest. "Now tell me why you're really here."

"I heard you're leaving and I wanted to confirm, in person, that there's no future of us working together. I wanted you to tell me face to face you're turning your back on the opportunity."

"That's not true." I match his smile. "I'm turning my back on you, Dad, not the opportunity."

"And your brother, too. You've just met him, yet you're pushing him away."

"I'm not pushing anything." We maintain our friendly facade despite the bitter meaning behind our calmly spoken words. "You're the one who kept his existence a secret."

"For his protection. You have no idea the safety risks you kids faced when you were young. You'll never understand the lengths I went to for all of my children."

My restraint vanishes as I sit forward, glaring my resentment. "What lengths did you go to when I told you your own brother molested your daughter? What fucking lengths were there then?"

"Is that what your badly bottled animosity has been about? You're holding a grudge over something you don't understand?"

"Something I don't understand? I was *there*. I dragged that son of a bitch off of her. And all you did to protect her was encourage Richard's fucking perversions."

He scoffs. "Did you ever think I was sating an addiction in a controlled environment so he wouldn't look elsewhere?"

"*You*—" I snap my mouth shut, my hands fisted.

"I handled your uncle," he reiterates. "I contained him."

"No, you only encouraged him to fuck other little girls."

He holds my gaze, the cogs turning in that messed up brain of his before he finally cuts his attention to Tobias.

Shit.

The fucking kid.

His tiny frame sits beside me, his shoulders curled inward, his head slumped. He clings to the cuffs of his long-sleeve shirt, trembling with quick breaths.

He's a mess.

"Tobias, have you got something to share with your brother?"

I scowl at my father. "Leave him alone. There's nothing he could say, about you or Richard that could cause me the slightest sense of vindication. I'm done."

I reach inside my jacket.

"*Tobias*," Luther warns.

I wish things were different and I didn't have to do this in front of the kid, but his life will be all the better without Luther in it. I curl my fingers around my gun when something stabs my thigh, a warm sensation spreading beneath my skin.

"*Fuck.*" I shove to my feet, my weapon drawn. "What the hell do you think you're doing?"

The kid stares up at me with wide eyes, his pupils tiny pinpricks. He clutches a plastic tube in his hand, his fingers white from the tight grip.

"Lower the weapon, son."

"No." My brain swells. It fucking tilts.

Everything slows—thoughts, breaths, heartbeats.

"What the fuck is this?" I snatch the plastic tube, the device similar to an EpiPen. "What the hell are you...?" My train of thought sways.

"It's a sedative. Don't worry. The effects will eventually wear off, but they're going to get worse before that happens."

A sedative.

A fucking sedative.

I bark out a laugh at the poetic justice.

"Burn in hell." I raise my gun and aim at my father's chest as my muscles stiffen. My body becomes heavy, each limb weighing a ton, my arm shaking.

"I didn't plunge it all." Tobias curls into himself. "I didn't do it right."

"What?" My father stands, his blurry frame barreling toward me.

He grabs my wrist, shoving it downward and twisting to lever my arm behind my back. He manipulates me like a puppet.

I have no control to stop him. No power to protest. All my strength goes into clinging to my weapon. It's all I focus on.

I won't let go.

I won't fucking fail.

"You're a piece of shit." My words are mumbled. "You steal from your own son. Then what? Attempt to kill him?"

"If I wanted you dead, I wouldn't waste time with theatrics." He speaks against my ear. "I told you I'd do anything to protect my children. This included. You're being softened by the people you surround yourself with. You've grown weak. It's time you went back to basics and learned what it's truly like to be a Torian."

"I know exactly what it's like. You're the one desecrating our name." I launch my elbow into his ribs and dive forward, hoping he'll release his hold. Instead, I lose my fucking balance. I stumble into the coffee table, the corner of my vision darkening.

Fuck.

I'm weighed down by air, the pressure intense.

But I don't lose my grip on the gun. I keep holding tight, fighting to tug it from Luther's grip. I close my eyes and force myself to focus. I concentrate everything on stopping the sway of consciousness.

The kid said it himself; he didn't succeed in injecting me with a full dose. I can pull myself out of this nosedive. I just might not be able to do it on my own.

"Luca." I'm a pathetic piece of shit for having to call for backup. "*Luc.*"

"He can't help you."

I climb to my feet, the gun held between me and my father. "You sedated him?"

"Out of courtesy, yes, but he's one of the pathetic men you've entrusted with my legacy, and you're going to need to cut him loose."

He doesn't struggle with his grip on my gun. He's confident. Strong, while I'm flailing to hold tight.

"Your guy was being *nice* to Penny yesterday." He scoffs. "Fucking nice. Is that the sort of pathetic weakness you want your men to portray? Have I taught you nothing?"

"*Luca,*" I roar.

Luther sighs. "Tobias, go get Penny."

The boy scampers from the sofa and runs for the hall.

I sway on my feet as I wait for hope. But there's no pounding steps coming in the opposite direction. I don't hear Luca or the sound of help on the way.

"It's time to go, son." My father grips my upper arm. "Let's make this as easy as possible."

"Fuck you." I launch a fist at his face and barely feel the connection. There's no pain in my knuckles. Only tightness.

He stumbles regardless, staggering backward, his grip leaving the gun.

Pull the fucking trigger.

My brain doesn't send the message fast enough. I'm stuck in a holding pattern as he rights himself and lunges at me, twisting the gun from my grip.

"*Luther*," Luca yells from behind me. "Drop it."

His voice is heaven to my ears. Fucking bliss… Until the shots ring out. My father fires.

Once.

Twice.

I turn to see Luca shove Penny down the hall before running in my direction, his large frame diving behind the sofa as more pops blast the room.

One minute he's there; the next he's gone. The only thing left behind is the blood splatter plastered against the wall.

He was hit.

Fucking shot.

Adrenaline consumes me. Anger and fear collide, clearing some of the fog from my head.

"Luther," Chris calls from outside. "You okay?"

My father grins. "Perfect. Couldn't be better."

I charge him, stumbling over my feet to drop my shoulder and send him flying. I reel with the onslaught of vertigo and struggle to remain upright as he collapses to the floor, the gun remaining tight in his hand.

"It's too late. I got him." He laughs as he pushes onto his elbows. "Penny, check to make sure he's dead."

"Don't go near him." I swing around to face her, my vision taking seconds to catch up. "Get the fuck away."

"Luther, I'm sorry." She creeps from the hall, the kid nowhere in sight. "I'm so sorry. I tried to stab him with the sedative but he stopped me. He was too quick." She rambles, one word tumbling over the other. "I didn't know what to do. I thought maybe I could—"

"Just check him."

Luther crawls to his feet as I latch onto the recliner for stability. If I could get my head to stop spinning, I'd be able to take control.

If the world didn't keep tilting on its axis, I'd kill him with my bare hands.

"There's blood." Her voice trembles. "It's coming from his head."

I can already hear the answer etched into her tone.

Whatever she's looking at is fucked up.

Then she crouches, descending out of my view.

"Penny," Luther warns. "What are you doing?"

"His pulse… I-I'm checking his pulse" She remains in hiding, the sentence held hostage for pained heartbeats. "I can't find it… He's… I think he's dead."

"Fuck." I raise my hands to my head, trying to keep all the crazy inside. "*Fuck.*"

I messed up.

I killed him, and Anissa will be next.

"Get his weapon." My father reclaims a harsh grip on my wrist. "Then unlock the door and hand it to Chris."

"Don't do it." I yank my arm back and stumble. "Don't fucking do it, Penny."

"She does what she's told," Luther seethes in my ear. "Otherwise she knows the consequences."

"What's to stop her shooting you?"

"She could try." He digs his fingers into the material of my suit. "But she'd be dead before she had time to aim. And then I'd kill all her friends just to spite her."

"I've got the gun." She stands, the weapon clutched in both hands, blood staining her fingertips.

"Keep it. Protect yourself. Don't give it to Chris." I should make a run for her. Tackle the pistol from her grip. Take charge of the situation.

"Don't even think about it." Luther jabs me in the shoulder with his gun. "You're predictable. Always have been."

"Too bad you've already admitted you won't kill me, old man."

"No, but I have no problem hurting you. It'll toughen you up."

I stagger to face him, my vision pixelated. "What do you hope to achieve? What the fuck are you going to do?"

I need to delay him.

If I slow things down, maybe I can draw this out until Hunt and Deck arrive. It's a fucking pussy's plan, but I can't get my brain to work out another option. I can't think.

"Tell Penny not to give him the gun and we can talk this out. That's what you want, right? To show me the error of my ways?"

Penny reaches the sheer curtain and pulls it wide.

"Tell her to stop," I repeat. "Do it."

Luther smiles at me. Chris does the same from the other side of the glass.

I can't let them get their hands on another gun.

"Penny. Don't." I keep my tone low. "Don't be stupid."

"Shut your mouth." Luther slams the butt of the gun against my cheek, connecting with bone.

Like a bitch, I fall to my knees, my ears ringing as Penny pulls the door wide.

"No."

Fuck. No.

I battle to get back up. I plant my hands and sway as she raises the gun, barrel first, her aim in the right direction, but her orders are clear.

I'm done for.

Anissa clouds my mind. All I can see is her and the torture she will endure. I can't let that happen.

I stumble to my feet as Chris reaches for the barrel.

"Don't fucking do it, Penny." I wobble with each step toward her.

"*Cole*," my father cautions.

I don't listen.

I don't stop. Not until the *pop, pop* shocks me still, her arm jolting with each pull of the trigger.

Chris turns white, all color seeping through the bullet wounds in his chest as he falls backward.

Penny sobs, the weapon slipping from her fingers to clatter to the floor.

"I'll fucking kill you," my father snarls.

I swing back to him, dazed, confused, but certain he will retaliate. "Get down," I yell at Penny and run to block Luther's aim. I sidestep when he does and struggle not to stumble. I tilt when necessary and fight to keep consciousness. I don't let him get a clear shot despite the shit affecting my brain. *"Hide."*

"I've got her." Luca lumbers to his feet from behind the sofa, his face strewn with blood.

"Luca?" He's alive.

He looks like he should be dead. But he's fucking alive.

Luther changes the focus of his aim, resetting his sights on Luca who shoves the sofa toward us, then rushes for Penny.

Pop. Pop.

The burst of noise from my father's gun assails me.

I hurry to get in front of the weapon, my steps faltering as Luca collides into Penny, taking her to the ground.

"Move," my father roars at me. "I'll fucking shoot you."

Luca scrambles behind the kitchen island, dragging Decker's sister with him.

"Do it. This will be your last chance." I raise my arms wide and smile when I realize I have the strength to hold them there. The shit poisoning my veins is wearing off. "It's over, Dad. Your new protégé failed to inject me properly. Your dog is dead. And you fucked up when you thought you took Luca out."

"You forget I'm the only one with a weapon, son."

There's a scrape of sound behind me. A shuffle of noise. Then I hear her. The most welcome reprieve and the greatest punishment all at once as Anissa says, "I'm sorry, motherfucker, but you're mistaken."

30

ANISSA

I clutch the gun in my hands, the metal warm against my palm as I aim at Luther over Cole's right shoulder.

My pulse pounds in my ears. My chest beats an agitated rhythm. It doesn't help when all eyes turn to me. Even Luca and Penny's, from where they're crouched behind the island counter.

But there's relief. The sight of Cole fills me with hope after torturous minutes spent thinking the worst.

I'd been trapped outside, weaponless, hopeless, and forced to hide behind the house yard shrubs while an unseen battle took place inside.

I hadn't known who instigated the gunfire. I wasn't sure if Cole was safe or if Luther had been taken down.

Then Penny pulled the curtain aside, opened the door, and dropped Chris like a domino, his head hitting the outdoor tile with a stomach-turning thwack.

"Lower your weapon, Luther." I fall back on my training and force the panic out of my system. "Hand it over and this may not have to end badly."

"Don't shoot, Niss," Cole demands. "He won't kill me."

I take stock of the room, knowing full well he's not my only concern.

There's blood on the far wall. Spots on the floor. A mass all over one side of Luca's face along with smears on Penny's cream pants.

Luther clucks his tongue. "I knew she wasn't a toy. You'll never understand the disgrace you've brought me, son. It's a fucking shame."

I continue my visual search of the room, but I don't see the boy. "Where's Tobias?"

I keep my aim on Luther's shoulder and remain thankful Cole isn't covering his father completely. I can take a clear shot from here. The only thing stopping me is the uncertainty of stealing Cole's closure from him.

"Don't concern yourself with my son." Luther takes a backward step, moving toward the kitchen. "If you were smart, you'd worry about your own life."

"He's safe, Anissa," Luca offers. "Give Cole your gun and let him finish this."

For a second, I contemplate compliance.

I could simply hand it over and remove myself from a position of power. But what if Cole can't follow through?

"He's right." Luther grins. "Give Cole the gun. Entrust my son to do what's right."

"Lower your weapon," I snap. "Put it down or I'll shoot."

"Your hesitation already speaks volumes, bitch."

He's wrong. I haven't pulled the trigger because this isn't my situation to finish. I'm risking my own life, and so many others because of my weakness for a man I never should've fallen for. I need to stop. "Cole, where's your gun?"

Luther chuckles and raises the weapon in his hand. "You're looking at it, Agent Fox. He got bested by his papa. And if you don't lower yours, I'll take pleasure in making you regret it."

"He's not going to kill me." Cole stumbles the tiniest step and exposes more of his father. "He won't fucking do it, Niss."

"You're hurt." It's not a question. Clearly, he's swaying on his feet.

"He's about to have a nap." Delight spreads across Luther's face. "And as soon as he falls, you're going to have nothing to shield you." He takes another retreating step and Cole follows, always keeping himself in front of the barrel. "But I think I might start the fun with the scared little piece of shit who would prefer to hide instead of helping his boss."

"I'm not hiding, asshole," Luca grates. "I'm giving Cole space to finish this his way. And if he can't, I'm on standby with a knife in my hand, ready and willing to slit your throat."

I glance at him to confirm.

He's not lying. A hunting knife is on the tile beside his thigh, lying in wait.

"A knife isn't going to help you. Not when I have a gun."

"Says the man who shot at me multiple times and still couldn't take me down." Luca scoffs out a laugh. "All Cole has to do is say the word and I'll happily fuck you up."

"It's over, Dad." Cole reaches out, his hand gliding toward the gun. "We're done here."

"Do you seriously think you've got the balls to kill me?" Luther brings voice to my fears. "You couldn't even kill your uncle when he messed around with your sister."

All the air leaves my lungs on a heave.

I'd questioned myself on who Cole's loved one could've been. I'd wondered and contemplated. Not once did I think his regret surrounded someone so close.

I hurt for him.

I'm pained by the betrayal.

"Don't worry. I'm still the monster you created. I always will be." Cole slaps his hand down to his side. "But your hold on me is over. I no longer believe family is everything. Not when it comes to you."

Luca waves at me from his hiding spot. "Give him your gun. Let him finish this." His tone is urgent. Demanding.

I ignore the instruction.

I still don't believe Cole is capable of killing his father. Not after he spoke of his hesitation last night. He may be brutal and malicious, but he also has a heart. One far bigger than I think anyone can imagine. And I won't risk all our lives on an uncertainty.

Luther retreats again, getting closer to the kitchen, encroaching on Luca and Penny's hiding spot.

"Cole, I'm going to shoot." I grip the gun tighter. "I can't let him take another step."

Cole stumbles again, his head swaying as he exposes Luther's chest. God, he's struggling to remain upright. He's giving me no choice.

"Cole?"

Luther takes another step, taunting me with a smile.

"Stop." I pin my aim to his body mass. "*Luther. Stop.*"

Cole rushes him, hauling him around the waist to slam him down to the floor.

They fight for the gun, chest to chest on the tile.

I have a clear shot. It's right there. Open. "Release the gun or I'll shoot."

They grapple. They grunt and heave and yell.

The direction of the barrel slowly pivots, pointing toward Cole. He's weakening. Luther's aim is so close.

"Cole?" I can't wait. I can't risk—

A burst of gunfire slams through the room, the shock making me stumble.

My ears ring. My pulse pounds.

Luther bucks, his mouth open, his eyes wide and rapidly blinking.

I got him. I shot him right through the side, the bullet hopefully piercing a mass of vital organs.

Cole scrambles backward, staring as his father gurgles and splutters while Luca and Penny rush to their feet.

They all stare at Luther as blood seeps from his mouth.

And still, he doesn't release the gun. He clings tight, inching his sights toward his son.

Pop.

Pop.

Pop.

I don't stop shooting until the clip is empty. Even then I keep pulling the trigger, over and over as he falls limp, never to move again.

But relief doesn't come.

The satisfaction I hoped would overwhelm me isn't there.

There's nothing. Only panic over Cole who rises to his feet to stare down at his father's lifeless body, unblinking, barely breathing.

I wait for him to break the silence. To react. To grieve. All he does is keep his focus on the pool of blood seeping its way across the tile.

"Cole?" I creep forward, my hand shaking with the need to reach for him.

He drags out the torture, the silence getting thicker.

"Baba?" Tobias's sweet voice wails from the hall entry. *"Baba?"*

"Tobias, no." Penny dashes across the room, maneuvering around Luca and Cole to scoop the boy into her arms and rush him back into the hall.

The boy's screams follow, the unending torture of a child losing a parent sinking into my ears and down to my heart.

And still, Cole doesn't move.

"Torian. You need to focus." Luca approaches him, the blood from his face soaking his shirt. "We've got stuff to do."

The closer he gets, the clearer the damage becomes. He was shot in the head, the bullet grazing his skull.

"Are you okay?" I start for him.

"It's a scratch." He waves me away. "Do us all a favor and grab the duffel from my room."

I nod, inching forward, bumping into the sofa before turning and fleeing down the hall toward the sound of a sobbing woman and child. I retrieve the duffel from Luca's room and drag it along the hall, the contents too heavy to carry with my protesting ribs and shoulder. "Here."

Luca rushes forward, falling to his knees to yank open the zipper and pull out tarps and numerous bottles of bleach.

"You need stitches." My voice is barely audible as I peer down at the side of his head. The gash has to be two inches long. The barest nudge to the right and he would've taken a bullet to the brain.

"Stitches are the last fucking thing on my mind." He bundles the items into his arms and stands. "Because unless this shit is cleaned up, you're going down for murder."

"It was self-defense."

"And how are you going to tell that story?" He scowls. "Are you going to throw Cole under the bus by saying you were a prisoner?"

"No. Of course not."

"So you're going to announce to the world you were working together? A Fed and a drug lord?" He scoffs. "Wake up, Anissa. These bodies need to fucking disappear. So if you're not going to help, get out of the fucking way."

I watch in a daze as he staggers to Luther's side and lays out the tarp along the tile.

Still, all Cole does is stare. No movement. No hint of what he's thinking.

"Cole." I start toward him, needing to be close. I don't care if he doesn't speak. His touch will be enough to tell me everything is all right.

I reach for him, about to run my fingers along his arm when he snaps from his daze and jerks away, his eyes filling with spite. "Back off."

All warmth seeps from my body. With two words and a scathing glare, he reduces me to nothing. "I—"

"Get away from me."

A panicked breath escapes my lips.

I don't understand. I saved his life. I saved *all* our lives, and now I've been reduced to a leper. If the feeling wasn't entirely familiar from my time in the Bureau, I'm not sure I could stop myself from breaking into a fit of sobs. "He was going to—"

"Get. The fuck. Away." His lip curls. "*Now*, Anissa."

My heart breaks.

Everything does—my strength, my pride, my confidence.

I shuffle back, placing more and more distance between us until I bump into a wall.

Maybe I should've waited… Listened… Ignored the building panic.

But I don't believe, not for one second, that Luther wouldn't have shot his own son. That monster was capable of killing anyone who stepped foot in his path. And if it wasn't Cole, it could've been anyone else.

I slither down the wall, sinking into a heap as Luca and Cole work together, lifting both bodies onto separate tarps, then wrapping them over and over. Then they carry one away, disappearing momentarily around the pool area before coming back for the next.

I should start cleaning up evidence, but I can't bring myself to do it. I can't move with the emotional pain leashing me in place.

Even when a boat revs to life, I remain shackled by invisible bonds.

I'm left alone for what feels like hours, staring at a pool of blood while unending suffering echoes from down the hall. I relive everything, over and over, the continuous loop punishing.

One minute I'd been asleep, the next, Luca woke me and demanded I get to the boat.

I hadn't had time to get the gun from under my pillow. *No.* I hadn't been fully awake to think about it until the open air hit my cheeks.

I'd sent Luca back to get it, leaving me to start the trek to the pier on my own.

That was when I'd heard them. The sound of voices in no way similar to the people I expected.

I hid, crouching behind the shrubs on the opposite side of the house yard, peeking through branches and leaves while I was locked outside with Chris.

I hadn't known what to do. But I was certain I didn't want to drag Cole's attention away from his task.

Then Penny had pulled the curtain aside, opened the door, and fired.

My world had shrunk to pure instinct.

That was when I ran for the open door, sidestepping the bloodbath at my feet to swipe the gun Penny dropped.

I hadn't spared a second thought about staying in my safe place. I'd risked my life to help Cole. I hadn't been able to spend another moment wondering if he was dead or alive. I'd needed to contradict my pessimism and see for myself that he was okay.

I scoff out a laugh.

I entered a war zone for him and now he hates me.

I pull my knees to my chest and bow my head.

I don't know how long I wait there, worrying about them never returning and even more concerned about what will happen if they do, until the familiar sound of shoes on gravel crunches outside.

I glance up to see Luca walk through the glass doorway, the blood now dried on his face, while Cole follows behind.

"What did you do with the bodies?"

"That's not your concern." Cole stalks to the kitchen, his face set in a tight scowl.

"Wait." I scramble to my feet. "Please talk to me."

He winces, a pained expression crossing his features for the briefest second before it turns to rage. "I don't think you want to know how I feel right now."

"Yes, I do. Tell me. Yell at me. But don't ignore me. Not now." Not when I'm drowning in guilt. "He was going to kill someone. You know that."

His jaw tics.

"Did I do the wrong thing?" My voice is a pathetic rasped plea. "Should I have let Luther keep aiming his gun at you?"

He ignores me and walks for the hall, not sparing me a backward glance.

"Why don't you wait outside?" Luca scoops a bottle of bleach from the floor and cracks the lid. "We need to focus on the cleanup."

"No. I'm not leaving him."

"I think you're doing more harm than good by staying." He pours the liquid onto the pool of blood where Luther fell, then places the bottle on the kitchen counter. "Come on. This shit is intense. You've gotta let the dust settle."

He indicates for me to follow him to the doors with a wave of his hand.

I still don't want to go.

I need to speak to Cole. He has to understand. "You can't tell me all our lives weren't in danger."

"We can talk outside." He stops at the glass doors.

Goddammit.

I feel sick. Worthless.

I follow after him on numb legs and walk outside, bypassing Chris's blood on the tiles. "What am I supposed to do?"

"Give him space." Luca moves into the doorway, blocking any possibility of my return inside. "You should be celebrating. This is over. You get to cut and run."

I don't want to cut and run.

I need closure.

I need Cole.

"Anissa..." Luca gives me a placating smile. A pathetic, deprecating curve of lips. "Being held here has fucked with your head. You've gotta realize the way you're feeling probably has a lot to do with Stockholm syndrome."

My world narrows to two words. One psychological condition.

No. The way I feel isn't dictated by mental instability.

"I think it's best if you wait at the pier," he continues. "We'll get word of Keira's arrival any minute now."

"I'm not going anywhere until I speak to Cole."

"I'm not giving you a choice." He jerks his chin toward the path. "I'm not Cole. You don't have me by the balls. This right here," he waves a hand between us, "is a kindness despite the mess you've made."

"The mess—"

"You took down a kingpin," he grates. "You just earned yourself a world of enemies. And who do you think is going to do everything in his power to protect your stupid ass when you fucking betrayed him?"

I suck in a breath. "I didn't—"

"Keep your mouth shut. Pretend Cole finished this. And go wait at the fucking pier."

My chest pounds with punishing beats. The way he looks at me—the disgust and annoyance—it's so fucking familiar.

I'm a pariah again.

"I don't need his protection," I whisper. "I can look after myself."

Luca scoffs. "We'll see."

A scream builds behind my sternum. I itch to lash out. To vent my frustration in a shriek. Instead, I turn and walk around the pool, hearing the slide of the glass door and the definitive *click* of the lock.

I don't stop along the path. I keep going, keep moving until I reach the end of the pier and sit to dangle my legs over the edge.

I did the right thing. I refuse to believe otherwise.

There was no other choice.

I continue to build on my argument as the sun creeps higher in the clear blue sky, beaming down on me from overhead.

The perfect weather mocks me. Everything does. And there's nothing I can do about it.

I remain in solitude, the numbness taking over through the passing morning until the low rumble of a boat approaches.

There's no motivation to panic anymore. I'm hollow. Empty.

I killed a man, thinking I was saving someone I care about, and instead, I've been accused of sabotage.

I don't even move when the boat approaches, the engine cut before it rocks into place beside the pier.

Decker climbs out first, his heavy boots thudding onto the wooden planks. "Sitting with all your friends, Agent Fox?"

He helps Keira from the vessel, Sarah and Hunter following close behind, all of them scowling their hatred at me.

I don't blame them. We have a convoluted history, especially Decker and I. Just like with Cole, they took opposing sides of the battlefield.

At least temporarily.

I no longer have any idea what team I'm on. There's no side for me.

I'm lost.

I push to my feet, wincing from the ache in my ribs as I face their judgment.

"You're beat up." Keira's scrutiny increases, her gaze trekking me up and down. "Cole didn't do this."

It sounds like a question. A pained plea for more information.

"No, he didn't touch me." Well, that's not technically true. We did a lot of touching, but not the kind she's referring to. And not the type I want to think about when he's made me an outcast.

"Are you all right?" she asks. "Who did this to you?"

"It doesn't matter."

She quirks a brow in offence. "Right… Okay, then. I'll leave you in peace."

I scoff as they start toward the house. There's no peace here. There never was. Not even in those precious moments spent alone with Cole.

But I was brought here for a reason. Cole dragged me into hell to tell Keira her father was dead, and now I understand why.

Luther's kids hated him. They despised everything he did. And they loved him in equal measure.

They didn't want his murder. They just had no other choice.

"Wait," I beg. "There's something Keira needs to know."

They pause collectively, then Hunt steps forward, his stance dominant. "If this is going to be some thinly veiled threat—"

"Quiet." Sarah claps him on the chest. "Let her speak."

They all stare, watching, waiting.

"He's dead, Keira." The admission lifts from the hollowness carving out my middle. "Luther is gone."

She stares at me without reaction. Without acknowledgement. As if I didn't speak.

"When?" Decker breaks the awkward silence.

"Earlier. Less than an hour ago. They're still cleaning up."

Keira turns, her stride determined as she continues for the house.

Her crew follow.

"Decker, wait."

He stiffens, his brutal glare hitting me from over his shoulder. "What?"

"Can I have a minute?"

He bares his teeth, not hiding an ounce of his hatred, then glances back at Keira. "Go ahead without me. I'll catch up." He crosses his muscled arms over his chest and stalks toward me. "What do you want?"

"There's something waiting for you inside."

He pulls a face—a mix of incredulity and annoyance. "Thanks for the ominous insight. Care to clarify?"

I open my mouth, but pause, unsure how to continue.

Maybe I'm not the person he should be hearing this from. The euphoric news shouldn't be tainted because it came from the lips of an enemy.

He deserves to believe the information as soon as he hears it. After everything he's been through, I want him to fully accept the relief without hesitation.

"It's something good."

His frown deepens. "Like a fucking present?"

I chuckle despite the seriousness. "Yeah, I guess."

"And you're not going to explain?"

He's such a strong man. A hero in his own right.

He went through hell with Penny's disappearance, then the misinformation of her murder. Thinking of his upcoming relief makes my eyes burn.

"I'll leave that up to Cole." I want to tell him everything. To salvage some of the memories from my time here with the purest glimpse of happiness. But it's not my place. "I just want you to know I'm happy for you."

31

TORIAN

I'M ON MY HANDS AND KNEES, SCRUBBING THE LAST VESTIGES OF MY FATHER'S BLOOD FROM the tile when the glass door slides open and my sister pulls aside the sheer curtain.

"Do my eyes deceive me?" she drawls. "Could my brother actually be cleaning?"

I sit back on my haunches and wipe the sweat from my brow with the back of my hand. "Macabre jokes aren't your style. I guess that's Decker's influence rubbing off on you."

"He's not rubbing anything off on me." She glances away, hiding the faint hint of tears in her eyes.

"I beg to differ." Hunter walks in behind her. "There was definitely a lot of rubbing on the flight here."

"It would've been a blessing if rubbing was all we had to witness." Sarah follows after him, shooting me a wink. "Congrats, Cole. It seems like you got the job done."

"I always get the job done." I shove to my feet, my head throbbing from the after-effects of whatever shit Tobias stabbed into my leg. "Luther's dead. His henchmen, too. Now all that's left is to dismantle the fucking huge operation he has going."

Keira nods, her attention turned toward the sterile kitchen. "Thank you."

I don't want her appreciation. Not when I should've done this a long time ago. And besides, she's giving me a front, and I don't appreciate the show.

She just lost her father after recently burying her uncle. Both of them betrayed her throughout her life. There's no way she's okay with any of this.

"Come here." I step forward and drag her into my chest, wrapping my arms around her. "I could've fucking killed you when the pilot told me what you'd done."

She leans into me, resting her head against my shoulder. "I know. The poor guy even tried to tell us we weren't allowed to board, but he didn't stand a chance."

"Not when I shoved a gun in his face." Hunter smiles, all teeth and no charm. "In his defense though, he did try to maintain a fake bravado for at least five seconds. He crumpled to shit after that."

"You'll haunt the guy's nightmares for years to come. All for nothing." Sarah glances around the crime scene, unperturbed by what's happened. "It looks like we didn't need to be here to help after all."

"If I needed anything, I would've asked." I place a kiss in Keira's hair and step back. "Where's Deck—"

"Right here." He slips between the curtains and makes his way to the front of the crowd. "I'm told I have some secret present waiting for me, but I swear to God, if that bitch was referring to the bloodbath that needs to be cleaned up, I'm not going to be happy."

"A present?" Keira frowns, glancing from me to Decker, then back again.

They all look at me. Silent. Even Luca stops cleaning his own blood off the wall to watch the show.

I shouldn't be the one to tell Decker the life-changing news. I'm not subtle. I don't have the patience or kindness to relay the information. It's not my thing.

"Hey, Luc." I jerk my chin at him. "Maybe you should explain the situation."

"Oh, no. *Fuck* no. You're on your own." He returns to cleaning, turning his back on me.

Asshole.

"What's the surprise?" Sarah cocks her hip against the sofa. "And do we all get one?"

"It isn't a fucking surprise or a present," I grate. "You all need to stop acting like this is all fun and games, because it's not the time for it."

"So the bitch *was* referring to the cleanup." Decker scoffs. "I fucking hate her."

"No, she wasn't."

Jesus Christ.

Any minute now Penny could walk down that hall. In fact, maybe I should just wait for that to happen and let nature take its course.

"Are we meant to guess?" Hunt asks.

"Just shut up, okay?" I huff out a breath and search for understanding that doesn't seem to exist.

"Oh, goodie." Decker rubs his hands together. "What delights do you have in store for me?"

"You might want to tone down the sarcasm," I grate. "This is serious."

"No shit. It's not like you get me presents on the daily. I'm kinda expecting to get shanked."

And I'd seriously prefer that alternative. "Fine," I huff. "I'm just going to spit it out."

"Don't worry. I tell Keira to do that all the time." He shrugs. "Honestly, if you spit or swallow it doesn't bother me either way."

"Oh, shit." Hunter snickers. "Blow job jokes with the boss man about his own sister. That's likely to get you killed."

Yeah. It fucking will.

I cock my fist and convince myself one swift uppercut will snap the sarcasm right out of him.

"Cole, just tell us." Keira begs with her eyes. "What's this all about?"

I throw my bloodstained cloth to the floor and look the sarcastic prick right in the eye. "Luther took me to his house yesterday."

Decker stiffens, the humor leaving his features. *About fucking time, asshole.*

"And?" Keira steps closer.

"And Penny was there."

The room erupts in chatter, multiple questions hurtled in every direction while Decker remains stone still.

"Are we talking about her remains?" Hunt asks. "What do you mean she was there?"

"I mean she was fucking there. Alive. Not necessarily well, because I've got no idea about her mental state, but she looked healthy enough."

Decker turns white, looking like a ghost of the man he was moments earlier. He rubs a hand over his mouth and sucks in a breath. "Where is she now?"

I loosen the top buttons on my shirt, needing more room to breathe. "Before we talk about that, you need to know—"

"Where. The fuck. Is she?" He storms forward, getting in my face, his chest rising and falling with heavy breaths.

There's nothing stopping me from putting a gun to his temple and telling him to back the fuck off. Not one damn thing after the shit I've gone through in the last twenty-four hours, but I'm smart enough to realize the next twenty-four he'll go through will be just as tough.

"Cole, please." Keira pushes between us, keeping her seething boyfriend at her back. "Where can we find her?"

"In one of the rooms down the hall. I don't know which one."

"She's here?" Decker storms past me.

I don't bother holding him back. He can work out his own way to deal with the reunion, but I latch onto Keira's arm as she tries to follow. "Wait."

She stops, tilts her head, and meets my gaze. "I need to go with him."

"I know. But first you need to know she's not alone."

"What does that mean?"

"There's a kid."

"That son of a bitch," Sarah hisses. "He knocked her up?"

"No. She hasn't been gone long enough. But I know he's ours."

"Ours?" A shaky breath escapes Keira's lips. "Meaning?"

"We have a half-brother. And to make matters worse, we just killed his father."

She clamps a trembling hand over her mouth. From fearless to faint-hearted in the space of minutes.

Yep. That's my sister.

She shakes her head, her eyes bleak with shock and confusion. "What do we do? Where's his mother? Is he okay?

"First, I don't know. Second, from what our father told me, the mother is dead.

And third, he was anxious as all hell when Luther made him stab me in the leg with a fucking sedative. But now I'm not so sure."

Her shock increases, the tremble in her hand turning to a full-blown shake.

"Just go to him." Luca walks toward us. "Try to show him as much support as possible. I'll come with you." He leads her to the hall and both of them continue out of sight.

I should probably follow, but I can't bring myself to face Tobias yet. Not until the evidence of our father's murder has been cleaned up. Maybe then we can both pretend he never existed.

"It sounds like Luca did good." Hunt focuses on the few remaining spots of blood on the floor. "Lucky for him."

I shrug. "He did okay. Who knows if you would've done better."

"*I know,*" he mutters. "We both fucking know."

I'd probably laugh at his wounded pride if I didn't feel like my time in Greece has been one big kick to the balls. My father may be dead, but his clusterfuck of a legacy is still left behind, his orphaned kid included.

"If only you hadn't stabbed me in the back, you could've been here."

"Don't fucking start." Hunt stalks for the kitchen. "Do you have more bleach around here somewhere?"

"In the duffel. Near the table."

He doesn't need any more instruction. He makes for the chemicals and starts cleaning, doing the job he's perfected for years, while he leaves me alone with his fiancée, one hand on her hip, her lips pursed.

I should throw my dirty cloth at her and demand she get to work. "Are you just going to stand there?"

"Probably." She cocks her head. "I'm trying to figure out what's going on in that messed up mind of yours. By any chance, does the big, bad Cole Torian need a cuddle?" She smirks, beating the emotional bullshit out of the room like she's wielding a stick.

"It's always great to see you, Sarah." I'm tempted to take her up on the offer only because I'm well aware she's not the comforting type. Even more so when it comes to me. "You can save the cuddle torture for Hunt. But I changed my mind about what I said earlier. I think I do need your help."

"I'm listening."

I contemplate my next move, hating the indecision I feel now more than I ever did when it came to the plans for my father's punishment.

"I want you to take Anissa to the jet and accompany her back to Portland."

She shrugs. "No problem. I can do that."

"Good, because I need you to do it now." Before I have to see her again. Before I have a chance to tell her all the messed-up shit going on in my head.

"Okay..." Sarah's eyes narrow. "And what do I do with her once we're Stateside?"

I stand a little taller, breathe a little deeper. "You let her go."

32

ANISSA

Weeks later

I RUN ALONG THE TRYON CREEK TRAIL, THE DENSE NATURE COMFORTABLY SURROUNDING ME as I push myself harder to pass two shirtless men jogging upfront.

I've taken this path for a while now, no longer appreciating the familiarity of the city streets. I need desolation. I can't even follow my early morning café routine because holding a brief conversation with the barista puts me on edge.

I want to be left alone. To quietly bathe in my mistakes. To hate the world from my darkened isolated corner.

Work hasn't been easy.

Taggert wasn't suspicious of the extra days I spent away from the office. Instead, he thought I was throwing a childish tantrum and used my disappearance to build bigger walls between me and my colleagues.

The entire department has made it clear they've grown tired of my drama.

All except Easton.

Anthony had my back the whole time—sending e-mails, leaving messages on my voicemail, hassling my apartment building manager for possible details of my whereabouts.

Even now, weeks later, he's the only person who checks on me.

There hasn't been one word from Cole.

I shake my head free from thoughts of him and punish myself harder, demanding more from my legs as I round the bare-chested male joggers and speed ahead.

It's a constant struggle not to suffocate in the past while also needing to analyze every second I spent on that island in an attempt to figure out where I went wrong.

I lost the game—that much is certain.

But it isn't all bad.

Numerous missing women have returned home. The stories they recounted to authorities and news outlets were clearly fictional—their disappearances explained by anything from running away, to going on drug benders, and even an elopement with a man who left a twenty-one-year-old high and dry in a foreign country—but regardless of whatever story Cole concocted to divert attention from his family, they're home.

And I'm thankful.

A snap of breaking undergrowth erupts from the bushes beside me, the hidden forest creature sending my hackles rising. I've been on edge since returning to Portland. Every shadow is Cole. Every bump in the night. Every private number that hangs up before I can connect the call.

Even now, surrounded by nature and calming solitude, my sixth sense is on alert.

I slow and glance over my shoulder, finding nothing. There're no shirtless men. No animals. Not even a bird flittering from tree to tree.

It's peaceful.

Too quiet.

I slide a hand over the canister of pepper spray held in the slim pocket of my skin-tight running pants and jog for the bend in the trail.

There's nothing to worry about out here.

Nothing but the waking nightmares I can't seem to shake.

I speed up, rounding the curve in the path only to skitter to a stop at the threat waiting in the small clearing.

My breathing catches. My pulse quickens.

Heat suffuses every single inch of me, the warm tingle a welcome sensation after weeks spent numb.

"Hello, little fox."

It feels like years have passed since his gorgeous face was more than a fading memory. A lifetime of misery since this foreboding man in his stunning suit, with his midnight eyes, stared at me.

I place my hands on my hips and straighten my back and shoulders, opening my lungs in an attempt to lessen the heaving gulps of air.

I don't speak. I can't. If I could, I wouldn't even know what to say. There's too much heartache.

And animosity.

Not to mention blinding rage.

He drags his gaze over me, slowly, the appraisal a tease even though his expression remains an emotionless mask. But he's not the only person with eyes on me. I can sense someone else, the tingle along my neck becoming a full-blown throb that descends down my spine.

I chance a glance over my shoulder, scrutinizing the mass of trees.

"It's Hunter," Cole murmurs. "He'll keep his distance and make sure we're not disturbed."

I continue to pant out my need for oxygen. "Is that meant to be comforting?"

A slow smile spreads across his gorgeous lips. The sight is punishing, the attack cutting deep. I'd almost forgotten how easily he lures his prey with that devilish appeal.

"I've missed your spite."

His admission rocks me, foundations and all.

The bliss lasts a split-second before I remember he was the one who discarded me like filthy garbage.

"What do you want, Cole?"

"You." He puts his hands in his pants pockets and lazily strolls toward me. "I think that's always been obvious, don't you?"

His lie doesn't warrant a response.

I refuse to participate in another game.

The way he played me still keeps me up at night.

I fell for him like a stone into murky waters, never to be seen again.

At one point, I couldn't picture returning to Portland without his protection wrapped around me. But that was before I came to terms with my Stockholm syndrome. Now, I know the sensation clawing beneath my sternum is nothing more than mental fuckery.

"What do you really want?" I cross my arms over my chest, building emotional barriers. "Because if you haven't noticed, I'm in the middle of something here."

"We were in the middle of something, too. Remember?" He raises a brow, continuing forward. He circles, walking behind me, setting me on edge. "We made a good team." His words brush my ear. "We were perfect together."

"You mean before you banished me?"

"I may have been quick to send you home, but don't forget that's exactly what you asked for." He continues around my other side, looking at me from the corner of his eye. "You wanted to get out of there as soon as possible. You made me promise to cut ties—no more games, no more flowers. Nothing. That was your stipulation, Nissa. Not mine."

He's manipulating the past, trying to rewrite history.

Yes, I made that deal with the devil, but that was before... Before he became the only air I wanted to breathe.

"You don't remember?" He stops in front of me, hands still in his pockets, his demeanor suave as hell. "It was after you tried to kill me with a loaded weights bar. We were in the panic room, and you were breathless and flushed. I'd wanted to fuck you up against—"

"Stop it," I snap. "You knew I didn't want to leave. Not after what I did. I was a mess."

A brief glimpse of regret pulls at his brows before quickly fading. "I needed time."

"And what about what I needed?" I slap a hand against my chest. "I was trying to save your life. Luca's and Penny's, and that little boy's, too. But you treated me as if I'd stabbed you in the back. The way you looked at me—" I shake my head, refusing to continue.

My recount doesn't matter.

Nothing does.

What I went through wasn't even reality. It was just another game.

"I needed time" he repeats, his voice softening. "When you shot him, I—"

"Regretted setting me up to take the fall?"

He turns quiet, cementing the suspicions that have torn me apart for weeks.

"Did you think I wouldn't work it out?" I glare. "You *wanted* me to kill him. You planned for it."

The silence stretches between us, building the anger I've kept tightly bottled.

"I admit it took me a while to put the clues together. I spent days locked in my apartment, staring at the ceiling, going over and over what I thought was a mistake on my behalf. But it was never a mistake, was it, Cole? It was your plan all along."

His mouth curves in a sad smile. "I should've known you'd figure it out."

The confirmation squeezes my heart before ripping it in two.

I'd known. God, how I'd known. But I didn't want to believe.

I'd hoped and prayed and begged to be wrong.

"Fuck you." I storm forward, grazing his shoulder, only to be stopped by the tight grip of his hand around my arm.

"You're not going to ask me why?"

I raise my chin. "I already know—it was a game."

"No, little fox. That part was never a game."

"Bullshit. You accused me of sleeping with you because of some fucked-up trickery. But it was really you who flipped the board that night."

"No."

"Yes. You worked me like a pro. That bullshit when you told me you weren't sure you could pull the trigger was pure gold." I tilt my head to face him. "But it was the day of reckoning where you really played your A-game. You kept repeating your father wouldn't shoot you—*you, Cole*—but you weren't the only victim in the room, and you would've known I was scared to death of Luther hurting any of us. And still, you kept saying it over and over. He won't shoot *me*, his own son. You predicted the subtlety would work its way into my psyche."

He doesn't answer.

I don't need him to.

Not anymore.

"And there was your strategic stance, too." I square my shoulders, thrilled to have the opportunity to get this shit off my chest. "You could've easily saved your father by blocking him with your body. You knew my aim. You were well aware I had an open shot. Yet you kept stumbling out of the way."

"You're a smart woman, Niss."

A sob inches its way up my throat, just waiting to be released.

I hate him. God, how I hate him. But I'd loved him, too.

It was a dizzying, heart-palpitating, Stockholm love. But love regardless.

"Not smart enough to understand why you continued the act after I pulled the trigger." I sniff and hate myself for the pathetic sound. "That part still has me stumped. Along with why you didn't just ask me to do it in the first place. But…" I shrug. "The past is in the past. And I no longer want to spare you a single thought, apart from wishing you all the best on your trip to hell."

I yank my arm from his grip and walk away, only to be hauled around the waist and pulled into his chest. Face to face. Hip to hip.

In an instant, I'm dragged back into fond memories, when I mistakenly thought the look in his eyes held hunger.

"Being away from you was hell on earth." He growls. "I have no plan to go through that again."

I fight his hold, shoving and scrambling.

He smothers me tighter, wrapping his arms around mine to hold them down at my sides.

"I'll scream."

He grins. "And you think I couldn't shut you up?"

I should be scared. Instead, the familiar burn of desire slides through me, scorching everything in its path.

I want him. After everything—all the pain, all the betrayal.

I.

Still.

Want.

Him.

"Scream, little fox," he whispers. "Give me the opportunity to silence that pretty mouth of yours."

My heart pounds beneath tightening ribs. My lips dry. My breathing becomes shallow.

I don't want to be like this, with every nerve in my body hyper aware of his touch.

I hate it. I loathe it. Yet, I no longer know how to feel alive when we're apart.

"You're going to listen to me." He leans in, his mouth a breath away from mine. "You're going to hear every word I have to say. Then, and only then, will you get to walk away from me."

I scoff and stare over his shoulder, refusing to submit. We both know he won't hurt me. The only thing he can break is my self-control.

I'm struggling to fight the need to have his mouth on mine. His hands on my body. His words in my ear.

I need it all, and the longer I remain captured against him, the more likely I am to succumb.

"I didn't break my promise to you," he murmurs. "I said no more games, and I meant it."

"Then why?" I focus on the trees, the leaves, the winding, weaving vines. "Why manipulate me?"

"Because you made it clear you hate who I am."

I turn rigid.

"After everything that happened, you still didn't understand my life, Nissa. You remained on that high horse, looking down on me."

I meet his gaze. "What does that have to do with me killing your father?"

"Everything." He stares at me, his eyes stony, his mouth tight. "I was determined to take Luther down. I would've killed anyone who dared take the closure away from me. But that day in Naxos changed everything. I wanted to torture Amar for what he did to you. I would've stripped the skin from his body, layer by layer, because of the part he played. But the horrified way you looked at me when I suggested punishment made it clear you were still stuck in your fairyland where justice is only served by someone holding a badge."

"That's not true."

"It's not?" He raises a brow. "Up until the very last night, you kept asking me how I could kill my own father. How I could possibly pull the fucking trigger on my own flesh and blood—"

"Because he was your father. At one time, he was everything to you."

"He was a fucking rapist," he snarls. "A sex trafficker. He ruined the lives of hundreds, and sending him six feet under would've brought me relief, *not* anguish." His anger is clear. His intent, too.

"Then why did you get me to do it?"

"Because of this." He jerks his head at me, narrowing his gaze. "Because of the way those judgmental eyes strip me to my core."

I shake my head. *No.*

"It's true, little fox. You messed with my mind. You, with your snappy mouth and perfect body, did things to me I couldn't undo. I knew I didn't want to let you go once my work in Greece was over. I couldn't stomach the thought of letting you out of my fucking sight, but I was also fully aware you and your high horse wouldn't be able to stand the sight of me once I murdered my own father."

I keep shaking my head. *No. That's not why.*

That couldn't be why.

"I manipulated you, Niss, because I couldn't let you go."

"Liar." I shove his chest. "You *did* let me go. You banished me in the blink of an eye. *You* looked at *me* with the same disgust you accused me of."

"Any disgust I had was for myself. Not you. I couldn't stand you looking at me when I'd been lowered to the point of letting a woman do my dirty work. And not just any woman. The *only* fucking woman I've ever given a shit about."

"Well, it's a bit damn late to tell me that now when I've lived with the guilt for weeks. I thought you hated me for what I'd done."

"I hated *me*," he snarls. "I hated being unable to get you out of my head. I hated my addiction to you and the inability to let go. I hated how your judgment tore me to fucking shreds. But most of all, I hated the fucking danger I put you in."

My pulse pounds in my throat, the thunderous beats wracking my body. I step back, not willing to believe him.

"I needed you." The admission is whispered from my lips. "I needed you to tell me you were okay. That I hadn't ruined your attempt to gain closure. And that the news reports of another mass grave of women found in Greece was untrue. But you wouldn't even speak to me. I called. So many times."

"I wasn't going to have this conversation with you over the phone."

I take another retreating step. "I went to your restaurant."

"I know." He nods. "They told me. But I was still in Greece tying up loose ends. I only returned Stateside an hour ago."

He's been gone this whole time?

I have so many questions. It kills me to keep my mouth closed and not bring voice to the curiosity surrounding those women. Surrounding *him*. It's pride that keeps my lips sewn shut.

"You're the first person I've seen since we landed, Nissa. I've thought of nothing else this entire time."

"Well, that's too bad, because I stopped thinking about you a while ago."

His lips kick up, silently calling me on my bullshit.

Asshole.

I look away, unable to face the truth. "How's Tobias?"

"I'm not entirely sure. He returned to the States a while ago. Keira and Layla have been helping to look after him. But they think he's feeding off Penny's trauma."

"And what do you think?" I whisper.

"I think I want to quit talking about shit that doesn't involve you. Instead, we should talk about your agent friend. I'm told Easton has been spending a lot of time at your apartment."

I bark out a laugh. "I'm not going to dignify you with a response."

"It's okay. You don't need to. I'm sure you're well aware he'll go missing if I find out he's laid hands on what's mine." He leans close, his mouth hovering near my ear. "And you're mine, Nissa, just in case you're confused about our situation."

I shudder, my entire body igniting with painful familiarity.

I want to be his. I ache for it every day. But the price is still too high.

I won't sell my soul for him.

"Like hell I am." I slide my arm away.

"You're mine," he repeats, his voice rough and ragged, the brutality filling my chest with a mass of tingles. "And I'm yours. It's always been that way. You know it as well as I do."

I shake my head, denying what I've tried to ignore for four weeks. Even longer. Since the day at the coffee shop. From the first day our eyes locked.

"I didn't report what happened in Greece," I admit. "I didn't tell anyone. Can't you be grateful and move on?"

"Can you move on?" It's not a question. It's a taunt. "Easton keeps hanging around at your apartment, but he never stays the night. He's made it clear he wants you. But you've never let him get grabby. Why's that?"

"Just how closely are you watching me?" I wish I was disgusted at the thought of him invading my privacy.

I wish.

I wish.

I wish.

Instead, my belly fills with butterflies. My lingering Stockholm issues have me concluding his stalking is a romantic gesture.

His lips lift in a lazy smirk. "He's not going to come around anymore."

"Because you say so?"

"Exactly." He inches away, leaving me cold. "I'll give you a week to let my return sink in. In that time, you need to tell him to walk away. Then you're going to meet me next Sunday morning at our coffee shop at eight."

"I'm not going to do any of that, Cole."

The smirk increases, the expression entirely devilish. "And why is that?"

"For starters, there are enough questions about my loyalties within the Bureau without being seen with you in public."

"Then quit and come work for me."

Everything inside me reacts. Stomach. Heart. Lungs.

Each organ squeezes. Twists.

I've thought long and hard about our differing morals. I've stewed on the way the FBI stabbed my father in the back. And yes, I've questioned whether I have what it takes to switch sides, ditching one corrupt organization for another. But the indecision over Cole has been everlasting. The frustration and confusion are always there. "Very funny."

"Funny?" He quirks a brow. "Do you know me to be the humorous type?"

No, I don't. He doesn't do jokes. He does taunts.

"Think about it." He takes a backward step. "Think about me. Think about how I haven't left your mind for a second all month. Then meet me next weekend. Eight o'clock. Sharp."

"I won't be there." My heart says otherwise, but I'm determine to succeed this time.

No more games. No more provoking.

I need to cut ties and move on.

"We'll see," he purrs.

I scoff and stalk along the path, my steps getting longer. "Goodbye, Cole."

This doesn't feel like goodbye. The tingling taking over my stomach resembles the excitement of a new beginning. A fresh start, despite the craziness.

"For now, Nissa. Goodbye for now."

EPILOGUE
TORIAN

One week later

SHE'S NOT COMING.

I knew she wouldn't.

That's why I'm sitting in my car out the front of her apartment building one minute before we're meant to meet.

I need to give her the opportunity to humiliate me. I get it. It's payback.

I did the same to her when I demanded she drop the sheet after we slept together. Then again after she killed my father.

I hurt her. And I sure as shit can man up enough to let her even the score—at least temporarily—because it's not like this thing between us is over.

While I'd been stuck in Greece, I hadn't been able to predict how she would react to my return. I'd wondered if she'd be angry. Would those handcuffs of hers be ready and waiting for a long-overdue arrest?

I'd thought about her every damn minute of every damn day. She'd clouded my vision while I'd spent weeks dismantling the intricate details of my father's operation. I'd even contemplated her placing me in the rearview and moving on with her life.

Then news got back to me about the visits from her agent friend, and the spiral of jealous rage I'd descended into made me work around the clock to get back to Portland earlier than predicted.

I'd needed to see her for myself. I couldn't keep questioning what she was thinking.

But that first glance on the trail in the woods had answered all the unknowns.

She'd caught sight of me and reacted with relief.

I'd seen her hope. Witnessed the brief glimpse of excitement.

Despite our differences, and the hell I'd dragged her through, it was clear she still wanted me.

She'd tried to hide the spark with tough words and tougher mental shields, but I'd seen the truth. I'd also felt her tremble under my touch, the same way she did on the island.

Nothing between us had changed.

"You said eight, right?" The young florist delivery woman leans against the window ledge of my Porsche and smiles down at me. "Are you ready for me to deliver the arrangement yet?"

"Give her one more minute."

As much as I previously enjoyed the predatory parts of my time with Niss, I'd prefer to set that aside and delve into new territory.

"Oh, gosh." The woman steps back and pats her pockets. "I forgot to write on the card. You said there was a message, right? What do you want me to put on it?"

She pulls an envelope from her jeans pocket, then continues to rummage until she finds a pen.

"Just wait a little while longer," I mutter.

If Anissa decides to meet me, the flowers will become redundant, which means the card isn't necessary. I just need to wait.

I know she'll show.

"No problem." The woman nods. "What made you decide to send an arrangement of poppies? Is the woman a veteran?"

I grin. "No. It's more of an inside story. One of those things that only has meaning to the people involved."

Her eyes light up. "I love those stories. It makes the gift so romantic. I live for that stuff. Would it be incredibly rude if I asked for details? How did poppies become the flower to symbolize your relationship?"

I bite back a laugh. The woman is in her early twenties and clearly spellbound by whimsical thoughts of romance. I'm sure she's expecting a tale filled with candlelit dinners and nights spent gazing at the stars.

I shrug. "It's simple, really. She's an FBI agent. I'm a notorious drug lord. The poppies are more of a taunt than anything. Alluring but deadly. Simplistic, yet the source of a multi-billion-dollar industry. The deep red color is also important because the temperamental times we've navigated together have been bathed in bloodshed."

She blinks at me, her face growing slack.

"We're a match made in heaven, don't you think?"

"Yes." The envelope and pen tremble in her grip. "Of course."

"Don't look so scared, sunshine. I'm only messing with you."

"Oh." She straightens and gives me a bashful smile. "For a minute, I thought you were serious. How crazy is that?"

"It's definitely crazy." I turn my attention back to the doors of the apartment building. "I just want to wait a few more seconds."

Thirty, to be exact.

I start the mental countdown, the tick of the metaphorical clock increasing my pulse.

Twenty-eight... Twenty-seven... Twenty-six...

Any moment now, my little fox is going to walk out those doors.

She's had her fun. She's inflicted her retaliation.

Now it's time to move forward.

Nineteen... Eighteen... Seventeen...

I can't wait to see her.

The last week has been torture. Watching her through the added security measures Decker put in place wasn't enough. I need to touch her. To fuck her. To hear her needy gasps against my ear.

Nine... Eight... Seven...

The doors swing wide and familiarity walks out.

Unwanted fucking familiarity.

An asshole in stone-washed jeans and a knitted goddamn sweater strides outside, not a care in the world as he increases my pulse, infusing my veins with a volatile dose of jealousy.

I shove the car door open, making the delivery woman scamper out of the way, and stalk toward the conceited prick. "Agent Easton, what brings you to the neighborhood?"

He pauses, his judgmental gaze trekking from my head to my toes. "I could ask you the same question."

I smile, hiding the venom surging to break free. "It's a beautiful day. I wanted to soak up the sunshine."

"What a coincidence. I'm about to do the same thing. I just had to check on my girl first. You know, priorities and all that."

His girl?

His fucking girl?

"You've got yourself a woman?" I want to kill him. Right here. In front of innocent witnesses and Sunday morning traffic. "Congratulations. She wouldn't happen to be the illustrious Agent Fox, would she?"

"How'd you know?" He smirks.

Fucking smirks.

My face heats, the need to act building like a furnace.

"Between you and me," he mock whispers, "she's been going through a tough time lately, and I'm enjoying spending every spare minute comforting her."

He's baiting me. And I'm devouring every morsel, even though it acts as poison.

"What a gentleman." I incline my head in approval. "I hope this tough time of hers isn't too serious."

"You know, Mr. Torian, it's a funny thing. She fell off the grid weeks ago. Just completely disappeared. Days later, she returned, battered and bruised on her arms, legs, and neck." His calm facade remains in place. "She claims it was an accident she received while vacationing on the coast. But I know her. Really well, in fact. So it's clear she's lying."

It's also clear he is, too.

If he's only aware of the damage on her limbs, this smug fucker hasn't had the pleasure of sleeping with her. No way in hell would the injury to her ribs have skipped his attention.

He might want to believe she's his girl, but that woman is most definitely still mine.

"I'm going to find out what happened to her, Mr. Torian." He steps forward, his sense of superiority all up in my face. "I'm going to break down those walls of hers until she tells me her juicy secrets. Then I'm going to go after the person responsible and tear him to pieces."

I raise my brows, impressed by his enthusiasm. "It sounds like you've got a tough task ahead of you."

"Not at all. It's only a matter of time." He leans closer, as if preparing to tell a secret. "Do you want to know the best part?"

I clench my jaw, growing tired of this cock-measuring competition.

"Once I make the arrest, I'll be her savior—the one she runs to in relief. Have you ever been someone's white knight, Cole? Do you know how generous a woman can be when all her demons have been slayed?"

"I'm more of a dark prince kinda guy," I growl.

"That's too bad, because unbreakable bonds are formed in those types of situations." He shrugs. "That's what I'm counting on, anyway."

Fuck him.

Fuck this straight-laced, badge-wearing prick.

He's not going to form any bond with Anissa. Not today. Not tomorrow. Not in a million fucking years. At least not while I'm around.

"Good luck." I clap him on the shoulder, my fingers digging into his jacket.

"Don't worry. I won't need it." He shrugs away from my grip and bumps into my shoulder as he starts down the cement path. "I'll see you around, Cole."

The poor bastard is delusional. Pathetic and fucking deranged.

He's no threat to what I have with Anissa.

I earned her trust under the harshest of conditions in only a matter of days. And by the sound of it, this asshole hasn't been able to get close in weeks.

"Be careful, Easton," I call over my shoulder. "You don't want to end up going off the grid like she did. Who knows if you'll return?"

I keep my focus on the building and raise my attention to her window, finding her staring back at me.

She doesn't retreat. She doesn't grant me a welcoming expression, either. But those gorgeous eyes drink me in. There's the faintest hint of hunger in her features. The tiniest glimpse. And that's enough for now.

I grin at her. I fucking beam my intentions her way.

Without a word, I let her know this isn't over. Her little mutt doesn't scare me. Not when she's made it clear she still wants me.

"Until next time, Niss."

I blow her a kiss, bidding her a silent farewell, then make my way back to the florist now waiting beside her white van.

"Are you ready for me to make the delivery?"

"Yes. It's time."

"And the card?" She holds out the crisp white envelope. "What would you like me to write on it?"

I contemplate my options, wondering if I should change my plan now Easton's entered the battlefield.

Should I approach her with caution? Maybe try a softer angle to beat the prick at his own game?

No. To hell with that.

I'm no white fucking knight.

Never have been. Never will be.

I hold out a hand. "Here, let me write on it."

The woman retrieves the slip of cardboard from the envelope and passes it over, allowing me to pen my message against the hood of the van.

If you want me to stalk you, then that's what I'll do.

Be careful, little fox. The big, bad wolf is coming for you.

Torian and Anissa will be continued…
But first comes Savior! *Click here to find out more.*
Or turn the page for a preview.

For more information on where this series is headed, join the Eden Summers' Newsletter or the super fun Facebook Reader Group.

You can also receive new release notifications from **BookBub**.

Turn the page for a preview of Savior.

ALSO BY EDEN SUMMERS

Hunting Her Series

Hunter

Decker

Torian

Savior

Luca

Cole

Reckless Beat Series

The Vault Series

Information on more of Eden's titles can be found at www.edensummers.com or your online book retailer.

ABOUT THE AUTHOR

Eden Summers is a bestselling author of contemporary romance with a side of sizzle and sarcasm.

She lives in Australia with a young family who are well aware she's circling the drain of insanity.
Eden can't resist alpha dominance, dark features and sarcasm in her fictional heroes and loves a strong heroine who knows when to bite her tongue but also serves retribution with a feminine smile on her face.

If you'd like access to exclusive information and giveaways, join Eden Summers' newsletter via the link on her website - www.edensummers.com

For more information:
www.edensummers.com
eden@edensummers.com

Printed in Great Britain
by Amazon

77405219R00426